CHRONICLES
OF THE
LENSMEN
VOLUME I

Books by E.E. "Doc" Smith

The Skylark Series

The Skylark of Space
Skylark of Valeron
Skylark Three
Skylark Duquesne

The Lensmen Series

Triplanetary
First Lensmen
Galactic Patrol
Gray Lensman
Second Stage Lensmen
Children of the Lens

An associational Lensman novel

Vortex Blaster

The Subspace Series

Subspace Explorers
Subspace Encounter

The Galaxy Primes
Master of Space (with E. Everett Evans)
The Best of E.E. "Doc" Smith

Chronicles of the Lensmen, *Volume I*

Triplanetary
First Lensman
Galactic Patrol

E.E. "DOC" SMITH

Foreword by
John Clute

FANTASY

First SFBC Science Fiction Printing: June 1998

Published by arrangement with:
Old Earth Books
Post Office Box 19951
Baltimore, MD 21211

Visit our website at *http://www.sfbc.com*

ISBN 1-56865-804-4

PRINTED IN THE UNITED STATES OF AMERICA.

CONTENTS

TRIPLANETARY 1

FIRST LENSMAN 241

GALACTIC PATROL 487

Triplanetary

To
Rod

Contents

Foreword 7

BOOK ONE: DAWN

1. Arisia and Eddore 13
2. The Fall of Atlantis 21
3. The Fall of Rome 38

BOOK TWO: THE WORLD WAR

4. 1918 55
5. 1941 65
6. 19—? 81

BOOK THREE: TRIPLANETARY

7. Pirates of Space 95
8. In Roger's Planetoid 109
9. Fleet Against Planetoid 122
10. Within the Red Veil 131
11. Nevian Strife 145
12. Worm, Submarine, and Freedom 159
13. The Hill 165
14. The Super-Ship Is Launched 175
15. Specimens 184
16. Super-Ship in Action 188
17. Roger Carries On 200
18. The Specimens Escape 215
19. Giants Meet 229

FOREWORD

by John Clute

We begin with a very big bang. "Two thousand million or so years ago," Doc Smith tells us in the first sentence of *Triplanetary*, "two galaxies were colliding." From this collision come almost all of the billions of planets that now circle the billions of stars of both galaxies. There are, however, two planets that date from before this Coalescence. In what becomes our own Home Galaxy, there is the planet of the Arisians, the almost infinitely wise predecessor race of all Civilization, which, in its wisdom, decides even before sentient life appears elsewhere that it must remain behind the arras of the worlds to come and secretly to Uplift—the Doc does not use this term, which David Brin brought into currency decades later, but his intention is similar—various promising races into the role of guardians of Civilization. The Arisians will act as mentors.

And in the Second Galaxy, there is the planet of the Eddorians, the vile but hugely competent race that represents a principle profoundly inimical (according to the Doc) to true Civilization: Eddorians are "intolerant, domineering, rapacious, insatiable, cold, callous, and brutal." They are also "keen, persevering, analytical, and efficient." Like Doc Smith himself, they show no signs of possessing a sense of humor. Eventually (though not in this first volume of the *Lensman* sequence), they create the vast interlocking two-galaxy-spanning hierarchy of piratical tyrannies known collectively as Boskone. Boskone is the arras Eddore hides behind and from the concealment of which Eddorians mean to rule the sevagram.

Given the hugeness of the scale of this first volume of the *Lensman* sequence, it is perhaps just as well that Doc Smith—however dilettantishly full of jokes he might have been in the privacy of his own home—does not do much smiling in his text. From its very first pages, the *Lensman* sequence never flags for an instant from the unrelenting *seriousness* of the story being told. Serious does not necessarily, of course, mean profound or subtle or wise, and there are many pages in the six large volumes in which a lack of intellectual rigor or a coarseness of style and apprehension or yet another moment in which men in uniform are numbingly adulated or an obliteratingly provincial vulgarity or a dumbfounding coyness about females, can nearly dislodge contemporary readers from the text. No, more than dislodge: *evict.* There are moments when it is very nearly impossible to believe that you belong in the same world Doc Smith seems to own. But these moments are rare. The seriousness underlying the bully-boy fun and games wins through, and any reader capable of a visceral response to the raw sound of Story being told will find the *Lensman* books ultimately irresistible. For—unlike a lot of sf—the *Lensman* books make precisely the sound of Story.

Unfortunately, the most dangerous part of the whole six volumes, the most unrelentingly "serious" part of the entire sequence, the most likely portion of the narrative to disengage the contemporary reader, is the introductory section that makes up the first six chapters of *Triplanetary.* The very first pages do constitute a grand panorama, during which the aeons-long conflict between the Arisians and the Eddorians is set in train, and we learn that Uplifted races on both sides (or, Civilization versus Boskone) will be pitted against each other in a universal war lasting millions of years, a conflict whose ultimate begetters will remain unrevealed to the leaders on either side, even to the Lensmen who comprise the corps elite of the Galactic Patrol, and who—in all but name—constitute the actual rulers of Civilization, maugre Democracy, which the Doc (almost certainly rightly) seems to think of as incompatible with the kinetic needs of space.

But then *Triplanetary* coasts into what must be described as back-story. There is a reason for this (for very rarely does Doc Smith allow his readers any respite from the bronze warhorn blare of his tale). The original *Lensman* sequence, as published in the 1930s and 1940s in *Astounding Science Fiction,* comprises only Volumes Three through Six of the sequence as published in book form by Fantasy Press between 1948 and 1954, because Smith, when he agreed to book publication, decided that the *in medias res* structure of the magazine sequence—by virtue of which everybody, Lensmen and readers alike, remain unaware of the true extent of the conflict before the last volume uncovers the arrases behind which the Arisians and the Eddorians have been hiding for hundreds of thousands of words—lacked gravitas.

He was almost certainly wrong. And, given the crudity of his concept of Civilization—basically, Civilization in the Doc's hands pretty closely models what might have happened had Lord Baden-Powell had the chance, with the aid of a clean-shaven thousand-strong unison of Boy Scouts, to clean up Des Moines: *Metropolis* as company town—this was not, perhaps, a wise decision. But he took it.

In any case, so as to transform this original story (we'll try to describe the genius of its structure in the foreword to *Galactic Patrol*) into a "History of Civilization," the Doc added not only an initial three chapters devoted to the overview (described above) but also another three, which are devoted to a cod history of Earth (here known as Tellus) up to the end of World War Three.

The most interesting sequences in these three chapters—which as a whole are a kind of gauntlet the reader must run in order to reach the genuine feast—are set in the 20th century and introduce the first of the Kinnison clan, who are half of the Arisian breeding program for Earthlings (eugenics presents no moral challenge to Doc Smith, and the fact that his chosen race is unmistakably Aryan needs to be assimilated by readers, and then—for the duration—completely and utterly ignored). Most interesting of all (for extrinsic reasons) is the chapter covering the civilian exploits of Ralph Kinnison, aged 51, in an ordnance plant in World War Two. The chapter is clumsily written, with far too many seemingly supererogatory walk-on characters, but when one realizes that the whole of this section is transparently autobiographical, it is impossible to stop reading. As the war began, Smith himself, like Kinnison, was 51; like the rambunctious but lovable Kinnison, he worked in an ordnance plant; and, like Kinnison, he was fired in 1944 because he refused to pass some shells as safe. This chapter of *Triplanetary* constitutes, therefore, both an act of revenge on Smith's part and an amusing revelation of the close identification he felt with his magnum opus. After all, Kinnison/Smith is a *Man*; he is a chosen carrier of Civilization; his great-great-great-grandchildren will *truly* rule the sevagram.

So even the "Civilization" chapters of *Triplanetary* can be read with interest. And (incidental to the sequence as a whole, but importantly to the history of sf) certain paragraphs of the Kinnison/Smith chapter uncannily adumbrate the peculiar, ingrown, freemasonical tone of hard sf as it has been written for the last 30 years or so. Read this:

> Kinnison was promoted again: to Chief Chemist. He and Sumner had never been friendly; he made no effort to find out why Cappy had quit, or had been terminated, whichever it was. This promotion made no difference. Barton, now Assistant, ran the whole Chemical Section save for one unit—Siberia—and did a superlative job. The Chief Chemist's secretary worked for Barton, not for Kinnison. Kinnison was the Czar of Siberia.

and so on. It is language which proclaims its isomorphic modelling of the inside of things: the non-stop momentum of the telling, the plethora of surnames (whose rhetorical function is to indicate functions, the individual bearers being substitutable), the can-do mercilessness of the verbing, the manipulative confusion of substantive (*i.e.*, Czar of Siberia) and the breath of life. It is the language of club minutes: club minutes as wetdream.

Once these six chapters are transacted, however, the language relaxes and expands, and we enter the true Smith world, which has little to do with individual planets (*Triplanetary* is set almost exclusively outside the solar system, which is governed by the Interplanetary Patrol that gives the book its title). Volume Three (where the real fun begins) reprints a previously independent serial, published in *Amazing Stories* in 1933, along with interpolated passages connecting it to the *Lensman* story, in which Arisians use their "zone of compulsion" to keep malignant Eddorians, the chief among them being Gharlane of Eddore, from realizing that their schemes for galactic domination have consistently been thwarted for millions of years.

We meet Conway Costigan, who does in Little what Kim Kinnison— who is one of the most convincingly ruthless heroes of all sf literature— does in Very Big. We meet Virgil Samms, who takes over the world for Democracy and runs it. We slingshot into the real story. Hold on. Once that story starts, it does not stop.

BOOK ONE

Dawn

1

ARISIA AND EDDORE

Two thousand million or so years ago two galaxies were colliding; or, rather, were passing through each other. A couple of hundreds of millions of years either way do not matter, since at least that much time was required for the inter-passage. At about that same time—within the same plus-or-minus ten percent margin of error, it is believed—practically all of the suns of both those galaxies became possessed of planets.

There is much evidence to support the belief that it was not merely a coincidence that so many planets came into being at about the same time as the galactic inter-passage. Another school of thought holds that it was pure coincidence; that all suns have planets as naturally and as inevitably as cats have kittens.

Be that as it may, Arisian records are clear upon the point that before the two galaxies began to coalesce, there were never more than three solar systems present in either; and usually only one. Thus, when the sun of the planet upon which their race originated grew old and cool, the Arisians were hard put to it to preserve their culture, since they had to work against time in solving the engineering problems associated with moving a planet from an older to a younger sun.

Since nothing material was destroyed when the Eddorians were forced into the next plane of existence, their historical records also have become available. Those records—folios and tapes and playable discs of platinum alloy, resistant indefinitely even to Eddore's noxious atmosphere—agree with those of the Arisians upon this point. Immediately before the Coalescence began there was one, and only one, planetary solar system in the Second Galaxy; and, until the advent of Eddore, the Second Galaxy was entirely devoid of intelligent life.

Thus for millions upon untold millions of years the two races, each the sole intelligent life of a galaxy, perhaps of an entire space-time continuum, remained completely in ignorance of each other. Both were already ancient at the time of the Coalescence. The only other respect in which the two were similar, however, was in the possession of minds of power.

Since Arisia was Earth-like in composition, atmosphere, and climate, the Arisians were at that time distinctly humanoid. The Eddorians were not. Eddore was and is large and dense; its liquid a poisonous, sludgy syrup; its atmosphere a foul and corrosive fog. Eddore was and is unique; so different from any other world of either galaxy that its very existence was inexplicable until its own records revealed the fact that it did not originate in normal space-time at all, but came to our universe from some alien and horribly different other.

As differed the planets, so differed the peoples. The Arisians went through the usual stages of savagery and barbarism on the way to Civilization. The Age of Stone. The Ages of Bronze, of Iron, of Steel, and of Electricity. Indeed, it is probable that it is because the Arisians went through these various stages that all subsequent Civilizations have done so, since the spores which burgeoned into life upon the cooling surfaces of all the planets of the commingling galaxies were Arisian, not Eddorian, in origin. Eddorian spores, while undoubtedly present, must have been so alien that they could not develop in any one of the environments, widely variant although they are, existing naturally or coming naturally into being in normal space and time.

The Arisians—especially after atomic energy freed them from physical labor—devoted themselves more and ever more intensively to the exploration of the limitless possibilities of the mind.

Even before the Coalescence, then, the Arisians had need neither of space-ships nor of telescopes. By power of mind alone they watched the lenticular aggregation of stars which was much later to be known to Tellurian astronomers as Lundmark's Nebula approach their own galaxy. They observed attentively and minutely and with high elation the occurrence of mathematical impossibility; for the chance of two galaxies ever meeting in direct, central, equatorial-plane impact and of passing completely through each other is an infinitesimal of such a high order as to be, even mathematically, practically indistinguishable from zero.

They observed the birth of numberless planets, recording minutely in their perfect memories every detail of everything that happened; in the hope that, as ages passed, either they or their descendants would be able to develop a symbology and a methodology capable of explaining the then inexplicable phenomenon. Carefree, busy, absorbedly intent, the

Arisian mentalities roamed throughout space—until one of them struck an Eddorian mind.

While any Eddorian could, if it chose, assume the form of a man, they were in no sense man-like. Nor, since the term implies a softness and a lack of organization, can they be described as being amoeboid. They were both versatile and variant. Each Eddorian changed, not only its shape, but also its texture, in accordance with the requirements of the moment. Each produced—extruded—members whenever and wherever it needed them; members uniquely appropriate to the task then in work. If hardness was indicated, the members were hard; if softness, they were soft. Small or large, rigid or flexible; jointed or tentacular— all one. Filaments or cables; fingers or feet; needles or mauls—equally simple. One thought and the body fitted the job.

They were asexual: sexless to a degree unapproached by any form of Tellurian life higher than the yeasts. They were not merely hermaphroditic, nor androgynous, nor parthenogenetic. They were completely without sex. They were also, to all intents and purposes and except for death by violence, immortal. For each Eddorian, as its mind approached the stagnation of saturation after a lifetime of millions of years, simply divided into two new-old beings. New in capacity and in zest; old in ability and in power, since each of the two "children" possessed in toto the knowledges and the memories of their one "parent."

And if it is difficult to describe in words the physical aspects of the Eddorians, it is virtually impossible to write or to draw, in any symbology of Civilization, a true picture of an Eddorian's—*any* Eddorian's—mind. They were intolerant, domineering, rapacious, insatiable, cold, callous, and brutal. They were keen, capable, persevering, analytical, and efficient. They had no trace of any of the softer emotions or sensibilities possessed by races adherent to Civilization. No Eddorian ever had anything even remotely resembling a sense of humor.

While not essentially bloodthirsty—that is, not loving bloodshed for its own sweet sake—they were no more averse to blood-letting than they were in favor of it. Any amount of killing which would or which might advance an Eddorian toward his goal was commendable; useless slaughter was frowned upon, not because it was slaughter, but because it was useless—and hence inefficient.

And, instead of the multiplicity of goals sought by the various entities of any race of Civilization, each and every Eddorian had only one. The same one: power. *Power!* P-O-W-E-R!!

Since Eddore was peopled originally by various races, perhaps as similar to each other as are the various human races of Earth, it is understandable that the early history of the planet—while it was still in its own space, that is—was one of continuous and ages-long war. And, since war always was and probably always will be linked solidly to technological advancement, the race now known simply as "The Eddorians" became technologists supreme. All other races disappeared. So did all other forms of life, however lowly, which interfered in any way with the Masters of the Planet.

Then, all racial opposition liquidated and overmastering lust as unquenched as ever, the surviving Eddorians fought among themselves: "push-button" wars employing engines of destruction against which the only possible defense was a fantastic thickness of planetary bed-rock.

Finally, unable either to kill or to enslave each other, the comparatively few survivors made a peace of sorts. Since their own space was practically barren of planetary systems, they would move their planet from space to space until they found one which so teemed with planets that each living Eddorian could become the sole Master of an ever-increasing number of worlds. This was a program very much worth while, promising as it did an outlet for even the recognizedly insatiable Eddorian craving for power. Therefore the Eddorians, for the first time in their prodigiously long history of fanatical non-cooperation, decided to pool their resources of mind and of material and to work as a group.

Union of a sort was accomplished eventually; neither peaceably nor without highly lethal friction. They knew that a democracy, by its very nature, was inefficient; hence a democratic form of government was not even considered. Any efficient government must of necessity be dictatorial. Nor were they all exactly alike or of exactly equal ability; perfect identity of any two such complex structures was in fact impossible, and any difference, however slight, was ample justification for stratification in such a society as theirs.

Thus one of them, fractionally more powerful and more ruthless than the rest, became the All-Highest—His Ultimate Supremacy—and a group of about a dozen others, only infinitesimally weaker, became his Council; a cabinet which was later to become known as the Innermost Circle. The tally of this cabinet varied somewhat from age to age; increasing by one when a member divided, decreasing by one when a jealous fellow or an envious underling managed to perpetrate a successful assassination.

And thus, at long last, the Eddorians began really to work together. There resulted, among other things, the hyper-spatial tube and the fully inertialess drive—the drive which was, millions of years later, to be given to Civilization by an Arisian operating under the name of Bergenholm. Another result, which occurred shortly after the galactic inter-passage had begun, was the eruption into normal space of the planet Eddore.

"I must now decide whether to make this space our permanent headquarters or to search farther," the All-Highest radiated harshly to his Council. "On the one hand, it will take some time for even those planets which have already formed to cool. Still more will be required for life to develop sufficiently to form a part of the empire which we have planned or to occupy our abilities to any great degree. On the other, we have already spent millions of years in surveying hundreds of millions of continua, without having found anywhere such a profusion of planets as will, in all probability, soon fill both of these galaxies. There may also be certain advantages inherent in the fact that these planets are not yet populated. As life develops, we can mold it as we please. Krongenes, what are your findings in regard to the planetary possibilities of other spaces?"

The term "Krongenes" was not, in the accepted sense, a name. Or, rather, it was more than a name. It was a key-thought, in mental shorthand; a condensation and abbreviation of the life-pattern or ego of that particular Eddorian.

"Not at all promising, Your Supremacy," Krongenes replied, promptly. "No space within reach of my instruments has more than a small fraction of the inhabitable worlds which will presently exist in this one."

"Very well. Have any of you others any valid objections to the establishment of our empire here in this space? If so, give me your thought now."

No objecting thoughts appeared, since none of the monsters then knew anything of Arisia or of the Arisians. Indeed, even if they had known, it is highly improbable that any objection would have been raised. First, because no Eddorian, from the All-Highest down, could conceive or would under any circumstances admit that any race, anywhere, had ever approached or ever would approach the Eddorians in any quality whatever; and second, because, as is routine in all dictatorships, disagreement with the All-Highest did not operate to lengthen the span of life.

"Very well. We will now confer as to . . . but hold! That thought is not one of ours! Who are you, stranger, to dare to intrude thus upon a conference of the Innermost Circle?"

"I am Enphilistor, a younger student, of the planet Arisia." This name, too, was a symbol. Nor was the young Arisian yet a Watchman, as he and so many of his fellows were so soon to become, for before Eddore's arrival Arisia had had no need of Watchmen. "I am not intruding, as you know. I have not touched any one of your minds; have not read any one of your thoughts. I have been waiting for you to notice my presence, so that we could become acquainted with each other. A surprising development, truly—we have thought for many cycles of time that we were the only highly advanced life in this universe . . .''

"Be silent, worm, in the presence of the Masters. Land your ship and surrender, and your planet will be allowed to serve us. Refuse, or even hesitate, and every individual of your race shall die."

"Worm? Masters? Land my ship?" The young Arisian's thought was pure curiosity, with no tinge of fear, dismay, or awe. "Surrender? Serve you? I seem to be receiving your thought without ambiguity, but your meaning is entirely . . ."

"Address me as 'Your Supremacy'," the All-Highest directed, coldly. "Land now or die now—this is your last warning."

"Your Supremacy? Certainly, if that is the customary form. But as to landing—and warning—and dying—surely you do not think that I am present in the flesh? And can it be possible that you are actually so aberrant as to believe that you can kill me—or even the youngest Arisian infant? What a peculiar—what an *extraordinary*—psychology!"

"Die, then, worm, if you must have it so!" the All-Highest snarled, and launched a mental bolt whose energies were calculated to slay any living thing.

Enphilistor, however, parried the vicious attack without apparent effort. His manner did not change. He did not strike back.

The Eddorian then drove in with an analyzing probe, only to be surprised again—the Arisian's thought could not be traced! And Enphilistor, while warding off the raging Eddorian with only a part of his mind, directed a quiet thought as though he were addressing someone close by his side:

"Come in, please, one or more of the Elders. There is a situation here which I am not qualified to handle."

"We, the Elders of Arisia in fusion, are here." A grave, deeply resonant pseudo-voice filled the Eddorians' minds; each perceived in three-dimensional fidelity an aged, white-bearded human face. "You of Eddore have been expected. The course of action which we must take has been determined long since. You will forget this incident completely. For cycles upon cycles of time to come no Eddorian shall know that we Arisians exist."

Even before the thought was issued the fused Elders had gone quietly and smoothly to work. The Eddorians forgot utterly the incident which had just happened. Not one of them retained in his conscious mind any inkling that Eddore did not possess the only intelligent life in space.

*   *   *

And upon distant Arisia a full meeting of minds was held.

"But why didn't you simply kill them?" Enphilistor asked. "Such action would be distasteful in the extreme, of course—almost impossible—but even I can perceive . . ." He paused, overcome by his thought.

"That which you perceive, youth, is but a very small fraction of the whole. We did not attempt to slay them because we could not have done so. Not because of squeamishness, as you intimate, but from sheer inability. The Eddorian tenacity of life is a thing far beyond your present understanding; to have attempted to kill them would have rendered it impossible to make them forget us. We must have time . . . cycles and cycles of time." The fusion broke off, pondered for minutes, then addressed the group as a whole:

"We, the Elder Thinkers, have not shared fully with you our visualization of the Cosmic All, because until the Eddorians actually appeared there was always the possibility that our findings might have been in error. Now, however, there is no doubt. The Civilization which has been pictured as developing peacefully upon all the teeming planets of two galaxies will not now of itself come into being. We of Arisia should be able to bring it eventually to full fruition, but the task will be long and difficult.

"The Eddorians' minds are of tremendous latent power. Were they to know of us now, it is practically certain that they would be able to develop powers and mechanisms by the use of which they would negate our every effort—they would hurl us out of this, our native space and time. We must have time . . . given time, we shall succeed. There shall be Lenses . . . and entities of Civilization worthy in every respect to wear them. But we of Arisia alone will never be able to conquer the Eddorians. Indeed, while this is not yet certain, the probability is exceedingly great that despite our utmost efforts at self-development our descendants will have to breed, from some people to evolve upon a planet not yet in existence, an entirely new race—a race tremendously more capable than ours—to succeed us as Guardians of Civilization."

Centuries passed. Millennia. Cosmic and geologic ages. Planets cooled to solidity and stability. Life formed and grew and developed. And as life evolved it was subjected to, and strongly if subtly affected by, the diametrically opposed forces of Arisia and Eddore.

2

THE FALL OF ATLANTIS

1. Eddore

"**M**embers of the Innermost Circle, wherever you are and whatever you may be doing, tune in!" the All-Highest broadcast. "Analysis of the data furnished by the survey just completed shows that in general the Great Plan is progressing satisfactorily. There seem to be only four planets which our delegates have not been or may not be able to control properly: Sol III, Rigel IV, Velantia III, and Palain VII. All four, you will observe, are in the other galaxy. No trouble whatever has developed in our own.

"Of these four, the first requires drastic and immediate personal attention. Its people, in the brief interval since our previous general survey, have developed nuclear energy and have fallen into a cultural pattern which does not conform in any respect to the basic principles laid down by us long since. Our deputies there, thinking erroneously that they could handle matters without reporting fully to or calling for help upon the next higher operating echelon, must be disciplined sharply. Failure, from whatever cause, can not be tolerated.

"Gharlane, as Master Number Two, you will assume control of Sol III immediately. This Circle now authorizes and instructs you to take whatever steps may prove necessary to restore order upon that planet. Examine carefully this data concerning the other three worlds which may very shortly become troublesome. Is it your thought that one or more others of this Circle should be assigned to work with you, to be sure that these untoward developments are suppressed?"

"It is not, Your Supremacy," that worthy decided, after a time of study. "Since the peoples in question are as yet of low intelligence; since one form of flesh at a time is all that will have to be energized; and since the techniques will be essentially similar; I can handle all four more efficiently alone than with the help or cooperation of others. If I read this data correctly, there will be need of only the most elementary precaution in the employment of mental force, since of the four races, only the Velantians have even a rudimentary knowledge of its uses. Right?"

"We so read the data." Surprisingly enough, the Innermost Circle agreed unanimously.

"Go, then. When finished, report in full."

"I go, All-Highest. I shall render a complete and conclusive report."

2. Arisia

"We, the Elder Thinkers in fusion, are spreading in public view, for study and full discussion, a visualization of the relationships existing and to exist between Civilization and its irreconcilable and implacable foe. Several of our younger members, particularly Eukonidor, who has just attained Watchmanship, have requested instruction in this matter. Being as yet immature, their visualizations do not show clearly why Nedanillor, Kriedigan, Drounli, and Brolenteen, either singly or in fusion, have in the past performed certain acts and have not performed certain others; or that the future actions of those Moulders of Civilization will be similarly constrained.

"This visualization, while more complex, more complete, and more detailed than the one set up by our forefathers at the time of the Coalescence, agrees with it in every essential. The five basics remain unchanged. First: the Eddorians can be overcome only by mental force. Second: the magnitude of the required force is such that its only possible generator is such an organization as the Galactic Patrol toward which we have been and are working. Third: since no Arisian or any fusion of Arisians will ever be able to spear-head that force, it was and is necessary to develop a race of mentality sufficient to perform that task. Fourth: this new race, having been instrumental in removing the menace of Eddore, will as a matter of course displace the Arisians as Guardians of Civilization. Fifth: the Eddorians must not become informed of us until such a time as it will be physically, mathematically impossible for them to construct any effective counter-devices."

"A cheerless outlook, truly," came a somber thought.

"Not so, daughter. A little reflection will show you that your present thinking is loose and turbid. When that time comes, every Arisian will be ready for the change. We know the way. We do not know to what that way leads; but the Arisian purpose in this phase of existence—this space-time continuum—will have been fulfilled and we will go eagerly and joyfully on to the next. Are there any more questions?"

There were none.

"Study this material, then, each of you, with exceeding care. It may be that some one of you, even a child, will perceive some facet of the truth which we have missed or have not examined fully; some fact or implication which may be made to operate to shorten the time of conflict or to lessen the number of budding Civilizations whose destruction seems to us at present to be sheerly unavoidable."

Hours passed. Days. No criticisms or suggestions were offered.

"We take it, then, that this visualization is the fullest and most accurate one possible for the massed intellect of Arisia to construct from the information available at the moment. The Moulders therefore, after describing briefly what they have already done, will inform us as to what they deem it necessary to do in the near future."

"We have observed, and at times have guided, the evolution of intelligent life upon many planets," the fusion began. "We have, to the best of our ability, directed the energies of these entities into the channels of Civilization; we have adhered consistently to the policy of steering as many different races as possible toward the intellectual level necessary for the effective use of the Lens, without which the proposed Galactic Patrol cannot come into being.

"For many cycles of time we have been working as individuals with the four strongest races, from one of which will be developed the people who will one day replace us as Guardians of Civilization. Blood lines have been established. We have encouraged matings which concentrate traits of strength and dissipate those of weakness. While no very great departure from the norm, either physically or mentally, will take place until after the penultimates have been allowed to meet and to mate, a definite general improvement of each race has been unavoidable.

"Thus the Eddorians have already interested themselves in our budding Civilization upon the planet Tellus, and it is inevitable that they will very shortly interfere with our work upon the other three. These four young Civilizations must be allowed to fall. It is to warn every Arisian against well-meant but inconsidered action that this conference was called. We ourselves will operate through forms of flesh of no higher intelligence than, and indistinguishable from, the natives of the planets affected. No traceable connection will exist between those forms and us. No other Arisians will operate within extreme range of any one of those four planets; they will from now on be given the same status as has been so long accorded Eddore itself. The Eddorians must not learn of us until after it is too late for them to act effectively upon that knowledge. Any chance bit of information obtained by any Eddorian must be obliterated at once. It is to guard against and to negate such accidental disclosures that our Watchmen have been trained."

"But if all of our Civilizations go down . . ." Eukonidor began to protest.

"Study will show you, youth, that the general level of mind, and hence of strength, is rising," the fused Elders interrupted. "The trend is ever upward; each peak and valley being higher than its predecessor. When the indicated level has been reached—the level at which the efficient use of the Lens will become possible—we will not only allow ourselves to become known to them; we will engage them at every point."

"One factor remains obscure." A Thinker broke the ensuing silence. "In this visualization I do not perceive anything to preclude the possibility that the Eddorians may at any time visualize us. Granted that the Elders of long ago did not merely visualize the Eddorians, but perceived them in time-space surveys; that they and subsequent Elders were able to maintain the status quo; and that the Eddorian way of thought is essentially mechanistic, rather than philosophic, in nature. There is still a possibility that the enemy may be able to deduce us by processes of logic alone. This thought is particularly disturbing to me at the present time because a rigid statistical analysis of the occurrences upon those four planets shows that they cannot possibly have been due to chance. With such an analysis as a starting point, a mind of even moderate ability could visualize us practically in toto. I assume, however, that this possibility has been taken into consideration, and suggest that the membership be informed."

"The point is well taken. The possibility exists. While the probability is very great that such an analysis will not be made until after we have declared ourselves, it is not a certainty. Immediately upon deducing our existence, however, the Eddorians would begin to build against us, upon the four planets and elsewhere. Since there is only one effective counter-structure possible, and since we Elders have long been alert to detect the first indications of that particular activity, we know that the situation remains unchanged. If it changes, we will call at once another full meeting of minds. Are there any other matters of moment? . . . If not, this conference will dissolve."

3. Atlantis

Ariponides, recently elected Faros of Atlantis for his third five-year term, stood at a window of his office atop the towering Farostery. His hands were clasped loosely behind his back. He did not really see the tremendous expanse of quiet ocean, nor the bustling harbor, nor the metropolis spread out so magnificently and so busily beneath him. He stood there, motionless, until a subtle vibration warned him that visitors were approaching his door.

"Come in, gentlemen . . . Please be seated." He sat down at one end of a table molded of transparent plastic. "Psychologist Talmonides, Statesman Cleto, Minister Philamon, Minister Marxes and Officer Artomenes, I have asked you to come here personally because I have every reason to believe that the shielding of this room is proof against eavesdroppers; a thing which can no longer be said of our supposedly private television channels. We must discuss, and if possible come to some decision concerning, the state in which our nation now finds itself.

"Each of us knows within himself exactly what he is. Of our own powers, we cannot surely know each other's inward selves. The tools and techniques of psychology, however, are potent and exact; and Talmonides, after exhaustive and rigorous examination of each one of us, has certified that no taint of disloyalty exists among us."

"Which certification is not worth a damn," the burly Officer declared. "What assurance do we have that Talmonides himself is not one of the ringleaders? Mind you, I have no reason to believe that he is not completely loyal. In fact, since he has been one of my best friends for over twenty years, I believe implicitly that he is. Nevertheless the plain fact is, Ariponides, that all the precautions you have taken, and any you can take, are and will be useless insofar as definite knowledge is concerned. The real truth is and will remain unknown."

"You are right," the Psychologist conceded. "And, such being the case, perhaps I should withdraw from the meeting."

"That wouldn't help, either." Artomenes shook his head. "Any competent plotter would be prepared for this, as for any other contingency. One of us others would be the real operator."

"And the fact that our Officer is the one who is splitting hairs so finely could be taken to indicate which one of us the real operator could be," Marxes pointed out, cuttingly.

"Gentlemen! Gentlemen!" Ariponides protested. "While absolute certainty is of course impossible to any finite mind, you all know how Talmonides was tested; you know that in his case there is no reasonable doubt. Such chance as exists, however, must be taken, for if we do not trust each other fully in this undertaking, failure is inevitable. With this word of warning I will get on with my report.

"This world-wide frenzy of unrest followed closely upon the controlled liberation of atomic energy and may be—probably is—traceable to it. It is in no part due to imperialistic aims or acts on the part of Atlantis. This fact cannot be stressed too strongly. We never have been and are not now interested in Empire. It is true that the other nations began as Atlantean colonies, but no attempt was ever made to hold any one of them in colonial status against the wish of its electorate. All nations were and are sister states. We gain or lose together. Atlantis, the parent, was and is a clearing-house, a co-ordinator of effort, but has never claimed or sought authority to rule; all decisions being based upon free debate and free and secret ballot.

"But now! Parties and factions everywhere, even in old Atlantis. Every nation is torn by internal dissensions and strife. Nor is this all. Uighar as a nation is insensately jealous of the Islands of the South, who in turn are jealous of Maya. Maya of Bantu, Bantu of Ekopt, Ekopt of Norheim, and Norheim of Uighar. A vicious circle, worsened by other jealousies and hatreds intercrossing everywhere. Each fears that some other is about to try to seize control of the entire world; and there seems to be spreading rapidly the utterly baseless belief that Atlantis itself is about to reduce all other nations of Earth to vassalage.

"This is a bald statement of the present condition of the world as I see it. Since I can see no other course possible within the constituted framework of our democratic government, I recommend that we continue our present activities, such as the international treaties and agreements upon which we are now at work, intensifying our effort wherever possible. We will now hear from Statesman Cleto."

"You have outlined the situation clearly enough, Faros. My thought, however, is that the principal cause of the trouble is the coming into being of this multiplicity of political parties, particularly those composed principally of crackpots and extremists. The connection with atomic energy is clear: since the atomic bomb gives a small group of people the power to destroy the world, they reason that it thereby confers upon them the authority to dictate to the world. My recommendation is merely a special case of yours; that every effort be made to influence the electorates of Norheim and of Uighar into supporting an effective international control of atomic energy."

"You have your data tabulated in symbolics?" asked Talmonides, from his seat at the keyboard of a calculating machine.

"Yes. Here they are."

"Thanks."

"Minister Philamon," the Faros announced.

"As I see it—as any intelligent man should be able to see it—the principal contribution of atomic energy to this world-wide chaos was the complete demoralization of labor," the gray-haired Minister of Trade stated, flatly. "Output per man-hour should have gone up at least twenty percent, in which case prices would automatically have come down. Instead, short-sighted guilds imposed drastic curbs on production, and now seem to be surprised that as production falls and hourly wages rise, prices also rise and real income drops. Only one course is possible, gentlemen; labor *must* be made to listen to reason. This feather-bedding, this protected loafing, this . . ."

"I protest!" Marxes, Minister of Work, leaped to his feet. "The blame lies squarely with the capitalists. Their greed, their rapacity, their exploitation of . . ."

"One moment, please!" Ariponides rapped the table sharply. "It is highly significant of the deplorable condition of the times that two Ministers of State should speak as you two have just spoken. I take it that neither of you has anything new to contribute to this symposium?"

Both claimed the floor, but both were refused it by vote.

"Hand your tabulated data to Talmonides," the Faros directed. "Officer Artomenes?"

"You, our Faros, have more than intimated that our defense program, for which I am primarily responsible, has been largely to blame for what has happened," the grizzled warrior began. "In part, perhaps it was—one must be blind indeed not to see the connection, and biased indeed not to admit it. But what should I have done, knowing that there is no practical defense against the atomic bomb? Every nation has them, and is manufacturing more and more. Every nation is infested with the agents of every other. Should I have tried to keep Atlantis toothless in a world bristling with fangs? And could I—or anyone else—have succeeded in doing so?"

"Probably not. No criticism was intended; we must deal with the situation as it actually exists. Your recommendations, please?"

"I have thought this thing over day and night, and can see no solution which can be made acceptable to our—or to any real—democracy. Nevertheless, I have one recommendation to make. We all know that Norheim and Uighar are the sore spots—particularly Norheim. We have more bombs as of now than both of them together. We know that Uighar's super-sonic jobs are ready. We don't know exactly what Norheim has, since they cut my Intelligence line a while back, but I'm sending over another operative—my best man, too—tonight. If he finds out that we have enough advantage in speed, and I'm pretty sure that we have,

I say hit both Norheim and Uighar right then, while we can, before they hit us. And hit them hard—pulverize them. Then set up a world government strong enough to knock out any nation—including Atlantis—that will not cooperate with it. This course of action is flagrantly against all international law and all the principles of democracy, I know; and even it might not work. It is, however, as far as I can see, the only course which *can* work."

"You—we all—perceive its weaknesses." The Faros thought for minutes. "You cannot be sure that your Intelligence has located all of the danger points, and many of them must be so far underground as to be safe from even our heaviest missiles. We all, including you, believe that the Psychologist is right in holding that the reaction of the other nations to such action would be both unfavorable and violent. Your report, please, Talmonides."

"I have already put my data into the integrator." The Psychologist punched a button and the mechanism began to whir and to click. "I have only one new fact of any importance; the name of one of the higher-ups and its corollary implication that there may be some degree of cooperation between Norheim and Uighar . . ."

He broke off as the machine stopped clicking and ejected its report.

"Look at that graph—up ten points in seven days!" Talmonides pointed a finger. "The situation is deteriorating faster and faster. The conclusion is unavoidable—you can see yourselves that this summation line is fast approaching unity—that the outbreaks will become uncontrollable in approximately eight days. With one slight exception—here—you will notice that the lines of organization and purpose are as random as ever. In spite of this conclusive integration I would be tempted to believe that this seeming lack of coherence was due to insufficient data—that back of this whole movement there is a carefully-set-up and completely-integrated plan—except for the fact that the factions and the nations are so evenly matched. But the data are sufficient. It is shown conclusively that no one of the other nations can possibly win, even by totally destroying Atlantis. They would merely destroy each other and our entire Civilization. According to this forecast, in arriving at which the data furnished by our Officer were prime determinants, that will surely be the outcome unless remedial measures be taken at once. You are of course sure of your facts, Artomenes?"

"I am sure. But you said you had a name, and that it indicated a Norheim-Uighar hookup. What is that name?"

"An old friend of yours . . ."

"Lo Sung!" The words as spoken were a curse of fury.

"None other. And, unfortunately, there is as yet no course of action indicated which is at all promising of success."

"Use mine, then!" Artomenes jumped up and banged the table with his fist. "Let me send two flights of rockets over right now that will blow Uigharstoy and Norgrad into radioactive dust and make a thousand square miles around each of them uninhabitable for ten thousand years! If that's the only way they can learn anything, let them learn!"

"Sit down, Officer," Ariponides directed, quietly. "That course, as you have already pointed out, is indefensible. It violates every Prime Basic of our Civilization. Moreover, it would be entirely futile, since this resultant makes it clear that every nation on Earth would be destroyed within the day."

"What, then?" Artomenes demanded, bitterly. "Sit still here and let them annihilate us?"

"Not necessarily. It is to formulate plans that we are here. Talmonides will by now have decided, upon the basis of our pooled knowledge, what must be done."

"The outlook is not good: not good at all," the Psychologist announced, gloomily. "The only course of action which carries any promise whatever of success—and its probability is only point one eight—is the one recommended by the Faros, modified slightly to include Artomenes' suggestion of sending his best operative on the indicated mission. For highest morale, by the way, the Faros should also interview this agent before he sets out. Ordinarily I would not advocate a course of action having so little likelihood of success; but since it is simply a continuation and intensification of what we are already doing, I do not see how we can adopt any other."

"Are we agreed?" Ariponides asked, after a short silence.

They were agreed. Four of the conferees filed out and a brisk young man strode in. Although he did not look at the Faros his eyes asked questions.

"Reporting for orders, sir." He saluted the Officer punctiliously.

"At ease, sir." Artomenes returned the salute. "You were called here for a word from the Faros. Sir, I present Captain Phryges."

"Not orders, son . . . no." Ariponides' right hand rested in greeting upon the captain's left shoulder, wise old eyes probed deeply into gold-flecked, tawny eyes of youth; the Faros saw, without really noticing, a flaming thatch of red-bronze-auburn hair. "I asked you here to wish you well; not only for myself, but for all our nation and perhaps for our entire race. While everything in my being rebels against an unprovoked and unannounced assault, we may be compelled to choose between our Officer's plan of campaign and the destruction of Civilization. Since you already know the vital importance of your mission, I need not enlarge upon it. But I want you to know fully, Captain Phryges, that all Atlantis flies with you this night."

"Th . . . thank you, sir." Phryges gulped twice to steady his voice. "I'll do my best, sir."

And later, in a wingless craft flying toward the airfield, young Phryges broke a long silence. "So *that* is the Faros . . . I like him, Officer . . . I have never seen him close up before . . . there's something about him . . . He isn't like my father, much, but it seems as though I have known him for a thousand years!"

"Hm . . . m . . . m. Peculiar. You two are a lot alike, at that, even though you don't look anything like each other. . . . Can't put a finger on exactly what it is, but it's there." Although Artomenes nor any other of his time could place it, the resemblance was indeed there. It was in and back of the eyes; it was the "look of eagles" which was long later to become associated with the wearers of Arisia's Lens. "But here we are, and your ship's ready. Luck, son."

"Thanks, sir. But one more thing. If it should—if I don't get back—will you see that my wife and the baby are . . . ?"

"I will, son. They will leave for North Maya tomorrow morning. They will live, whether you and I do or not. Anything else?"

"No, sir. Thanks. Goodbye."

The ship was a tremendous flying wing. A standard commercial job. Empty—passengers, even crewmen, were never subjected to the brutal accelerations regularly used by unmanned carriers. Phryges scanned the panel. Tiny motors were pulling tapes through the controllers. Every light showed green. Everything was set. Donning a water-proof coverall, he slid through a flexible valve into his acceleration-tank and waited.

A siren yelled briefly. Black night turned blinding white as the harnessed energies of the atom were released. For five and six-tenths seconds the sharp, hard, beryllium-bronze leading edge of the back-sweeping V sliced its way through ever-thinning air.

The vessel seemed to pause momentarily; paused and bucked viciously. She shuddered and shivered, tried to tear herself into shreds and chunks; but Phryges in his tank was unconcerned. Earlier, weaker ships went to pieces against the solid-seeming wall of atmospheric incompressibility at the velocity of sound; but this one was built solidly enough, and powered to hit that wall hard enough, to go through unharmed.

The hellish vibration ceased; the fantastic violence of the drive subsided to a mere shove; Phryges knew that the vessel had leveled off at its cruising speed of two thousand miles per hour. He emerged, spilling the least possible amount of water upon the polished steel floor. He took off his coverall and stuffed it back through the valve into the tank. He mopped and polished the floor with towels, which likewise went into the tank.

He drew on a pair of soft gloves and, by manual control, jettisoned the acceleration tank and all the apparatus which had made that unloading possible. This junk would fall into the ocean; would sink; would never be found. He examined the compartment and the hatch minutely. No scratches, no scars, no mars; no tell-tale marks or prints of any kind. Let the Norskies search. So far, so good.

Back toward the trailing edge then, to a small escape-hatch beside which was fastened a dull black ball. The anchoring devices went out first. He gasped as the air rushed out into near-vacuum, but he had been trained to take sudden and violent fluctuations in pressure. He rolled the ball out upon the hatch, where he opened it; two hinged hemispheres, each heavily padded with molded composition resembling sponge rubber. It seemed incredible that a man as big as Phryges, especially when wearing a parachute, could be crammed into a space so small; but that lining had been molded to fit.

This ball *had* to be small. The ship, even though it was on a regularly-scheduled commercial flight, would be scanned intensively and continuously from the moment of entering Norheiman radar range. Since the ball would be invisible on any radar screen, no suspicion would be aroused; particularly since—as far as Atlantean Intelligence had been able to discover—the Norheimans had not yet succeeded in perfecting any device by the use of which a living man could bail out of a supersonic plane.

Phryges waited—and waited—until the second hand of his watch marked the arrival of zero time. He curled up into one half of the ball; the other half closed over him and locked. The hatch opened. Ball and closely-prisoned man plummeted downward; slowing abruptly, with a horrible deceleration, to terminal velocity. Had the air been any trifle thicker the Atlantean captain would have died then and there; but that, too, had been computed accurately and Phryges lived.

And as the ball bulleted downward on a screaming slant, it *shrank!*

This, too, the Atlanteans hoped, was new—a synthetic which air-friction would erode away, molecule by molecule, so rapidly that no perceptible fragment of it would reach ground.

The casing disappeared, and the yieldingly porous lining. And Phryges, still at an altitude of over thirty thousand feet, kicked away the remaining fragments of his cocoon and, by judicious planing, turned himself so that he could see the ground, now dimly visible in the first dull gray of dawn. There was the highway, paralleling his line of flight; he wouldn't miss it more than a hundred yards.

He fought down an almost overwhelming urge to pull his rip-cord too soon. He had to wait—wait until the last possible second—because parachutes were big and Norheiman radar practically swept the ground. Low enough at last, he pulled the ring. Z-r-r-e-e-k—WHAP! The chute banged open; his harness tightened with a savage jerk, mere seconds before his hard-sprung knees took the shock of landing.

That was close—too close! He was white and shaking, but unhurt, as he gathered in the billowing, fighting sheet and rolled it, together with his harness, into a wad. He broke open a tiny ampoule, and as the drops of liquid touched it the stout fabric began to disappear. It did not burn; it simply disintegrated and vanished. In less than a minute there remained only a few steel snaps and rings, which the Atlantean buried under a meticulously-replaced circle of sod.

He was still on schedule. In less than three minutes the signal would be on the air and he would know where he was—unless the Norsks had succeeded in finding and eliminating the whole Atlantean under-cover group. He pressed a stud on a small instrument; held it down. A line burned green across the dial—flared red—vanished.

"Damn!" he breathed, explosively. The strength of the signal told him that he was within a mile or so of the hide-out—first-class computation—but the red flash warned him to keep away. Kinnexa—*it had better be Kinnexa!*—would come to him.

How? By air? Along the road? Through the woods on foot? He had no way of knowing—talking, even on a tight beam, was out of the question. He made his way to the highway and crouched behind a tree. Here she could come at him by any route of the three. Again he waited, pressing infrequently a stud of his sender.

A long, low-slung ground-car swung around the curve and Phryges' binoculars were at his eyes. It *was* Kinnexa—or a duplicate. At the thought he dropped the glasses and pulled his guns—blaster in right hand, air-pistol in left. But no, that wouldn't do. She'd be suspicious, too—she'd have to be—and that car probably mounted heavy stuff. If he stepped out ready for business she'd fry him, and quick. Maybe not—she might have protection—but he couldn't take the chance.

The car slowed; stopped. The girl got out, examined a front tire, straightened up, and looked down the road, straight at Phryges' hiding place. This time the binoculars brought her up to little more than arm's length. Tall, blonde, beautifully built; the slightly crooked left eyebrow. The thread-line of gold betraying a one-tooth bridge and the tiny scar on her upper lip, for both of which he had been responsible—she always did insist on playing cops-and-robbers with boys older and bigger than herself—it *was* Kinnexa! Not even Norheim's science could imitate so perfectly every personalizing characteristic of a girl he had known ever since she was knee-high to a duck!

The girl slid back into her seat and the heavy car began to move. Open-handed, Phryges stepped out into its way. The car stopped.

"Turn around. Back up to me, hands behind you," she directed, crisply.

The man, although surprised, obeyed. Not until he felt a finger exploring the short hair at the back of his neck did he realize what she was seeking—the almost imperceptible scar marking the place where she bit him when she was seven years old!

"Oh, Fry! It *is* you! *Really* you! Thank the gods! I've been ashamed of that all my life, but now . . ."

He whirled and caught her as she slumped, but she did not quite faint.

"Quick! Get in . . . drive on . . . not too fast!" she cautioned, sharply, as the tires began to scream. "The speed limit along here is seventy, and we can't be picked up."

"Easy it is, Kinny. But *give!* What's the score? Where's Kolanides? Or rather, what happened to him?"

"Dead. So are the others, I think. They put him on a psycho-bench and turned him inside out."

"But the blocks?"

"Didn't hold—over here they add such trimmings as skinning and salt to the regular psycho routine. But none of them knew anything about me, nor about how their reports were picked up, or I'd have been dead, too. But it doesn't make any difference, Fry—we're just one week too late."

"What do you mean, too late? Speed it up!" His tone was rough, but the hand he placed on her arm was gentleness itself.

"I'm telling you as fast as I can. I picked up his last report day before yesterday. They have missiles just as big and just as fast as ours— maybe more so—and they are going to fire one at Atlantis tonight at exactly seven o'clock."

"Tonight! Holy gods!" The man's mind raced.

"Yes." Kinnexa's voice was low, uninflected. "And there was nothing in the world that I could do about it. If I approached any one of our places, or tried to use a beam strong enough to reach anywhere, I would simply have got picked up, too. I've thought and thought, but could figure out only one thing that might possibly be of any use, and I couldn't do that alone. But two of us, perhaps . . ."

"Go on. Brief me. Nobody ever accused you of not having a brain, and you know this whole country like the palm of your hand."

"Steal a ship. Be over the ramp at exactly Seven Pay Emma. When the lid opens, go into a full-power dive, beam Artomenes—if I had a second before they blanketed my wave—and meet their rocket head-on in their own launching-tube."

This was stark stuff, but so tense was the moment and so highly keyed up were the two that neither of them saw anything out of the ordinary in it.

"Not bad, if we can't figure out anything better. The joker being, of course, that you didn't see how you could steal a ship?"

"Exactly. I can't carry blasters. No woman in Norheim is wearing a coat or a cloak now, so I can't either. And just look at this dress! Do you see any place where I could hide even one?"

He looked, appreciatively, and she had the grace to blush.

"Can't say that I do," he admitted. "But I'd rather have one of our own ships, if we could make the approach. Could both of us make it, do you suppose?"

"Not a chance. They'd keep at least one man inside all the time. Even if we killed everybody outside, the ship would take off before we could get close enough to open the port with the outside controls."

"Probably. Go on. But first, are you sure that you're in the clear?"

"Positive." She grinned mirthlessly. "The fact that I am still alive is conclusive evidence that they didn't find out anything about me. But I don't want you to work on that idea if you can think of a better one. I've got passports and so on for you to be anything you want to be, from a tube-man up to an Ekoptian banker. Ditto for me, and for us both, as Mr. and Mrs."

"Smart girl." He thought for minutes, then shook his head. "No possible way out that I can see. The sneak-boat isn't due for a week, and from what you've said it probably won't get here. But you might make it, at that. I'll drop you somewhere . . ."

"You will not," she interrupted, quietly but definitely. "Which would *you* rather—go out in a blast like that one will be, beside a good Atlantean, or, after deserting him, be psychoed, skinned, salted, and—still alive—drawn and quartered?"

"Together, then, all the way," he assented. "Man and wife. Tourists—newlyweds—from some town not too far away. Pretty well fixed, to match what we're riding in. Can do?"

"Very simple." She opened a compartment and selected one of a stack of documents. "I can fix this one up in ten minutes. We'll have to dispose of the rest of these, and a lot of other stuff, too. And you had better get out of that leather and into a suit that matches this passport photo.''

"Right. Straight road for miles, and nothing in sight either way. Give me the suit and I'll change now. Keep on going or stop?''

"Better stop, I think,'' the girl decided. "Quicker, and we'll have to find a place to hide or bury this evidence.''

While the man changed clothes, Kinnexa collected the contraband, wrapping it up in the discarded jacket. She looked up just as Phryges was adjusting his coat. She glanced at his armpits, then stared.

"Where are your blasters?'' she demanded. "They ought to show, at least a little, and even I can't see a sign of them.''

He showed her.

"But they're so tiny! I never saw blasters like that!''

"I've got a blaster, but it's in the tail pocket. These aren't. They're air-guns. Poisoned needles. Not worth a damn beyond a hundred feet, but deadly close up. One touch anywhere and the guy dies right then. Two seconds max.''

"Nice!'' She was no shrinking violet, this young Atlantean spy. "You have spares, of course, and I can hide two of them easily enough in leg-holsters. Gimme, and show me how they work.''

"Standard controls, pretty much like blasters. Like so.'' He demonstrated, and as he drove sedately down the highway the girl sewed industriously.

The day wore on, nor was it uneventful. One incident, in fact—the detailing of which would serve no useful purpose here—was of such a nature that at its end:

"Better pin-point me, don't you think, on that ramp?'' Phryges asked, quietly. "Just in case you get scragged in one of these brawls and I don't?''

"Oh! Of course! Forgive me, Fry—it slipped my mind completely that you didn't know where it was. Area six; pin-point four seven three dash six oh five.''

"Got it.'' He repeated the figures.

But neither of the Atlanteans was "scragged,'' and at six P.M. an allegedly honeymooning couple parked their big roadster in the garage at Norgrad Field and went through the gates. Their papers, tickets included, were in perfect order; they were as inconspicuous and as undemonstrative as newlyweds are wont to be. No more so, and no less.

Strolling idly, gazing eagerly at each new thing, they made their circuitous way toward a certain small hangar. As the girl had said, this field boasted hundreds of super-sonic fighters, so many that servicing was a round-the-clock routine. In that hangar was a sharp-nosed, stubby-V'd flyer, one of Norheim's fastest. It was serviced and ready.

It was too much to hope, of course, that the visitors could actually get into the building unchallenged. Nor did they.

"Back, you!" A guard waved them away. "Get back to the Concourse, where you belong—no visitors allowed out here!"

F-f-t! F-f t! Phryges' air-guns broke into soft but deadly coughing. Kinnexa whirled—hands flashing down, skirt flying up—and ran. Guards tried to head her off; tried to bring their own weapons to bear. Tried—failed—died.

Phryges, too, ran; ran backward. His blaster was out now and flaming, for no living enemy remained within needle range. A rifle bullet w-h-i-n-g-e-d past his head, making him duck involuntarily and uselessly. Rifles were bad; but their hazard, too, had been considered and had been accepted.

Kinnexa reached the fighter's port, opened it, sprang in. He jumped. She fell against him. He tossed her clear, slammed and dogged the door. He looked at her then, and swore bitterly. A small, round hole marred the bridge of her nose: the back of her head was gone.

He leaped to the controls and the fleet little ship screamed skyward. He cut in transmitter and receiver, keyed and twiddled briefly. No soap. He had been afraid of that. They were already blanketing every frequency he could employ; using power through which he could not drive even a tight beam a hundred miles.

But he could still crash that missile in its tube. Or—could he? He was not afraid of other Norheiman fighters; he had a long lead and he rode one of their very fastest. But since they were already so suspicious, wouldn't they launch the bomb *before* seven o'clock? He tried vainly to coax another knot out of his wide-open engines.

With all his speed, he neared the pin-point just in time to see a trail of super-heated vapor extending up into and disappearing beyond the stratosphere. He nosed his flyer upward, locked the missile into his sights, and leveled off. Although his ship did not have the giant rocket's acceleration, he could catch it before it got to Atlantis, since he did not need its altitude and since most of its journey would be made without power. What he could do about it after he caught it he did not know, but he'd do *something*.

He caught it; and, by a feat of piloting to be appreciated only by those who have handled planes at super-sonic speeds, he matched its course and velocity. Then, from a distance of barely a hundred feet, he poured his heaviest shells into the missile's war-head. He *couldn't* be missing! It was worse than shooting sitting ducks—it was like dynamiting fish in a bucket! Nevertheless, nothing happened. The thing wasn't fuzed for impact, then, but for time; and the activating mechanism would be shell- and shock-proof.

But there was still a way. He didn't need to call Artomenes now, even if he could get through the interference which the fast-approaching pursuers were still sending out. Atlantean observers would have lined this stuff up long since; the Officer would know exactly what was going on.

Driving ahead and downward, at maximum power, Phryges swung his ship slowly into a right-angle collision course. The fighter's needle nose struck the war-head within a foot of the Atlantean's point of aim, and as he died Phryges knew that he had accomplished his mission. Norheim's missile would not strike Atlantis, but would fall at least ten miles short, and the water there was very deep. Very, *very* deep. Atlantis would not be harmed.

It might have been better, however, if Phryges had died with Kinnexa on Norgrad Field; in which case the continent would probably have endured. As it was, while that one missile did not reach the city, its frightful atomic charge exploded under six hundred fathoms of water, ten scant miles from Atlantis' harbor, and very close to an ancient geological fault.

Artomenes, as Phryges had surmised, had had time in which to act, and he knew much more than Phryges did about what was coming toward Atlantis. Too late, he knew that not one missile, but seven, had been launched from Norheim, and at least five from Uighar. The retaliatory rockets which were to wipe out Norgrad, Uigharstoy, and thousands of square miles of environs were on their way long before either bomb or earthquake destroyed all of the Atlantean launching ramps.

But when equilibrium was at last restored, the ocean rolled serenely where a minor continent had been.

3

THE FALL OF ROME

1. Eddore

Like two high executives of a Tellurian corporation discussing business affairs during a chance meeting at one of their clubs, Eddore's All Highest and Gharlane, his second in command, were having the Eddorian equivalent of an after-business-hours chat.

"You did a nice job on Tellus," the All-Highest commended. "On the other three, too, of course, but Tellus was so far and away the worst of the lot that the excellence of the work stands out. When the Atlantean nations destroyed each other so thoroughly I thought that this thing called 'democracy' was done away with forever, but it seems to be mighty hard to kill. However, I take it that you have this Rome situation entirely under control?"

"Definitely. Mithradates of Pontus was mine. So were both Sulla and Marius. Through them and others I killed practically all of the brains and ability of Rome, and reduced that so-called 'democracy' to a howling, aimless mob. My Nero will end it. Rome will go on by momentum—outwardly, will even appear to grow—for a few generations, but what Nero will do can never be undone."

"Good. A difficult task, truly."

"Not difficult, exactly . . . but it's so damned *steady*." Gharlane's thought was bitter. "But that's the hell of working with such short-lived races. Since each creature lives only a minute or so, they change so fast that a man can't take his mind off of them for a second. I've been wanting to take a little vacation trip back to our old time-space, but it doesn't look as though I'll be able to do it until after they get some age and settle down.''

"That won't be too long. Life-spans lengthen, you know, as races approach their norms."

"Yes. But none of the others is having half the trouble that I am. Most of them, in fact, have things coming along just about the way they want them. My four planets are raising more hell than all the rest of both galaxies put together, and I know that it isn't me—next to you, I'm the most efficient operator we've got. What I'm wondering about is why I happen to be the goat."

"Precisely because you *are* our most efficient operator." If an Eddorian can be said to smile, the All-Highest smiled. "You know, as well as I do, the findings of the Integrator."

"Yes, but I am wondering more and more as to whether to believe them unreservedly or not. Spores from an extinct life-form—suitable environments—operation of the laws of chance—Tommyrot! I am beginning to suspect that chance is being strained beyond its elastic limit, for my particular benefit, and as soon as I can find out who is doing that straining there will be one empty place in the Innermost Circle.''

"Have a care, Gharlane!" All levity, all casualness disappeared. "Whom do you suspect? Whom do you accuse?''

"Nobody, as yet. The true angle never occurred to me until just now, while I have been discussing the thing with you. Nor shall I either suspect or accuse, ever. I shall determine, then I shall act."

"In defiance of *me? Of my* orders?" the All-Highest demanded, his short temper flaring.

"Say, rather, in support," the lieutenant shot back, unabashed. "If some one is working on me through my job, what position are you probably already in, without knowing it? Assume that I am right, that these four planets of mine got the way they are because of monkey business inside the Circle. Who would be next? And how sure are you that there isn't something similar, but not so far advanced, already aimed at you? It seems to me that serious thought is in order."

"Perhaps so . . . You may be right . . . There have been a few non-conformable items. Taken separately, they did not seem to be of any importance; but together, and considered in this new light . . ."

Thus was borne out the conclusion of the Arisian Elders that the Eddorians would not at that time deduce Arisia; and thus Eddore lost its chance to begin in time the forging of a weapon with which to oppose effectively Arisia's—Civilization's—Galactic Patrol, so soon to come into being.

If either of the two had been less suspicious, less jealous, less arrogant and domineering—in other words, had not been Eddorians—this History of Civilization might never have been written; or written very differently and by another hand.

Both were, however, Eddorians.

2. Arisia

In the brief interval between the fall of Atlantis and the rise of Rome to the summit of her power, Eukonidor of Arisia had aged scarcely at all. He was still a youth. He was, and would be for many centuries to come, a Watchman. Although his mind was powerful enough to understand the Elders' visualization of the course of Civilization—in fact, he had already made significant progress in his own visualization of the Cosmic All—he was not sufficiently mature to contemplate unmoved the events which, according to all Arisian visualizations, were bound to occur.

"Your feeling is but natural, Eukonidor." Drounli, the Moulder principally concerned with the planet Tellus, meshed his mind smoothly with that of the young Watchman. "We do not enjoy it ourselves, as you know. It is, however, *necessary*. In no other way can the ultimate triumph of Civilization be assured."

"But can nothing be done to alleviate . . . ?" Eukonidor paused.

Drounli waited. "Have you any suggestions to offer?"

"None," the younger Arisian confessed. "But I thought . . . you, or the Elders, so much older and stronger . . . could . . ."

"We can not. Rome will fall. It must be allowed to fall."

"It will be Nero, then? And we can do nothing?"

"Nero. We can do little enough. Our forms of flesh—Petronius, Acte, and the others—will do whatever they can; but their powers will be exactly the same as those of other human beings of their time. They must be and will be constrained, since any show of unusual powers, either mental or physical, would be detected instantly and would be far too revealing. On the other hand, Nero—that is, Gharlane of Eddore—will be operating much more freely."

"Very much so. Practically unhampered, except in purely physical matters. But, if nothing can be done to stop it . . . If Nero must be allowed to sow his seeds of ruin . . ."

And upon that cheerless note the conference ended.

3. Rome

"But what have you, Livius, or any of us, for that matter, got to live for?" demanded Patroclus the gladiator of his cell-mate. "We are well fed, well kept, well exercised; like horses. But, like horses, we are lower than slaves. Slaves have some freedom of action; most of us have none. We fight—fight whoever or whatever our cursed owners send us against. Those of us who live fight again; but the end is certain and comes soon. I had a wife and children once. So did you. Is there any chance, however slight, that either of us will ever know them again; or learn even whether they live or die? None. At this price, is your life worth living? Mine is not."

Livius the Bithynian, who had been staring out past the bars of the cubicle and over the smooth sand of the arena toward Nero's garlanded and purple-bannered throne, turned and studied his fellow gladiator from toe to crown. The heavily-muscled legs, the narrow waist, the sharply-tapering torso, the enormous shoulders. The leonine head, surmounted by an unkempt shock of red-bronze-auburn hair. And, lastly, the eyes—gold-flecked, tawny eyes—hard and cold now with a ferocity and a purpose not to be concealed.

"I have been more or less expecting something of this sort," Livius said then, quietly. "Nothing overt—you have builded well, Patroclus—but to one who knows gladiators as I know them there has been something in the wind for weeks past. I take it that someone swore his life for me and that I should not ask who that friend might be."

"One did. You should not."

"So be it. To my unknown sponsor, then, and to the gods, I give thanks, for I am wholly with you. Not that I have any hope. Although your tribe breeds men—from your build and hair and eyes you descend from Spartacus himself—you know that even he did not succeed. Things now are worse, infinitely worse, than they were in his day. No one who has ever plotted against Nero has had any measure of success; not even his scheming slut of a mother. All have died, in what fashions you know. Nero is vile, the basest of the base. Nevertheless, his spies are the most efficient that the world has ever known. In spite of that, I feel as you do. If I can take with me two or three of the Praetorians, I die content. But by your look, your plan is not what I thought, to storm vainly Nero's podium yonder. Have you, by any chance, some trace of hope of success?"

"More than a trace; much more." The Thracian's teeth bared in a wolfish grin. "His spies are, as you say, very good. But, this time, so are we. Just as hard and just as ruthless. Many of his spies among us have died; most, if not all, of the rest are known. They, too, shall die. Glatius, for instance. Once in a while, by the luck of the gods, a man kills a better man than he is; but Glatius has done it six times in a row, without getting a scratch. But the next time he fights, in spite of Nero's protection, Glatius dies. Word has gone out, and there are gladiators' tricks that Nero never heard of."

"Quite true. One question, and I too may begin to hope. This is not the first time that gladiators have plotted against Ahenobarbus. Before the plotters could accomplish anything, however, they found themselves matched against each other and the signal was always for death, never for mercy. Has this . . . ?" Livius paused.

"It has not. It is that which gives me the hope I have. Nor are we gladiators alone in this. We have powerful friends at court; one of whom has for days been carrying a knife sharpened especially to slip between Nero's ribs. That he still carries that knife and that we still live are proofs enough for me that Ahenobarbus, the matricide and incendiary, has no suspicion whatever of what is going on."

(At this point Nero on his throne burst into a roar of laughter, his gross body shaking with a merriment which Petronius and Tigellinus ascribed to the death-throes of a Christian woman in the arena.)

"Is there any small thing which I should be told in order to be of greatest use?" Livius asked.

"Several. The prisons and the pits are so crowded with Christians that they die and stink, and a pestilence threatens. To mend matters, some scores of hundreds of them are to be crucified here tomorrow."

"Why not? Everyone knows that they are poisoners of wells and murderers of children, and practitioners of magic. Wizards and witches."

"True enough." Patroclus shrugged his massive shoulders. "But to get on, tomorrow night, at full dark, the remaining hundreds who have not been crucified are to be—have you ever seen sarmentitii and semaxii?"

"Once only. A gorgeous spectacle, truly, almost as thrilling as to feel a man die on your sword. Men and women, wrapped in oil-soaked garments smeared with pitch and chained to posts, make splendid torches indeed. You mean, then, that . . . ?"

"Aye. In Caesar's own garden. When the light is brightest Nero will ride in parade. When his chariot passes the tenth torch our ally swings his knife. The Praetorians will rush around, but there will be a few moments of confusion during which we will go into action and the guards will die. At the same time others of our party will take the palace and kill every man, woman, and child adherent to Nero."

"Very nice—in theory." The Bithynian was frankly skeptical. "But just how are we going to get there? A few gladiators—such champions as Patroclus of Thrace—are at times allowed to do pretty much as they please in their free time, and hence could possibly be on hand to take part in such a brawl, but most of us will be under lock and guard."

"That too, has been arranged. Our allies near the throne and certain other nobles and citizens of Rome, who have been winning large sums by our victories, have prevailed upon our masters to give a grand banquet to *all* gladiators tomorrow night, immediately following the mass crucifixion. It is going to be held in the Claudian Grove, just across from Caesar's Gardens."

"Ah!" Livius breathed deep; his eyes flashed. "By Baal and Bacchus! By the round, high breasts of Isis! For the first time in years I begin to live! Our masters die first, then and there . . . but hold—weapons?"

"Will be provided. Bystanders will have them, and armor and shields, under their cloaks. Our owners first, yes; and then the Praetorians. But note, Livius, that Tigellinus, the Commander of the Guard, is mine—mine alone. I, personally, am going to cut his heart out."

"Granted. I heard that he had your wife for a time. But you seem quite confident that you will still be alive tomorrow night. By Baal and Ishtar, I wish I could feel so! With something to live for at last, I can feel my guts turning to water—I can hear Charon's oars. Like as not, now, some toe-dancing stripling of a retiarius will entangle me in his net this very afternoon, and no mercy signal has been or will be given this day. Such is the crowd's temper, from Caesar down, that even you will get 'Pollice verso' if you fall."

"True enough. But you had better get over that feeling, if you want to live. As for me, I'm safe enough. I have made a vow to Jupiter, and he who has protected me so long will not desert me now. Any man or any thing who faces me during these games, dies."

"I hope so, sin . . . but listen! The horns . . . and someone is coming!"

The door behind them swung open. A lanista, or master of gladiators, laden with arms and armor, entered. The door swung to and was locked from the outside. The visitor was obviously excited, but stared wordlessly at Patroclus for seconds.

"Well, Iron-heart," he burst out finally, "aren't you even curious about what you have got to do today?"

"Not particularly," Patroclus replied, indifferently. "Except to dress to fit. Why? Something special?"

"*Extra* special. The sensation of the year. Fermius himself. Unlimited. Free choice of weapons and armor."

"Fermius!" Livius exclaimed. "Fermius the Gaul? May Athene cover you with her shield!"

"You can say that for me, too," the lanista agreed, callously. "Before I knew who was entered, like a fool, I bet a hundred sesterces on Patroclus here, at odds of only one to two, against the field. But listen, Bronze-head. If you get the best of Fermius, I'll give you a full third of my winnings."

"Thanks. You'll collect. A good man, Fermius, and smart. I've heard a lot about him, but never saw him work. He has seen me, which isn't so good. Both heavy and fast—somewhat lighter than I am, and a bit faster. He knows that I always fight Thracian, and that I'd be a fool to try anything else against him. He fights either Thracian or Samnite, depending upon the opposition. Against me his best bet would be to go Samnite. Do you know?"

"No. They didn't say. He may not decide until the last moment."

"Unlimited, against me, he'll go Samnite. He'll have to. These unlimiteds are tough, but it gives me a chance to use a new trick I've been working on. I'll take that sword there—no scabbard—and two daggers, besides my gladius. Get me a mace; the lightest real mace they've got in their armory."

"A *mace!* Fighting *Thracian*, against a *Samnite?*"

"Exactly. A mace. Am I going to fight Fermius, or do you want to do it yourself?"

The mace was brought and Patroclus banged it, with a two-handed roundhouse swing, against a stone of the wall. The head remained solid upon the shaft. Good. They waited.

Trumpets blared; the roar of the vast assemblage subsided almost to silence.

"Grand Champion Fermius versus Grand Champion Patroclus," came raucous announcement. "Single combat. Any weapons that either chooses to use, used in any way possible. No rest, no intermission. Enter!"

Two armored figures strode toward the center of the arena. Patroclus' armor, from towering helmet down, and including the shield, was of dully-gleaming steel, completely bare of ornament. Each piece was marred and scarred; very plainly that armor was for use and had been used. On the other hand, the Samnite half-armor of the Gaul was resplendent with the decorations affected by his race. Fermius' helmet sported three brilliantly-colored plumes, his shield and cuirass, enameled in half the colors of the spectrum, looked as though they were being worn for the first time.

Five yards apart, the gladiators stopped and wheeled to face the podium upon which Nero lolled. The buzz of conversation—the mace had excited no little comment and speculation—ceased. Patroclus heaved his ponderous weapon into the air; the Gaul whirled up his long, sharp sword. They chanted in unison:

"Ave, Caesar Imperator!
Morituri te salutant!"

The starting-flag flashed downward; and at its first sight, long before it struck the ground, both men moved. Fermius whirled and leaped; but, fast as he was, he was not quite fast enough. That mace, which had seemed so heavy in the Thracian's hands a moment before, had become miraculously maneuverable—it was hurtling through the air directly toward the middle of his body! It did not strike its goal—Patroclus hoped that he was the only one there who suspected that he had not expected it to touch his opponent—but in order to dodge the missile Fermius had to break his stride; lost momentarily the fine coordination of his attack. And in that moment Patroclus struck. Struck, and struck again.

But, as has been said, Fermius was both strong and fast. The first blow, aimed backhand at his bare right leg, struck his shield instead. The left-handed stab, shield-encumbered as the left arm was, ditto. So did the next trial, a vicious forehand cut. The third of the mad flurry of swordcuts, only partially deflected by the sword which Fermius could only then get into play, sheared down and a red, a green, and a white plume floated toward the ground. The two fighters sprang apart and studied each other briefly.

From the gladiators' standpoint, this had been the veriest preliminary skirmishing. That the Gaul had lost his plumes and that his armor showed great streaks of missing enamel meant no more to either than that the Thracian's supposedly surprise attack had failed. Each knew that he faced the deadliest fighter of his world; but if that knowledge affected either man, the other could not perceive it.

But the crowd went wild. Nothing like that first terrific passage-at-arms had ever before been seen. Death, sudden and violent, had been in the air. The arena was saturated with it. Hearts had been ecstatically in throats. Each person there, man or woman, had felt the indescribable thrill of death—vicariously, safely—and every fiber of their lusts demanded more. More! Each spectator knew that one of those men would die that afternoon. None wanted, or would permit, them both to live. This was to the death, and death there would be.

Women, their faces blotched and purple with emotion, shrieked and screamed. Men, stamping their feet and waving their arms, yelled and swore. And many, men and women alike, laid wagers.

"Five hundred sesterces on Fermius!" one shouted, tablet and stylus in air.

"Taken!" came answering yell. "The Gaul is done—Patroclus all but had him there!"

"One thousand, you!" came another challenge. "Patroclus missed his chance and will never get another—a thousand on Fermius!"

"Two thousand!"

"Five thousand!"

"Ten!"

The fighters closed—swung—stabbed. Shields clanged vibrantly under the impact of fended strokes, swords whined and snarled. Back and forth—circling—giving and taking ground—for minute after endless minute that desperately furious exhibition of skill, of speed and of power and of endurance, went on. And as it went on, longer and longer past the time expected by even the most optimistic, tension mounted higher and higher.

Blood flowed crimson down the Gaul's bare leg and the crowd screamed its approval. Blood trickled out of the joints of the Thracian's armor and it became a frenzied mob.

No human body could stand that pace for long. Both men were tiring fast, and slowing. With the drive of his weight and armor, Patroclus forced the Gaul to go where he wanted him to go. Then, apparently gathering his every resource for a final effort, the Thracian took one short, choppy step forward and swung straight down, with all his strength.

The blood-smeared hilt turned in his hands; the blade struck flat and broke, its length whining viciously away. Fermius, although staggered by the sheer brute force of the abortive stroke, recovered almost instantly; dropping his sword and snatching at his gladius to take advantage of the wonderful opportunity thus given him.

But that breaking had not been accidental; Patroclus made no attempt to recover his balance. Instead, he ducked *past* the surprised and shaken Gaul. Still stooping, he seized the mace, which everyone except he had forgotten, and swung; swung with all the totalized and synchronized power of hands, wrists, arms, shoulders, and magnificent body.

The iron head of the ponderous weapon struck the center of the Gaul's cuirass, which crunched inward like so much cardboard. Fermius seemed to leave the ground and, folded around the mace, to fly briefly through the air. As he struck the ground, Patroclus was upon him. The Gaul was probably already dead—that blow would have killed an elephant—but that made no difference. If that mob knew that Fermius was dead, they might start yelling for his life, too. Hence, by lifting his head and poising his dirk high in air, he asked of Caesar his Imperial will.

The crowd, already frantic, had gone stark mad at the blow. No thought of mercy could or did exist in that insanely bloodthirsty throng; no thought of clemency for the man who had fought such a magnificent fight. In cooler moments they would have wanted him to live, to thrill them again and yet again; but now, for almost half an hour, they had been loving the hot, the suffocating thrill of death in their throats. Now they wanted, and would have, the ultimate thrill.

"Death!" The solid structure rocked to the crescendo roar of the demand. "*Death!* DEATH!"

Nero's right thumb pressed horizontally against his chest. Every vestal was making the same sign. Pollice verso. Death. The strained and strident yelling of the mob grew even louder.

Patroclus lowered his dagger and delivered the unnecessary and unfelt thrust; and—

"Peractum est!" arose one deafening yell.

Thus the red-haired Thracian lived; and also, somewhat to his own surprise, did Livius.

"I'm glad to see you, Bronze-heart, by the white thighs of Ceres, I am!" that worthy exclaimed, when the two met, the following day. Patroclus had never seen the Bithynian so buoyant. "Pallas Athene covered you, like I asked her to. But by the red beak of Thoth and the sacred Zaimph of Tanit, it gave me the horrors when you made that throw so quick and missed it, and I went as crazy as the rest of them when you pulled the real coup. But now, curse it, I suppose that we'll all have to be on the lookout for it—or no, unlimiteds aren't common, thank Ninib the Smiter and his scarlet spears!"

"I hear you didn't do so badly, yourself," Patroclus interrupted his friend's loquacity. "I missed your first two, but I saw you take Kalendios. He's a high-rater—one of the best of the locals—and I was afraid he might snare you, but from the looks of you, you got only a couple of stabs. Nice work."

"Prayer, my boy. Prayer is the stuff. I prayed to 'em in order, and hit the jackpot with Shamash. My guts curled up again, like they belong, and I knew that the portents were all in my favor. Besides, when you were walking out to meet Fermius, did you notice that red-headed Greek posturer making passes at you?"

"Huh? Don't be a fool. I had other things to think of."

"So I figured. So did she, probably, because after while she came around behind with a lanista and made eyes at me. I must have the next best shape to you here, I guess. What a wench! Anyway, I felt better and better, and before she left I knew that no damn retiarius that ever waved a trident could put a net past my guard. And they couldn't, either. A couple more like that and I'll be a Grand Champion myself. But they're digging the holes for the crosses and there's the horn that the feast is ready. This show is going to be really good.''

They ate, hugely and with unmarred appetite, of the heaped food which Nero had provided. They returned to their assigned places to see crosses, standing as close together as they could be placed and each bearing a suffering Christian, filling the whole vast expanse of the arena.

And, if the truth must be told, those two men enjoyed thoroughly every moment of that long and sickeningly horrible afternoon. They were the hardest products of the hardest school the world has ever known: trained rigorously to deal out death mercilessly at command; to accept death unflinchingly at need. They should not and can not be judged by the higher, finer standards of a softer, gentler day.

The afternoon passed; evening approached. All the gladiators then in Rome assembled in the Claudian Grove, around tables creaking under their loads of food and wine. Women, too, were there in profusion; women for the taking and yearning to be taken; and the tide of revelry ran open, wide, and high. Although all ate and apparently drank with abandon, most of the wine was in fact wasted. And as the sky darkened, most of the gladiators, one by one, began to get rid of their female companions upon one pretext or another and to drift toward the road which separated the festivities from the cloaked and curious throng of lookers-on.

At full dark, a red glare flared into the sky from Caesar's garden and the gladiators, deployed now along the highway, dashed across it and seemed to wrestle briefly with cloaked figures. Then armed, more-or-less-armored men ran back to the scene of their reveling. Swords, daggers, and gladii thrust, stabbed, and cut. Tables and benches ran red; ground and grass grew slippery with blood.

The conspirators turned then and rushed toward the Emperor's brilliantly torch-lit garden. Patroclus, however, was not in the van. He had had trouble in finding a cuirass big enough for him to get into. He had been delayed further by the fact that he had had to kill three strange lanistae before he could get at his owner, the man he really wanted to slay. He was therefore some little distance behind the other gladiators when Petronius rushed up to him and seized him by the arm.

White and trembling, the noble was not now the exquisite Arbiter Elegantiae; nor the imperturbable Augustian.

"Patroclus! In the name of Bacchus, Patroclus, why do the men go there now? No signal was given—I could not get to Nero!"

"What?" the Thracian blazed. "Vulcan and his fiends! It *was* given—I heard it myself! What went wrong?"

"Everything." Petronius licked his lips. "I was standing right beside him. No one else was near enough to interfere. It was—should have been—easy. But after I got my knife out I couldn't move. It was his *eyes*, Patroclus—I swear it, by the white breasts of Venus! He has the evil eye—I couldn't move a muscle, I tell you! Then, although I didn't want to, I turned and ran!"

"How did you find *me* so quick?"

"I—I—I—don't know," the frantic Arbiter stuttered. "I ran and ran, and there you were. But what are we—you—going to do?"

Patroclus' mind raced. He believed implicitly that Jupiter guarded him personally. He believed in the other gods and goddesses of Rome. He more than half believed in the multitudinous deities of Greece, of Egypt, and even of Babylon. The other world was real and close; the evil eye only one of the many inexplicable facts of every-day life. Nevertheless, in spite of his credulity—or perhaps in part because of it—he also believed firmly in himself; in his own powers. Wherefore he soon came to a decision.

"Jupiter, ward from me Ahenobarbus' evil eye!" he called aloud, and turned.

"Where are you going?" Petronius, still shaking, demanded.

"To do the job *you* swore to do, of course—to kill that bloated toad. And then to give Tigellinus what I have owed him so long."

At full run, he soon overtook his fellows, and waded resistlessly into the fray. He was Grand Champion Patroclus, working at his trade; the hard-learned trade which he knew so well. No Praetorian or ordinary soldier could stand before him save momentarily. He did not have all of his Thracian armor, but he had enough. Man after man faced him, and man after man died.

And Nero, sitting at ease with a beautiful boy at his right and a beautiful harlot at his left, gazed appreciatively through his emerald lens at the flaming torches; the while, with a very small fraction of his Eddorian mind, he mused upon the matter of Patroclus and Tigellinus.

Should he let the Thracian kill the Commander of his Guard? Or not? It didn't really matter, one way or the other. In fact, nothing about this whole foul planet—this ultra-microscopic, if offensive, speck of cosmic dust in the Eddorian Scheme of Things—really mattered at all. It would be mildly amusing to watch the gladiator consummate his vengeance by carving the Roman to bits. But, on the other hand, there was such a thing as pride of workmanship. Viewed in that light, the Thracian could not kill Tigellinus, because that bit of corruption had a few more jobs to do. He must descend lower and lower into unspeakable depravity, finally to cut his own throat with a razor. Although Patroclus would not know it—it was better technique not to let him know it—the Thracian's proposed vengeance would have been futility itself compared with that which the luckless Roman was to wreak on himself.

Wherefore a shrewdly-placed blow knocked the helmet from Patroclus' head and a mace crashed down, spattering his brains abroad.

Thus ended the last significant attempt to save the civilization of Rome; in a fiasco so complete that even such meticulous historians as Tacitus and Suetonius mention it merely as a minor disturbance of Nero's garden party.

The planet Tellus circled its sun some twenty hundred times. Sixty-odd generations of men were born and died, but that was not enough. The Arisian program of genetics required more. Therefore the Elders, after due deliberation, agreed that that Civilization, too, must be allowed to fall. And Gharlane of Eddore, recalled to duty from the middle of a much-too-short vacation, found things in very bad shape indeed and went busily to work setting them to rights. He had slain one fellow-member of the Innermost Circle, but there might very well have been more than one Master involved.

BOOK TWO

The World War

4

1918

Sobbing furiously, Captain Ralph Kinnison wrenched at his stick—with half of his control surfaces shot away the crate was hellishly logy. He could step out, of course, the while saluting the victorious Jerries, but he wasn't on fire—yet—and hadn't been hit—yet. He ducked and flinched sidewise as another burst of bullets stitched another seam along his riddled fuselage and whanged against his dead engine. Afire? Not yet—good! Maybe he could land the heap, after all!

Slowly—oh, *so* sluggishly—the Spad began to level off, toward the edge of the wheatfield and that friendly, inviting ditch. If the krauts didn't get him with their next pass . . .

He heard a chattering beneath him—Brownings, by God!—and the expected burst did not come. He knew that he had been just about over the front when they conked his engine; it was a toss-up whether he would come down in enemy territory or not. But now, for the first time in ages, it seemed, there were machine-guns going that were not aimed at him!

His landing-gear swished against stubble and he fought with all his strength of body and of will to keep the Spad's tail down. He almost succeeded; his speed was almost spent when he began to nose over. He leaped, then, and as he struck ground he curled up and rolled—he had been a motorcycle racer for years—feeling as he did so a wash of heat: a tracer had found his gas-tank at last! Bullets were thudding into the ground; one shrieked past his head as, stooping over, folded into the smallest possible target, he galloped awkwardly toward the ditch.

The Brownings still yammered, filling the sky with cupro-nickeled lead; and while Kinnison was flinging himself full length into the pro-tecting water and mud, he heard a tremendous crash. One of those Huns had been too intent on murder; had stayed a few seconds too long; had come a few meters too close.

The clamor of the guns stopped abruptly.

"We got one! We got one!" A yell of exultation.

"Stay down! Keep low, you boneheads!" roared a voice of authority, quite evidently a sergeant's. "Wanna get your blocks shot off? Take down them guns; we gotta get to hell out of here. Hey, you flyer! Are you O.K., or wounded, or maybe dead?"

Kinnison spat out mud until he could talk. "O.K.!" he shouted, and started to lift an eye above the low bank. He stopped, however, as whistling metal, sheeting in from the north, told him that such action would be decidedly unsafe. "But I ain't leaving this ditch right now— sounds mighty hot out there!"

"You said it, brother. It's hotter than the hinges of hell, from behind that ridge over there. But ooze down that ditch a piece, around the first bend. It's pretty well in the clear there, and besides, you'll find a ledge of rocks running straight across the flat. Cross over there and climb the hill—join us by that dead snag up there. We got to get out of here. That sausage over there must have seen this shindig and they'll blow this whole damn area off the map. Snap it up! And you, you goldbricks, get the lead out of your pants!"

Kinnison followed directions. He found the ledge and emerged, scraping thick and sticky mud from his uniform. He crawled across the little plain. An occasional bullet whined through the air, far above him; but, as the sergeant had said, this bit of terrain was "in the clear." He climbed the hill, approached the gaunt, bare tree-trunk. He heard men moving, and cautiously announced himself.

"O.K., fella," came the sergeant's deep bass. "Yeah, it's us. Shake a leg!"

"That's easy!" Kinnison laughed for the first time that day. "I'm shaking already, like a hula-hula dancer's empennage. What outfit is this, and where are we?"

"B R R O O M!" The earth trembled, the air vibrated. Below and to the north, almost exactly where the machine-guns had been, an awe-inspiring cloud billowed majestically into the air; a cloud composed of smoke, vapor, pulverized earth, chunks of rock, and debris of what had been trees. Nor was it alone.

"Crack! Bang! Tweet! Boom! Wham!" Shell of all calibers, high explosive and gas, came down in droves. The landscape disappeared. The little company of Americans, in complete silence and with one mind, devoted themselves to accumulating distance. Finally, when they had to stop for breath:

"Section B, attached to the 76th Field Artillery," the sergeant answered the question as though it had just been asked. "As to where we are, somewhere between Berlin and Paris is about all I can tell you. We got hell knocked out of us yesterday, and have been running around lost ever since. They shot off a rally signal on top of this here hill, though, and we was just going to shove off when we seen the krauts chasing you."

"Thanks. I'd better rally with you, I guess—find out where we are, and what's the chance of getting back to my own outfit."

"Damn slim, I'd say. Boches are all around us here, thicker than fleas on a dog."

They approached the summit, were challenged, were accepted. They saw a gray-haired man—an old man, for such a location—seated calmly upon a rock, smoking a cigarette. His smartly-tailored uniform, which fitted perfectly his not-so-slender figure, was muddy and tattered. One leg of his breeches was torn half away, revealing a blood-soaked bandage. Although he was very evidently an officer, no insignia were visible. As Kinnison and the gunners approached, a first lieutenant—practically spic-and-span—spoke to the man on the rock.

"First thing to do is to settle the matter of rank," he announced, crisply. "I'm First Lieutenant Randolph, of . . ."

"Rank, eh?" The seated one grinned and spat out the butt of his cigarette. "But then, it was important to me, too, when I was a first lieutenant—about the time that you were born. Slayton, Major-General."

"Oh . . . excuse me, sir . . ."

"Skip it. How many men you got, and what are they?"

"Seven, sir. We brought in a wire from Inf . . ."

"A *wire!* Hellandamnation, why haven't you got it with you, then? Get it!"

The crestfallen officer disappeared; the general turned to Kinnison and the sergeant.

"Have you got any ammunition, sergeant?"

"Yes, sir. About thirty belts."

"Thank God! We can use it, and you. As for you, Captain, I don't know . . ."

The wire came up. The general seized the instrument and cranked.

"Get me Spearmint . . . Spearmint? Slayton—give me Weatherby . . . This is Slayton . . . yes, but . . . No, but I want . . . Hellandamnation, Weatherby, shut up and let me talk—don't you know that this wire's apt to be cut any second? We're on top of Hill Fo-wer, Ni-yun, Sev-en—that's right—about two hundred men; maybe three. Composite—somebody, apparently, from half the outfits in France. Too fast and too far—both flanks wide open—cut off . . . Hello! Hello! Hello!'' he dropped the instrument and turned to Kinnison. "You want to go back, Captain, and I need a runner—bad. Want to try to get through?''

"Yes, sir.''

"First phone you come to, get Spearmint—General Weatherby. Tell him Slayton says that we're cut off, but the Germans aren't in much force nor in good position, and for God's sake to get some air and tanks in here to keep them from consolidating. Just a minute. Sergeant, what's your name?'' He studied the burly non-com minutely.

"Wells, sir.''

"What would you say ought to be done with the machine-guns?''

"Cover that ravine, there, first. Then set up to enfilade if they try to come up over there. Then, if I could find any more guns, I'd . . .''

"Enough. Second Lieutenant Wells, from now. GHQ will confirm. Take charge of all the guns we have. Report when you have made disposition. Now, Kinnison, listen. I can probably hold out until tonight. The enemy doesn't know yet that we're here, but we are due for some action pretty quick now, and when they locate us—if there aren't too many of their own units here, too—they'll flatten this hill like a table. So tell Weatherby to throw a column in here as soon as it gets dark, and to advance Eight and Sixty, so as to consolidate this whole area. Got it?''

"Yes, sir.''

"Got a compass?''

"Yes, sir.''

"Pick up a tin hat and get going. A hair north of due west, about a kilometer and a half. Keep cover, because the going will be tough. Then you'll come to a road. It's a mess, but it's ours—or was, at last accounts—so the worst of it will be over. On that road, which goes southwest, about two kilometers further, you'll find a Post—you'll know it by the motorcycles and such. Phone from there. Luck!''

Bullets began to whine and the general dropped to the ground and crawled toward a coppice, bellowing orders as he went. Kinnison crawled, too, straight west, availing himself of all possible cover, until he encountered a sergeant-major reclining against the south side of a great tree.

"Cigarette, buddy?'' that wight demanded.

"Sure. Take the pack. I've got another that'll last me—maybe more. But what the hell goes on here? Who ever heard of a major general getting far enough up front to get shot in the leg, and he talks as though he were figuring on licking the whole German army. Is the old bird nuts, or what?''

"Not so you would notice it. Didn'cha ever hear of 'Hellandamnation' Slayton? You will, buddy, you will. If Pershing doesn't give him three stars after this, he's crazier than hell. He ain't supposed to be on combat at all—he's from GHQ and can make or break anybody in the AEF. Out here on a look-see trip and couldn't get back. But you got to hand it to him—he's getting things organized in great shape. I came in with him—I'm about all that's left of them that did—just waiting for this breeze to die down, but it's getting worse. We'd better duck—over there!''

Bullets whistled and stormed, breaking more twigs and branches from the already shattered, practically denuded trees. The two slid precipitately into the indicated shell-hole, into stinking mud. Wells' guns burst into action.

"Damn! I hated to do this," the sergeant grumbled, "On accounta I just got half dry.''

"Wise me up," Kinnison directed. "The more I know about things, the more apt I am to get through.''

"This is what is left of two battalions, and a lot of casuals. They made objective, but it turns out the outfits on their right and left couldn't, leaving their flanks right out in the open air. Orders come in by blinker to rectify the line by falling back, but by then it couldn't be done. Under observation.''

Kinnison nodded. He knew what a barrage would have done to a force trying to cross such open ground in daylight.

"One man could prob'ly make it, though, if he was careful and kept his eyes wide open," the sergeant-major continued. "But you ain't got binoculars, have you?''

"No.''

"Get a pair easy enough. You saw them boots without any hobnails in 'em, sticking out from under some blankets?''

"Yes. I get you." Kinnison knew that combat officers did not wear hobnails, and usually carried binoculars. "How come so many at once?''

"Just about all the officers that got this far. Conniving, my guess is, behind old Slayton's back. Anyway, a kraut aviator spots 'em and dives. Our machine-guns got him, but not until after he heaved a bomb. Dead center. Christ, what a mess! But there's six-seven good glasses in there. I'd grab one myself, but the general would see it—he can see right through the lid of a mess-kit. Well, the boys have shut those krauts up, so I'll hunt the old man up and tell him what I found out. *Damn* this mud!''

Kinnison emerged sinuously and snaked his way to a row of blanket-covered forms. He lifted a blanket and gasped: then vomited up everything, it seemed, that he had eaten for days. But he *had* to have binoculars.

He got them.

Then, still retching, white and shaken, he crept westward; availing himself of every possible item of cover.

For some time, from a point somewhere north of his route, a machine-gun had been intermittently at work. It was close; but the very loudness of its noise, confused as it was by resounding echoes, made it impossible to locate at all exactly the weapon's position. Kinnison crept forward inchwise; scanning every foot of visible terrain through his powerful glass. He knew by the sound that it was German. More, since what he did not know about machine-guns could have been printed in bill-poster type upon the back of his hand, he knew that it was a Maxim, Model 1907—a mean, mean gun. He deduced that it was doing plenty of damage to his fellows back on the hill, and that they had not been able to do much of anything about it. And it was beautifully hidden; even he, close as he must be, couldn't see it. But damn it, there *had* to be a . . .

Minute after minute, unmoving save for the traverse of his binoculars, he searched, and finally he found. A tiny plume—the veriest wisp—of vapor, rising from the surface of the brook. Steam! Steam from the cooling jacket of that Maxim 1907! And there was the tube!

Cautiously he moved around until he could trace that tube to its business end—the carefully-hidden emplacement. There it was! He couldn't maintain his westward course without them spotting him; nor could he go around far enough. And besides . . . and besides that, there would be at least a patrol, if it hadn't gone up the hill already. And there were grenades available, right close . . .

He crept up to one of the gruesome objects he had been avoiding, and when he crept away he half-carried, half-dragged three grenades in a canvas bag. He wormed his way to a certain boulder. He straightened up, pulled three pins, swung his arm three times.

Bang! Bam! Pow! The camouflage disappeared; so did the shrubbery for yards around. Kinnison had ducked behind the rock, but he ducked still deeper as a chunk of something, its force pretty well spent, clanged against his steel helmet. Another object thudded beside him—a leg, gray-clad and wearing a heavy field boot!

Kinnison wanted to be sick again, but he had neither the time nor the contents.

And damn! What *lousy* throwing! He had never been any good at baseball, but he had supposed that he could hit a thing as big as that gun-pit—but not one of his grenades had gone in. The crew would probably be dead—from concussion, if nothing else—but the gun probably wasn't even hurt. He would have to go over there and cripple it himself.

He went—not exactly boldly—forty-five in hand. The Germans looked dead. One of them sprawled on the parapet, right in his way. He gave the body a shove, watched it roll down the slope. As it rolled, however, it came to life and yelled; and at that yell there occurred a thing at which young Kinnison's hair stood straight up inside his iron helmet. On the gray of the blasted hillside hitherto unseen gray forms moved; moved toward their howling comrade. And Kinnison, blessing for the first time in his life his inept throwing arm, hoped fervently that the Maxim was still in good working order.

A few seconds of inspection showed him that it was. The gun had practically a full belt and there was plenty more. He placed a box—he would have no Number Two to help him here—took hold of the grips, shoved off the safety, and squeezed the trip. The gun roared—what a gorgeous, what a heavenly racket that Maxim made! He traversed until he could see where the bullets were striking: then swung the stream of metal to and fro. One belt and the Germans were completely disorganized; two belts and he could see no signs of life.

He pulled the Maxim's block and threw it away; shot the water-jacket full of holes. That gun was done. Nor had he increased his own hazard. Unless more Germans came very soon, nobody would ever know who had done what, or to whom.

He slithered away; resumed earnestly his westward course: going as fast as—sometimes a trifle faster than—caution would permit. But there were no more alarms. He crossed the dangerously open ground; skulked rapidly through the frightfully shattered wood. He reached the road, strode along it around the first bend, and stopped, appalled. He had heard of such things, but he had never seen one; and mere description has always been and always will be completely inadequate. Now he was walking right into it—the thing he was to see in nightmare for all the rest of his ninety-six years of life.

Actually, there was very little to see. The road ended abruptly. What had been a road, what had been wheatfields and farms, what had been woods, were practically indistinguishable, one from the other; were fantastically and impossibly the same. The entire area had been churned.

Worse—it was as though the ground and its every surface object had been run through a gargantuan mill and spewed abroad. Splinters of wood, riven chunks of metal, a few scraps of bloody flesh. Kinnison screamed, then, and ran; ran back and around that blasted acreage. And as he ran, his mind built up pictures; pictures which became only the more vivid because of his frantic efforts to wipe them out.

That road, the night before, had been one of the world's most heavily traveled highways. Motorcycles, trucks, bicycles. Ambulances. Kitchens. Staff-cars and other automobiles. Guns; from seventy-fives up to the big boys, whose tremendous weight drove their wide caterpillar treads inches deep into solid ground. Horses. Mules. And people—*especially* people—like himself. Solid columns of men, marching as fast as they could step—there weren't trucks enough to haul them all. That road had been crowded—jammed. Like State and Madison at noon, only more so. Over-jammed with all the personnel, all the instrumentation and incidentalia, all the weaponry, of war.

And upon that teeming, seething highway there had descended a rain of steel-encased high explosive. Possibly some gas, but probably not. The German High Command had given orders to pulverize that particular area at that particular time; and hundreds, or perhaps thousands, of German guns, in a micrometrically-synchronized symphony of fire-power, had pulverized it. Just that. Literally. Precisely. No road remained; no farm, no field, no building, no tree or shrub. The bits of flesh might have come from horse or man or mule; few indeed were the scraps of metal which retained enough of their original shape to show what they had once been.

Kinnison ran—or staggered—around that obscene blot and struggled back to the road. It was shell-pocked, but passable. He hoped that the shell-holes would decrease in number as he went along, but they did not. The enemy had put this whole road out of service. And that farm, the P.C., ought to be around the next bend.

It was, but it was no longer a Post of Command. Either by directed fire—star-shell illumination—or by uncannily accurate chart-work, they had put some heavy shell exactly where they would do the most damage. The buildings were gone; the cellar in which the P.C. had been was now a gaping crater. Parts of motorcycles and of staff cars littered the ground. Stark treetrunks—all bare of leaves, some riven of all except the largest branches, a few stripped even of bark—stood gauntly. In a crotch of one, Kinnison saw with rising horror, hung the limp and shattered naked torso of a man; blown completely out of his clothes.

Shells were—had been, right along—coming over occasionally. Big ones, but high; headed for targets well to the west. Nothing close enough to worry about. Two ambulances, a couple of hundred meters apart, were coming; working their way along the road, between the holes. The first one slowed . . . stopped.

"Seen anybody—Look out! Duck!"

Kinnison had already heard that unmistakable, unforgettable screech, was already diving headlong into the nearest hole. There was a crash as though the world were falling apart. Something smote him; seemed to drive him bodily into the ground. His light went out. When he recovered consciousness he was lying upon a stretcher; two men were bending over him.

"What hit me?" he gasped. "Am I . . . ?" He stopped. He was afraid to ask: afraid even to try to move, lest he should find that he didn't have any arms or legs.

"A wheel, and maybe some of the axle, of the other ambulance, is all," one of the men assured him. "Nothing much; you're practically as good as ever. Shoulder and arm bunged up a little and something— maybe shrapnel, though—poked you in the guts. But we've got you all fixed up, so take it easy and . . ."

"What we want to know is," his partner interrupted, "Is there anybody else alive up here?"

"Uh-uh," Kinnison shook his head.

"O.K. Just wanted to be sure. Lots of business back there, and it won't do any harm to have a doctor look at you."

"Get me to a 'phone, as fast as you can," Kinnison directed, in a voice which he thought was strong and full of authority, but which in fact was neither. "I've got an important message for General Weatherby, at Spearmint."

"Better tell us what it is, hadn't you?" The ambulance was now jolting along what had been the road. "They've got phones at the hospital where we're going, but you might faint or something before we get there."

Kinnison told; but fought to retain what consciousness he had. Throughout that long, rough ride he fought. He won. He himself spoke to General Weatherby—the doctors, knowing him to be a Captain of Aviation and realizing that his message should go direct, helped him telephone. He himself received the General's sizzlingly sulphurous assurance that relief would be sent and that that quadruply-qualified line would be rectified that night.

Then someone jabbed him with a needle and he lapsed into a dizzy, fuzzy coma, from which he did not emerge completely for weeks. He had lucid intervals at times, but he did not, at the time or ever, know surely what was real and what was fantasy.

There were doctors, doctors, doctors; operations, operations, operations. There were hospital tents, into which quiet men were carried; from which still quieter men were removed. There was a larger hospital, built of wood. There was a machine that buzzed and white-clad men who studied films and papers. There were scraps of conversation.

"Belly wounds are bad," Kinnison thought—he was never sure—that he heard one of them say. "And such contusions and multiple and compound fractures as those don't help a bit. Prognosis unfavorable—distinctly so—but we'll soon see what we can do. Interesting case . . . fascinating. What would you do, Doctor, if you were doing it?"

"I'd let it alone!" A younger, stronger voice declared, fervently. "Multiple perforations, infection, extravasation, oedema—uh-uh! I am watching, Doctor, and learning!"

Another interlude, and another. Another. And others. Until finally, orders were given which Kinnison did not hear at all.

"Adrenalin! Massage! Massage hell out of him!"

Kinnison again came to—partially to, rather—anguished in every fiber of his being. Somebody was sticking barbed arrows into every square inch of his skin; somebody else was pounding and mauling him all over, taking particular pains to pummel and to wrench at all the places where he hurt the worst. He yelled at the top of his voice; yelled and swore bitterly: "QUIT IT!" being the expurgated gist of his luridly profane protests. He did not make nearly as much noise as he supposed, but he made enough.

"Thank God!" Kinnison heard a lighter, softer voice. Surprised, he stopped swearing and tried to stare. He couldn't see very well, either, but he was pretty sure that there was a middle-aged woman there. There was, and her eyes were not dry. "He is going to live, after all!"

As the days passed, he began really to sleep, naturally and deeply.

He grew hungrier and hungrier, and they would not give him enough to eat. He was by turns sullen, angry, and morose.

In short, he was convalescent.

For Captain Ralph K. Kinnison, THE WAR was over.

5

1941

Chubby, brownette Eunice Kinnison sat in a rocker, reading the Sunday papers and listening to her radio. Her husband Ralph lay sprawled upon the davenport, smoking a cigarette and reading the current issue of EX-TRAORDINARY STORIES against an unheard background of music. Mentally, he was far from Tellus, flitting in his super-dreadnaught through parsec after parsec of vacuous space.

The music broke off without warning and there blared out an announcement which yanked Ralph Kinnison back to Earth with a violence almost physical. He jumped up, jammed his hands into his pockets.

"Pearl Harbor!" he blurted. "How in . . . How could they have let them get *that* far?"

"But *Frank!*" the woman gasped. She had not worried much about her husband; but Frank, her son . . . "He'll have to go . . ." Her voice died away.

"Not a chance in the world." Kinnison did not speak to soothe, but as though from sure knowledge. "Designing Engineer for Lockwood? He'll want to, all right, but anyone who was ever even exposed to a course in aeronautical engineering will sit this war out."

"But they say it can't last very long. It can't, can it?"

"I'll say it can. Loose talk. Five years minimum is my guess—not that my guess is any better than anybody else's."

He prowled around the room. His somber expression did not lighten.

"I knew it," the woman said at length. "You, too—even after the last one . . . You haven't said anything, so I thought, perhaps . . ."

"I know I didn't. There was always the chance that we wouldn't get drawn into it. If you say so, though, I'll stay home."

"Am I apt to? I let you go when you were really in danger . . ."

"What do you mean by *that* crack?" he interrupted.

"Regulations. One year too old—Thank Heaven!"

"So what? They'll need technical experts, bad. They'll make exceptions."

"Possibly. Desk jobs. Desk officers don't get killed in action—or even wounded. Why, perhaps, with the children all grown up and married, we won't even have to be separated."

"Another angle—financial."

"Pooh! Who cares about that? Besides, for a man out of a job . . ."

"From you, I'll let that one pass. Thanks, Eunie—you're an ace. I'll shoot 'em a wire."

The telegram was sent. The Kinnisons waited. And waited. Until, about the middle of January, beautifully-phrased and beautifully-mimeographed letters began to arrive.

"The War Department recognizes the value of your previous military experience and appreciates your willingness once again to take up arms in defense of the country . . . Veteran Officer's Questionnaire . . . please fill out completely . . . Form 191A . . . Form 170 in duplicate . . . Form 315 . . . Impossible to forecast the extent to which the War Department may ultimately utilize the services which you and thousands of others have so generously offered . . . Form . . . Form . . . Not to be construed as meaning that you have been permanently rejected . . . Form . . . Advise you that while at the present time the War Department is unable to use you . . ."

"Wouldn't that fry you to a crisp?" Kinnison demanded. "What in hell have they got in their heads—sawdust? They think that because I'm fifty one years old I've got one foot in the grave—I'll bet four dollars that I'm in better shape than that cursed Major General and his whole damned staff!"

"I don't doubt it, dear." Eunice's smile was, however, mostly of relief. "But here's an ad—it's been running for a week."

"CHEMICAL   ENGINEERS . . . shell   loading   plant . . . within seventy-five miles of Townville . . . over five years experience . . . organic chemistry . . . technology . . . explosives . . ."

"They want *you*," Eunice declared, soberly.

"Well, I'm a Ph.D. in Organic. I've had more than five years experience in both organic chemistry and technology. If I don't know something about explosives I did a smart job of fooling Dean Montrose, back at Gosh Whatta University. I'll write 'em a letter."

He wrote. He filled out a form. The telephone rang.

"Kinnison speaking . . . yes . . . Dr. Sumner? Oh, yes, Chief Chemist . . . That's it—one year over age, so I thought . . . Oh, that's a minor matter. We won't starve. If you can't pay a hundred and fifty I'll come for a hundred, or seventy five, or fifty . . . That's all right, too. I'm well enough known in my own field so that a title of Junior Chemical Engineer wouldn't hurt me a bit . . . O.K., I'll see you about one o'clock . . . Stoner and Black, Inc., Operators, Entwhistle Ordnance Plant, Entwhistle, Missikota . . . What! Well, maybe I could, at that . . . Goodbye."

He turned to his wife. "You know what? They want me to come down right away and go to work. Hot Dog! *Am* I glad that I told that louse Hendricks exactly where he could stick that job of mine!"

"He must have known that you wouldn't sign a straight-salary contract after getting a share of the profits so long. Maybe he believed what you always say just before or just after kicking somebody's teeth down their throats; that you're so meek and mild—a regular Milquetoast. Do you really think that they'll want you back, after the war?" It was clear that Eunice was somewhat concerned concerning Kinnison's joblessness; but Kinnison was not.

"Probably. That's the gossip. And I'll come back—when hell freezes over." His square jaw tightened. "I've heard of outfits stupid enough to let their technical brains go because they could sell—for a while—anything they produced, but I didn't know that I was working for one. Maybe I'm not exactly a Timid Soul, but you'll have to admit that I never kicked anybody's teeth out unless they tried to kick mine out first."

Entwhistle Ordnance Plant covered twenty-odd square miles of more or less level land. Ninety-nine percent of its area was "Inside the Fence." Most of the buildings within that restricted area, while in reality enormous, were dwarfed by the vast spaces separating them; for safety-distances are not small when TNT and tetryl by the ton are involved. Those structures were built of concrete, steel, glass, transite, and tile.

"Outside the Fence" was different. This was the Administration Area. Its buildings were tremendous wooden barracks, relatively close together, packed with the executive, clerical, and professional personnel appropriate to an organization employing over twenty thousand men and women.

Well inside the fence, but a safety-distance short of the One Line—Loading Line Number One—was a long, low building, quite inadequately named the Chemical Laboratory. "Inadequately" in that the Chief Chemist, a highly capable—if more than a little cantankerous—Explosives Engineer, had already gathered into his Chemical Section most of Development, most of Engineering, and all of Physics, Weights and Measures, and Weather.

One room of the Chemical Laboratory—in the corner most distant from Administration—was separated from the rest of the building by a sixteen-inch wall of concrete and steel extending from foundation to roof without a door, window, or other opening. This was the laboratory of the Chemical Engineers, the boys who played with explosives high and low; any explosion occurring therein could not affect the Chemical Laboratory proper or its personnel.

Entwhistle's main roads were paved; but in February of 1942, such minor items as sidewalks existed only on the blueprints. Entwhistle's soil contained much clay, and at that time the mud was approximately six inches deep. Hence, since there were neither inside doors nor sidewalks, it was only natural that the technologists did not visit at all frequently the polished-tile cleanliness of the Laboratory. It was also natural enough for the far larger group to refer to the segregated ones as exiles and outcasts; and that some witty chemist applied to that isolated place the name "Siberia".

The name stuck. More, the Engineers seized it and acclaimed it. They were Siberians, and proud of it, and Siberians they remained; long after Entwhistle's mud turned into dust. And within the year the Siberians were to become well and favorably known in every ordnance plant in the country, to many high executives who had no idea of how the name originated.

Kinnison became a Siberian as enthusiastically as the youngest man there. The term "youngest" is used in its exact sense, for not one of them was a recent graduate. Each had had at least five years of responsible experience, and "Cappy" Sumner kept on building. He hired extravagantly and fired ruthlessly—to the minds of some, senselessly. But he knew what he was doing. He knew explosives, and he knew men. He was not liked, but he was respected. His building was good.

Being one of the only two "old" men there—and the other did not stay long—Kinnison, as a Junior Chemical Engineer, was not at first accepted without reserve. Apparently he did not notice that fact, but went quietly about his assigned duties. He was meticulously careful with, but very evidently not in any fear of, the materials with which he worked. He pelleted and tested tracer, igniter, and incendiary compositions; he took his turn at burning out rejects. Whenever asked, he went out on the lines with any one of them.

His experimental tetryls always "miked" to size, his TNT melt-pours—introductory to loading forty-millimeter on the Three Line—came out solid, free from checks and cavitations. It became evident to those young but keen minds that he, alone of them all, was on familiar ground. They began to discuss their problems with him. Out of his years of technological experience, and by bringing everyone present into the discussion, he either helped them directly or helped them to help themselves. His stature grew.

Black-haired, black-eyed "Tug" Tugwell, two hundred pounds of ex-football-player in charge of tracer on the Seven Line, called him "Uncle" Ralph, and the habit spread. And in a couple of weeks—at about the same time that "Injun" Abernathy was slightly injured by being blown through a door by a minor explosion of his igniter on the Eight line—he was promoted to full Chemical Engineer; a promotion which went unnoticed, since it involved only changes in title and salary.

Three weeks later, however, he was made Senior Chemical Engineer, in charge of Melt-Pour. At this there was a celebration, led by "Blondie" Wanacek, a sulphuric-acid expert handling tetryl on the Two. Kinnison searched minutely for signs of jealousy or antagonism, but could find none. He went blithely to work on the Six line, where they wanted to start pouring twenty-pound fragmentation bombs, ably assisted by Tug and by two new men. One of these was "Doc" or "Bart" Barton, who, the grapevine said, had been hired by Cappy to be his Assistant. His motto, like that of Rikki-Tikki-Tavi, was to run and find out, and he did so with glee and abandon. He was a good egg. So was the other newcomer, "Charley" Charlevoix, a prematurely gray paint-and-lacquer expert who had also made the Siberian grade.

A few months later, Sumner called Kinnison into the office. The latter went, wondering what the old hard-shell was going to cry about now; for to be called into that office meant only one thing—censure.

"Kinnison, I like your work," the Chief Chemist began, gruffly, and Kinnison's mouth almost dropped open. "Anybody who ever got a Ph.D. under Montrose would have to know explosives, and the F.B.I. report on you showed that you had brains, ability, and guts. But none of that explains how you can get along so well with those damned Siberians. I want to make you Assistant Chief and put you in charge of Siberia. Formally, I mean—actually, you have been for months."

"Why, no . . . I didn't . . . Besides, how about Barton? He's too good a man to kick in the teeth that way."

"Admitted." This *did* surprise Kinnison. He had never thought that the irascible and tempestuous Chief would ever confess to a mistake. This was a Cappy he had never known. "I discussed it with him yesterday. He's a damned good man—but it's decidedly questionable whether he has got whatever it is that made Tugwell, Wanacek and Charlevoix work straight through for seventy two hours, napping now and then on benches and grabbing coffee and sandwiches when they could, until they got that frag bomb straightened out.''

Sumner did not mention the fact that Kinnison had worked straight through, too. That was taken for granted.

"Well, I don't know.'' Kinnison's head was spinning. "I'd like to check with Barton first. O.K.?''

"I expected that. O.K.''

Kinnison found Barton and led him out behind the testing shed.

"Bart, Cappy tells me that he figures on kicking you in the face by making me Assistant and that you O.K.'d it. One word and I'll tell the old buzzard just where to stick the job and exactly where to go to do it.''

"Reaction, perfect. Yield, one hundred percent.'' Barton stuck out his hand. "Otherwise, I would tell him all that myself and more. As it is, Uncle Ralph, smooth out the ruffled plumage. They'd go to hell for you, wading in standing straight up—they might do the same with me in the driver's seat, and they might not. Why take a chance? You're IT. Some things about the deal I don't like, of course—but at that, it makes me about the only man working for Stoner and Black who can get a release any time a good permanent job breaks. I'll stick until then. O.K.?'' It was unnecessary for Barton to add that as long as he was there he would really work.

"I'll say it's O.K.!'' and Kinnison reported to Sumner.

"All right, Chief, I'll try it—if you can square it with the Siberians.''

"That will not be too difficult.''

Nor was it. The Siberians' reaction brought a lump to Kinnison's throat.

"Ralph the First, Czar of Siberia!'' they yelled. "Long live the Czar! Kowtow, serfs and vassals, to Czar Ralph the First!''

Kinnison was still glowing when he got home that night, to the Government Housing Project and to the three-room "mansionette'' in which he and Eunice lived. He would never forget the events of that day.

"What a gang! *What* a gang! But listen, ace—they work under their own power—you couldn't *keep* those kids from working. Why should I get the credit for what they do?''

"I haven't the foggiest.'' Eunice wrinkled her forehead—and her nose—but the corners of her mouth quirked up. "Are you quite sure that you haven't had *anything* to do with it? But supper is ready—let's eat.''

More months passed. Work went on. Absorbing work, and highly varied; the details of which are of no importance here. Paul Jones, a big, hard, top-drawer chicle technologist, set up the Four line to pour demolition blocks. Frederick Hinton came in, qualified as a Siberian, and went to work on anti-personnel mines.

Kinnison was promoted again: to Chief Chemist. He and Sumner had never been friendly; he made no effort to find out why Cappy had quit, or had been terminated, whichever it was. This promotion made no difference. Barton, now Assistant, ran the whole Chemical Section save for one unit—Siberia—and did a superlative job. The Chief Chemist's secretary worked for Barton, not for Kinnison. Kinnison was the Czar of Siberia.

The Anti-Personnel mines had been giving trouble. Too many men were being killed by prematures, and nobody could find out why. The problem was handed to Siberia. Hinton tackled it, missed, and called for help. The Siberians rallied 'round. Kinnison loaded and tested mines. So did Paul and Tug and Blondie. Kinnison was testing, out in the Firing Area, when he was called to Administration to attend a Staff Meeting. Hinton relieved him. He had not reached the gate, however, when a guard car flagged him down.

"Sorry, sir, but there has been an accident at Pit Five and you are needed out there."

"Accident! Fred Hinton! Is he . . . ?"

"I'm afraid so, sir."

It is a harrowing thing to have to help gather up what fragments can be found of one of your best friends. Kinnison was white and sick as he got back to the firing station, just in time to hear the Chief Safety Officer say:

"Must have been carelessness—rank carelessness. I warned this man Hinton myself, on one occasion."

"Carelessness, hell!" Kinnison blazed. "You had the guts to warn *me* once, too, and I've forgotten more about safety in explosives than you ever will know. Fred Hinton was *not* careless—if I hadn't been called in, that would have been me."

"What is it, then?"

"I don't know—yet. I tell you now, though, Major Moulton, that I *will* know, and the minute I find out I'll talk to you again."

He went back to Siberia, where he found Tug and Paul, faces still tear-streaked, staring at something that looked like a small piece of wire.

"This is it, Uncle Ralph," Tug said, brokenly. "Don't see how it could be, but it is."

"What is what?" Kinnison demanded.

"Firing pin. Brittle. When you pull the safety, the force of the spring must break it off at this constricted section here."

"But damn it, Tug, it doesn't make sense. It's tension . . . but wait—

there'd be some horizontal component, at that. But they'd have to be brittle as glass.''

"I know it. It doesn't seem to make much sense. But we were there, you know—and I assembled every one of those God damned mines myself. Nothing else could possibly have made that mine go off just when it did.''

"O.K., Tug. We'll test 'em. Call Bart in—he can have the scale-lab boys rig us up a gadget by the time we can get some more of those pins in off the line.''

They tested a hundred, under the normal tension of the spring, and three of them broke. They tested another hundred. Five broke. They stared at each other.

"That's it,'' Kinnison declared. "But this will stink to high Heaven—have Inspection break out a new lot and we'll test a thousand.''

Of that thousand pins, thirty two broke.

"Bart, will you dictate a one-page preliminary report to Vera and rush it over to Building One as fast as you can? I'll go over and tell Moulton a few things.''

Major Moulton was, as usual, "in conference,'' but Kinnison was in no mood to wait.

"Tell him,'' he instructed the Major's private secretary, who had barred his way, "that either he will talk to me right now or I will call District Safety over his head. I'll give him sixty seconds to decide which.''

Moulton decided to see him. "I'm very busy, Doctor Kinnison, but . . .''

"I don't give a swivel-eyed tinker's damn how busy you are. I told you that the minute I found out what was the matter with the M2 mine I'd talk to you again. Here I am. Brittle firing pins. Three and two-tenths percent defective. So I'm . . .''

"Very irregular, Doctor. The matter will have to go through channels . . .''

"Not this one. The formal report is going through channels, but as I started to tell you, this is an emergency report to you as Chief of Safety. Since the defect is not covered by specs, neither Process nor Ordnance can reject except by test, and whoever does the testing will very probably be killed. Therefore, as every employee of Stoner and Black is not only authorized but positively instructed to do upon discovering an unsafe condition, I am reporting it direct to Safety. Since my whiskers are a trifle longer than an operator's, I am reporting it direct to the Head of the Safety Division; and I am telling you that if you don't do something about it damned quick—stop production and slap a HOLD order on all the M2AP's you can reach—I'll call District and make you personally responsible for every premature that occurs from now on."

Since any safety man, anywhere, would much rather stop a process than authorize one, and since this particular safety man loved to throw his weight around, Kinnison was surprised that Moulton did not act instantly. The fact that he did not so act should have, but did not, give the naive Kinnison much information as to conditions existing Outside the Fence.

"But they need those mines very badly; they are an item of very heavy production. If we stop them . . . how long? Have you any suggestions?"

"Yes. Call District and have them rush through a change of spec— include heat-treat and a modified Charpy test. In the meantime, we can get back into full production tomorrow if you have District slap a hundred-per-cent inspection onto those pins."

"Excellent! We can do that—very fine work, Doctor! Miss Morgan, get District at once!"

This, too, should have warned Kinnison, but it did not. He went back to the Laboratory.

Tempus fugited.

Orders came to get ready to load M67 H.E., A.T. (105 m/m High Explosive, Armor Tearing) shell on the Nine, and the Siberians went joyously to work upon the new load. The explosive was to be a mixture of TNT and a polysyllabic compound, everything about which was highly confidential and restricted.

"But what the hell's so hush-hush about *that* stuff?" demanded Blondie, who, with five or six others, was crowding around the Czar's desk. Unlike the days of Cappy Sumner, the private office of the Chief Chemist was now as much Siberia as Siberia itself. "The Germans developed it originally, didn't they?"

"Yes, and the Italians used it against the Ethiopians—which was why their bombs were so effective. But it says 'hush-hush', so that's the way it will be. And if you talk in your sleep, Blondie, tell Betty not to listen."

The Siberians worked. The M67 was put into production. It was such a success that orders for it came in faster than they could be filled. Production was speeded up. Small cavitations began to appear. Nothing serious, since they passed Inspection. Nevertheless, Kinnison protested, in a formal report, receipt of which was formally acknowledged.

General Somebody-or-other, Entwhistle's Commanding Officer, whom none of the Siberians had ever met, was transferred to more active duty, and a colonel—Snodgrass or some such name—took his place. Ordnance got a new Chief Inspector.

An M67, Entwhistle loaded, prematured in a gun-barrel, killing twenty seven men. Kinnison protested again, verbally this time, at a staff meeting. He was assured—verbally—that a formal and thorough investigation was being made. Later he was informed—verbally and without witnesses—that the investigation had been completed and that the loading was not at fault. A new Commanding Officer—Lieutenant-Colonel Franklin—appeared.

The Siberians, too busy to do more than glance at newspapers, paid very little attention to a glider-crash in which several notables were killed. They heard that an investigation was being made, but even the Czar did not know until later that Washington had for once acted fast in correcting a bad situation; that Inspection, which had been under Production, was summarily divorced therefrom. And gossip spread abroad that Stillman, then Head of the Inspection Division, was not a big enough man for the job. Thus it was an entirely unsuspecting Kinnison who was called into the innermost private office of Thomas Keller, the Superintendent of Production.

"Kinnison, how in hell do you handle those Siberians? I never saw anything like them before in my life."

"No, and you never will again. Nothing on Earth except a war could get them together or hold them together. I don't 'handle' them—they can't be 'handled'. I give them a job to do and let them do it. I back them up. That's all."

"Umngpf." Keller grunted. "That's a hell of a formula—if I want anything done right I've got to do it myself. But whatever your system is, it works. But what I wanted to talk to you about is, how'd you like to be Head of the Inspection Division, which would be enlarged to include your present Chemical Section?"

"Huh?" Kinnison demanded, dumbfounded.

"At a salary well up on the confidential scale." Keller wrote a figure upon a piece of paper, showed it to his visitor, then burned it in an ashtray.

Kinnison whistled. "I'd like it—for more reasons than that. But I didn't know that you—or have you already checked with the General and Mr. Black?"

"Naturally," came the smooth reply. "In fact, I suggested it to them and have their approval. Perhaps you are curious to know why?"

"I certainly am."

"For two reasons. First, because you have developed a crew of technical experts that is the envy of every technical man in the country.

Second, you and your Siberians have done every job I ever asked you to, and done it fast. As a Division Head, you will no longer be under me, but I am right, I think, in assuming that you will work with me just as efficiently as you do now?''

"I can't think of any reason why I wouldn't.'' This reply was made in all honesty; but later, when he came to understand what Keller had meant, how bitterly Kinnison was to regret its making!

He moved into Stillman's office, and found there what he thought was ample reason for his predecessor's failure to make good. To his way of thinking it was tremendously over-staffed, particularly with Assistant Chief Inspectors. Delegation of authority, so widely preached throughout Entwhistle Ordnance Plant, had not been given even lip service here. Stillman had not made a habit of visiting the lines; nor did the Chief Line Inspectors, the boys who really knew what was going on, ever visit him. They reported to the Assistants, who reported to Stillman, who handed down his Jovian pronouncements.

Kinnison set out, deliberately this time, to mold his key Chief Line Inspectors into just such a group as the Siberians already were. He released the Assistants to more productive work; retaining of Stillman's office staff only a few clerks and his private secretary, one Celeste de St. Aubin, a dynamic, vivacious—at times explosive—brunette. He gave the boys on the Lines full authority; the few who could not handle the load he replaced with men who could. At first the Chief Line Inspectors simply could not believe; but after the affair of the forty millimeter, in which Kinnison rammed the decision of his subordinate past Keller, past the General, past Stoner and Black, and clear up to the Commanding Officer before he made it stick, they were his to a man.

Others of his Section Heads, however, remained aloof. Pettler, whose Technical Section was now part of Inspection, and Wilson, of Gages, were two of those who talked largely and glowingly, but acted obstructively if they acted at all. As weeks went on, Kinnison became wiser and wiser, but made no sign. One day, during a lull, his secretary hung out the "In Conference" sign and went into Kinnison's private office.

"There isn't a reference to any such Investigation anywhere in Central Files.'' She paused, as if to add something, then turned to leave.

"As you were, Celeste. Sit down. I expected that. Suppressed—if made at all. You're a smart girl, Celeste, and you know the ropes. You know that you can talk to me, don't you?''

"Yes, but this is ... well, the word is going around that they are going to break you, just as they have broken every other good man on the Reservation.''

"I expected that, too." The words were quiet enough, but the man's jaw tightened. "Also, I know how they are going to do it."

"How?"

"This speed-up on the Nine. They know that I won't stand still for the kind of casts that Keller's new procedure, which goes into effect tonight, is going to produce . . . and this new C.O. probably will."

Silence fell, broken by the secretary.

"General Sanford, our first C.O., was a soldier, and a good one," she declared finally. "So was Colonel Snodgrass. Lieutenant Colonel Franklin wasn't; but he was too much of a man to do the dir . . ."

"Dirty work," dryly. "Exactly. Go on."

"And Stoner, the New York half—ninety five percent, really—of Stoner and Black, Inc., is a Big Time Operator. So we get this damned nincompoop of a major, who doesn't know a f-u-s-e from a f-u-z-e, direct from a Wall Street desk."

"So what?" One must have heard Ralph Kinnison say those two words to realize how much meaning they can be made to carry.

"So what!" the girl blazed, wringing her hands. "Ever since you have been over here I have been expecting you to blow up—to smash something—in spite of the dozens of times you have told me 'a fighter can not slug effectively, Celeste, until he gets both feet firmly planted.' When—*when*—are you going to get your feet planted?"

"Never, I'm afraid," he said glumly, and she stared. "So I'll have to start slugging with at least one foot in the air."

That startled her. "Explain, please?"

"I wanted *proof.* Stuff that I could take to the District—that I could use to tack some hides out flat on a barn door with. Do I get it? I do not. Not a shred. Neither can you. What chance do you think there is of ever getting any real proof?"

"Very little," Celeste admitted. "But you can at least smash Pettler, Wilson, and that crowd. *How* I hate those slimy snakes! I wish that you could smash Tom Keller, the poisonous moron!"

"Not so much moron—although he acts like one at times—as an ignorant puppet with a head swelled three sizes too big for his hat. But you can quit yapping about slugging—fireworks are due to start at two o'clock tomorrow afternoon, when Drake is going to reject tonight's run of shell."

"Really? But I don't see how either Pettler or Wilson come in."

"They don't. A fight with those small fry—even smashing them—wouldn't make enough noise. Keller."

"Keller!" Celeste squealed. "But you'll . . ."

"I know I'll get fired. So what? By tackling him I can raise enough hell so that the Big Shots will have to cut out at least some of the rough stuff. You'll probably get fired too, you know—you've been too close to me for your own good.''

"Not me." She shook her head vigorously. "The minute they terminate you, I quit. Poof! Who cares? Besides, I can get a better job in Townville."

"Without leaving the Project. That's what I figured. It's the boys I'm worried about. I've been getting them ready for this for weeks."

"But they will quit, too. Your Siberians—your Inspectors—of a surety they will quit, every one!"

"They won't release them; and what Stoner and Black will do to them, even after the war, if they quit without releases, shouldn't be done to a dog. They won't quit, either—at least, if they don't try to push them around too much. Keller's mouth is watering to get hold of Siberia, but he'll never make it, nor any one of his stooges . . . I'd better dictate a memorandum to Black on that now, while I'm calm and collected; telling him what he'll have to do to keep my boys from tearing Entwhistle apart."

"But do you think he will pay any attention to it?"

"I'll say he will!" Kinnison snorted. "Don't kid yourself about Black, Celeste. He's a smart man, and before this is done he'll know that he'll have to keep his nose clean."

"But you—how can you do it?" Celeste marveled. "Me, I would urge them on. Few would have the patriotism . . ."

"Patriotism, hell! If that were all, I would have stirred up a revolution long ago. It's for the boys, in years to come. They've got to keep *their* noses clean, too. Get your notebook, please, and take this down. Rough draft—I'm going to polish it up until it has teeth and claws in every line."

And that evening, after supper, he informed Eunice of all the new developments.

"Is it still O.K. with you," he concluded, "for me to get myself fired off of this high-salaried job of mine?"

"Certainly. Being you, how can you do anything else? Oh, how I wish I could wring their necks!" That conversation went on and on, but additional details are not necessary here.

Shortly after two o'clock of the following afternoon, Celeste took a call; and listened shamelessly.

"Kinnison speaking."

"Tug, Uncle Ralph. The casts sectioned just like we thought they would. Dead ringers for Plate D. So Drake hung a red ticket on every tray. Piddy was right there, waiting, and started to raise hell. So I chipped in, and he beat it so fast that I looked to see his coat-tail catch fire. Drake didn't quite like to call you, so I did. If Piddy keeps on going at the rate he left here, he'll be in Keller's office in nothing flat.''

"O.K., Tug. Tell Drake that the shell he rejected are going to stay rejected, and to come in right now with his report. Would you like to come along?''

"*Would* I!'' Tugwell hung up, and:

"But do you want *him* here, Doc?'' Celeste asked, anxiously, without considering whether or not her boss would approve of her eavesdropping.

"I certainly do. If I can keep Tug from blowing his top, the rest of the boys will stay in line.''

A few minutes later Tugwell strode in, bringing with him Drake, the Chief Line Inspector of the Nine Line. Shortly thereafter the office door was wrenched open. Keller had come to Kinnison, accompanied by the Superintendent whom the Siberians referred to, somewhat contemptuously, as "Piddy.''

"Damn your soul, Kinnison, come out here—I want to talk to you!'' Keller roared, and doors snapped open up and down the long corridor.

"Shut up, you God damned louse!'' This from Tugwell, who, black eyes almost emitting sparks, was striding purposefully forward. "I'll sock you so damned hard that . . .''

"Pipe down, Tug, I'll handle this.'' Kinnison's voice was not loud, but it had then a peculiarly carrying and immensely authoritative quality. "Verbally or physically; however he wants to have it.''

He turned to Keller, who had jumped backward into the hall to avoid the young Siberian.

"As for you, Keller, if you had the brains that God gave bastard geese in Ireland, you would have had this conference in private. Since you started it in public, however, I'll finish it in public. How you came to pick *me* for a yes-man I'll never know—just one more measure of your stupidity, I suppose.''

"Those shell are perfect!'' Keller shouted. "Tell Drake here to pass them, right now. If you don't, by God, I'll . . .''

"Shut up!'' Kinnison's voice cut. "I'll do the talking—you listen. The spec says quote shall be free from objectionable cavitation unquote. The Line Inspectors, who know their stuff, say that those cavitations are objectionable. So do the Chemical Engineers. Therefore, as far as I am concerned, they are objectionable. Those shell are rejected, and they will *stay* rejected.''

"That's what *you* think,'' Keller raged. "But there'll be a new Head of Inspection, who will pass them, tomorrow morning!''

"In that you may be half right. When you get done licking Black's boots, tell him that I am in my office."

Kinnison re-entered his suite. Keller, swearing, strode away with Piddy. Doors clicked shut.

"I *am* going to quit, Uncle Ralph, law or no law!" Tugwell stormed. "They'll run that bunch of crap through, and then . . .''

"Will you promise not to quit until they do?" Kinnison asked, quietly.

"Huh?" "What?" Tugwell's eyes—and Celeste's—were pools of astonishment. Celeste, being on the inside, understood first.

"Oh—to keep his nose clean—I see!" she exclaimed.

"Exactly. Those shell will not be accepted, nor any like them. On the surface, we got licked. I will get fired. You will find, however, that we won this particular battle. And if you boys stay here and hang together and keep on slugging, you can win a lot more."

"Maybe, if we raise enough hell, we can make them fire us, too?" Drake suggested.

"I doubt it. But unless I'm wrong, you can just about write your own ticket from now on, if you play it straight." Kinnison grinned to himself, at something which the young people could not see.

"You told me what Stoner and Black would do to us," Tugwell said, intensely. "What I'm afraid of is that they'll do it to you."

"They can't. Not a chance in the world," Kinnison assured him. "You fellows are young—not established. But I'm well-enough known in my own field so that if they tried to blackball me they'd just get themselves laughed at, and they know it. So beat it back to the Nine, you kids, and hang red tickets on everything that doesn't cross-section up to standard. Tell the gang goodbye for me—I'll keep you posted."

In less than an hour Kinnison was called into the Office of the President. He was completely at ease; Black was not.

"It has been decided to . . . uh . . . ask for your resignation," the President announced at last.

"Save your breath," Kinnison advised. "I came down here to do a job, and the only way you can keep me from doing that job is to fire me."

"That was not . . . uh . . . entirely unexpected. A difficulty arose, however, in deciding what reason to put on your termination papers."

"I can well believe that. You can put down anything you like," Kinnison shrugged, "with one exception. Any implication of incompetence and you'll have to prove it in court."

"Incompatibility, say?"

"O.K."

"Miss Briggs—'Incompatibility with the highest echelon of Stoner and Black, Inc.,' please. You may as well wait, Dr. Kinnison; it will take only a moment."

"Fine. I've got a couple of things to say. First, I know as well as you do that you're between Scylla and Charybdis—damned if you do and damned if you don't."

"Certainly not! Ridiculous!" Black blustered, but his eyes wavered. "Where did you get such a preposterous idea? What do you mean?"

"If you ram those sub-standard H.E.A.T. shell through, you are going to have some more prematures. Not many—the stuff is actually almost good enough—one in ten thousand, say: perhaps one in fifty thousand. But you know damned well that you can't afford *any*. What my Siberians and Inspectors know about you and Keller and Piddy and the Nine Line would be enough; but to cap the climax that brainless jackal of yours let the cat completely out of the bag this afternoon, and everybody in Building One was listening. One more premature would blow Entwhistle wide open—would start something that not all the politicians in Washington could stop. On the other hand, if you scrap those lots and go back to pouring good loads, your Mr. Stoner, of New York and Washington, will be very unhappy and will scream bloody murder. I'm sure, however, that you won't offer any Plate D loads to Ordnance—in view of the temper of my boys and girls, and the number of people who heard your dumb stooge give you away, you won't dare to. In fact, I told some of my people that you wouldn't; that you are a smart enough operator to keep your nose clean."

"You *told* them!" Black shouted, in anger and dismay.

"Yes? Why not?" The words were innocent enough, but Kinnison's expression was full of meaning. "I don't want to seem trite, but you are just beginning to find out that honesty and loyalty are a hell of a hard team to beat."

"Get out! Take these termination papers and GET OUT!"

And Doctor Ralph K. Kinnison, head high, strode out of President Black's office and out of Entwhistle Ordnance Plant.

6

19—?

"Theodore K. Kinnison!" A crisp, clear voice snapped from the speaker of an apparently cold, ordinary-enough-looking radio-television set.

A burly young man caught his breath sharply as he leaped to the instrument and pressed an inconspicuous button.

"Theodore K. Kinnison acknowledging!" The plate remained dark, but he knew that he was being scanned.

"Operation Bullfinch!" the speaker blatted.

Kinnison gulped. "Operation Bullfinch—Off!" he managed to say.

"Off!"

He pushed the button again and turned to face the tall, trim honey-blonde who stood tensely poised in the archway. Her eyes were wide and protesting; both hands clutched at her throat.

"Uh-huh, sweets, they're coming—over the Pole," he gritted. "Two hours, more or less."

"Oh, Ted!" She threw herself into his arms. They kissed, then broke away.

The man picked up two large suit-cases, already packed—everything else, including food and water, had been in the car for weeks—and made strides. The girl rushed after him, not bothering even to close the door of the apartment, scooping up *en passant* a leggy boy of four and a chubby, curly-haired girl of two or thereabouts. They ran across the lawn toward a big, low-slung sedan.

"Sure you got your caffeine tablets?" he demanded as they ran.

"Uh—huh."

"You'll need 'em. Drive like the devil—*stay ahead!* You can—this heap has got the legs of a centipede and you've got plenty of gas and oil. Eleven hundred miles from anywhere and a population of one-tenth per square mile—you'll be safe there if anybody is."

"It isn't us I'm worried about—it's you!" she panted. "Technos' wives get a few minutes' notice ahead of the H-blast—I'll be ahead of the rush and I'll stay ahead. It's you, Ted—*you!*"

"Don't worry, keed. That popcycle of mine has got legs, too, and there won't be so much traffic, the way I'm going."

"Oh, blast! I didn't mean that, and you know it!"

They were at the car. While he jammed the two bags into an exactly-fitting space, she tossed the children into the front seat, slid lithely under the wheel, and started the engine.

"I know you didn't, sweetheart. I'll be back." He kissed her and the little girl, the while shaking hands with his son. "Kidlets, you and mother are going out to visit Grand-dad Kinnison, like we told you all about. Lots of fun. I'll be along later. Now, Lady Lead-Foot, scram—and shovel on the coal!"

The heavy vehicle backed and swung; gravel flew as the accelerator-pedal hit the floor.

Kinnison galloped across the alley and opened the door of a small garage, revealing a long, squat motorcycle. Two deft passes of his hands and two of his three spotlights were no longer white—one flashed a brilliant purple, the other a searing blue. He dropped a perforated metal box into a hanger and flipped a switch—a peculiarly-toned siren began its ululating shriek. He took the alley turn at an angle of forty-five degrees; burned the pavement toward Diversey.

The light was red. No matter—everybody had stopped—that siren could be heard for miles. He barreled into the intersection; his step-plate ground the concrete as he made a screaming left turn.

A siren—creeping up from behind. City tone. Two red spots—city cop—so soon—good! He cut his gun a trifle, the other bike came along-side.

"Is this IT?" the uniformed rider yelled, over the coughing thunder of the competing exhausts.

"Yes!" Kinnison yelled back. "Clear Diversey to the Outer Drive, and the Drive south to Gary and north to Waukegan. Snap it up!"

The white-and-black motorcycle slowed; shot over toward the curb. The officer reached for his microphone.

Kinnison sped on. At Cicero Avenue, although he had a green light, traffic was so heavy that he had to slow down; at Pulaski two policemen waved him through a red. Beyond Sacramento nothing moved on wheels.

Seventy . . . seventy five . . . he took the bridge at eighty, both wheels in air for forty feet. Eighty five . . . ninety . . . that was about all he could do and keep the heap on so rough a road. Also, he did not have Diversey all to himself any more; blue-and-purple-flashing bikes were coming in from every side-street. He slowed to a conservative fifty and went into close formation with the other riders.

The H-blast—the city-wide warning for the planned and supposedly orderly evacuation of all Chicago—sounded, but Kinnison did not hear it.

Across the Park, edging over to the left so that the boys going south would have room to make the turn—even such riders as those need *some* room to make a turn at fifty miles per hour!

Under the viaduct—biting brakes and squealing tires at that sharp, narrow, right-angle left turn—north on the wide, smooth Drive!

That highway was made for speed. So were those machines. Each rider, as he got into the flat, lay down along his tank, tucked his chin behind the cross-bar, and twisted both throttles out against their stops. They were in a hurry. They had a long way to go; and if they did not get there in time to stop those trans-polar atomic missiles, all hell would be out for noon.

Why was all this necessary? This organization, this haste, this split-second timing, this city-wide exhibition of insane hippodrome riding? Why were not all these motorcycle-racers stationed permanently at their posts, so as to be ready for any emergency? Because America, being a democracy, could not strike first, but had to wait—wait in instant readiness—until she was actually attacked. Because every good Techno in America had his assigned place in some American Defense Plan; of which Operation Bullfinch was only one. Because, without the presence of those Technos at their every-day jobs, all ordinary technological work in America would perforce have stopped.

A branch road curved away to the right. Scarcely slowing down, Kinnison bulleted into the turn and through an open, heavily-guarded gate. Here his mount and his lights were passwords enough: the real test would come later. He approached a towering structure of alloy—jammed on his brakes—stopped beside a soldier who, as soon as Kinnison jumped off, mounted the motorcycle and drove it away.

Kinnison dashed up to an apparently blank wall, turned his back upon four commissioned officers holding cocked forty-fives at the ready, and fitted his right eye into a cup. Unlike fingerprints, retinal patterns cannot be imitated, duplicated, or altered; any imposter would have died instantly, without arrest or question. For every man who belonged aboard that rocket had been checked and tested—*how* he had been checked and tested!—since one spy, in any one of those Technos' chairs, could wreak damage untellable.

The port snapped open. Kinnison climbed a ladder into the large, but crowded, Operations Room.

"Hi, Teddy!" a yell arose.

"Hi, Walt! Hi-ya, Red! What-ho, Baldy!" and so on. These men were friends of old.

"Where are they?" he demanded. "Is our stuff getting away? Lemme take a peek at the Ball!"

"I'll say it is! O.K., Ted, squeeze in here!"

He squeezed in. It was not a ball, but a hemisphere, slightly oblate and centered approximately by the North Pole. A multitude of red dots moved slowly—a hundred miles upon that map was a small distance— northward over Canada; a closer-packed, less numerous group of yellowish-greens, already on the American side of the Pole, was coming south.

As had been expected, the Americans had more missiles than did the enemy. The other belief, that America had more adequate defenses and better-trained, more highly skilled defenders, would soon be put to test.

A string of blue lights blazed across the continent, from Nome through Skagway and Wallaston and Churchill and Kaniapiskau to Belle Isle; America's First Line of Defense. Regulars all. Ambers almost blanketed those blues; their combat rockets were already grabbing altitude. The Second Line, from Portland, Seattle, and Vancouver across to Halifax, also showed solid green, with some flashes of amber. Part Regulars; part National Guard.

Chicago was in the Third Line, all National Guard, extending from San Francisco to New York. Green—alert and operating. So were the Fourth, the Fifth, and the Sixth. Operation Bullfinch was clicking; on schedule to the second.

A bell clanged; the men sprang to their stations and strapped down. Every chair was occupied. Combat Rocket Number One Oh Six Eight Five, full-powered by the disintegrating nuclei of unstable isotopes, took off with a whooshing roar which even her thick walls could not mute.

The Technos, crushed down into their form-fitting cushions by three G's of acceleration, clenched their teeth and took it.

Higher! Faster! The rocket shivered and trembled as it hit the wall at the velocity of sound, but it did not pause.

Higher! Faster! Higher! Fifty miles high. One hundred . . . five hundred . . . a thousand . . . fifteen hundred . . . two thousand! Half a radius— the designated altitude at which the Chicago Contingent would go into action.

Acceleration was cut to zero. The Technos, breathing deeply in relief, donned peculiarly-goggled helmets and set up their panels.

Kinnison stared into his plate with everything he could put into his optic nerve. This was not like the Ball, in which the lights were electronically placed, automatically controlled, clear, sharp, and steady. This was radar. A radar considerably different from that of 1948, of course, and greatly improved, but still pitifully inadequate in dealing with objects separated by hundreds of miles and traveling at velocities of thousands of miles per hour!

Nor was this like the practice cruises, in which the targets had been harmless barrels or equally harmless dirigible rockets. This was the real thing; the targets today would be lethal objects indeed. Practice gunnery, with only a place in the Proficiency List at stake, had been exciting enough: this was too exciting—*much* too exciting—for the keenness of brain and the quickness and steadiness of eye and of hand so soon to be required.

A target? Or was it? Yes—three or four of them!

"Target One—zone Ten," a quiet voice spoke into Kinnison's ear and one of the white specks upon his plate turned yellowish green. The same words, the same lights, were heard and seen by the eleven other Technos of Sector A, of which Kinnison, by virtue of standing at the top of his Combat Rocket's Proficiency List, was Sector Chief. He knew that the voice was that of Sector A's Fire Control Officer, whose duty it was to determine, from courses, velocities, and all other data to be had from ground and lofty observers, the order in which his Sector's targets should be eliminated. And Sector A, an imaginary but sharply-defined cone, was in normal maneuvering the hottest part of the sky. Fire Control's "Zone Ten" had informed him that the object was at extreme range and hence there would be plenty of time. Nevertheless:

"Lawrence—two! Doyle—one! Drummond—stand by with three!" he snapped, at the first word.

In the instant of hearing his name each Techno stabbed down a series of studs and there flowed into his ears a rapid stream of figures—the up-to-the-second data from every point of observation as to every element of motion of his target. He punched the figures into his calculator, which would correct automatically for the motion of his own vessel—glanced once at the printed solution of the problem—tramped down upon a pedal once, twice, or three times, depending upon the number of projectiles he had been directed to handle.

Kinnison had ordered Lawrence, a better shot than Doyle, to launch two torpedoes; neither of which, at such long range, was expected to strike its mark. His second, however, should come close; so close that the instantaneous data sent back to both screens—and to Kinnison's—by the torpedo itself would make the target a sitting duck for Doyle, the less proficient follower.

Drummond, Kinnison's Number Three, would not launch his missiles unless Doyle missed. Nor could both Drummond and Harper, Kinnison's Number Two, be "out" at once. One of the two had to be "in" at all times, to take Kinnison's place in charge of the Sector if the Chief were ordered out. For while Kinnison could order either Harper or Drummond on target, he could not send himself. He could go out only when ordered to do so by Fire Control: Sector Chiefs were reserved for emergency use only.

"Target Two—Zone Nine," Fire Control said.

"Carney, two. French, one. Day, stand by with three!" Kinnison ordered.

"Damn it—missed!" This from Doyle. "Buck fever—no end."

"O.K., boy—that's why we're starting so soon. I'm shaking like a vibrator myself. We'll get over it . . ."

The point of light which represented Target One bulged slightly and went out. Drummond had connected and was back "in".

"Target Three—Zone Eight. Four—eight," Fire Control remarked.

"Target Three—Higgins and Green; Harper stand by. Four—Case and Santos: Lawrence."

After a minute or two of actual combat the Technos of Sector A began to steady down. Stand-by men were no longer required and were no longer assigned.

"Target Forty-one—six," said Fire Control; and:

"Lawrence, two. Doyle, two," ordered Kinnison. This was routine enough, but in a moment:

"Ted!" Lawrence snapped. "Missed—wide—both barrels. Forty-one's dodging—manned or directed—coming like hell—watch it, Doyle—WATCH IT!"

"Kinnison, take it!" Fire Control barked, voice now neither low nor steady, and without waiting to see whether Doyle would hit or miss. "It's in Zone Three already—collision course!"

"Harper! Take over!"

Kinnison got the data, solved the equations, launched five torpedoes at fifty gravities of acceleration. One . . . two—three-four-five; the last three as close together as they could fly without setting off their proximity fuzes.

Communications and mathematics and the electronic brains of calculating machines had done all that they could do; the rest was up to human skill, to the perfection of coordination and the speed of reaction of human mind, nerve, and muscle.

Kinnison's glance darted from plate to panel to computer-tape to meter to galvanometer and back to plate; his left hand moved in tiny arcs the knobs whose rotation varied the intensities of two mutually perpendicular components of his torpedoes' drives. He listened attentively to the reports of triangulating observers, now giving him data covering his own missiles, as well as the target object. The fingers of his right hand punched almost constantly the keys of his computer; he corrected almost constantly his torpedoes' course.

"Up a hair," he decided. "Left about a point."

The target moved away from its predicted path.

Down two—left three—down a hair—*Right!* The thing was almost through Zone Two; was blasting into Zone One.

He thought for a second that his first torp was going to connect. It almost did—only a last-instant, full-powered side thrust enabled the target to evade it. Two numbers flashed white upon his plate; his actual error, exact to the foot of distance and to the degree on the clock, measured and transmitted back to his board by instruments in his torpedo.

Working with instantaneous and exact data, and because the enemy had so little time in which to act, Kinnison's second projectile made a very near miss indeed. His third was a graze; so close that its proximity fuze functioned, detonating the cyclonite-packed warhead. Kinnison knew that his third went off, because the error-figures vanished, almost in the instant of their coming into being, as its detecting and transmitting instruments were destroyed. That one detonation might have been enough; but Kinnison had had one glimpse of his error—how small it was!—and had a fraction of a second of time. Hence Four and Five slammed home; dead center. Whatever that target had been, it was no longer a threat.

"Kinnison, in," he reported briefly to Fire Control, and took over from Harper the direction of the activities of Sector A.

The battle went on. Kinnison sent Harper and Drummond out time after time. He himself was given three more targets. The first wave of the enemy—what was left of it—passed. Sector A went into action, again at extreme range, upon the second. Its remains, too, plunged downward and onward toward the distant ground.

The third wave was really tough. Not that it was actually any worse than the first two had been, but the CR10685 was no longer getting the data which her Technos ought to have to do a good job; and every man aboard her knew why. Some enemy stuff had got through, of course;

and the observatories, both on the ground and above it—the eyes of the whole American Defense—had suffered heavily.

Nevertheless, Kinnison and his fellows were not too perturbed. Such a condition was not entirely unexpected. They were now veterans; they had been tried and had not been found wanting. They had come unscathed through a bath of fire the like of which the world had never before known. Give them any kind of computation at all—or no computation at all except old CR10685's own radar and their own torps, of which they still had plenty—and they could and would take care of anything that could be thrown at them.

The third wave passed. Targets became fewer and fewer. Action slowed down . . . stopped.

The Technos, even the Sector Chiefs, knew nothing whatever of the progress of the battle as a whole. They did not know where their rocket was, or whether it was going north, east, south, or west. They knew when it was going up or down only by the "seats of their pants." They did not even know the nature of the targets they destroyed, since upon their plates all targets looked alike—small, bright, greenish-yellow spots. Hence:

"Give us the dope, Pete, if we've got a minute to spare," Kinnison begged of his Fire Control Officer. "You know more than we do—give!"

"It's coming in now," came prompt reply. "Six of those targets that did such fancy dodging were atomics, aimed at the Lines. Five were dirigibles, with our number on 'em. You fellows did a swell job. Very little of their stuff got through—not enough, they say, to do much damage to a country as big as the U.S.A. On the other hand, they stopped scarcely any of ours—they apparently didn't have anything to compare with you Technos.

"But all hell seems to be busting loose, all over the world. Our east and west coasts are both being attacked, they say; but are holding. Operation Daisy and Operation Fairfield are clicking, just like we did. Europe, they say, is going to hell—everybody is taking pot-shots at everybody else. One report says that the South American nations are bombing each other . . . Asia, too . . . nothing definite; as straight dope comes in I'll relay it to you.

"We came through in very good shape, considering . . . losses less than anticipated, only seven percent. The First Line—as you know already—took a God-awful shellacking; in fact, the Churchill-Belcher section was practically wiped out, which was what lost us about all of our Observation . . . We are now just about over the southern end of Hudson Bay, heading down and south to join in making a vertical Fleet

Formation . . . no more waves coming, but they say to expect attacks from low-flying combat rockets—there goes the alert! On your toes, fellows—but there isn't a thing on Sector A's scree . . ."

There wasn't. Since the CR10685 was diving downward and southward, there wouldn't be. Nevertheless, some observer aboard that rocket saw that atomic missile coming. Some Fire Control Officer yelled orders; some Technos did their best—and failed.

And such is the violence of nuclear fission; so utterly incomprehensible is its speed, that Theodore K. Kinnison died without realizing that anything whatever was happening to his ship or to him.

Gharlane of Eddore looked upon ruined Earth, his handiwork, and found it good. Knowing that it would be many hundreds of Tellurian years before that planet would again require his personal attention, he went elsewhere; to Rigel Four, to Palain Seven, and to the solar system of Velantia, where he found that his creatures the Overlords were not progressing according to schedule. He spent quite a little time there, then searched minutely and fruitlessly for evidence of inimical activity within the Innermost Circle.

And upon far Arisia a momentous decision was made: the time had come to curb sharply the hitherto unhampered Eddorians.

"We are ready, then, to war openly upon them?" Eukonidor asked, somewhat doubtfully. "Again to cleanse the planet Tellus of dangerous radioactives and of too-noxious forms of life is of course a simple matter. From our protected areas in North America a strong but democratic government can spread to cover the world. That government can be extended easily enough to include Mars and Venus. But Gharlane, who is to operate as Roger, who has already planted, in the Adepts of North Polar Jupiter, the seeds of the Jovian Wars . . ."

"Your visualization is sound, youth. Think on."

"Those interplanetary wars are of course inevitable, and will serve to strengthen and to unify the government of the Inner Planets . . . provided that Gharlane does not interfere . . . Oh, I see. Gharlane will not at first know; since a zone of compulsion will be held upon him. When he or some Eddorian fusion perceives that compulsion and breaks it— at some such time of high stress as the Nevian incident—it will be too late. Our fusions will be operating. Roger will be allowed to perform only such acts as will be for Civilization's eventual good. Nevia was selected as Prime Operator because of its location in a small region of the galaxy which is almost devoid of solid iron and because of its watery nature; its aquatic forms of life being precisely those in which the Eddorians are least interested. They will be given partial neutralization of inertia; they will be able to attain velocities a few times greater than that of light. That covers the situation, I think?"

"Very good, Eukonidor," the Elders approved. "A concise and accurate summation."

Hundreds of Tellurian years passed. The aftermath. Reconstruction. Advancement. One world—two worlds—three worlds—united, harmonious, friendly. The Jovian Wars. A solid, unshakeable union.

Nor did any Eddorian know that such fantastically rapid progress was being made. Indeed, Gharlane knew, as he drove his immense ship of space toward Sol, that he would find Tellus inhabited by peoples little above savagery.

And it should be noted in passing that not once, throughout all those centuries, did a man named Kinnison marry a girl with red-bronze-auburn hair and gold-flecked, tawny eyes.

BOOK THREE

Triplanetary

7

PIRATES OF SPACE

Apparently motionless to her passengers and crew, the Interplanetary liner *Hyperion* bored serenely onward through space at normal acceleration. In the railed-off sanctum in one corner of the control room a bell tinkled, a smothered whirr was heard, and Captain Bradley frowned as he studied the brief message upon the tape of the recorder—a message flashed to his desk from the operator's panel. He beckoned, and the second officer, whose watch it now was, read aloud:

"Reports of scout patrols still negative."

"Still negative." The officer scowled in thought. "They've already searched beyond the widest possible location of wreckage, too. Two unexplained disappearances inside a month—first the *Dione*, then the *Rhea*—and not a plate nor a lifeboat recovered. Looks bad, sir. One might be an accident; two might possibly be a coincidence..." His voice died away.

"But at three it would get to be a habit," the captain finished the thought. "And whatever happened, happened quick. Neither of them had time to say a word—their location recorders simply went dead. But of course they didn't have our detector screens nor our armament. According to the observatories we're in clear ether, but I wouldn't trust them from Tellus to Luna. You have given the new orders, of course?"

"Yes, sir. Detectors full out, all three courses of defensive screen on the trips, projectors manned, suits on the hooks. Every object detected to be investigated immediately—if vessels, they are to be warned to stay beyond extreme range. Anything entering the fourth zone is to be rayed."

"Right—we are going through!"

"But no known type of vessel could have made away with them

without detection," the second officer argued. "I wonder if there isn't something in those wild rumors we've been hearing lately?"

"Bah! Of course not!" snorted the captain. "Pirates in ships faster than light—sub-ethereal rays—nullification of gravity—mass without inertia—ridiculous! Proved impossible, over and over again. No, sir, if pirates are operating in space—and it looks very much like it—they won't get far against a good big battery full of kilowatt-hours behind three courses of heavy screen, and good gunners behind multiplex projectors. They're good enough for anybody. Pirates, Neptunians, angels, or devils—in ships or on broomsticks—if they tackle the *Hyperion* we'll burn them out of the ether!"

Leaving the captain's desk, the watch officer resumed his tour of duty. The six great lookout plates into which the alert observers peered were blank, their far-flung ultra-sensitive detector screens encountering no obstacle—the ether was empty for thousands upon thousands of kilometers. The signal lamps upon the pilot's panel were dark, its warning bells were silent. A brilliant point of white light in the center of the pilot's closely ruled micrometer grating, exactly upon the cross-hairs of his directors, showed that the immense vessel was precisely upon the calculated course, as laid down by the automatic integrating course plotters. Everything was quiet and in order.

"All's well, sir," he reported briefly to Captain Bradley—but all was not well.

Danger—more serious far in that it was not external—was even then, all unsuspected, gnawing at the great ship's vitals. In a locked and shielded compartment, deep down in the interior of the liner, was the great air purifier. Now a man leaned against the primary duct—the aorta through which flowed the stream of pure air supplying the entire vessel. This man, grotesque in full panoply of space armor, leaned against the duct, and as he leaned a drill bit deeper and deeper into the steel wall of the pipe. Soon it broke through, and the slight rush of air was stopped by the insertion of a tightly fitting rubber tube. The tube terminated in a heavy rubber balloon, which surrounded a frail glass bulb. The man stood tense, one hand holding before his silica-and-steel-helmeted head a large pocket chronometer, the other lightly grasping the balloon. A sneering grin was upon his face as he awaited the exact second of action—the carefully predetermined instant when his right hand, closing, would shatter the fragile flask and force its contents into the primary air stream of the *Hyperion!*

Far above, in the main saloon, the regular evening dance was in full swing. The ship's orchestra crashed into silence, there was a patter of applause, and Clio Marsden, radiant belle of the voyage, led her partner out into the promenade and up to one of the observation plates.

"Oh, we can't see the Earth any more!" she exclaimed. "Which way do you turn this, Mr. Costigan?"

"Like this," and Conway Costigan, burly young First Officer of the liner, turned the dials. "There—this plate is looking back, or down, at Tellus; this other one is looking ahead."

Earth was a brilliantly shining crescent far beneath the flying vessel. Above her, ruddy Mars and silvery Jupiter blazed in splendor ineffable against a background of utterly indescribable blackness—a background thickly besprinkled with dimensionless points of dazzling brilliance which were the stars.

"Oh, isn't it wonderful!" breathed the girl, awed. "Of course, I suppose that it's old stuff to you, but I'm a ground-gripper, you know, and I could look at it forever, I think. That's why I want to come out here after every dance. You know, I . . ."

Her voice broke off suddenly, with a queer, rasping catch, as she seized his arm in a frantic clutch and as quickly went limp. He stared at her sharply, and understood instantly the message written in her eyes—eyes now enlarged, staring, hard, brilliant, and full of soul-searing terror as she slumped down, helpless but for his support. In the act of exhaling as he was, lungs almost entirely empty, yet he held his breath until he had seized the microphone from his belt and had snapped the lever to "emergency."

"Control room!" he gasped then, and every speaker throughout the great cruiser of the void blared out the warning as he forced his already evacuated lungs to absolute emptiness. "Vee-Two Gas! Get tight!"

Writhing and twisting in his fierce struggle to keep his lungs from gulping in a draft of that noxious atmosphere, and with the unconscious form of the girl draped limply over his left arm, Costigan leaped toward the portal of the nearest lifeboat. Orchestra instruments crashed to the floor and dancing couples fell and sprawled inertly while the tortured First Officer swung the door of the lifeboat open and dashed across the tiny room to the air-valves. Throwing them wide open, he put his mouth to the orifice and let his laboring lungs gasp their eager fill of the cold blast roaring from the tanks. Then, air-hunger partially assuaged, he again held his breath, broke open the emergency locker, donned one of the space-suits always kept there, and opened its valves wide in order to flush out of his uniform any lingering trace of the lethal gas.

He then leaped back to his companion. Shutting off the air, he released a stream of pure oxygen, held her face in it, and made shift to force some of it into her lungs by compressing and releasing her chest against his own body. Soon she drew a spasmodic breath, choking and coughing, and he again changed the gaseous stream to one of pure air, speaking urgently as she showed signs of returning consciousness.

"Stand up!" he snapped. "Hang onto this brace and keep your face in this air-stream until I get a suit around you! Got me?"

She nodded weakly, and, assured that she could hold herself at the valve, it was the work of only a minute to encase her in one of the protective coverings. Then, as she sat upon a bench, recovering her strength, he flipped on the lifeboat's visiphone projector and shot its invisible beam up into the control room, where he saw space-armored figures furiously busy at the panels.

"Dirty work at the cross-roads!" he blazed to his captain, man to man—formality disregarded, as it so often was in the Triplanetary service. "There's skulduggery afoot somewhere in our primary air! Maybe that's the way they got those other two ships—pirates! Might have been a timed bomb—don't see how anybody could have stowed away down there through the inspections, and nobody but Franklin can neutralize the shield of the air room—but I'm going to look around, anyway. Then I'll join you fellows up there."

"What was it?" the shaken girl asked. "I think that I remember your saying 'Vee-Two gas.' That's forbidden! Anyway, I owe you my life, Conway, and I'll never forget it—never. Thanks—but the others—how about all the rest of us?"

"It was Vee-Two, and it is forbidden," Costigan replied grimly, eyes fast upon the flashing plate, whose point of projection was now deep in the bowels of the vessel. "The penalty for using it or having it is death on sight. Gangsters and pirates use it, since they have nothing to lose, being on the death list already. As for your life, I haven't saved it yet—you may wish I'd let it ride before we get done. The others are too far gone for oxygen—couldn't have brought even you around in a few more seconds, quick as I got to you. But there's a sure antidote—we all carry it in a lockbox in our armor—and we all know how to use it, because crooks all use Vee-Two and so we're always expecting it. But since the air will be pure again in half an hour we'll be able to revive the others easily enough if we can get by with whatever is going to happen next. There's the bird that did it, right in the air-room. It's the Chief Engineer's suit, but that isn't Franklin that's in it. Some passenger—disguised—slugged the Chief—took his suit and projectors—hole in duct—p-s-s-t! All washed out! Maybe that's all he was scheduled to do to us in this performance, but he'll do nothing else in this life!"

"Don't go down there!" protested the girl. "His armor is *so* much better than that emergency suit you are wearing, and he's got Mr. Franklin's Lewiston, besides!''

"Don't be an idiot!" he snapped. "We can't have a live pirate aboard—we're going to be altogether too busy with outsiders directly. Don't worry, I'm not going to give him a break. I'll take a Standish—I'll rub him out like a blot. Stay right here until I come back after you," he commanded, and the heavy door of the lifeboat clanged shut behind him as he leaped out into the promenade.

Straight across the saloon he made his way, paying no attention to the inert forms scattered here and there. Going up to a blank wall, he manipulated an almost invisible dial set flush with its surface, swung a heavy door aside, and lifted out the Standish—a fearsome weapon. Squat, huge, and heavy, it resembled somewhat an overgrown machine rifle, but one possessing a thick, short telescope, with several opaque condensing lenses and parabolic reflectors. Laboring under the weight of the thing, he strode along corridors and clambered heavily down short stairways. Finally he came to the purifier room, and grinned savagely as he saw the greenish haze of light obscuring the door and walls—the shield was still in place; the pirate was still inside, still flooding with the terrible Vee-Two the *Hyperion*'s primary air.

He set his peculiar weapon down, unfolded its three massive legs, crouched down behind it, and threw in a switch. Dull red beams of frightful intensity shot from the reflectors and sparks, almost of lightning proportions, leaped from the shielding screen under their impact. Roaring and snapping, the conflict went on for seconds, then, under the superior force of the Standish, the greenish radiance gave way. Behind it the metal of the door ran the gamut of color—red, yellow, blinding white—then literally exploded; molten, vaporized, burned away. Through the aperture thus made Costigan could plainly see the pirate in the space-armor of the chief engineer—an armor which was proof against rifle fire and which could reflect and neutralize for some little time even the terrific beam Costigan was employing. Nor was the pirate unarmed—a vicious flare of incandescence leaped from his Lewiston, to spend its force in spitting, crackling pyrotechnics against the ether-wall of the squat and monstrous Standish. But Costigan's infernal engine did not rely only upon vibratory destruction. At almost the first flash of the pirate's weapon the officer touched a trigger, there was a double report, ear-shattering in that narrowly confined space, and the pirate's body literally flew into mist as a half-kilogram shell tore through his armor and exploded. Costigan shut off his beam, and with not the slightest softening of one hard lineament stared around the air-room;

making sure that no serious damage had been done to the vital machinery of the air-purifier—the very lungs of the great space-ship.

Dismounting the Standish, he lugged it back up to the main saloon, replaced it in its safe, and again set the combination lock. Thence to the lifeboat, where Clio cried out in relief as she saw that he was unhurt.

"Oh, Conway, I've been so afraid something would happen to you!" she exclaimed, as he led her rapidly upward toward the control room. "Of course you . . ." she paused.

"Sure," he replied, laconically. "Nothing to it. How do you feel—about back to normal?"

"All right, I think, except for being scared to death and just about out of control. I don't suppose that I'll be good for anything, but whatever I can do, count me in on."

"Fine—you may be needed, at that. Everybody's out, apparently, except those like me, who had a warning and could hold their breath until they got to their suits."

"But how did you know what it was? You can't see it, nor smell it, nor anything."

"You inhaled a second before I did, and I saw your eyes. I've been in it before—and when you see a man get a jolt of that stuff just once, you never forget it. The engineers down below got it first, of course—it must have wiped them out. Then we got it in the saloon. Your passing out warned me, and luckily I had enough breath left to give the word. Quite a few of the fellows up above should have had time to get away—we'll see 'em all in the control room."

"I suppose that was why you revived me—in payment for so kindly warning you of the gas attack?" The girl laughed; shaky, but game.

"Something like that, probably," he answered, lightly. "Here we are—now we'll soon find out what's going to happen next."

In the control room they saw at least a dozen armored figures; not now rushing about, but seated at their instruments, tense and ready. Fortunate it was that Costigan—veteran of space as he was, though young in years—had been down in the saloon; fortunate that he had been familiar with that horrible outlawed gas; fortunate that he had had presence of mind enough and sheer physical stamina enough to send his warning without allowing one paralyzing trace to enter his own lungs. Captain Bradley, the men on watch, and several other officers in their quarters or in the ward-rooms—space-hardened veterans all—had obeyed instantly and without question the amplifiers' gasped command to "get tight." Exhaling or inhaling, their air-passages had snapped shut as that dread "Vee-Two" was heard, and they had literally jumped into their armored suits of space—flushing them out with volume after volume of unquestionable air; holding their breath to the last possible second, until their straining lungs could endure no more.

Costigan waved the girl to a vacant bench, cautiously changed into his own armor from the emergency suit he had been wearing, and approached the captain.

"Anything in sight, sir?" he asked, saluting. "They should have started something before this."

"They've started, but we can't locate them. We tried to send out a general sector alarm, but had hardly started when they blanketed our wave. Look at that!"

Following the captain's eyes, Costigan stared at the high powered set of the ship's operator. Upon the plate, instead of a moving, living, three-dimensional picture, there was a flashing glare of blinding white light; from the speaker, instead of intelligible speech, was issuing a roaring, crackling stream of noise.

"It's impossible!" Bradley burst out, violently. "There's not a gram of metal inside the fourth zone—within a hundred thousand kilometers—and yet they must be close to send such a wave as that. But the Second thinks not—what do you think, Costigan?" The bluff commander, reactionary and of the old school as was his breed, was furious—baffled, raging inwardly to come to grips with the invisible and indetectable foe. Face to face with the inexplicable, however, he listened to the younger men with unusual tolerance.

"It's not only possible; it's quite evident that they've got something we haven't." Costigan's voice was bitter. "But why shouldn't they have? Service ships never get anything until it's been experimented with for years, but pirates and such always get the new stuff as soon as it's discovered. The only good thing I can see is that we got part of a message away, and the scouts can trace that interference out there. But the pirates know that, too—it won't be long now," he concluded, grimly.

He spoke truly. Before another word was said the outer screen flared white under a beam of terrific power, and simultaneously there appeared upon one of the lookout plates a vivid picture of the pirate vessel—a huge, black torpedo of steel, now emitting flaring offensive beams of force.

Instantly the powerful weapons of the *Hyperion* were brought to bear, and in the blast of full-driven beams the stranger's screens flamed incandescent. Heavy guns, under the recoil of whose fierce salvos the frame of the giant globe trembled and shuddered, shot out their tons of high-explosive shell. But the pirate commander had known accurately the strength of the liner, and knew that her armament was impotent against the forces at his command. His screens were invulnerable, the giant shells were exploded harmlessly in mid-space, miles from their objective. And suddenly a frightful pencil of flame stabbed brilliantly from the black hulk of the enemy. Through the empty ether it tore, through the mighty defensive screens, through the tough metal of the outer and inner walls. Every ether-defense of the *Hyperion* vanished, and her acceleration dropped to a quarter of its normal value.

"Right through the battery room!" Bradley groaned. "We're on the emergency drive now. Our rays are done for, and we can't seem to put a shell anywhere near her with our guns!"

But ineffective as the guns were, they were silenced forever as a frightful beam of destruction stabbed relentlessly through the control room, whiffing out of existence the pilot, gunnery, and lookout panels and the men before them. The air rushed into space, and the suits of the three survivors bulged out into drum-head tightness as the pressure in the room decreased.

Costigan pushed the captain lightly toward a wall, then seized the girl and leaped in the same direction.

"Let's get out of here, quick!" he cried, the miniature radio instruments of the helmets automatically taking up the duty of transmitting speech as the sound disks refused to function. "They can't see us—our ether wall is still up and their spy-rays can't get through it from the outside, you know. They're working from blue-prints, and they'll probably take your desk next," and even as they bounded toward the door, now become the outer seal of an airlock, the pirates' beam tore through the space which they had just quitted.

Through the airlock, down through several levels of passengers' quarters they hurried, and into a lifeboat, whose one doorway commanded the full length of the third lounge—an ideal spot, either for defense or for escape outward by means of the miniature cruiser. As they entered their retreat they felt their weight begin to increase. More and more force was applied to the helpless liner, until it was moving at normal acceleration.

"What do you make of that, Costigan?" asked the captain. "Tractor beams?"

"Apparently. They've got something, all right. They're taking us somewhere, fast. I'll go get a couple of Standishes, and another suit of armor—we'd better dig in," and soon the small room became a veritable fortress, housing as it did those two formidable engines of destruction. Then the first officer made another and longer trip, returning with a complete suit of Triplanetary space armor, exactly like those worn by the two men, but considerably smaller.

"Just as an added factor of safety, you'd better put this on, Clio—those emergency suits aren't good for much in a battle. I don't suppose that you ever fired a Standish, did you?"

"No, but I can soon learn how to do it," she replied pluckily.

"Two is all that can work here at once, but you should know how to take hold in case one of us goes out. And while you're changing suits you'd better put on some stuff I've got here—Service Special phones and detectors. Stick this little disk onto your chest with this bit of tape; low down, out of sight. Just under your wishbone is the best place. Take off your wrist watch and wear this one *continuously*—never take it off for a second. Put on these pearls, and wear them all the time, too. Take this capsule and hide it against your skin, some place where it can't be found except by the most rigid search. Swallow it in an emergency—it goes down easily and works just as well inside as outside. It is the most important thing of all—you can get along with it alone if you lose everything else, but without that capsule the whole system's shot to pieces. With that outfit, if we should get separated, you can talk to us—we're both wearing 'em, although in somewhat different forms. You don't need to talk loud—just a mutter will be enough. They're handy little outfits—almost impossible to find, and capable of a lot of things."

"Thanks, Conway—I'll remember that, too," Clio replied, as she turned toward the tiny locker to follow his instructions. "But won't the scouts and patrols be catching us pretty quick? The operator sent a warning."

"Afraid the ether's empty, as far as we're concerned."

Captain Bradley had stood by in silent astonishment during this conversation. His eyes had bulged slightly at Costigan's "we're both wearing 'em," but he had held his peace and as the girl disappeared a look of dawning comprehension came over his face.

"Oh, I see, sir," he said, respectfully—far more respectfully than he had ever before addressed a mere first officer. "Meaning that we both *will be* wearing them shortly, I assume. 'Service Specials'—but you didn't specify exactly *what* Service, did you?"

"Now that you mention it, I don't believe that I did," Costigan grinned.

"That explains several things about you—particularly your recognition of Vee-Two and your uncanny control and speed of reaction. But aren't you . . . ."

"No," Costigan interrupted. "This situation is apt to get altogether too serious to overlook any bets. If we get away, I'll take them away from her and she'll never know that they aren't routine equipment. As for you, I know that you can and do keep your mouth shut. That's why I'm hanging this junk on you—I had a lot of stuff in my kit, but I flashed it all with the Standish except what I brought in here for us three. Whether you think so or not, we're in a real jam—our chance of getting away is mighty close to zero . . ."

He broke off as the girl came back, now to all appearances a small Triplanetary officer, and the three settled down to a long and eventless wait. Hour after hour they flew through the ether, but finally there was a lurching swing and an abrupt increase in their acceleration. After a short consultation Captain Bradley turned on the visiray set and, with the beam at its minimum power, peered cautiously downward, in the direction opposite to that in which he knew the pirate vessel must be. All three stared into the plate, seeing only an infinity of emptiness, marked only by the infinitely remote and coldly brilliant stars. While they stared into space a vast area of the heavens was blotted out and they saw, faintly illuminated by a peculiar blue luminescence, a vast ball—a sphere so large and so close that they seemed to be dropping downward toward it as though it were a world! They came to a stop— paused, weightless—a vast door slid smoothly aside—they were drawn *upward* through an airlock and floated quietly in the air above a small, but brightly-lighted and orderly city of metallic buildings! Gently the *Hyperion* was lowered, to come to rest in the embracing arms of a regulation landing cradle.

"Well, wherever it is, we're here," remarked Captain Bradley, grimly, and:

"And now the fireworks start," assented Costigan, with a questioning glance at the girl.

"Don't mind me," she answered his unspoken question. "I don't believe in surrendering, either."

"Right," and both men squatted down behind the ether-walls of their terrific weapons; the girl prone behind them.

They had not long to wait. A group of human beings—men and to all appearances Americans—appeared unarmed in the little lounge. As soon as they were well inside the room, Bradley and Costigan released upon them without compunction the full power of their frightful projectors. From the reflectors, through the doorway, there tore a concentrated double beam of pure destruction—but that beam did not reach its goal. Yards from the men it met a screen of impenetrable density. Instantly the gunners pressed their triggers and a stream of high-explosive shells issued from the roaring weapons. But shells, also, were futile. They struck the shield and vanished—vanished without exploding and without leaving a trace to show that they had ever existed.

Costigan sprang to his feet, but before he could launch his intended attack a vast tunnel appeared beside him—something had gone through the entire width of the liner, cutting effortlessly a smooth cylinder of emptiness. Air rushed in to fill the vacuum, and the three visitors felt themselves seized by invisible forces and drawn into the tunnel. Through it they floated, up to and over buildings, finally slanting downward toward the door of a great high-towered structure. Doors opened before them and closed behind them, until at last they stood upright in a room which was evidently the office of a busy executive. They faced a desk which, in addition to the usual equipment of the business man, carried also a bewilderingly complete switchboard and instrument panel.

Seated impassively at the desk there was a gray man. Not only was he dressed entirely in gray, but his heavy hair was gray, his eyes were gray, and even his tanned skin seemed to give the impression of grayness in disguise. His overwhelming personality radiated an aura of grayness—not the gentle gray of the dove, but the resistless, driving gray of the super-dreadnought; the hard, inflexible, brittle gray of the fracture of high-carbon steel.

"Captain Bradley, First Officer Costigan, Miss Marsden," the man spoke quietly, but crisply. "I had not intended you two men to live so long. That is a detail, however, which we will pass by for the moment. You may remove your suits."

Neither officer moved, but both stared back at the speaker, unflinchingly.

"I am not accustomed to repeating instructions," the man at the desk continued; voice still low and level, but instinct with deadly menace. "You may choose between removing those suits and dying in them, here and now."

Costigan moved over to Clio and slowly took off her armor. Then, after a flashing exchange of glances and a muttered word, the two officers threw off their suits simultaneously and fired at the same instant; Bradley with his Lewiston, Costigan with a heavy automatic pistol whose bullets were explosive shells of tremendous power. But the man in gray, surrounded by an impenetrable wall of force, only smiled at the fusillade, tolerantly and maddeningly. Costigan leaped fiercely, only to be hurled backward as he struck that unyielding, invisible wall. A vicious beam snapped him back into place, the weapons were snatched away, and all three captives were held in their former positions.

"I permitted that, as a demonstration of futility," the gray man said, his hard voice becoming harder, "but I will permit no more foolishness. Now I will introduce myself. I am known as Roger. You probably have heard nothing of me: very few Tellurians have, or ever will. Whether or not you two live depends solely upon yourselves. Being something of a student of men, I fear that you will both die shortly. Able and resourceful as you have just shown yourselves to be, you could be valuable to me, but you probably will not—in which case you shall, of course, cease to exist. That, however, in its proper time—you shall be of some slight service to me in the process of being eliminated. In your case, Miss Marsden, I find myself undecided between two courses of action; each highly desirable, but unfortunately mutually exclusive. Your father will be glad to ransom you at an exceedingly high figure, but in spite of that fact I may decide to use you in a research upon sex."

"Yes?" Clio rose magnificently to the occasion. Fear forgotten, her courageous spirit flashed from her clear young eyes and emanated from her taut young body, erect in defiance. "You may think that you can do anything with me that you please, but you can't!"

"Peculiar—highly perplexing—why should that one stimulus, in the case of young females, produce such an entirely disproportionate reaction?" Roger's eyes bored into Clio's; the girl shivered and looked away. "But sex itself, primal and basic, the most widespread concomitant of life in this continuum, is completely illogical and paradoxical. Most baffling—decidedly, this research on sex must go on."

Roger pressed a button and a tall, comely woman appeared—a woman of indefinite age and of uncertain nationality.

"Show Miss Marsden to her apartment," he directed, and as the two women went out a man came in.

"The cargo is unloaded, sir," the newcomer reported. "The two men and the five women indicated have been taken to the hospital."

"Very well, dispose of the others in the usual fashion." The minion went out, and Roger continued, emotionlessly;

"Collectively, the other passengers may be worth a million or so, but it would not be worth while to waste time upon them."

"What are you, anyway?" blazed Costigan, helpless but enraged beyond caution. "I have heard of mad scientists who tried to destroy the Earth, and of equally mad geniuses who thought themselves Napoleons capable of conquering even the Solar System. Whichever you are, you should know that you can't get away with it."

"I am neither. I am, however, a scientist, and I direct many other scientists. I am not mad. You have undoubtedly noticed several peculiar features of this place?"

"Yes, particularly the artificial gravity and those screens. An ordinary ether-wall is opaque in one direction, and doesn't bar matter—yours are transparent both ways and something more than impenetrable to matter. How do you do it?"

"You could not understand them if I explained them to you, and they are merely two of our smaller developments. I do not intend to destroy your planet Earth; I have no desire to rule over masses of futile and brainless men. I have, however, certain ends of my own in view. To accomplish my plans I require hundreds of millions in gold and other hundreds of millions in uranium, thorium, and radium; all of which I shall take from the planets of this Solar System before I leave it. I shall take them in spite of the puerile efforts of the fleets of your Triplanetary League.

"This structure was designed by me and built under my direction. It is protected from meteorites by forces of my devising. It is indetectable and invisible—ether waves are bent around it without loss or distortion. I am discussing these points at such length so that you may realize exactly your position. As I have intimated, you can be of assistance to me if you will."

"Now just what could you offer any *man* to make him join your outfit?" demanded Costigan, venomously.

"Many things," Roger's cold tone betrayed no emotion, no recognition of Costigan's open and bitter contempt. "I have under me many men, bound to me by many ties. Needs, wants, longings, and desires differ from man to man, and I can satisfy practically any of them. Many men take delight in the society of young and beautiful women, but there are other urges which I have found quite efficient. Greed, thirst for fame, longing for power, and so on, including many qualities usually regarded as 'noble'. And what I promise, I deliver. I demand only loyalty to me, and that only in certain things and for a relatively short period. In all else, my men do as they please. In conclusion, I can use you two conveniently, but I do not need you. Therefore you may choose now between my service and—the alternative."

"Exactly what is the alternative?"

"We will not go into that. Suffice it to say that it has to do with a minor research, which is not progressing satisfactorily. It will result in your extinction, and perhaps I should mention that that extinction will not be particularly pleasant."

"I say NO, you . . . ." Bradley roared. He intended to give an unexpurgated classification, but was rudely interrupted.

"Hold on a minute!" snapped Costigan. "How about Miss Marsden?"

"She has nothing to do with this discussion," returned Roger, icily. "I do not bargain—in fact, I believe that I shall keep her for a time.

She has it in mind to destroy herself if I do not allow her to be ransomed, but she will find that door closed to her until I permit it to open.''

"In that case, I string along with the Chief—take what he started to say about you and run it clear across the board for me!" barked Costigan.

"Very well. That decision was to be expected from men of your type." The gray man touched two buttons and two of his creatures entered the room. "Put these men into two separate cells on the second level," he ordered. "Search them; all their weapons may not have been in their armor. Seal the doors and mount special guards, tuned to me here."

Imprisoned they were, and carefully searched; but they bore no arms, and nothing had been said concerning communicators. Even if such instruments could be concealed, Roger would detect their use instantly. At least, so ran his thought. But Roger's men had no inkling of the possibility of Costigan's "Service Special" phones, detectors, and spyray—instruments of minute size and of infinitesimal power, but yet instruments which, working as they were below the level of the ether, were effective at great distances and caused no vibrations in the ether by which their use could be detected. And what could be more innocent than the regulation personal equipment of every officer of space? The heavy goggles, the wrist-watch and its supplementary pocket chronometer, the flash-lamp, the automatic lighter, the sender, the money-belt?

All these items of equipment were examined with due care; but the cleverest minds of the Triplanetary Service had designed those communicators to pass any ordinary search, however careful, and when Costigan and Bradley were finally locked into the designated cells they still possessed their ultra-instruments.

8

IN ROGER'S PLANETOID

In the hall Clio glanced around her wildly, seeking even the narrowest avenue of escape. Before she could act, however, her body was clamped as though in a vise, and she struggled, motionless.

"It is useless to attempt to escape, or to do anything except what Roger wishes," the guide informed her somberly, snapping off the instrument in her hand and thus restoring to the thoroughly cowed girl her freedom of motion.

"His lightest wish is law," she continued as they walked down a long corridor. "The sooner you realize that you must do exactly as he pleases, in all things, the easier your life will be."

"But I wouldn't *want* to keep on living!" Clio declared, with a flash of spirit. "And I can *always* die, you know."

"You will find that you cannot," the passionless creature returned, monotonously. "If you do not yield, you will long and pray for death, but you will not die unless Roger wills it. Look at me: I cannot die. Here is your apartment. You will stay here until Roger gives further orders concerning you."

The living automaton opened a door and stood silent and impassive while Clio, staring at her in horror, shrank past her and into the sumptuously furnished suite. The door closed soundlessly and utter silence descended as a pall. Not an ordinary silence, but the indescribable perfection of the absolute, complete absence of all sound. In that silence Clio stood motionless. Tense and rigid, hopeless, despairing, she stood there in that magnificent room, fighting an almost overwhelming impulse to scream. Suddenly she heard the cold voice of Roger, speaking from the empty air.

"You are over-wrought, Miss Marsden. You can be of no use to yourself or to me in that condition. I command you to rest; and, to insure that rest, you may pull that cord, which will establish about this room an ether wall: a wall to cut off even this my voice..."

The voice ceased as she pulled the cord savagely and threw herself upon a divan in a torrent of gasping, strangling, but rebellious sobs. Then again came a voice, but not to her ears. Deep within her, pervading every bone and muscle, it made itself felt rather than heard.

"Clio?" it asked. "Don't talk yet..."

"Conway!" she gasped in relief, every fiber of her being thrilled into new hope at the deep, well-remembered voice of Conway Costigan.

"Keep still!" he snapped. "Don't act so happy! He may have a spy-ray on you. He can't hear me, but he may be able to hear you. When he was talking to you you must have noticed a sort of rough, sandpapery feeling under that necklace I gave you? Since he's got an ether-wall around you the beads are dead now. If you feel anything like that under the wrist-watch, breathe deeply, twice. If you don't feel anything there, it's safe for you to talk, as loud as you please."

"I don't feel a thing, Conway!" she rejoiced. Tears forgotten, she was her old, buoyant self again. "So that wall *is* real, after all? I only about half believed it."

"Don't trust it too much, because he can cut it off from the outside any time he wants to. Remember what I told you: that necklace will warn you of any spy-ray in the ether, and the watch will detect anything below the level of the ether. It's dead now, of course, since our three phones are direct-connected; I'm in touch with Bradley, too. Don't be too scared; we've got a lot better chance than I thought we had."

"What? You don't mean it!"

"Absolutely. I'm beginning to think that maybe we've got something he doesn't know exists—our ultra-wave. Of course I wasn't surprised when his searchers failed to find our instruments, but it never occurred to me that I might have a clear field to use them in! I can't quite believe it yet, but I haven't been able to find any indication that he can even detect the bands we are using. I'm going to look around over there with my spy-ray... I'm looking at you now—feel it?"

"Yes, the watch feels that way, now."

"Fine! Not a sign of interference over here, either. I can't find a trace of ultra-wave—anything below ether-level, you know—anywhere in the whole place. He's got so much stuff that we've never heard of that I supposed of course he'd have ultra-wave, too; but if he hasn't, that gives us the edge. Well, Bradley and I've got a lot of work to do... Wait a minute, I just had a thought. I'll be back in about a second."

There was a brief pause, then the soundless, but clear voice went on:

"Good hunting! That woman that gave you the blue willies isn't alive—she's full of the prettiest machinery and circuits you ever saw!"

"Oh, Conway!" and the girl's voice broke in an engulfing wave of thanksgiving and relief. "It was so unutterably horrible, thinking of what must have happened to her and to others like her!"

"He's running a colossal bluff, I think. He's good, all right, but he lacks quite a lot of being omnipotent. But don't get too cocky, either. Plenty has happened to plenty of women here, and men too—and plenty may happen to us unless we put out a few jets. Keep a stiff upper lip, and if you want us, yell. 'Bye!"

The silent voice ceased, the watch upon Clio's wrist again became an unobtrusive timepiece, and Costigan, in his solitary cell far below her tower room, turned his peculiarly goggled eyes toward other scenes. His hands, apparently idle in his pockets, manipulated tiny controls; his keen, highly-trained eyes studied every concealed detail of mechanism of the great globe. Finally, he took off the goggles and spoke in a low voice to Bradley, confined in another windowless room across the hall.

"I think I've got dope enough, Captain. I've found out where he put our armor and guns, and I've located all the main leads, controls, and generators. There are no ether-walls around us here, but every door is shielded, and there are guards outside our doors—one to each of us. They're robots, not men. That makes it harder, since they're undoubtedly connected direct to Roger's desk and will give an alarm at the first hint of abnormal performance. We can't do a thing until he leaves his desk. See that black panel, a little below the cord-switch to the right of your door? That's the conduit cover. When I give you the word, tear that off and you'll see one red wire in the cable. It feeds the shield-generator of your door. Break that wire and join me out in the hall. Sorry I had only one of these ultra-wave spies, but once we're together it won't be so bad. Here's what I thought we could do," and he went over in detail the only course of action which his survey had shown to be possible.

"There, he's left his desk!" Costigan exclaimed after the conversation had continued for almost an hour. "Now as soon as we find out where he's going, we'll start something . . . he's going to see Clio, the swine! This changes things, Bradley!" His hard voice was a curse.

"Somewhat!" blazed the captain. "I know how you two have been getting on all during the cruise. I'm with you, but what can we do?"

"We'll do something," Costigan declared grimly. "If he makes a pass at her I'll get him if I have to blow this whole sphere out of space, with us in it!"

"Don't do that, Conway," Clio's low voice, trembling but determined, was felt by both men. "If there's a chance for you to get away and do anything about fighting him, don't mind me. Maybe he only wants to talk about the ransom, anyway."

"He wouldn't talk ransom to *you*—he's going to talk something else entirely," Costigan gritted, then his voice changed suddenly. "But say, maybe it's just as well this way. They didn't find our specials when they searched us, you know, and we're going to do plenty of damage right soon now. Roger probably isn't a fast worker—more the cat-and-mouse type, I'd say—and after we get started he'll have something on his mind besides you. Think you can stall him off and keep him interested for about fifteen minutes?"

"I'm sure I can—I'll do *anything* to help us, or you, get away from this horrible . . .." her voice ceased as Roger broke the ether-wall of her apartment and walked toward the divan, upon which she crouched in wide-eyed, helpless, trembling terror.

"Get ready, Bradley!" Costigan directed tersely. "He left Clio's ether-wall off, so that any abnormal signals would be relayed to him from his desk—he knows that there's no chance of anyone disturbing him in that room. But I'm holding a beam on that switch, so that the wall is on, full strength. No matter what we do now, he can't get a warning. I'll have to hold the beam exactly in place, though, so you'll have to do the dirty work. Tear out that red wire and kill those two guards. You know how to kill a robot, don't you?"

"Yes—break his eye-lenses and his ear-drums and he'll stop whatever he's doing and send out distress calls . . . Got 'em both. Now what?"

"Open my door—the shield switch is to the right."

Costigan's door flew open and the Triplanetary captain leaped into the room.

"Now for our armor!" he cried.

"Not yet!" snapped Costigan. He was standing rigid, goggled eyes staring immovably at a spot upon the ceiling. "I can't move a millimeter until you've closed Clio's ether-wall switch. If I take this ray off it for a second we're sunk. Five floors up, straight ahead down a corridor—fourth door on right. When you're at the switch you'll feel my ray on your watch. Snap it up!"

"Right," and the captain leaped away at a pace to be equalled by few men of half his years.

Soon he was back, and after Costigan had tested the ether-wall of the "bridal suite" to make sure that no warning signal from his desk or his servants could reach Roger within it, the two officers hurried away toward the room in which their space-armor was.

"Too bad they don't wear uniforms," panted Bradley, short of breath from the many flights of stairs. "Might have helped some as disguise."

"I doubt it—with so many robots around, they've probably got signals that we couldn't understand anyway. If we meet anybody it'll mean a battle. Hold it!" Peering through walls with his spy-ray, Costigan had seen two men approaching, blocking an intersecting corridor into which they must turn. "Two of 'em, a man and a robot—the robot's on your side. We'll wait here, right at the corner—when they round it take 'em!" and Costigan put away his goggles in readiness for strife.

All unsuspecting, the two pirates came into view, and as they appeared the two officers struck. Costigan, on the inside, drove a short, hard right low into the human pirate's abdomen. The fiercely-driven fist sank to the wrist into the soft tissues and the stricken man collapsed. But even as the blow landed Costigan had seen that there was a third enemy, following close behind the two he had been watching, a pirate who was even then training a ray projector upon him. Reacting automatically, Costigan swung his unconscious opponent around in front of him, so that it was into an enemy's body that the vicious ray tore, and not into his own. Crouching down into the smallest possible compass, he straightened out with the lashing force of a mighty steel spring, hurling the corpse straight at the flaming mouth of the projector. The weapon crashed to the floor and dead pirate and living went down in a heap. Upon that heap Costigan hurled himself, feeling for the pirate's throat. But the fellow had wriggled clear, and countered with a gouging thrust that would have torn out the eyes of a slower man, following it up instantly with a savage kick for the groin. No automaton this, geared and set to perform certain fixed duties with mechanical precision, but a lithe, strong man in hard training, fighting with every foul trick known to his murderous ilk.

But Costigan was no tyro in the art of dirty fighting. Few indeed were the maiming tricks of foul combat unknown to even the rank and file of the highly efficient under-cover branch of the Triplanetary Service; and Costigan, a Sector Chief, knew them all. Not for pleasure, sportsmanship, nor million-dollar purses did those secret agents use Nature's weapons. They came to grips only when it could not possibly be avoided, but when they were forced to fight in that fashion they went in with but one grim purpose—to kill, and to kill in the shortest possible space of time. Thus it was that Costigan's opening soon came. The pirate launched a vicious *coup de sabot*, which Costigan avoided by a lightning shift. It was a slight shift, barely enough to make the kicker miss, and two powerful hands closed upon that flying foot in midair like the sprung jaws of a bear-trap. Closed and twisted viciously, in the same fleeting instant. There was a shriek, smothered as a heavy boot crashed to its carefully predetermined mark—the pirate was out, definitely and permanently.

The struggle had lasted scarcely ten seconds, coming to its close just as Bradley finished blinding and deafening the robot. Costigan picked up the projector, again donned his spy-ray goggles, and the two hurried on.

"Nice work, Chief—it must be a gift to rough-house the way you do," Bradley exclaimed. "That's why you took the live one?"

"Practice helps some, too—I've been in brawls before, and I'm a lot younger and maybe a bit faster than you are," Costigan explained briefly, penetrant gaze rigidly to the fore as they ran along one corridor after another.

Several more guards, both living and mechanical, were encountered on the way, but they were not permitted to offer any opposition. Costigan saw them first. In the furious beam of the projector of the dead pirate they were riven into nothingness, and the two officers sped on to the room which Costigan had located from afar. The three suits of Triplanetary space armor had been locked up in a cabinet; a cabinet whose doors Costigan literally blew off with a blast of force rather than consume time in tracing the power leads.

"I feel like something now!" Costigan, once more encased in his own armor, heaved a great sigh of relief. "Rough-and-tumble's all right with one or two, but that generator room is full of grief, and we won't have any too much stuff as it is. We've got to take Clio's suit along—we'll carry it down to the door of the power room, drop it there, and pick it up on the way back."

Contemptuous now of possible guards, the armored pair strode toward the power plant—the very heart of the immense fortress of space. Guards were encountered, and captains—officers who signaled frantically to their chief, since he alone could unleash the frightful forces at his command, and who profanely wondered at his unwonted silence—but the enemy beams were impotent against the ether walls of that armor; and the pirates, without armor in the security of their own planetoid as they were, vanished utterly in the ravening beams of the twin Lewistons. As they paused before the door of the power room, both men felt Clio's voice raised in her first and last appeal, an appeal wrung from her against her will by the extremity of her position.

"Conway! Hurry! His eyes—they're tearing me apart! Hurry, dear!" In the horror-filled tones both men read clearly—however inaccurately—the girl's dire extremity. Each saw plainly a happy, carefree young Earth-girl, upon her first trip into space, locked inside an ether-wall with an over-brained, under-conscienced human machine—a super-intelligent, but lecherous and unmoral mechanism of flesh and blood, acknowledging no authority, ruled by nothing save his own scientific drivings and the almost equally powerful urges of his desires and passions! She must have fought with every resource at her command. She must have wept and pleaded, stormed and raged, feigned submission and played for time— and her torment had not touched in the slightest degree the merciless and gloating brain of the being who called himself Roger. Now his tantalizing, ruthless cat-play would be done, the horrible gray-brown face would be close to hers—she wailed her final despairing message to Costigan and attacked that hideous face with the fury of a tigress.

Costigan bit off a bitter imprecation. "Hold him just a second longer, sweetheart!" he cried, and the power room door vanished.

Through the great room the two Lewistons swept at full aperture and at maximum power, two rapidly-opening fans of death and destruction. Here and there a guard, more rapid than his fellows, trained a futile projector—a projector whose magazine exploded at the touch of that frightful field of force, liberating instantaneously its thousands upon thousands of kilowatt-hours of stored-up energy. Through the delicately adjusted, complex mechanisms the destroying beams tore. At their touch armatures burned out, high-tension leads volatilized in crashing, high-voltage arcs, masses of metal smoked and burned in the path of vast forces now seeking the easiest path to neutralization, delicate instruments blew up, copper ran in streams. As the last machine subsided into a semi-molten mass of metal the two wreckers, each grasping a brace, felt themselves become weightless and knew that they had accomplished the first part of their program.

Costigan leaped for the outer door. His the task to go to Clio's aid— Bradley would follow more slowly, bringing the girl's armor and taking care of any possible pursuit. As he sailed through the air he spoke.

"Coming, Clio! All right, girl?" Questioningly, half fearfully.

"All right, Conway." Her voice was almost unrecognizable, broken in retching agony. "When everything went crazy he . . . found out that the ether-wall was up and . . . forgot all about me. He shut it off . . . and seemed to go crazy too . . . he is floundering around like a wild man now . . . I'm trying to keep . . . him from . . . going down-stairs."

"Good girl—keep him busy one minute more—he's getting all the warnings at once and wants to get back to his board. But what's the matter with you? Did he . . . hurt you, after all?"

"Oh, no, not that—he didn't do anything but look at me—but that was bad enough—but I'm sick—horribly sick. I'm falling . . . I'm so dizzy that I can scarcely see . . . my head is breaking up into little pieces . . . I just *know* I'm going to die, Conway! Oh . . . oh!"

"Oh, is *that* all!" In his sheer relief that they had been in time, Costigan did not think of sympathizing with Clio's very real present distress of mind and body. "I forgot that you're a ground-gripper—that's just a little touch of space-sickness. It'll wear off directly . . . All right, I'm coming! Let go of him and get as far away from him as you can!"

He was now in the street. Perhaps two hundred feet distant and a hundred feet above him was the tower room in which were Clio and Roger. He sprang directly toward its large window, and as he floated "upward" he corrected his course and accelerated his pace by firing backward at various angles with his heavy service pistol, uncaring that at the point of impact of each of those shells a small blast of destruction erupted. He missed the window a trifle, but that did not matter—his flaming Lewiston opened a way for him, partly through the window, partly through the wall. As he soared through the opening he trained projector and pistol upon Roger, now almost to the door, noticing as he did so that Clio was clinging convulsively to a lamp-bracket upon the wall. Door and wall vanished in the Lewiston's terrific beam, but the pirate stood unharmed. Neither ravening ray nor explosive shell could harm him—he had snapped on the protective shield whose generator was always upon his person.

When Clio reported that Roger seemed to go crazy and was floundering around like a wild man, she had no idea of how she was understating the actual situation; for Gharlane of Eddore, then energizing the form of flesh that was Roger, had for the first time in his prodigiously long life met in direct conflict an overwhelmingly superior force.

Roger had been sublimely confident that he could detect the use, anywhere in or around his planetoid, of ultra-wave. He had been equally sure that he could control directly and absolutely the physical activities of any number of these semi-intelligent "human beings."

But four Arisians in fusion—Drounli, Brolenteen, Nedanillor, and Kriedigan—had been on guard for weeks. When the time came to act, they acted.

Roger's first thought, upon discovering what tremendous and inexplicable damage had already been done, was to destroy instantly the two men who were doing it. He could not touch them. His second was to blast out of existence this supposedly human female, but no more could he touch her. His fiercest mental bolts spent themselves harmlessly three millimeters away from her skin; she gazed into his eyes completely unaware of the torrents of energy pouring from them. He could not even aim a weapon at her! His third was to call for help to Eddore. He could not. The sub-ether was closed; nor could he either discover the manner of its closing or trace the power which was keeping it closed!

His Eddorian body, even if he could recreate it here, could not withstand the environment—this Roger-thing would have to do whatever it could, unaided by Gharlane's mental powers. And, physically, it was a very capable body indeed. Also, it was armed and armored with mechanisms of Gharlane's own devising; and Eddore's second-in-command was in no sense a coward.

But Roger, while not exactly a ground-gripper, did not know how to handle himself without weight; whereas Costigan, given six walls against which to push, was even more efficient in weightless combat than when handicapped by the force of gravitation. Keeping his projector upon the pirate, he seized the first club to hand—a long, slender pedestal of metal—and launched himself past the pirate chief. With all the momentum of his mass and velocity and all the power of his good right arm he swung the bar at the pirate's head. That fiercely-driven mass of metal should have taken head from shoulders, but it did not. Roger's shield of force was utterly rigid and impenetrable; the only effect of the frightful blow was to set him spinning, end over end, like the flying baton of an acrobatic drum-major. As the spinning form crashed against the opposite wall of the room Bradley floated in, carrying Clio's armor. Without a word the captain loosened the helpless girl's grip upon the bracket and encased her in the suit. Then, supporting her at the window, he held his Lewiston upon the captive's head while Costigan propelled him toward the opening. Both men knew that Roger's shield of force must be threatened every instant—that if he were allowed to release it he probably would bring to bear a hand-weapon even superior to their own.

Braced against the wall, Costigan sighted along Roger's body toward the most distant point of the lofty dome of the artificial planet and gave him a gentle push. Then, each grasping Clio by an arm, the two officers shoved mightily with their feet and the three armored forms darted away toward their only hope of escape—an emergency boat which could be launched through the shell of the great globe. To attempt to reach the *Hyperion* and to escape in one of her lifeboats would have been useless; they could not have forced the great gates of the main airlocks and no other exits existed. As they sailed onward through the air, Costigan keeping the slowly-floating form of Roger enveloped in his beam, Clio began to recover.

"Suppose they get their gravity fixed?" she asked, apprehensively. "And they're raying us and shooting at us!"

"They may have it fixed already. They undoubtedly have spare parts and duplicate generators, but if they turn it on the fall will kill Roger too, and he wouldn't like that. They'll have to get him down with a helicopter or something, and they know that we'll get them as fast as they come up. They can't hurt us with hand-weapons, and before they can bring up any heavy stuff they'll be afraid to use it, because we'll be too close to their shell.

"I wish we could have brought Roger along," he continued, savagely, to Bradley. "But you were right, of course—it'd be altogether too much like a rabbit capturing a wildcat. My Lewiston's about done right now, and there can't be much left of yours—what he'd do to us would be a sin and a shame."

Now at the great wall, the two men heaved mightily upon a lever, the gate of the emergency port swung slowly open, and they entered the miniature cruiser of the void. Costigan, familiar with the mechanism of the craft from careful study from his prison cell, manipulated the controls. Through gate after massive gate they went, until finally they were out in open space, shooting toward distant Tellus at the maximum acceleration of which their small craft was capable.

Costigan cut the other two phones out of circuit and spoke, his attention fixed upon some extremely distant point.

"Samms!" he called, sharply. "Costigan. We're out . . . all right . . . yes . . . sure . . . absolutely . . . you tell 'em, Sammy, I've got company here."

Through the sound-disks of their helmets the girl and the captain had heard Costigan's share of the conversation. Bradley stared at his erstwhile first officer in amazement, and even Clio had often heard that mighty, half-mythical name. Surely that bewildering young man must rank high, to speak so familiarly to Virgil Samms, the all-powerful head of the space-pervading Service of the Triplanetary League!

"You've turned in a general call-out," Bradley stated, rather than asked.

"Long ago—I've been in touch right along," Costigan answered. "Now that they know what to look for and know that ether-wave detectors are useless, they can find it. Every vessel in seven sectors, clear down to the scout patrols, is concentrating on this point, and the call is out for all battleships and cruisers afloat. There are enough operatives out there with ultra-waves to locate that globe, and once they spot it they'll point it out to all the other vessels."

"But how about the other prisoners?" asked the girl. "They'll be killed, won't they?"

"Hard telling," Costigan shrugged. "Depends on how things turn out. We lack a lot of being safe ourselves yet."

"What's worrying me mostly is our own chance," Bradley assented. "They will chase us, of course."

"Sure, and they'll have more speed than we have. Depends on how far away the nearest Triplanetary vessels are. But we've done everything we can do, for now."

Silence fell, and Costigan cut in Clio's phone and came over to the seat upon which she was reclining, white and stricken—worn out by the horrible and terrifying ordeals of the last few hours. As he seated himself beside her she blushed vividly, but her deep blue eyes met his gray ones steadily.

"Clio, I . . . we . . . you . . . that is," he flushed hotly and stopped. This secret agent, whose clear, keen brain no physical danger could cloud; who had proved over and over again that he was never at a loss in any emergency, however desperate—this quick-witted officer floundered in embarrassment like any schoolboy; but continued, doggedly: "I'm afraid that I gave myself away back there, but . . ."

"We gave ourselves away, you mean," she filled in the pause. "I did my share, but I won't hold you to it if you don't want—but I *know* that you love me, Conway!"

"*Love* you!" The man groaned, his face lined and hard, his whole body rigid. "That doesn't half tell it, Clio. You don't need to hold me— I'm held for life. There never was a woman who meant anything to me before, and there never will be another. You're the only woman that ever existed. It isn't that. Can't you see that it's impossible?"

"Of course I can't—it isn't impossible, at all." She released her shields, four hands met and tightly clasped, and her low voice thrilled with feeling as she went on: "You love me and I love you. That is all that matters."

"I wish it were," Costigan returned bitterly, "but you don't know what you'd be letting yourself in for. It's who and what you are and who and what I am that's griping me. You, Clio Marsden, Curtis Marsden's daughter. Nineteen years old. You think you've been places and done things. You haven't. You haven't seen or done anything—you don't know what it's all about. And who am I to love a girl like you? A homeless spacehound who hasn't been on any planet three weeks in three years. A hard-boiled egg. A trouble-shooter and a brawler by instinct and training. A sp . . ." he bit off the word and went on quickly: "Why, you don't know me at all, and there's a lot of me that you never *will* know—that I can't let you know! You'd better lay off me, girl, while you can. It'll be best for you, believe me.''

"But I can't, Conway, and neither can you," the girl answered softly, a glorious light in her eyes. "It's too late for that. On the ship it was just another of those things, but since then we've come really to know each other, and we're sunk. The situation is out of control, and we both know it—and neither of us would change it if we could, and you know that, too. I don't know very much, I admit, but I do know what you thought you'd have to keep from me, and I admire you all the more for it. We all honor the Service, Conway dearest—it is only you men who have made and are keeping the Three Planets fit places to live in—and I know that any one of Virgil Samms' assistants would have to be a man in a thousand million . . .''

"What makes you think that?" he demanded sharply.

"You told me so yourself, indirectly. Who else in the three worlds could possibly call him 'Sammy'? You are hard, of course, but you must be so—and I never did like soft men, anyway. And you brawl in a good cause. You are very much a *man*, my Conway; a real, *real* man, and I love you! Now, if they catch us, all right—we'll die together, at least!" she finished, intensely.

"You're right, sweetheart, of course," he admitted. "I don't believe that I *could* really let you let me go, even though I know you ought to," and their hands locked together even more firmly than before. "If we ever get out of this jam I'm going to kiss you, but this is no time to be taking off your helmet. In fact, I'm taking too many chances with you in keeping your shields off. Snap 'em on again—they ought to be getting fairly close by this time.''

Hands released and armor again tight, Costigan went over to join Bradley at the control board.

"How're they coming, Captain?" he asked.

"Not so good. Quite a ways off yet. At least an hour, I'd say, before a cruiser can get within range.''

"I'll see if I can locate any of the pirates chasing us. If I do it'll be by accident; this little spy-ray isn't good for much except close work. I'm afraid the first warning we'll have will be when they take hold of us with a tractor or spear us with a needle. Probably a beam, though; this is one of their emergency lifeboats and they wouldn't want to destroy it unless they have to. Also, I imagine that Roger wants us alive pretty badly. He has unfinished business with all three of us, and I can well believe that his 'not particularly pleasant extinction' will be even less so after the way we rooked him.''

"I want you to do me a favor, Conway." Clio's face was white with horror at the thought of facing again that unspeakable creature of gray. "Give me a gun or something, please. I don't want him ever to look at me that way again, to say nothing of what else he might do, while I'm alive."

"He won't," Costigan assured her, narrow of eye and grim of jaw. He was, as she had said, hard. "But you don't want a gun. You might get nervous and use it too soon. I'll take care of you at the last possible moment, because if he gets hold of us we won't stand a chance of getting away again."

For minutes there was silence, Costigan surveying the ether in all directions with his ultra-wave device. Suddenly he laughed, and the others stared at him in surprise.

"No, I'm not crazy," he told them. "This is really funny; it had never occurred to me that the ether-walls of all these ships make them invisible. I can see them, of course, with this sub-ether spy, but they can't see us! I knew that they should have overtaken us before this. I've finally found them. They've passed us, and are now tacking around, waiting for us to do something so that they can see us! They're heading right into the Fleet—they think they're safe, of course, but what a surprise they've got coming to them!"

But it was not only the pirates who were to be surprised. Long before the pirate ship had come within extreme visibility range of the Triplanetary Fleet it lost its invisibility and was starkly outlined upon the lookout plates of the three fugitives. For a few seconds the pirate craft seemed unchanged, then it began to glow redly, with a red that seemed to become darker as it grew stronger. Then the sharp outlines blurred, puffs of air burst outward, and the metal of the hull became a viscous, fluid-like something, flowing away in a long, red streamer into seemingly empty space. Costigan turned his ultra-gaze into that space and saw that it was actually far from empty. There lay a vast something, formless and indefinite even to his sub-ethereal vision; a something into which the viscid stream of transformed metal plunged. Plunged, and vanished.

Powerful interference blanketed his ultra-wave and howled throughout his body; but in the hope that some part of his message might get through he called Samms, and calmly and clearly he narrated everything that had just happened. He continued his crisp report, neglecting not the smallest detail, while their tiny craft was drawn inexorably toward a redly impermeable veil; continued it until their lifeboat, still intact, shot through that veil and he found himself unable to move. He was conscious, he was breathing normally, his heart was beating; but not a voluntary muscle would obey his will!

9

FLEET AGAINST PLANETOID

One of the newest and fleetest of the Patrol Vessels of the Triplanetary League, the heavy cruiser *Chicago*, of the North American Division of the Tellurian Contingent, plunged stolidly through interplanetary vacuum. For five long weeks she had patrolled her allotted volume of space. In another week she would report back to the city whose name she bore, where her space-weary crew, worn by their long "tour" in the awesomely oppressive depths of the limitless void, would enjoy to the full their fortnight of refreshing planetary leave.

She was performing certain routine tasks—charting meteorites, watching for derelicts and other obstructions to navigation, checking in constantly with all scheduled spaceships in case of need, and so on— but primarily she was a warship. She was a mighty engine of destruction, hunting for the unauthorized vessels of whatever power or planet it was that had not only defied the Triplanetary League, but was evidently attempting to overthrow it; attempting to plunge the Three Planets back into the ghastly sink of bloodshed and destruction from which they had so recently emerged. Every space-ship within range of her powerful detectors was represented by two brilliant, slowly-moving points of light; one upon a great micrometer screen, the other in the "tank," the immense, three-dimensional, minutely cubed model of the entire Solar System.

A brilliantly intense red light flared upon a panel and a bell clanged brazenly the furious signals of the sector alarm. Simultaneously a speaker roared forth its message of a ship in dire peril.

"Sector alarm! N. A. T. *Hyperion* gassed with Vee-Two. Nothing detectable in space, but . . ."

The half-uttered message was drowned out in a crackling roar of meaningless noise, the orderly signals of the bell became a hideous clamor, and the two points of light which had marked the location of the liner disappeared in widely spreading flashes of the same high-powered interference. Observers, navigators, and control officers were alike dumbfounded. Even the captain, in the shell-proof, shock-proof, and doubly ray-proof retreat of his conning compartment, was equally at a loss. No ship or thing could *possibly* be close enough to be sending out interfering waves of such tremendous power—yet there they were!

"Maximum acceleration, straight for the point where the *Hyperion* was when her tracers went out," the captain ordered, and through the fringe of that widespread interference he drove a solid beam, reporting concisely to GHQ. Almost instantly the emergency call-out came roaring in—every vessel of the Sector, of whatever class or tonnage, was to concentrate upon the point in space where the ill-fated liner had last been known to be.

Hour after hour the great globe drove on at maximum acceleration, captain and every control officer alert and at high tension. But in the Quartermaster's Department, deep down below the generator rooms, no thought was given to such minor matters as the disappearance of a *Hyperion*. The inventory did not balance, and two Q.M. privates were trying, profanely and without success, to find the discrepancy.

"Charged calls for Mark Twelve Lewistons, none requisitioned, on hand eighteen thous . . ." The droning voice broke off short in the middle of a word and the private stood rigid, in the act of reaching for another slip, every faculty concentrated upon something imperceptible to his companion.

"Come on, Cleve—snap it up!" the second commanded, but was silenced by a vicious wave of the listener's hand.

"What!" the rigid one exclaimed. "Reveal ourselves! Why, it's . . . Oh, all right . . . Oh, that's it . . . uh-huh . . . I see . . . yes, I've got it solid. So long!"

The inventory sheets fell unheeded from his hand, and his fellow private stared after him in amazement as he strode over to the desk of the officer in charge. That officer also stared as the hitherto easy-going and gold-bricking Cleve saluted crisply, showed him something flat in the palm of his left hand, and spoke.

"I've just got some of the funniest orders ever put out, lieutenant, but they came from 'way, 'way up. I'm to join the brass hats in the Center. You'll know all about it directly, I imagine. Cover me up as much as you can, will you?" and he was gone.

Unchallenged he made his way to the control room, and his curt "urgent report for the Captain" admitted him there without question.

But when he approached the sacred precincts of the captain's own and inviolate room, he was stopped in no uncertain fashion by no less a personage than the Officer of the Day.

". . . and report yourself under arrest immediately!" the O.D. concluded his brief but pointed speech.

"You were right in stopping me, of course," the intruder conceded, unmoved. "I wanted to get in there without giving everything away, if possible, but it seems that I can't. Well, I've been ordered by Virgil Samms to report to the Captain, at once. See this? Touch it!" He held out a flat, insulated disk, cover thrown back to reveal a tiny golden meteor, at the sight of which the officer's truculent manner altered markedly.

"I've heard of them, of course, but I never saw one before," and the officer touched the shining symbol lightly with his finger, jerking backward as there shot through his whole body a thrilling surge of power, shouting into his very bones an unpronounceable syllable—the password of the Triplanetary Service. "Genuine or not, it gets you to the Captain. He'll know, and if it's a fake you'll be breathing space in five minutes."

Projector at the ready, the Officer of the Day followed Cleve into the Holy of Holies. There the grizzled four-striper touched the golden meteor lightly, then drove his piercing gaze deep into the unflinching eyes of the younger man. But that captain had won his high rank neither by accident nor by "pull"—he understood at once.

"It *must* be an emergency," he growled, half-audibly, still staring at his lowly Q-M clerk, "to make Samms uncover this way." He turned and curtly dismissed the wondering O.D. Then: "All right! Out with it!"

"Serious enough so that every one of us afloat has just received orders to reveal himself to his commanding officer and to anyone else, if necessary to reach that officer at once—orders never before issued. The enemy have been located. They have built a base, and have ships better than our best. Base and ships cannot be seen nor detected by any ether wave. However, the Service has been experimenting for years with a new type of communicator beam; and, while pretty crude yet, it was given to us when the *Dione* went out without leaving a trace. One of our men was in the *Hyperion*, managed to stay alive, and has been sending data. I am instructed to attach my new phone set to one of the universal plates in your conning room, and to see what I can find."

"Go to it!" The captain waved his hand and the operative bent to his task.

"Commanders of all vessels of the Fleet!" The Headquarters speaker, receiver sealed upon the wave-length of the Admiral of the Fleet, broke the long silence. "All vessels in sectors L to R, inclusive, will interlock location signals. Some of you have received, or will receive shortly, certain communications from sources which need not be mentioned. Those commanders will at once send out red K4 screens. Vessels so marked will act as temporary flagships. Unmarked vessels will proceed at maximum to the nearest flagship, grouping about it in the regulation squadron cone in order of arrival. Squadrons most distant from objective point designated by flagship observers will proceed toward it at maximum; squadrons nearest it will decelerate or reverse velocity—that point must not be approached until full Fleet formation has been accomplished. Heavy and light cruisers of all other sectors inside the orbit of Mars . . ." the orders went on, directing the mobilization of the stupendous forces of the League, so that they would be in readiness in the highly improbable event of the failure of the massed power of seven sectors to reduce the pirate base.

In those seven sectors perhaps a dozen vessels threw out enormous spherical screens of intense red light, and as they did so their tracer points upon all the interlocked lookout plates also became ringed about with red. Toward those crimson markers the pilots of the unmarked vessels directed their courses at their utmost power; and while the white lights upon the lookout plates moved slowly toward and clustered about the red ones the ultra-instruments of the Service operatives were probing into space, sweeping the neighborhood of the computed position of the pirate's stronghold.

But the object sought was so far away that the small spy-ray sets of the Service men, intended as they were for close-range work, were unable to make contact with the invisible planetoid for which they were seeking. In the captain's sanctum of the *Chicago*, the operative studied his plate for only a minute or two, then shut off his power and fell into a brown study, from which he was rudely aroused.

"Aren't you even going to *try* to find them?" demanded the captain.

"No," Cleve returned shortly. "No use—not half enough power or control. I'm trying to think . . . maybe . . . say, Captain, will you please have the Chief Electrician and a couple of radio men come in here?"

They came, and for hours, while the other ultra-wave men searched the apparently empty ether with their ineffective beams, the three technical experts and the erstwhile Quartermaster's clerk labored upon a huge and complex ultra-wave projector—the three blindly and with doubtful questions; the one with sure knowledge at least of what he was trying to do. Finally the thing was done, the crude, but efficient graduated circles were set, and the tubes glowed redly as their massed output drove into a tight beam of ultra-vibration.

"There it is, sir," Cleve reported, after some ten minutes of manip- ulation, and the vast structure of the miniature world flashed into being upon his plate. "You may notify the fleet—coordinates H II.62, RA 124–31–16, and Dx about 173.2."

The report made and the assistants out of the room, the captain turned to the observer and saluted gravely.

"We have always known, sir, that the Service had *men*; but I had no idea that any one man could possibly do, on the spur of the moment, what you have just done—unless that man happened to be Lyman Cleveland."

"Oh, it doesn't . . ." the observer began, but broke off, muttering unintelligibly at intervals; then swung the visiray beam toward the Earth. Soon a face appeared upon the plate; the keen, but careworn face of Virgil Samms!

"Hello, Lyman," his voice came clearly from the speaker, and the Captain gasped—his ultra-wave observer and sometime clerk was Ly- man Cleveland himself, probably the greatest living expert in beam transmission! "I knew that you'd do something, if it could be done. How about it—can the others install similar sets on their ships? I'm betting that they can't."

"Probably not," Cleveland frowned in thought. "This is a patchwork affair, made of gunny sacks and hay-wire. I'm holding it together by main strength and awkwardness, and even at that, it's apt to go to pieces any minute."

"Can you rig it up for photography?"

"I think so. Just a minute—yes, I can. Why?"

"Because there's something going on out there that neither we nor apparently the pirates know anything about. The Admiralty seems to think that it's the Jovians again, but we don't see how it can be—if it is, they have developed a lot of stuff that none of our agents has even suspected," and he recounted briefly what Costigan had reported to him, concluding: "Then there was a burst of interference—on the *ultra-band*, mind you—and I've heard nothing from him since. Therefore I want you to stay out of the battle entirely. Stay as far away from it as you can and still get good pictures of everything that happens. I will see that orders are issued to the *Chicago* to that effect."

"But listen . . ."

"Those are orders!" snapped Samms. "It is of the utmost importance that we know every detail of what is going to happen. The answer is pictures. The only possibility of obtaining pictures is that machine you have just developed. If the fleet wins, nothing will be lost. If the fleet loses—and I am not half as confident of success as the Admiral is— the *Chicago* doesn't carry enough power to decide the issue, and we will have the pictures to study, which is all-important. Besides, we have probably lost Conway Costigan today, and we don't want to lose *you*, too.''

Cleveland remained silent, pondering this startling news, but the grizzled Captain, veteran of the Fourth Jovian War that he was, was not convinced.

"We'll blow them out of space, Mr. Samms!" he declared.

"You just think you will, Captain. I have suggested, as forcibly as possible, that the general attack be withheld until after a thorough investigation is made, but the Admiralty will not listen. They see the advisibility of withdrawing a camera ship, but that is as far as they will go."

"And that's plenty far enough!" growled the *Chicago*'s commander, as the beam snapped off. "Mr. Cleveland, I don't like the idea of running away under fire, and I won't do it without direct orders from the Admiral."

"Of course you won't—that's why you are going . . ."

He was interrupted by a voice from the Headquarters speaker. The captain stepped up to the plate and, upon being recognized, he received the exact orders which had been requested by the Chief of the Triplanetary Service.

Thus it was that the *Chicago* reversed her acceleration, cut off her red screen, and fell rapidly behind, while the vessels following her shot away toward another crimson-flaring loader. Farther and farther back she dropped, back to the limiting range of the mechanism upon which Cleveland and his highly-trained assistants were hard at work. And during all this time the forces of the seven sectors had been concentrating. The pilot vessels, with their flaming red screens, each followed by a cone of space-ships, drew closer and closer together, approaching the *Fearless*—the British super-dreadnought which was to be the flagship of the Fleet—the mightiest and heaviest space-ship which had yet lifted her stupendous mass into the ether.

Now, systematically and precisely, the great Cone of Battle was coming into being; a formation developed during the Jovian Wars while the forces of the Three Planets were fighting in space for their very civilizations' existence, and one never used since the last space-fleets of Jupiter's murderous hordes had been wiped out.

The mouth of that enormous hollow cone was a ring of scout patrols, the smallest and most agile vessels of the fleet. Behind them came a somewhat smaller ring of light cruisers, then rings of heavy cruisers and of light battleships, and finally of heavy battleships. At the apex of the cone, protected by all the other vessels of the formation and in best position to direct the battle, was the flagship. In this formation every vessel was free to use her every weapon, with a minimum of danger to her sister ships; and yet, when the gigantic main projectors were operated along the axis of the formation, from the entire vast circle of the cone's mouth there flamed a cylindrical field of force of such intolerable intensity that in it no conceivable substance could endure for a moment!

The artificial planet of metal was now close enough so that it was visible to the ultra-vision of the Service men, so plainly visible that the cigar-shaped warships of the pirates were seen issuing from the enormous air-locks. As each vessel shot out into space it sped straight for the approaching fleet without waiting to go into any formation—gray Roger believed his structures invisible to Triplanetary eyes, thought that the presence of the fleet was the result of mathematical calculations, and was convinced that his mighty vessels of the void would destroy even that vast fleet without themselves becoming known. He was wrong. The foremost vessels were allowed actually to enter the mouth of that conical trap before an offensive move was made. Then the vice-admiral in command of the fleet touched a button, and simultaneously every generator in every Triplanetary vessel burst into furious activity. Instantly the hollow volume of the immense cone became a coruscating hell of resistless energy, an inferno which with the velocity of light extended itself into a far-reaching cylinder of rapacious destruction. Ether-waves they were, it is true, but vibrations driven with such fierce intensity that the screens of deflection surrounding the pirate vessels could not handle even a fraction of their awful power. Invisibility lost, their defensive screens flared briefly; but even the enormous force backing Roger's inventions, greater far than that of any single Triplanetary vessel, could not hold off the incredible violence of the massed attack of the hundreds of mighty vessels composing the Fleet. Their defensive screens flared briefly, then went down; their great hulls first glowing red, then shining white, then in a brief moment exploding into flying masses of red hot, molten, and gaseous metal.

A full two-thirds of Roger's force was caught in that raging, incandescent beam; caught and obliterated: but the remainder did not retreat to the planetoid. Darting out around the edge of the cone at a stupendous acceleration, they attacked its flanks and the engagement became general. But now, since enough beams were kept upon each ship of the enemy so that invisibility could not be restored, each Triplanetary war vessel could attack with full efficiency. Magnesium flares and star-shells illuminated space for a thousand miles, and from every unit of both fleets was being hurled every item of solid, explosive, and vibratory destruction known to the warfare of that age. Offensive beams, rods and daggers of frightful power struck and were neutralized by defensive screens equally capable; the long range and furious dodging made ordinary solid, or even atomic-explosive projectiles useless; and both sides were filling all space with such a volume of blanketing frequencies that such radio-dirigible atomics as were launched could not be controlled, but darted madly and erratically hither and thither, finally to be exploded or volatilized harmlessly in mid-space by the touch of some fiercely insistant, probing beam of force.

Individually, however, the pirate vessels were far more powerful than those of the fleet, and that superiority soon began to make itself felt. The power of the smaller ships began to fail as their accumulators became discharged under the awful drain of the battle, and vessel after vessel of the Triplanetary fleet was hurled into nothingness by the concentrated blasts of the pirates' rays. But the Triplanetary forces had one great advantage. In furious haste the Service men had been altering the controls of the dirigible atomic torpedoes, so that they would respond to ultra-wave control; and, few in number though they were, each was highly effective.

A hard-eyed observer, face almost against his plate and both hands and both feet manipulating controls, hurled the first torpedo. Propelling rockets viciously aflame, it twisted and looped around the incandescent rods of destruction so thickly and starkly outlined, under perfect control; unaffected by the hideous distortion of all ether-borne signals. Through a pirate screen it went, and under the terrific blast of its detonation the entire midsection of the stricken battleship vanished. It should have been out, cold—but to the amazement of the observers, both ends kept on fighting with scarcely lessened power! Two more of the frightful bombs had to be launched—each remaining section had to be blown to bits—before those terrible beams went out! Not a man in that great fleet had even an inkling of the truth; that those great vessels, those awful engines of destruction, did not contain a single living creature: that they were manned and fought by automatons; robots controlled by keen-eyed, space-hardened veterans inside the pirates' planetoid!

But they were to receive an inkling of it. As ship after ship of the pirate fleet was destroyed, Roger realized that his navy was beaten, and forthwith all his surviving vessels darted toward the apex of the cone, where the heaviest battleships were stationed. There each hurled itself upon a Triplanetary warship, crashing to its own destruction, but in that destruction ensuring the loss of one of the heaviest vessels of the enemy.

Thus passed the *Fearless*, and twenty of the finest space-ships of the fleet as well. But the ranking officer assumed command, the war-cone was re-formed, and, yawning maw to the fore, the great formation shot toward the pirate stronghold, now near at hand. It again launched its stupendous cylinder of annihilation, but even as the mighty defensive screens of the planetoid flared into incandescently furious defense, the battle was interrupted and pirates and Triplanetarians learned alike that they were not alone in the ether.

Space became suffused with a redly impenetrable opacity, and through that indescribable pall there came reaching huge arms of force incredible; writhing, coruscating beams of power which glowed a baleful, although almost imperceptible, red. A vessel of unheard-of armament and power, hailing from the then unknown solar system of Nevia, had come to rest in that space. For months her commander had been searching for one ultra-precious substance. Now his detectors had found it; and, feeling neither fear of Triplanetarian weapons nor reluctance to sacrifice those thousands of Triplanetarian lives, he was about to take it!

10

WITHIN THE RED VEIL

Nevia, the home planet of the marauding space-ship, would have appeared peculiar indeed to Terrestrial senses. High in the deep red heavens a fervent blue sun poured down its flood of brilliant purplish light upon a world of water. Not a cloud was to be seen in that flaming sky, and through that dustless atmosphere the eye could see the horizon—a horizon three times as distant as the one to which we are accustomed—with a distinctness and clarity impossible in our Terra's dust-filled air. As that mighty sun dropped below the horizon the sky would fill suddenly with clouds and rain would fall violently and steadily until midnight. Then the clouds would vanish as suddenly as they had come into being, the torrential downpour would cease, and through that huge world's wonderfully transparent gaseous envelope the full glory of the firmament would be revealed. Not the firmament as we know it—for that hot blue sun and Nevia, her one planet-child, were light-years distant from Old Sol and his numerous brood—but a strange and glorious firmament containing few constellations familiar to Earthly eyes.

Out of the vacuum of space a fish-shaped vessel of the void—the vessel that was to attack so boldly both the massed fleet of Triplanetary and Roger's planetoid—plunged into the rarefied outer atmosphere, and crimson beams of force tore shriekingly through the thin air as it braked its terrific speed. A third of the circumference of Nevia's mighty globe was traversed before the velocity of the craft could be reduced sufficiently to make a landing possible. Then, approaching the twilight zone, the vessel dived vertically downward, and it became evident that Nevia was neither entirely aqueous nor devoid of intelligent life. For the blunt nose of the space-ship was pointing toward what was evidently a half-submerged city, a city whose buildings were flat-topped, hexagonal towers, exactly alike in size, shape, color, and material. These buildings were arranged as the cells of a honeycomb would be if each cell were separated from its neighbors by a relatively narrow channel of water, and all were built of the same white metal. Many bridges and more tubes extended through the air from building to building, and the watery "streets" teemed with swimmers, with surface craft, and with submarines.

The pilot, stationed immediately below the conical prow of the spaceship, peered intently through thick windows which afforded unobstructed vision in every direction. His four huge and contractile eyes were active, each operating independently in sending its own message to his peculiar but capable brain. One was watching the instruments, the others scanned narrowly the immense, swelling curve of the ship's belly, the water upon which his vessel was to land, and the floating dock to which it was to be moored. Four hands—if hands they could be called— manipulated levers and wheels with infinite delicacy of touch, and with scarcely a splash the immense mass of the Nevian vessel struck the water and glided to a stop within a foot of its exact berth.

Four mooring bars dropped neatly into their sockets and the captain-pilot, after locking his controls in neutral, released his safety straps and leaped lightly from his padded bench to the floor. Scuttling across the floor and down a runway upon his four short, powerful, heavily scaled legs, he slipped smoothly into the water and flashed away, far below the surface. For Nevians are true amphibians. Their blood is cold; they use with equal comfort and efficiency gills and lungs for breathing; their scaly bodies are equally at home in the water or in the air; their broad, flat feet serve equally well for running about upon a solid surface or for driving their streamlined bodies through the water at a pace few fishes can equal.

Through the water the Nevian commander darted along, steering his course accurately by means of his short, vaned tail. Through an opening in a wall he sped and along a submarine hallway, emerging upon a broad ramp. He scurried up the incline and into an elevator which lifted him to the top floor of the hexagon, directly into the office of the Secretary of Commerce of all Nevia.

"Welcome, Captain Nerado!" The Secretary waved a tentacular arm and the visitor sprang lightly upon a softly cushioned bench, where he lay at ease, facing the official across his low, flat "desk." "We congratulate you upon the success of your final trial flight. We received all your reports, even while you were traveling at ten times the velocity of light. With the last difficulties overcome, you are now ready to start?"

"We are ready," the captain-scientist replied, soberly. "Mechanically, the ship is as nearly perfect as our finest minds can make her. She is stocked for two years. All the iron-bearing suns within reach have been plotted. Everything is ready except the iron. Of course the Council refused to allow us any of the national supply—how much were you able to purchase for us in the market?''

"Nearly ten pounds . . ."

"Ten pounds! Why, the securities we left with you could not have bought two pounds, even at the price then prevailing!''

"No, but you have friends. Many of us believe in you, and have dipped into our own resources. You and your fellow scientists of the expedition have each contributed his entire personal fortune; why should not some of the rest of us also contribute, as private citizens?''

"Wonderful—we thank you. Ten pounds!" The captain's great triangular eyes glowed with an intense violet light. "At least a year of cruising. But . . . what if, after all, we should be wrong?''

"In that case you shall have consumed ten pounds of irreplaceable metal." The Secretary was unmoved. "That is the viewpoint of the Council and of almost everyone else. It is not the waste of treasure they object to; it is the fact that ten pounds of iron will be forever lost.''

"A high price, truly," the Columbus of Nevia assented. "And after all, I may be wrong.''

"You probably are wrong," his host made startling answer. "It is practically certain—it is almost a demonstrable mathematical fact—that no other sun within hundreds of thousands of light-years of our own has a planet. In all probability Nevia is the only planet in the entire Universe. We are very probably the only intelligent life in the Universe. There is only one chance in numberless millions that anywhere within the cruising range of your newly perfected space-ship there may be an iron-bearing planet upon which you can effect a landing. There is a larger chance, however, that you may be able to find a small, cold, iron-bearing cosmic body—small enough so that you can capture it. Although there are no mathematics by which to evaluate the probability of such an occurrence, it is upon that larger chance that some of us are staking a portion of our wealth. We expect no return whatever, but if you *should* by some miracle happen to succeed, what then? Deep seas being made shallow, civilization extending itself over the globe, science advancing by leaps and bounds, Nevia becoming populated as she should be peopled—that, my friend, is a chance well worth taking!''

The Secretary called in a group of guards, who escorted the small package of priceless metal to the space-ship. Before the massive door was sealed the friends bade each other farewell.

". . . I will keep in touch with you on the ultra-wave," the Captain

concluded. "After all, I do not blame the Council for refusing to allow
the other ship to go out. Ten pounds of iron will be a fearful loss to the
world. If we *should* find iron, however, see to it that she loses no time
in following us."

"No fear of that! If you find iron she will set out at once, and all
space will soon be full of vessels. Good-bye."

The last opening was sealed and Nerado shot the great vessel into the
air. Up and up, out beyond the last tenuous trace of atmosphere, on and
on through space it flew with ever-increasing velocity until Nevia's
gigantic blue sun had been left so far behind that it became a splendid
blue-white star. Then, projectors cut off to save the precious iron whose
disintegration furnished them power, for week after week Captain Nerado and his venturesome crew of scientists drifted idly through the illimitable void.

There is no need to describe in detail Nerado's tremendous voyage.
Suffice it to say that he found a G-type dwarf star possessing planets—
not one planet only, but six . . . seven . . . eight . . . yes, at least nine!
And most of those worlds were themselves centers of attraction around
which were circling one or more worldlets! Nerado thrilled with joy as
he applied a full retarding force, and every creature aboard that great
vessel had to peer into a plate or through a telescope before he could
believe that planets other than Nevia did in reality exist!

Velocity checked to the merest crawl, as space-speeds go, and with
electro-magnetic detector screens full out, the Nevian vessel crept toward our sun. Finally the detectors encountered an obstacle, a
conductive substance which the patterns showed conclusively to be
practically pure iron. Iron—an enormous mass of it—floating alone out
in space! Without waiting to investigate the nature, appearance, or structure of the precious mass, Nerado ordered power into the converters and
drove an enormous softening field of force upon the object—a force of
such a nature that it would condense the metallic iron into an allotropic
modification of much smaller bulk; a red, viscous, extremely dense and
heavy liquid which could be stored conveniently in his tanks.

No sooner had the precious fluid been stored away than the detectors
again broke into an uproar. In one direction was an enormous mass of
iron, scarcely detectable; in another a great number of smaller masses;
in a third an isolated mass, comparatively small in size. Space seemed
to be full of iron, and Nerado drove his most powerful beam toward
distant Nevia and sent an exultant message.

"We have found iron—easily obtained and in unthinkable quantity—
not in fractions of milligrams, but in millions upon unmeasured millions
of tons! Send our sister ship here at once!"

"Nerado!" The captain was called to one of the observation plates as soon as he had opened his key. "I have been investigating the mass of iron now nearest us, the small one. It is an artificial structure, a small space-boat, and there are three creatures in it—monstrosities certainly, but they must possess some intelligence or they could not be navigating space."

"What? Impossible!" exclaimed the chief explorer. "Probably, then, the other was—but no matter, we had to have the iron. Bring the boat in without converting it, so that we may study at our leisure both the beings and their mechanisms," and Nerado swung his own visiray beam into the emergency boat, seeing there the armored figures of Clio Marsden and the two Triplanetary officers.

"They are indeed intelligent," Nerado commented, as he detected and silenced Costigan's ultra-beam communicator. "Not, however, as intelligent as I had supposed," he went on, after studying the peculiar creatures and their tiny spaceship more in detail. "They have immense stores of iron, yet use it for nothing other than building material. They make little and inefficient use of atomic energy. They apparently have a rudimentary knowledge of ultra-waves, but do not use them intelligently—they cannot neutralize even these ordinary forces we are now employing. They are of course more intelligent than the lower ganoids, or even than some of the higher fishes, but by no stretch of the imagination can they be compared to us. I am quite relieved—I was afraid that in my haste I might have slain members of a highly developed race."

The helpless boat, all her forces neutralized, was brought up close to the immense flying fish. There flaming knives of force sliced her neatly into sections and the three rigid armored figures, after being bereft of their external weapons, were brought through the airlocks and into the control room, while the pieces of their boat were stored away for future study. The Nevian scientists first analyzed the air inside the space-suits of the Terrestrials, then carefully removed the protective coverings of the captives.

Costigan—fully conscious through it all and now able to move a little, since the peculiar temporary paralysis was wearing off—braced himself for he knew not what shock, but it was needless; their grotesque captors were not torturers. The air, while somewhat more dense than Earth's and of a peculiar odor, was eminently breatheable, and even though the vessel was motionless in space an almost-normal gravitation gave them a large fraction of their usual weight.

After the three had been relieved of their pistols and other articles which the Nevians thought might prove to be weapons, the strange paralysis was lifted entirely. The Earthly clothing puzzled the captors immensely, but so strenuous were the objections raised to its removal that they did not press the point, but fell back to study their find in detail.

Then faced each other the representatives of the civilizations of two widely separated solar systems. The Nevians studied the human beings with interest and curiosity blended largely with loathing and repulsion; the three Terrestrials regarded the unmoving, expressionless "faces"— if those coned heads could be said to possess such things—with horror and disgust, as well as with other emotions, each according to his type and training. For to human eyes the Nevian is a fearful thing. Even today there are few Terrestrials—or Solarians, for that matter—who can look at a Nevian, eye to eye, without feeling a creeping of the skin and experiencing a "gone" sensation in the pit of the stomach. The horny, wrinkled, drought-resisting Martian, whom we all know and rather like, is a hideous being indeed. The bat-eyed, colorless, hairless, practically skinless Venerian is worse. But they both are, after all, remote cousins of Terra's humanity, and we get along with them quite well whenever we are compelled to visit Mars or Venus. But the Nevians—

The horizontal, flat, fish-like body is not so bad, even supported as it is by four short, powerful, scaly, flat-footed legs; and terminating as it does in the weird, four-vaned tail. The neck, even, is endurable, although it is long and flexible, heavily scaled, and is carried in whatever eye-wringing loops or curves the owner considers most convenient or ornamental at the time. Even the smell of a Nevian—a maladorous reek of over-ripe fish—does in time become tolerable, especially if sufficiently disguised with creosote, which purely Terrestrial chemical is the most highly prized perfume of Nevia. But the head! It is that member that makes the Nevian so appalling to Earthly eyes, for it is a thing utterly foreign to all Solarian history or experience. As most Tellurians already know, it is fundamentally a massive cone, covered with scales, based spearhead-like upon the neck. Four great sea-green, triangular eyes are spaced equidistant from each other about half way up the cone. The pupils are contractile at will, like the eyes of the cat, permitting the Nevian to see equally well in any ordinary extreme of light or darkness. Immediately below each eye springs out a long, jointless, boneless, tentacular arm; an arm which at its extremity divides into eight delicate and sensitive, but very strong, "fingers." Below each arm is a mouth: a beaked, needle-tusked orifice of dire potentialities. Finally, under the overhanging edge of the cone-shaped head are the delicately-frilled organs which serve either as gills or as nostrils and lungs, as may be desired. To other Nevians the eyes and other features are highly expressive, but to us they appear utterly cold and unmoving. Terrestrial senses can detect no changes of expression in a Nevian's "face." Such were the frightful beings at whom the three prisoners stared with sinking hearts.

But if we human beings have always considered Nevians grotesque and repulsive, the feeling has always been mutual. For those "monstrous" beings are a highly intelligent and extremely sensitive race, and our—to us—trim and graceful human forms seem to them the very quintessence of malformation and hideousness.

"Good Heavens, Conway!" Clio exclaimed, shrinking against Costigan as his left arm flashed around her. "What horrible monstrosities! And they can't talk—not one of them has made a sound—suppose they can be deaf and dumb?"

But at the same time Nerado was addressing his fellows.

"What hideous, deformed creatures they are! Truly a low form of life, even though they do possess some intelligence. They cannot talk, and have made no signs of having heard our words to them—do you suppose that they communicate by sight? That those weird contortions of their peculiarly placed organs serve as speech?"

Thus both sides, neither realizing that the other had spoken. For the Nevian voice is pitched so high that the lowest note audible to them is far above our limit of hearing. The shrillest note of a Terrestrial piccolo is to them so profoundly low that it cannot be heard.

"We have much to do." Nerado turned away from the captives. "We must postpone further study of the specimens until we have taken aboard a full cargo of the iron which is so plentiful here."

"What shall we do with them, sir?" asked one of the Nevian officers. "Lock them in one of the storage rooms?"

"Oh, no! They might die there, and we must by all means keep them in good condition, to be studied most carefully by the fellows of the College of Science. What a commotion there will be when we bring in this group of strange creatures, living proof that there are other suns possessing planets; planets which are supporting organic and intelligent life! You may put them in three communicating rooms, say in the fourth section—they will undoubtedly require light and exercise. Lock all the exits, of course, but it would be best to leave the doors between the rooms unlocked, so that they can be together or apart, as they choose. Since the smallest one, the female, stays so close to the larger male, it may be that they are mates. But since we know nothing of their habits or customs, it will be best to give them all possible freedom compatible with safety."

Nerado turned back to his instruments and three of the frightful crew came up to the human beings. One walked away, waving a couple of arms in an unmistakeable signal that the prisoners were to follow him. The three obediently set out after him, the other two guards falling behind.

"Now's our best chance!" Costigan muttered, as they passed through a low doorway and entered a narrow corridor. "Watch that one ahead of you, Clio—hold him for a second if you can. Bradley, you and I will take the two behind us—now!"

Costigan stooped and whirled. Seizing a cable-like arm, he pulled the outlandish head down, while the full power of his mighty right leg drove a heavy service boot into the place where scaly neck and head joined. The Nevian fell, and instantly Costigan leaped at the leader, ahead of the girl. Leaped; but dropped to the floor, again paralyzed. For the Nevian leader had been alert, his four eyes covering the entire circle of vision, and he had acted rapidly. Not in time to stop Costigan's first berserk attack—the First Officer's reactions were practically instantaneous and he moved fast—but in time to retain command of the situation. Another Nevian appeared, and while the stricken guard was recovering, all four arms wrapped tightly around his convulsively looping, writhing neck, the three helpless Terrestrials were lifted into the air and carried bodily into the quarters to which Nerado had assigned them. Not until they had been placed upon cushions in the middle room and the heavy metal doors had been locked upon them did they again find themselves able to use arms or legs.

"Well, that's another round we lose," Costigan commented, cheerfully. "A guy can't mix it very well when he can neither kick, strike, nor bite. I expected those lizards to rough me up then, but they didn't."

"They don't want to hurt us. They want to take us home with them, wherever that is, as curiosities, like wild animals or something," decided the girl, shrewdly. "They're pretty bad, of course, but I like them a lot better than I do Roger and his robots, anyway."

"I think you have the right idea, Miss Marsden," Bradley rumbled. "That's it, exactly. I feel like a bear in a cage. I should think you'd feel worse than ever. What chance has an animal of escaping from a menagerie?"

"These animals, lots. I'm feeling better and better all the time," Clio declared, and her serene bearing bore out her words. "You two got us out of that horrible place of Roger's, and I'm pretty sure that you will get us away from here, somehow or other. They may think we're stupid animals, but before you two and the Triplanetary Patrol and the Service get done with them they'll have another think coming."

"That's the old fight, Clio!" cheered Costigan. "I haven't got it figured out as close as you have, but I get about the same answer. These four-legged fish carry considerably heavier stuff than Roger did, I'm thinking; but they'll be up against something themselves pretty quick that is *no* light-weight, believe me!''

"Do you know something, or are you just whistling in the dark?'' Bradley demanded.

"I know a little; not much. Engineering and Research have been working on a new ship for a long time; a ship to travel so much faster than light that it can go anywhere in the Galaxy and back in a month or so. New sub-ether drive, new atomic power, new armament, new everything. Only bad thing about it is that it doesn't work so good yet— it's fuller of bugs than a Venerian's kitchen. It has blown up five times that I know of, and has killed twenty-nine men. But when they get it licked they'll *have something!*''

"When, or if?'' asked Bradley, pessimistically.

"I said *when!*'' snapped Costigan, his voice cutting. "When the Service goes after anything they get it, and when they get it it *stays* . . .'' He broke off abruptly and his voice lost its edge. "Sorry. Didn't mean to get high, but I think we'll have help, if we can keep our heads up a while. And it looks good—these are first-class cages they've given us. All the comforts of home, even to lookout plates. Let's see what's going on, shall we?''

After some experimenting with the unfamiliar controls Costigan learned how to operate the Nevian visiray, and upon the plate they saw the Cone of Battle hurling itself toward Roger's planetoid. They saw the pirate fleet rush out to do battle with Triplanetary's massed forces, and with bated breath they watched every maneuver of that epic battle to its savagely sacrificial end. And that same battle was being watched, also with the most intense interest, by the Nevians in their control room.

"It is indeed a bloodthirsty combat,'' mused Nerado at his observation plate. "And it is peculiar—or rather, probably only to be expected from a race of such a low stage of development—that they employ only ether-borne forces. Warfare seems universal among primitive types— indeed, it is not so long ago that our own cities, few in number though they are, ceased fighting each other and combined against the semi-civilized fishes of the greater deeps.''

He fell silent, and for many minutes watched the furious battle between the two navies of the void. That conflict ended, he watched the Triplanetary fleet reform its battle cone and rush upon the planetoid.

"Destruction, always destruction,'' he sighed, adjusting his power switches. "Since they are bent upon mutual destruction I can see no purpose in refraining from destroying all of them. We need the iron, and they are a useless race.''

He launched his softening, converting field of dull red energy. Vast as that field was, it could not encompass the whole fleet, but half of the lip of the gigantic cone soon disappeared, its component vessels subsiding into a sluggishly flowing stream of allotropic iron. The fleet, abandoning its attack upon the planetoid, swung its cone around, to bring the flame-erupting axis to bear upon the formless something dimly perceptible to the ultra-vision of Samms' observers. Furiously the gigantic composite beam of the massed fleet was hurled, nor was it alone.

For Gharlane had known, ever since the easy escape of his human prisoners, that something was occurring which was completely beyond his experience, although not beyond his theoretical knowledge. He had found the sub-ether closed; he had been unable to make his sub-ethereal weapons operative against either the three captives or the war-vessels of the Triplanetary Patrol. Now, however, he could work in the sub-ethereal murk of the newcomers; a light trial showed him that if he so wished he could use sub-ethereal offenses against them. What was the real meaning of those facts?

He had become convinced that those three persons were no more human than was Roger himself. Who or what was activating them? It was definitely not Eddorian workmanship; no Eddorian would have developed those particular techniques, nor could possibly have developed them without his knowledge. What, then? To do what had been done necessitated the existence of a race as old and as capable as the Eddorians, but of an entirely different nature; and, according to Eddore's vast Information Center, no such race existed or ever had existed.

Those visitors, possessing mechanisms supposedly known only to the science of Eddore, would also be expected to possess the mental powers which had been exhibited. Were they recent arrivals from some other space-time continuum? Probably not—Eddorian surveys had found no trace of any such life in any reachable plenum. Since it would be utterly fantastic to postulate the unheralded appearance of two such races at practically the same moment, the conclusion seemed unavoidable that these as yet unknown beings were the protectors—the activators, rather—of the two Triplanetary officers and the woman. This view was supported by the fact that while the strangers had attacked Triplanetary's fleet and had killed thousands of Triplanetary's men, they had actually rescued those three supposedly human beings. The planetoid, then, would be attacked next. Very well, he would join Triplanetary in attacking them—with weapons no more dangerous to them than Triplanetary's own—the while preparing his real attack, which would come later. Roger issued orders; and waited; and thought more and more intensely upon one point which remained obscure—why, when the strangers themselves destroyed Triplanetary's fleet, had Roger been unable to use his most potent weapons against that fleet?

Thus, then, for the first time in Triplanetary's history, the forces of law and order joined hands with those of piracy and banditry against a common foe. Rods, beams, planes, and stilettos of unbearable energy the doomed fleet launched, in addition to its terrifically destructive main beam: Roger hurled every material weapon at his command. But bombs, high-explosive shells, even the ultra-deadly atomic torpedoes, alike were ineffective; alike simply vanished in that redly murky veil of nothingness. And the fleet was being melted. In quick succession the vessels flamed red, shrank together, gave out their air, and merged their component iron into the intensely crimson, sullenly viscous stream which was flowing through the impenetrable veil against which both Triplanetarians and pirates were directing their terrific offense.

The last vessel of the attacking cone having been converted and the resulting metal stored away, the Nevians—as Roger had anticipated—turned their attention toward the planetoid. But that structure was no feeble warship. It had been designed by, and built under the personal supervision of, Gharlane of Eddore. It was powered, equipped, and armed to meet any emergency which Gharlane's tremendous mind had been able to envision. Its entire bulk was protected by the shield whose qualities had so surprised Costigan; a shield far more effective than any Tellurian scientist or engineer would have believed possible.

The voracious converting beam of the Nevians, below the level of the ether though it was, struck that shield and rebounded; defeated and futile. Struck again, again rebounded; then struck and clung hungrily, licking out over that impermeable surface in darting tongues of flame as the surprised Nerado doubled and then quadrupled his power. Fiercer and fiercer the Nevian flood of force drove in. The whole immense globe of the planetoid became one scintillant ball of raw, red energy; but still the pirates' shield remained intact.

Gray Roger sat coldly motionless at his great desk, the top of which was now swung up to become a panel of massed and tiered instruments and controls. He could carry this load forever—but unless he was very wrong, this load would change shortly. What then? The essence that was Gharlane could not be killed—could not even be hurt—by any physical, chemical, or nuclear force. Should he stay with the planetoid to its end, and thus perforce return to Eddore with no material evidence whatever? He would not. Too much remained undone. Any report based upon his present information could be neither complete nor conclusive, and reports submitted by Gharlane of Eddore to the coldly cynical and ruthlessly analytical innermost Circle had always been and always would be both.

It was a fact that there existed at least one non-Eddorian mind which was the equal of his own. If one, there would be a race of such minds. The thought was galling; but to deny the existence of a fact would be the essence of stupidity. Since power of mind was a function of time, that race must be of approximately the same age as his own. Therefore the Eddorian Information Center, which by the inference of its completeness denied the existence of such a race, was wrong. It was not complete.

Why was it not complete? The only possible reason for two such races remaining unaware of the existence of each other would be the deliberate intent of one of them. Therefore, at some time in the past, the two races had been in contact for at least an instant of time. All Eddorian knowledge of that meeting had been suppressed and no more contacts had been allowed to occur.

The conclusion reached by Gharlane was a disturbing thing indeed; but, being an Eddorian, he faced it squarely. He did not have to wonder how such a suppression could have been accomplished—he knew. He also knew that his own mind contained everything known to his every ancestor since the first Eddorian was: the probability was exceedingly great that if any such contact had ever been made his mind would still contain at least some information concerning it, however carefully suppressed that knowledge had been.

He thought. Back . . . back . . . farther back . . . farther still . . .

And as he thought, an interfering force began to pluck at him; as though palpable tongs were pulling out of line the mental probe with which he was exploring the hitherto unplumbed recesses of his mind.

"Ah . . . so you do not want me to remember?" Roger asked aloud, with no change in any lineament of his hard, gray face. "I wonder . . . do you really believe that you can keep me from remembering? I must abandon this search for the moment, but rest assured that I shall finish it very shortly."

"Here is the analysis of his screen, sir." A Nevian computer handed his chief a sheet of metal, bearing rows of symbols.

"Ah, a polycyclic . . . complete coverage . . . a screen of that type was scarcely to have been expected from such a low form of life," Nerado commented, and began to adjust dials and controls.

As he did so the character of the clinging mantle of force changed. From red it flamed quickly through the spectrum, became unbearably violet, then disappeared; and as it disappeared the shielding wall began to give way. It did not cave in abruptly, but softened locally, sagging into a peculiar grouping of valleys and ridges—contesting stubbornly every inch of position lost.

Roger experimented briefly with inertialessness. No use. As he had expected, they were prepared for that. He summoned a few of the ablest of his scientist-slaves and issued instructions. For minutes a host of robots toiled mightily, then a portion of the shield bulged out and became a tube extending beyond the attacking layers of force; a tube from which there erupted a beam of violence incredible. A beam behind which was every erg of energy that the gigantic mechanisms of the planetoid could yield. A beam that tore screamingly through the sub-ether; that by the very vehemence of its incalculable energy tore a hole through the redly impenetrable Nevian field and hurled itself upon the inner screen of the fish-shaped cruiser in frenzied incandesence. And was there, or was there not, a lesser eruption upon the other side—an almost imperceptible flash, as though something had shot from the doomed planetoid out into space?

Nerado's neck writhed convulsively as his tortured drivers whined and shrieked at the terrific overload; but Roger's effort was far too intense to be long maintained. Generator after generator burned out, the defensive screen collapsed, and the red converter beam attacked voraciously the unresisting metal of those prodigious walls. Soon there was a terrific explosion as the pent-up air of the planetoid broke through its weakening container, and the sluggish river of allotropic iron flowed in an ever larger stream, ever faster.

"It is well that we had an unlimited supply of iron." Nerado almost tied a knot in his neck as he spoke in huge relief. "With but the seven pounds remaining of our original supply, I fear that it would have been difficult to parry that last thrust."

"Difficult?" asked the second in command. "We would now be free atoms in space. But what shall I do with this iron? Our reservoirs will not hold more than half of it. And how about that one ship which remains untouched?"

"Jettison enough supplies from the lower holds to make room for this lot. As for that one ship, let it go. We will be overloaded as it is, and it is of the utmost importance that we get back to Nevia as soon as possible."

This, if Gharlane could have heard it, would have answered his question. All Arisia knew that it was *necessary* for the camera-ship to survive. The Nevians were interested only in iron; but the Eddorian, being a perfectionist, would not have been satisfied with anything less than the complete destruction of every vessel of Triplanetary's fleet.

The Nevian space-ship moved away, sluggishly now because of its prodigious load. In their quarters in the fourth section the three Terrestrials, who had watched with strained attention the downfall and absorption of the planetoid, stared at each other with drawn faces. Clio broke the silence.

"Oh, Conway, this is ghastly! It's . . . it's just simply too damned perfectly horrible!" she gasped, then recovered a measure of her customary spirit as she stared in surprise at Costigan's face. For it was thoughtful, his eyes were bright and keen—no trace of fear or disorganization was visible in any line of his hard young face.

"It's not so good," he admitted frankly. "I wish I wasn't such a dumb cluck—if Lyman Cleveland or Fred Rodebush were here they could help a lot, but I don't know enough about any of their stuff to flag a hand-car. I can't even interpret that funny flash—if it really was a flash—that we saw."

"Why bother about one little flash, after all that really did happen?" asked Clio, curiously.

"You think Roger launched something? He couldn't have—I didn't see a thing," Bradley argued.

"I don't know what to think. I've never seen anything material sent out so fast that I couldn't trace it with an ultra-wave—but on the other hand, Roger's got a lot of stuff that I never saw anywhere else. However, I don't see that it has anything to do with the fix we're in right now—but at that, we might be worse off. We're still breathing air, you notice, and if they don't blanket my wave I can still talk."

He put both hands into his pockets and spoke.

"Samms? Costigan. Put me on a recorder, quick—I probably haven't got much time," and for ten minutes he talked, concisely and as rapidly as he could utter words, reporting clearly and exactly everything that had transpired. Suddenly he broke off, writhing in agony. Frantically he tore his shirt open and hurled a tiny object across the room.

"Wow!" he exclaimed. "They may be deaf, but they can certainly detect an ultra-wave, and what an interference they can set up on it! No, I'm not hurt," he reassured the anxious girl, now at his side, "but it's a good thing I had you out of circuit—it would have jolted you loose from six or seven of your back teeth."

"Have you any idea where they're taking us?" she asked soberly.

"No," he answered flatly, looking deep into her steadfast eyes. "No use lying to you—if I know you at all you'd rather take it standing up. That talk of Jovians or Neptunians is the bunk—nothing like that ever grew in our Solarian system. All the signs say that we're going for a long ride."

11

NEVIAN STRIFE

The Nevian space-ship was hurtling upon its way. Space-navigators both, the two Terrestrial officers soon discovered that it was even then moving with a velocity far above that of light and that it must be accelerating at a high rate, even though to them it seemed stationary—they could feel only a gravitational force somewhat less than that of their native Earth.

Bradley, seasoned old campaigner that he was, had retired promptly as soon as he had completed a series of observations, and was sleeping soundly upon a pile of cushions in the first of the three inter-connecting rooms. In the middle room, which was to be Clio's, Costigan was standing very close to the girl, but was not touching her. His body was rigid, his face was tense and drawn.

"You are wrong, Conway; all wrong," Clio was saying, very seriously. "I know how you feel, but it's false chivalry."

"That isn't it, at all," he insisted, stubbornly. "It isn't only that I've got you out here in space, in danger and alone, that's stopping me. I know you and I know myself well enough to know that what we start now we'll go through with for life. It doesn't make any difference, that way, whether I start making love to you now or whether I wait until we're back on Tellus; but I'm telling you that for your own good you'd better pass me up entirely. I've got enough horsepower to keep away from you if you tell me to—not otherwise."

"I know it, both ways, dear, but . . . ."

"But nothing!" he interrupted. "Can't you get it into your skull what you'll be letting yourself in for if you marry me? Assume that we get back, which isn't sure, by any means. But even if we do, some day—

and maybe soon, too, you can't tell—somebody is going to collect fifty grams of radium for my head.''

"Fifty grams—and everybody knows that Samms himself is rated at only sixty? I *knew* that you were somebody, Conway!'' Clio exclaimed, undeterred. "But at that, something tells me that any pirate will earn even that much reward several times over before he collects it. Don't be silly, my dear—goodnight.''

She tipped her head back, holding up to him her red, sweetly curved, smiling lips, and his arms swept around her. Her arms went up around his neck and they stood, clasped together in the motionless ecstasy of love's first embrace.

"Girl, girl, how I love you!'' Costigan's voice was husky, his usually hard eyes were glowing with a tender light. "That settles that. I'll really *live* now, anyway, while . . .''

"Stop it!'' she commanded, sharply. "You're going to live until you die of old age—see if you don't. You'll simply *have* to, Conway!''

"That's so, too—no percentage in dying now. All the pirates between Tellus and Andromeda couldn't take me after this—I've got too much to live for. Well, goodnight, sweetheart, I'd better beat it—you need some sleep.''

The lovers' parting was not as simple and straightforward a procedure as Costigan's speech would indicate, but finally he did seek his own room and relaxed upon a pile of cushions, his stern visage transformed. Instead of the low metal ceiling he saw a beautiful, oval, tanned young face, framed in a golden-blonde corona of hair. His gaze sank into the depths of loyal, honest, dark blue eyes; and looking deeper and deeper into those blue wells he fell asleep. Upon his face, too set and grim by far for a man of his years—the lives of Sector Chiefs of the Triplanetary Service were not easy, nor as a rule were they long—there lingered as he slept that newly-acquired softness of expression, the reflection of his transcendent happiness.

For eight hours he slept soundly, as was his wont, then, also according to his habit and training he came wide awake, with no intermediate stage of napping.

"Clio?'' he whispered. "Awake, girl?''

"Awake!'' her voice come through the ultra phone, relief in every syllable. "Good heavens, I thought you were going to sleep until we got to wherever it is that we're going! Come on in, you two—I don't see how you can possibly sleep, just as though you were home in bed.''

"You've got to learn to sleep anywhere if you expect to keep in . . .'' Costigan broke off as he opened the door and saw Clio's wan face. She had evidently spent a sleepless and wracking eight hours. "Good Lord, Clio, why didn't you call me?"

"Oh, I'm all right, except for being a little jittery. No need of asking how *you* feel, is there?"

"No—I feel hungry," he answered cheerfully. "I'm going to see what we can do about it—or say, guess I'll see whether they're still interfering on Samms' wave."

He took out the small, insulated case and touched the contact stud lightly with his finger. His arm jerked away powerfully.

"Still at it," he gave the unnecessary explanation. "They don't seem to want us to talk outside, but his interference is as good as my talking—they can trace it, of course. Now I'll see what I can find out about our breakfast."

He stepped over to the plate and shot its projector beam forward into the control room, where he saw Nerado lying, doglike, at his instrument panel. As Costigan's beam entered the room a blue light flashed on and the Nevian turned an eye and an arm toward his own small observation plate. Knowing that they were now in visual communication, Costigan beckoned an invitation and pointed to his mouth in what he hoped was the universal sign of hunger. The Nevian waved an arm and fingered controls, and as he did so a wide section of the floor of Clio's room slid aside. The opening thus made revealed a table which rose upon its low pedestal, a table equipped with three softly-cushioned benches and spread with a glittering array of silver and glassware.

Bowls and platters of a dazzlingly white metal, narrow-waisted goblets of sheerest crystal; all were hexagonal, beautifully and intricately carved or etched in apparently conventional marine designs. And the table utensils of this strange race were peculiar indeed. There were tearing forceps of sixteen needle-sharp curved teeth; there were flexible spatulas; there were deep and shallow ladles with flexible edges; there were many other peculiarly-curved instruments at whose uses the Terrestrials could not even guess; all having delicately-fashioned handles to fit the long slender fingers of the Nevians.

But if the table and its appointments were surprising to the Terrestrials, revealing as they did a degree of culture which none of them had expected to find in a race of beings so monstrous, the food was even more surprising, although in another sense. For the wonderful crystal goblets were filled with a grayish-green slime of a nauseous and overpowering odor, the smaller bowls were full of living sea spiders and other such delicacies; and each large platter contained a fish fully a foot long, raw and whole, garnished tastefully with red, purple, and green strands of seaweed!

Clio looked once, then gasped, shutting her eyes and turning away from the table, but Costigan flipped the three fish into a platter and set it aside before he turned back to the visiplate.

"They'll go good fried," he remarked to Bradley, signaling vigorously to Nerado that the meal was not acceptable and that he wanted to talk to him, *in person*. Finally he made himself clear, the table sank down out of sight, and the Nevian commander cautiously entered the room.

At Costigan's insistence, he came up to the visiplate, leaving near the door three alert and fully-armed guards. The man then shot the beam into the galley of the pirate's lifeboat, suggesting that they should be allowed to live there. For some time the argument of arms and fingers raged—though not exactly fluent conversation, both sides managed to convey their meanings quite clearly. Nerado would not allow the Terrestrials to visit their own ship—he was taking no chances—but after a thorough ultra-ray inspection he did finally order some of his men to bring into the middle room the electric range and a supply of Terrestrial food. Soon the Nevian fish were sizzling in a pan and the appetizing odors of coffee and browning biscuit permeated the room. But at the first appearance of those odors the Nevians departed hastily, content to watch the remainder of the curious and repulsive procedure in their visiray plates.

Breakfast over and everything made tidy and ship-shape, Costigan turned to Clio.

"Look here, girl; you've got to learn how to sleep. You're all in. Your eyes look like you've been on a Martian picnic and you didn't eat half enough breakfast. You've got to sleep and eat to keep fit. We don't want you passing out on us, so I'll put out this light, and you'll lie down here and sleep until noon."

"Oh, no, don't bother. I'll sleep tonight. I'm quite . . ."

"You'll sleep now," he informed her, levelly. "I never thought of you being nervous, with Bradley and me on each side of you. We're both right here now, though, and we'll stay here. We'll watch over you like a couple of old hens with one chick between them. Come on; lie down and go bye-bye."

Clio laughed at the simile, but lay down obediently. Costigan sat upon the edge of the great divan, holding her hand, and they chatted idly. The silences grew longer, Clio's remarks became fewer, and soon her long-lashed eyelids fell and her deep, regular breathing showed that she was sound asleep. The man stared at her, his very heart in his eyes. So young, so beautiful, so lovely—and *how* he did love her! He was not formally religious, but his every thought was a prayer. If he could only get her out of this mess . . . he wasn't fit to live on the same planet with her, but . . . just give him one chance, God . . . just one!

But Costigan had been laboring for days under a terrific strain, and had been going very short on sleep. Half hypnotized by his own mixed emotions and by his staring at the smooth curves of Clio's cheek, his own eyes closed and, still holding her hand, he sank down into the soft cushions beside her and into oblivion.

Thus sleeping hand in hand like two children Bradley found them, and a tender, fatherly expression came over his face as he looked down at them.

"Nice little girl, Clio," he mused, "and when they made Costigan they broke the mold. They'll do—about as fine a couple of kids as old Tellus ever produced. I could do with some more sleep myself." He yawned prodigiously, lay down at Clio's left, and in minutes was himself asleep.

Hours later, both men were awakened by a merry peal of laughter. Clio was sitting up, regarding them with sparkling eyes. She was refreshed, buoyant, ravenously hungry and highly amused. Costigan was amazed and annoyed at what he considered a failure in a self-appointed task; Bradley was calm and matter-of-fact.

"Thanks for being such a nice body-guard, you two." Clio laughed again, but sobered quickly. "I slept wonderfully well, but I wonder if I can sleep tonight without making you hold my hand all night?"

"Oh, he doesn't mind doing that," Bradley commented.

"Mind it!" Costigan exclaimed, and his eyes and his tone spoke volumes.

They prepared and ate another meal, one to which Clio did full justice. Rested and refreshed, they had begun to discuss possibilities of escape when Nerado and his three armed guards entered the room. The Nevian scientist placed a box upon a table and began to make adjustments upon its panels, eyeing the Terrestrials attentively after each setting. After a time a staccato burst of articulate speech issued from the box, and Costigan saw a great light.

"You've got it—hold it!" he exclaimed, waving his arms excitedly. "You see, Clio, their voices are pitched either higher or lower than ours—probably higher—and they've built an audio-frequency changer. He's nobody's fool, that lizard!"

Nerado heard Costigan's voice, there was no doubt of that. His long neck looped and twisted in Nevian gratification; and although neither side could understand the other, both knew that intelligent speech and hearing were attributes common to the two races. This fact altered markedly the relations between captors and captives. The Nevians admitted among themselves that the strange bipeds might be quite intelligent, after all; and the Terrestrials at once became more hopeful.

"It isn't so bad, if they can talk," Costigan summed up the situation. "We might as well take it easy and make the best of it, particularly since we haven't been able to figure out any possible way of getting away from them. They can talk and hear, and we can learn their language in time. Maybe we can make some kind of a deal with them to take us back to our own system, if we can't make a break."

The Nevians being as eager as the Terrestrials to establish communication, Nerado kept the newly devised frequency-changer in constant use. There is no need of describing at length the details of that interchange of languages. Suffice it to say that starting at the very bottom they learned as babies learn, but with the great advantage over babies of possessing fully developed and capable brains. And while the human beings were learning the tongue of Nevia, several of the amphibians (and incidentally Clio Marsden) were learning Triplanetarian; the two officers knowing well that it would be much easier for the Nevians to learn the logically-built common language of the Three Planets than to master the senseless intricacies of English.

In a short time the two parties were able to understand each other after a fashion, by using a weird mixture of both languages. As soon as a few ideas had been exchanged, the Nevian scientists built transformers small enough to be worn collar-like by the Terrestrials, and the captives were allowed to roam at will throughout the great vessel; only the compartment in which was stored the dismembered pirate lifeboat being sealed to them. Thus it was that they were not left long in doubt when another fish-shaped cruiser of the void was revealed upon their lookout plates in the awful emptiness of interstellar space.

"That is our sister-ship going to your Solarian system for a cargo of the iron which is so plentiful there," Nerado explained to his involuntary guests.

"I hope the gang has got the bugs worked out of our super-ship!" Costigan muttered savagely to his companions as Nerado turned away. "If they have, that outfit will get something more than a load of iron when they get there!"

More time passed, during which a blue-white star separated itself from the infinitely distant firmament and began to show a perceptible disk. Larger and larger it grew, becoming bluer and bluer as the flying space-ship approached it, until finally Nevia could be seen, apparently close beside her parent orb.

Heavily laden though the vessel was, such was her power that she was soon dropping vertically downward toward a large lagoon in the middle of the Nevian city. That bit of open water was devoid of life, for this was to be no ordinary landing. Under the terrific power of the beams braking the descent of that unimaginable load of allotropic iron the water seethed and boiled; and instead of floating gracefully upon the surface of the sea, this time the huge ship of space sank like a plummet to the bottom. Having accomplished the delicate feat of docking the vessel safely in the immense cradle prepared for her, Nerado turned to the Tellurians, who, now under guard, had been brought before him.

"While our cargo of iron is being discharged, I am to take you three specimens to the College of Science, where you are to undergo a thorough physical and psychological examination. Follow me."

"Wait a minute!" protested Costigan, with a quick and furtive wink at his companions. "Do you expect us to go through *water*, and at this frightful depth?"

"Certainly," replied the Nevian, in surprise. "You are air-breathers, of course, but you must be able to swim a little, and this slight depth—but little more than thirty of your meters—will not trouble you."

"You are wrong, twice," declared the Terrestrial, convincingly. "If by 'swimming' you mean propelling yourself in or through the water, we know nothing of it. In water over our heads we drown helplessly in a minute or two, and the pressure at this depth would kill us instantly."

"Well, I could take a lifeboat, of course, but that . . ." the Nevian Captain began, doubtfully, but broke off at the sound of a staccato call from his signal panel.

"Captain Nerado, attention!"

"Nerado," he acknowledged into a microphone.

"The Third City is being attacked by the fishes of the greater deeps. They have developed new and powerful mobile fortresses mounting unheard-of weapons and the city reports that it cannot long withstand their attack. They are asking for all possible help. Your vessel not only has vast stores of iron, but also mounts weapons of power. You are requested to proceed to their aid at the earliest possible moment."

Nerado snapped out orders and the liquid iron fell in streams from wide-open ports, forming a vast, red pool in the bottom of the dock. In a short time the great vessel was in equilibrium with the water she displaced, and as soon as she had attained a slight buoyancy the ports snapped shut and Nerado threw on the power.

"Go back to your own quarters and stay there until I send for you," the Nevian directed, and as the Terrestrials obeyed the curt orders the cruiser tore herself from the water and flashed up into the crimson sky.

"What a barefaced liar!" Bradley exclaimed. The three, transformers

cut off, were back in the middle room of their suite. "You can outswim
an otter, and I happen to know that you came up out of the old DZ83
from a depth of . . ."

"Maybe I did exaggerate a trifle," Costigan interrupted, "but the
more helpless he thinks we are the better for us. And we want to stay
out of any of their cities as long as we can, because they may be hard
places to get out of. I've got a couple of ideas, but they aren't ripe
enough to pick yet . . . Wow! How this bird's been traveling! We're
there already! If he hits the water going like this, he'll split himself,
sure!"

With undiminished velocity they were flashing downward in a long
slant toward the beleaguered Third City, and from the flying vessel there
was launched toward the city's central lagoon a torpedo. No missile
this, but a capsule containing a full ton of allotropic iron, which would
be of more use to the Nevian defenders than millions of men. For the
Third City was sore pressed indeed. Around it was one unbroken ring
of boiling, exploding water—water billowing upward in searing, blinding bursts of super-heated steam, or being hurled bodily in all directions
in solid masses by the cataclysmic forces being released by the embattled fishes of the greater deeps. Her outer defenses were already down,
and even as the Terrestrials stared in amazement another of the immense
hexagonal buildings burst into fragments; its upper structure flying
wildly into scrap metal, its lower half subsiding drunkenly below the
surface of the boiling sea.

The three Earth-people seized whatever supports were at hand as the
Nevian space-ship struck the water with undiminished speed, but the
precaution was needless—Nerado knew thoroughly his vessel, its
strength and its capabilities. There was a mighty splash, but that was
all. The artificial gravity was unchanged by the impact; to the passengers
the vessel was still motionless and on even keel as, now a submarine,
she snapped around like a very fish and attacked the rear of the nearest
fortress.

For fortresses they were; vast structures of green metal, plowing forward implacably upon immense caterpillar treads. And as they crawled
they destroyed, and Costigan, exploring the strange submarine with his
visiray beam, watched and marveled. For the fortresses were full of
water; water artificially cooled and aerated, entirely separate from the
boiling flood through which they moved. They were manned by fish
some five feet in length. Fish with huge, goggling eyes; fish plentifully
equipped with long, armlike tentacles; fish poised before control panels
or darting about intent upon their various duties. Fish with brains, wag-
ing war!

Nor was their warfare ineffectual. Their heat-rays boiled the water for hundreds of yards before them and their torpedoes were exploding against the Nevian defenses in one appallingly continuous concussion. But most potent of all was a weapon unknown to Triplanetary warfare. From a fortress there would shoot out, with the speed of a meteor, a long, jointed, telescopic rod; tipped with a tiny, brilliantly-shining ball. Whenever that glowing tip encountered any obstacle, that obstacle disappeared in an explosion world-wracking in its intensity. Then what was left of the rod, dark now, would be retracted into the fortress—only to emerge again in a moment with a tip once more shining and potent.

Nerado, apparently as unfamiliar with the peculiar weapon as were the Terrestrials, attacked cautiously; sending out far to the fore his murkily impenetrable screens of red. But the submarine was entirely non-ferrous, and its officers were apparently quite familiar with the Nevian beams which licked at and clung to the green walls in impotent fury. Through the red veil came stabbing ball after ball, and only the most frantic dodging saved the space-ship from destruction in those first few furious seconds. And now the Nevian defenders of the Third City had secured and were employing the vast store of allotropic iron so opportunely delivered by Nerado.

From the city there pushed out immense nets of metal, extending from the surface of the ocean to its bottom; nets radiating such terrific forces that the very water itself was beaten back and stood motionless in vertical, glassy walls. Torpedoes were futile against that wall of energy. The most fiercely driven rays of the fishes flamed incandescent against it, in vain. Even the incredible violence of a concentration of every available force-ball against one point could not break through. At that unimaginable explosion water was hurled for miles. The bed of the ocean was not only exposed, but in it there was blown a crater at whose dimensions the Terrestrials dared not even guess. The crawling fortresses themselves were thrown backward violently and the very world was rocked to its core by the concussion, but that iron-driven wall held. The massive nets swayed and gave back, and tidal waves hurled their mountainously destructive masses through the Third City, but the mighty barrier remained intact. And Nerado, still attacking two of the powerful tanks with his every weapon, was still dodging those flashing balls charged with the quintessence of destruction. The fishes could not see through the subethereal veil, but all the gunners of the two fortresses were combing it thoroughly with ever-lengthening, ever-thrusting rods, in a desperate attempt to wipe out the new and apparently all-powerful

Nevian submarine whose sheer power was slowly but inexorably crushing even their gigantic walls.

"Well, I think that right now's the best chance we'll ever have of doing something for ourselves." Costigan turned away from the absorbing scenes pictured upon the visiplate and faced his two companions.

"But what can we possibly do?" asked Clio.

"Whatever it is, we'll try it!" Bradley exclaimed.

"Anything's better than staying here and letting them analyze us—no telling what they'd do to us," Costigan went on. "I know a lot more about things than they think I do. They never did catch me using my spy-ray—it's on an awfully narrow beam, you know, and uses almost no power at all—so I've been able to dope out quite a lot of stuff. I can open most of their locks, and I know how to run their small boats. This battle, fantastic as it is, is deadly stuff, and it isn't one-sided, by any means, either, so that every one of them, from Nerado down, seems to be on emergency duty. There are no guards watching us, or stationed where we want to go—our way out is open. And once out, this battle is giving us our best possible chance to get away from them. There's so much emission out there already that they probably couldn't detect the driving force of the lifeboat, and they'll be too busy to chase us, anyway."

"Once out, then what?" asked Bradley.

"We'll have to decide that before we start, of course. I'd say make a break back for Earth. We know the direction and we'll have plenty of power."

"But good Heavens, Conway, it's so far!" exclaimed Clio. "How about food, water, and air—would we ever get there?"

"You know as much about that as I do. I think so, but of course anything might happen. This ship is none too big, is considerably slower than the big space-ship, and we're a long ways from home. Another bad thing is the food question. The boat is well stocked according to Nevian ideas, but it's pretty foul stuff for us to eat. However, it's nourishing, and we'll have to eat it, since we can't carry enough of our own supplies to the boat to last long. Even so, we may have to go on short rations, but I think that we'll be able to make it. On the other hand, what happens if we stay here? They will find us sooner or later, and we don't know any too much about these ultra-weapons. We are land-dwellers, and there is little if any land on this planet. Then, too, we don't know where to look for what land there may be, and even if we could find it, we know that it is all overrun with amphibians already. There's a lot of things that might be better, but they might be a lot worse, too. How about it? Do we try it or do we stay here?"

"We try it!" exclaimed Clio and Bradley, as one.

"All right. I'd better not waste any more time talking—let's go!"

Stepping up to the locked and shielded door, he took out a peculiarly built torch and pointed it at the Nevian lock. There was no light, no noise, but the massive portal swung smoothly open. They stepped out and Costigan relocked and reshielded the entrance.

"How . . . what . . ." Clio demanded.

"I've been going to school for the last few weeks," Costigan grinned, "and I've picked up quite a few things here and there—literally, as well as figuratively. Snap it up, guys! Our armor is stored with the pieces of the pirates' lifeboat, and I'll feel a lot better when we've got it on and have hold of a few Lewistons."

They hurried down corridors, up ramps, and along hallways, with Costigan's spy-ray investigating the course ahead for chance Nevians. Bradley and Clio were unarmed, but the operative had found a piece of flat metal and had ground it to a razor edge.

"I think I can throw this thing straight enough and fast enough to chop off a Nevian's head before he can put a paralyzing ray on us," he explained grimly, but he was not called upon to show his skill with the improvised cleaver.

As he had concluded from his careful survey, every Nevian was at some control or weapon, doing his part in that frightful combat with the denizens of the greater deeps. Their path was open; they were neither molested nor detected as they ran toward the compartment within which was sealed all their belongings. The door of that room opened, as had the other, to Costigan's knowing beam; and all three set hastily to work. They made up packs of food, filled their capacious pockets with emergency rations, buckled on Lewistons and automatics, donned their armor, and clamped into their external holsters a full complement of additional weapons.

"Now comes the ticklish part of the business," Costigan informed the others. His helmet was slowly turning this way and that, and the others knew that through his spy-ray goggles he was studying their route. "There's only one boat we stand a chance of reaching, and somebody's mighty apt to see us. There's a lot of detectors up there, and we'll have to cross a corridor full of communicator beams. There, that line's off—scoot!"

At his word they dashed out into the hall and hurried along for minutes, dodging sharply to right or left as the leader snapped out orders. Finally he stopped.

"Here's those beams I told you about. We'll have to roll under 'em. They're less than waist high—right there's the lowest one. Watch me do it, and when I give you the word, one at a time, you do the same. *Keep low*—don't let an arm or a leg get up into a ray or they may see us."

He threw himself flat, rolled upon the floor a yard or so, and scrambled to his feet. He gazed intently at the blank wall for a space.

"Bradley—now!" he snapped, and the captain duplicated his performance.

But Clio, unused to the heavy and cumbersome space-armor she was wearing, could not roll in it with any degree of success. When Costigan barked his order she tried, but stopped, floundering almost directly below the network of invisible beams. As she struggled one mailed arm went up, and Costigan saw in his ultra-goggles the faint flash as the beam encountered the interfering field. But already he had acted. Crouching low, he struck down the arm, seized it, and dragged the girl out of the zone of visibility. Then in furious haste he opened a nearby door and all three sprang into a tiny compartment.

"Shut off all the fields of your suits, so that they can't interfere!" he hissed into the utter darkness. "Not that I'd mind killing a few of them, but if they start an organized search we're sunk. But even if they did get a warning by touching your glove, Clio, they probably won't suspect us. Our rooms are still shielded, and the chances are that they're too busy to bother much about us, anyway."

He was right. A few beams darted here and there, but the Nevians saw nothing amiss and ascribed the interference to the falling into the beam of some chance bit of charged metal. With no further misadventures the fugitives gained entrance to the Nevian lifeboat, where Costigan's first act was to disconnect one steel boot from his armor of space. With a sigh of relief he pulled his foot out of it, and from it carefully poured into the small power-tank of the craft fully thirty pounds of allotropic iron!

"I pinched it off them," he explained, in answer to amazed and inquiring looks, "and maybe you don't think it's a relief to get it out of that boot! I couldn't steal a flask to carry it in, so this was the only place I could put it. These lifeboats are equipped with only a couple of grams of iron apiece, you know, and we couldn't get half-way back to Tellus on that, even with smooth going; and we may have to fight. With this much to go on, though, we could go to Andromeda, fighting all the way. Well, we'd better break away."

Costigan watched his plate closely; and, when the maneuvering of the great vessel brought his exit port as far away as possible from the

Third City and the warring tanks, he shot the little cruiser out and away. Straight out into the ocean it sped, through the murky red veil, and darted upward toward the surface. The three wanderers sat tense, hardly daring to breathe, staring into the plates—Clio and Bradley pushing at mental levers and stepping down hard upon mental brakes in unconscious efforts to help Costigan dodge the beams and rods of death flashing so appallingly close upon all sides. Out of the water and into the air the darting, dodging lifeboat flashed in safety; but in the air, supposedly free from menace, came disaster. There was a crunching, grating shock and the vessel was thrown into a dizzy spiral, from which Costigan finally leveled it into headlong flight away from the scene of battle. Watching the pyrometers which recorded the temperature of the outer shell, he drove the lifeboat ahead at the highest safest atmospheric speed while Bradley went to inspect the damage.

"Pretty bad, but better than I thought," the captain reported. "Outer and inner plates broken away on a seam. We wouldn't hold cotton waste, let alone air. Any tools aboard?"

"Some—and what we haven't got we'll make," Costigan declared. "We'll put a lot of distance behind us, then we'll fix her up and get away from here."

"What are those fish, anyway, Conway?" Clio asked, as the lifeboat tore along. "The Nevians are bad enough, Heaven knows, but the very idea of intelligent and educated *fish* is enough to drive one mad!"

"You know Nerado mentioned several times the 'semi-civilized fishes of the greater deeps'?" he reminded her. "I gather that there are at least three intelligent races here. We know two—the Nevians, who are amphibians, and the fishes of the greater deeps. The fishes of the lesser deeps are also intelligent. As I get it, the Nevian cities were originally built in very shallow water, or perhaps were upon islands. The development of machinery and tools gave them a big edge on the fish; and those living in the shallow seas, nearest the islands, gradually became tributary nations, if not actually slaves. Those fish not only serve as food, but work in the mines, hatcheries, and plantations, and do all kinds of work for the Nevians. Those so-called 'lesser deeps' were conquered first, of course, and all their races of fish are docile enough now. But the deep-sea breeds, who live in water so deep that the Nevians can hardly stand the pressure down there, were more intelligent to start with, and more stubborn besides. But the most valuable metals here are deep down—this planet is very light for its size, you know—so the Nevians kept at it until they conquered some of the deep-sea fish, too, and put 'em to work. But those high-pressure boys were nobody's fools. They realized that as time went on the amphibians would get further and

further ahead of them in development, so they let themselves be conquered, learned how to use the Nevians' tools and everything else they
could get hold of, developed a lot of new stuff of their own, and now
they're out to wipe the amphibians off the map completely, before they
get too far ahead of them to handle.''

"And the Nevians are afraid of them, and want to kill them all, as
fast as they possibly can," guessed Clio.

"That would be the logical thing, of course," commented Bradley.
"Got pretty nearly enough distance now, Costigan?"

"There isn't enough distance on the planet to suit me," Costigan
replied. "We'll need all we can get. A full diameter away from that
crew of amphibians is too close for comfort—their detectors are keen."

"Then they can detect us?" Clio asked. "Oh, I wish they hadn't hit
us—we'd have been away from here long ago."

"So do I," Costigan agreed, feelingly. "But they did—no use
squawking. We can rivet and weld those seams, and things could be a
lot worse—we are still breathing air!"

In silence the lifeboat flashed onward, and half of Nevia's mighty
globe was traversed before it was brought to a halt. Then in furious
haste the two officers set to work, again to make their small craft sound
and spaceworthy.

12

WORM, SUBMARINE, AND FREEDOM

Since both Costigan and Bradley had often watched their captors at work during the long voyage from the Solar System to Nevia, they were quite familiar with the machine tools of the amphibians. Their stolen lifeboat, being an emergency craft, of course carried full repair equipment; and to such good purpose did the two officers labor that even before their air-tanks were fully charged, all the damage had been repaired.

The lifeboat lay motionless upon the mirror-smooth surface of the ocean. Captain Bradley had opened the upper port and the three stood in the opening, gazing in silence toward the incredibly distant horizon, while powerful pumps were forcing the last possible ounces of air into the storage cylinders. Mile upon strangely flat mile stretched that waveless, unbroken expanse of water, merging finally into the violent redness of the Nevian sky. The sun was setting; a vast ball of purple flame dropping rapidly toward the horizon. Darkness came suddenly as that seething ball disappeared, and the air became bitterly cold, in sharp contrast to the pleasant warmth of a moment before. And as suddenly clouds appeared in blackly banked masses and a cold, driving rain began to beat down.

"Br-r-r, it's cold! Let's go in—Oh! *Shut the door!*" Clio shrieked, and leaped wildly down into the compartment below, out of Costigan's way, for he and Bradley had also seen slithering toward them the frightful arm of the Thing.

Almost before the girl had spoken Costigan had leaped to the controls, and not an instant too soon; for the tip of that horrible tentacle flashed into the rapidly narrowing crack just before the door clanged shut. As the powerful toggles forced the heavy wedges into engagement and drove the massive disk home, that grisly tip fell severed to the floor of the compartment and lay there, twitching and writhing with a loathesome and unearthly vigor. Two feet long the piece was, and larger than a strong man's leg. It was armed with spiked and jointed metallic scales, and instead of sucking disks it was equipped with a series of *mouths*— mouths filled with sharp metallic teeth which gnashed and ground together furiously, even though sundered from the horrible organism which they were designed to feed.

The little submarine shuddered in every plate and member as monstrous coils encircled her and tightened inexorably in terrific, rippling surges eloquent of mastodonic power; and a strident vibration smote sickeningly upon Terrestrial eardrums as the metal spikes of the monstrosity crunched and ground upon the outer plating of their small vessel. Costigan stood unmoved at the plate, watching intently; hands ready upon the controls. Due to the artificial gravity of the lifeboat it seemed perfectly stationary to its occupants. Only the weird gyrations of the pictures upon the lookout screens showed that the craft was being shaken and thrown about like a rat in the jaws of a terrier; only the gauges revealed that they were almost a mile below the surface of the ocean already, and were still going downward at an appalling rate. Finally Clio could stand no more.

"Aren't you going to do something, Conway?" she cried.

"Not unless I have to," he replied, composedly. "I don't believe that he can really hurt us, and if I use force of any kind I'm afraid that it will kick up enough disturbance to bring Nerado down on us like a hawk onto a chicken. However, if he takes us much deeper I'll have to go to work on him. We're getting down pretty close to our limit, and the bottom's a long ways down yet."

Deeper and deeper the lifeboat was dragged by its dreadful opponent, whose spiked teeth still tore savagely at the tough outer plating of the craft, until Costigan reluctantly threw in his power switches. Against the full propellant thrust the monster could draw them no lower, but neither could the lifeboat make any headway toward the surface. The pilot then turned on his beams, but found that they were ineffective. So closely was the creature wrapped around the submarine that his weapons could not be brought to bear upon it.

"What can it possibly be, anyway, and what can we do about it?" Clio asked.

"I thought at first it was something like a devilfish, or possibly an overgrown starfish, but it isn't," Costigan made answer. "It must be a kind of flat worm. That doesn't sound reasonable—the thing must be all of a hundred meters long—but there it is. The only thing left to do that I can think of is to try to boil him alive.''

He closed other circuits, diffusing a terrific beam of pure heat, and the water all about them burst into furious clouds of steam. The boat leaped upward as the metallic fins of the gigantic worm fanned vapor instead of water, but the creature neither released its hold nor ceased its relentlessly grinding attack. Minute after minute went by, but finally the worm dropped limply away—cooked through and through; vanquished only by death.

"Now we've put our foot in it, clear to the neck!" Costigan exclaimed, as he shot the lifeboat upward at its maximum power. "Look at that! I knew that Nerado could trace us, but I didn't have any idea that *they* could!"

Staring with Costigan into the plate, Bradley and the girl saw, not the Nevian sky-rover they had expected, but a fast submarine cruiser, manned by the frightful fishes of the greater deeps. It was coming directly toward the lifeboat, and even as Costigan hurled the little vessel off at an angle and then sped upward into the air, one of the deadly offensive rods, tipped with its glowing ball of pure destruction, flashed through the spot where they would have been had they held their former course.

But powerful as were the propellant forces of the lifeboat and fiercely though Costigan applied them, the denizens of the deep clamped a tractor beam upon the flying vessel before it had gained a mile of altitude. Costigan aligned his every driving projector as his vessel came to an abrupt halt in the invisible grip of the beam, then experimented with various dials.

"There ought to be some way of cutting that beam," he pondered audibly, "but I don't know enough about their system to do it, and I'm afraid to monkey around with things too much, because I might accidentally release the screens we've already got out, and they're stopping altogether too much stuff for us to do without them right now."

He frowned as he studied the flaring defensive screens, now radiating an incandescent violet under the concentration of forces being hurled against them by the warlike fishes, then stiffened suddenly.

"I thought so—they *can* shoot 'em!" he exclaimed, throwing the lifeboat into a furious corkscrew turn, and the very air blazed into flaming splendor as a dazzlingly scintillating ball of energy sped past them and high into the air beyond.

Then for minutes a spectacular battle raged. The twisting, turning, leaping airship, small as she was and agile, kept on eluding the explosive projectiles of the fishes, and her screens neutralized and re-radiated the

full power of the attacking beams. More—since Costigan did not need
to think of sparing his iron, the ocean around the great submarine began
furiously to boil under the full-driven offensive beams of the tiny Nevian ship. But escape Costigan could not. He could not cut that tractor
beam and the utmost power of his drivers could not wrest the lifeboat
from its tenacious clutch. And slowly but inexorably the ship of space
was being drawn downward toward the ship of ocean's depths. Downward, in spite of the utmost possible effort of every projector and generator; and Clio and Bradley, sick at heart, looked once at each other.
Then they looked at Costigan, who, jaw hard set and eyes unflinchingly
upon his plate, was concentrating his attack upon one turret of the green
monster as they settled lower and lower.

"If this is . . . if our number is going up, Conway," Clio began, un-
steadily.

"Not yet, it isn't!" he snapped. "Keep a stiff upper lip, girl. We're
still breathing air, and the battle's not over yet!"

Nor was it; but it was not Costigan's efforts, mighty though they
were, that ended the attack of the fishes of the greater deeps. The tractor
beam snapped without warning, and so prodigious were the forces being
exerted by the lifeboat that as it hurled itself away the three passengers
were thrown violently to the floor, in spite of the powerful gravity controls. Scrambling up on hands and knees, bracing himself as best he
could against the terrific forces, Costigan managed finally to force a
hand up to his panel. He was barely in time; for even as he cut the
driving power to its normal value the outer shell of the lifeboat was
blazing at white heat from the friction of the atmosphere through which
it had been tearing with such an insane acceleration!

"Oh, I see—Nerado to the rescue," Costigan commented, after a
glance into the plate. "I hope that those fish blow him clear out of the
Galaxy!"

"Why?" demanded Clio. "I should think that you'd . . ."

"Think again," he advised her. "The worse Nerado gets licked the
better for us. I don't really expect that, but if they can keep him busy
long enough, we can get far enough away so that he won't bother about
us any more."

As the lifeboat tore upward through the air at the highest permissible
atmospheric velocity Bradley and Clio peered over Costigan's shoulders
into the plate, watching in fascinated interest the scene which was being
kept in focus upon it. The Nevian ship of space was plunging downward
in a long, slanting dive, her terrific beams of force screaming out ahead
of her. The beams of the little lifeboat had boiled the waters of the
ocean; those of the parent craft seemed literally to blast them out of

existence. All about the green submarine there had been volumes of furiously-boiling water and dense clouds of vapor; now water and fog alike disappeared, converted into transparent superheated steam by the blasts of Nevian energy. Through that tenuous gas the enormous mass of the submarine fell like a plummet, her defensive screens flaming an almost invisible violet, her every offensive weapon vomiting forth solid and vibratory destruction toward the Nevian cruiser so high in the angry, scarlet heavens.

For miles the submarine dropped, until the frightful pressure of the depth drove water into Nerado's beam faster than his forces could volatilize it. Then in that seething funnel there was waged a starkly fantastic conflict. At its wildly turbulent bottom lay the submarine, now apparently trying to escape, but held fast by the tractors of the spaceship; at its top, smothered almost to the point of invisibility by billowing masses of steam, hung poised the Nevian cruiser.

As the atmosphere had grown thinner and thinner with increasing altitude Costigan had regulated his velocity accordingly, keeping the outer shell of the vessel at the highest temperature consistent with safety. Now beyond measurable atmospheric pressure, the shell cooled rapidly and he applied full touring acceleration. At an appalling and constantly increasing speed the miniature space-ship shot away from the strange, red planet; and smaller and smaller upon the plate became its picture. The great vessel of the void had long since plunged beneath the surface of the sea, to come more closely to grips with the vessel of the fishes; for a long time nothing of the battle had been visible save immense clouds of steam, blanketing hundreds of square miles of the ocean's surface. But just before the picture became too small to reveal details a few tiny dark spots appeared above the banks of cloud, now brilliantly illuminated by the rays of the rising sun—dots which might have been fragments of either vessel, blown bodily from the depths of the ocean and, riven asunder, hurled high into the air by the incredible forces at the command of the other.

Nevia a tiny moon and the fierce blue sun rapidly growing smaller in the distance, Costigan swung his visiray beam into the line of travel and turned to his companions.

"Well, we're off," he said, scowling. "I hope it was Nerado that got blown up back there, but I'm afraid it wasn't. He whipped two of those submarines that we know of, and probably half their fleet besides. There's no particular reason why that one should be able to take him, so it's my idea that we should get ready for great gobs of trouble. They'll chase us, of course; and I'm afraid that with their power, they'll catch us."

"But what can we do, Conway?" asked Clio.

"Several things," he grinned. "I managed to get quite a lot of dope on that paralyzing ray and some of their other stuff, and we can install the necessary equipment in our suits easily enough."

They removed their armor, and Costigan explained in detail the changes which must be made in the Triplanetary field generators. All three set vigorously to work—the two officers deftly and surely; Clio uncertainly and with many questions, but with undaunted spirit. Finally, having done everything they could do to strengthen their position, they settled down to the watchful routine of the flight, with every possible instrument set to detect any sign of the pursuit they so feared.

13

THE HILL

The heavy cruiser Chicago hung motionless in space, thousands of miles distant from the warring fleets of space-ships so viciously attacking and so stubbornly defending Roger's planetoid. In the captain's sanctum Lyman Cleveland crouched tensely above his ultra-cameras, his sensitive fingers touching lightly their micro-metric dials. His body was rigid, his face was set and drawn. Only his eyes moved; flashing back and forth between his instruments and the smoothly-running strands of spring-steel wire upon which were being magnetically recorded the frightful scenes of carnage and destruction.

Silent and bitterly absorbed, though surrounded by staring officers whose fervent, almost unconscious cursing was prayerful in its intensity, the visiray expert kept his ultra-instruments upon that awful struggle to its dire conclusion. Flawlessly those instruments noted every detail of the destruction of Roger's fleet, of the transformation of the armada of Triplanetary into an unknown fluid, and finally of the dissolution of the gigantic planetoid itself. Then furiously Cleveland drove his beam against the crimsonly opaque obscurity into which the peculiar, viscous stream of substance was disappearing. Time after time he applied his every watt of power, with no result. A vast volume of space, roughly ellipsoidal in shape, was closed to him by forces entirely beyond his experience or comprehension. But suddenly, while his rays were still trying to pierce that impenetrable murk, it disappeared instantly and without warning: the illimitable infinity of space once more lay revealed upon his plates and his beams flashed unimpeded through the void.

"Back to Tellus, sir?" The *Chicago's* captain broke the strained silence.

"I wouldn't say so, if I had the say." Cleveland, baffled and frustrated, straightened up and shut off his cameras. "We should report back as soon as possible, of course, but there seems to be a lot of wreckage out there yet that we can't photograph in detail at this distance. A close study of it might help us a lot in understanding what they did and how they did it. I'd say that we should get close-ups of whatever is left, and do it right away, before it gets scattered all over space; but of course I can't give you orders."

"You can, though," the captain made surprising answer. "My orders are that you are in command of this vessel."

"In that case we will proceed at full emergency acceleration to investigate the wreckage," Cleveland replied, and the cruiser—sole survivor of Triplanetary's supposedly invincible force—shot away with every projector delivering its maximum blast.

As the scene of the disaster was approached there was revealed upon the plates a confused mass of debris; a mass whose individual units were apparently moving at random, yet which was as a whole still following the orbit of Roger's planetoid. Space was full of machine parts, structural members, furniture, flotsam of all kinds; and everywhere were the bodies of men. Some were encased in space-suits, and it was to these that the rescuers turned first—space-hardened veterans though the men of the *Chicago* were, they did not care even to look at the others. Strangely enough, however, not one of the floating figures spoke or moved, and spaceline men were hurriedly sent out to investigate.

"All dead." Quickly the dread report came back. "Been dead a long time. The armor is all stripped off the suits, and all the generators and other apparatus are all shot. Something funny about it, too—none of them seem to have been touched, but the machinery of the suits seems to be about half missing."

"I've got it all on the reels, sir." Cleveland, his close-up survey of the wreckage finished, turned to the captain. "What they've just reported checks up with what I have photographed everywhere. I've got an idea of what might have happened, but it's so new that I'll have to have some evidence before I'll believe it myself. You might have them bring in a few of the armored bodies, a couple of those switchboards and panels floating around out there, and half a dozen miscellaneous pieces of junk—the nearest things they get hold of, whatever they happen to be."

"Then back to Tellus at maximum?"

"Right—back to Tellus, as fast as we can possibly get there."

While the *Chicago* hurtled through space at full power, Cleveland and the ranking officers of the vessel grouped themselves about the salvaged wreckage. Familiar with space-wrecks as were they all, none of them had ever seen anything like the material before them. For every part and instrument was weirdly and meaninglessly disintegrated. There were no breaks, no marks of violence, and yet nothing was intact. Bolt-holes stared empty, cores, shielding cases and needles had disappeared, the vital parts of every instrument hung awry, disorganization reigned rampant and supreme.

"I never imagined such a mess," the captain said, after a long and silent study of the objects. "If you have a theory to cover *that*, Cleveland, I would like to hear it!"

"I want you to notice something first," the expert replied. "But don't look for what's there—look for what *isn't* there."

"Well, the armor is gone. So are the shielding cases, shafts, spindles, the housings and stems . . ." the captain's voice died away as his eyes raced over the collection. "Why, everything that was made of wood, bakelite, copper, aluminum, silver, bronze, or anything but steel hasn't been touched, and every bit of that is gone. But that doesn't make sense—what does it mean?"

"I don't know—yet," Cleveland replied, slowly. "But I'm afraid that there's more, and worse." He opened a spacesuit reverently, revealing the face; a face calm and peaceful, but utterly, sickeningly white. Still reverently, he made a deep incision in the brawny neck, severing the jugular vein, then went on, soberly:

"You never imagined such a thing as *white* blood, either, but it all checks up. Someway, somehow, every atom of free or combined iron in this whole volume of space was made off with."

"Huh? How come? And above all, *why?*" from the amazed and staring officers.

"You know as much as I do," grimly, ponderingly. "If it were not for the fact that there are solid asteroids of iron out beyond Mars, I would say that somebody wanted iron badly enough to wipe out the fleet and the planetoid to get it. But anyway, whoever they were, they carried enough power so that our armament didn't bother them at all. They simply took the metal they wanted and went away with it—so fast that I couldn't trace them with an ultra-beam. There's only one thing plain; but that's so plain that it scares me stiff. This whole affair spells intelligence, with a capital 'I', and that intelligence is anything but friendly. I want to put Fred Rodebush at work on this just as fast as I can get him."

He stepped over to his ultra-projector and put in a call for Virgil Samms, whose face soon appeared upon his screen.

"We got it all, Virgil," he reported. "It's something extraordinary—bigger, wider, and deeper than any of us dreamed. It may be urgent, too, so I think I had better shoot the stuff in on an ultra-beam and save some time. Fred has a telemagneto recorder there that he can synchronize with this outfit easily enough. Right?''

"Right. Good work, Lyman—thanks," came back terse approval and appreciation, and soon the steel wires were again flashing from reel to reel. This time, however, their varying magnetic charges were so modulating ultra-waves that every detail of that calamitous battle of the void was being screened and recorded in the innermost private laboratory of the Triplanetary Service.

Eager though he naturally was to join his fellow-scientists, Cleveland was not impatient during the long, but uneventful journey back to Earth. There was much to study, many improvements to be made in his comparatively crude first ultra-camera. Then, too, there were long conferences with Samms, and particularly with Rodebush, the nuclear physicist, who would have to do much of the work involved in solving the riddles of the energies and weapons of the Nevians. Thus it did not seem long before green Terra grew large beneath the flying sphere of the *Chicago*.

"Going to have to circle it once, aren't you?" Cleveland asked the chief pilot. He had been watching that officer closely for minutes, admiring the delicacy and precision with which the great vessel was being maneuvered preliminary to entering the Earth's atmosphere.

"Yes," the pilot replied. "We had to come in in the shortest possible time, and that meant a velocity here that we can't check without a spiral. However, even at that we saved a lot of time. You can save quite a bit more, though, by having a rocket-plane come out to meet us somewhere around fifteen or twenty thousand kilometers, depending upon where you want to land. With their drives they can match our velocity and still make the drop direct."

"Guess I'll do that—thanks," and the operative called his chief, only to learn that his suggestion had already been acted upon.

"We beat you to it, Lyman," Samms smiled. "The *Silver Sliver* is out there now, looping to match your course, acceleration, and velocity at twenty-two thousand kilometers. You'll be ready to transfer?"

"I'll be ready." And the Quartermaster's ex-clerk went to his quarters and packed his dunnage-bag.

In due time the long, slender body of the rocket-plane came into view, creeping "down" upon the space-ship from "above", and Cleveland bade his friends goodbye. Donning a space-suit, he stationed himself in the starboard airlock. Its atmosphere was withdrawn, the outer door opened, and he glanced across a bare hundred feet of space at the rocket-plane which, keel ports fiercely aflame, was braking her terrific speed to match the slower pace of the gigantic sphere of war. Shaped like a toothpick, needle-pointed fore and aft, with ultra-stubby wings and vanes, with flush-set rocket ports everywhere, built of a lustrous, silvery alloy of noble and almost infusible metals—such was the private speed-boat of Triplanetary's head man. The fastest thing known, whether in planetary air, the stratosphere, or the vacuous depth of interplanetary space, her first flashing trial spins had won her the nickname of the *Silver Sliver*. She had had a more formal name, but that title had long since been buried in the Departmental files.

Lower and lower dropped the speed-boat, her rockets flaming ever brighter, until her slender length lay level with the airlock door. Then her blasting discharges subsided to the power necessary to match exactly the *Chicago*'s acceleration.

"Ready to cut, *Chicago!* Give me a three-second call!" snapped from the pilot room of the *Sliver*.

"Ready to cut!" the pilot of the *Chicago* replied. "Seconds! Three! Two! One! CUT!"

At the last word the power of both vessels was instantly cut off and everything in them became weightless. In the tiny airlock of the slender plane crouched a space-line man with coiled cable in readiness, but he was not needed. As the flaring exhausts ceased Cleveland swung out his heavy bag and stepped lightly off into space, and in a right line he floated directly into the open port of the rocket-plane. The door clanged shut behind him and in a matter of moments he stood in the control room of the racer, divested of his armor and shaking hands with his friend and co-laborer, Frederick Rodebush.

"Well, Fritz, what do you know?" Cleveland asked, as soon as greetings had been exchanged. "How do the various reports dovetail together? I know that you couldn't tell me anything on the wave, but there's no danger of eavesdroppers *here.*"

"You can't tell," Rodebush soberly replied. "We're just beginning to wake up to the fact that there are a lot of things we don't know anything about. Better wait until we're back at the Hill. We have a full set of ultra screens around there now. There's a couple of other good reasons, too—it would be better for both of us to go over the whole thing with Virgil, from the ground up; and we can't do any more talking, anyway. Our orders are to get back there at maximum, and you know what that means aboard the *Sliver*. Strap yourself solid in that shock-absorber there, and here's a pair of ear-plugs."

"When the *Sliver* really cuts loose it means a rough party, all right." Cleveland assented, snapping about his body the heavy spring-straps of his deeply cushioned seat, "but I'm just as anxious to get back to the Hill as anybody can be to get me there. All set."

Rodebush waved his hand at the pilot and the purring whisper of the exhausts changed instantly to a deafening, continuous explosion. The men were pressed deeply into their shock-absorbing chairs as the *Silver Sliver* spun around her longitudinal axis and darted away from the *Chicago* with such a tremendous acceleration that the spherical warship seemed to be standing still in space. In due time the calculated midpoint was reached, the slim space-plane rolled over again, and, mad acceleration now reversed, rushed on toward the Earth, but with constantly diminishing speed. Finally a measurable atmospheric pressure was encountered, the needle prow dipped downward, and the *Silver Sliver* shot forward upon her tiny wings and vanes, nose-rockets now drumming in staccato thunder. Her metal grew hot; dull red, bright red, yellow, blinding white; but it neither melted nor burned. The pilot's calculations had been sound, and though the limiting point of safety of temperature was reached and steadily held, it was not exceeded. As the density of the air increased so decreased the velocity of the man-made meteorite. So it was that a dazzling lance of fire sped high over Seattle, lower over Spokane, and hurled itself eastward, a furiously flaming arrow; slanting downward in a long, screaming dive toward the heart of the Rockies. As the now rapidly cooling greyhound of the skies passed over the western ranges of the Bitter Roots it became apparent that her goal was a vast, flat-topped, conical mountain, shrouded in violet light; a mountain whose height awed even its stupendous neighbors.

While not artificial, the Hill had been altered markedly by the engineers who had built into it the headquarters of the Triplanetary Service. Its mile-wide top was a jointless expanse of gray armor steel; the steep, smooth surface of the truncated cone was a continuation of the same immensely thick sheet of metal. No known vehicle could climb that smooth, hard, forbidding slope of steel; no known projectile could mar that armor; no known craft could even approach the Hill without detection. Could not approach it at all, in fact, for it was constantly inclosed in a vast hemisphere of lambent violet flame through which neither material substance nor destructive ray could pass.

As the *Silver Sliver*, crawling along at a bare five hundred miles an hour, approached that transparent, brilliantly violet wall of destruction, a light of the same color filled her control room and as suddenly went out; flashing on and off again and again.

"Giving us the once-over, eh?" Cleveland asked. "That something new, isn't it?"

"Yes, it's a high-powered ultra-wave spy," Rodebush returned. "The light is simply a warning, which can be carried if desired. It can also carry voice and vision . . ."

"Like this," Samms' voice interrupted from a speaker upon the pilot's panel and his clear-cut face appeared upon the television screen. "I don't suppose Fred thought to mention it, but this is one of his inventions of the last few days. We are just trying it out on you. It doesn't mean a thing though, as far as the *Sliver* is concerned. Come ahead!"

A circular opening appeared in the wall of force, an opening which disappeared as soon as the plane had darted through it; and at the same time her landing-cradle rose into the air through a great trap-door. Slowly and gracefully the space-plane settled downward into that cushioned embrace. Then cradle and nestled *Sliver* sank from view and, turning smoothly upon mighty trunnions, the plug of armor drove solidly back into its place in the metal pavement of the mountain's lofty summit. The cradle-elevator dropped rapidly, coming to rest many levels down in the heart of the Hill, and Cleveland and Rodebush leaped lightly out of their transport, through her still hot outer walls. A door opened before them and they found themselves in a large room of unshadowed daylight illumination; the office of the Chief of the Triplanetary Service. Calmly efficient executives sat at their desks, concentrating upon problems or at ease, according to the demands of the moment; agents, secretaries, and clerks, men and women, went about their wonted tasks; televisotypes and recorders flashed busily but silently—each person and machine an integral part of the Service which for so many years had been carrying an ever-increasing share of the load of governing the three planets.

"Right of way, Norma?" Rodebush paused before the desk of Virgil Samms' private secretary. She pressed a button and the door behind her swung wide.

"You two do not need to be announced," the attractive young woman smiled. "Go right in."

Samms met them at the door eagerly, shaking hands particularly vigorously with Cleveland.

"Congratulations on that camera, Lyman!" he exclaimed. "You did a wonderful piece of work on that. Help yourselves to smokes and sit down—there are a lot of things we want to talk over. Your pictures carried most of the story, but they would have left us pretty much at sea without Costigan's reports. But as it was, Fred here and his crew worked out most of the answers from the dope the two of you got; and what few they haven't got yet they soon will have."

"Nothing new on Conway?" Cleveland was almost afraid to ask the question.

"No." A shadow came over Samms' face. "I'm afraid . . . but I'm hoping it's only that those creatures, whatever they are, have taken him so far away he can't reach us."

"They certainly are so far away that we can't reach them," Rodebush volunteered. "We can't even get their ultra-wave interference any more."

"Yes, that's a hopeful sign," Samms went on. "I hate to think of Conway Costigan checking out. There, fellows, was a real observer. He was the only man I have ever known who combined the two qualities of the perfect witness. He could actually see everything he looked at, and could report it truly, to the last, least detail. Take all this stuff, for instance; especially their ability to transform iron into a fluid allotrope, and in that form to use its atomic—nuclear?—energy as power. Something brand new, and yet he described their converters and projectors so minutely that Fred was able to work out the underlying theory in three days, and to tie it in with our own super-ship. My first thought was that we'd have to rebuild it iron-free, but Fred showed me my error—you found it first yourself, of course."

"It wouldn't do any good to make the ship non-ferrous unless you could so change our blood chemistry that we could get along without hemoglobin, and that would be quite a feat," Cleveland agreed. "Then, too, our most vital electrical machinery is built around iron cores. We'll also have to develop a screen for those forces—screens, rather, so powerful that they can't drive anything through them."

"We've been working along those lines ever since you reported," Rodebush said, "and we're beginning to see light. And in that same connection it's no wonder that we couldn't handle our super-ship. We had some good ideas, but they were wrongly applied. However, things look quite promising now. We have that transformation of iron all worked out in theory, and as soon as we get a generator going we can straighten out everything else in short order. And think what that unlimited power means! All the power we want—power enough even to try out such hitherto purely theoretical possibilities as the neutralization of the inertia of matter!"

"Hold on!" protested Samms. "You certainly can't do *that!* Inertia is—*must* be—a basic attribute of matter, and surely cannot be done away with without destroying the matter itself. Don't start anything like that, Fred—I don't want to lose you and Lyman, too."

"Don't worry about us, Chief," Rodebush replied with a smile. "If you will tell me what matter is, fundamentally, I may agree with you

... No? Well, then, don't be surprised at anything that happens. We are going to do a lot of things that nobody on the Three Planets ever thought of doing before."

Thus for a long time the argument and discussion went on, to be interrupted by the voice of the secretary.

"Sorry to disturb you, Mr. Samms, but some things have come up that you will have to handle. Knobos is calling from Mars. He has caught the *Endymion*, and has killed about half her crew doing it. Milton has finally reported from Venus, after being out of touch for five days. He trailed the Wintons into Thalleron swamp. They crashed him there, but he won out and has what he went after. And just now I got a flash from Fletcher, in the asteroid belt. I think that he has finally traced that dope line. But Knobos is on now—what do you want him to do about the *Endymion?*"

"Tell him to—no, put him on here, I'd better tell him myself," Samms directed, and his face hardened in ruthless decision as the horny, misshapen face of the Martian lieutenant appeared upon the screen. "What do you think, Knobos? Shall they come to trial or not?"

"Not."

"I don't think so, either. It is better that a few gangsters should disappear in space than that the Patrol should have to put down another uprising. See to it."

"Right." The screen darkened and Samms spoke to his secretary. "Put Milton and Fletcher on whenever they come in." He turned to his guests. "We've covered the ground quite thoroughly. Goodbye—I wish I could go with you, but I'll be pretty well tied up for the next week or two."

" 'Tied up' doesn't half express it," Rodebush remarked as the two scientists walked along a corridor toward an elevator. "He probably is the busiest man on three planets."

"As well as the most powerful," Cleveland supplemented. "And very few men could use his power as fairly—but he's welcome to it, as far as I'm concerned. I'd have the pink fantods for a month if I had to do only once what he's just done—and to him it's just part of a day's work."

"You mean the *Endymion?* What else could he do?"

"Nothing—that's the hell of it. It had to be done, since bringing them to trial would mean killing half the people of Morseca; but at the same time it's a ghastly thing to order a job of deliberate, cold-blooded, and illegal murder."

"You're right, of course, but you would ..." he broke off, unable to put his thoughts into words. For while inarticulate, manlike, concerning their deepest emotions, in both men was ingrained the code of their organization; both knew that to every man chosen for it THE SERVICE was everything, himself nothing.

"But enough of that, we'll have plenty of grief of our own right here." Rodebush changed the subject abruptly as they stepped into a vast room, almost filled by the immense bulk of the *Boise*—the sinister space-ship which, although never flown, had already lined with black so many pages of Triplanetary's roster. She was now, however, the center of a furious activity. Men swarmed over her and through her, in the orderly confusion of a fiercely driven but carefully planned program of reconstruction.

"I hope your dope is right, Fritz!" Cleveland called, as the two scientists separated to go to their respective laboratories. "If it is, we'll make a perfect lady out of this unmanageable man-killer yet!"

14

THE SUPER-SHIP IS LAUNCHED

After weeks of ceaseless work, during which was lavished upon her every resource of mind and material afforded by three planets, the *Boise* was ready for her maiden flight. As nearly ready, that is, as the thought and labor of man could make her. Rodebush and Cleveland had finished their last rigid inspection of the craft and, standing beside the center door of the main airlock, were talking with their chief.

"You say that you think that it's safe, and yet you won't take a crew," Samms argued. "In that case it isn't safe enough for you two, either. We need you too badly to permit you to take such chances."

"You've *got* to let us go, because we are the only ones who are at all familiar with her theory," Rodebush insisted. "I said, and I still say, that I *think* it is safe. I can't prove it, however, even mathematically; because she's altogether too full of too many new and untried mechanisms, too many extrapolations beyond all existing or possible data. Theoretically, she is sound, but you know that theory can go only so far, and that mathematically negligible factors may become operative at those velocities. We do not need a crew for a short trip. We can take care of any minor mishaps, and if our fundamental theories are wrong, all the crews between here and Jupiter wouldn't do any good. Therefore we two are going—alone."

"Well, be very careful, anyway. I wish that you could start out slow and take it easy."

"In a way, so do I, but she wasn't designed to neutralize half of gravity, nor half of the inertia of matter—it's got to be everything or nothing, as soon as the neutralizers go on. We could start out on the projectors, of course, instead of on the neutralizers, but that wouldn't prove anything and would only prolong the agony."

"Well, then, be as careful as you can."

"We'll do that, Chief," Cleveland put in. "We think as much of us as anybody else does—maybe more—and we aren't committing suicide if we can help it. And remember about everybody staying inside when we take off—it's barely possible that we'll take up a lot of room. Good-bye!"

"Goodbye, fellows!"

The massive insulating doors were shut, the metal side of the mountain opened, and huge, squat caterpillar tractors came roaring and clanking into the room. Chains and cables were made fast and, mighty steel rails groaning under the load, the space-ship upon her rolling ways was dragged out of the Hill and far out upon the level floor of the valley before the tractors cast off and returned to the fortress.

"Everybody is under cover," Samms informed Rodebush. The Chief was staring intently into his plate, upon which was revealed the control room of the untried supership. He heard Rodebush speak to Cleveland; heard the observer's brief reply; saw the navigator push the switch-button—then the communicator plate went blank. Not the ordinary blankness of a cut-off, but a peculiarly disquieting fading out into darkness. And where the great space-ship had rested there was for an instant nothing. Exactly nothing—a vacuum. Vessel, falsework, rollers, trucks, the enormous steel I-beams of the tracks, even the deep-set concrete piers and foundations and a vast hemisphere of the solid ground; all disappeared utterly and instantaneously. But almost as suddenly as it had been formed the vacuum was filled by a cyclonic rush of air. There was a detonation as of a hundred vicious thunderclaps made one, and through the howling, shrieking blasts of wind there rained down upon valley, plain, and metaled mountain a veritable avalanche of debris; bent, twisted, and broken rails and beams, splintered timbers, masses of concrete, and thousands of cubic yards of soil and rock. For the atomic-powered "Rodebush-Cleveland" neutralizers were more powerful by far, and had a vastly greater radius of action, than the calculations of their designers had shown; and for a moment everything within a hundred yards or so of the *Boise* behaved as though it were an integral part of the vessel. Then, left behind immediately by the super-ship's almost infinite velocity, all this material had again become subject to all of Nature's everyday laws and had crashed back to the ground.

"Could you hold your beam, Randolph?" Samms' voice cut sharply through the daze of stupefaction which held spellbound most of the denizens of the Hill. But all were not so held—no conceivable emergency could take the attention of the chief ultra-wave operator from his instruments.

"No, sir," Radio Center shot back. "It faded out and I couldn't recover it. I put everything I've got behind a tracer on that beam, but haven't been able to lift a single needle off the pin."

"And no wreckage of the vessel itself," Samms went on, half audibly. "Either they have succeeded far beyond their wildest hopes or else . . . more probably . . ." He fell silent and switched off the plate. Were his two friends, those intrepid scientists, alive and triumphant, or had they gone to lengthen the list of victims of that man-killing space-ship? Reason told him that they were gone. They *must* be gone, or else the ultra-beams—energies of such unthinkable velocity of propagation that man's most sensitive instruments had never been able even to estimate it—would have held the ship's transmitter in spite of any velocity attainable by matter under any conceivable conditions. The ship must have been disintegrated as soon as Rodebush released his forces. And yet, had not the physicist dimly foreseen the possibility of such an actual velocity—or had he? However, individuals could come and go, but the Service went on. Samms squared his shoulders unconsciously; and slowly, grimly, made his way back to his private office.

"Mr. Fairchild would like to have a moment as soon as possible, sir," his secretary informed him even before he sat down. "Senator Morgan has been here all day, you know, and he insists on seeing you personally."

"Oh, that kind, eh? All right, I'll see him. Get Fairchild, please . . . Dick? Can you talk, or is he there listening?"

"No, he's heckling Saunders at the moment. He's been here long enough. Can you take a minute and throw him out?"

"Of course, if you say so, but why not throw the hooks into him yourself, as usual?"

"He wants to lay down the law to you, personally. He's a Big Shot, you know, and his group is kicking up quite a row, so it might be better to have it come straight from the top. Besides, you've got a unique knack—when you throw a harpoon, the harpoonee doesn't forget it."

"All right. He's the uplifter and leveler-off. Down with Triplanetary, up with National Sovereignty. We're power-mad dictators—iron-heel-on-the-necks-of-the-people, and so on. But what's he like, personally? Thick-skinned, of course—got a brain?"

"Rhinoceros. He's got a brain, but it's definitely weaseloid. Bear down—sink it in full length, and then twist it."

"O.K. You've got a harpoon, of course?"

"Three of 'em!" Fairchild, Head of Triplanetary's Public Relations, grinned with relish. "Boss Jim Towne owns him in fee simple. The number of his hot lock box is N469T414. His subbest sub-rosa girl-friend is Fi-Chi le Bay . . . yes, everything that the name implies. She got a superdeluxe fur coat—Martian tekkyl, no less—out of that Mackenzie River power deal. Triple play, you might say—Clander to Morgan to le Bay.''

"Nice. Bring him in."

"Senator Morgan, Mr. Samms," Fairchild made the introduction and the two men sized each other up in lightning glances. Samms saw a big man, florid, somewhat inclined toward corpulence, with the surface geniality—and the shrewd, calculating eyes—of the successful politician. The senator saw a tall, hard-trained man in his forties; a lean, keen, smooth-shaven face; a shock of red-bronze-auburn hair a couple of weeks overdue for a cutting; a pair of gold-flecked tawny eyes too penetrant for comfort.

"I trust, Senator, that Fairchild has taken care of you satisfactorily?"

"With one or two exceptions, yes." Since Samms did not ask what the exceptions could be, Morgan was forced to continue. "I am here, as you know, in my official capacity as Chairman of the Pernicious Activities Committee of the North American Senate. It has been observed for years that the published reports of your organization have left much unsaid. It is common knowledge that high-handed outrages have been perpetrated; if not by your men themselves, in such circumstances that your agents could not have been ignorant of them. Therefore it has been decided to make a first-hand and comprehensive investigation, in which matter your Mr. Fairchild has not been at all cooperative."

"Who decided to make this investigation?"

"Why, the North American Senate, of course, through its Pernicious Activities . . ."

"I thought so." Samms interrupted. "Don't you know, Senator, that the Hill is not a part of the North American Continent? That the Triplanetary Service is responsible only to the Triplanetary Council?"

"Quibbling, sir, and outmoded! This, sir, is a democracy!" the Senator began to orate. "All that will be changed very shortly, and if you are as smart as you are believed to be, I need only say that you and those of your staff who cooperate . . ."

"You need say nothing at all." Samms' voice cut. "It has not been changed yet. The Government of North America rules its continent, as do the other Continental Governments. The combined Continental Governments of the Three Planets form the Triplanetary Council, which is a non-political body, the members of which hold office for life and which is the supreme authority in any matter, small or large, affecting more than one Continental Government. The Council has two principal operating agencies; the Triplanetary Patrol, which enforces its decisions, rules, and regulations, and the Triplanetary Service, which performs such other tasks as the Council directs. We have no interest in the purely internal affairs of North America. Have you any information to the contrary?''

''More quibbling!'' the Senator thundered. ''This is not the first time in history that a ruthless dictatorship has operated in the disguise of a democracy. Sir, I *demand* full access to your files, so that I can spread before the North American Senate the full facts of the various matters which I mentioned to Fairchild—one of which was the affair of the *Pelarion*. In a democracy, sir, facts should not be hidden; the people must and shall be kept completely informed upon any matter which affects their welfare or their political lives!''

''Is that so? If I should ask, then, for the purpose of keeping the Triplanetary Council, and through it your constituents, fully informed as to the political situation in North America, you would undoubtedly give me the key to safe-deposit box N469T414? For it is common knowledge, in the Council at least, that there is a certain amount of— shall we say turbidity?—in the supposedly pellucid reaches of North American politics.''

''What? Preposterous!'' Morgan made a heroic effort, but could not quite maintain his poise. ''Private papers only, sir!''

''Perhaps. Certain of the Councillors believe, however mistakenly, that there are several things of interest there: such as the record of certain transactions involving one James F. Towne; references to and details concerning dealings—not to say deals—with Mackenzie Power, specifically with Mackenzie Power's Mr. Clander; and perhaps a juicy bit or two concerning a person known as le Bay and a tekkyl coat. Of interest no end, don't you think, to the dear people of North America?''

As Samms drove the harpoon in and twisted it, the big man suffered visibly. Nevertheless:

''You refuse to cooperate, eh?'' he blustered. ''Very well, I will go— but you have not heard the last of me, Samms!''

''No? Probably not. But remember, before you do any more rabble-rousing, that this lock-box thing is merely a sample. We of the Service know a lot of things that we do not mention to anybody—except in self-defense.''

''I am holding Fletcher, Mr. Samms. Shall I put him on now?'' Norma asked, as the completely deflated Morgan went out.

''Yes, please . . . Hello, Sid; mighty glad to see you—we were scared for a while. How did you make out, and what was it?''

''Hi, Chief! Mostly hadive. Some heroin, and quite a bit of Martian ladolian. Lousy job, though—three of the gang got away, and took about a quarter of the loot with them. That was what I want to talk to you about in such a hurry—fake meteors; the first I ever saw."

Samms straightened up in his chair.

"Just a second. Norma, put Redmond on here with us . . . Listen, Harry. Now, Fletcher, did you see that fake meteor yourself? Touch it?"

"Both. In fact, I've still got it. One of the runners, pretending to be a Service man, flashed it on *me*. It's really good, too, Chief. Even now, I can't tell it from my own except that mine is in my pocket. Shall I send it in?"

"By all means; to Dr. H. D. Redmond, Head of Research. Keep on slugging, Sid—goodbye. Now, Harry, what do you think? It *could* be one of our own, you know."

"Could be, but probably isn't. We'll know as soon as we get it in the lab. Chances are, though, that they have caught up with us again. After all, that was to be expected—anything that science can synthesize, science can analyze; and whatever the morals and ethics of the pirates may be, they have got brains."

"And you haven't been able to devise anything better?"

"Variations only, which wouldn't take much time to solve. Fundamentally, the present meteor is the best we know."

"Got anybody you would like to put on it, immediately?"

"Of course. One of the new boys will be perfect for the job, I think. Name of Bergenholm. Quite a character. Brilliant, erratic, flashes of sheer genius that he can't explain, even to us. I'll put him on it right away."

"Thanks a lot. And now, Norma, please keep everybody off my neck that you can. I want to think."

And think he did; keen eyes clouded, staring unseeingly at the papers littering his desk. Triplanetary needed a symbol—a something—which would identify a Service man anywhere, at any time, under any circumstances, without doubt or question . . . something that could not be counterfeited or imitated, to say nothing of being duplicated . . . something that no scientist not of Triplanetary Service could *possibly* imitate . . . better yet, something that no one not of Triplanetary could even wear . . .

Samms grinned fleetingly at that thought. A tall order—one calling for a *deus ex machina* with a vengeance . . . But damn it, there ought to be *some* way to . . .

"Excuse me, sir." His secretary's voice, usually so calm and cool, trembled as she broke in on his thinking. "Commissioner Kinnison is calling. Something terrible is going on again, out toward Orion. Here he is," and there appeared upon Samms' screen the face of the Commissioner of Public Safety, the commander-in-chief of Triplanetary's every armed force; whether of land or of water, of air or of empty space.

"They've come back, Virgil!" The Commissioner rapped out, without preliminary or greeting. ".'Four vessels gone—a freighter and a passenger liner, with her escort of two heavy cruisers. All in Sector M, Dx about 151. I have ordered all traffic out of space for the duration of the emergency, and since even our warships seem useless, every ship is making for the nearest dock at maximum. How about that new flyer of yours—got anything that will do us any good?" No one beyond the "Hill's" shielding screens knew that the *Boise* had already been launched.

"I don't know. We don't even know whether we have a super-ship or not," and Samms described briefly the beginning—and very probably the ending—of the trial flight, concluding: "It looks bad, but if there was any possible way of handling her, Rodebush and Cleveland did it. All our tracers are negative yet, so nothing definite has . . ."

He broke off as a frantic call came in from the Pittsburgh station for the Commissioner; a call which Samms both heard and saw.

"The city is being attacked!" came the urgent message. "We need all the reenforcements you can send us!" and a picture of the beleagured city appeared in ghastly detail upon the screens of the observers; a view being recorded from the air. It required only seconds for the commissioner to order every available man and engine of war to the seat of conflict; then, having done everything they could do, Kinnison and Samms stared in helpless, fascinated horror into their plates, watching the scenes of carnage and destruction depicted there.

The Nevian vessel—the sister-ship, the craft which Costigan had seen in mid-space as it hurtled Earthward in response to Nerado's summons—hung poised in full visibility high above the metropolis. Scornful of the pitiful weapons wielded by man, she hung there, her sinister beauty of line sharply defined against the cloudless sky. From her shining hull there reached down a tenuous but rigid rod of crimson energy; a rod which slowly swept hither and thither as the Nevians searched out the richest deposits of the precious metal for which they had come so far. Iron, once solid, now a viscous red liquid, was sluggishly flowing in an ever-thickening stream up that intangible crimson duct and into the capacious storage tanks of the Nevian raider; and wherever that flaming beam went there went also ruin, destruction, and death. Office buildings, skyscrapers towering majestically in their architectural symmetry and beauty, collapsed into heaps of debris as their steel skeletons were abstracted. Deep into the ground the beam bored; flood, fire, and explosion following in its wake as the mazes of underground piping disappeared. And the humanity of the buildings died: instantaneously and painlessly, never knowing what struck them, as the life-bearing iron of their bodies went to swell the Nevian stream.

Pittsburgh's defenses had been feeble indeed. A few antiquated railway rifles had hurled their shells upward in futile defiance, and had been quietly absorbed. The district planes of Triplanetary, newly armed with iron-driven ultra-beams, had assembled hurriedly and had attacked the invader in formation, with but little more success. Under the impact of their beams, the stranger's screens had flared white, then poised ship and flying squadron had alike been lost to view in a murkily opaque shroud of crimson flame. The cloud had soon dissolved, and from the place where the planes had been there had floated or crashed down a litter of non-ferrous wreckage. And now the cone of space-ships from the Buffalo base of Triplanetary was approaching Pittsburgh, hurling itself toward the Nevian plunderer and toward known, gruesome, and hopeless defeat.

"Stop them, Rod!" Samms cried. "It's sheer slaughter! They haven't got a thing—they aren't even equipped yet with the iron drive!"

"I know it," the commissioner groaned, "and Admiral Barnes knows it as well as we do, but it can't be helped—wait a minute! The Washington cone is reporting. They're as close as the other, and they have the new armament. Philadelphia is close behind, and so is New York. Now perhaps we can do something!"

The Buffalo flotilla slowed and stopped, and in a matter of minutes the detachments from the other bases arrived. The cone was formed and, iron-driven vessels in the van, the old-type craft far in the rear, it bore down upon the Nevian, vomiting from its hollow front a solid cylinder of annihilation. Once more the screens of the Nevian flared into brilliance, once more the red cloud of destruction was flung abroad. But these vessels were not entirely defenseless. Their iron-driven ultra-generators threw out screens of the Nevians' own formulae, screens of prodigious power to which the energies of the amphibians clung and at which they clawed and tore in baffled, wildly coruscant displays of power unthinkable. For minutes the furious conflict raged, while the inconceivable energy being dissipated by those straining screens hurled itself in terribly destructive bolts of lightning upon the city far beneath.

No battle of such incredible violence could long endure. Triplanetary's ships were already exerting their utmost power, while the Nevians, contemptuous of Solarian science, had not yet uncovered their full strength. Thus the last desperate effort of mankind was proved futile as the invaders forced their beams deeper and deeper into the overloaded defensive screens of the war-vessels; and one by one the supposedly invincible space-ships of humanity dropped in horribly dismembered ruin upon the ruins of what had once been Pittsburgh.

15

SPECIMENS

Only too well founded was Costigan's conviction that the submarine of the deep-sea fishes had not been able to prevail against Nerado's formidable engines of destruction. For days the Nevian lifeboat with its three Terrestrial passengers hurtled through the interstellar void without incident, but finally the operative's fears were realized—his far-flung detector screens reacted; upon his observation plate they could see Nerado's mammoth space-ship, in full pursuit of its fleeing life-boat!

"On your toes, folks—it won't be long now!" Costigan called, and Bradley and Clio hurried into the tiny control room.

Armor donned and tested, the three Terrestrials stared into the observation plates, watching the rapidly-enlarging picture of the Nevian space-ship. Nerado had traced them and was following them, and such was the power of the great vessel that the now inconceivable velocity of the lifeboat was the veriest crawl in comparison to that of the pursuing cruiser.

"And we've hardly started to cover the distance back to Tellus. Of course you couldn't get in touch with anybody yet?" Bradley stated, rather than asked.

"I kept trying, of course, until they blanketed my wave, but all negative. Thousands of times too far for my transmitter. Our only hope of reaching anybody was the mighty slim chance that our super-ship might be prowling around out here already, but it isn't, of course. Here they are!"

Reaching out to the control panel, Costigan viciously shot out against the great vessel wave after wave of lethal vibrations, under whose fiercely clinging impacts the Nevian defensive screens flared white; but, strangely enough, their own screens did not radiate. As if contemptuous of any weapons the lifeboat might wield, the mother ship simply defended herself from the attacking beams, in much the same fashion as a wildcat mother wards off the claws and teeth of her spitting, snarling kitten who is resenting a touch of needed maternal discipline.

"They probably wouldn't fight us, at that," Clio first understood the situation. "This is their own lifeboat, and they want us alive, you know."

"There's one more thing we can try—hang on!" Costigan snapped, as he released his screens and threw all his power into one enormous pressor beam.

The three were thrown to the floor and held there by an awful weight as the lifeboat darted away at the stupendous acceleration of the beam's reaction against the unimaginable mass of the Nevian sky-rover; but the flight was of short duration. Along that pressor beam there crept a dull red rod of energy, which surrounded the fugitive shell and brought it slowly to a halt. Furiously then Costigan set and reset his controls, launching his every driving force and his every weapon, but no beam could penetrate that red murk, and the lifeboat remained motionless in space. No, not motionless—the red rod was shortening, drawing the truant craft back toward the launching port from which she had so hopefully emerged a few days before. Back and back it was drawn; Costigan's utmost efforts futile to affect by a hair's breadth its line of motion. Through the open port the boat slipped neatly, and as it came to a halt in its original position within the multi-layered skin of the monster, the prisoners heard the heavy doors clang shut behind them, one after another.

And then sheets of blue fire snapped and crackled all about the three suits of Triplanetary armor—the two large human figures and the small one were outlined starkly in blinding blue flame.

"That's the first thing that has come off according to schedule." Costigan laughed, a short, fierce bark. "That is their paralyzing ray, we've got it stopped cold, and we've each got enough iron to hold it forever."

"But it looks as though the best we can do is a stalemate," Bradley argued. "Even if they can't paralyze us, we can't hurt them, and we are heading back for Nevia."

"I think Nerado will come in for a conference, and we'll be able to make terms of some kind. He must know what these Lewistons will do, and he knows that we'll get a chance to use them, some way or other, before he gets to us again," Costigan asserted, confidently—but again he was wrong.

The door opened, and through it there waddled, rolled, or crawled a metal-clad monstrosity—a thing with wheels, legs and writhing tentacles of jointed bronze; a thing possessed of defensive screens sufficiently powerful to absorb the full blast of the Triplanetary projectors without effort. Three brazen tentacles reached out through the ravening beams of the Lewistons, smashed them to bits, and wrapped themselves in unbreakable shackles about the armored forms of the three human beings. Through the door the machine or creature carried its helpless load, and out into and along a main corridor. And soon the three Terrestrials, without arms, without armor, and almost without clothing, were standing in the control room, again facing the calm and unmoved Nerado. To the surprise of the impetuous Costigan, the Nevian commander was entirely without rancor.

"The desire for freedom is perhaps common to all forms of animate life," he commented, through the transformer. "As I told you before, however, you are specimens to be studied by the College of Science, and you shall be so studied in spite of anything you may do. Resign yourselves to that."

"Well, say that we don't try to make any more trouble; that we cooperate in the examination and give you whatever information we can," Costigan suggested. "Then you will probably be willing to give us a ship and let us go back to our own world?"

"You will not be allowed to cause any more trouble," the amphibian declared, coldly. "Your cooperation will not be required. We will take from you whatever knowledge and information we wish. In all probability you will never be allowed to return to your own system, because as specimens you are too unique to lose. But enough of this idle chatter—take them back to their quarters!"

Back to their three inter-communicating rooms the prisoners were led under heavy guard; and, true to his word, Nerado made certain that they had no more opportunities to escape. To Nevia the space-ship sped without incident, and in manacles the Terrestrials were taken to the College of Science, there to undergo the physical and psychical examinations which Nerado had promised them.

Nor had the Nevian scientist-captain erred in stating that their cooperation was neither needed nor desired. Furious but impotent, the human beings were studied in laboratory after laboratory by the coldly analytical, unfeeling scientists of Nevia, to whom they were nothing more nor less than specimens; and in full measure they came to know what it meant to play the part of an unknown, lowly organism in a biological research. They were photographed, externally and internally. Every bone, muscle, organ, vessel, and nerve was studied and charted. Every reflex and reaction was noted and discussed. Meters registered every impulse and recorders filmed every thought, every idea, and every sensation. Endlessly, day after day, the nerve-wracking torture went on, until the frantic subjects could bear no more. White-faced and shaking, Clio finally screamed wildly, hysterically, as she was being strapped down upon a laboratory bench; and at the sound Costigan's nerves, already at the breaking point, gave way in an outburst of berserk fury.

The man's struggles and the girl's shrieks were alike futile, but the surprised Nevians, after a consultation, decided to give the specimens a vacation. To that end they were installed, together with their Earthly belongings, in a three-roomed structure of transparent metal, floating in the large central lagoon of the city. There they were left undisturbed for a time—undisturbed, that is, except by the continuous gaze of the crowd of hundreds of amphibians which constantly surrounded the floating cottage.

"First we're bugs under a microscope," Bradley growled, "then we're goldfish in a bowl. I don't know that . . ."

He broke off as two of their jailers entered the room. Without a word into the transformers they seized Bradley and Clio. As those tentacular arms stretched out toward the girl, Costigan leaped. A vain attempt. In midair the paralyzing beam of the Nevians touched him and he crashed heavily to the crystal floor; and from that floor he looked on in helpless, raging fury while his sweetheart and his captain were carried out of their prison and into a waiting submarine.

16

SUPER-SHIP IN ACTION

Doctor Frederick Rodebush sat at the control panel of Triplanetary's newly reconstructed super-ship, one finger poised over a small black button. Facing the unknown though the physicist was, yet he grinned whimsically at his friend.

"Something, whatever it is, is about to occur. The *Boise* is about to take off. Ready, Cleve?"

"Shoot!" laconically. Cleveland also was constitutionally unable to voice his deeper sentiments in time of stress.

Rodebush drove his finger down, and instantly over both men there came a sensation akin to a tremendously intensified vertigo; but a vertigo as far beyond the space-sickness of weightlessness as that horrible sensation is beyond mere Earthly dizziness. The pilot reached weakly toward the board, but his leaden hands refused utterly to obey the dictates of his reeling mind. His brain was a writhing, convulsive mass of torment indescribable; expanding, exploding, swelling out with an unendurable pressure against its confining skull. Fiery spirals, laced with streaming, darting lances of black and green, flamed inside his bursting eyeballs. The Universe spun and whirled in mad gyrations about him as he reeled drunkenly to his feet, staggering and sprawling. He fell. He realized that he was falling, yet he could not fall! Thrashing wildly, grotesquely in agony, he struggled madly and blindly across the room, directly toward the thick steel wall. The tip of one hair of his unruly thatch touched the wall, and the slim length of that single hair did not even bend as its slight strength brought to an instant halt the hundred-and-eighty-odd pounds of mass—mass now entirely without inertia—that was his body.

But finally the sheer brain power of the man began to triumph over his physical torture. By force of will he compelled his grasping hands to seize a life-line, almost meaningless to his dazed intelligence; and through that nightmare incarnate of hellish torture he fought his way back to the control board. Hooking one leg around a standard, he made a seemingly enormous effort and depressed a red button; then fell flat upon the floor, weakly but in a wave of relief and thankfulness, as his racked body felt again the wonted phenomena of weight and of inertia. White, trembling, frankly and openly sick, the two men stared at each other in half-amazed joy.

"It worked," Cleveland smiled wanly as he recovered sufficiently to speak, then leaped to his feet. "Snap it up, Fred! We must be falling fast—we'll be wrecked when we hit!"

"We're not falling anywhere." Rodebush, foreboding in his eyes, walked over to the main observation plate and scanned the heavens. "However, it's not as bad as I was afraid it might be. I can still recognize a few of the constellations, even though they are all pretty badly distorted. That means that we can't be more than a couple of light-years or so away from the Solar System. Of course, since we had so little thrust on, practically all of our energy and time was taken up in getting out of the atmosphere. Even at that, though, it's a good thing that space isn't a perfect vacuum, or we would have been clear out of the Universe by this time."

"Huh? What are you talking about? Impossible! Where are we, anyway? Then we must be making mil . . . Oh, I see!" Cleveland exclaimed, somewhat incoherently, as he also stared into the plate.

"Right. We aren't traveling at all—*now*." Rodebush replied. "We are perfectly stationary relative to Tellus, since we made that hop without inertia. We must have attained one hundred percent neutralization—one hundred point oh oh oh oh oh—which we didn't quite expect. Therefore we must have stopped instantaneously when our inertia was restored. Incidentally, that original, pre-inertialess velocity—'intrinsic' velocity, suppose we could call it?—is going to introduce plenty of complications, but we don't have to worry about them right now. Also, it isn't *where* we are that is worrying me—we can get fixes on enough recognizable stars to find that out in short order—it's *when*."

"That's right, too. Say we're two light years away from home. You think maybe that we're two years older now than we were ten minutes ago? Interesting no end—and distinctly possible. Maybe even probable—I wouldn't know—there's been a lot of discussion on that theory, and as far as I know we're the first ones who ever had a chance to prove or disprove it absolutely. Let's snap back to Tellus and find out, right now."

"We'll do that, after a little more experimenting. You see, I had no intention of giving us such a long push. I was going to throw the switches in and out, but you know what happened. However, there's one good thing about it—it's worth two years of anybody's life to settle that relativity-time thing definitely, one way or the other."

"I'll say it is. But say, we've got a lot of power on our ultra-wave; enough to reach Tellus, I think. Let's locate the sun and get in touch with Samms."

"Let's work on these controls a little first, so we'll have something to report. Out here's a fine place to try the ship out—nothing in the way."

"All right with me. But I *would* like to find out whether I'm two years older than I think I am, or not!"

Then for four hours they put the great super-ship through her paces, just as test-pilots check up on every detail of performance of an airplane of new and radical design. They found that the horrible vertigo could be endured, perhaps in time even conquered as space-sickness could be conquered, by a strong will in a sound body; and that their new conveyance had possibilities of which even Rodebush had never dreamed. Finally, their most pressing questions answered, they turned their most powerful ultra-beam communicator toward the yellowish star which they knew to be Old Sol.

"Samms . . . Samms." Cleveland spoke slowly and distinctly. "Rodebush and Cleveland reporting from the 'Space-Eating Wampus', now directly in line with Beta Ursae Minoris from the sun, distance about two point two light years. It will take six bands of tubes on your tightest beam, LSV3, to reach us. Barring a touch of an unusually severe type of space-sickness, everything worked beautifully; even better than either of us dared to believe. There's something we want to know right away—have we been gone four hours and some odd minutes, or better than two years?"

He turned to Rodebush and went on:

"Nobody knows how fast this ultra-wave travels, but if it goes as fast as we did coming out it's no creeper. I'll give him about thirty minutes, then shoot in another . . ."

But, interrupting Cleveland's remark, the care-ravaged face of Virgil Samms appeared sharp and clear upon the plate and his voice snapped curtly from the speaker.

"Thank God you're alive, and twice that that the ship works!" he exclaimed. "You've been gone four hours, eleven minutes, and forty-one seconds, but never mind about abstract theorizing. Get back here, to Pittsburgh, as fast as you can drive. That Nevian vessel or another one like her is mopping up the city, and has destroyed half the Fleet already!''

"We'll be back there in nine minutes!'' Rodebush snapped into the transmitter. ''Two to get from here to atmosphere, four from atmosphere down to the Hill, and three to cool off. Notify the full four-shift crew—everybody we've picked out. Don't need anybody else. Ship, equipment, and armament are *ready*!''

"Two minutes to atmosphere? Think you can do it?'' Cleveland asked, as Rodebush flipped off the power and leaped to the control panel. "You might, though, at that.''

"We could do it in less than that if we had to. We used scarcely any power at all coming out, and I'm going to use quite a lot going back,'' the physicist explained rapidly, as he set the dials which would determine their flashing course.

The master switches were thrown and the pangs of inertialessness again assailed them—but weaker far this time than ever before—and upon their lookout plates they beheld a spectacle never before seen by eye of man. For the ultrabeam, with its heterodyned vision, is not distorted by any velocity yet attained, as are the ether-borne rays of light. Converted into light only at the plate, it showed their progress as truly as though they had been traveling at a pace to be expressed in the ordinary terms of miles per hour. The yellow star that was the sun detached itself from the firmament and leaped toward them, swelling visibly, momently, into a blinding monster of incandescence. And toward them also flung the Earth, enlarging with such indescribable rapidity that Cleveland protested involuntarily, in spite of his knowledge of the peculiar mechanics of the vessel in which they were.

"Hold it, Fred, hold it! Way 'nuff!'' he exclaimed.

"I'm using only a few thousand kilograms of thrust, and I'll cut that as soon as we touch atmosphere, long before she can even begin to heat,'' Rodebush explained. "Looks bad, but we'll stop without a jar.''

"What would you call this kind of flight, Fritz?'' Cleveland asked. "What's the opposite of 'inert'?''

"Damned if I know. Isn't any, I guess. Light? No . . . how would 'free' be?''

"Not bad. 'Free' and 'Inert' maneuvering, eh? O.K.''

Flying "free'', then, the super-ship came from her practically infinite velocity to an almost instantaneous halt in the outermost, most tenuous layer of the Earth's atmosphere. Her halt was but momentary. Inertia restored, she dropped at a sharp angle downward. More than dropped; she was forced downward by one full battery of projectors; projectors driven by iron-powered generators. Soon they were over the Hill, whose violet screens went down at a word.

Flaming a dazzling white from the friction of the atmosphere through which she had torn her way, the *Boise* slowed abruptly as she neared the ground, plunging toward the surface of the small but deep artificial lake below the Hill's steel apron. Into the cold waters the space-ship dove, and even before they could close over her, furious geysers of steam and boiling water erupted as the stubborn alloy gave up its heat to the cooling liquid. Endlessly the three necessary minutes dragged their slow way into time, but finally the water ceased boiling and Rodebush tore the ship from the lake and hurled her into the gaping doorway of her dock. The massive doors of the air-locks opened, and while the full crew of picked men hurried aboard with their personal equipment, Samms talked earnestly to the two scientists in the control room.

". . . and about half the fleet is still in the air. They aren't attacking; they are just trying to keep her from doing much more damage until you can get there. How about your take-off? We can't launch you again—the tracks are gone—but you handled her easily enough coming in?"

"That was all my fault," Rodebush admitted. "I had no idea that the fields would extend beyond the hull. We'll take her out on the projectors this time, though, the same as we brought her in—she handles like a bicycle. The projector blast tears things up a little, but nothing serious. Have you got that Pittsburgh beam for me yet? We're about ready to go."

"Here it is, Doctor Rodebush," came Norma's voice, and upon the screen there flashed into being the view of the events transpiring above that doomed city. "The dock is empty and sealed against your blast."

"Goodbye, and power to your tubes!" came Samms' ringing voice.

As the words were being spoken mighty blasts of power raved from the driving projectors, and the immense mass of the super-ship shot out through the portals and upward into the stratosphere. Through the tenuous atmosphere the huge globe rushed with ever-mounting speed, and while the hope of Triplanetary drove eastward Rodebush studied the everchanging scene of battle upon his plate and issued detailed instructions to the highly trained specialists manning every offensive and defensive weapon.

But the Nevians did not wait to join battle until the newcomers arrived. Their detectors were sensitive—operative over untold thousands of miles—and the ultra-screen of the Hill had already been noted by the invaders as the Earth's only possible source of trouble. Thus the departure of the *Boise* had not gone unnoticed, and the fact that not even with his most penetrant rays could he see into her interior had already given the Nevian commander some slight concern. Therefore as soon as it was determined that the great globe was being directed toward Pittsburgh the fish-shaped cruiser of the void went into action.

High in the stratosphere, speeding eastward, the immense mass of the *Boise* slowed abruptly, although no projector had slackened its effort. Cleveland, eyes upon interferometer grating and spectrophotometer charts, fingers flying over calculator keys, grinned as he turned toward Rodebush.

"Just as you thought, Skipper; an ultra-band pusher. C4V63L29. Shall I give him a little pull?"

"Not yet; let's feel him out a little before we force a close-up. We've got plenty of mass. See what he does when I put full push on the projectors."

As the full power of the Tellurian vessel was applied the Nevian was forced backward, away from the threatened city, against the full drive of her every projector. Soon, however, the advance was again checked, and both scientists read the reason upon their plates. The enemy had put down reenforcing rods of tremendous power. Three compression members spread out fanwise behind her, bracing her against a low mountainside, while one huge tractor beam was thrust directly downward, holding in an unbreakable grip a cylinder of earth extending deep down into bedrock.

"Two can play at that game!" and Rodebush drove down similar beams, and forward-reaching tractors as well. "Strap yourselves in solid, everybody!" he sounded a general warning. "Something is going to give way somewhere soon, and when it does we'll get a jolt!"

And the promised jolt did indeed come soon. Prodigiously massive and powerful as the Nevian was, the *Boise* was even more massive and more powerful; and as the already enormous energy feeding the tractors, pushers, and projectors was raised to its inconceivable maximum, the vessel of the enemy was hurled upward, backward; and that of Earth shot ahead with a bounding leap that threatened to strain even her mighty members. The Nevian anchor rods had not broken; they had simply pulled up the vast cylinders of solid rock that had formed their anchorages.

"Grab him now!" Rodebush yelled, and even while an avalanche of falling rock was burying the countryside Cleveland snapped a tractor ray upon the flying fish and pulled tentatively.

Nor did the Nevian now seem averse to coming to grips. The two warring super-dreadnoughts darted toward each other, and from the invader there flooded out the dread crimson opacity which had theretofore meant the doom of all things Solarian. Flooded out and engulfed the immense globe of humanity's hope in its spreading cloud of redly impenetrable murk. But not for long. Triplanetary's supership boasted no ordinary Terrestrial defense, but was sheathed in screen after screen of ultra-vibrations: imponderable walls, it is true, but barriers impenetrable to any unfriendly wave. To the outer screen the red veil of the Nevians clung tenaciously, licking greedily at every square inch of the shielding sphere of force, but unable to find an opening through which to feed upon the steel of the *Boise*'s armor.

"Get back—'way back! Go back and help Pittsburgh!" Rodebush drove an ultra communicator beam through the murk to the instruments of the Terrestrial admiral; for the surviving warships of the fleet—its most powerful units—were hurling themselves forward, to plunge into that red destruction. "None of you will last a second in this red field. And watch out for a violet field pretty soon—it'll be worse than this. We can handle them alone, I think; but if we can't, there's nothing in the System that can help us!"

And now the hitherto passive screen of the super-ship became active. At first invisible, it began to glow in fierce violet light, and as the glow brightened to unbearable intensity the entire spherical shield began to increase in size. Driven outward from the super-ship as a center, its advancing surface of seething energy consumed the crimson murk as a billow of blast-furnace heat consumes the cloud of snowflakes in the air above its cupola. Nor was the red death-mist all that was consumed. Between that ravening surface and the armor skin of the *Boise* there was nothing. No debris, no atmosphere, no vapor, no single atom of material substance—the first time in Terrestrial experience that an absolute vacuum had ever been attained!

Stubbornly contesting every foot of way lost, the Nevian fog retreated before the violet sphere of nothingness. Back and back it fell, disappearing altogether from all space as the violet tide engulfed the enemy vessel; but the flying fish did not disappear. Her triple screens flashed into furiously incandescent splendor and she entered unscathed that vacuous sphere, which collapsed instantly into an enormously elongated ellipsoid, at each focus a madly warring ship of space.

Then in that tube of vacuum was waged a spectacular duel of ultra-weapons—weapons impotent in air, but deadly in empty space. Beams, rays, and rods of Titantic power smote cracklingly against ultra-screens equally capable. Time after time each contestant ran the gamut of the spectrum with his every available ultra-force, only to find all channels closed. For minutes the terrible struggle went on, then:

"Cooper, Adlington, Spencer, Dutton!" Rodebush called into his transmitter. "Ready? Can't touch him on the ultra, so I'm going onto the macro-bands. Give him everything you have as soon as I collapse the violet. Go!"

At the word the violet barrier went down, and with a crash as of a disrupting Universe the atmosphere rushed into the void. And through the hurricane there shot out the deadliest material weapons of Triplanetary. Torpedoes—non-ferrous, ultra-screened, beam-dirigible torpedoes charged with the most effective forms of material destruction known to man. Cooper hurled his canisters of penetrating gas, Adlington his allotropic-iron atomic bombs, Spencer his indestructible armor-piercing projectiles, and Dutton his shatterable flasks of the quintessence of corrosion—a sticky, tacky liquid of such dire potency that only one rare Solarian element could contain it. Ten, twenty, fifty, a hundred were thrown as fast as the automatic machinery could launch them; and the Nevians found them adversaries not to be despised. Size for size, their screens were quite as capable as those of the *Boise*. The Nevians' destructive rays glanced harmlessly from their shields, and the Nevians' elaborate screens, neutralized at impact by those of the torpedoes, were impotent to impede their progress. Each projectile must needs be caught and crushed individually by beams of the most prodigious power; and while one was being annihilated dozens more were rushing to the attack. Then, while the twisting, dodging invader was busiest with the tiny but relentless destroyers, Rodebush launched his heaviest weapon.

The macro-beams! Prodigious streamers of bluish-green flame which tore savagely through course after course of Nevian screen! Malevolent fangs, driven with such power and velocity that they were biting into the very walls of the enemy vessel before the amphibians knew that their defensive shells of force had been punctured! And the emergency screens of the invaders were equally futile. Course after course was sent out, only to flare viciously through the spectrum and to go black.

Outfought at every turn, the now frantically dodging Nevian leaped away in headlong flight, only to be brought to a staggering, crashing halt as Cleveland nailed her with a tractor beam. But the Tellurians were to learn that the Nevians held in reserve a means of retreat. The tractor snapped—sheared off squarely by a sizzling plane of force—and the fish-shaped cruiser faded from Cleveland's sight, just as the *Boise* had disappeared from the communicator plates of Radio Center, back in the Hill, when she was launched. But though the plates in the control room could not hold the Nevian, she did not vanish beyond the ken of Randolph, now Communications Officer in the super-ship. For, warned and humiliated by his losing one speeding vessel from his plates in Radio Center, he was now ready for any emergency. Therefore as the

Nevian fled Randolph's spy-ray held her, automatically behind it as there was the full output of twelve special banks of iron-driven power tubes; and thus it was that the vengeful Earthmen flashed immediately along the Nevians' line of flight. Inertialess now, pausing briefly from time to time to enable the crew to accustom themselves to the new sensations, Triplanetary's super-ship pursued the invader; hurtling through the void with a velocity unthinkable.

"He was easier to take than I thought he would be," Cleveland grunted, staring into the plate.

"I thought he had more stuff, too," Rodebush assented, "but I guess Costigan got almost everything they had. If so, with all our own stuff and most of theirs besides, we should be able to take them. Conway's data indicated that they have only partial neutralization of inertia—if it's one hundred percent we'll never catch them—but it isn't—there they are!"

"And this time I'm going to hold her or burn out all our generators trying," Cleveland declared, grimly. "Are you fellows down there able to handle yourselves yet? Fine! Start throwing out your cans!"

Space-hardened veterans all, the other Tellurian officers had fought off the horrible nausea of inertialessness, just as Rodebush and Cleveland had done. Again the ravening green macro-beams tore at the flying cruiser, again the mighty frames of the two space-ships shuddered sickeningly as Cleveland clamped on his tractor rod, again the highly dirigible torpedoes dashed out with their freights of death and destruction. And again the Nevian shear-plane of force slashed at the *Boise*'s tractor beam; but this time the mighty puller did not give way. Sparkling and spitting high-tension sparks, the plane bit deeply into the stubborn rod of energy. Brighter, thicker, and longer grew the discharges as the gnawing plane drew more and more power; but in direct ratio to that power the rod grew larger, denser, and ever harder to cut. More and more vivid became the pyrotechnic display, until suddenly the entire tractor rod disappeared. At the same instant a blast of intolerable flame erupted from the *Boise*'s flank and the whole enormous fabric of her shook and quivered under the force of a terrific detonation.

"Randolph! I don't see them! Are they attacking or running?" Rodebush demanded. He was the first to realize what had happened.

"Running—fast!"

"Just as well, perhaps, but get their line. Adlington!"

"Here!"

"Good! Was afraid you were gone—that was one of your bombs, wasn't it?"

"Yes. Well launched, just inside the screens. Don't see how it could have detonated unless something hot and hard struck it in the tube; it would need about that much time to explode. Good thing it didn't go off any sooner, or none of us would have been here. As it is, Area Six is pretty well done in, but the bulkheads held the damage to Six. What happened?''

"We don't know, exactly. Both generators on the tractor beam went out. At first, I thought that was all, but my neutralizers are dead and I don't know what else. When the G-4's went out the fusion must have shorted the neutralizers. They would make a mess; it must have burned a hole down into number six tube. Cleveland and I will come down, and we'll all look around.''

Donning space-suits, the scientists let themselves into the damaged compartment through the emergency air-locks, and what a sight they saw! Both outer and inner walls of alloy armor had been blown away by the awful force of the explosion. Jagged plates hung awry; bent, twisted and broken. The great torpedo tube, with all its intricate automatic machinery, had been driven violently backward and lay piled in hideous confusion against the backing bulkheads. Practically nothing remained whole in the entire compartment.

"Nothing much we can do here,'' Rodebush said finally, through his transmitter. "Let's go see what number four generator looks like.''

That room, although not affected by the explosion from without, had been quite as effectively wrecked from within. It was still stiflingly hot; its air was still reeking with the stench of burning lubricant, insulation, and metal; its floor was half covered by a semi-molten mass of what had once been vital machinery. For with the burning out of the generator bars the energy of the disintegrating allotropic iron had had no outlet, and had built up until it had broken through its insulation and in an irresistible flood of power had torn through all obstacles in its path to neutralization.

"Hm . . . m . . . m. Should have had an automatic shut-off—one detail we overlooked,'' Rodebush mused. "The electricians can rebuild this stuff here, though—that hole in the hull is something else again.''

"I'll say it's something else,'' the grizzled Chief Engineer agreed. "She's lost all her spherical strength—anchoring a tractor with this ship now would turn her inside out. Back to the nearest Triplanetary shop for us, I would say.''

"Come again, Chief!'' Cleveland advised the engineer. "None of us would live long enough to get there. We can't travel inertialess until the repairs are made, so if they can't be made without very much traveling, it's just too bad.''

"I don't see how we could support our jacks . . .'' the engineer paused, then went on: "If you can't give me Mars or Tellus, how about some other planet? I don't care about atmosphere, or about anything but mass. I can stiffen her up in three or four days if I can sit down on something heavy enough to hold our jacks and presses; but if we have to rig up space-cradles around the ship herself it'll take a long time—months, probably. Haven't got a spare planet on hand, have you?"

"We might have, at that," Rodebush made surprising answer. "A couple of seconds before we engaged we were heading toward a sun with at least two planets. I was just getting ready to dodge them when we cut the neutralizers, so they should be fairly close somewhere—yes, there's the sun, right over there. Rather pale and small; but it's close, comparatively speaking. We'll go back up into the control room and find out about the planets."

The strange sun was found to have three large and easily located children, and observation showed that the crippled space-ship could reach the nearest of these in about five days. Power was therefore fed to the driving projectors, and each scientist, electrician, and mechanic bent to the task of repairing the ruined generators; rebuilding them to handle any load which the converters could possibly put upon them. For two days the *Boise* drove on, then her acceleration was reversed, and finally a landing was effected upon the forbidding, rocky soil of the strange world.

It was larger than the Earth, and of a somewhat stronger gravitation. Although its climate was bitterly cold, even in its short daytime, it supported a luxuriant but outlandish vegetation. Its atmosphere, while rich enough in oxygen and not really poisonous, was so rank with indescribably fetid vapors as to be scarcely breatheable. But these things bothered the engineers not at all. Paying no attention to temperature or to scenery and without waiting for chemical analysis of the air, the space-suited mechanics leaped to their tasks; and in only a little more time than had been mentioned by the chief engineer the hull and giant frame of the super-ship were as staunch as of yore.

"All right, Skipper!" came finally the welcome word. "You might try her out with a fast hop around this world before you shove off in earnest."

Under the fierce blast of her projectors the vessel leaped ahead, and time after time, as Rodebush hurled her mass upon tractor beam or pressor, the engineers sought in vain for any sign of weakness. The strange planet half girdled and the severest tests passed flawlessly, Rodebush reached for his neutralizer switches. Reached and paused, dumbfounded, for a brilliant purple light had sprung into being upon his panel and a bell rang out insistently.

"What the hell!" Rodebush shot out an exploring beam along the detector line and gasped. He stared, mouth open, then yelled:

"*Roger* is here, rebuilding his planetoid! STATIONS ALL!"

17

ROGER CARRIES ON

As has been intimated, Gray Roger did not perish in the floods of Nevian energy which destroyed his planetoid. While those terrific streamers of force emanating from the crimson obscurity surrounding the amphibians' space-ship were driving into his defensive screens he sat impassive and immobile at his desk, his hard gray eyes moving methodically over his instruments and recorders.

When the clinging mantle of force changed from deep red into shorter and ever shorter wave-lengths, however:

"Baxter, Hartkopf, Chatelier, Anandrusung, Penrose, Nishimura, Mirsky . . ." he called off a list of names. "Report to me here at once!"

"The planetoid is lost," he informed his select group of scientists when they had assembled, "and we must abandon it in exactly fifteen minutes, which will be the time required for the robots to fill this first section with our most necessary machinery and instruments. Pack each of you one box of the things he most wishes to take with him, and report back here in not more than thirteen minutes. Say nothing to anyone else."

They filed out calmly, and as they passed out into the hall Baxter, perhaps a trifle less case-hardened than his fellows, at least voiced a thought for those they were so brutally deserting.

"I say, it seems a bit thick to dash off this way and leave the rest of them; but still, I suppose . . ."

"You suppose correctly." Bland and heartless Nishimura filled in the pause. "A small part of the planetoid may be able to escape; which, to me at least, is pleasantly surprising news. It cannot carry all our men and mechanisms, therefore only the most important of both are saved.

What would you? For the rest it is simply what you call 'the fortune of war', no?''

"But the beautiful . . .'' began the amorous Chatelier.

"Hush, fool!'' snorted Hartkopf. "One word of that to the ear of Roger and you too left behind are. Of such nonessentials the Universe full is, to be collected in times of ease, but in times hard to be disregarded. Und this is a time of *schrecklichkeit* indeed!''

The group broke up, each man going to his own quarters; to meet again in the First Section a minute or so before the zero time. Roger's "office'' was now packed so tightly with machinery and supplies that but little room was left for the scientists. The gray monstrosity still sat unmoved behind his dials.

"But of what use is it, Roger?'' the Russian physicist demanded. "Those waves are of some ultra-band, of a frequency immensely higher than anything heretofore known. Our screens should not have stopped them for an instant. It is a mystery that they have held so long, and certainly this single section will not be permitted to leave the planetoid without being destroyed.''

"There are many things you do not know, Mirsky,'' came the cold and level answer. "Our screens, which you think are of your own devising, have several improvements of my own in the formulae, and would hold forever had I the power to drive them. The screens of this section, being smaller, can be held as long as will be found necessary.''

"Power!'' the dumbfounded Russian exclaimed. "Why, we have almost infinite power—unlimited—sufficient for a lifetime of high expenditure!''

But Roger made no reply, for the time of departure was at hand. He pressed down a tiny lever, and a mechanism in the power room threw in the gigantic plunger switches which launched against the Nevians the stupendous beam which so upset the complacence of Nerado the amphibian—the beam into which was poured recklessly every resource of power afforded by the planetoid, careless alike of burnout and of exhaustion. Then, while all of the attention of the Nevians and practically all of their maximum possible power output was being devoted to the neutralization of that last desperate thrust, the metal wall of the planetoid opened and the First Section shot out into space. Full-driven as they were, Roger's screens flared white as he drove through the temporarily lessened attack of the Nevians; but in their preoccupation the amphibians did not notice the additional disturbance and the section tore on, unobserved and undetected.

Far out in space, Roger raised his eyes from the instrument panel and continued the conversation as though it had not been interrupted.

"Everything is relative, Mirsky, and you have misused gravely the term 'unlimited'. Our power was, and is, very definitely limited. True, it then seemed ample for our needs, and is far superior to that possessed by the inhabitants of any solar system with which I am familiar; but the beings behind that red screen, whoever they are, have sources of power as far above ours as ours are above those of the Solarians."

"How do you know?"

"That power, what is it?"

"We have, then, the analyses of those fields recorded!" came simultaneous questions and exclamations.

"Their source of power is the intra-atomic energy of iron. Complete; not the partial liberation incidental to the nuclear fission of such unstable isotopes as those of thorium, uranium, plutonium, and so on. Therefore much remains to be done before I can proceed with my plan—I must have the most powerful structure in the macrocosmic universe."

Roger thought for minutes, nor did any one of his minions break the silence. Gharlane of Eddore did not have to wonder why such incredible advancement could have been made without his knowledge: after the fact, he knew. He had been and was still being hampered by a mind of power; a mind with which, in due time, he would come to grips.

"I now know what to do," he went on presently. "In the light of what I have learned, the losses of time, life, and treasure—even the loss of the planetoid—are completely insignificant."

"But what can you do about it?" growled the Russian.

"Many things. From the charts of the recorders we can compute their fields of force, and from that point it is only a step to their method of liberating the energy. We shall build robots. They shall build other robots, who shall in turn construct another planetoid; one this time that, wielding the theoretical maximum of power, will be suited to my needs."

"And where will you build it? We are marked. Invisibility now is useless. Triplanetary will find us, even if we take up an orbit beyond that of Pluto!"

"We have already left your Solarian system far behind. We are going to another system; one far enough removed so that the spy-rays of Triplanetary will never find us, and yet one that we can reach in a reasonable length of time with the energies at our command. Some five days will be required for the journey, however, and our quarters are cramped. Therefore make places for yourselves wherever you can, and lessen the tedium of those days by working upon whatever problems are most pressing in your respective researches."

The gray monster fell silent, immersed in what thoughts no one knew, and the scientists set out to obey his orders. Baxter, the British chemist, followed Penrose, the lantern-jawed, saturnine American engineer and inventor, as he made his way to the furthermost cubicle of the section.

"I say, Penrose, I'd like to ask you a couple of questions, if you don't mind?"

"Go ahead. Ordinarily it's dangerous to be a cackling hen anywhere around *him*, but I don't imagine that he can hear anything here now. His system must be pretty well shot to pieces. You want to know all I know about Roger?"

"Exactly so. You have been with him so much longer than I have, you know. In some ways he impresses one as being scarcely human, if you know what I mean. Ridiculous, of course, but of late I have been wondering whether he really *is* human. He knows too much, about too many things. He seems to be acquainted with many solar systems, to visit which would require lifetimes. Then, too, he has dropped remarks which would imply that he actually saw things that happened long before any living man could possibly have been born. Finally, he looks—well, peculiar—and certainly does not act human. I have been wondering, and have been able to learn nothing about him; as you have said, such talk as this aboard the planetoid was not advisable."

"You needn't worry about being paid your price; that's one thing. If we live—and that was part of the agreement, you know—we will get what we sold out for. You will become a belted earl. I have already made millions, and shall make many more. Similarly, Chatelier has had and will have his women, Anandrusung and Nishimura their cherished revenges, Hartkopf his power, and so on." He eyed the other speculatively, then went on:

"I might as well spill it all, since I'll never have a better chance and since you should know as much as the rest of us do. You're in the same boat with us and tarred with the same brush. There's a lot of gossip, that may or may not be true, but I know one very startling fact. Here it is. My great-great-grandfather left some notes which, taken in connection with certain things I myself saw on the planetoid, prove beyond question that our Roger went to Harvard University at the same time he did. Roger was a grown man then, and the elder Penrose noted that he was marked, like this," and the American sketched a cabalistic design.

"What!" Baxter exclaimed. "An adept of North Polar Jupiter—*then?*"

"Yes. That was before the First Jovian War, you know, and it was those medicine-men—really high-caliber scientists—that prolonged that war so . . ."

"But I say, Penrose, that's really a bit thick. When they were wiped out it was proved a lot of hocus-pocus . . ."

"*If* they were wiped out," Penrose interrupted in turn. "Some of it may have been hocus-pocus, but most of it certainly was not. I'm not asking you to believe anything except that one fact; I'm just telling you the rest of it. But it is also a fact that those adepts knew things and did things that take a lot of explaining. Now for the gossip, none of which is guaranteed. Roger is supposed to be of Tellurian parentage, and the story is that his father was a moon-pirate, his mother a Greek adventuress. When the pirates were chased off the moon they went to Ganymede, you know, and some of them were captured by the Jovians. It seems that Roger was born at an instant of time sacred to the adepts, so they took him on. He worked his way up through the Forbidden Society as all adepts did, by various kinds of murder and job lots of assorted deviltries, until he got clear to the top—the seventy-seventh mystery . . ."

"The secret of eternal youth!" gasped Baxter, awed in spite of himself.

"Right, and he stayed Chief Devil, in spite of all the efforts of all his ambitious sub-devils to kill him, until the turning-point of the First Jovian War. He cut away then in a space-ship, and ever since then he has been working—and working hard—on some stupendous plan of his own that nobody else has ever got even an inkling of. That's the story. True or not, it explains a lot of things that no other theory can touch. And now I think you'd better shuffle along; enough of this is a great plenty!"

Baxter went to his own cubby, and each man of gray Roger's cold-blooded crew methodically took up his task. True to prediction, in five days a planet loomed beneath them and their vessel settled through a reeking atmosphere toward a rocky and forbidding plain. Then for hours they plunged along, a few thousand feet above the surface of that strange world, while Roger with his analytical detectors sought the most favorable location from which to wrest the materials necessary for his program of construction.

It was a world of cold; its sun was distant, pale, and wan. It had monstrous forms of vegetation, of which each branch and member writhed and fought with a grotesque and horrible individual activity. Ever and anon a struggling part broke from its parent plant and darted away in independent existence; leaping upon and consuming or being consumed by a fellow creature equally monstrous. This flora was of a uniform color, a lurid, sickly yellow. In form some of it was fern-like, some cactus-like, some vaguely tree-like; but it was all outrageous, inherently repulsive to all Solarian senses. And no less hideous were the animal-like forms of life which slithered and slunk rapaciously through that fantastic pseudo-vegetation. Snake-like, reptile-like, bat-like, the creatures squirmed, crawled, and flew; each covered with a dankly oozing yellow hide and each motivated by twin common impulses—to kill and insatiably and indiscriminately to devour. Over this reeking wilderness Roger drove his vessel, untouched by its disgusting, its appalling ferocity and horror.

"There should be intelligence, of a kind," he mused, and swept the surface of the planet with an exploring beam. "Ah, yes, there is a city, of sorts," and in a few minutes the outlaws were looking down upon a metal-walled city of roundly conical buildings.

Inside these structures and between and around them there scuttled formless blobs of matter, one of which Roger brought up into his vessel by means of a tractor. Held immovable by the beam it lay upon the floor, a strangely extensile, amoeba-like, metal-studded mass of leathery substance. Of eyes, ears, limbs, or organs it apparently had none, yet it radiated an intensely hostile aura; a mental effluvium concentrated of rage and of hatred.

"Apparently the ruling intelligence of the planet," Roger commented. "Such creatures are useless to us; we can build machines in half the time that would be required for their subjugation and training. Still, it should not be permitted to carry back what it may have learned of us." As he spoke the adept threw the peculiar being out into the air and dispassionately rayed it out of existence.

"That thing reminds me of a man I used to know, back in Penobscot." Penrose was as coldly callous as his unfeeling master. "The evenest-tempered man in town—mad all the time!"

Eventually Roger found a location which satisfied his requirements of raw materials, and made a landing upon that unfriendly soil. Sweeping beams denuded a great circle of life, and into that circle leaped robots. Robots requiring neither rest nor food, but only lubricants and power; robots insensible alike to that bitter cold and to that noxious atmosphere.

But the outlaws were not to win a foothold upon that inimical planet easily, nor were they to hold it without effort. Through the weird vegetation of the circle's bare edge there scuttled and poured along a horde of the metal-studded men—if "men" they might be called—who, ferocity incarnate, rushed the robot line. Mowed down by hundreds, still they came on; willing, it seemed, to spend any number of lives in order that one living creature might once touch a robot with one outthrust metallic stud. Whenever that happened there was a flash as of lightning, the heavy smoke of burning insulation, grease, and metal, and the robot went down out of control. Recalling his remaining automatons, Roger sent out a shielding screen, against which the defenders of their planet raged in impotent fury. For days they hurled themselves and their every force against that impenetrable barrier, then withdrew: temporarily stopped, but by no means acknowledging defeat.

Then while Roger and his cohorts directed affairs from within their comfortable and now sufficiently roomy vessel, there came into being around it an industrial city of metal, peopled by metallic and insensate mechanisms. Mines were sunk, furnaces were blown in, smelters belched forth into the already unbearable air their sulphurous fumes, rolling mills and machine shops were built and were equipped; and as fast as new enterprises were completed, additional robots were ready to man them. In record time the heavy work of girders, members, and plates was well under way; and shortly thereafter light, deft, multi-fingered mechanisms began to build and to install the prodigious amount of precise machinery required by the vastness of the structure.

As soon as he was sure that he would be completely free for a sufficient length of time, Roger-Gharlane assembled, boiled down and concentrated, his every mental force. He probed then, very gently, for whatever it was that had been and was still blocking him. He found it—synchronized with it—and in the instant hurled against it the fiercest thrust possible for his Eddorian mind to generate: a bolt whose twin had slain more than one member of Eddore's Innermost Circle; a bolt whose energies, he had previously felt sure, would slay any living thing save only His Ultimate Supremacy, the All-Highest of Eddore.

Now, however, and not completely to his surprise, that blast of force was ineffective; and the instantaneous riposte was of such intensity as to require for its parrying everything that Gharlane had. He parried it, however barely, and directed a thought at his unknown opponent.

"You, whoever you may be, have found out that you cannot kill me. No more can I kill you. So be it. Do you still believe that you can keep me from remembering whatever it was that my ancestor was compelled to forget?"

"Now that you have obtained a focal point we cannot prevent you from remembering; and merely to hinder you would be pointless. You may remember in peace."

Back and back went Gharlane's mind. Centuries ... millenia ... cycles ... eons. The trace grew dim, almost imperceptible, deeply buried beneath layer upon layer of accretions of knowledge, experience, and sensation which no one of many hundreds of his ancestors had even so much as disturbed. But every iota of knowledge that any of his progenitors had ever had was still his. However dim, however deeply buried, however suppressed and camouflaged by inimical force, he could now find it.

He found it, and in the instant of its finding it was as though Enphilistor the Arisian spoke directly to him; as though the fused Elders of Arisia tried—vainly now—to erase from his own mind all knowledge of Arisia's existence. The fact that such a race as the Arisians had existed so long ago was bad enough. That the Arisians had been aware throughout all those ages of the Eddorians, and had been able to keep their own existence secret, was worse. The crowning fact that the Arisians had had all this time in which to work unopposed against his own race made even Gharlane's indomitable ego quail.

This was *important*. Such minor matters as the wiping out of nonconforming cultures—the extraordinarily rapid growth of which was now explained—must wait. Eddore must revise its thinking completely; the pooled and integrated mind of the Innermost Circle must scrutinize every fact, every implication and connotation, of this new-old knowledge. Should he flash back to Eddore, or should he wait and take the planetoid, with its highly varied and extremely valuable contents? He would wait; a few moments more would be a completely negligible addition to the eons of time which had already elapsed since action should have been begun.

The rebuilding of the planetoid, then, went on. Roger had no reason to suspect that there was anything physically dangerous within hundreds of millions of miles. Nevertheless, since he knew that he could no longer depend upon his own mental powers to keep him informed as to all that was going on around him, it was his custom to scan, from time to time, all nearby space by means of ether-borne detectors. Thus it came about that one day, as he sent out his beam, his hard gray eyes grew even harder.

"Mirsky! Nishimura! Penrose! Come here!" he ordered, and showed them upon his plate an enormous sphere of steel, its offensive beams flaming viciously. "Is there any doubt whatever in your minds as to the System to which that ship belongs?"

"None at all—Solarian," replied the Russian. "To narrow it still further, Triplanetarian. While larger than any I have ever seen before, its construction is unmistakeable. They managed to trace us, and are testing out their weapons before attacking. Do we attack or do we run away?"

"If Triplanetarian, and it surely is, we attack," coldly. "This one section is armed and powered to defeat Triplanetary's entire navy. We shall take that ship, and shall add its slight resources to our own. And it may even be that they have picked up the three who escaped me . . . I have never yet been balked for long. Yes, we shall take that vessel. And those three sooner or later. Except for the fact that their escape from me is a matter which should be corrected, I care nothing whatever about either Bradley or the woman. Costigan, however, is in a different category . . . Costigan *handled* me . . ." Diamond-hard eyes glared balefully at the urge of thoughts to a clean and normal mind unthinkable.

"To your posts," he ordered. "The machines will continue to function under their automatic controls during the short time it will require to abate this nuisance."

"One moment!" A strange voice roared from the speakers. "Consider yourselves under arrest, by order of the Triplanetary Council! Surrender and you shall receive impartial hearing; fight us and you shall never come to trial. From what we have learned of Roger, we do not expect him to surrender, but if any of you other men wish to avoid immediate death, leave your vessel at once. We will come back for you later."

"Any of you wishing to leave this vessel have my full permission to do so," Roger announced, disdaining any reply to the challenge of the *Boise*. "Any such, however, will not be allowed inside the planetoid area after the rest of us return from wiping out that patrol. We attack in one minute."

"Would not one do better by stopping on?" Baxter, in the quarters of the American, was in doubt as to the most profitable course to pursue. "I should leave immediately if I thought that that ship could win; but I do not fancy that it can, do you?"

"That ship? *One* Triplanetary ship against *us?*" Penrose laughed raucously. "Do as you please. I'd go in a minute if I thought that there was any chance of us losing; but there isn't, so I'm staying. I know which side *my* bread's buttered on. Those cops are bluffing, that's all. Not bluffing exactly, either, because they'll go through with it as long as they last. Foolish, but it's a way they have—they'll die trying every time instead of running away, even when they know they're licked before they start. They don't use good judgment."

"None of you are leaving? Very well, you each know what to do," came Roger's emotionless voice. The stipulated minute having elapsed, he advanced a lever and the outlaw cruiser slid quietly into the air.

Toward the poised *Boise* Roger steered. Within range, he flung out a weapon new-learned and supposedly irresistible to any ferrous thing or creature, the red converter-field of the Nevians. For Roger's analytical detectors had stood him in good stead during those frightful minutes in the course of which the planetoid had borne the brunt of Nerado's superhuman attack; in such good stead that from the records of those ingenious instruments he and his scientists had been able to reconstruct not only the generators of the attacking forces, but also the screens employed by the amphibians in the neutralization of similar beams. With a vastly inferior armament the smallest of Roger's vessels had defeated the most powerful battleships of Triplanetary; what had he to fear in such a heavy craft as the one he now was driving, one so superlatively armed and powered? It was just as well for his peace of mind that he had no inkling that the harmless-looking sphere he was so blithely attacking was in reality the much-discussed, half-mythical super-ship upon which the Triplanetary Service had been at work so long; nor that its already unprecedented armament had been reenforced, thanks to that hated Costigan, with Roger's own every worthwhile idea, as well as with every weapon and defense known to that arch-Nevian, Nerado!

Unknowing and contemptuous, Roger launched his converter field, and instantly found himself fighting for his very life. For from Rodebush at the controls down, the men of the *Boise* countered with wave after wave and with salvo after salvo of vibratory and material destruction. No thought of mercy for the men of the pirate ship could enter their minds. The outlaws had each been given a chance to surrender, and each had refused it. Refusing, they knew, as the Triplanetarians knew and as all modern readers know, meant that they were staking their lives upon victory. For with modern armaments few indeed are the men who live through the defeat in battle of a war-vessel of space.

Roger launched his field of red opacity, but it did not reach even the *Boise*'s screens. All space seemed to explode into violet splendor as Rodebush neutralized it, drove it back with his obliterating zone of force; but even that all-devouring zone could not touch Roger's peculiarly efficient screen. The outlaw vessel stood out, unharmed. Ultra-violet, infra-red, pure heat, infra-sound, solid beams of high-tension, high-frequency stuff in whose paths the most stubborn metals would be volatilized instantly, all iron-driven; every deadly and torturing vibration known was hurled against that screen: but it, too, was iron-driven, and it held. Even the awful force of the macro-beam was dissipated by it—reflected, hurled away on all sides in coruscating torrents of blinding, dazzling energy. Cooper, Adlington, Spencer, and Dutton hurled against it their bombs and torpedoes—and still it held. But Roger's fiercest blasts and heaviest projectiles were equally impotent against the force-shields of the super-ship. The adept, having no liking for a battle upon equal terms, then sought safety in flight, only to be brought to a crashing, stunning halt by a massive tractor beam.

"That must be that polycyclic screen that Conway reported on."

Cleveland frowned in thought. "I've been doing a lot of work on that, and I think I've calculated an opener for it, Fred, but I'll have to have number ten projector and the whole output of number ten power room. Can you let me play with that much juice for a while? All right, Blake, tune her up to fifty-five thousand—there, hold it! Now, you other fellows, listen! I'm going to try to drill a hole through that screen with a hollow, quasi-solid beam; like a diamond drill cutting out a core. You won't be able to shove anything into the hole from outside the beam, so you'll have to steer your cans out through the central orifice of number ten projector—that'll be cold, since I'm going to use only the outer ring. I don't know how long I'll be able to hold the hole open, though, so shoot them along as fast as you can. Ready? Here goes!"

He pressed a series of contacts. Far below, in number ten converter room, massive switches drove home and the enormous mass of the vessel quivered under the terrific reaction of the newly-calculated, semimaterial beam of energy that was hurled out, backed by the mightiest of all the mighty converters and generators of Triplanetary's superdreadnaught. That beam, a pipe-like hollow cylinder of intolerable energy, flashed out, and there was a rending, tearing crash as it struck Roger's hitherto impenetrable wall. Struck and clung, grinding, boring in, while from the raging inferno that marked the circle of contact of cylinder and shield the pirate's screen radiated scintillating torrents of crackling, streaming sparks, lightning-like in length and in intensity.

Deeper and deeper the gigantic drill was driven. It was through! Pierced Roger's polycyclic screen; exposed the bare metal of Roger's walls! And now, concentrated upon one point, flamed out in seemingly redoubled fury Triplanetary's raging beams—in vain. For even as they could not penetrate the screen, neither could they penetrate the wall of Cleveland's drill, but rebounded from it in the cascaded brilliance of thwarted lightning.

"Oh, what a dumb-bell I am!" groaned Cleveland. "Why, oh *why* didn't I have somebody rig up a secondary SX7 beam on Ten's inner rings? Hop to it, will you, Blake, so that we'll have it in case they are able to stop the cans?"

But the pirates could not stop all of Triplanetary's projectiles, now hurrying along inside the pipe as fast as they could be driven. In fact, for a few minutes gray Roger, knowing that he faced the first real defeat of his long life, paid no attention to them at all, nor to any of his useless offensive weapons: he struggled only to break away from the savage grip of the *Boise*'s tractor rod. Futile. He could neither cut nor stretch that inexorably anchoring beam. Then he devoted his every resource to the closing of that unbelievable breach in his shield. Equally futile. His most desperate efforts resulted only in more frenzied displays of incandescence along the curved surface of contact of that penetrant cylinder. And through that terrific conduit came speeding package after package of destruction. Bombs, armor-piercing shells, gas shells, and shells of poisonous and corrosive fluids followed each other in close succession. The surviving scientists of the planetoid, expert gunners and ray-men all, destroyed many of the projectiles, but it was not humanly possible to cope with them all. And the breach could not be forced shut against the all but irresistible force of Cleveland's "opener". And with all his power Roger could not shift his vessel's position in the grip of Triplanetary's tractors sufficiently to bring a projector to bear upon the super-ship along the now unprotected axis of that narrow, but deadly tube.

Thus it was that the end came soon. A war-head touched steel plating and there ensued a space-wracking explosion of atomic iron. Gaping wide, helpless, with all defenses down, other torpedoes entered the stricken hulk and completed its destruction even before they could be recalled. Atomic bombs literally volatilized most of the pirate vessel; vials of pure corrosion began to dissolve the solid fragments of her substance into dripping corruption. Reeking gases filled every cranny of circumambient space as what was left of Roger's battle cruiser began the long plunge to the ground. The super-ship followed the wreckage down, and Rodebush sent out an exploring spy-ray.

". . . resistance was such that it was necessary to employ corrosive, and ship and contents were completely disintegrated," he dictated, a little later, into his vessel's log. "While there were of course no remains recognizable as human, it is certain that Roger and his last eleven men died; since it is clear that the circumstances and conditions were such that no life could possibly have survived."

It is true that the form of flesh which had been known as Roger was destroyed. The solids and liquids of its substance were resolved into their component molecules or atoms. That which had energized that form of flesh, however, could not be harmed by any physical force, however applied. Therefore that which made Roger what he was; the essence which was Gharlane of Eddore; was actually back upon his native planet even before Rodebush completed his study of what was left of the pirates' vessel.

The Innermost Circle met, and for a space of time which would have been very long indeed for any Earthly mind those monstrous beings considered as one multi-ply intelligence every newly-exposed phase and facet of the truth. At the end, they knew the Arisians as well as the

Arisians knew them. The All-Highest then called a meeting of all the minds of Eddore.

". . . hence it is clear that these Arisians, while possessing minds of tremendous latent capability, are basically soft, and therefore inefficient," he concluded. "Not weak, mind you, but scrupulous and unrealistic; and it is by taking advantage of these characteristics that we shall ultimately triumph."

"A few details, All-Highest, if Your Ultimate Supremacy would deign," a lesser Eddorian requested. "Some of us have not been able to perceive at all clearly the optimum lines of action."

"While detailed plans of campaign have not yet been worked out, there will be several main lines of attack. A purely military undertaking will of course be one, but it will not be the most important. Political action, by means of subversive elements and obstructive minorities, will prove much more useful. Most productive of all, however, will be the operations of relatively small but highly organized groups whose functions will be to negate, to tear down and destroy, every bulwark of what the weak and spineless adherents of Civilization consider the finest things in life—love, truth, honor, loyalty, purity, altruism, decency, and so on."

"Ah, love . . . extremely interesting, Supremacy, this thing they call sex," Gharlane offered. "What a silly, what a meaningless thing it is! I have studied it intensively, but am not yet fully enough informed to submit a complete and conclusive report. I do know, however, that we can and will use it. In our hands, vice will become a potent weapon indeed.   Vice . . . drugs . . . greed . . . gambling . . . extortion . . . blackmail . . . lust . . . abduction . . . assassination . . . ah-h-h!"

"Exactly. There will be room, and need, for the fullest powers of every Eddorian. Let me caution you all, however, that little or none of this work is to be done by any of us in person. We must work through echelon upon echelon of higher and lower executives and supervisors if we are to control efficiently the activities of the thousands of billions of operators which we must and will have at work. Each echelon of control will be vastly greater in number than the one immediately above it, but correspondingly lower in the individual power of its component personnel. The sphere of activity of each supervisor, however small or great, will be clearly and sharply defined. Rank, from the operators at planetary-population levels up to and including the Eddorian Directorate, will be a linear function of ability. Absolute authority will be delegated. Full responsibility will be assumed. Those who succeed will receive advancement and satisfaction of desire; those who fail will die.

"Since the personnel of the lower echelons will be of small value and easy of replacement, it is of little moment whether or not they become involved in reverses affecting the still lower echelons whose activities they direct. The echelon immediately below us of Eddore, however—and incidentally, it is my thought that the Ploorans will best serve as our immediate underlings—must never, under any conditions, allow any hint of any of its real business to become known either to any member of any lower echelon or to any adherent of Civilization. This point is vital; everyone here must realize that only in that way can our own safety remain assured, and must take pains to see to it that any violator of this rule is put instantly to death.

"Those of you who are engineers will design ever more powerful mechanisms to use against the Arisians. Psychologists will devise and put into practice new methods and techniques, both to use against the able minds of the Arisians and to control the activities of mentally weaker entities. Each Eddorian, whatever his field or his ability, will be given the task he is best fitted to perform. That is all."

And upon Arisia, too, while there was no surprise, a general conference was held. While some of the young Watchmen may have been glad that the open conflict for which they had been preparing so long was now about to break, Arisia as a whole was neither glad nor sorry. In the Great Scheme of Things which was the Cosmic All, this whole affair was an infinitesimal incident. It had been foreseen. It had come. Each Arisian would do to the fullest extent of his ability that which the very fact of his being an Arisian would compel him to do. It would pass.

"In effect, then, our situation has not really changed," Eukonidor stated, rather than asked, after the Elders had again spread their Visualization for public inspection and discussion. "This killing, it seems, must go on. This stumbling, falling, and rising; this blind groping; this futility; this frustration; this welter of crime, disaster, and bloodshed. Why? It seems to me that it would be much better—cleaner, simpler, faster, more efficient, and involving infinitely less bloodshed and suffering—for us to take now a direct and active part, as the Eddorians have done and will continue to do."

"Cleaner, youth, yes; and simpler. Easier; less bloody. It would not, however, be better; or even good; because no end-point would ever be attained. Young civilizations advance only by overcoming obstacles. Each obstacle surmounted, each step of progress made, carries its suffering as well as its reward. We could negate the efforts of any echelon below the Eddorians themselves, it is true. We could so protect and shield each one of our protégé races that not a war would be waged and not a law would be broken. But to what end? Further contemplation will show you immature thinkers that in such a case not one of our races would develop into what the presence of the Eddorians has made it necessary for them to become.

"From this it follows that we would never be able to overcome Eddore; nor would our conflict with that race remain indefinitely at stalemate. Given sufficient time during which to work against us, they will be able to win. However, if every Arisian follows his line of action as it is laid out in this Visualization, all will be well. Are there any more questions?"

"None. The blanks which you may have left can be filled in by a mind of very moderate power."

"Look here, Fred." Cleveland called attention to the plate, upon which was pictured a horde of the peculiar inhabitants of that ghastly planet, wreaking their frenzied electrical wrath upon everything within the circle bared of native life by Roger's destructive beams. "I was just going to suggest that we clean up the planetoid that Roger started to build, but I see that the local boys and girls are attending to it."

"Just as well, perhaps. I would like to stay and study these people a little while, but we must get back onto the trail of the Nevians," and the *Boise* leaped away into space, toward the line of flight of the amphibians.

They reached that line and along it they traveled at full normal blast. As they traveled their detecting receivers and amplifiers were reaching out with their utmost power; ultra-instruments capable of rendering audible any signal originating within many light-years of them, upon any possible communications band. And constantly at least two men, with every sense concentrated in their ears, were listening to those instruments.

Listening—straining to distinguish in the deafening roar of background noise from the over-driven tubes any sign of voice or of signal:

Listening—while, millions upon millions of miles beyond even the prodigious reach of those ultra-instruments, three human beings were even then sending out into empty space an almost hopeless appeal for the help so desperately needed!

18

THE SPECIMENS ESCAPE

Knowing well that conversation with its fellows is one of the greatest needs of any intelligent being, the Nevians had permitted the Terrestrial specimens to retain possession of their ultra-beam communicators. Thus it was that Costigan had been able to keep in touch with his sweetheart and with Bradley. He learned that each had been placed upon exhibition in a different Nevian city; that the three had been separated in response to an insistent popular demand for such a distribution of the peculiar, but highly interesting creatures from a distant solar system. They had not been harmed. In fact, each was visited daily by a specialist, who made sure that his charge was being kept in the pink of condition.

As soon as he became aware of this condition of things Costigan became morose. He sat still, drooped, and pined away visibly. He refused to eat, and of the worried specialist he demanded liberty. Then, failing in that as he knew he would fail, he demanded something to *do*. They pointed out to him, reasonably enough, that in such a civilization as theirs there was nothing he *could* do. They assured him that they would do anything they could to alleviate his mental suffering, but that since he was a museum piece he must see, himself, that he must be kept on display for a short time. Wouldn't he please behave himself and eat, as a reasoning being should? Costigan sulked a little longer, then wavered. Finally he agreed to compromise. He would eat and exercise if they would fit up a laboratory in his apartment, so that he could continue the studies he had begun upon his own native planet. To this they agreed, and thus it came about that one day the following conversation was held:

"Clio? Bradley? I've got something to tell you this time. Haven't said anything before, for fear things might not work out, but they did.

I went on a hunger strike and made them give me a complete laboratory. As a chemist I'm a damn good electrician; but luckily, with the seawater they've got here, it's a very simple thing to make . . ."

"Hold on!" snapped Bradley. "Somebody may be listening in on us!"

"They aren't. They can't, without my knowing it, and I'll cut off the second anybody tries to synchronize with my beam. To resume—making Vee-Two is a very simple process, and I've got everything around here that's hollow clear full of it . . ."

"How come they let you?" asked Clio.

"Oh, they don't know what I'm doing. They watched me for a few days, and all I did was make up and bottle the weirdest messes imaginable. Then I finally managed to separate oxygen and nitrogen, after trying hard all of one day; and when they saw that I didn't know anything about either one of them or what to do with them after I had them, they gave me up in disgust as a plain dumb ape and haven't paid any attention to me since. So I've got me plenty of kilograms of liquid Vee-Two, all ready to touch off. I'm getting out of here in about three minutes and a half, and I'm coming over after you folks, in a new, iron-powered space-speedster that they don't know I know anything about. They've just given it its final tests, and it's the slickest thing you ever saw."

"But Conway, dearest, you can't possibly rescue me," Clio's voice broke. "Why, there are thousands of them, all around here. If you can get away, go, dear, but don't . . ."

"I said I was coming after you, and if I get away I'll be there. A good whiff of this stuff will lay out a thousand of them just as easily as it will one. Here's the idea. I've made a gas mask for myself, since I'll be in it where it's thick, but you two won't need any. It's soluble enough in water so that three or four thicknesses of wet cloth over your noses will be enough. I'll tell you when to wet down. We're going to break away or go out trying—there aren't enough amphibians between here and Andromeda to keep us humans cooped up like menagerie animals forever! But here comes my specialist with the keys to the city; time for the overture to start. See you later!"

The Nevian physician directed his key tube upon the transparent wall of the chamber and an opening appeared, an opening which vanished as soon as he had stepped through it; Costigan kicked a valve open; and from various innocent tubes there belched forth into the water of the central lagoon and into the air over it a flood of deadly vapor. As the Nevian turned toward the prisoner there was an almost inaudible hiss and a tiny jet of the frightful, outlawed stuff struck his open gills, just below his huge, conical head. He tensed momentarily, twitched convulsively just once, and fell motionless to the floor. And outside, the streams of avidly soluble liquefied gas rushed out into air and into water. It spread, dissolved, and diffused with the extreme mobility which is one of its characteristics; and as it diffused and was borne outward the Nevians in their massed hundreds died. Died not knowing what killed them, not knowing even that they died. Costigan, bitterly resentful of the inhuman treatment accorded the three and fiercely anxious for the success of his plan of escape, held his breath and, grimly alert, watched the amphibians die. When he could see no more motion anywhere he donned his gas-mask, strapped upon his back a large canister of the poison—his capacious pockets were already full of smaller containers—and two savagely exultant sentences escaped him.

"I am a poor, ignorant specimen of ape that can be let play with apparatus, am I?" he rasped, as he picked up the key tube of the specialist and opened the door of his prison. "They'll learn now that it ain't safe to judge by the looks of a flea how far he can jump!"

He stepped out through the opening into the water, and, burdened as he was, made shift to swim to the nearest ramp. Up it he ran, toward a main corridor. But ahead of him there was wafted a breath of dread Vee-Two, and where that breath went, went also unconsciousness—an unconsciousness which would deepen gradually into permanent oblivion save for the prompt intervention of one who possessed, not only the necessary antidote, but the equally important knowledge of exactly how to use it. Upon the floor of that corridor were strewn Nevians, who had dropped in their tracks. Past or over their bodies Costigan strode, pausing only to direct a jet of lethal vapor into whatever branching corridor or open door caught his eye. He was going to the intake of the city's ventilation plant, and no unmasked creature dependent for life upon oxygen could bar his path. He reached the intake, tore the canister from his back, and released its full, vast volume of horrid contents into the primary air stream of the entire city.

And all throughout that doomed city Nevians dropped; quietly and without a struggle, unknowing. Busy executives dropped upon their cushioned, flat-topped desks; hurrying travelers and messengers dropped upon the floors of the corridors or relaxed in the noxious waters of the ways; lookouts and observers dropped before their flashing screens; central operators of communications dropped under the winking lights of their panels. Observers and centrals in the outlying sections of the city wondered briefly at the unwonted universal motionlessness and stagnation; then the racing taint in water and in air reached them, too, and they ceased wondering—forever.

Then through those quiet halls Costigan stalked to a certain storage room, where with all due precaution he donned his own suit of Triplanetary armor. Making an ungainly bundle of the other Solarian equipment stored there, he dragged it along behind him as he clanked back toward his prison, until he neared the dock at which was moored the Nevian space-speedster which he was determined to take. Here, he knew, was the first of many critical points. The crew of the vessel was aboard, and, with its independent air-supply, unharmed. They had weapons, were undoubtedly alarmed, and were very probably highly suspicious. They, too, had ultra-beams and might see him, but his very closeness to them would tend to protect him from ultra-beam observation. Therefore he crouched tensely behind a buttress, staring through his spy-ray goggles, waiting for a moment when none of the Nevians would be near the entrance, but grimly resolved to act instantly should he feel any touch of a spying ultra-beam.

"Here's where the pinch comes," he growled to himself. "I know the combinations, but if they're suspicious enough and act quick enough they can seal that door on me before I can get it open, and then rub me out like a blot; but . . . ah!"

The moment had arrived, before the touch of any revealing ray. He trained the key-tube, the entrance opened, and through that opening in the instant of its appearance there shot a brittle bulb of glass, whose breaking meant death. It crashed into fragments against a metallic wall and Costigan, entering the vessel, consigned its erstwhile crew one by one to the already crowded waters of the lagoon. He then leaped to the controls and drove the captured speedster through the air, to plunge it down upon the surface of the lagoon beside the door of the isolated structure which had for so long been his prison. Carefully he transferred to the vessel the motley assortment of containers of Vee-Two, and after a quick check-up to make sure that he had overlooked nothing, he shot his craft straight up into the air. Then only did he close his ultra-wave circuits and speak.

"Clio, Bradley—I got away clean, without a bit of trouble. Now I'm coming after you, Clio."

"Oh, it's wonderful that you got away, Conway!" the girl exclaimed. "But hadn't you better get Captain Bradley first? Then, if anything should happen, he would be of some use, while I . . ."

"I'll knock him into an outside loop if he does!" the captain snorted, and Costigan went on:

"You won't need to. You come first, Clio, of course. But you're too far away for me to see you with my spy, and I don't want to use the high-powered beam of this boat for fear of detection; so you'd better keep on talking, so that I can trace you."

"That's one thing I *am* good at!" Clio laughed in sheer relief. "If talking were music, I'd be a full brass band!" and she kept up a flow of inconsequential chatter until Costigan told her that it was no longer necessary; that he had established the line.

"Any excitement around there yet?" he asked her then.

"Nothing unusual that I can see," she replied. "Why? Should there be some?"

"I hope not, but when I made my getaway I couldn't kill them all, of course, and I thought maybe they might connect things up with my jail-break and tell the other cities to take steps about you two. But I guess they're pretty well disorganized back there yet, since they can't know who hit them, or what with, or why. I must have got about every-body that wasn't sealed up somewhere, and it doesn't stand to reason that those who are left can check up very closely for a while yet. But they're nobody's fools—they'll certainly get conscious when I snatch you, maybe before . . . there, I see your city, I think."

"What are you going to do?"

"Same as I did back there, if I can. Poison their primary air and all the water I can reach . . ."

"Oh, Conway!" Her voice rose to a scream. "They must know— they're all getting out of the water and are rushing inside the buildings as fast as they possibly can!"

"I see they are," grimly. "I'm right over you now, 'way up. Been locating their primary intake. They've got a dozen ships around it, and have guards posted all along the corridors leading to it; and *those guards are wearing masks!* They're clever birds, all right, those amphibians— they know what they got back there and how they got it. That changes things, girl! If we use gas here we won't stand a chance in the world of getting old Bradley. Stand by to jump when I open that door!"

"Hurry, dear! They are coming out here after me!"

"Sure they are." Costigan had already seen the two Nevians swim-ming out toward Clio's cage, and had hurled his vessel downward in a screaming power dive. "You're too valuable a specimen for them to let you be gassed, but if they can get there before I do they're traveling fools!"

He miscalculated slightly, so that instead of coming to a halt at the surface of the liquid medium the speedster struck with a crash that hurled solid masses of water for hundreds of yards. But no ordinary crash could harm that vessel's structure, her gravity controls were not overloaded, and she shot back to the surface; gallant ship and reckless pilot alike unharmed. Costigan trained his key-tube upon the doorway of Clio's cell, then tossed it aside.

"Different combination over here!" he barked. "Got to cut you out—lie down in that far corner!"

His hands flashed over the panel, and as Clio fell prone without hesitation or question a heavy beam literally blasted away a large portion of the roof of the structure. The speedster shot into the air and dropped down until she rested upon the tops of opposite walls; walls still glowing, semi-molten. The girl piled a stool upon the table and stood upon it, reached upward and seized the mailed hands extended downward toward her. Costigan heaved her up into the vessel with a powerful jerk, slammed the door shut, leaped to the controls, and the speedster darted away.

"Your armor's in that bundle there. Better put it on, and check your Lewistons and pistols—no telling what kind of jams we'll get into," he snapped, without turning. "Bradley, start talking . . . all right, I've got your line. Better get your wet rags ready and get organized generally—every second will count by the time we get there. We're coming so fast that our outer plating's white hot, but it may not be fast enough, at that."

"It isn't fast enough, quite," Bradley announced, calmly. "They're coming out after me now."

"Don't fight them and probably they won't paralyze you. Keep on talking, so that I can find out where they take you."

"No good, Costigan." The voice of the old spacehound did not reveal a sign of emotion as he made his dread announcement. "They have it all figured out. They're not taking any chances at all—they're going to paral . . ." His voice broke off in the middle of the word.

With a bitter imprecation Costigan flashed on the powerful ultra-beam projector of the speedster and focused the plate upon Bradley's prison; careless now of detection, since the Nevians were already warned. Upon that plate he watched the Nevians carry the helpless body of the captain into a small boat, and continued to watch as they bore it into one of the largest buildings of the city. Up a series of ramps they took the still form, placing it finally upon a soft couch in an enormous and heavily guarded central hall. Costigan turned to his companion, and even through the helmets she could see plainly the white agony of his expression. He moistened his lips and tried twice to speak—tried and failed; but he made no move either to cut off their power or to change their direction.

"Of course," she approved steadily. "We are going through. I know that you *want* to run with me, but if you actually did it I would never want to see you or hear of you again, and you would hate me forever.''

"Hardly that.'' The anguish did not leave his eyes and his voice was hoarse and strained, but his hands did not vary the course of the speedster by so much as a hair's breadth. "You're the finest little fellow that ever waved a plume, and I would love you no matter what happened. I'd trade my immortal soul to the devil if it would get you out of this mess, but we're both in it up to our necks and we can't back out now. If they kill him we beat it—he and I both knew that it was on the chance of that happening that I took you first—but as long as all three of us are alive it's all three or none.''

"Of course,'' she said again, as steadily, thrilled this time to the depths of her being by the sheer manhood of him who had thus simply voiced his Code; a man of such fiber that neither love of life nor his infinitely greater love for her could make him lower its high standard. "We are going through. Forget that I am a woman. We are three human beings, fighting a world full of monsters. I am simply one of us three. I will steer your ship, fire your projectors, or throw your bombs. What can I do best?''

"Throw bombs,'' he directed, briefly. He knew what must be done were they to have even the slightest chance of winning clear. "I'm going to blast a hole down into that auditorium, and when I do you stand by that port and start dropping bottles of perfume. Throw a couple of big ones right down the shaft I make, and the rest of them most anywhere, after I cut the wall open. They'll do good wherever they hit, land or water.''

"But Captain Bradley—he'll be gassed, too.'' Her fine eyes were troubled.

"Can't be helped. I've got the antidote, and it'll work any time under an hour. That'll be lots of time—if we aren't gone in less than ten minutes we'll be staying here. They're bringing in platoons of militia in full armor, and if we don't beat those boys to it we're in for plenty of grief. All right—start throwing!''

The speedster had come to a halt directly over the imposing edifice within which Bradley was incarcerated, and a mighty beam had flared downward, digging a fiery well through floor after floor of stubborn metal. The ceiling of the amphitheater was pierced. The beam expired. Down into that assembly hall there dropped two cannisters of Vee-Two, to crash and to fill its atmosphere with imperceptible death. Then the beam flashed on again, this time at maximum power, and with it Costigan burned away half of the entire building. Burned it away until room above room gaped open, shelf-like, to outer atmosphere; the great hall now resembling an over-size pigeon-hole surrounded by smaller ones. Into that largest pigeon-hole the speedster darted, and cushioned desks and benches crashed down; crushed flat under its enormous weight as it came to rest upon the floor.

Every available guard had been thrown into that room, regardless of customary occupation or of equipment. Most of them had been ordinary watchmen, not even wearing masks, and all such were already down. Many, however, were masked, and a few were dressed in full armor. But no portable armor could mount defenses of sufficient power to withstand the awful force of the speedster's weapons, and one flashing swing of a projector swept the hall almost clear of life.

"Can't shoot very close to Bradley with this big beam, but I'll mop up on the rest of them by hand. Stay here and cover me, Clio!" Costigan ordered, and went to open the port.

"I can't—I won't!" Clio replied instantly. "I don't know the controls well enough. I'd kill you or Captain Bradley, sure; but I *can* shoot, and I'm going to!" and she leaped out, close upon his heels.

Thus, flaming Lewiston in one hand and barking automatic in the other, the two mailed figures advanced toward Bradley, now doubly helpless; paralyzed by his enemies and gassed by his friends. For a time the Nevians melted away before them, but as they approached more nearly the couch upon which the captain was they encountered six figures encased in armor fully as capable as their own. The beams of the Lewistons rebounded from that armor in futile pyrotechnics, the bullets of the automatics spattered and exploded impotently against it. And behind that single line of armored guards were massed perhaps twenty unarmored, but masked, soldiers; and scuttling up the ramps leading into the hall were coming the platoons of heavily armored figures which Costigan had previously seen.

Decision instantly made, Costigan ran back toward the speedster, but he was not deserting his companions.

"Keep the good work up!" he instructed the girl as he ran. "I'll pick those jaspers off with a pencil and then stand off the bunch that's coming while you rub out the rest of that crew there and drag Bradley back here."

Back at the control panel, he trained a narrow, but intensely dense beam—quasi-solid lightning—and one by one the six armored figures fell. Then, knowing that Clio could handle the remaining opposition, he devoted his attention to the reenforcements so rapidly approaching from the sides. Again and again the heavy beam lashed out, now upon this side, now upon that, and in its flaming path Nevians disappeared. And not only Nevians—in the incredible energy of that beam's blast, floor, walls, ramps, and every material thing vanished in clouds of thick and brilliant vapor. The room temporarily clear of foes, he sprang again to Clio's assistance, but her task was nearly done. She had "rubbed out" all opposition and, tugging lustily at Bradley's feet, had already dragged him almost to the side of the speedster.

" 'At-a-girl, Clio!'' cheered Costigan, as he picked up the burly captain and tossed him through the doorway. "Highly useful, girl of my dreams, as well as ornamental. In with you, and we'll go places!''

But getting the speedster out of the now completely ruined hall proved to be much more of a task than driving it in had been, for scarcely had Costigan closed his locks than a section of the building collapsed behind them, cutting off their retreat. Nevian submarines and airships were beginning to arrive upon the scene, and were beaming the building viciously in an attempt to entrap or to crush the foreigners in its ruins. Costigan managed finally to blast his way out, but the Nevians had had time to assemble in force and he was met by a concentrated storm of beams and of metal from every inimical weapon within range.

But not for nothing had Conway Costigan selected for his dash for liberty the craft which, save only for the two immense interstellar cruisers, was the most powerful vessel ever built upon red Nevia. And not for nothing had he studied minutely and to the last, least detail every item of its controls and of its armament during wearily long days and nights of solitary imprisonment. He had studied it under test, in action, and at rest; studied it until he knew thoroughly its every possibility—and what a ship it was! The atomic-powered generators of his shielding screens handled with ease the terrific load of the Nevians' assault, his polycyclic screens were proof against any material projectile, and the machines supplying his offensive weapons with power were more than equal to their tasks. Driven now at full rating those frightful beams lashed out against the Nevian blocking the way, and under their impacts her screens flared brilliantly through the spectrum and went down. And in the instant of their failure the enemy vessel was literally blown into nothingness—no unprotected metal, however resistant, could exist for a moment in the pathway of those iron-driven tornadoes of pure energy.

Ship after ship of the Nevians plunged toward the speedster in desperately suicidal attempts to ram her down, but each met the same flaming fate before it could reach its target. Then from the grouped submarines far below there reached up red rods of force, which seized the space-ship and began relentlessly to draw her down.

"What are they doing that for, Conway? *They* can't fight us!''

"They don't want to fight us. They want to hold us, but I know what to do about that, too,'' and the powerful tractor rods snapped as a plane of pure force knifed through them. Upward now at the highest permissible velocity the speedster leaped, and past the few ships remaining above her she dodged; nothing now between her and the freedom of boundless space.

"You did it, Conway; you did it!" Clio exulted. "Oh, Conway, you're just simply wonderful!"

"I haven't done it yet," Costigan cautioned her. "The worst is yet to come. Nerado. He's why they wanted to hold us back, and why I was in such a hurry to get away. That boat of his is bad medicine, girl, and we want to put plenty of kilometers behind us before he gets started."

"But do you think he will chase us?"

"*Think* so? I *know* so! The mere facts that we are rare specimens and that he told us that we were going to stay there all the rest of our lives would make him chase us clear to Lundmark's Nebula. Besides that, we stepped on their toes pretty heavily before we left. We know altogether too much now to be let get back to Tellus; and finally, they'd all die of acute enlargement of the spleen if we get away with this prize ship of theirs. I hope to tell you they'll chase us!"

He fell silent, devoting his whole attention to his piloting, driving his craft onward at such velocity that its outer plating held steadily at the highest point of temperature compatible with safety. Soon they were out in open space, hurtling toward the sun under the drive of every possible watt of power, and Costigan took off his armor and turned toward the helpless body of the captain.

"He looks so . . . so . . . so *dead*, Conway! Are you really sure that you can bring him to?"

"Absolutely. Lots of time yet. Just three simple squirts in the right places will do the trick." He took from a locked compartment of his armor a small steel box, which housed a surgeon's hypodermic and three vials. One, two, three, he injected small, but precisely measured amounts of the fluids into the three vital localities, then placed the inert form upon a deeply cushioned couch.

"There! That'll take care of the gas in five or six hours. The paralysis will wear off long before that, so he'll be all right when he wakes up; and we're going away from here with everything we can put out. I've done everything I know how to do, for the present."

Then only did Costigan turn and look down, directly into Clio's eyes. Wide, eloquent blue eyes that gazed back up into his, tender and unafraid; eyes freighted with the oldest message of woman to chosen man. His hard young face softened wonderfully as he stared at her; there were two quick steps and they were in each other's arms. Lips upon eager lips, blue eyes to gray, motionless they stood clasped in ecstasy; thinking nothing of the dreadful past, nothing of the fearful future, conscious only of the glorious, wonderful present.

"Clio mine . . . darling . . . girl, girl, how I love you!" Costigan's deep voice was husky with emotion. "I haven't kissed you for seven thousand years! I don't rate you, by a million steps; but if I can just get you out of this mess, I swear by all the gods of interplanetary space . . ."

"You needn't, lover. Rate *me?* Good Heavens, Conway! It's just the other way . . ."

"Stop it!" he commanded in her ear. "I'm still dizzy at the idea of your loving me at all, to say nothing of loving me *this* way! But you do, and that's all I ask, here or hereafter."

"Love you? *Love* you!" Their mutual embrace tightened and her low voice thrilled brokenly as she went on: "Conway dearest . . . I can't say a thing, but you know . . . Oh, Conway!"

After a time Clio drew a long and tremulous, but supremely happy breath as the realities of their predicament once more obtruded themselves upon her consciousness. She released herself gently from Costigan's arms.

"Do you really think that there is a chance of us getting back to the Earth, so that we can be together . . . always?"

"A chance, yes. A probability, no," he replied, unequivocally. "It depends upon two things. First, how much of a start we got on Nerado. His ship is the biggest and fastest thing I ever saw, and if he strips her down and drives her—which he will—he'll catch us long before we can make Tellus. On the other hand, I gave Rodebush a lot of data, and if he and Lyman Cleveland can add it to their own stuff and get that super-ship of ours rebuilt in time, they'll be out here on the prowl; and they'll have what it takes to give even Nerado plenty of argument. No use worrying about it, anyway. We won't know anything until we can detect one or the other of them, and then will be the time to do something about it."

"If Nerado catches us, will you . . ." She paused.

"Rub you out? I will not. Even if he does catch us, and takes us back to Nevia, I won't. There's lots more time coming onto the clock. Nerado won't hurt either of us badly enough to leave scars, either physical, mental, or moral. I'd kill you in a second if it were Roger; he's dirty. He's mean—he's thoroughly bad. But Nerado's a good enough old scout, in his way. He's big and he's clean. You know, I could really like that fish if I could meet him on terms of equality sometime?"

"*I* couldn't!" she declared vigorously. "He's crawly and scaly and snaky; and he smells so . . . so . . ."

"So rank and fishy?" Costigan laughed deeply. "Details, girl; mere details. I've seen people who looked like money in the bank and who smelled like a bouquet of violets that you couldn't trust half the length of Nerado's neck."

"But look what he did to us!" she protested. "And they weren't trying to recapture us back there; they were trying to kill us."

"That was perfectly all right, what he did and what they did—what else could they have done?" he wanted to know. "And while you're looking, look at what we did to them—plenty, I'd say. But we all had it to do, and neither side will blame the other for doing it. He's a square shooter, I tell you."

"Well, maybe, but I don't like him a bit, and let's not talk about him any more. Let's talk about us. Remember what you said once, when you advised me to 'let you lay,' or whatever it was?" Woman-like, she wished to dip again lightly into the waters of pure emotion, even though she had such a short time before led the man out of their profoundest depths. But Costigan, into whose hard life love of woman had never before entered, had not yet recovered sufficiently from his soul-shaking plunge to follow her lead. Inarticulate, distrusting his newly found supreme happiness, he must needs stay out of those enchanted waters or plunge again. And he was afraid to plunge—diffident, still deeming himself unworthy of the miracle of this wonder-girl's love—even though every fiber of his being shrieked its demand to feel again that slender body in his arms. He did not consciously think those thoughts. He acted them without thinking; they were prime basics in that which made Conway Costigan what he was.

"I do remember, and I still think it's a sound idea, even though I am too far gone now to let you put it into effect," he assured her, half seriously. He kissed her, tenderly and reverently, then studied her carefully. "But you look as though you'd been on a Martian picnic. When did you eat last?"

"I don't remember, exactly. This morning, I think."

"Or maybe last night, or yesterday morning? I thought so! Bradley and I can eat anything that's chewable, and drink anything that will pour, but you can't. I'll scout around and see if I can't fix up something that you'll be able to eat."

He rummaged through the store-rooms, emerging with sundry viands from which he prepared a highly satisfactory meal.

"Think you can sleep now, sweetheart?" After supper, once more within the circle of Costigan's arms, Clio nodded her head against his shoulder.

"Of course I can, dear. Now that you are with me, out here alone,

I'm not a bit afraid any more. You will get us back to Earth some way, sometime; I just know that you will. Good-night, Conway."

"Good-night, Clio . . . little sweetheart," he whispered, and went back to Bradley's side.

In due time the captain recovered consciousness, and slept. Then for days the speedster flashed on toward our distant solar system; days during which her wide-flung detector screens remained cold.

"I don't know whether I'm afraid they'll hit something or afraid that they won't," Costigan remarked more than once, but finally those tenuous sentinels did in fact encounter an interfering vibration. Along the detector line a visibeam sped, and Costigan's face hardened as he saw the unmistakeable outline of Nerado's interstellar cruiser, far behind them.

"Well, a stern chase always was a long one," Costigan said finally. "He can't catch us for plenty of days yet . . . now what?" for the alarms of the detectors had broken out anew. There was still another point of interference to be investigated. Costigan traced it, and there, almost dead ahead of them, between them and their sun, nearing them at the incomprehensible rate of the sum of the two vessels' velocities, came another cruiser of the Nevians!

"Must be the sister-ship, coming back from our System with a load of iron," Costigan deduced. "Heavily loaded as she is, we may be able to dodge her; and she's coming so fast that if we can stay out of her range we'll be all right—she won't be able to stop for probably three or four days. But if our super-ship is anywhere in these parts, now's the time for her to rally 'round!"

He gave the speedster all the side-thrust she would take; then, putting every available communicator tube behind a tight beam, he aimed it at Sol and began sending out a long-continued call to his fellows of the Triplanetary Service.

Nearer and nearer the Nevian flashed, trying with all her power to intercept the speedster; and it soon became evident that, heavily laden though she was, she could make enough sideway to bring her within range at the time of meeting.

"Of course, they've got partial neutralization of inertia, the same as we have," Costigan cogitated, "and by the way he's coming I'd say that he had orders to blow us out of the ether—he knows as well as we do that he can't capture us alive at anything like the relative velocities we've got now. I can't give her any more side thrust without overloading the gravity controls, so overloaded they've got to be. Strap down, you two, because they may go out entirely!"

"Do you think that you can pull away from them, Conway?" Clio was staring in horrified fascination into the plate, watching the pictured vessel increase in size, moment by moment.

"I don't know whether I can or not, but I'm going to try. Just in case we don't, though, I'm going to keep on yelling for help. In solid? All right, boat, DO YOUR STUFF!"

19

GIANTS MEET

"**C**heck your blast, Fred, I think that I hear something trying to come through!" Cleveland called out, sharply. For days the *Boise* had torn through the illimitable reaches of empty space, and now the long vigil of the keen-eared listeners was to be ended. Rodebush cut off his power, and through the crackling roar of tube-noise an almost inaudible voice made itself heard.

"... all the help you can give us. Samms—Cleveland—Rodebush—anybody of Triplanetary who can hear me, listen! This is Costigan, with Miss Marsden and Captain Bradley, heading for where we think the sun is, from right ascension about six hours, declination about plus fourteen degrees. Distance unknown, but probably a good many light-years. Trace my call. One Nevian ship is overhauling us slowly, another is coming toward us from the sun. We may or may not be able to dodge it, but we need all the help you can give us. Samms—Rodebush—Cleveland—anybody of Triplanetary . . ."

Endlessly the faint, faint voice went on, but Rodebush and Cleveland were no longer listening. Sensitive ultra-loops had been swung, and along the indicated line shot Triplanetary's super-ship at a velocity which she had never before even approached; the utterly incomprehensible, almost incalculable velocity attained by inertialess matter driven through an almost perfect vacuum by the *Boise's* maximum projector blast—a blast which would lift her stupendous normal tonnage against a gravity five times that of Earth. At the full frightful measure of that velocity the super-ship literally annihilated distance, while ahead of her the furiously driven spy-ray beam fanned out in quest of the three Triplanetarians who were calling for help.

"Got any idea how fast we're going?" Rodebush demanded, glancing up for an instant from the observation plate. "We should be able to see him, since we could hear him, and our range is certainly as great as anything he can have."

"No. Can't figure velocity without any reliable data on how many atoms of matter exist per cubic meter out here." Cleveland was staring at the calculator. "It's constant, of course, at the value at which the friction of the medium is equal to our thrust. Incidentally, we can't hold it too long. We're running a temperature, which shows that we're stepping along faster than anybody ever computed before. Also, it points out the necessity for something that none of us ever anticipated needing in an open-space drive—refrigerators or radiating wall-shields or repellers or something of the sort. But to get back to our velocity—taking Throckmorton's estimates it figures somewhere near the order of magnitude of ten to the twenty-seventh. Fast enough, anyway, so that you'd better bend an eye on that plate. Even after you see them you won't know where they really are, because we don't know any of the velocities involved—our own, theirs, or that of the beam—and we may be right on top of them."

"Or, if we happen to be outrunning the beam, we won't see them at all. That makes it nice piloting."

"How are you going to handle things when we get there?"

"Lock to them and take them aboard, if we're in time. If not, if they are fighting already—*there they are!*"

The picture of the speedster's control room flashed upon the plate and Costigan's voice greeted them from the speaker.

"Hi, Fritz! Hi, Cleve! Welcome to our city! Where are you?"

"We don't know," Cleveland snapped back, "and we don't know where you are, either. Can't figure anything without data. I see you're still breathing air. Where are the Nevians? How much time have we got yet?"

"Not enough, I'm afraid. By the looks of things they will be within range of us in a couple of hours, and you haven't even touched our detector screen yet."

"A couple of *hours!*" In his relief Cleveland shouted the words. "That's time to burn—we can be just about out of the Galaxy in that . . ." He broke off at a yell from Rodebush.

"Broadcast, Spud, BROADCAST!" the physicist had cried, as Costigan's image had disappeared utterly from his plate.

He cut off the *Boise's* power, stopping her instantaneously in midspace, but the connection had been broken. Costigan could not possibly have heard the orders to change his beam signal to a broadcast, so that they could pick it up; nor would it have done any good if he had heard

and had obeyed. So immeasurably great had been their velocity that
they had flashed past the speedster and were now unknown thousands—
or millions—of miles beyond the fugitives they had come so far to help;
far beyond the range of any possible broadcast. But Cleveland understood instantly what had happened. He now had a little data upon which
to work, and his hands flew over the keys of the calculator.

"Back blast, at maximum, seventeen seconds!" he directed crisply.
"Not exact, of course, but that will put us close enough so that we can
find 'em with our detectors."

For the calculated seventeen seconds the super-ship retraced her path,
at the same awful speed with which she had come so far. The blast
expired and there, plainly limned upon the observation plates, was the
Nevian speedster.

"As a computer, you're good, Cleve," Rodebush applauded. "So
close that we can't use the neutralizers to catch him. If we use one dyne
of drive we'll overshoot a million kilometers before I could snap the
switch."

"And yet he's so far away and going so fast that if we keep our
inertia on it'll take all day at full blast to overtake—no, wait a minute—
we could *never* catch him." Cleveland was puzzled. "What to do?
Shunt in a potentiometer?"

"No, we don't need it." Rodebush turned to the transmitter. "Costigan! We are going to take hold of you with a very light tractor—a
tracer, really—and whatever you do, DON'T CUT IT, or we can't reach
you in time. It may look like a collision, but it won't be—we'll just
touch you, without even a jar."

"A tractor—inertialess?" Cleveland wondered.

"Sure. Why not?" Rodebush set up the beam at its absolute minimum
of power and threw in the switch.

While hundreds of thousands of miles separated the two vessels and
the attractor was exerting the least effort of which it was capable, yet
the super-ship leaped toward the smaller craft at a pace which covered
the intervening distance in almost no time at all. So rapidly were the
objectives enlarging upon the plates that the automatic focusing devices
could scarcely function rapidly enough to keep them in place. Cleveland
flinched involuntarily and seized his arm-rests in a spasmodic clutch as
he watched this, the first inertialess space-approach; and even Rodebush,
who knew better than anyone else what to expect, held his breath and
swallowed hard at the unbelieveable rate at which the two vessels were
rushing together.

And if these two, who had rebuilt the super-ship, could hardly control
themselves, what of the three in the speedster, who knew nothing what-

ever of the wonder-craft's potentialities? Clio, staring into the plate with Costigan, uttered one piercing shriek as she sank her fingers into his shoulders. Bradley swore a mighty deep-space oath and braced himself against certain annihilation. Costigan stared for an instant, unable to believe his eyes; then, in spite of the warning, his hand darted toward the studs which would cut the beam. Too late. Before his flying fingers could reach the buttons the *Boise* was upon them; had struck the speedster in direct central impact. Moving at the full measure of her unthinkable velocity though the super-ship was in the instant of impact, yet the most delicate recording instruments of the speedster could not detect the slightest shock as the enormous globe struck the comparatively tiny torpedo and clung to it; accommodating instantaneously and effortlessly her own terrific pace to that of the smaller and infinitely slower craft. Clio sobbed in relief and Costigan, one arm around her, sighed hugely.

"Hey, you spacelugs!" he cried. "Glad to see you, and all that, but you might as well kill a man outright as scare him to death! So *that's* the super-ship, huh? *Some* ship!"

"Hi-ya, Murf! Hi, Spud!" came from the speaker.

"Murf? Spud? How come?" Clio, practically recovered now, glanced upward questioningly. It was plain that she did not quite know whether or not to like the nicknames which the rescuers were calling her Conway.

"My middle name is Murphy, so they've called me things like that ever since I was so high." Costigan indicated a length of approximately twelve inches. "And now you'll probably live long enough—I hope—to hear me called a lot worse stuff than that."

"Don't *talk* that way—we're safe now, Con . . . Spud? It's nice that they like you so much—but they would, of course." She snuggled even closer, and both listened to what Rodebush was saying.

". . . realize myself that it would look so bad; it scared me as much as it did anybody. Yes, this is IT. She really works—thanks more than somewhat to Conway Costigan, by the way. But you had better transfer. If you'll get your things . . ."

" 'Things' is good!" Costigan laughed, and Clio giggled sunnily.

"We've made so many transfers already that what you see is all we've got," Bradley explained. "We'll bring ourselves, and we'll hurry. That Nevian is coming up fast."

"Is there anything on this ship you fellows want?" Costigan asked.

"There may be, but we haven't any locks big enough to let her inside and we haven't time to study her now. You might leave her controls in neutral, so that we can calculate her position if we should want her later on."

"All right." The three armor-clad figures stepped into the *Boise*'s open lock, the tractor beam was cut off, and the speedster flashed away from the now stationary super-ship.

"Better let formalities go for a while," Captain Bradley interrupted the general introductions taking place. "I was scared out of nine years' growth when I saw you coming at us, and maybe I've still got the humps; but that Nevian is coming up fast, and if you don't already know it I can tell you that she's *no* light cruiser."

"That's so, too," Costigan agreed. "Have you fellows got enough stuff so that you think you can take him? You've got the legs on him, anyway—you can certainly run if you want to!"

"Run?" Cleveland laughed. "We have a bone of our own to pick with that ship. We licked her to a standstill once, until we burned out a set of generators, and since we got them fixed we've been chasing her all over space. We were chasing her when we picked up your call. See there? She's doing the running."

The Nevian was running, in truth. Her commander had seen and had recognized the great vessel which had flashed out of nowhere to the rescue of the three fugitives from Nevia; and, having once been at grips with that vengeful super-dreadnaught, he had little stomach for another encounter. Therefore his side-thrust was now being exerted in the opposite direction; he was frankly trying to put as much distance as possible between himself and Triplanetary's formidable warship. In vain. A light tractor was clamped on and the *Boise* flashed up to close range before Rodebush restored her inertia and Cleveland brought the two vessels relatively to rest by increasing gradually his tractor's pull. And this time the Nevian could not cut the tractor. Again that shearing plane of force bit into it and tore at it, but it neither yielded nor broke. The rebuilt generators of Number Four were designed to carry the load, and they carried it. And again Triplanetary's every mighty weapon was brought into play.

The "cans" were thrown, ultra-and infra-beams were driven, the furious macro-beam gnawed hungrily at the Nevian's defenses; and one by one those defenses went down. In desperation the enemy commander threw his every generator behind a polycyclic screen; only to see Cleveland's even more powerful drill bore relentlessly through it. After that puncturing, the end came soon. A secondary SX7 beam was now in place on mighty Ten's inner rings, and one fierce blast blew a hole completely through the Nevian cruiser. Into that hole entered Adlington's terrific bombs and their gruesome fellows, and where they entered, life departed. All defenses vanished, and under the blasts of the *Boise*'s batteries, now unopposed, the metal of the Nevian vessel exploded into a widely spreading cloud of vapor. Sparkling vapor, with perhaps here and there a droplet or two of material which had been only liquified.

So passed the sister-ship, and Rodebush turned his plates upon the vessel of Nerado. But that highly intelligent amphibian had seen all that had occurred. He had long since given over the pursuit of the speedster, and he did not rush in to do hopeless battle beside his fellow Nevians against the Tellurians. His analytical detectors had written down each detail of every weapon and of every screen employed; and even while prodigious streamers of force were raving out from his vessel, braking her terrific progress and swinging her around in an immense circle back toward far Nevia, his scientists and mechanics were doubling and redoubling the power of his already Titanic installations, to match and if possible to overmatch those of Triplanetary's super-dreadnaught.

"Do we kill him now or do we let him suffer a while longer?" Costigan demanded.

"I don't think so, yet," Rodebush replied. "Would you, Cleve?"

"Not yet," said Cleveland, grimly, reading the other's thought and agreeing with it. "Let him pilot us to Nevia; we might not be able to find it without a guide. While we're at it we want to so pulverize that crowd that if they never come near the Solarian system again they'll think it's twenty minutes too soon."

Thus it was that the *Boise*, increasing her few dynes of driving force at a rate just sufficient to match her quarry's acceleration, pursued the Nevian ship. Apparently exerting every effort, she never came quite within range of the fleeing raider; yet never was she so far behind that the Nevian space-ship was not in clear register upon her observation plates.

Nor was Nerado alone in strengthening his vessel. Costigan knew well and respected highly the Nevian scientist-captain, and at his suggestion much time was spent in reenforcing the super-ship's armament to the iron-driven limit of theoretical and mechanical possibility.

In mid-space, however, the Nevian slowed down.

"What gives?" Rodebush demanded of the group at large. "Not turnover time already, is it?"

"No." Cleveland shook his head. "Not for at least a day yet."

"Cooking up something on Nevia, is my guess," Costigan put in. "If I know that lizard at all, he wired ahead—specifications for the welcoming committee. We're getting there too fast, so he's stalling. Check?"

"Check." Rodebush agreed. "But there's no use of us waiting, if you're sure you know which one of those stars up ahead is Nevia. Do you, Cleve?"

"Definitely."

"The only other thing is, then, shall we blow them out of the ether first?"

"You might try," Costigan remarked. "That is, if you're damned sure that you can run if you have to."

"Huh? *Run?*" demanded Rodebush.

"Just that. It's spelled R-U-N, run. I know those freaks better than you do. Believe me, Fritz, they've got what it takes."

"Could be, at that," Rodebush admitted. "We'll play it safe."

The *Boise* leaped upon the Nevian, every weapon aflame. But, as Costigan had expected, Nerado's vessel was completely ready for any emergency. And, unlike her sister-ship, she was manned by scientists well versed in the fundamental theory of the weapons with which they fought. Beams, rods, and lances of energy flamed and flared; planes and pencils cut, slashed, and stabbed; defensive screens glowed redly or flashed suddenly into intensely brilliant, coruscating incandescence. Crimson opacity struggled sullenly against violet curtain of annihilation. Material projectiles and torpedoes were launched under full beam control; only to be exploded harmlessly in mid-space, to be blasted into nothingness, or to disappear innocuously against impenetrable polycyclic screens. Even Cleveland's drill was ineffective. Both vessels were equipped completely with iron-driven mechanisms; both were manned by scientists capable of wringing the highest possible measure of power from their installations. Neither could harm the other.

The *Boise* flashed away; reached Nevia in minutes. Down into the crimson atmosphere she dropped, down toward the city which Costigan knew was Nerado's home port.

"Hold up a bit!" Costigan cautioned, sharply. "There's something down there that I don't like!"

As he spoke there shot upward from the city a multitude of flashing balls. The Nevians had mastered the secret of the explosive of the fishes of the greater deeps, and were launching it in a veritable storm against the Tellurian visitor.

"Those?" asked Rodebush, calmly. The detonating balls of destruction were literally annihilating even the atmosphere beyond the polycyclic screen, but that barrier was scarcely affected.

"No. That." Costigan pointed out a hemispherical dome which, redly translucent, surrounded a group of buildings towering high above their neighbors. "Neither those high towers nor those screens were there the last time I was in this town. Nerado *was* stalling for time, and that's what they're doing down there—that's all those fire-balls are for. Good sign, too—they aren't ready for us yet. We'd better take 'em while the taking's good. If they *were* ready for us, our play would be to get out of here while we're all in one piece.''

Nerado had been in touch with the scientists of his city; he had been instructing them in the construction of converters and generators of such weight and power that they could crush even the defenses of the super-ship. The mechanisms were not, however, ready; the entirely unsus-pected possibilities of speed inherent in absolute inertialessness had not entered into Nerado's calculations.

"Better drop a few cans down onto that dome, fellows," Rodebush suggested to his gunners.

"We can't," came Adlington's instant reply. "No use trying it—that's a polycyclic screen. Can you drill it? If you can, I've got a real bomb here—that special we built—that will do the trick if you can protect it from them until it gets down into the water."

"I'll try it," Cleveland answered, at a nod from the physicist. "I couldn't drill Nerado's polycyclics, but I couldn't use any momentum on him. Couldn't ram him—he fell back with my thrust. But that screen down there can't back away from us, so maybe I can work on it. Get your special ready. Hang on, everybody!"

The *Boise* looped upward, and from an altitude of miles dove straight down through a storm of force-balls, beams, and shells; a dive checked abruptly as the hollow tube of energy which was Cleveland's drill snarled savagely down ahead of her and struck the shielding hemisphere with a grinding, lightning-spitting shock. As it struck, backed by all the enormous momentum of the plunging space-ship and driven by the full power of her prodigious generators it bored in, clawing and gouging viciously through the tissues of that rigid and unyielding barrier of pure energy. Then, mighty drill and plunging mass against iron-driven wall, eye-tearing and furiously spectacular warfare was waged.

Well it was for Triplanetary that day that its super-ship carried ample supplies of allotropic iron; well it was that her originally Gargantuan converters and generators had been doubled and quadrupled in power on the long Nevian way! For that ocean-girdled fortress was powered to withstand any conceivable assault—but the *Boise*'s power and mo-mentum were now inconceivable; and every watt and every dyne was solidly behind that hellishly flaming, that voraciously tearing, that irre-sistibly ravening cylinder of energy incredible!

Through the Nevian shield that cylinder gnawed its frightful way, and down its protecting length there drove Adlington's "Special" bomb. "Special" it was indeed; so great of girth that it could barely pass through the central orifice of Ten's mighty projector, so heavily charged with sensitized atomic iron that its detonation upon any planet would not have been considered for an instant if that planet's integrity meant anything to its attackers. Down the shielding pipe of force the "Special" screamed under full propulsion, and beneath the surface of Nevia's ocean it plunged.

"Cut!" yelled Adlington, and as the scintillating drill expired the bomber pressed his detonating switch.

For moments the effect of the explosion seemed unimportant. A dull, low rumble was all that was to be heard of a concussion that jarred red Nevia to her very center; and all that could be seen was a slow heaving of the water. But that heaving did not cease. Slowly, *so* slowly it seemed to the observers now high in the heavens, the waters rose up and parted; revealing a vast chasm blown deep into the ocean's rocky bed. Higher and higher the lazy mountains of water reared; effortlessly to pick up, to smash, to grind into fragments, and finally to toss aside every building, every structure, every scrap of material substance pertaining to the whole Nevian city.

Flattened out, driven backward for miles, the buffeted waters were pressed, leaving exposed bare ground and broken rock where once had been the ocean's busy floor. Tremendous blasts of incandescent gas raved upward, jarring even the enormous mass of the super-ship poised so high above the site of the explosion. Then the displaced millions of tons of water rushed back into that newly rived pit, seeming to seek in that mad rush to make even more complete the already total destruction of the city. The raging torrents poured into that yawning cavern, filled it, and piled mountainously above it; receding and piling up, again and again; causing tidal waves which swept a full half of Nevia's mighty, watery globe. That city was silenced—forever.

"MY ... GOD!" Cleveland was the first to break the awed, the stunned, silence. He licked his lips. "But we had it to do ... and at that, it's not as bad as what they did to Pittsburgh—they would have evacuated all except military personnel."

"Of course ... what next?" asked Rodebush. "Look around, I suppose, to see if they have any more ..."

"Oh, no, Conway—no! Don't let them!" Clio was sobbing openly. "I'm going to my room and crawl under the bed—I'll see that sight all the rest of my life!"

"Steady, Clio." Costigan's arm tightened around her. "We'll have to look, but we won't find any more. One—if they could have finished it—would have been enough."

Again and again the *Boise* circled the world. No more super-powered installations were being built. And, surprisingly enough, the Nevians made no demonstration of hostility.

"I wonder why?" Rodebush mused. "Of course, we aren't attacking them, either, but you'd think . . . do you suppose that they are waiting for Nerado?"

"Probably." Costigan paused in thought. "We'd better wait for him, too. We can't leave things this way."

"But if we can't force engagement . . . a stalemate . . ." Cleveland's voice was troubled.

"We'll do *something!*" Costigan declared. "This thing has got to be settled, some way or other, before we leave here. First, try talking. I've got an idea that . . . anyway, it can't do any harm, and I know that he can hear and understand you."

Nerado arrived. Instead of attacking, his ship hung quietly poised, a mile or two away from the equally undemonstrative *Boise*. Rodebush directed a beam.

"Captain Nerado, I am Rodebush of Triplanetary. What do you wish to do about this situation?"

"I wish to talk to you." The Nevian's voice came clearly from the speaker. "You are, I now perceive, a much higher form of life than any of us had thought possible; a form perhaps as high in evolution as our own. It is a pity that we did not take the time for a full meeting of minds when we first neared your planet, so that much life, both Tellurian and Nevian, might have been spared. But what is past cannot be recalled. As reasoning beings, however, you will see the futility of continuing a combat in which neither is capable of winning victory over the other. You may, of course, destroy more of our Nevian cities, in which case I should be compelled to go and destroy similarly upon your Earth; but, to reasoning minds, such a course would be sheerest stupidity."

Rodebush cut the communicator beam.

"Does he mean it?" he demanded of Costigan. "It sounds perfectly reasonable, but . . ."

"But fishy!" Cleveland broke in. "Altogether too reasonable to be true!"

"He means it. He means every word of it," Costigan assured his fellows. "I had an idea that he would take it that way. That's the way they are. Reasonable; passionless. Funny—they lack a lot of things that we have; but they've got stuff that I wish more of us Tellurians had, too. Give me the plate—I'll talk for Triplanetary," and the beam was restored.

"Captain Nerado," he greeted the Nevian commander. "Having been with you and among your people, I know that you mean what you say and that you speak for your race. Similarly, I believe that I can speak for the Triplanetary Council—the governing body of three of the planets of our solar system—in saying that there is no need for any more conflict between our peoples. I also was compelled by circumstances to do certain things which I now wish could be undone; but as you have said, the past is past. Our two races have much to gain from each other by friendly exchanges of materials and of ideas, while we can expect nothing except mutual extermination if we elect to continue this warfare. I offer you the friendship of Triplanetary. Will you release your screens and come aboard to sign a treaty?''

''My screens are down. I will come.'' Rodebush likewise cut off his power, although somewhat apprehensively, and a Nevian lifeboat entered the main air-lock of the *Boise*.

Then, at a table in the control room of Triplanetary's first super-ship, there was written the first Inter-Systemic Treaty. Upon one side were the three Nevians; amphibious, cone-headed, loop-necked, scaly, four-legged things to us monstrosities: upon the other were human beings; air-breathing, round-headed, short-necked, smooth-bodied, two-legged creatures equally monstrous to the fastidious Nevians. Yet each of these representatives of two races so different felt respect for the other race increase within him minute by minute as the conversation went on.

The Nevians had destroyed Pittsburgh, but Adlington's bomb had blown an important Nevian city completely out of existence. One Nevian vessel had wiped out a Triplanetarian fleet; but Costigan had depopulated one Nevian city, had seriously damaged another, and had beamed down many Nevian ships. Therefore loss of life and material damage could be balanced off. The Solarian System was rich in iron, to which the Nevians were welcome; red Nevia possessed abundant stores of substances which upon Earth were either rare or of vital importance, or both. Therefore commerce was to be encouraged. The Nevians had knowledges and skills unknown to Earthly science, but were entirely ignorant of many things commonplace to us. Therefore interchange of students and of books was highly desirable. And so on.

Thus was signed the Triplanetario-Nevian Treaty of Eternal Peace. Nerado and his two companions were escorted ceremoniously to their vessel, and the *Boise* took off inertialess for Earth, bearing the good news that the Nevian menace was no more.

Clio, now a hardened spacehound, immune even to the horrible nausea of inertialessness, wriggled lithely in the curve of Costigan's arm and laughed up at him.

''You can talk all you want to, Conway Murphy Spud Costigan, but

I don't like them the least little bit. They give me goose-bumps all over. I suppose that they are really estimable folks; talented, cultured, and everything; but just the same I'll bet that it will be a long, long time before anybody on Earth will really, truly *like* them!' '

First
Lensman

To
E. Everett Evans

Contents

1. Arisia and Eddore 247
2. Go to Arisia! 256
3. The Lens 266
4. Bribery 280
5. Rigel Four 292
6. Operation Zwilnik—Thionite 302
7. Battle of The Hill 315
8. Examination Zwilnik, Oral 330
9. Trenco 342
10. Palainians on Pluto 356
11. Zabriskan Fontema 366
12. Thionite and Uranium 376
13. Candidate Kinnison 387
14. Mining and Disaster 402
15. Department Q 415
16. Olmstead Goes Fishing 427
17. Bennett the Arsenal 439
18. Operation Zunk 449
19. Cylinder of Battle 461
20. The Election 473
Epilogue *482*

1

ARISIA AND EDDORE

The visitor, making his way unobserved through the crowded main laboratory of *The Hill*, stepped up to within six feet of the back of a big Norwegian seated at an electrono-optical bench. Drawing an automatic pistol, he shot the apparently unsuspecting scientist seven times, as fast as he could pull the trigger; twice through the brain, five times, closely spaced, through the spine.

"Ah, Gharlane of Eddore, I have been expecting you to look me up. Sit down." Blonde, blue-eyed Dr. Nels Bergenholm, completely undisturbed by the passage of the stream of bullets through his head and body, turned and waved one huge hand at a stool beside his own.

"But those were not ordinary projectiles!" the visitor protested. Neither person—or rather, entity—was in the least surprised that no one else had paid any attention to what had happened, but it was clear that the one was taken aback by the failure of his murderous attack. "They should have volatilized that form of flesh—should at least have blown you back to Arisia, where you belong."

"Ordinary or extraordinary, what matter? As you, in the guise of Gray Roger, told Conway Costigan a short time since, 'I permitted that, as a demonstration of futility.' Know, Gharlane, once and for all, that you will no longer be allowed to act directly against any adherent of Civilization, wherever situate. We of Arisia will not interfere in person with your proposed conquest of the two galaxies as you have planned it, since the stresses and conflicts involved are necessary—and, I may add, sufficient—to produce the Civilization which must and shall come into being. Therefore, neither will you, or any other Eddorian, so interfere. You will go back to Eddore and you will stay there."

"Think you so?" Gharlane sneered. "You, who have been so afraid of us for over two thousand million Tellurian years that you dared not let us even learn of you? So afraid of us that you dared not take any action to avert the destruction of any one of your budding Civilizations upon any one of the worlds of either galaxy? So afraid that you dare not, even now, meet me mind to mind, but insist upon the use of this slow and unsatisfactory oral communication between us?''

"Either your thinking is loose, confused, and turbid, which I do not believe to be the case, or you are trying to lull me into believing that you are stupid." Bergenholm's voice was calm, unmoved. "I do not *think* that you will go back to Eddore; I know it. You, too, as soon as you have become informed upon certain matters, will know it. You protest against the use of spoken language because it is, as you know, the easiest, simplest, and surest way of preventing you from securing any iota of the knowledge for which you are so desperately searching. As to a meeting of our two minds, they met fully just before you, operating as Gray Roger, remembered that which your entire race forgot long ago. As a consequence of that meeting I so learned every line and vibration of your life pattern as to be able to greet you by your symbol, Gharlane of Eddore, whereas you know nothing of me save that I am an Arisian, a fact which has been obvious from the first."

In an attempt to create a diversion, Gharlane released the zone of compulsion which he had been holding; but the Arisian took it over so smoothly that no human being within range was conscious of any change.

"It is true that for many cycles of time we concealed our existence from you," Bergenholm went on without a break. "Since the reason for that concealment will still further confuse you, I will tell you what it was. Had you Eddorians learned of us sooner you might have been able to forge a weapon of power sufficient to prevent the accomplishment of an end which is now certain.

"It is true that your operations as Lo Sung of Uighar were not constrained. As Mithradates of Pontus—as Sulla, Marius, and Nero of Rome—as Hannibal of Carthage—as those self-effacing wights Alcixerxes of Greece and Menocoptes of Egypt—as Genghis Khan and Attila and the Kaiser and Mussolini and Hitler and the Tyrant of Asia— you were allowed to do as you pleased. Similar activities upon Rigel Four, Velantia, Palain Seven, and elsewhere were also allowed to proceed without effective opposition. With the appearance of Virgil Samms, however, the time arrived to put an end to your customary pernicious, obstructive, and destructive activities. I therefore interposed a barrier between you and those who would otherwise be completely defenseless against you."

"But why now? Why not thousands of cycles ago? And why Virgil Samms?"

"To answer those questions would be to give you valuable data. You may—too late—be able to answer them yourself. But to continue: you accuse me, and all Arisia, of cowardice; an evidently muddy and inept thought. Reflect, please, upon the completeness of your failure in the affair of Roger's planetoid; upon the fact that you have accomplished nothing whatever since that time; upon the situation in which you now find yourself.

"Even though the trend of thought of your race is basically materialistic and mechanistic, and you belittle ours as being 'philosophic' and 'impractical', you found—much to your surprise—that your most destructive physical agencies are not able to affect even this form of flesh which I am now energizing, to say nothing of affecting the reality which is I.

"If this episode is the result of the customary thinking of the second-in-command of Eddore's Innermost Circle . . . but no, my visualization cannot be that badly at fault. Overconfidence—the tyrant's innate proclivity to underestimate an opponent—these things have put you into a false position; but I greatly fear that they will not operate to do so in any really important future affair."

"Rest assured that they will not!" Gharlane snarled. "It may not be—exactly—cowardice. It is, however, something closely akin. If you could have acted effectively against us at any time in the past, you would have done so. If you could act effectively against us now, you would be acting, not talking. That is elementary—self-evidently true. So true that you have not tried to deny it—nor would you expect me to believe you if you did." Cold black eyes stared level into icy eyes of Norwegian blue.

"Deny it? No. I am glad, however, that you used the word 'effectively' instead of 'openly'; for we have been acting effectively against you ever since these newly-formed planets cooled sufficiently to permit of the development of intelligent life."

"What? You have? How?"

"That, too, you may learn—too late. I have now said all I intend to say. I will give you no more information. Since you already know that there are more adult Arisians than there are Eddorians, so that at least one of us can devote his full attention to blocking the direct effort of any one of you, it is clear to you that it makes no difference to me whether you elect to go or to stay. I can and I will remain here as long as you do; I can and I will accompany you whenever you venture out

of the volume of space protected by Eddorian screen, wherever you go.
The election is yours."

Gharlane disappeared. So did the Arisian—instantaneously. Dr. Nels
Bergenholm, however, remained. Turning, he resumed his work where
he had left off, knowing exactly what he had been doing and exactly
what he was going to do to finish it. He released the zone of compulsion,
which he had been holding upon every human being within sight or
hearing, so dextrously that no one suspected, then or ever, that anything
out of the ordinary had happened. He knew these things and did these
things in spite of the fact that the form of flesh which his fellows of the
Triplanetary Service knew as Nels Bergenholm was then being energized, not by the stupendously powerful mind of Drounli the Molder,
but by an Arisian child too young to be of any use in that which was
about to occur.

Arisia was ready. Every Arisian mind capable of adult, or of even
near-adult thinking was poised to act when the moment of action should
come. They were not, however, tense. While not in any sense routine,
that which they were about to do had been foreseen for many cycles of
time. They knew exactly what they were going to do, and exactly how
to do it. They waited.

"My visualization is not entirely clear concerning the succession of
events stemming from the fact that the fusion of which Drounli is a part
did not destroy Gharlane of Eddore while he was energizing Gray
Roger," a young Watchman, Eukonidor by symbol, thought into the
assembled mind. "May I take a moment of this idle time in which to
spread my visualization, for enlargement and instruction?"

"You may, youth." The Elders of Arisia—the mightiest intellects of
that tremendously powerful race—fused their several minds into one
mind and gave approval. "That will be time well spent. Think on."

"Separated from the other Eddorians by inter-galactic distance as he
then was, Gharlane could have been isolated and could have been destroyed," the youth pointed out, as he somewhat diffidently spread his
visualization in the public mind. "Since it is axiomatic that his destruction would have weakened Eddore somewhat and to that extent would
have helped us, it is evident that some greater advantage will accrue
from allowing him to live. Some points are clear enough: that Gharlane
and his fellows will believe that the Arisian fusion could not kill him,
since it did not; that the Eddorians, contemptuous of our powers and
thinking us vastly their inferiors, will not be driven to develop such
things as atomic-energy-powered mechanical screens against third-level
thought until such a time as it will be too late for even those devices
to save their race from extinction; that they will, in all probability, never

even suspect that the Galactic Patrol which is so soon to come into being will in fact be the prime operator in that extinction. It is not clear, however, in view of the above facts, why it has now become necessary for us to slay one Eddorian upon Eddore. Nor can I formulate or visualize with any clarity the techniques to be employed in the final wiping out of the race; I lack certain fundamental data concerning events which occurred and conditions which obtained many, many cycles before my birth. I am unable to believe that my perception and memory could have been so imperfect—can it be that none of that basic data is, or ever has been available?"

"That, youth, is the fact. While your visualization of the future is of course not as detailed nor as accurate as it will be after more cycles of labor, your background of knowledge is as complete as that of any other of our number."

"I see." Eukonidor gave the mental equivalent of a nod of complete understanding. "It is necessary, and the death of a lesser Eddorian—a Watchman—will be sufficient. Nor will it be either surprising or alarming to Eddore's Innermost Circle that the integrated total mind of Arisia should be able to kill such a relatively feeble entity. I see."

Then silence; and waiting. Minutes? Or days? Or weeks? Who can tell? What does time mean to any Arisian?

Then Drounli arrived; arrived in the instant of his leaving the Hill— what matters even intergalactic distance to the speed of thought? He fused his mind with those of the three other Molders of Civilization. The massed and united mind of Arisia, poised and ready, awaiting only his coming, launched itself through space. That tremendous, that theretofore unknown concentration of mental force arrived at Eddore's outer screen in practically the same instant as did the entity that was Gharlane. The Eddorian, however, went through without opposition; the Arisians did not.

Some two thousand million years ago, when the Coalescence occurred—the event which was to make each of the two interpassing galaxies teem with planets—the Arisians were already an ancient race; so ancient that they were even then independent of the chance formation of planets. The Eddorians, it is believed, were older still. The Arisians were native to this, our normal space-time continuum; the Eddorians were not.

Eddore was—and is—huge, dense, and hot. Its atmosphere is not air, as we of small, green Terra know air, but is a noxious mixture of gaseous substances known to mankind only in chemical laboratories. Its hydrosphere, while it does contain some water, is a poisonous, stinking, foully corrosive, slimy and sludgy liquid.

And the Eddorians were as different from any people we know as Eddore is different from the planets indigenous to our space and time. They were, to our senses, utterly monstrous; almost incomprehensible. They were amorphous, amoeboid, sexless. Not androgynous or parthenogenetic, but absolutely sexless; with a sexlessness unknown in any Earthly form of life higher than the yeasts. Thus they were, to all intents and purposes and except for death by violence, immortal; for each one, after having lived for hundreds of thousands of Tellurian years and having reached its capacity to live and to learn, simply divided into two new individuals, each of which, in addition to possessing in full its parent's mind and memories and knowledges, had also a brand-new zest and a greatly increased capacity.

And, since life was, there had been competition. Competition for power. Knowledge was worth while only insofar as it contributed to power. Warfare began, and raged, and continued; the appallingly efficient warfare possible only to such entities as those. Their minds, already immensely powerful, grew stronger and stronger under the stresses of internecine struggle.

But peace was not even thought of. Strife continued, at higher and ever higher levels of violence, until two facts became apparent. First, that every Eddorian who could be killed by physical violence had already died; that the survivors had developed such tremendous powers of mind, such complete mastery of things physical as well as mental, that they could not be slain by physical force. Second, that during the ages through which they had been devoting their every effort to mutual extermination, their sun had begun markedly to cool; that their planet would very soon become so cold that it would be impossible for them ever again to live their normal physical lives.

Thus there came about an armistice. The Eddorians worked together—not without friction—in the development of mechanisms by the use of which they moved their planet across light-years of space to a younger, hotter sun. Then, Eddore once more at its hot and reeking norm, battle was resumed. Mental battle, this time, that went on for more than a hundred thousand Eddorian years; during the last ten thousand of which not a single Eddorian died.

Realizing the futility of such unproductive endeavor, the relatively few survivors made a peace of sorts. Since each had an utterly insatiable lust for power, and since it had become clear that they could neither conquer nor kill each other, they would combine forces and conquer enough planets—enough galaxies—so that each Eddorian could have as much power and authority as he could possibly handle.

What matter that there were not that many planets in their native space? There were other spaces, an infinite number of them; some of which, it was mathematically certain, would contain millions upon millions of planets instead of only two or three. By mind and by machine they surveyed the neighboring continua; they developed the hyperspatial tube and the inertialess drive; they drove their planet, spaceshipwise, through space after space after space.

And thus, shortly after the Coalescence began, Eddore came into our space-time; and here, because of the multitudes of planets already existing and the untold millions more about to come into existence, it stayed. Here was what they had wanted since their beginnings; here were planets enough, here were fields enough for the exercise of power, to sate even the insatiable. There was no longer any need for them to fight each other; they could now cooperate whole-heartedly—as long as each was getting more—and *more*—and MORE!

Enphilistor, a young Arisian, his mind roaming eagerly abroad as was its wont, made first contact with the Eddorians in this space. Inoffensive, naive, innocent, he was surprised beyond measure at their reception of his friendly greeting; but in the instant before closing his mind to their vicious attacks, he learned the foregoing facts concerning them.

The fused mind of the Elders of Arisia, however, was not surprised. The Arisians, while not as mechanistic as their opponents, and innately peaceful as well, were far ahead of them in the pure science of the mind. The Elders had long known of the Eddorians and of their lustful wanderings through plenum after plenum. Their Visualizations of the Cosmic All had long since forecast, with dreadful certainty, the invasion which had now occurred. They had long known what they would have to do. They did it. So insidiously as to set up no opposition they entered the Eddorians' minds and sealed off all knowledge of Arisia. They withdrew, tracelessly.

They did not have much data, it is true; but no more could be obtained at that time. If any one of those touchy, suspicious minds had been given any cause for alarm, any focal point of doubt, they would have had time in which to develop mechanisms able to force the Arisians out of this space before a weapon to destroy the Eddorians—the as yet incompletely designed Galactic Patrol—could be forged. The Arisians could, even then, have slain by mental force alone all the Eddorians except the All-Highest and his Innermost Circle, safe within their then impenetrable shield; but as long as they could not make a clean sweep they could not attack—then.

Be it observed that the Arisians were not fighting for themselves. As individuals or as a race they had nothing to fear. Even less than the Eddorians could they be killed by any possible application of physical force. Past masters of mental science, they knew that no possible concentration of Eddorian mental force could kill any one of them. And if they were to be forced out of normal space, what matter? To such mentalities as theirs, any given space would serve as well as any other.

No, they were fighting for an ideal; for the peaceful, harmonious, liberty-loving Civilization which they had envisaged as developing throughout, and eventually entirely covering the myriads of planets of, two tremendous Island Universes. Also, they felt a heavy weight of responsibility. Since all these races, existing and yet to appear, had sprung from and would spring from the Arisian life-spores which permeated this particular space, they all were and would be, at bottom, Arisian. It was starkly unthinkable that Arisia would leave them to the eternal dominance of such a rapacious, such a tyrannical, such a hellishly insatiable breed of monsters.

Therefore the Arisians fought; efficiently if insidiously. They did not—they could not—interfere openly with Eddore's ruthless conquest of world after world; with Eddore's ruthless smashing of Civilization after Civilization. They did, however, see to it, by selective matings and the establishment of blood-lines upon numberless planets, that the trend of the level of intelligence was definitely and steadily upward.

Four Molders of Civilization—Drounli, Kriedigan, Nedanillor, and Brolenteen, who, in fusion, formed the "Mentor of Arisia" who was to become known to every wearer of Civilization's Lens—were individually responsible for the Arisian program of development upon the four planets of Tellus, Rigel IV, Velantia, and Palain VII. Drounli established upon Tellus two principal lines of blood. In unbroken male line of descent the Kinnisons went back to long before the dawn of even mythical Tellurian history. Kinnexa of Atlantis, daughter of one Kinnison and sister of another, is the first of the blood to be named in these annals; but the line was then already old. So was the other line; characterized throughout its tremendous length, male and female, by peculiarly spectacular red-bronze-auburn hair and equally striking gold-flecked, tawny eyes.

Nor did these strains mix. Drounli had made it psychologically impossible for them to mix until the penultimate stage of development should have been reached.

While that stage was still in the future Virgil Samms appeared, and all Arisia knew that the time had come to engage the Eddorians openly, mind to mind. Gharlane-Roger was curbed, savagely and sharply. Every

Eddorian, wherever he was working, found his every line of endeavor solidly blocked.

Gharlane, as has been intimated, constructed a supposedly irresistible weapon and attacked his Arisian blocker, with results already told. At that failure Gharlane knew that there was something terribly amiss; that it had been amiss for over two thousand million Tellurian years. Really alarmed for the first time in his long life, he flashed back to Eddore; to warn his fellows and to take counsel with them as to what should be done. And the massed and integrated force of all Arisia was only an instant behind him.

Arisia struck Eddore's outermost screen, and in the instant of impact that screen went down. And then, instantaneously and all unperceived by the planet's defenders, the Arisian forces split. The Elders, including all the Molders, seized the Eddorian who had been handling that screen—threw around him an impenetrable net of force—yanked him out into intergalactic space.

Then, driving in resistlessly, they turned the luckless wight inside out. And before the victim died under their poignant probings, the Elders of Arisia learned everything that the Eddorian and all of his ancestors had ever known. They then withdrew to Arisia, leaving their younger, weaker, partially-developed fellows to do whatever they could against mighty Eddore.

Whether the attack of these lesser forces would be stopped at the second, the third, the fourth, or the innermost screen; whether they would reach the planet itself and perhaps do some actual damage before being driven off; was immaterial. Eddore must be allowed and would be allowed to repel that invasion with ease. For cycles to come the Eddorians must and would believe that they had nothing really to fear from Arisia.

The real battle, however, had been won. The Arisian visualizations could now be extended to portray every essential element of the climactic conflict which was eventually to come. It was no cheerful conclusion at which the Arisians arrived, since their visualizations all agreed in showing that the only possible method of wiping out the Eddorians would also of necessity end their own usefulness as Guardians of Civilization.

Such an outcome having been shown necessary, however, the Arisians accepted it, and worked toward it, unhesitatingly.

2

GO TO ARISIA!

As has been said, The Hill, which had been built to be the Tellurian headquarters of the Triplanetary Service and which was now the headquarters of the half-organized Solarian Patrol, was—and is—a truncated, alloy-sheathed, honeycombed mountain. But, since human beings do not like to live eternally underground, no matter how beautifully lighted or how carefully and comfortably air-conditioned the dungeon may be, the Reservation spread far beyond the foot of that gray, forbidding, mirror-smooth cone of metal. Well outside that far-flung Reservation there was a small city; there were hundreds of highly productive farms; and, particularly upon this bright May afternoon, there was a Recreation Park, containing, among other things, dozens of tennis courts.

One of these courts was three-quarters enclosed by stands, from which a couple of hundred people were watching a match which seemed to be of some little local importance. Two men sat in a box which had seats for twenty, and watched admiringly the pair who seemed in a fair way to win in straight sets the mixed-doubles championship of the Hill.

"Fine-looking couple, Rod, if I do say so myself, as well as being smooth performers." Solarian Councillor Virgil Samms spoke to his companion as the opponents changed courts. "I still think, though, the young hussy ought to wear some clothes—those white nylon shorts make her look nakeder even than usual. I told her so, too, the jade, but she keeps on wearing less and less."

"Of course," Commissioner Roderick K. Kinnison laughed quietly. "What did you expect? She got her hair and eyes from you, why not your hard-headedness, too? One thing, though, that's all to the good—

she's got what it takes to strip ship that way, and most of 'em haven't. But what I can't understand is why they don't..." He paused.

"I don't either. Lord knows we've thrown them at each other hard enough, and Jack Kinnison and Jill Samms would certainly make a pair to draw to. But if they won't... but maybe they will yet. They're still youngsters, and they're friendly enough."

If Samms pere could have been out on the court, however, instead of in the box, he would have been surprised; for young Kinnison, although smiling enough as to face, was addressing his gorgeous partner in terms which carried little indeed of friendliness.

"Listen, you bird-brained, knot-headed, grand-standing half-wit!" he stormed, voice low but bitterly intense. "I ought to beat your alleged brains out! I've told you a thousand times to watch your own territory and *stay out of mine!* If you had been where you belonged, or even taken my signal, Frank couldn't have made that thirty-all point; and if Lois hadn't netted she'd've caught you flat-footed, a kilometer out of position, and made it deuce. What do you think you're doing, anyway— playing tennis or seeing how many innocent bystanders you can bring down out of control?"

"What do *you* think?" the girl sneered, sweetly. Her tawny eyes, only a couple of inches below his own, almost emitted sparks. "And just look at who's trying to tell who how to do what! For your infor- mation, Master Pilot John K. Kinnison, I'll tell you that just because you can't quit being 'Killer' Kinnison even long enough to let two good friends of ours get a point now and then, or maybe even a game, is no reason why I've got to turn into 'Killer' Samms. And I'll also tell you..."

"You'll tell me nothing, Jill—I'm telling *you!* Start giving away points in anything and you'll find out some day that you've given away too many. I'm not having any of that kind of game—and as long as you're playing with me you aren't either—or else. If you louse up this match just once more, the next ball I serve will hit the tightest part of those fancy white shorts of yours—right where the hip pocket would be if they had any—and it'll raise a welt that will make you eat off of the mantel for three days. So watch your step!"

"You insufferable lug! I'd like to smash this racket over your head! I'll do it, too, and walk off the court, if you don't..."

The whistle blew. Virgilia Samms, all smiles, toed the base-line and became the personification and embodiment of smoothly flowing mo- tion. The ball whizzed over the net, barely clearing it—a sizzling service ace. The game went on.

And a few minutes later, in the shower room, where Jack Kinnison was caroling lustily while plying a towel, a huge young man strode up and slapped him ringingly between the shoulder blades.

"Congratulations, Jack, and so forth. But there's a thing I want to ask you. Confidential, sort of. O.K.?"

"Shoot! Haven't we been eating out of the same dish for lo, these many moons? Why the diffidence all of a sudden, Mase? It isn't in character."

"Well . . . it's . . . I'm a lip-reader, you know."

"Sure. We all are. What of it?"

"It's only that . . . well, I saw what you and Miss Samms said to each other out there, and if that was lovers' small talk I'm a Venerian mud-puppy."

"*Lovers!* Who the hell ever said we were lovers? . . . Oh, you've been inhaling some of dad's balloon-juice. *Lovers!* Me and that red-headed skinker—that jelly-brained sapadilly? *Hardly!*"

"Hold it, Jack!" The big officer's voice was slightly edged. "You're off course—a hell of a long flit off. That girl has got everything. She's the class of the Reservation—why, she's a regular twelve-nineteen!"

"Huh?" Amazed, young Kinnison stopped drying himself and stared. "You mean to say you've been giving her a miss just because . . ." He had started to say "because you're the best friend I've got in the System," but he did not.

"Well, it would have smelled slightly cheesy, I thought." The other man did not put into words, either, what both of them so deeply knew to be the truth. "But if you haven't got . . . if it's O.K. with you, of course . . ."

"Stand by for five seconds—I'll take you around."

Jack threw on his uniform, and in a few minutes the two young officers, immaculate in the space-black-and-silver of the Patrol, made their way toward the women's dressing rooms.

". . . but she's all right, at that . . . in most ways . . . I guess." Kinnison was half-apologizing for what he had said. "Outside of being chicken-hearted and pig-headed, she's a good egg. She really qualifies . . . most of the time. But I wouldn't have her, bonus attached, any more than she would have me. It's strictly mutual. You won't fall for her, either, Mase; you'll want to pull one of her legs off and beat the rest of her to death with it inside of a week—but there's nothing like finding things out for yourself."

In a short time Miss Samms appeared; dressed somewhat less revealingly than before in the blouse and kilts which were the mode of the moment.

"Hi, Jill! This is Mase—I've told you about him. My boatmate. Master Electronicist Mason Northrop."

"Yes, I've heard about you, 'Troncist—a lot." She shook hands warmly.

"He hasn't been putting tracers on you, Jill, on accounta he figured he'd be poaching. Can you feature that? I straightened him out, though, in short order. Told him why, too, so he ought to be insulated against any voltage you can generate."

"Oh, you did? How sweet of you! But how . . . oh, those?" She gestured at the powerful prism binoculars, a part of the uniform of every officer of space.

"Uh-huh." Northrop wriggled, but held firm.

"If I'd only been as big and husky as you are," surveying admiringly some six feet two of altitude and two hundred-odd pounds of hard meat, gristle, and bone, "I'd have grabbed him by one ankle, whirled him around my head, and flung him into the fifteenth row of seats. What's the matter with him, Mase, is that he was born centuries and centuries too late. He should have been an overseer when they built the pyramids—flogging slaves because they wouldn't step just so. Or better yet, one of those people it told about in those funny old books they dug up last year—liege lords, or something like that, remember? With the power of life and death—'high, middle, and low justice', whatever that was—over their vassals and their families, serfs, and serving-wenches. *Especially* serving-wenches! He likes little, cuddly baby-talkers, who pretend to be utterly spineless and completely brainless—eh, Jack?"

"Ouch! Touché, Jill—but maybe I had it coming to me, at that. Let's call it off, shall we? I'll be seeing you two, hither or yon." Kinnison turned and hurried away.

"Want to know why he's doing such a quick flit?" Jill grinned up at her companion; a bright, quick grin. "Not that he was giving up. The blonde over there—the one in rocket red. Very few blondes can wear such a violent shade. Dimples Maynard."

"And is she . . . er . . . ?"

"Cuddly and baby-talkish? Uh-uh. She's a grand person. I was just popping off; so was he. You know that neither of us really meant half of what we said . . . or . . . at least . . ." Her voice died away.

"I don't know whether I do or not," Northrop replied, awkwardly but honestly. "That was savage stuff if there ever was any. I can't see for the life of me why you two—two of the world's finest people—should have to tear into each other that way. Do you?"

"I don't know that I ever thought of it like that." Jill caught her lower lip between her teeth. "He's splendid, really, and I like him a lot—usually. We get along perfectly most of the time. We don't fight at all except when we're too close together . . . and then we fight about anything and everything . . . say, suppose that that could be it? Like charges, repelling each other inversely as the square of the distance? That's about the way it seems to be."

"Could be, and I'm glad." The man's face cleared. "And I'm a charge of the opposite sign. Let's go!"

And in Virgil Samms' deeply-buried office, Civilization's two strongest men were deep in conversation.

". . . troubles enough to keep four men of our size awake nights." Samms' voice was light, but his eyes were moody and somber. "You can probably whip yours, though, in time. They're mostly in one solar system; a short flit covers the rest. Languages and customs are known. But how—*how*—can legal processes work efficiently—work at all, for that matter—when a man can commit a murder or a pirate can loot a space-ship and be a hundred parsecs away before the crime is even discovered? How can a Tellurian John Law find a criminal on a strange world that knows nothing whatever of our Patrol, with a completely alien language—maybe no language at all—where it takes months even to find out who and where—if any—the native police officers are? But there must be a way, Rod—there's *got* to be a way!" Samms slammed his open hand resoundingly against his desk's bare top. "And by God I'll find it—the Patrol *will* come out on top!"

" 'Crusader' Samms, now and forever!" There was no trace of mockery in Kinnison's voice or expression, but only friendship and admiration. "And I'll bet you do. Your Interstellar Patrol, or whatever . . ."

"Galactic Patrol. I know what the name of it is going to be, if nothing else."

". . . is just as good as in the bag, right now. You've done a job so far, Virge. This whole system, Nevia, the colonies on Aldebaran II and other planets, even Valeria, as tight as a drum. Funny about Valeria, isn't it . . ."

There was a moment of silence, then Kinnison went on:

"But wherever diamonds are, there go Dutchmen. And Dutch women go wherever their men do. And, in spite of medical advice, Dutch babies arrive. Although a lot of the adults died—three G's is no joke—practically all of the babies keep on living. Developing bones and muscles to fit—walking at a year and a half old—living normally—they say that the third generation will be perfectly at home there."

"Which shows that the human animal is more adaptable than some ranking medicos had believed, is all. Don't try to side-track me, Rod.

You know as well as I do what we're up against; the new headaches that interstellar commerce is bringing with it. New vices—drugs—thionite, for instance; we haven't been able to get an inkling of an idea as to where that stuff is coming from. And I don't have to tell you what piracy has done to insurance rates."

"I'll say not—look at the price of Aldebaranian cigars, the only kind fit to smoke! You've given up, then, on the idea that Arisia is the pirates' GHQ?"

"Definitely. It isn't. The pirates are even more afraid of it than tramp spacemen are. It's out of bounds—absolutely forbidden territory, apparently—to everybody, my best operatives included. All we know about it is the name—Arisia—that our planetographers gave it. It is the first completely incomprehensible thing I have ever experienced. I am going out there myself as soon as I can take the time—not that I expect to crack a thing that my best men couldn't touch, but there have been so many different and conflicting reports—no two stories agree on anything except in that no one could get anywhere near the planet—that I feel the need of some first-hand information. Want to come along?"

"Try to keep me from it!"

"But at that, we shouldn't be too surprised," Samms went on, thoughtfully. "Just beginning to scratch the surface as we are, we should expect to encounter peculiar, baffling—even completely inexplicable things. Facts, situations, events, and beings for which our one-system experience could not possibly have prepared us. In fact, we already have. If, ten years ago, anyone had told you that such a race as the Rigellians existed, what would you have thought? One ship went there, you know—once. One hour in any Rigellian city—one minute in a Rigellian automobile—drives a Tellurian insane."

"I see your point." Kinnison nodded. "Probably I would have ordered a mental examination. And the Palainians are even worse. People—if you can call them that—who live on Pluto and *like* it! Entities so alien that nobody, as far as I know, understands them. But you don't have to go even that far from home to locate a job of unscrewing the inscrutable. Who, what, and why—and for how long—was Gray Roger? And, not far behind him, is this young Bergenholm of yours. And by the way, you never did give me the low-down on how come it was the 'Bergenholm', and not the 'Rodebush-Cleveland', that made transgalactic commerce possible and caused nine-tenths of our headaches. As I get the story, Bergenholm wasn't—isn't—even an engineer."

"Didn't I? Thought I did. He wasn't, and isn't. Well, the original Rodebush-Cleveland free drive was a killer, you know . . ."

"*How* I know!" Kinnison exclaimed, feelingly.

"They beat their brains out and ate their hearts out for months, without getting it any better. Then, one day, this kid Bergenholm ambles into their shop—big, awkward, stumbling over his own feet. He gazes innocently at the thing for a couple of minutes, then says:

" 'Why don't you use uranium instead of iron and rewind it so it will put out a wave-form like this, with humps here, and here; instead of there, and there?' and he draws a couple of free-hand, but really beautiful curves.

" 'Why should we?' they squawk at him.

" 'Because it will work that way,' he says, and ambles out as unconcernedly as he came in. Can't—or won't—say another word.

"Well, in sheer desperation, they tried it—and it WORKED! And nobody has ever had a minutes' trouble with a Bergenholm since. That's why Rodebush and Cleveland both insisted on the name."

"I see; and it points up what I just said. But if he's such a mental giant, why isn't he getting results with his own problem, the meteor? Or is he?"

"No . . . or at least he wasn't as of last night. But there's a note on my pad that he wants to see me sometime today—suppose we have him come in now?"

"Fine! I'd like to talk to him, if it's O.K. with you and with him."

The young scientist was called in, and was introduced to the Commissioner.

"Go ahead, Doctor Bergenholm," Samms suggested then. "You may talk to both of us, just as freely as though you and I were alone."

"I have, as you already know, been called psychic," Bergenholm began, abruptly. "It is said that I dream dreams, see visions, hear voices, and so on. That I operate on hunches. That I am a genius. Now I very definitely am *not* a genius—unless my understanding of the meaning of that word is different from that of the rest of mankind."

Bergenholm paused. Samms and Kinnison looked at each other. The latter broke the short silence.

"The Councillor and I have just been discussing the fact that there are a great many things we do not know; that with the extension of our activities into new fields, the occurrence of the impossible has become almost a commonplace. We are able, I believe, to listen with open minds to anything you have to say."

"Very well. But first, please know that I am a scientist. As such, I am trained to observe; to think calmly, clearly, and analytically; to test every hypothesis. I do not believe at all in the so-called supernatural. This universe did not come into being, it does not continue to be, except by the operation of natural and immutable laws. And I mean *immutable*, gentlemen. Everything that has ever happened, that is happening now, or that ever is to happen, was, is, and will be statistically connected with its predecessor event and with its successor event. If I did not believe that implicitly, I would lose all faith in the scientific method. For if one single 'supernatural' event or thing had ever occurred or existed it would have constituted an entirely unpredictable event and would have initiated a series—a succession—of such events; a state of things which no scientist will or can believe possible in an orderly universe.

"At the same time, I recognize the fact that I myself have done things—caused events to occur, if you prefer—that I cannot explain to you or to any other human being in any symbology known to our science; and it is about an even more inexplicable—call it 'hunch' if you like—that I asked to have a talk with you today."

"But you are arguing in circles," Samms protested. "Or are you trying to set up a paradox?"

"Neither. I am merely clearing the way for a somewhat startling thing I am to say later on. You know, of course, that any situation with which a mind is unable to cope; a really serious dilemma which it cannot resolve; will destroy that mind—frustration, escape from reality, and so on. You also will realize that I must have become cognizant of my own peculiarities long before anyone else did or could?"

"Ah. I see. Yes, of course." Samms, intensely interested, leaned forward. "Yet your present personality is adequately, splendidly integrated. How could you possibly have overcome—reconciled—a situation so full of conflict?"

"You are, I think, familiar with my parentage?" Samms, keen as he was, did not consider it noteworthy that the big Norwegian answered his question only by asking one of his own.

"Yes . . . oh, I'm beginning to see . . . but Commissioner Kinnison has not had access to your dossier. Go ahead."

"My father is Dr. Hjalmar Bergenholm. My mother, before her marriage, was Dr. Olga Bjornson. Both were, and are, nuclear physicists—very good ones. Pioneers, they have been called. They worked, and are still working, in the newest, outermost fringes of the field."

"Oh!" Kinnison exclaimed. "A mutant? Born with second sight—or whatever it is?"

"Not second sight, as history describes the phenomenon, no. The records do not show that any such faculty was ever demonstrated to the satisfaction of any competent scientific investigator. What I have is something else. Whether or not it will breed true is an interesting topic of speculation, but one having nothing to do with the problem now in hand. To return to the subject, I resolved my dilemma long since. There is, I am absolutely certain, a science of the mind which is as definite, as positive, as immutable of law, as is the science of the physical. While I will make no attempt to prove it to you, I *know* that such a science exists, and that I was born with the ability to perceive at least some elements of it.

"Now to the matter of the meteor of the Patrol. That emblem was and is purely physical. The pirates have just as able scientists as we have. What physical science can devise and synthesize, physical science can analyze and duplicate. There is a point, however, beyond which physical science cannot go. It can neither analyze nor imitate the tangible products of that which I have so loosely called the science of the mind.

"I know, Councillor Samms, what the Triplanetary Service needs; something vastly more than its meteor. I also know that the need will become greater and greater as the sphere of action of the Patrol expands. Without a really efficient symbol, the Solarian Patrol will be hampered even more than the Triplanetary Service; and its logical extension into the Space Patrol, or whatever that larger organization may be called, will be definitely impossible. We need something which will identify any representative of Civilization, positively and unmistakably, wherever he may be. It must be impossible of duplication, or even of imitation, to which end it must kill any unauthorized entity who attempts imposture. It must operate as a telepath between its owner and any other living intelligence, of however high or low degree, so that mental communication, so much clearer and faster than physical, will be possible without the laborious learning of language; or between us and such peoples as those of Rigel Four or of Palain Seven, both of whom we know to be of high intelligence and who must already be conversant with telepathy."

"Are you or have you been, reading my mind?" Samms asked quietly.

"No," Bergenholm replied flatly. "It is not and has not been necessary. Any man who can think, who has really considered the question, and who has the good of Civilization at heart, must have come to the same conclusions."

"Probably so, at that. But no more side issues. You have a solution of some kind worked out, or you would not be here. What is it?"

"It is that you, Solarian Councillor Samms, should go to Arisia as soon as possible."

"Arisia!" Samms exclaimed, and:

"Arisia! Of all the hells in space, why Arisia?" Kinnison demanded.

"What's he supposed to do there? And how can we make the approach? Don't you know that *nobody* can get anywhere near that damn planet?"

Bergenholm shrugged his shoulders and spread both arms wide in a patomime of complete helplessness.

"How do you know—another of your hunches?" Kinnison went on. "Or did somebody tell you something? *Where* did you get it?"

"It is not a hunch," the Norwegian replied, positively. "No one told me anything. But I *know*—as definitely as I know that the combustion of hydrogen in oxygen will yield water—that the Arisians are very well versed in that which I have called the science of the mind; that if Virgil Samms goes to Arisia he will obtain the symbol he needs; that he will never obtain it otherwise. As to *how* I know these things . . . I can't . . . I just . . . I *know* it, I tell you!"

Without another word, without asking permission to leave, Bergenholm whirled around and hurried out. Samms and Kinnison stared at each other.

"Well?" Kinnison asked, quizzically.

"I'm going. Now. Whether I can be spared or not, and whether you think I'm out of control or not. I believe him, every word—and besides, there's the Bergenholm. How about you? Coming?"

"Yes. Can't say that I'm sold one hundred percent; but, as you say, the Bergenholm is a hard fact to shrug off. And at minimum rating, it's got to be tried. What are you taking? Not a fleet, probably—the *Boise?* Or the *Chicago?*" It was the Commissioner of Public Safety speaking now, the Commander-in-Chief of the Armed Forces. "The *Chicago*, I'd say—the fastest and strongest thing in space."

"Recommendation approved. Blast-off; twelve hundred hours tomorrow!"

3

THE LENS

The superdreadnought *Chicago*, as she approached the imaginary but nevertheless sharply defined boundary which no other ship had been allowed to pass, went inert and crept forward, mile by mile. Every man, from Commissioner and Councillor down, was taut and tense. So widely variant, so utterly fantastic, were the stories going around about this Arisia that no one knew what to expect. They expected the unexpected—and got it.

"Ah, Tellurians, you are precisely on time." A strong, assured, deeply resonant pseudo-voice made itself heard in the depths of each mind aboard the tremendous ship of war. "Pilots and navigating officers, you will shift course to one seventy eight dash seven twelve fifty three. Hold that course, inert, at one Tellurian gravity of acceleration. Virgil Samms will now be interviewed. He will return to the consciousnesses of the rest of you in exactly six of your hours."

Practically dazed by the shock of their first experience with telepathy, not one of the *Chicago's* crew perceived anything unusual in the phraseology of that utterly precise, diamond-clear thought. Samms and Kinnison, however, precisionists themselves, did. But, warned although they were and keyed up although they were to detect any sign of hypnotism or of mental suggestion, neither of them had the faintest suspicion, then or ever, that Virgil Samms did not as a matter of fact leave the *Chicago* at all.

Samms *knew* that he boarded a lifeboat and drove it toward the shimmering haze beyond which Arisia was. Commissioner Kinnison *knew*, as surely as did every other man aboard, that Samms did those things, because he and the other officers and most of the crew watched Samms do them. They watched the lifeboat dwindle in size with distance;

watched it disappear within the peculiarly iridescent veil of force which their most penetrant ultra-beam spy-rays could not pierce.

They waited.

And, since every man concerned *knew*, beyond any shadow of doubt and to the end of his life, that everything that seemed to happen actually did happen, it will be so described.

Virgil Samms, then, drove his small vessel through Arisia's innermost screen and saw a planet so much like Earth that it might have been her sister world. There were the white ice-caps, the immense blue oceans, the verdant continents partially obscured by fleecy banks of cloud.

Would there, or would there not, be cities? While he had not known at all exactly what to expect, he did not believe that there would be any large cities upon Arisia. To qualify for the role of *deus ex machina*, the Arisian with whom Samms was about to deal would have to be a superman indeed—a being completely beyond man's knowledge or experience in power of mind. Would such a race of beings have need of such things as cities? They would not. There would be no cities.

Nor were there. The lifeboat flashed downward—slowed—landed smoothly in a regulation dock upon the outskirts of what appeared to be a small village surrounded by farms and woods.

"This way, please." An inaudible voice directed him toward a two-wheeled vehicle which was almost, but not quite, like a Dillingham roadster.

This car, however, took off by itself as soon as Samms closed the door. It sped smoothly along a paved highway devoid of all other traffic, past farms and past cottages, to stop of itself in front of the low, massive structure which was the center of the village and, apparently, its reason for being.

"This way, please," and Samms went through an automatically-opened door; along a short, bare hall; into a fairly large central room containing a vat and one deeply-holstered chair.

"Sit down, please." Samms did so, gratefully. He did not know whether he could have stood up much longer or not.

He had expected to encounter a tremendous mentality; but this was a thing far, far beyond his wildest imaginings. This was a brain—just that—nothing else. Almost globular; at least ten feet in diameter; immersed in and in perfect equilibrium with a pleasantly aromatic liquid— a BRAIN!

"Relax," the Arisian ordered, soothingly, and Samms found that he *could* relax. "Through the one you know as Bergenholm I heard of your need and have permitted you to come here this once for instruction."

"But this . . . none of this . . . it isn't . . . it *can't* be real!" Samms blurted. "I am—I *must* be—imagining it . . . and yet I know that I *can't* be hypnotized—I've been psychoed against it!"

"What is reality?" the Arisian asked, quietly. "Your profoundest thinkers have never been able to answer that question. Nor, although I am much older and a much more capable thinker than any member of your race, would I attempt to give you its true answer. Nor, since your experience has been so limited, is it to be expected that you could believe without reservation any assurances I might give you in thoughts or in words. You must, then, convince yourself—definitely, by means of your own five senses—that I and everything about you are real, as you understand reality. You saw the village and this building; you see the flesh that houses the entity which is I. You feel your own flesh; as you tap the woodwork with your knuckles you feel the impact and hear the vibrations as sound. As you entered this room you must have perceived the odor of the nutrient solution in which and by virtue of which I live. There remains only the sense of taste. Are you by any chance either hungry or thirsty?"

"Both."

"Drink of the tankard in the niche yonder. In order to avoid any appearance of suggestion I will tell you nothing of its content except the one fact that it matches perfectly the chemistry of your tissues."

Gingerly enough, Samms brought the pitcher to his lips—then, seizing it in both hands, he gulped down a tremendous draught. It was GOOD! It smelled like all appetizing kitchen aromas blended into one; it tasted like all of the most delicious meals he had ever eaten; it quenched his thirst as no beverage had ever done. But he could not empty even that comparatively small container—whatever the stuff was, it had a satiety value immensely higher even than old, rare, roast beef! With a sigh of repletion Samms replaced the tankard and turned again to his peculiar host.

"I am convinced. That was real. No possible mental influence could so completely and unmistakably satisfy the purely physical demands of a body as hungry and as thirsty as mine was. Thanks, immensely, for allowing me to come here, Mr. . . . ?"

"You may call me Mentor. I have no name, as you understand the term. Now, then, please think fully—you need not speak—of your problems and of your difficulties; of what you have done and of what you have it in mind to do."

Samms thought, flashingly and cogently. A few minutes sufficed to cover Triplanetary's history and the beginning of the Solarian Patrol; then, for almost three hours, he went into the ramifications of the Galactic Patrol of his imaginings. Finally he wrenched himself back to reality. He jumped up, paced the floor, and spoke.

"But there's a vital flaw, one inherent and absolutely ruinous fact that makes the whole thing impossible!" he burst out, rebelliously. "No one man, or group of men, no matter who they are, can be or should be trusted with that much power. The Council and I have already been called everything imaginable; and what we have done so far is literally nothing at all in comparison with what the Galactic Patrol could and must do. Why, I myself would be the first to protest against the granting of such power to *anybody*. Every dictator in history, from Philip of Macedon to the Tyrant of Asia, claimed to be—and probably was, in his beginnings—motivated solely by benevolence. How am I to think that the proposed Galactic Council, or even I myself, will be strong enough to conquer a thing that has corrupted utterly every man who has ever won it? Who is to watch the watchmen?"

"The thought does you credit, youth," Mentor replied, unmoved. "That is one reason why you are here. You, of your own force, can not know that you are in fact incorruptible. I, however, know. Moreover, there is an agency by virtue of which that which you now believe to be impossible will become commonplace. Extend your arm."

Samms did so, and there snapped around his wrist a platinum-iridium bracelet carrying, wrist-watch-wise, a lenticular something at which the Tellurian stared in stupified amazement. It seemed to be composed of thousands—millions—of tiny gems, each of which emitted pulsatingly all the colors of the spectrum; it was throwing out—broadcasting—a turbulent flood of writhing, polychromatic light!

"The successor to the golden meteor of the Triplanetary Service," Mentor said, calmly. "The Lens of Arisia. You may take my word for it, until your own experience shall have convinced you of the fact, that no one will ever wear Arisia's Lens who is in any sense unworthy. Here also is one for your friend, Commissioner Kinnison; it is not necessary for him to come physically to Arisia. It is, you will observe, in an insulated container, and does not glow. Touch its surface, but lightly and very fleetingly, for the contact will be painful."

Samms' finger-tip barely touched one dull, gray, lifeless jewel: his whole arm jerked away uncontrollably as there swept through his whole being the intimation of an agony more poignant by far than any he had ever known.

"Why—it's *alive*!" he gasped.

"No, it is not really alive, as you understand the term . . ." Mentor paused, as though seeking a way to describe to the Tellurian a thing which was to him starkly incomprehensible. "It is, however, endowed with what you might call a sort of pseudo-life; by virtue of which it gives off its characteristic radiation while, and only while, it is in physical circuit with the living entity—the ego, let us say—with whom it is in exact resonance. Glowing, the Lens is perfectly harmless; it is complete—saturated—satiated—fulfilled. In the dark condition it is, as you have learned, dangerous in the extreme. It is then incomplete—unfulfilled—frustrated—you might say seeking or yearning or demanding. In that condition its pseudo-life interferes so strongly with any life to which it is not attuned that that life, in a space of seconds, is forced out of this plane or cycle of existence."

"Then I—I alone—of all the entities in existence, can wear this particular Lens?" Samms licked his lips and stared at it, glowing so satisfyingly and contentedly upon his wrist. "But when I die, will it be a perpetual menace?"

"By no means. A Lens cannot be brought into being except to match some one living personality; a short time after you pass into the next cycle your Lens will disintegrate."

"Wonderful!" Samms breathed, in awe. "But there's one thing . . . these things are . . . priceless, and there will be millions of them to make . . . and you don't . . ."

"What will we get out of it, you mean?" The Arisian seemed to smile.

"Exactly." Samms blushed, but held his ground. "Nobody does anything for nothing. Altruism is beautiful in theory, but it has never been known to work in practice. I will pay a tremendous price—any price within reason or possibility—for the Lens; but I will have to know what that price is to be."

"It will be heavier than you think, or can at present realize; although not in the sense you fear." Mentor's thought was solemnity itself. "Whoever wears the Lens of Arisia will carry a load that no weaker mind could bear. The load of authority; of responsibility; of knowledge that would wreck completely any mind of lesser strength. Altruism? No. Nor is it a case of good against evil, as you so firmly believe. Your mental picture of glaring white and of unrelieved black is not a true picture. Neither absolute evil nor absolute good do or can exist."

"But that would make it still worse!" Samms protested. "In that case, I can't see any reason at all for your exerting yourselves—putting yourselves out—for us."

"There is, however, reason enough; although I am not sure that I can make it as clear to you as I would wish. There are in fact three reasons; any one of which would justify us in exerting—would compel us to exert—the trivial effort involved in the furnishing of Lenses to your

Galactic Patrol. First, there is nothing either intrinsically right or intrinsically wrong about liberty or slavery, democracy or autocracy, freedom of action or complete regimentation. It seems to us, however, that the greatest measure of happiness and of well-being for the greatest number of entities, and therefore the optimum advancement toward whatever sublime Goal it is toward which this cycle of existence is trending in the vast and unknowable Scheme of Things, is to be obtained by securing for each and every individual the greatest amount of mental and physical freedom compatible with the public welfare. We of Arisia are only a small part of this cycle; and, as goes the whole, so goes in greater or lesser degree each of the parts. Is it impossible for you, a fellow citizen of this cycle-universe, to believe that such fulfillment alone would be ample compensation for a much greater effort?''

"I never thought of it in that light . . ." It was hard for Samms to grasp the concept; he never did understand it thoroughly. "I begin to see, I think . . . at least, I believe you."

"Second, we have a more specific obligation in that the life of many, many worlds has sprung from Arisian seed. Thus, *in loco parentis*, we would be derelict indeed if we refused to act. And third, you yourself spend highly valuable time and much effort in playing chess. Why do you do it? What do you get out of it?"

"Why, I . . . uh . . . mental exercise, I suppose . . . I *like* it!''

"Just so. And I am sure that one of your very early philosophers came to the conclusion that a fully competent mind, from a study of one fact or artifact belonging to any given universe, could construct or visualize that universe, from the instant of its creation to its ultimate end?''

"Yes. At least, I have heard the proposition stated, but I have never believed it possible."

"It is not possible simply because no fully competent mind ever has existed or ever will exist. A mind can become fully competent only by the acquisition of infinite knowledge, which would require infinite time as well as infinite capacity. Our equivalent of your chess, however, is what we call the 'Visualization of the Cosmic All.' In my visualization a descendant of yours named Clarrissa MacDougall will, in a store called Brenleer's upon the planet . . . but no, let us consider a thing nearer at hand and concerning you personally, so that its accuracy will be subject to check. Where you will be and exactly what you will be doing, at some definite time in the future. Five years, let us say?''

"Go ahead. If you can do that you're *good*."

"Five Tellurian calendar years then, from the instant of your passing through the screen of 'The Hill' on this present journey, you will be . . .

allow me, please, a moment of thought . . . you will be in a barber shop
not yet built; the address of which is to be fifteen hundred fifteen
Twelfth Avenue, Spokane, Washington, North America, Tellus. The
barber's name will be Antonio Carbonero and he will be lefthanded. He
will be engaged in cutting your hair. Or rather, the actual cutting will
have been done and he will be shaving, with a razor trade-marked
'Jensen-King-Byrd,' the short hairs in front of your left ear. A comparatively small, quadrupedal, grayish-striped entity, of the race called
'cat'—a young cat, this one will be, and called Thomas, although
actually of the female sex—will jump into your lap, addressing you
pleasantly in a language with which you yourself are only partially
familiar. You call it mewing and purring, I believe?"

"Yes," the flabbergasted Samms managed to say. "Cats do purr—
especially kittens."

"Ah—very good. Never having met a cat personally, I am gratified
at your corroboration of my visualization. This female youth erroneously
called Thomas, somewhat careless in computing the elements of her
trajectory, will jostle slightly the barber's elbow with her tail; thus causing him to make a slight incision, approximately three millimeters long,
parallel to and just above your left cheekbone. At the precise moment
in question, the barber will be applying a styptic pencil to this insignificant wound. This forecast is, I trust, sufficiently detailed so that you
will have no difficulty in checking its accuracy or its lack thereof?"

"Detailed! *Accuracy!*" Samms could scarcely think. "But listen—
not that I want to cross you up deliberately, but I'll tell you now that a
man doesn't like to get sliced by a barber, even such a little nick as
that. I'll remember that address—and the cat—and I'll never go into
the place!"

"Every event does affect the succession of events," Mentor acknowledged, equably enough. "Except for this interview, you would have
been in New Orleans at that time, instead of in Spokane. I have considered every pertinent factor. You will be a busy man. Hence, while
you will think of this matter frequently and seriously during the near
future, you will have forgotten it in less than five years. You will remember it only at the touch of the astringent, whereupon you will give
voice to certain self-derogatory and profane remarks."

"I ought to." Samms grinned; a not-too-pleasant grin. He had been
appalled by the quality of mind able to do what Mentor had just done;
he was now more than appalled by the Arisian's calm certainty that
what he had foretold in such detail would in every detail come to pass.
"If, after all this warning, I go into a barber shop at fifteen fifteen
Twelfth, Spokane—let a tiger-striped kitten jump into my lap—let a

left-handed Tony Carbonero nick me—uh-uh, Mentor, UH-UH! *If* I do, I'll deserve to be called everything I can think of!''

"These that I have mentioned, the gross occurrences, are problems only for inexperienced thinkers.'' Mentor paid no attention to Samms' determination never to enter that shop. "The real difficulties lie in the fine detail, such as the length, mass, and exact place and position of landing, upon apron or floor, of each of your hairs as it is severed. Many factors are involved. Other clients passing by—opening and shutting doors—air currents—sunshine—wind—pressure, temperature, humidity. The exact fashion in which the barber will flick his shears, which in turn depends upon many other factors—what he will have been doing previously, what he will have eaten and drunk, whether or not his home life will have been happy . . . you little realize, youth, what a priceless opportunity this will be for me to check the accuracy of my visualization. I shall spend many periods upon the problem. I cannot attain perfect accuracy, of course. Ninety nine point nine nines percent, let us say . . . or perhaps ten nines . . . is all that I can reasonably expect . . .''

"But, Mentor!'' Samms protested. "I can't help you on a thing like that! How can I know or report the exact mass, length, and orientation of single hairs?''

"You cannot; but, since you will be wearing your Lens, I myself can and will compare minutely my visualization with the actuality. For know, youth, that wherever any Lens is, there can any Arisian be if he so desires. And now, knowing that fact, and from your own knowledge of the satisfactions to be obtained from chess and other such mental activities, and from the glimpses you have had into my own mind, do you retain any doubts that we Arisians will be fully compensated for the trifling effort involved in furnishing whatever number of Lenses may be required?''

"I have no more doubts. But this Lens . . . I'm getting more afraid of it every minute. I see that it is a perfect identification; I can understand that it can be a perfect telepath. But is it something else, as well? If it has other powers . . . what are they?''

"I cannot tell you; or, rather, I will not. It is best for your own development that I do not, except in the most general terms. It has additional qualities, it is true; but, since no two entities ever have the same abilities, no two Lenses will ever be of identical qualities. Strictly speaking, a Lens has no real power of its own; it merely concentrates, intensifies, and renders available whatever powers are already possessed by its wearer. You must develop your own powers and your own abilities; we of Arisia, in furnishing the Lens, will have done everything that we should do.''

"Of course, sir; and much more than we have any right to expect. You have given me a Lens for Roderick Kinnison; how about the others? Who is to select them?"

"You are, for a time." Silencing the man's protests, Mentor went on: "You will find that your judgment will be good. You will send to us only one entity who will not be given a Lens, and it is necessary that that one entity should be sent here. You will begin a system of selection and training which will become more and more rigorous as time goes on. This will be necessary; not for the selection itself, which the Lensmen themselves could do among babies in their cradles, but because of the benefits thus conferred upon the many who will not graduate, as well as upon the few who will. In the meantime you will select the candidates; and you will be shocked and dismayed when you discover how few you will be able to send.

"You will go down in history as First Lensman Samms; the Crusader, the man whose wide vision and tremendous grasp made it possible for the Galactic Patrol to become what it is to be. You will have highly capable help, of course. The Kinnisons, with their irresistible driving force, their indomitable will to do, their transcendent urge; Costigan, back of whose stout Irish heart lie Erin's best of brains and brawn; your cousins George and Ray Olmstead; your daughter Virgilia . . ."

"Virgilia! Where does *she* fit into this picture? What do you know about her—and how?"

"A mind would be incompetent indeed who could not visualize, from even the most fleeting contact with you, a fact which has been in existence for some twenty three of your years. Her doctorate in psychology; her intensive studies under Martian and Venerian masters—even under one reformed Adept of North Polar Jupiter—of the involuntary, uncontrollable, almost unknown and hence highly revealing muscles of the face, the hands, and other parts of the human body. You will remember that poker game for a long time."

"I certainly will." Samms grinned, a bit shamefacedly. "She gave us clear warning of what she was going to do, and then cleaned us out to the last millo."

"Naturally. She has, all unconsciously, been training herself for the work she is destined to do. But to resume; you will feel yourself incompetent, unworthy—that, too, is a part of Lensman's Load. When you first scan the mind of Roderick Kinnison you will feel that he, not you, should be the prime mover in the Galactic Patrol. But know now that no mind, not even the most capable in the universe, can either visualize truly or truly evaluate itself. Commissioner Kinnison, upon scanning your mind as he will scan it, will know the truth and will be well content. But time presses; in one minute you leave."

"Thanks a lot . . . thanks." Samms got to his feet and paused, hesitantly. "I suppose that it will be all right . . . that is, I can call on you again, if . . . ?"

"No," the Arisian declared, coldly. "My visualization does not indicate that it will ever again be either necessary or desirable for you to visit or to communicate with me or with any other Arisian."

Communication ceased as though a solid curtain had been drawn between the two. Samms strode out and stepped into the waiting vehicle, which whisked him back to his lifeboat. He blasted off; arriving in the control room of the *Chicago* precisely at the end of the sixth hour after leaving it.

"Well, Rod, I'm back . . ." he began, and stopped; utterly unable to speak. For at the mention of the name Samms' Lens had put him fully en rapport with his friend's whole mind; and what he perceived struck him—literally and precisely—dumb.

He had always liked and admired Rod Kinnison. He had always known that he was tremendously able and capable. He had known that he was big; clean; a square shooter; the world's best. Hard; a driver who had little more mercy on his underlings in selected undertakings than he had on himself. But now, as he saw spread out for his inspection Kinnison's ego in its entirety; as he compared in fleeting glances that terrific mind with those of the other officers—good men, too, all of them—assembled in the room; he knew that he had never even begun to realize what a giant Roderick Kinnison really was.

"What's the matter, Virge?" Kinnison exclaimed, and hurried up, both hands outstretched. "You look like you're seeing ghosts! What did they do to you?"

"Nothing—much. But 'ghosts' doesn't half describe what I'm seeing right now. Come into my office, will you, Rod?"

Ignoring the curious stares of the junior officers, the Commissioner and the Councillor went into the latter's quarters, and in those quarters the two Lensmen remained in close consultation during practically all of the return trip to Earth. In fact, they were still conferring deeply, via Lens, when the *Chicago* landed and they took a ground-car into the Hill.

"But who are you going to send first, Virge?" Kinnison demanded. "You must have decided on at least some of them, by this time."

"I know of only five, or possibly six, who are ready," Samms replied, glumly. "I would have sworn that I knew of a hundred, but they don't measure up. Jack, Mason Northrop, and Conway Costigan, for the first load. Lyman Cleveland, Fred Rodebush, and perhaps Bergenholm—I haven't been able to figure him out, but I'll know when I get him under my Lens—next. That's all.''

''Not quite. How about your identical-twin cousins, Ray and George Olmstead, who have been doing such a terrific job of counter-spying?''

''Perhaps . . . Quite possibly.''

''And if I'm good enough, Clayton and Schweikert certainly are, to name only two of the commodores. And Knobos and DalNalten. And above all, how about Jill?''

''Jill Why, I don't . . . she measures up, of course, but . . . but at that, there was nothing said against it, either . . . I wonder . . .''

''Why not have the boys in—Jill, too—and thrash it out?''

The young people were called in; the story was told; the problem stated. The boys' reaction was instantaneous and unanimous. Jack Kinnison took the lead.

''Of course Jill's going, if anybody does!'' he burst out, vehemently. ''Count *her* out, with all the stuff she's got? *Hardly!*''

''Why, Jack! This, from *you?*'' Jill seemed highly surprised. ''I have it on excellent authority that I'm a skinker; a half-witted one, at that. A jelly-brain, with come-hither eyes.''

''You are, and a lot of other things besides.'' Jack Kinnison did not back up a millimeter, even before their fathers. ''But even at your sapadilliest your half wits are better than most other people's whole ones; and I never said or thought that your brain couldn't function, whenever it wanted to, back of those sad eyes. Whatever it takes to be a Lensman, sir,'' he turned to Samms, ''she's got just as much of as the rest of us. Maybe more.''

''I take it, then, that there is no objection to her going?'' Samms asked.

There was no objection.

''What ship shall we take, and when?''

''The *Chicago*. Now.'' Kinnison directed. ''She's hot and ready. We didn't strike any trouble going or coming, so she didn't need much servicing. Flit!''

They flitted, and the great battleship made the second cruise as uneventfully as she had made the first. The *Chicago's* officers and crew knew that the young people left the vessel separately; that they returned separately, each in his or her lifeboat. They met, however, not in the control room, but in Jack Kinnison's private quarters; the three young Lensmen and the girl. The three were embarrassed; ill at ease. The Lenses were—definitely—not working. No one of them would put his Lens on Jill, since she did not have one . . . The girl broke the short silence.

"Wasn't she the most perfectly *beautiful* thing you ever saw?" she breathed. "In spite of being over seven feet tall? She looked to be about twenty—except her eyes—but she must have been a hundred, to know so much—but what are you boys staring so about?"

"*She!*" Three voices blurted as one.

"Yes. She. Why? I know we weren't together, but I got the impression, some way or other, that there was only the one. What did *you* see?"

All three men started to talk at once, a clamor of noise; then all stopped at once.

"You first, Spud. Whom did you talk to, and what did he, she, or it say?" Although Conway Costigan was a few years older than the other three, they all called him by nickname as a matter of course.

"National Police Headquarters—Chief of the Detective Bureau," Costigan reported, crisply. "Between forty three and forty five; six feet and half an inch; one seventy five. Hard, fine, keen, a Big Time Operator if there ever was one. Looked a lot like your father, Jill; the same dark auburn hair, just beginning to gray, and the same deep orange-yellow markings in his eyes. He gave me the works; then took this Lens out of his safe, snapped it onto my wrist, and gave me two orders—get out and stay out."

Jack and Mase stared at Costigan, at Jill, and at each other. Then they whistled in unison.

"I see this is not going to be a unanimous report, except possibly in one minor detail," Jill remarked. "Mase, you're next."

"I landed on the campus of the University of Arisia," Northrop stated, flatly. "Immense place—hundreds of thousands of students. They took me to the Physics Department—to the private laboratory of the Department Head himself. He had a panel with about a million meters and gauges on it; he scanned and measured every individual component element of my brain. Then he made a pattern, on a milling router just about as complicated as his panel. From there on, of course, it was simple—just like a dentist making a set of china choppers or a metallurgist embedding a test-section. He snapped a couple of sentences of directions at me, and then said 'Scram!' That's all."

"Sure that was all?" Costigan asked. "Didn't he add 'and *stay* scrammed'?"

"He didn't *say* it, exactly, but the implication was clear enough."

"The one point of similarity," Jill commented. "Now you, Jack. You have been looking as though we were all candidates for canvas jackets that lace tightly up the back."

"Uh-uh. As though maybe *I* am. I didn't see anything at all. Didn't even land on the planet. Just floated around in an orbit inside that screen. The thing I talked with was a pattern of pure force. This Lens simply appeared on my wrist, bracelet and all, out of thin air. He told me plenty, though, in a very short time—his last word being for me not to come back or call back.''

"Hm . . . m . . . m.'' This of Jack's was a particularly indigestible bit, even for Jill Samms.

"In plain words,'' Costigan volunteered, "we all saw exactly what we expected to see.''

"Uh-uh,'' Jill denied. "I certainly did not expect to see a woman . . . no; what each of us saw, I think, was what would do us the most good— give each of us the highest possible lift. I am wondering whether or not there was anything at all really there.''

"That might be it, at that.'' Jack scowled in concentration. "But there must have been *something* there—these Lenses are real. But what makes me mad is that they wouldn't give you a Lens. You're just as good a man as any one of us—if I didn't know it wouldn't do a damn bit of good I'd go back there right now and . . .''

"Don't pop off so, Jack!'' Jill's eyes, however, were starry. "I know you mean it, and I could almost love you, at times—but I don't need a Lens. As a matter of fact, I'll be much better off without one.''

"Jet back, Jill!'' Jack Kinnison stared deeply into the girl's eyes— but still did not use his Lens. "Somebody must have done a terrific job of selling, to make you believe that . . . or *are* you sold, actually?''

"Actually. Honestly. That Arisian was a thousand times more of a woman than I ever will be, and she didn't wear a Lens—never had worn one. Women's minds and Lenses don't fit. There's a sex-based incompatibility. Lenses are as masculine as whiskers—and at that, only a very few men can ever wear them, either. Very special men, like you three and Dad and Pops Kinnison. Men with tremendous force, drive, and scope. Pure killers, all of you; each in his own way, of course. No more to be stopped than a glacier, and twice as hard and ten times as cold. A woman simply *can't* have that kind of a mind! There is going to be a woman Lensman some day—just one—but not for years and years; and I wouldn't be in her shoes for anything. In this job of mine, of . . .''

"Well, go on. What is this job you're so sure you are going to do?''

"Why, I don't know!'' Jill exclaimed, startled eyes wide. "I thought I knew all about it, but I don't! Do you, about yours?''

They did not, not one of them; and they were all as surprised at that fact as the girl had been.

"Well, to get back to this Lady Lensman who is going to appear some day, I gather that she is going to be some kind of a freak. She'll have to be, practically, because of the sex-based fundamental nature of the Lens. Mentor didn't say so, in so many words, but she made it perfectly clear that . . ."

"Mentor!" the three men exclaimed.

Each of them had dealt with Mentor!

"I am beginning to see," Jill said, thoughtfully. "Mentor. Not a real name at all. To quote the Unabridged verbatim—I had occasion to look the word up the other day and I am appalled now at the certainty that there was a connection—quote; Mentor, a wise and faithful counselor; unquote. Have any of you boys anything to say? I haven't; and I am beginning to be scared blue."

Silence fell; and the more they thought, those three young Lensmen and the girl who was one of the two human women ever to encounter knowingly an Arisian mind, the deeper that silence became.

4

BRIBERY

"**S**o you didn't find anything on Nevia." Roderick Kinnison got up, deposited the inchlong butt of his cigar in an ashtray, lit another, and prowled about the room; hands jammed deep into breeches pockets. "I'm surprised. Nerado struck me as being a B.T.O. . . . I thought sure he'd qualify."

"So did I." Samms' tone was glum. "He's Big Time, and an Operator; but not big enough, by far. I'm—we're both—finding out that Lensman material is *damned* scarce stuff. There's none on Nevia, and no indication whatever that there ever will be any."

"Tough . . . and you're right, of course, in your stand that we'll have to have Lensmen from as many different solar systems as possible on the Galactic Council or the thing won't work at all. So damned much jealousy—which is one reason why we're here in New York instead of out at the Hill, where we belong—we've found that out already, even in such a small and comparatively homogeneous group as our own system—the Solarian Council will not only have to be made up mostly of Lensmen, but each and every inhabited planet of Sol will have to be represented—even Pluto, I suppose, in time. And by the way, your Mr. Saunders wasn't any too pleased when you took Knobos of Mars and DalNalten of Venus away from him and made Lensmen out of them—and put them miles over his head."

"Oh, I wouldn't say that . . . exactly. I convinced him . . . but at that, since Saunders is not Lensman grade himself, it was a trifle difficult for him to understand the situation completely."

"You say it easy—'difficult' is not the word I would use. But back to the Lensman hunt." Kinnison scowled blackly. "I agree, as I said before, that we need non-human Lensmen, the more the better, but I don't think much of your chance of finding any. What makes you think ... Oh, I see ... but I don't know whether you're justified or not in assuming a high positive correlation between a certain kind of mental ability and technological advancement.''

"No such assumption is necessary. Start anywhere you please, Rod, and take it from there; including Nevia.''

"I'll start with known facts, then. Interstellar flight is new to us. We haven't spread far, or surveyed much territory. But in the eight solar systems with which we are most familiar there are seven planets—I'm not counting Valeria—which are very much like Earth in point of mass, size, climate, atmosphere, and gravity. Five of the seven did not have any intelligent life and were colonized easily and quickly. The Tellurian worlds of Procyon and Vega became friendly neighbors—thank God we learned something on Nevia—because they were already inhabited by highly advanced races: Procia by people as human as we are, Vegia by people who would be so if it weren't for their tails. Many other worlds of these systems are inhabited by more or less intelligent non-human races. Just how intelligent they are we don't know, but the Lens-men will soon find out.

"My point is that no race we have found so far has had either atomic energy or any form of space-drive. In any contact with races having space-drives we have not been the discoverers, but the discovered. *Our* colonies are all within twenty six light-years of Earth except Aldebaran II, which is fifty seven, but which drew a lot of people, in spite of the distance, because it was so nearly identical with Earth. On the other hand, the Nevians, from a distance of over a hundred light-years, found *us* ... implying an older race and a higher development ... but you just told me that they would *never* produce a Lensman!''

"That point stopped me, too, at first. Follow through; I want to see if you arrive at the same conclusion I did.''

"Well ... 1 ... 1 ...'' Kinnison thought intensely, then went on: "Of course, the Nevians were not colonizing; nor, strictly speaking, exploring. They were merely hunting for iron—a highly organized, intensively specialized operation to find a raw material they needed desperately.''

"Precisely,'' Samms agreed.

"The Rigellians, however, were *surveying*, and Rigel is about four hundred and forty light-years from here. We didn't have a thing they needed or wanted. They nodded at us in passing and kept on going. I'm still on your track?''

"Dead center. And just where does that put the Palainians?''

"I see ... you may have something there, at that. Palain is so far away that nobody knows even where it is—probably thousands of light-years. Yet they have not only explored this system; they colonized Pluto long before our white race colonized America. But damn it, Virge, I don't like it—any part of it. Rigel Four you may be able to take, with your Lens . . . even one of their damned automobiles, if you stay solidly en rapport with the driver. But *Palain*, Virge! Pluto is bad enough, but the home planet! You can't. Nobody can. It simply can't be done!''

"I know it won't be easy," Samms admitted, bleakly, "but if it's got to be done, I'll do it. And I have a little information that I haven't had time to tell you yet. We discussed once before, you remember, what a job it was to get into any kind of communication with the Palainians on Pluto. You said then that nobody could understand them, and you were right—then. However, I re-ran those brain-wave tapes, wearing my Lens, and could understand them—the thoughts, that is—as well as though they had been recorded in precisionist-grade English.''

"*What?*" Kinnison exclaimed, then fell silent. Samms remained silent. What they were thinking of Arisia's Lens cannot be expressed in words.

"Well, go on," Kinnison finally said. "Give me the rest of it—the stinger that you've been holding back.''

"The messages—*as messages*—were clear and plain. The backgrounds, however, the connotations and implications, were not. Some of their codes and standards seem to be radically different from ours—so utterly and fantastically different that I simply cannot reconcile either their conduct or their ethics with their obviously high intelligence and their advanced state of development. However, they have at least some minds of tremendous power, and none of the peculiarities I deduced were of such a nature as to preclude Lensmanship. Therefore I am going to Pluto; and from there—I hope—to Palain Seven. If there's a Lensman there, I'll get him.''

"You will, at that," Kinnison paid quiet tribute to what he, better than anyone else, knew that his friend had.

"But enough of me—how are you doing?''

"As well as can be expected at this stage of the game. The thing is developing along three main lines. First, the pirates. Since that kind of thing is more or less my own line I'm handling it myself, unless and until you find someone better qualified. I've got Jack and Costigan working on it now.

"Second; drugs, vice, and so on. I hope you find somebody to take this line over, because, frankly, I'm in over my depth and want to get out. Knobos and DalNalten are trying to find out if there's anything to the idea that there may be a planetary, or even inter-planetary, ring involved. Since Sid Fletcher isn't a Lensman I couldn't disconnect him openly from his job, but he knows a lot about the dope-vice situation and is working practically full time with the other two.

"Third; pure—or rather, decidedly impure—politics. The more I studied *that* subject, the clearer it became that politics would be the worst and biggest battle of the three. There are too many angles I don't know a damned thing about, such as what to do about the succession of foaming, screaming fits your friend Senator Morgan will be throwing the minute he finds out what our Galactic Patrol is going to do. So I ducked the whole political line.

"Now you know as well as I do—better, probably—that Morgan is only the Pernicious Activities Committee of the North American Senate. Multiply him by the thousands of others, all over space, who will be on our necks before the Patrol can get its space-legs, and you will see that all that stuff will have to be handled by a Lensman who, as well as being a mighty smooth operator, will have to know *all* the answers and will have to have plenty of guts. I've got the guts, but none of the other prime requisites. Jill hasn't, although she's got everything else. Fairchild, your Relations ace, isn't a Lensman and can never become one. So you can see quite plainly who has got to handle politics himself."

"You may be right . . . but this Lensman business comes first . . ." Samms pondered, then brightened. "Perhaps—probably—I can find somebody on this trip—a Palainian, say—who is better qualified than any of us."

Kinnison snorted. "If you can, I'll buy you a week in any Venerian relaxerie you want to name."

"Better start saving up your credits, then, because from what I already know of the Palainian mentality such a development is distinctly more than a possibility." Samms paused, his eyes narrowing. "I don't know whether it would make Morgan and his kind more rabid or less so to have a non-Solarian entity possess authority in our affairs political—but at least it would be something new and different. But in spite of what you said about 'ducking' politics, what have you got Northrop, Jill and Fairchild doing?"

"Well, we had a couple of discussions. I couldn't give either Jill or Dick orders, of course . . ."

"Wouldn't, you mean," Samms corrected.

"Couldn't," Kinnison insisted. "Jill, besides being your daughter and Lensman grade, has no official connection with either the Triplanetary Service or the Solarian Patrol. And the Service, including Fairchild, is still Triplanetary; and it will have to stay Triplanetary until you have found enough Lensmen so that you can spring your twin surprises—

Galactic Council and Galactic Patrol. However, Northrop and Fairchild are keeping their eyes and ears open and their mouths shut, and Jill is finding out whatever she can about drugs and so on, as well as the various political angles. They'll report to you—facts, deductions, guesses, and recommendations—whenever you say the word."

"Nice work, Rod. Thanks. I think I'll call Jill now, before I go—wonder where she is? . . . but I wonder . . . with the Lens perhaps telephones are superflous? I'll try it."

"JILL!" he thought intensely into his Lens, forming as he did so a mental image of his gorgeous daughter as he knew her. But he found, greatly to his surprise, that neither elaboration nor emphasis was necessary.

"Ouch!" came almost instantaneous answer, long before his thought was complete. "Don't think so hard, Dad, it hurts—I almost missed a step." Virgilia was actually there with him; inside his own mind; in closer touch with him than she had ever before been. "Back so soon? Shall we report now, or aren't you ready to go to work yet?"

"Skipping for the moment your aspersions on my present activities—not quite." Samms moderated the intensity of his thought to a conversational level. "Just wanted to check with you. Come in, Rod." In flashing thoughts he brought her up to date. "Jill, do you agree with what Rod here has just told me?"

"Yes. Fully. So do the boys."

"That settles it, then—unless, of course, I can find a more capable substitute."

"Of course—but we will believe that when we see it."

"Where are you and what are you doing?"

"Washington, D.C. European Embassy. Dancing with Herkimer Herkimer Third, Senator Morgan's Number One secretary. I was going to make passes at him—in a perfectly lady-like way, of course—but it wasn't necessary. He thinks he can break down my resistance."

"Careful, Jill! That kind of stuff . . ."

"Is very old stuff indeed, Daddy dear. Simple. And Herkimer Herkimer Third isn't really a menace; he just thinks he is. Take a look—you can, can't you, with your Lens?"

"Perhaps . . . Oh, yes. I see him as well as you do." Fully en rapport with the girl as he was, so that his mind received simultaneously with hers any stimulus which she was willing to share, it seemed as though a keen, handsome, deeply tanned face bent down from a distance of inches toward his own. "But I don't like it a bit—and him even less."

"That's because you aren't a girl." Jill giggled mentally. "This is fun; and it won't hurt him a bit, except maybe for a slightly bruised vanity, when I don't fall down flat at his feet. And I'm learning a lot that he hasn't any suspicion he's giving away.''

''Knowing you, I believe that. But don't . . . that is . . . well, be *very* careful not to get your fingers burned. The job isn't worth it—yet.''

''Don't worry, Dad.'' She laughed unaffectedly. ''When it comes to playboys like this one, I've got millions and skillions and whillions of ohms of resistance. But here comes Senator Morgan himself, with a fat and repulsive Venerian—he's calling my boy-friend away from me, with what he thinks is an imperceptible high-sign, into a huddle—and my olfactory nerves perceive a rich and fruity aroma, as of skunk—so . . . I hate to seem to be giving a Solarian Councillor the heave-ho, but if I want to read what goes on—and I certainly do—I'll have to concentrate. As soon as you get back give us a call and we'll report. Take it easy, Dad!''

''You're the one to be told that, not me. Good hunting, Jill!''

Samms, still seated calmly at his desk, reached out and pressed a button marked ''GARAGE''. His office was on the seventieth floor; the garage occupied level after level of sub-basement. The screen brightened; a keen young face appeared.

''Good evening, Jim. Will you please send my car up to the Wright Skyway feeder?''

''At once, sir. It will be there in seventy five seconds.''

Samms cut off; and, after a brief exchange of thought with Kinnison, went out into the hall and along it to the ''DOWN'' shaft. There, going free, he stepped through a doorless, unguarded archway into over a thousand feet of air. Although it was long after conventional office hours the shaft was still fairly busy, but that made no difference—inertialess collisions cannot even be felt. He bulleted downward to the sixth floor, where he brought himself to an instantaneous halt.

Leaving the shaft, he joined the now thinning crowd hurrying toward the exit. A girl with meticulously plucked eyebrows and an astounding hair-do, catching sight of his Lens, took her hands out of her breeches pockets—skirts went out, as office dress, when up-and-down open-shaft velocities of a hundred or so miles per hour replaced elevators—nudged her companion, and whispered excitedly:

''Look there! Quick! I never saw one close up before, did you? That's him—himself! First Lensman Samms!''

At the Portal, the Lensman as a matter of habit held out his car-check, but such formalities were no longer necessary, or even possible. Everybody knew, or wanted to be thought of as knowing, Virgil Samms.

''Stall four sixty five, First Lensman, sir,'' the uniformed gateman told him, without even glancing at the extended disk.

"Thank you, Tom."

"This way, please, sir, First Lensman," and a youth, teeth gleaming white in a startlingly black face, strode proudly to the indicated stall and opened the vehicle's door.

"Thank you, Danny," Samms said, as appreciatively as though he did not know exactly where his ground-car was.

He got in. The door jammed itself gently shut. The runabout—a Dillingham eleven-forty—shot smoothly forward upon its two fat, soft tires. Half-way to the exit archway he was doing forty; he hit the steeply-banked curve leading into the lofty "street" at ninety. Nor was there shock or strain. Motorcycle-wise, but automatically, the "Dilly" leaned against its gyroscopes at precisely the correct angle; the huge low-pressure tires clung to the resilient synthetic of the pavement as though integral with it. Nor was there any question of conflicting traffic, for this thoroughfare, six full levels above Varick street proper, was not, strictly speaking, a street at all. It had only one point of access, the one which Samms had used; and only one exit—it was simply and only a feeder into Wright Skyway, a limited-access superhighway.

Samms saw, without noting particularly, the maze of traffic-ways of which this feeder was only one tiny part; a maze which extended from ground-level up to a point well above even the towering buildings of New York's metropolitan district.

The way rose sharply; Samms' right foot went down a little farther; the Dillingham began to pick up speed. Moving loud-speakers sang to him and yelled and blared at him, but he did not hear them. Brilliant signs, flashing and flaring all the colors of the spectrum—sheer triumphs of the electrician's art—blazed in or flamed into arresting words and eye-catching pictures, but he did not see them. Advertising—advertising designed by experts to sell everything from aard-varks to Martian zyzmol ("bottled ecstacy")—but the First Lensman was a seasoned big-city dweller. His mind had long since become a perfect filter, admitting to his consciousness only things which he wanted to perceive: only so can big-city life be made endurable.

Approaching the Skyway, he cut in his touring roadlights, slowed down a trifle, and insinuated his low-flyer into the stream of traffic. Those lights threw fifteen hundred watts apiece, but there was no glare—polarized lenses and windshields saw to that.

He wormed his way over to the left-hand, high-speed lane and opened up. At the edge of the skyscraper district, where Wright Skyway angles sharply downward to ground level, Samms' attention was caught and held by something off to his right—a blue-white, whistling something that hurtled upward into the air. As it ascended it slowed down; its monotone shriek became lower and lower in pitch; its light went down through the spectrum toward the red. Finally it exploded, with an earth-shaking crash; but the lightning-like flash of the detonation, instead of vanishing almost instantaneously, settled itself upon a low-hanging artificial cloud and became a picture and four words—two bearded faces and "SMITH BROS. COUGH DROPS"!

"Well, I'll be damned!" Samms spoke aloud, chagrined at having been compelled to listen to and to look at an advertisement. "I thought I had seen everything, but *that* is really new!"

Twenty minutes—fifty miles—later, Samms left the Skyway at a point near what had once been South Norwalk, Connecticut; an area transformed now into the level square miles of New York Spaceport.

New York Spaceport; then, and until the establishment of Prime Base, the biggest and busiest field in existence upon any planet of Civilization. For New York City, long the financial and commercial capital of the Earth, had maintained the same dominant position in the affairs of the Solar System and was holding a substantial lead over her rivals, Chicago, London, and Stalingrad, in the race for interstellar supremacy.

And Virgil Samms himself, because of the ever-increasing menace of piracy, had been largely responsible for the policy of basing the war-vessels of the Triplanetary Patrol upon each space-field in direct ratio to the size and importance of that field. Hence he was no stranger in New York Spaceport; in fact, master psychologist that he was, he had made it a point to know by first name practically everyone connected with it.

No sooner had he turned his Dillingham over to a smiling attendant, however, than he was accosted by a man whom he had never seen before.

"Mr. Samms?" the stranger asked.

"Yes." Samms did not energize his Lens; he had not yet developed either the inclination or the technique to probe instantaneously every entity who approached him, upon any pretext whatever, in order to find out what that entity *really* wanted.

"I'm Isaacson . . ." the man paused, as though he had supplied a world of information.

"Yes?" Samms was receptive, but not impressed.

"Interstellar Spaceways, you know. We've been trying to see you for two weeks, but we couldn't get past your secretaries, so I decided to buttonhole you here, myself. But we're just as much alone here as we would be in either one of our offices—yes, more so. What I want to talk to you about is having our exclusive franchise extended to cover the outer planets and the colonies."

"Just a minute, Mr. Isaacson. Surely you know that I no longer have even a portfolio in the Council; that practically all of my attention is, and for some time to come will be, directed elsewhere?"

"Exactly—*officially*." Isaacson's tone spoke volumes. "But you're still the Boss; they'll do anything you tell them to. We couldn't try to do business with you before, of course, but in your present position there is nothing whatever to prevent you from getting into the biggest thing that will ever be. We are the biggest corporation in existence now, as you know, and we are still growing—fast. We don't do business in a small way, or with small men; so here's a check for a million credits, or I will deposit it to your account . . ."

"I'm not interested."

"As a binder," the other went on, as smoothly as though his sentence had not been interrupted, "with twenty five million more to follow on the day that our franchise goes through."

"I'm still not interested."

"No . . . o . . . o . . . ?" Isaacson studied the Lensman narrowly: and Samms, Lens now wide awake, studied the enterpreneur. "Well . . . I . . . while I admit that we want you pretty badly, you are smart enough to know that we'll get what we want anyway, with or without you. With you, though, it will be easier and quicker, so I am authorized to offer you, besides the twenty six million credits . . ." he savored the words as he uttered them: "twenty two and one-half percent of Spaceways. On today's market that is worth fifty million credits; ten years from now it will be worth fifty *billion*. That's my high bid; that's as high as we can possibly go."

"I'm glad to hear that—I'm *still* not interested," and Samms strode away, calling his friend Kinnison as he did so.

"Rod? Virgil." He told the story.

"Whew!" Kinnison whistled expressively. "They're not pikers, anyway, are they? What a *sweet* set-up—and you could wrap it up and hand it to them like a pound of coffee . . ."

"Or you could, Rod."

"Could be . . ." The big Lensman ruminated. "But *what* a hookup! Perfectly legitimate, and with plenty of precedents—and arguments, of a sort—in its favor. The outer planets. Then Alpha Centauri and Sirius and Procyon and so on. Monopoly—all the traffic will bear . . ."

"Slavery, you mean!" Samms stormed. "It would hold Civilization back for a thousand years!"

"Sure, but what do *they* care?"

"That's it . . . and he said—and actually believed—that they would get it without my help . . . I can't help wondering about that."

"Simple enough, Virge, when you think about it. He doesn't know yet what a Lensman is. Nobody does, you know, except Lensmen. It will take some time for that knowledge to get around . . ."

"And still longer for it to be *believed*."

"Right. But as to the chance of Interstellar Spaceways ever getting the monopoly they're working for, I didn't think I would have to remind you that it was not entirely by accident that over half of the members of the Solarian Council are Lensmen, and that any Galactic Councillor will automatically *have* to be a Lensman. So go right ahead with what you started, my boy, and don't give Isaacson and Company another thought. We'll bend an optic or two in that direction while you are gone."

"I was overlooking a few things, at that, I guess." Samms sighed in relief as he entered the main office of the Patrol.

The line at the receptionist's desk was fairly short, but even so, Samms was not allowed to wait. That highly decorative, but far-from-dumb blonde, breaking off in mid-sentence her business of the moment, turned on her charm as though it had been a battery of floodlights, pressed a stud on her desk, and spoke to the man before her and to the Lensman:

"Excuse me a moment, please. First Lensman Samms, sir . . . ?"

"Yes, Miss Regan?" her communicator—"squawk-box," in every day parlance—broke in.

"First Lensman Samms is here, sir," the girl announced, and broke the circuit.

"Good evening, Sylvia. Lieutenant-Commander Wagner, please, or whoever else is handling clearances," Samms answered what he thought was to have been her question.

"Oh, no, sir; you are cleared. Commodore Clayton has been waiting for you . . . here he is, now."

"Hi, Virgil!" Commodore Clayton, a big, solid man with a scarred face and a shock of iron-gray hair, whose collar bore the two silver stars which proclaimed him to be the commander-in-chief of a continental contingent of the Patrol, shook hands vigorously. "I'll zip you out. Miss Regan, call a bug, please."

"Oh, that isn't necessary, Alex!" Samms protested. "I'll pick one up outside."

"Not in any Patrol base in North America, my friend; nor, unless I am very badly mistaken, anywhere else. From now on, Lensmen have absolute priority, and the quicker everybody realizes exactly what that means, the better."

The "bug"—a vehicle something like a jeep, except more so—was waiting at the door. The two men jumped aboard.

"The *Chicago*—and blast!" Clayton ordered, crisply.

The driver obeyed—literally. Gravel flew from beneath skidding tires as the highly maneuverable little ground-car took off. A screaming turn into the deservedly famous Avenue of Oaks. Along the Avenue. Through the Gate, the guards saluting smartly as the bug raced past them. Past the barracks. Past the airport hangars and strips. Out into the space-field, the scarred and blackened area devoted solely to the widely-spaced docks of the tremendous vessels which plied the vacuous reaches of interplanetary and interstellar space. Space-docks were, and are, huge and sprawling structures; built of concrete and steel and asbestos and ultra-stubborn refractory and insulation and vacuum-breaks; fully air-conditioned and having refrigeration equipment of thousands of tons per hour of ice; designed not only to expedite servicing, unloading, and loading, but also to protect material and personnel from the raving, searing blasts of take-off and of landing.

A space-dock is a squat and monstrous cylinder, into whose hollow top the lowermost one-third of a space-ship's bulk fits as snugly as does a baseball into the "pocket" of a veteran fielder's long-seasoned glove. And the tremendous distances between those docks minimize the apparent size, both of the structures themselves and of the vessels surmounting them. Thus, from a distance, the *Chicago* looked little enough, and harmless enough; but as the bug flashed under the overhanging bulk and the driver braked savagely to a stop at one of the dock's entrances, Samms could scarcely keep from flinching. That featureless, gray, smoothly curving wall of alloy steel loomed so incredibly high above them—extended so terrifyingly far outward beyond its visible means of support! It *must* be on the very verge of crashing!

Samms stared deliberately at the mass of metal towering above him, then smiled—not without effort—at his companion.

"You'd think, Alex, that a man would get over being afraid that a ship was going to fall on him, but I haven't—yet."

"No, and you probably never will. I never have, and I'm one of the old hands. Some claim not to mind it—but not in front of a lie detector. That's why they had to make the passenger docks bigger than the liners—too many passengers fainted and had to be carried aboard on stretchers—or cancelled passage entirely. However, scaring hell out of them on the ground had one big advantage; they felt so safe inside that they didn't get the colly-wobbles so bad when they went free."

"Well, I've got over *that*, anyway. Good-bye, Alex; and thanks."

Samms entered the dock, shot smoothly upward, followed an escort-

ing officer to the captain's own cabin, and settled himself into a cushioned chair facing an ultra-wave viewplate. A face appeared upon his
communicator screen and spoke.

"Winfield to First Lensman Samms—you will be ready to blast off
at twenty one hundred?"

"Samms to Captain Winfield," the Lensman replied. "I will be
ready."

Sirens yelled briefly; a noise which Samms knew was purely a formality. Clearance had been issued; Station PiXNY was filling the air
with warnings. Personnel and material close enough to the *Chicago*'s
dock to be affected by the blast were under cover and safe.

The blast went on; the plate showed, instead of a view of the space-
field, a blaze of blue-white light. The warship was inertialess, it is true;
but so terrific were the forces released that incandescent gases, furiously
driven, washed the dock and everything for hundreds of yards around
it.

The plate cleared. Through the lower, denser layers of atmosphere
the *Chicago* bored in seconds; then, as the air grew thinner and thinner,
she rushed upward faster and faster. The terrain below became concave
... then convex. Being completely without inertia, the ship's velocity
was at every instant that at which the friction of the medium through
which she blasted her way equaled precisely the force of her driving
thrust.

Wherefore, out in open space, the Earth a fast-shrinking tiny ball and
Sol himself growing smaller, paler, and weaker at a startling rate, the
Chicago's speed attained an almost constant value; a value starkly im-
possible for the human mind to grasp.

5

RIGEL FOUR

For hours Virgil Samms sat motionless, staring almost unseeing into his plate. It was not that the view was not worth seeing—the wonder of space, the ever-changing, constantly-shifting panorama of incredibly brilliant although dimensionless points of light, against that wondrous background of mist-besprinkled black velvet, is a thing that never fails to awe even the most seasoned observer—but he had a tremendous load on his mind. He had to solve an apparently insoluble problem. How ... how ... HOW could he do what he had to do?

Finally, knowing that the time of landing was approaching, he got up, unfolded his fans, and swam lightly through the air of the cabin to a hand-line, along which he drew himself into the control room. He could have made the trip in that room, of course, if he had so chosen; but, knowing that officers of space do not really like to have strangers in that sanctum, he did not intrude until it was necessary.

Captain Winfield was already strapped down at his master conning plate. Pilots, navigators, and computers worked busily at their respective tasks.

"I was just going to call you, First Lensman." Winfield waved a hand in the general direction of a chair near his own. "Take the Lieutenant-Captain's station, please." Then, after a few minutes: "Go inert, Mr. White."

"Attention, all personnel," Lieutenant-Captain White spoke conversationally into a microphone. "Prepare for inert maneuvering, Class Three. Off."

A bank of tiny red lights upon a panel turned green practically as one. White cut the Bergenholm, whereupon Virgil Samms' mass changed instantly from a weight of zero to one of five hundred and twenty five pounds—ships of war then had no space to waste upon such non-essentials as artificial gravity. Although he was braced for the change and cushioned against it, the Lensman's breath *whooshed!* out sharply; but, being intensely interested in what was going on, he swallowed convulsively a couple of times, gasped a few deep breaths, and fought his way back up to normalcy.

The Chief Pilot was now at work, with all the virtuoso's skill of his rank and grade; one of the hall-marks of which is to make difficult tasks look easy. He played trills and runs and arpeggios—at times veritable glissades—upon keyboards and pedals, directing with micrometric precision the tremendous forces of the superdreadnaught to the task of matching the intrinsic velocity of New York Spaceport at the time of his departure to the I. V. of the surface of the planet so far below.

Samms stared into his plate; first at the incredibly tiny apparent size of that incredibly hot sun, and then at the barren-looking world toward which they were dropping at such terrific speed.

"It doesn't seem possible . . ." he remarked, half to Winfield, half to himself, "that a sun could be that big and that hot. Rigel Four is almost two hundred times as far away from it as Earth is from Sol—something like eighteen billion miles—it doesn't look much, if any, bigger than Venus does from Luna—yet this world is hotter than the Sahara Desert."

"Well, blue giants are both big and hot," the captain replied, matter-of-factly, "and their radiation, being mostly invisible, is deadly stuff. And Rigel is about the biggest in this region. There are others a lot worse, though. Doradus S, for instance, would make Rigel, here, look like a tallow candle. I'm going out there, some of these days, just to take a look at it. But that's enough of astronomical chit-chat—we're down to twenty miles of altitude and we've got your city just about stopped."

The *Chicago* slowed gently to a halt; perched motionless upon softly hissing jets. Samms directed his visibeam downward and sent along it an exploring, questing thought. Since he had never met a Rigellian in person, he could not form the mental image or pattern necessary to become en rapport with any one individual of the race. He did know, however, the type of mind which must be possessed by the entity with whom he wished to talk, and he combed the Rigellian city until he found one. The rapport was so incomplete and imperfect as to amount almost to no contact at all, but he could, perhaps, make himself understood.

"If you will excuse this possibly unpleasant and certainly unwarranted intrusion," he thought, carefully and slowly, "I would like very much to discuss with you a matter which should become of paramount importance to all the intelligent peoples of all the planets in space."

"I welcome you, Tellurian." Mind fused with mind at every one of uncountable millions of points and paths. This Rigellian professor of sociology, standing at his desk, was physically a monster . . . the oil-drum of a body, the four blocky legs, the multi-branchiate tentacular arms, that immobile dome of a head, the complete lack of eyes and of ears . . . nevertheless Samms' mind fused with the monstrosity's as smoothly, as effortlessly, and almost as completely as it had with his own daughter's!

And *what* a mind! The transcendent poise; the staggeringly tremendous range and scope—the untroubled and unshakeable calm; the sublime quietude; the vast and placid certainty; the ultimate stability, unknown and forever unknowable to any human or near-human race!

"Dismiss all thought of intrusion, First Lensman Samms . . . I have heard of you human beings, of course, but have never considered seriously the possibility of meeting one of you mind to mind. Indeed, it was reported that none of our minds could make any except the barest and most unsatisfactory contact with any of yours they chanced to encounter. It is, I now perceive, the Lens which makes this full accord possible, and it is basically about the Lens that you are here?"

"It is," and Samms went on to cover in flashing thoughts his conception of what the Galactic Patrol should be and should become. That was easy enough; but when he tried to describe in detail the qualifications necessary for Lensmanship, he began to bog down. "Force, drive, scope, of course . . . range . . . power . . . but above all, an absolute integrity . . . an ultimate incorruptibility . . ." He could recognize such a mind after meeting it and studying it, but as to finding it . . . It might not be in any place of power or authority. His own, and Rod Kinnison's, happened to be; but Costigan's was not . . . and both Knobos and DalNalten had made inconspicuousness a fine art . . .

"I see," the native stated, when it became clear that Samms could say no more. "It is evident, of course, that I cannot qualify; nor do I know anyone personally who can. However . . ."

"What?" Samms demanded. "I was sure, from the feel of your mind, that you . . . but with a mind of such depth and breadth, such tremendous scope and power, you must be incorruptible!"

"I am," came the dry rejoinder. "We all are. No Rigellian is, or ever will be or can be, what you think of as 'corrupt' or 'corruptible.' Indeed, it is only by the narrowest, most intense concentration upon every line of your thought that I can translate your meaning into a concept possible for any of us even to understand."

"Then what . . . Oh, I see. I was starting at the wrong end. Naturally enough, I suppose, I looked first for the qualities rarest in my own race."

"Of course. Our minds have ample scope and range; and, perhaps, sufficient power. But those qualities which you refer to as 'force' and 'drive' are fully as rare among us as absolute mental integrity is among you. What you know as 'crime' is unknown. We have no police, no government, no laws, no organized armed forces of any kind. We take, practically always, the line of least resistance. We live and let live, as your thought runs. We work together for the common good."

"Well . . . I don't know what I expected to find here, but certainly not *this* . . ." If Samms had never before been completely thunderstruck, completely at a loss, he was then. "You don't think, then, that there is any chance?"

"I have been thinking, and there may be a chance . . . a slight one, but still a chance," the Rigellian said, slowly. "For instance, that youth, so full of curiosity, who first visited your planet. Thousands of us have wondered, to ourselves and to each other, about the peculiar qualities of mind which compelled him and others to waste so much time, effort, and wealth upon a project so completely useless as exploration. Why, he had even to develop energies and engines theretofore unknown, and which can never be of any real use!"

Samms was shaken by the calm finality with which the Rigellian dismissed all possibility of the usefulness of interstellar exploration, but stuck doggedly to his purpose.

"However slight the chance, I must find and talk to this man. I suppose he is now out in deep space somewhere. Have you any idea where?"

"He is now in his home city, accumulating funds and manufacturing fuel with which to continue his pointless activities. That city is named . . . that is, in your English you might call it . . . Suntown? Sunberg? No, it must be more specific . . . Rigelsville? Rigel City?"

"Rigelston, I would translate it?" Samms hazarded.

"Exactly—Rigelston." The professor marked its location upon a globular mental map far more accurate and far more detailed than the globe which Captain Winfield and his lieutenant were then studying.

"Thanks. Now, can you and will you get in touch with this explorer and ask him to call a meeting of his full crew and any others who might be interested in the project I have outlined?"

"I can. I will. He and his kind are not quite sane, of course, as you know; but I do not believe that even they are so insane as to be willing to subject themselves to the environment of your vessel."

"They will not be asked to come here. The meeting will be held in Rigelston. If necessary, I shall insist that it be held there."

"You would? I perceive that you would. It is strange ... yes, fantastic ... you are quarrelsome, pugnacious, antisocial, vicious, small-bodied and small-brained; timid, nervous, and highly and senselessly excitable; unbalanced and unsane; as sheerly monstrous mentally as you are physically ..." These outrageous thoughts were sent as casually and as impersonally as though the sender were discussing the weather. He paused, then went on: "And yet, to further such a completely visionary project, you are eager to subject yourself to conditions whose counterparts I could not force myself, under any circumstances whatever, to meet. It may be ... it must be true that there is an extension of the principle of working together for the common good which my mind, for lack of pertinent data, has not been able to grasp. I am now en rapport with Dronvire the explorer."

"Ask him, please, not to identify himself to me. I do not want to go into that meeting with any preconceived ideas."

"A balanced thought," the Rigellian approved. "Someone will be at the airport to point out to you the already desolated area in which the space-ship of the explorers makes its so-frightful landings; Dronvire will ask someone to meet you at the airport and bring you to the place of meeting."

The telepathic line snapped and Samms turned a white and sweating face to the *Chicago*'s captain.

"God, what a strain! Don't ever try telepathy unless you positively have to—especially not with such an outlandishly *different* race as these Rigellians are!"

"Don't worry; I won't." Winfield's words were not at all sympathetic, but his tone was. "You looked as though somebody was beating your brains out with a spiked club. Where next, First Lensman?"

Samms marked the location of Rigelston upon the vessel's chart, then donned ear-plugs and a special, radiation-proof suit of armor, equipped with refrigerators and with extra-thick blocks of lead glass to protect the eyes.

The airport, an extremely busy one well outside the city proper, was located easily enough, as was the spot upon which the Tellurian ship was to land. Lightly, slowly, she settled downward, her jets raving out against a gravity fully twice that of her native Earth. Those blasts, however, added little or nothing to the destruction already accomplished by the craft then lying there—a torpedo-shaped cruiser having perhaps one-twentieth of the *Chicago*'s mass and bulk.

The superdreadnaught landed, sinking into the hard, dry ground to a depth of some ten or fifteen feet before she stopped. Samms, en rapport with the entity who was to be his escort, made a flashing survey of the mind so intimately in contact with his own. No use. This one was not and never could become Lensman material. He climbed heavily down the ladder. This double-normal gravity made the going a bit difficult, but he could stand that a lot better than some of the other things he was going to have to take. The Rigellian equivalent of an automobile was there, waiting for him, its door invitingly open.

Samms had known—in general—what to expect. The two-wheeled chassis was more or less similar to that of his own Dillingham. The body was a narrow torpedo of steel, bluntly pointed at both ends, and without windows. Two features, however, were both unexpected and unpleasant—the hard, tough steel of which that body was forged was an inch and a half thick, instead of one-sixteenth; and even that extraordinarily armored body was dented and scarred and marred, especially about the fore and rear quarters, as deeply and as badly and as casually as are the fenders of an Earthly jalopy!

The Lensman climbed, not easily or joyously, into that grimly forbidding black interior. Black? It was so black that the port-hole-like doorway seemed to admit no light at all. It was blacker than a witch's cat in a coal cellar at midnight! Samms flinched; then, stiffening, thought at the driver.

"My contact with you seems to have slipped. I'm afraid that I will have to cling to you rather more tightly than may be either polite or comfortable. Deprived of sight, and without your sense of perception, I am practically helpless."

"Come in, Lensman, by all means. I offered to maintain full engagement, but it seemed to me that you declined it; quite possibly the misunderstanding was due to our unfamiliarity with each others' customary mode of thought. Relax, please, and come in . . . there! Better?"

"Infinitely better. Thanks."

And it was. The darkness vanished; through the unexplainable perceptive sense of the Rigellian he could "see" everything—he had a practically perfect three-dimensional view of the entire circumambient sphere. He could see both the inside and the outside of the ground car he was in and of the immense space-ship in which he had come to Rigel IV. He could see the bearings and the wrist-pins of the internal-combustion engine of the car, the interior structure of the welds that held the steel plates together, the busy airport outside, and even deep into the ground. He could see and study in detail the deepest-buried, most heavily shielded parts of the atomic engines of the *Chicago*.

But he was wasting time. He could also plainly see a deeply-cushioned chair, designed to fit a human body, welded to a stanchion and equipped with half a dozen padded restraining straps. He sat down quickly; strapped himself in.

"Ready?"

"Ready."

The door banged shut with a clangor which burst through space-suit and ear-plugs with all the violence of a nearby thunderclap. And that was merely the beginning. The engine started—an internal-combustion engine of well over a thousand horsepower, designed for maximum efficiency by engineers in whose lexicon there were no counterparts of any English words relating to noise, or even to sound. The car took off; with an acceleration which drove the Tellurian backward, deep into the cushions. The scream of tortured tires and the crescendo bellowing of the engine combined to form an uproar which, amplified by and reverberating within the resonant shell of metal, threatened to addle the very brain inside the Lensman's skull.

"You suffer!" the driver exclaimed, in high concern. "They cautioned me to start and stop gently, to drive slowly and carefully, to bump softly. They told me you are frail and fragile, a fact which I perceived for myself and which has caused me to drive with the utmost possible care and restraint. Is the fault mine? Have I been too rough?"

"Not at all. It isn't that. It's the ungodly noise." Then, realizing that the Rigellian could have no conception of his meaning, he continued quickly:

"The vibrations in the atmosphere, from sixteen cycles per second up to about nine or ten thousand." He explained what a second was. "My nervous system is very sensitive to those vibrations. But I expected them and shielded myself against them as adequately as I could. Nothing can be done about them. Go ahead."

"Atmospheric vibrations? *Atmospheric* vibrations? Atmospheric *vibrations?*" The driver marveled, and concentrated upon this entirely new concept while he—

1. Swung around a steel-sheathed concrete pillar at a speed of at least sixty miles per hour, grazing it so closely that he removed one layer of protective coating from the metal.

2. Braked so savagely to miss a wildly careening truck that the restraining straps almost cut Samms' body, spacesuit and all, into slices.

3. Darted into a hole in the traffic so narrow that only tiny fractions of inches separated his hurtling Juggernaut from an enormous steel column on one side and another speeding vehicle on the other.

4. Executed a double-right-angle reverse curve, thus missing by

hair's breadths two vehicles traveling in the opposite direction and one in his own.

5. As a grand climax to this spectacular exhibition of insane driving, he plunged at full speed into a traffic artery which seemed so full already that it could not hold even one more car. But it could—just barely could. However, instead of near misses or grazing hits, this time there were bumps, dents—little ones, nothing at all, really, only an inch or so deep—and an utterly hellish concatenation and concentration of noise.

"I fail completely to understand what effect such vibrations could have," the Rigellian announced finally, sublimely unconscious that anything at all out of the ordinary had occurred. For him, nothing had. "But surely they cannot be of any use?"

"On this world, I am afraid not. No," Samms admitted, wearily. "Here, too, apparently, as everywhere, the big cities are choking themselves to death with their own traffic."

"Yes. We build and build, but never have roads enough."

"What are those mounds along the streets?" For some time Samms had been conscious of those long, low, apparently opaque structures; attracted to them because they were the only non-transparent objects within range of the Rigellian's mind. "Or is it something I should not mention?"

"What? Oh, those? By no means."

One of the near-by mounds lost its opacity. It was filled with swirling, gyrating bands and streamers of energy so vivid and so solid as to resemble fabric; with wildly hurtling objects of indescribable shapes and contours; with brilliantly flashing symbols which Samms found, greatly to his surprise, made sense—not through the Rigellian's mind, but through his own Lens:

"EAT TEEGMEE'S FOOD!"

"Advertising!" Samms' thought was a snort.

"Advertising. You do not perceive yours, either, as you drive?" This was the first bond to be established between two of the most highly advanced races of the First Galaxy!

The frightful drive continued; the noise grew worse and worse. Imagine, if you can, a city of fifteen millions of people, throughout whose entire length, breadth, height, and depth no attempt whatever had ever been made to abate any noise, however violent or piercing! If your imagination has been sufficiently vivid and if you have worked understandingly enough, the product may approximate what First Lensman Samms was forced to listen to that day.

Through ever-thickening traffic, climbing to higher and ever higher roadways between towering windowless walls of steel, the massive Rigellian automobile barged and banged its way. Finally it stopped, a thousand feet or so above the ground, beside a building which was still under construction. The heavy door clanged open. They got out.

And then—it chanced to be daylight at the time—Samms saw a tangle of fighting, screaming *colors* whose like no entity possessing the sense of sight had ever before imagined. Reds, yellows, blues, greens, purples, and every variation and inter-mixture possible; laid on or splashed on or occurring naturally at perfect random, smote his eyes as violently as the all-pervading noise had been assailing his ears.

He realized then that through his guide's sense of perception he had been "seeing" only in shades of gray, that to these people "visible" light differed only in wave-length from any other band of the complete electromagnetic spectrum of vibration.

Strained and tense, the Lensman followed his escort along a narrow catwalk, through a wall upon which riveters and welders were busily at work, into a room practically without walls and ceiled only by story after story of huge I-beams. Yet *this* was the meeting-place; almost a hundred Rigellians were assembled there!

And as Samms walked toward the group a craneman dropped a couple of tons of steel plate, from a height of eight or ten feet, upon the floor directly behind him.

"I just about jumped right out of my armor," is the way Samms himself described his reactions; and that description is perhaps as good as any.

At any rate, he went briefly out of control, and the Rigellian sent him a steadying, inquiring, wondering thought. He could no more understand the Tellurian's sensitivity than Samms could understand the fact that to these people, even the concept of physical intrusion was absolutely in-comprehensible. These builders were not workmen, in the Tellurian sense. They were Rigellians, each working his few hours per week for the common good. They would be no more in contact with the meeting than would their fellows on the other side of the planet.

Samms closed his eyes to the riot of clashing colors, deafened himself by main strength to the appalling clangor of sound, forced himself to concentrate every fiber of his mind upon his errand.

"Please synchronize with my mind, as many of you as possible," he thought at the group as a whole, and went en rapport with mind after mind after mind. And mind after mind after mind lacked something. Some were stronger than others, had more initiative and drive and urge, but none would quite do. Until—

"Thank God!" In the wave of exultant relief, of fulfillment, Samms no longer saw the colors or heard the din. "You, sir, are of Lensman grade. I perceive that you are Dronvire."

"Yes, Virgil Samms, I am Dronvire; and at long last I know what it is that I have been seeking all my life. But how of these, my other friends? Are not some of them . . . ?"

"I do not know, nor is it necessary that I find out. You will select . . ." Samms paused, amazed. The other Rigellians were still in the room, but mentally, he and Dronvire were completely alone.

"They anticipated your thought, and, knowing that it was to be more or less personal, they left us until one of us invites them to return."

"I like that, and appreciate it. You will go to Arisia. You will receive your Lens. You will return here. You will select and send to Arisia as many or as few of your fellows as you choose. These things I require you, by the Lens of Arisia, to do. Afterward—please note that this is in no sense obligatory—I would like very much to have you visit Earth and accept appointment to the Galactic Council. Will you?"

"I will." Dronvire needed no time to consider his decision.

The meeting was dismissed. The same entity who had been Samms' chauffeur on the in-bound trip drove him back to the *Chicago*, driving as "slowly" and as "carefully" as before. Nor, this time, did the punishment take such toll, even though Samms knew that each terrific lunge and lurch was adding one more bruise to the already much-too-large collection discoloring almost every square foot of his tough hide. He had succeeded, and the thrill of success had its usual analgesic effect.

The *Chicago*'s captain met him in the air-lock and helped him remove his suit.

"Are you *sure* you're all right, Samms?" Winfield was no longer the formal captain, but a friend. "Even though you didn't call, we were beginning to wonder . . . you look as though you'd been to a Valerian clambake, and I sure as hell don't like the way you're favoring those ribs and that left leg. I'll tell the boys you got back in A-prime shape, but I'll have the doctors look you over, just to make sure."

Winfield made the announcement, and through his Lens Samms could plainly feel the wave of relief and pleasure that spread throughout the great ship with the news. It surprised him immensely. Who was *he*, that all these boys should care so much whether he lived or died?

"I'm perfectly all right," Samms protested. "There's nothing at all the matter with me that twenty hours of sleep won't fix as good as new."

"Maybe; but you'll go to the sick-bay first, just the same," Winfield insisted. "And I suppose you want me to blast back to Tellus?"

"Right. And fast. The Ambassadors' Ball is next Tuesday evening, you know, and that's one function I can't stay away from, even with a Class A Double Prime excuse."

6
OPERATION ZWILNIK—THIONITE

The Ambassadors' Ball, one of the most ultra-ultra functions of the year, was well under way. It was not that everyone who was anyone was there; but everyone who was there was, in one way or another, very emphatically someone. Thus, there were affairs at which there were more young and beautiful women, and more young and handsome men; but none exhibiting newer or more expensive gowns, more ribbons and decorations, more or costlier or more refined jewelry, or a larger acreage of powdered and perfumed epidermis.

And even so, the younger set was well enough represented. Since pioneering appeals more to youth than to age, the men representing the colonies were young; and their wives, together with the daughters and the second (or third or fourth, or occasionally the fifth) wives of the human personages practically balanced the account.

Nor was the throng entirely human. The time had not yet come, of course, when warm-blooded, oxygen-breathing monstrosities from hundreds of other solar systems would vie in numbers with the humanity present. There were, however, a few Martians on the floor, wearing their light "robes du convention" and dancing with meticulously mathematical precision. A few Venerians, who did not dance, sat in state or waddled importantly about. Many worlds of the Solarian System, and not a few other systems, were represented.

One couple stood out, even against that opulent and magnificent background. Eyes followed them wherever they went.

The girl was tall, trim, supple; built like a symphony. Her Callistan vexto-silk gown, of the newest and most violent shade of "radioactive" green, was phosphorescently luminous; fluorescent; gleaming and glowing. Its hem swept the floor, but above the waist it vanished mysteriously except for wisps which clung to strategic areas here and there with no support, apparently, except the personal magnetism of the wearer. She, almost alone of all the women there, wore no flowers. Her only jewelry was a rosette of huge, perfectly-matched emeralds, perched precariously upon her bare left shoulder. Her hair, unlike the other womens' flawless coiffures, was a flamboyant, artistically-disarranged, red-bronze-auburn mop. Her soft and dewy eyes—Virgilia Samms could control her eyes as perfectly as she could her highly educated hands—were at the moment gold-flecked, tawny wells of girlish innocence and trust.

"But I *can't* give you this next dance, too, Herkimer—*Honestly* I can't!" she pleaded, snuggling just a trifle closer into the embrace of the young man who was just as much man, physically, as she was woman. "I'd just *love* to, really, but I just simply *can't*, and you know why, too."

"You've got some duty-dances, of course . . ."

"*Some?* I've got a list as long as from here to there! Senator Morgan first, of course, then Mr. Isaacson, then I sat one out with Mr. Ossmen— I can't *stand* Venerians, they're so slimy and fat and repulsive!—and that leathery horned toad from Mars and that Jovian hippopotamus . . ."

She went down the list, and as she named or characterized each entity another finger of her left hand pressed down upon the back of her partner's right, to emphasize the count of her social obligations. But those talented fingers were doing more—far, far more—than that.

Herkimer Herkimer Third, although no little of a Don Juan, was a highly polished, smoothly finished, thoroughly seasoned diplomat. As such, his eyes and his other features—particularly his eyes—had been schooled for years to reveal no trace of whatever might be going on inside his brain. If he had entertained any suspicion of the beautiful girl in his arms, if anyone had suggested that she was trying her best to pump him, he would have smiled the sort of smile which only the top-drawer diplomat can achieve. He was not suspicious of Virgilia Samms. However, simply because she was Virgil Samms' daughter, he took an extra bit of pains to betray no undue interest in any one of the names she recited. And besides, she was not looking at his eyes, nor even at his face. Her glance, demurely downcast, was all too rarely raised above the level of his chin.

There were some things, however, that Herkimer Herkimer Third did not know. That Virgilia Samms was the most accomplished muscle-reader of her times. That she was so close to him, not because of his manly charm, but because only in that position could she do her pro-digious best. That she could work with her eyes alone, but in emergen-cies, when fullest possible results were imperative, she had to use her exquisitely sensitive fingers and her exquisitely tactile skin. That she had studied intensively, and had tabulated the reactions of, each of the entities on her list. That she was now, with his help, fitting those reactions into a pattern. And finally, that that pattern was beginning to assume the grim shape of MURDER!

And Virgilia Samms, working now for something far more urgent and vastly more important than a figmental Galactic Patrol, hoped desperately that this Herkimer was not a muscle-reader too; for she knew that she was revealing her secrets even more completely than was he. In fact, if things got much worse, he could not help but feel the pounding of her heart . . . but she could explain that easily enough, by a few appropriate wriggles . . . No, he wasn't a reader, definitely not. He wasn't watching the right places; he was looking where that gown had been designed to make him look, and nowhere else . . . and no tell-tale muscles lay beneath any part of either of his hands.

As her eyes and her fingers and her lovely torso sent more and more information to her keen brain, Jill grew more and more anxious. She was sure that murder was intended, but who was to be the victim? Her father? Probably. Pops Kinnison? Possibly. Somebody else? Barely possibly. And when? And where? And how? *She didn't know!* And she would have to be *sure* . . . Mentioning names hadn't been enough, but a personal appearance . . . Why *didn't* dad show up—or did she wish he wouldn't come at all . . . ?

Virgil Samms entered the ball-room.

"And dad told me, Herkimer," she cooed sweetly, gazing up into his eyes for the first time in over a minute, "that I must dance with every one of them. So you see . . . Oh, there he is now, over there! I've been wondering where he's been keeping himself." She nodded toward the entrance and prattled on artlessly. "He's almost *never* late, you know, and I've . . ."

He looked, and as his eyes met those of the First Lensman, Jill learned three of the facts she needed so badly to know. Her father. Here. Soon. She never knew how she managed to keep herself under control; but, some way and just barely, she did.

Although nothing showed, she was seething inwardly: wrought up as she had never before been. What could she do? She *knew*, but she did not have a scrap or an iota of visible or tangible evidence; and if she made one single slip, however slight, the consequences could be immediate and disastrous.

After this dance might be too late. She could make an excuse to leave the floor, but that would look very bad, later . . . and none of them would Lens her, she knew, while she was with Herkimer—*damn* such chivalry!

... She *could* take the chance of waving at her father, since she hadn't seen him for so long ... no, the smallest risk would be with Mase. He looked at her every chance he got, and she'd *make* him use his Lens ...

Northrop looked at her; and over Herkimer's shoulder, for one fleeting instant, she allowed her face to reveal the terrified appeal she so keenly felt.

"Want me, Jill?" His Lensed thought touched only the outer fringes of her mind. Full rapport is more intimate than a kiss: no one except her father had ever really put a Lens on Virgilia Samms. Nevertheless:

"*Want* you! I never wanted anybody so much in my life! Come in, Mase—quick—*please!*"

Diffidently enough, he came; but at the first inkling of the girl's news all thought of diffidence or of privacy vanished.

"Jack! Spud! Mr. Kinnison! Mr. Samms!" he Lensed sharp, imperative, almost frantic thoughts. "Listen in!"

"Steady, Mase, I'll take over," came Roderick Kinnison's deeper, quieter mental voice. "First, the matter of guns. Anybody except me wearing a pistol? You are, Spud?"

"Yes, sir."

"You would be. But you and Mase, Jack?"

"We've got our Lewistons!"

"You would have. Blasters, my sometimes-not-quite-so-bright son, are fine weapons indeed for certain kinds of work. In emergencies, it is of course permissible to kill a few dozen innocent bystanders. In such a crowd as this, though, it is much better technique to kill only the one you are aiming at. So skip out to my car, you two, right now, and change—and make it *fast.*" Everyone knew that Roderick Kinnison's car was at all times an arsenal on wheels. "Wish you were in uniform, too, Virge, but it can't be helped now. Work your way—*slowly*—around to the northwest corner. Spud, do the same."

"It's impossible—starkly unthinkable!" and "I'm not *sure* of anything, really ..." Samms and his daughter began simultaneously to protest.

"Virgil, you talk like a man with a paper nose. Keep still until after you've used your brain. And I'm sure enough of what you know, Jill, to take plenty of steps. You can relax now—take it easy. We're covering Virgil and I called up support in force. You *can* relax a little, I see. Good! I'm not trying to hide from anybody that the next few minutes may be critical. Are you pretty sure, Jill, that Herkimer is a key man?"

"Pretty sure, Pops." *How* much better she felt, now that the Lensmen were on guard! "In this one case, at least."

"Good! Then let him talk you into giving him every dance, right straight through until something breaks. Watch him. He must know the signal and who is going to operate, and if you can give us a fraction of a second of warning it will help no end. Can do?''

"I'll say I can—and I would love to, the big, slimy, stinking skinker!" As transliterated into words, the girl's thought may seem a trifle confused, but Kinnison knew exactly what she meant.

"One more thing, Jill; a detail. The boys are coming back in and are working their partners over this way. See if Herkimer notices that they have changed their holsters.''

"No, he didn't notice," Jill reported, after a moment. "But I don't notice any difference, either, and I'm looking for it.''

"Nevertheless, it's there, and the difference between a Mark Seventeen and a Mark Five is something more than that between Tweedledum and Tweedledee," Kinnison returned, dryly. "However, it may not be as obvious to nonmilitary personnel as it is to us. That's far enough, boys, don't get too close. Now, Virge, keep solidly en rapport with Jill on one side and with us on the other, so that she won't have to give herself and the show away by yelling and pointing, and . . ."

"But this is preposterous!" Samms stormed.

"Preposterous, hell," Roderick Kinnison's thought was still coldly level; only the fact that he was beginning to use non-ballroom language revealed any sign of the strain he was under. "Stop being so goddam heroic and start using your brain. You turned down fifty billion credits. Why do you suppose they offered that much, when they can get anybody killed for a hundred? And what would they do about it?''

"But they couldn't get away with it, Rod, at an Ambassadors' Ball. They *couldn't*, possibly.''

"Formerly, no. That was my first thought, too. But it was you who pointed out to me, not so long ago, that the techniques of crime have changed of late. In the new light, the swankier the brawl the greater the confusion and the better the chance of getting away clean. Comb *that* out of your whiskers, you red-headed mule!''

"Well . . . there might be something in it, after all . . ." Samms' thought showed apprehension at last.

"You know damn well there is. But you boys—Jack and Mase especially—loosen up. You can't do good shooting while you're strung up like a couple of cocoons. Do something—talk to your partners or think at Jill . . ."

"That won't be hard, sir." Mason Northrop grinned feebly. "And that reminds me of something, Jill. Mentor certainly bracketed the target when he—or she, or it, maybe—said that you would never need a Lens.''

"Huh?" Jill demanded, inelegantly. "I don't see the connection, if any."

"No? Everybody else does, I'll bet. How about it?" The other Lensmen, even Samms, agreed enthusiastically. "Well, do you think that any of those characters, particularly Herkimer Herkimer Third, would let a harness bull in harness—even such a beautiful one as you—get close enough to him to do such a Davey the Dip act on his mind?"

"Oh . . . I never thought of that, but it's right, and I'm glad . . . but Pops, you said something about 'support in force'. Have you any idea how long it will be? I *hope* I can hold out, with you all supporting me, but . . ."

"You can, Jill. Two or three minutes more, at most."

"Support? In force? What do you mean?" Samms snapped.

"Just that. The whole damned army," Kinnison replied. "I sent Two-Star Commodore Alexander Clayton a thought that lifted him right out of his chair. Everything he's got, at full emergency blast. Armor—mark eighty fours—six by six extra heavies—a ninety sixty for an ambulance—full escort, upstairs and down—way-friskers—'copters—cruisers and big stuff—in short, the works. I would have run with you before this, if I dared; but the minute the relief party shows up, we do a flit."

"If you *dared?*" Jill asked, shaken by the thought.

"Exactly, my dear. I don't dare. If they start anything we'll do our damndest, but I'm praying they won't."

But Kinnison's prayers—if he made any—were ignored. Jill heard a sharp, but very usual and insignificant sound; someone had dropped a pencil. She felt an inconspicuous muscle twitch slightly. She saw the almost imperceptible tensing of a neck-muscle which would have turned Herkimer's head in a certain direction if it had been allowed to act. Her eyes flashed along that line, searched busily for milliseconds. A man was reaching unobstrusively, as though for a handkerchief. But men at Ambassadors' Balls do not carry blue handkerchiefs; nor does any fabric, however dyed, resemble at all closely the blued steel of an automatic pistol.

Jill would have screamed, then, and pointed; but she had time to do neither. Through her rapport with her father the Lensmen saw everything that she saw, in the instant of her seeing it. Hence five shots blasted out, practically as one, before the girl could scream, or point, or even move. She did scream, then; but since dozens of other women were screaming, too, it made no difference—then.

Conway Costigan, trigger-nerved spacehound that he was and with years of gun-fighting and of hand-to-hand brawling in his log, shot first; even before the gunman did. It was Costigan's blinding speed that saved

Virgil Samms' life that day; for the would-be assassin was dying, with a heavy slug crashing through his brain, before he finished pulling the trigger. The dying hand twitched upward. The bullet intended for Samms' heart went high; through the fleshy part of the shoulder.

Roderick Kinnison, because of his age, and his son and Northrop, because of their inexperience, were a few milliseconds slow. They, however, were aiming for the body, not for the head; and any of those three resulting wounds would have been satisfactorily fatal. The man went down, and stayed down.

Samms staggered, but did not go down until the elder Kinnison, as gently as was consistent with the maximum of speed, threw him down. "Stand back! Get back! Give him air!" Men began to shout, the while pressing closer themselves.

"You men, stand back. Some of you go get a stretcher. You women, come here." Kinnison's heavy, parade-ground voice smashed down all lesser noises. "Is there a doctor here?"

There was; and, after being "frisked" for weapons, he went busily to work.

"Joy—Betty—Jill—Clio," Kinnison called his own wife and their daughter, Virgilia Samms, and Mrs. Costigan. "You four first. Now you—and you—and you—and you . . ." he went on, pointing out large, heavy women wearing extremely extreme gowns, "Stand here, right over him. Cover him up, so that nobody else can get a shot at him. You other women, stand behind and between these—closer yet—fill those spaces up solid—there! Jack, stand there. Mase, there. Costigan, the other end; I'll take this one. Now, everybody, listen. I know damn well that none of you women are wearing guns above the waist, and you've all got long skirts—thank God for ballgowns! Now, fellows, if any one of these women makes a move to lift her skirt, blow her brains out, right then, without waiting to ask questions."

"Sir, I protest! This is outrageous!" one of the dowagers exclaimed.

"Madam, I agree with you fully. It is." Kinnison smiled as genuinely as he could under the circumstances. "It is, however, *necessary*. I will apologize to all you ladies, and to you, doctor—in writing if you like— after we have Virgil Samms aboard the *Chicago*; but until then I would not trust my own grandmother."

The doctor looked up. "The *Chicago*? This wound does not appear to be a very serious one, but this man is going to a hospital at once. Ah, the stretcher. So . . . please . . . easy . . . there, that is excellent. Call an ambulance, please, immediately."

"I did. Long ago. But no hospital, doctor. All those windows—open to the public—or the whole place bombed—by no means. I'm taking no chances whatever.''

"Except with your own life!'' Jill put in sharply, looking up from her place at her father's side. Assured that the First Lensman was in no danger of dying, she had begun to take interest in other things. "You are important, too, you know, and you're standing right out there in the open. Get another stretcher, lie down on it, and we'll guard you, too . . . and don't be too stiff-necked to take your own advice!'' she flared, as he hesitated.

"I'm not, if it were necessary, but it isn't. If they had killed him, yes. I'd probably be next in line. But since he got only a scratch, there'd be no point at all in killing even a *good* Number Two.''

"A *scratch!*'' Jill fairly seethed. "Do you call that horrible wound a *scratch?*''

"Huh? Why, certainly—that's all it is—thanks to you,'' he returned, in honest and complete surprise. "No bones shattered—no main arteries cut—missed the lung—he'll be as good as new in a couple of weeks.''

"And now,'' he went on aloud, "if you ladies will please pick up this stretcher we will move en masse, and *slowly*, toward the door.''

The women, no longer indignant but apparently enjoying the sensation of being the center of interest, complied with the request.

"Now, boys,'' Kinnison Lensed a thought. "Did any of you—Costigan?—see any signs of a concerted rush, such as there would have been to get the killer away if we hadn't interfered?''

"No, sir,'' came Costigan's brisk reply. "None within sight of me.''

"Jack and Mase—I don't suppose you looked?''

They hadn't—had not thought of it in time.

"You'll learn. It takes a few things like this to make it automatic. But I couldn't see any, either, so I'm fairly certain there wasn't any. Smart operators—quick on the uptake.''

"I'd better get at this, sir, don't you think, and let Operation Boskone go for a while?'' Costigan asked.

"I don't think so.'' Kinnison frowned in thought. "This operation was *planned*, son, by people with brains. Any clues you could find now would undoubtedly be plants. No, we'll let the regulars look; we'll stick to our own . . .''

Sirens wailed and screamed outside. Kinnison sent out an exploring thought.

"Alex?''

"Yes. Where do you want this ninety-sixty with the doctors and nurses? It's too wide for the gates.''

"Go through the wall. Across the lawn. Right up to the door, and never mind the frippery they've got all over the place—have your adjutant tell them to bill us for damage. Samms is shot in the shoulder. Not too serious, but I'm taking him to the Hill, where I know he'll be safe. What have you got on top of the umbrella, the *Boise* or the *Chicago?* I haven't had time to look up yet."

"Both."

"Good man."

Jack Kinnison stared at the monstrous tank, which was smashing statues, fountains, and ornamental trees flat into the earth as it moved ponderously across the grounds, and licked his lips. He looked at the companies of soldiers "frisking" the route, the grounds, and the crowd—higher up, at the hovering helicopters—still higher, at the eight light cruisers so evidently and so viciously ready to blast—higher still, at the long streamers of fire which, he now knew, marked the locations of the two most powerful engines of destruction ever built by man—and his face turned slowly white.

"Good Lord, Dad!" he swallowed twice. "I had no idea . . . but they might, at that."

"Not 'might', son. They damn well would, if they could get here soon enough with heavy enough stuff." The elder Kinnison's jaw-muscles did not loosen, his darting eyes did not relax their vigilance for a fraction of a second as he Lensed the thought. "You boys can't be expected to know it all, but right now you're learning fast. Get this— paste it in your iron hats. *Virgil Samms' life is the most important thing in this whole damned universe!* If they had got him then it would not, strictly speaking, have been my fault, but if they get him now, it will be."

The land cruiser crunched to a stop against the very entrance, and a white-clad man leaped out.

"Let me look at him, please . . ."

"Not yet!" Kinnison denied, sharply. "Not until he's got four inches of solid steel between him and whoever wants to finish the job they started. Get your men around him, and get him aboard—fast!"

Samms, protected at every point at every instant, was lifted into the maw of the ninety-sixty; and as the massive door clanged shut Kinnison heaved a tremendous sigh of relief. The cavalcade moved away.

"Coming with us, Rod?" Commodore Clayton shouted.

"Yes, but got a couple minutes' work here yet. Have a staff car wait for me, and I'll join you." He turned to the three young Lensmen and the girl. "This fouls up our plans a little, but not too much—I hope. No change in Mateese or Boskone; you and Costigan, Jill, can go ahead as planned. Northrop, you'll have to brief Jill on Zwilnik and find out what she knows. Virgil was going to do it tonight, after the brawl here, but you know as much about it now as any of us. Check with Knobos, DalNalten, and Fletcher—while Virgil is laid up you and Jack may have to work on both Zabriska and Zwilnik—he'll Lens you. Get the dope, then do as you think best. Get going!" He strode away toward the waiting staff-car.

"Boskone? Zwilnik?" Jill demanded. "What gives? What are they, Jack?"

"We don't know yet—maybe we're going to name a couple of planets . . ."

"Piffle!" she scoffed. "Can *you* talk sense, Mase? What's Boskone?"

"A simple, distinctive, pronounceable coined word; suggested, I believe, by Dr. Bergenholm . . ." he began.

"You know what I mean, you . . ." she broke in, but was silenced by a sharply Lensed thought from Jack. His touch was very light, barely sufficient to make conversation possible; but even so, she flinched.

"Use your brain, Jill; you aren't thinking a lick—not that you can be blamed for it. Stop talking; there may be lip-readers or high-powered listeners around. This feels funny, doesn't it?" He twitched mentally and went on: "You already know what Operation Mateese is, since it's your own dish—politics. Operation Zwilnik is drugs, vice, and so on. Operation Boskone is pirates; Spud is running that. Operation Zabriska is Mase and me checking some peculiar disturbances in the sub-ether. Come in, Mase, and do your stuff—I'll see you later, aboard. Clear ether, Jill!"

Young Kinnison vanished from the fringes of her mind and Northrop appeared. And what a difference! His mind touched hers as gingerly as Jack's had done; as skittishly, as instantaneously ready to bolt away from anything in the least degree private. However, Jack's mind had rubbed hers the wrong way, right from the start—and Mase's didn't!

"Now, about this Operation Zwilnik," Jill began.

"Something else first. I couldn't help noticing, back there, that you and Jack . . . well, not out of phase, exactly, or really out of sync, but sort of . . . well, as though . . ."

" 'Hunting'?" she suggested.

"Not exactly . . . 'forcing' might be better—like holding a tight beam together when it wants to fall apart. So you noticed it yourself?"

"Of course, but I thought Jack and I were the only ones who did. Like scratching a blackboard with your fingernails—you *can* do it, but you're awfully glad to stop . . . and I *like* Jack, too, darn it—at a distance."

"And you and I fit like precisely tuned circuits. Jack really meant it, then, when he said that you ... that is, he ... I didn't quite believe it until now, but if ... you know, of course, what you've already done to me."

Jill's block went on, full strength. She arched her eyebrows and spoke aloud—"why, I haven't the *faintest* idea!"

"Of course not. That's why you're using voice. I've found out, too, that I can't lie with my mind. I feel like a heel and a louse, with so much job ahead, but you've simply got to tell me something. Then—whatever you say—I'll hit the job with everything I've got. Do I get heaved out between planets without a space-suit, or not?"

"I don't think so." Jill blushed vividly, but her voice was steady. "You would rate a space-suit, and enough oxygen to reach another plan—another goal. And now we'd better get to work, don't you think?"

"Yes. Thanks, Jill, a million. I know as well as you do that I was talking out of turn, and how much—but I had to know." He breathed deep. "And that's all I ask—for now. Cut your screens."

She lowered her mental barriers, finding it surprisingly easy to do so in this case; let them down almost as far as she was in the habit of doing with her father. He explained in flashing thoughts everything he knew of the four Operations, concluding:

"I'm not assigned to Zabriska permanently; I'll probably work with you on Mateese after your father gets back into circulation. I'm to act more as a liaison man—neither Knobos nor DalNalten knows you well enough to Lens you. Right?"

"Yes, I've met Mr. Knobos only once, and have never even seen Dr. DalNalten."

"Ready to visit them, via Lens?"

"Yes. Go ahead."

The two Lensmen came in. They came into his mind, not hers. Nevertheless their thoughts, superimposed upon Northrop's, came to the girl as clearly as though all four were speaking to each other face to face.

"What a *weird* sensation!" Jill exclaimed. "Why, I never *imagined* anything like it!"

"We are sorry to trouble you, Miss Samms ..." Jill was surprised anew. The silent voice deep within her mind was of characteristically Martian timber, but instead of the harshly guttural consonants and the hissing sibilants of any Martian's best efforts at English, pronunciation and enunciation were flawless.

"Oh, I didn't mean that. It's no trouble at all, really, I just haven't got used to this telepathy yet."

"None of us has, to any noticeable degree. But the reason for this call is to ask you if you have anything new, however slight, to add to our very small knowledge of Zwilnik?"

"Very little, I'm afraid; and that little is mostly guesses, deductions, and jumpings at conclusions. Father told you about the way I work, I suppose?"

"Yes. Exact data is not to be expected. Hints, suggestions, possible leads, will be of inestimable value."

"Well, I met a very short, very fat Venerian, named Ossmen, at a party at the European Embassy. Do either of you know him?"

"I know of him," DalNalten replied. "A highly reputable merchant, with such large interests on Tellus that he has to spend most of his time here. He is not in any one of our books . . . although there is nothing at all surprising in that fact. Go on, please, Miss Samms."

"He didn't come to the party with Senator Morgan; but he came to some kind of an agreement with him that night, and I am pretty sure that it was about thionite. That's the only new item I have."

"*Thionite!*" The three Lensmen were equally surprised.

"Yes. Thionite. Definitely."

"How *sure* are you of this, Miss Samms?" Knobos asked, in deadly earnest.

"I am not *sure* that this particular agreement was about thionite, no; but the probability is roughly nine-tenths. I *am* sure, however, that both Senator Morgan and Ossmen know a lot about thionite that they want to hide. Both gave very high positive reactions—well beyond the six-sigma point of virtual certainty."

There was a pause, broken by the Martian, but not by a thought directed at any one of the three.

"Sid!" he called, and even Jill could feel the Lensed thought speed.

"Yes, Knobos? Fletcher."

"That haul-in you made, out in the asteroids. Heroin, hadive, and ladolian, wasn't it? No thionite involved anywhere?"

"No thionite. However, you must remember that part of the gang got away, so all I can say positively is that we didn't see, or hear about, any thionite. There was some gossip, of course; but you know there always is."

"Of course. Thanks, Sid." Jill could feel the brilliant Martian's mental gears whirl and click. Then he went into such a flashing exchange of thought with the Venerian that the girl lost track in seconds.

"One more question, Miss Samms?" DalNalten asked. "Have you detected any indications that there may be some connection between either Ossmen or Morgan and any officer or executive of Interctellar Spaceways?''

"*Spaceways!* Isaacson?'' Jill caught her breath. "Why . . . nobody even thought of such a thing—at least, nobody ever mentioned it to me—I never thought of making any such tests.''

"The possibility occurred to me only a moment ago, at your mention of thionite. The connection, if any exists, will be exceedingly difficult to trace. But since most, if not all, of the parties involved will probably be included in your Operation Mateese, and since a finding, either positive or negative, would be tremendously significant, we feel emboldened to ask you to keep this point in mind.''

"Why, of course I will. I'll be very glad to.''

"We thank you for your courtesy and your help. One or both of us will get in touch with you from time to time, now that we know the pattern of your personality. May immortal Grolossen speed the healing of your father's wound.''

7

BATTLE OF THE HILL

Late that night—or, rather, very early the following morning—Senator Morgan and his Number One secretary were closeted in the former's doubly spy-ray-proofed office. Morgan's round, heavy, florid face had perhaps lost a little of its usual color; the fingers of his left hand drummed soundlessly upon the glass top of his desk. His shrewd gray eyes, however, were as keen and as calculating as ever.

"This things smells, Herkimer ... it *reeks* ... but I *still* can't figure any of the angles. That operation was *planned*. Sure fire, it *couldn't* miss. Right up to the last split second it worked perfectly. Then—blooie! A flat bust. The Patrol landed and everything was under control. There *must* have been a leak somewhere—but where in hell could it have been?''

"There couldn't have been a leak, Chief; it doesn't make sense.'' The secretary uncrossed his long legs, recrossed them in the other direction, threw away a half-smoked cigarette, lit another. "If there'd been any kind of a leak they would have done a lot more than just kill the low man on the ladder. You know as well as I do that Rocky Kinnison is the hardest-boiled character this side of hell. If he had known anything, he would have killed everybody in sight, including you and me. Besides, if there had been a leak, he would not have let Samms get within ten thousand miles of the place—that's one sure thing. Another is he wouldn't have waited until after it was all over to get his army there. No Chief, there couldn't have been a leak. Whatever Samms or Kinnison found out—probably Samms, he's a hell of a lot smarter than Kinnison is, you know—he learned right there and then. He must have seen Brainerd start to pull his gun.''

"I thought of that. I'd buy it, except for one fact. Apparently you didn't time the interval between the shots and the arrival of the tanks."

"Sorry, Chief." Herkimer's face was a study in chagrin. "I made a bad slip there."

"I'll say you did. One minute and fifty eight seconds."

"*What!*"

Morgan remained silent.

"The patrol is fast, of course . . . and always ready . . . and they would yank the stuff in on tractor beams, not under their own power . . . but even so . . . five minutes, is my guess, Chief. Four and a half, absolute minimum."

"Check. And where do you go from there?"

"I see your point. I don't. That blows everything wide open. One set of facts says there was a leak, which occurred between two and a half and three minutes before the signal was given. I ask you, Chief, does that make sense?"

"No. That's what is bothering me. As you say, the facts seem to be contradictory. Somebody must have learned something before anything happened; but if they did, why didn't they do more? And Murgatroyd. If they didn't know about him, why the ships—especially the big battlewagons? If they did think he might be out there somewhere, why didn't they go and find out?"

"Now I'll ask one. Why didn't our Mr. Murgatroyd do something? Or wasn't the pirate fleet supposed to be in on this? Probably not, though."

"My guess would be the same as yours. Can't see any reason for having a fleet cover a one-man operation, especially as well-planned a one as this was. But that's none of our business. These Lensmen are. I was watching them every second. Neither Samms nor Kinnison did anything whatever during that two minutes."

"Young Kinnison and Northrop each left the hall about that time."

"I know it. So they did. Either one of them *could* have called the Patrol—but what has that to do with the price of beef C.I.F. Valeria?"

Herkimer refrained tactfully from answering the savage question. Morgan drummed and thought for minutes, then went on slowly:

"There are two, and only two, possibilities; neither of which seem even remotely possible. It was—*must* have been—either the Lens or the girl."

"The girl? Act your age, Senator. I knew where *she* was, and what she was doing, every second."

"That was evident." Morgan stopped drumming and smiled cynically. "I'm getting a hell of a kick out of seeing you taking it, for a change, instead of dishing it out."

"Yes?" Herkimer's handsome face hardened. "That game isn't over, my friend."

"That's what *you* think," the Senator jibed. "Can't believe that any woman *can* be Herkimer-proof, eh? You've been working on her for six weeks now, instead of the usual six hours, and you haven't got anywhere yet."

"I will, Senator." Herkimer's nostrils flared viciously. "I'll get her, one way or another, if it's the last thing I ever do."

"I'll give you eight to five you don't; and a six-month time limit."

"I'll take five thousand of that. But what makes you think that she's anything to be afraid of? She's a trained psychologist, yes; but so am I; and I'm older and more experienced than she is. That leaves that yoga stuff—her learning how to sit cross-legged, how to contemplate her navel, and how to try to get in tune with the infinite. How do you figure *that* puts her in my class?"

"I told you, I don't. Nothing makes sense. But she *is* Virgil Samms' daughter."

"What of it? You didn't gag on George Olmstead—you picked him yourself for one of the toughest jobs we've got. By blood he's just about as close to Virgil Samms as Virgilia is. They might as well have been hatched out of the same egg."

"Physically, yes. Mentally and psychologically, no. Olmstead is a realist, a materialist. He wants his reward in this world, not the next, and is out to get it. Furthermore, the job will probably kill him, and even if it doesn't, he will never be in a position of trust or where he can learn much of anything. On the other hand, Virgil Samms is—but I don't need to tell you what *he* is like. But you don't seem to realize that she's just like him—she isn't playing around with you because of your overpowering charm . . ."

"Listen, Chief. She didn't know anything and she didn't do anything. I was dancing with her all the time, as close as that," he clasped his hands tightly together, "so I know what I'm talking about. And if you think she could *ever* learn anything from me, skip it. You know that nobody on Earth, or anywhere else, can read my face; and besides, she was playing coy right then—wasn't even looking at me. So count her out."

"We'll have to, I guess." Morgan resumed his quiet drumming. "If there were any possibility that she pumped you I'd send you to the mines, but there's no sign . . . that leaves the Lens. It has seemed, right

along, more logical than the girl—but a lot more fantastic. Been able
to find out anything more about it?''

"No. Just what they've been advertising. Combination radio-phone,
automatic language-converter, telepath, and so on. Badge of the top
skimmings of the top-bracket cops. But I began to think, out there on
the floor, that they aren't advertising everything they know.''

"So did I. You tell me.''

"Take the time zero minus three minutes. Besides the five Lensmen—
and Jill Samms—the place was full of top brass; scrambled eggs all
over the floor. Commodores and lieutenant-Commodores from all continental governments of the Earth, the other planets, and the colonies,
all wearing full-dress side-arms. Nobody knew anything then; we agree
on that. But within the next few seconds, somebody found out something and called for help. One of the Lensmen could possibly have done
that without showing signs. BUT—at zero time all four Lensmen had
their guns out—and *not* Lewistons, please note—and were shooting;
whereas none of the other armed officers knew that anything was going
on until after it was all over. That puts the finger on the Lens.''

"That's the way I figured it. But the difficulties remain unchanged.
How? Mind-reading?''

"Space-drift!'' Herkimer snorted. "My mind can't be read.''

"Nor mine.''

"And besides, if they could read minds, they wouldn't have waited
until the last possible split second to do it, unless . . . say, wait a minute!
. . . Did Brainerd act or look nervous, toward the last? I wasn't to look
at him, you know.''

"Not nervous, exactly; but he did get a little tense.''

"There you are, then. Hired murderers aren't smart. A Lensman saw
him tighten up and got suspicious. Turned in the alarm on general principles. Warned the others to keep on their toes. But even so, it doesn't
look like mind-reading—they'd have killed him sooner. They were
watchful, and mighty quick on the draw.''

"That could be it. That's about as thin and as specious an explanation
as I ever saw cooked up, but it *does* cover the facts . . . and the two of
us will be able to make it stick . . . but take notice, pretty boy, that
certain parties are not going to like this at all. In fact, they are going to
be very highly put out.''

"That's a nice hunk of understatement, boss. But notice one beautiful
thing about this story?'' Herkimer grinned maliciously. "It lets us pass
the buck to Big Jim Towne. We can be—and will be—sore as hell
because he picks such weak-sister characters to do his killings!''

*   *   *

In the heavily armored improvised ambulance, Virgil Samms sat up and directed a thought at his friend Kinnison, finding his mind a turmoil of confusion.

"What's the matter, Rod?"

"Plenty!" the big Lensman snapped back. "They were—maybe still are—too damn far ahead of us. Something has been going on that we haven't even suspected. I stood by, as innocent as a three-year-old girl baby, and let you walk right into that one—and I emphatically do not enjoy getting caught with my pants down that way. It makes me jumpy. This may be all, but it may not be—not by eleven thousand light-years—and I'm trying to dope out what is going to happen next."

"And what have you deduced?"

"Nothing. I'm stuck. So I'm tossing it into your lap. Besides, that's what you are getting paid for, thinking. So go ahead and think. What would you be doing, if you were on the other side?"

"I see. You think, then, that it might not be good technique to take the time to go back to the spaceport?"

"You get the idea. But—can you stand transfer?"

"Certainly. They got my shoulder dressed and taped, and my arm in a sling. Shock practically all gone. Some pain, but not much. I can walk without falling down."

"Fair enough. Clayton!" He Lensed a vigorous thought. "Have any of the observers spotted anything, high up or far off?"

"No, sir."

"Good. Kinnison to Commodore Clayton, orders. Have a 'copter come down and pick up Samms and myself on tractors. Instruct the *Boise* and the cruisers to maintain utmost vigilance. Instruct the *Chicago* to pick us up. Detach the *Chicago* and the *Boise* from your task force. Assign them to me. Off."

"Clayton to Commissioner Kinnison. Orders received and are being carried out. Off."

The transfers were made without incident. The two superdreadnaughts leaped into the high stratosphere and tore westward. Half-way to the Hill, Kinnison called Dr. Frederick Rodebush.

"Fred? Kinnison. Have Cleve and Bergenholm link up with us. Now—how are the Geigers on the outside of the Hill behaving?"

"Normal, all of them," the physicist-Lensman reported after a moment. "Why?"

Kinnison detailed the happenings of the recent past. "So tell the boys to unlimber all the stuff the Hill has got."

"My God!" Cleveland exclaimed. "Why, that's putting us back to the days of the Interplanetary Wars!"

"With one notable exception," Kinnison pointed out. "The attack, if any, will be strictly modern. I hope we'll be able to handle it. One good thing, the old mountain's got a lot of sheer mass. How much radioactivity will it stand?"

"Allotropic iron, U-235, or plutonium?" Rodebush seized his slide-rule.

"What difference does it make?"

"From a practical standpoint . . . perhaps none. But with a task force defending, not many bombs could get through, so I'd say . . ."

"I wasn't thinking so much of bombs."

"What, then?"

"Isotopes. A good, thick blanket of dust. Slow-speed, fine stuff that neither our ships nor the Hill's screens could handle. We've got to decide, first, whether Virgil will be safer there in the Hill or out in space in the *Chicago;* and second, for how long."

"I see . . . I'd say here, *under* the Hill. Months, perhaps years, before anything could work down this far. And we can *always* get out. No matter how hot the surface gets, we've got enough screen, heavy water, cadmium, lead, mercury, and everything else necessary to get him out through the locks."

"That's what I was hoping you'd say. And now, about the defense . . . I wonder . . . I don't want everybody to think I've gone completely hysterical, but I'll be damned if I want to get caught again with . . ." His thought faded out.

"May I offer a suggestion, sir?" Bergenholm's thought broke the prolonged silence.

"I'd be very glad to have it—your suggestions so far haven't been idle vaporings. Another hunch?"

"No, sir, a logical procedure. It has been some months since the last emergency call-out drill was held. If you issue such another call now, and nothing happens, it can be simply another surprise drill; with credit, promotion, and monetary awards for the best performances; further practice and instruction for the less proficient units."

"Splendid, Dr. Bergenholm!" Samms' brilliant and agile mind snatched up the thought and carried it along. "And what a chance, Rod, for something vastly larger and more important than a Continental, or even a Tellurian, drill—make it the first maneuver of the Galactic Patrol!"

"I'd like to, Virge, but we can't. My boys are ready, but you aren't. No top appointments and no authority."

"That can be arranged in a very few minutes. We have been waiting for the psychological moment. This, especially if trouble should develop, is the time. You yourself expect an attack, do you not?''

"Yes. I would not start anything unless and until I was ready to finish it, and I see no reason for assuming that whoever it was that tried to kill you is not at least as good a planner as I am.''

"And the rest of you . . . ? Dr. Bergenholm?''

"My reasoning, while it does not exactly parallel that of Commissioner Kinnison, leads to the same conclusion; that an attack in great force is to be expected.''

"Not *exactly* parallel?'' Kinnison demanded. "In what respects?''

"You do not seem to have considered the possibility, Commissioner, that the proposed assassination of First Lensman Samms could very well have been only the first step in a comprehensive operation.''

"I didn't . . . and it *could* have been. So go ahead, Virge, with . . .''

The thought was never finished, for Samms had already gone ahead. Simultaneously, it seemed, the minds of eight other Lensmen joined the group of Tellurians. Samms, intensely serious, spoke aloud to his friend:

"The Galactic Council is now assembled. Do you, Roderick K. Kinnison, promise to uphold, in as much as you conscientiously can and with all that in you lies, the authority of this Council throughout all space?''

"I promise.''

"By virtue of the authority vested in me its president by the Galactic Council, I appoint you Port Admiral of the Galactic Patrol. My fellow councillors are now inducting the armed forces of their various solar systems into the Galactic Patrol . . . It will not take long . . . There, you may make your appointments and issue orders for the mobilization.''

The two superdreadnaughts were now approaching the Hill. The *Boise* stayed "up on top''; the *Chicago* went down. Kinnison, however, paid very little attention to the landing or to Samms' disembarkation, and none whatever to the *Chicago's* reascent into the high heavens. He knew that everything was under control; and, now alone in his cabin, he was busy.

"All personnel of all armed forces just inducted into the Galactic Patrol, attention!'' He spoke into an ultra-wave microphone, the familiar parade-ground rasp very evident in his deep and resonant voice. "Kinnison of Tellus, Port Admiral, speaking. Each of you has taken oath to the Galactic Patrol?''

They had.

"At ease. The organization chart already in your hands is made effective as of now. Enter in your logs the date and time. Promotions: Commodore Clayton of North America, Tellus . . .''

In his office at New York Spaceport Clayton came to attention and saluted crisply; his eyes shining, his deeply-scarred face alight.

". . . to be Admiral of the First Galactic Region. Commodore Schweikert of Europe, Tellus . . ."

In Berlin a narrow-waisted, almost foppish-seeming man, with roached blond hair and blue eyes, bowed stiffly from the waist and saluted punctiliously.

". . . to be Lieutenant-Admiral of the First Galactic Region."

And so on, down the list. A marshal and a lieutenant-marshal of the Solarian System; a general and a lieutenant-general of the planet Sol Three. Promotions, agreed upon long since, to fill the high offices thus vacated. Then the list of commodores upon other planets—Guindlos of Redland, Mars; Sesseffsen of Thalleron, Venus; Raymond of the Jovian Sub-System; Newman of Alphacent; Walters of Sirius; vanMeeter of Valeria; Adams of Procyon; Roberts of Altair; Barrtell of Fomalhout; Armand of Vega; and Coigne of Aldebaran—each of whom was actually the commander-in-chief of the armed forces of a world. Each of these was made general of his planet.

"Except for lieutenant-commodores and up, who will tune their minds to me—dismissed!" Kinnison stopped talking and went onto his Lens.

"That was for the record. I don't need to tell you, fellows, how glad I am to be able to do this. You're tops, all of you—I don't know of anybody I'd rather have at my back when the ether gets rough . . ."

"Right back at you, chief!" "Same to you, Rod!" "Rocky Rod, Port Admiral!" "Now we're blasting!" came a melange of thoughts. Those splendid men, with whom he had shared so much of danger and of stress, were all as jubilant as schoolboys.

"But the thing that makes this possible may also make it necessary for us to go to work; to earn your extra stars and my wheel." Kinnison smothered the welter of thoughts and outlined the situation, concluding: "So you see it may turn out to be only a drill—but on the other hand, since the outfit is big enough to have built a war-fleet alone, if it wanted one, and since it may have had a lot of first-class help that none of us knows anything about, we may be in for the damndest battle that any of us ever saw. So come prepared for *anything*. I am now going back onto voice, for the record.

"Kinnison to the commanding officers of all fleets, subfleets, and task-forces of the Galactic Patrol. Information. Subject, tactical problem; defense of the Hill against a postulated Black Fleet of unknown size, strength, and composition; of unknown nationality or origin; coming from an unknown direction in space at an unknown time.

"Kinnison to Admiral Clayton. Orders. Take over. I am relinquishing command of the *Boise* and the *Chicago.*"

"Clayton to Port Admiral Kinnison. Orders received. Taking over. I am at the *Chicago*'s main starboard lock. I have instructed Ensign Masterson, the commanding officer of this gig, to wait; that he is to take you down to the Hill."

"WHAT? Of all the damned..." This was a thought, and unrecorded.

"Sorry, Rod—I'm sorry as hell, and I'd like no end to have you along." This, too, was a thought. "But that's the way it is. Ordinary Admirals ride the ether with their fleets. Port Admirals stay aground. I report to you, and you run things—in broad—by remote control."

"I see." Kinnison then Lensed a fuming thought at Samms. "Alex *couldn't* do this to me—and wouldn't—and knows damn well that I'd burn him to a crisp if he had the guts to try it. So it's *your* doing—what in hell's the big idea?"

"Who's being heroic now, Rod?" Samms asked, quietly. "Use *your* brain. And then come down here, where you belong."

And Kinnison, after a long moment of rebellious thought and with as much grace as he could muster, came down. Down not only to the Patrol's familiar offices, but down into the deepest crypts beneath them. He was glum enough, and bitter, at first: but he found much to do. Grand Fleet Headquarters—*his* headquarters—was being organized, and the best efforts of the best minds and of the best technologists of three worlds were being devoted to the task of strengthening the already extremely strong defenses of THE HILL. And in a very short time the plates of GFHQ showed that Admiral Clayton and Lieutenant-Admiral Schweikert were doing a very nice job.

All of the really heavy stuff was of Earth, the Mother Planet, and was already in place; as were the less numerous and much lighter contingents of Mars, of Venus, and of Jove. And the fleets of the outlying solar systems—cutters, scouts, and a few light cruisers—were neither maintaining fleet formation nor laying course for Sol. Instead, each individual vessel was blasting at maximum for the position in space in which it would form one unit of a formation englobing at a distance of light-years the entire Solarian System, and each of those hurtling hundreds of ships was literally combing all circumambient space with its furiously-driven detector beams.

"Nice." Kinnison turned to Samms, now beside him at the master plate. "Couldn't have done any better myself."

"After you get it made, what are you going to do with it in case nothing happens?'' Samms was still somewhat skeptical. ''How long can you make a drill last?''

''Until all the ensigns have long gray whiskers if I have to, but don't worry—if we have time to get the preliminary globe made I'll be the surprisedest man in the system.''

And Kinnison was not surprised; before full englobement was accomplished, a loud-speaker gave tongue.

''Flagship *Chicago* to Grand Fleet Headquarters!'' it blatted, sharply. ''The Black Fleet has been detected. RA twelve hours, declination plus twenty degrees, distance about thirty light-years . . .''

Kinnison started to say something; then, by main force, shut himself up. He wanted intensely to take over, to tell the boys out there exactly what to do, but he couldn't. He was now a Big Shot—damn the luck! He could be and must be responsible for broad policy and for general strategy, but, once those vitally important decisions had been made, the actual work would have to be done by others. He didn't like it—but there it was. Those flashing thoughts took only an instant of time.

''. . . which is such extreme range that no estimate of strength or composition can be made at present. We will keep you informed.''

''Acknowledge,'' he ordered Randolph; who, wearing now the five silver bars of major, was his Chief Communications Officer. ''No instructions.''

He turned to his plate. Clayton hadn't had to be told to pull in his light stuff; it was all pelting hell-for-leather for Sol and Tellus. Three general plans of battle had been mapped out by Staff. Each had its advantages—and its disadvantages. Operation Acorn—long distance—would be fought at, say, twelve light-years. It would keep everything, particularly the big stuff, away from the Hill, and would make automatics *useless* . . . unless some got past, or *unless* the automatics were coming in on a sneak course, or *unless* several other things—in any one of which cases *what* a God-awful shellacking the Hill would take!

He grinned wryly at Samms, who had been following his thought, and quoted: ''A vast hemisphere of lambent violet flame, through which neither material substance nor destructive ray can pass.''

''Well, that dedicatory statement, while perhaps a bit florid, was strictly true at the time—before the days of allotropic iron and of polycyclic drills. Now I'll quote one: 'Nothing is permanent except change.' ''

''Uh-huh,'' and Kinnison returned to his thinking. Operation Adack. Middle distance. Uh-uh. He didn't like it any better now than he had before, even though some of the Big Brains of Staff thought it the ideal solution. A compromise. All of the disadvantages of both of the others, and none of the advantages of either. It *still* stunk, and unless the Black fleet had an utterly fantastic composition Operation Adack was out.

And Virgil Samms, quietly smoking a cigarette, smiled inwardly. Rod the Rock could scarcely be expected to be in favor of any sort of compromise.

That left Operation Affick. Close up. It had three tremendous advantages. First, the Hill's own offensive weapons—as long as they lasted. Second, the new Rodebush-Bergenholm fields. Third, no sneak attack could be made without detection and interception. It had one tremendous disadvantage; some stuff, and probably a lot of it, would get through. Automatics, robots, guided missiles equipped with superspeed drives, with polycyclic drills, and with atomic warheads strong enough to shake the whole world.

But with those new fields, shaking the world wouldn't be enough; in order to get deep enough to reach Virgil Samms they would damn near have to destroy the world. Could *anybody* build a bomb that powerful? He didn't think so. Earth technology was supreme throughout all known space; of Earth technologists the North Americans were, and always had been, tops. Grant that the Black Fleet was, basically, North American. Grant further that they had a man as good as Adlington—or that they could spy-ray Adlington's brain and laboratories and shops—a tall order. Adlington himself was several months away from a world-wrecker, unless he could put one a hundred miles down before detonation, which simply was not feasible. He turned to Samms.

"It'll be Affick, Virge, unless they've got a composition that is radically different from anything I ever saw put into space."

"So? I can't say that I am very much surprised."

The calm statement and the equally calm reply were beautifully characteristic of the two men. Kinnison had not asked, nor had Samms offered, advice. Kinnison, after weighing the facts, made his decision. Samms, calmly certain that the decision was the best that could be made upon the data available, accepted it without question or criticism.

"We've still got a minute or two," Kinnison remarked. "Don't quite know what to make of their line of approach. Coma Berenices. I don't know of anything at all out that way, do you? They could have detoured, though."

"No, I don't." Samms frowned in thought. "Probably a detour."

"Check." Kinnison turned to Randolph. "Tell them to report whatever they know; we can't wait any . . ."

As he was speaking the report came in.

The Black Fleet was of more or less normal make-up; considerably larger than the North American contingent, but decidedly inferior to the Patrol's present Grand Fleet. Either three or four capital ships . . .

"And we've got six!" Kinnison said, exultantly. "Our own two, Asia's *Himalaya*, Africa's *Johannesburg*, South America's *Bolivar*, and Europe's *Europa*."

. . . Battle cruisers and heavy cruisers, about in the usual proportions; but an unusually high ratio of scouts and light cruisers. There were either two or three large ships which could not be classified definitely at that distance; long-range observers were going out to study them.

"Tell Clayton," Kinnison instructed Randolph, "that it is to be Operation Affick, and for him to fly at it."

"Report continued," the speaker came to life again. "There are three capital ships, apparently of approximately the *Chicago* class, but teardrop-shaped instead of spherical . . ."

"Ouch!" Kinnison flashed a thought at Samms. "I don't like that. They can both fight and run."

". . . The battle cruisers are also tear-drops. The small vessels are torpedo-shaped. There are three of the large ships, which we are still not able to classify definitely. They are spherical in shape, and very large, but do not seem to be either armed or screened, and are apparently carriers—possibly of automatics. We are now making contact—off!"

Instead of looking at the plates before them, the two Lensmen went en rapport with Clayton, so that they could see everything he saw. The stupendous Cone of Battle had long since been formed; the word to fire was given in a measured two-second call. Every firing officer in every Patrol ship touched his stud in the same split second. And from the gargantuan mouth of the Cone there spewed a miles-thick column of energy so raw, so stark, so incomprehensibly violent that it must have been seen to be even dimly appreciated. It simply cannot be described.

Its prototype, Triplanetary's Cylinder of Annihilation, had been a highly effective weapon indeed. The offensive beams of the fish-shaped Nevian cruisers of the void were even more powerful. The Cleveland-Rodebush projectors, developed aboard the original *Boise* on the long Nevian way, were stronger still. The composite beam projected by this fleet of the Galactic Patrol, however, was the sublimation and quintessence of each of these, redesigned and redesigned by scientists and engineers of ever-increasing knowledge, rebuilt and rebuilt by technologists of ever-increasing skill.

Capital ships and a few of the heaviest cruisers could mount screen generators able to carry that frightful load; but every smaller ship caught in that semi-solid rod of indescribably incandescent fury simply flared into nothingness.

But in the instant before the firing order was given—as though precisely timed, which in all probability was the case—the ever-watchful observers picked up two items of fact which made the new Admiral of the First Galactic Region cut his almost irresistible weapon and break up his Cone of Battle after only a few seconds of action. One: those three enigmatic cargo scows had fallen apart *before* the beam reached them, and hundreds—yes, thousands—of small objects had hurtled radially outward, out well beyond the field of action of the Patrol's beam, at a speed many times that of light. Two: Kinnison's forebodings had been prophetic. A swarm of Blacks, all small—must have been hidden right on Earth somewhere!—were already darting at the Hill from the south.

"Cease firing!" Clayton rapped into his microphone. The dreadful beam expired. "Break cone formation! Independent action—light cruisers and scouts, *get those bombs!* Heavy cruisers and battle cruisers, engage similar units of the Blacks, two to one if possible. *Chicago* and *Boise*, attack Black Number One. *Bolivar* and *Himalaya*, Number Two. *Europa* and *Johannesburg*, Number Three!"

Space was full of darting, flashing, madly warring ships. The three Black superdreadnaughts leaped forward as one. Their massed batteries of beams, precisely synchronized and aimed, lashed out as one at the nearest Patrol super heavy, the *Boise*. Under the vicious power of that beautifully-timed thrust that warship's first, second, and third screens, her very wall-shield, flared through the spectrum and into the black. Her Chief Pilot, however, was fast—*very* fast—and he had a fraction of a second in which to work. Thus, practically in the instant of her wall-shield's failure, she went free; and while she was holed badly and put out of action, she was not blown out of space. In fact, it was learned later that she lost only forty men.

The Blacks were not as fortunate. The *Chicago*, now without a partner, joined beams with the *Bolivar* and the *Himalaya* against Number Two; then, a short half-second later, with her other two sister-ships against Number Three. And in that very short space of time two Black super-dreadnaughts ceased utterly to be.

But also, in that scant second of time, Black Number One had all but disappeared! Her canny commander, with no stomach at all for odds of five to one against, had ordered flight at max; she was already one-sixtieth of a light-year—about one hundred thousand million miles—away from the Earth and was devoting her every energy to the accumulation of still more distance.

"Bolivar! Himalaya!" Clayton barked savagely. "Get him!" He wanted intensely to join the chase, but he couldn't. He had to stay here.

And he didn't have time even to swear. Instead, without a break, the words tripping over each other against his teeth: "*Chicago! Johannesburg! Europa!* Act at will against heaviest craft left. Blast 'em down!"

He gritted his teeth. The scouts and light cruisers were doing their damndest, but they were outnumbered three to one—Christ, what a lot of stuff was getting through! The Blacks wouldn't last long, between the Hill and the heavies . . . but maybe long enough, at that—the Patrol globe was leaking like a sieve! He voiced a couple of bursts of deep-space profanity and, although he was almost afraid to look, sneaked a quick peek to see how much was left of the Hill. He looked—and stopped swearing in the middle of a four-letter Anglo-Saxon word.

What he saw simply did not make sense. Those Black bombs should have peeled the armor off of that mountain like the skin off of a nectarine and scattered it from the Pacific to the Mississippi. By now there should be a hole a mile deep where the Hill had been. But there wasn't. The Hill was still there! It might have shrunk a little—Clayton couldn't see very well because of the worse-than-incandescent radiance of the practically continuous, sense-battering, world-shaking atomic detonations—*but the Hill was still there!*

And as he stared, chilled and shaken, at that indescribably terrific spectacle, a Black cruiser, holed and helpless, fell toward that armored mountain with an acceleration starkly impossible to credit. And when it struck it did not penetrate, and splash, and crater, as it should have done. Instead, it simply spread out, *in a thin layer,* over an acre or so of the fortress' steep and apparently still armored surface!

"You saw that, Alex? Good. Otherwise you could scarcely believe it," came Kinnison's silent voice. "Tell all our ships to stay away. There's a force of over a hundred thousand G's acting in a direction normal to every point of our surface. The boys are giving it all the decrement they can—somewhere between distance cube and fourth power—but even so it's pretty fierce stuff. How about the *Bolivar* and the *Himalaya?* Not having much luck catching Mr. Black, are they?"

"Why, I don't know. I'll check . . . No, sir, they aren't. They report that they are losing ground and will soon lose trace."

"I was afraid so, from that shape. Rodebush was about the only one who saw it coming . . . well, we'll have to redesign and rebuild . . ."

Port Admiral Kinnison, shortly after directing the foregoing thought, leaned back in his chair and smiled. The battle was practically over. The Hill had come through. The Rodebush-Bergenholm fields had held her together through the most God-awful session of saturation atomic bombing that any world had ever seen or that the mind of man had ever conceived. And the counter-forces had kept the interior rock from flowing like water. So far, so good.

Her original armor was gone. Converted into . . . what? For hundreds of feet inward from the surface she was hotter than the reacting slugs of the Hanfords. Delousing her would be a project, not an operation; millions of cubic yards of material would have to be hauled off into space with tractors and allowed to simmer for a few hundred years; but what of that?

Bergenholm had said that the fields would tend to prevent the radioactives from spreading, as they otherwise would—and *Virgil, Samms was still safe!*

"Virge, my boy, come along." He took the First Lensman by his good arm and lifted him out of his chair. "Old Doctor Kinnison's peerless prescription for you and me is a big, thick, juicy, porterhouse steak."

8

EXAMINATION ZWILNIK, ORAL

That murderous attack upon Virgil Samms, and its countering by those new super-lawmen, the Lensmen, and by an entire task force of the North American Armed Forces, was news of Civilization-wide importance. As such, it filled every channel of Universal Telenews for an hour. Then, in stunning and crescendo succession, came the staccato reports of the creation of the Galactic Patrol, the mobilization—allegedly for maneuvers!—of Galactic Patrol's Grand Fleet, and the ultimately desperate and all-too-nearly successful attack upon The Hill.

"Just a second, folks; we'll have it very shortly. You'll see something that nobody ever saw before and that nobody will ever see again. We're getting in as close as the Law will let us." The eyes of Telenews' ace reporter and the telephoto lens of his cameraman stared down from a scooter at the furiously smoking, sputteringly incandescent surface of Triplanetary's ancient citadel; while upon dozens of worlds thousands of millions of people packed themselves tighter and tighter around tens of millions of visiplates and loudspeakers in order to see and to hear the tremendous news.

"There it is, folks, look at it—the only really impregnable fortress ever built by man! A good many of our experts had it written off as obsolete, long ago, but it seems these Lensmen had something up their sleeves besides their arms, heh-heh! And speaking of Lensmen, they haven't been throwing their weight around, so most of us haven't noticed them very much, but this reporter wants to go on record right now as saying there must be a lot more to the Lens than any of us has thought, because otherwise nobody would have gone to all that trouble and expense, to say nothing of the tremendous loss of life, just to kill the Chief Lensman, which seems to have been what they were after.

"We told you a few minutes ago, you know, that every Continent of Civilization sent official messages denying most emphatically any connection with this outrage. It's still a mystery, folks; in fact, it is getting more and more mysterious all the time. *Not one single man of the Black Fleet was taken alive!* Not even in the ships that were only holed—they blew themselves up! And there were no uniforms or books or anything of the kind to be found in any of the wrecks—no identification whatever!

"And now for the scoop of all time! Universal Telenews has obtained permission to interview the two top Lensmen, both of whom you all know—Virgil Samms and 'Rod the Rock' Kinnison—personally for this beam. We are now going down, by remote control, of course, right into the Galactic Patrol office, right in The Hill itself. Here we are. Now if you will step just a little closer to the ike, please, Mr. Samms; or should I say . . . ?"

"You should say 'First Lensman Samms,' " Kinnison said bruskly.

"Oh, yes, First Lensman Samms. Thank you, Mr. Kinnison. Now, First Lensman Samms, our clients all want to know all about the Lens. We all know what it *does*, but what, really, *is* it? Who invented it? How does it work?"

Kinnison started to say something, but Samms silenced him with a thought.

"I will answer those questions by asking you one." Samms smiled disarmingly. "Do you remember what happened because the pirates learned to duplicate the golden meteor of the Triplanetary Service?"

"Oh, I see." The Telenews ace, although brash and not at all thin-skinned, was quick on the uptake. "Hush-hush? T. S.?"

"Top Secret. Very much so," Samms confirmed, "and we are going to keep some things about the Lens secret as long as we possibly can."

"Fair enough. Sorry folks, but you will agree that they're right on that. Well, then, Mr. Samms, who do you think it was that tried to kill you, and where do you think the Black Fleet came from?"

"I have no idea," Samms said, slowly and thoughtfully. "No. No idea whatever."

"What? Are you *sure* of that? Aren't you holding back maybe just a little bit of a suspicion, for diplomatic reasons?"

"I am holding nothing back; and through my Lens I can make you certain of the fact. Lensed thoughts come from the mind itself, direct, not through such voluntary muscles as the tongue. The mind does not lie—even such lies as you call 'diplomacy.' "

The Lensman demonstrated and the reporter went on:

"He is *sure*, folks, which fact knocked me speechless for a second or two—which is quite a feat in itself. Now, Mr. Samms, one last question. What is all this Lens stuff really about? What are all you Lensmen—the Galactic Council and so on—really up to? What do you expect to get out of it? And why would anybody want to make such an all-out effort to get rid of you? And give it to me on the Lens, please, if you can do it and talk at the same time—that was a wonderful sensation, folks, of getting the dope straight and *knowing* that it was straight.''

''I can and will answer both by voice and by Lens. Our basic purpose is . . .'' and he quoted verbatim the resounding sentences which Mentor had impressed so ineradicably upon his mind. ''You know how little happiness, how little real well-being, there is upon any world today. We propose to increase both. What we expect to get out of it is happiness and well-being for ourselves, the satisfaction felt by any good workman doing the job for which he is best fitted and in which he takes pride. As to why anyone should want to kill me, the logical explanation would seem to be that some group or organization or race, opposed to that for which we Lensmen stand, decided to do away with us and started with me.''

''Thank you, Mr. Samms. I am sure that we all enjoyed this interview very much. Now, folks, you all know 'Rocky Rod,' 'Rod the Rock,' Kinnison . . . just a little closer, please . . . thank you. I don't suppose you have any suspicions, either, any more than . . .''

''I certainly have!'' Kinnison barked, so savagely that five hundred million people jumped as one. ''How do you want it; voice, or Lens, or both?'' Then, on the Lens: ''Think it over, son, because *I suspect everybody!*''

''Bub-both, please, Mr. Kinnison.'' Even Universal's star reporter was shaken by the quiet but deadly fury of the big Lensman's thought, but he rallied so quickly that his hesitation was barely noticeable. ''Your Lensed thought to me was that you suspect *everybody*, Mr. Kinnison?''

''Just that. Everybody. I suspect every continental government of every world we know, including that of North America of Tellus. I suspect political parties and organized minorities. I suspect pressure groups. I suspect capital and I suspect labor. I suspect an organization of criminals. I suspect nations and races and worlds that no one of us has as yet heard of—not even you, the top-drawer newshawk of the universe.''

''But you have nothing concrete to go on, I take it?''

''If I did have, do you think I'd be standing here talking to you?''

*   *   *

First Lensman Samms sat in his private quarters and thought.

Lensman Dronvire of Rigel Four stood behind him and helped him think.

Port Admiral Kinnison, with all his force and drive, began a comprehensive program of investigation, consolidation, expansion, redesigning, and rebuilding.

Virgilia Samms went to a party practically every night. She danced, she flirted, she talked. *How* she talked! Meaningless small talk for the most part—but interspersed with artless questions and comments which, while they perhaps did not put her partner of the moment completely at ease, nevertheless did not quite excite suspicion.

Conway Costigan, Lens under sleeve, undisguised but inconspicuous, rode the ether-lanes; observing minutely and reporting fully.

Jack Kinnison piloted and navigated and computed for his friend and boatmate:

Mason Northrop; who, completely surrounded by breadboard hookups of new and ever-more-fantastic complexity, listened and looked; listened and tuned; listened and rebuilt; listened and—finally—took bearings and bearings and bearings with his ultra-sensitive loops.

DalNalten and Knobos, with dozens of able helpers, combed the records of three worlds in a search which produced as a by-product a monumental "who's who" of crime.

Skilled technicians fed millions of cards, stack by stack, into the most versatile and most accomplished machines known to the statisticians of the age.

And Dr. Nels Bergenholm, abandoning temporarily his regular line of work, devoted his peculiar talents to a highly abstruse research in the closely allied field of organic chemistry.

The walls of Virgil Samms' quarters became covered with charts, diagrams, and figures. Tabulations and condensations piled up on his desk and overflowed into baskets upon the floor. Until:

"Lensman Olmstead, of Alphacent, sir," his secretary announced.

"Good! Send him in, please."

The stranger entered. The two men, after staring intently at each other for half a minute, smiled and shook hands vigorously. Except for the fact that the newcomer's hair was brown, they were practically identical!

"I'm certainly glad to see you, George. Bergenholm passed you, of course?"

"Yes. He says that he can match your hair to mine, even the individual white ones. And he has made me a wigmaker's dream of a wig."

"Married?" Samms' mind leaped ahead to possible complications.

"Widower, same as you. And . . ."

"Just a minute—going over this once will be enough." He Lensed call after call. Lensmen in various parts of space became en rapport with him and thus with each other.

"Lensmen—especially you, Rod—George Olmstead is here, and his brother Ray is available. I am going to work."

"I *still* don't like it!" Kinnison protested. "It's too dangerous. I told the Universe I was going to keep you covered, and I *meant* it!"

"That's what makes it perfectly safe. That is, if Bergenholm is *sure* that the duplication is close enough . . ."

"I am sure." Bergenholm's deeply resonant pseudovoice left no doubt at all in any one of the linked minds. "The substitution will not be detected."

". . . and that nobody knows, George, or even suspects, that you got your Lens."

"I am sure of that." Olmstead laughed quietly. "Also, nobody except us and your secretary knows that I am here. For a good many years I have made a specialty of that sort of thing. Photos, fingerprints, and so on have all been taken care of."

"Good. I simply can not work efficiently here," Samms expressed what all knew to be the simple truth. "Dronvire is a much better analyst-synthesist than I am; as soon as any significant correlation is possible he will know it. We have learned that the Towne-Morgan crowd, Mackenzie Power, Ossmen Industries, and Interstellar Spaceways are all tied in together, and that thionite is involved, but we have not been able to get any further. There is a slight correlation—barely significant—between deaths from thionite and the arrival in the Solarian System of certain Spaceways liners. The fact that certain officials of the Earth-Screen Service have been and are spending considerably more than they earn sets up a slight but definite probability that they are allowing space-ships or boats from space-ships to land illegally. These smugglers carry contraband, which may or may not be thionite. In short, we lack fundamental data in every department, and it is high time for me to begin doing my share in getting it."

"I don't check you, Virge." None of the Kinnisons ever did give up without a struggle. "Olmstead is a mighty smooth worker, and you are our prime coordinator. Why not let him keep up the counter-espionage—do the job you were figuring on doing yourself—and you stay here and boss it?"

"I have thought of that, a great deal, and have . . ."

"Because Olmstead can not do it," a hitherto silent mind cut in, decisively. "I, Rularion of North Polar Jupiter, say so. There are psychological factors involved. The ability to separate and to evaluate the constituent elements of a complex situation; the ability to make correct decisions without hesitation; as well as many others not as susceptible to concise statement, but which collectively could be called power of mind. How say you, Bergenholm of Tellus? For I have perceived in you a mind approximating in some respects the philosophical and psychological depth of my own.'' This outrageously egotistical declaration was, to the Jovian, a simple statement of an equally simple truth, and Bergenholm accepted it as such.

"I agree. Olmstead probably could not succeed."

"Well, then, can Samms?" Kinnison demanded.

"Who knows?" came Bergenholm's mental shrug, and simultaneously:

"Nobody knows whether I can or not, but I am going to try," and Samms ended—almost—the argument by asking Bergenholm and a couple of other Lensmen to come into his office and by taking off his Lens.

"And that's another thing I don't like." Kinnison offered one last objection. "Without your Lens, *anything* can happen to you."

"Oh, I won't have to be without it very long. And besides, Virgilia isn't the only one in the Samms family who can work better—sometimes—without a Lens."

The Lensmen came in and, in a surprisingly short time, went out. A few minutes later, two Lensmen strolled out of Samms' inner office into the outer one.

"Good-bye, George," the red-headed man said aloud, "and good luck."

"Same to you, Chief," and the brown-haired one strode out.

Norma the secretary was a smart girl, and observant. In her position, she had to be. Her eyes followed the man out, then scanned the Lensman from toe to crown.

"I've never seen anything like it, Mr. Samms," she remarked then. "Except for the difference in coloring, and a sort of . . . well, stoopiness . . . he could be your identical twin. You two must have had a common ancestor—or several—not too far back, didn't you?"

"We certainly did. Quadruple second cousins, you might call it. We have known of each other for years, but this is the first time we have met."

"Quadruple second cousins? What does that mean? How come?"

"Well, say that once upon a time there were two men named Albert and Chester . . ."

"What? Not two Irishmen named Pat and Mike? You're slipping, boss." The girl smiled roguishly. During rush hours she was always the fast, cool, efficient secretary, but in moments of ease such persiflage as this was the usual thing in the First Lensman's private office. "Not at all up to your usual form."

"Merely because I am speaking now as a genealogist, not as a raconteur. But to continue, we will say that Chester and Albert had four children apiece, two boys and two girls, two pairs of identical twins, each. And when they grew up—half way up, that is . . ."

"Don't tell me that we are going to suppose that all those identical twins married each other?"

"Exactly. Why not?"

"Well, it would be stretching the laws of probability all out of shape. But go ahead—I can see what's coming, I think."

"Each of those couples had one, and only one, child. We will call those children Jim Samms and Sally Olmstead; John Olmstead and Irene Samms."

The girl's levity disappeared. "James Alexander Samms and Sarah Olmstead Samms. Your parents. I didn't see what was coming, after all. This George Olmstead; then, is your . . ."

"Whatever it is, yes. I can't name it, either—maybe you had better call Genealogy some day and find out. But it's no wonder we look alike. And there are three of us, not two—George has an identical twin brother."

The red-haired Lensman stepped back into the inner office, shut the door, and Lensed a thought at Virgil Samms.

"It worked, Virgil! I talked to her for five solid minutes, practically leaning on her desk, and she didn't tumble! And if this wig of Bergenholm's fooled *her* so completely, the job he did on you would fool *anybody!*"

"Fine! I've done a little testing myself, on the keenest men I know, without a trace of recognition so far."

His last lingering doubt resolved, Samms boarded the ponderous, radiation-proof, neutron-proof shuttle-scow which was the only possible means of entering or leaving the Hill. A fast cruiser whisked him to Nampa, where Olmstead's "accidentally" damaged transcontinental transport was being repaired, and from which city Olmstead had been gone so briefly that no one had missed him. He occupied Olmstead's space; he surrendered the remainder of Olmstead's ticket. He reached New York. He took a 'copter to Senator Morgan's office. He was escorted into the private office of Herkimer Herkimer Third.

"Olmstead. Of Alphacent."

"Yes?" Herkimer's hand moved, ever so little, upon his desk's top.

"Here." The Lensman dropped an envelope upon the desk in such fashion that it came to rest within an inch of the hand.

"Prints. Here." Samms made prints. "Wash your hands, over there." Herkimer pressed a button. "Check all these prints, against each other and the files. Check the two halves of the torn sheet, fiber to fiber." He turned to the Lensless Lensman, now standing quietly before his desk. "Routine; a formality, in your case, but necessary."

"Of course."

Then for long seconds the two hard men stared into the hard depths of each other's eyes.

"You may do, Olmstead. We have had very good reports of you. But you have never been in thionite?"

"No. I have never even seen any."

"What do you want to get into it for?"

"Your scouts sounded me out; what did they tell you? The usual thing—promotion from the ranks into the brass—to get to where I can do myself and the organization some good."

"Yourself first, the organization second?"

"What else? Why should I be different from the rest of you?"

This time the locked eyes held longer; one pair smoldering, the other gold-flecked, tawny ice.

"Why, indeed?" Herkimer smiled thinly. "We do not advertise it, however."

"Outside, I wouldn't, either; but here I'm laying my cards flat on the table."

"I see. You *will* do, Olmstead, if you live. There's a test, you know."

"They told me there would be."

"Well, aren't you curious to know what it is?"

"Not particularly. *You* passed it, didn't you?"

"What do you mean by *that* crack?" Herkimer leaped to his feet; his eyes, smoldering before, now ablaze.

"Exactly what I said, no more and no less. You may read into it anything you please." Samms' voice was as cold as were his eyes. "You picked me out because of what I am. Did you think that moving upstairs would make a boot-licker out of me?"

"Not at all." Herkimer sat down and took from a drawer two small, transparent, vaguely capsule-like tubes, each containing a few particles of purple dust. "You know what this is?"

"I can guess."

"Each of these is a good, heavy jolt; about all that a strong man with a strong heart can stand. Sit down. Here is one dose. Pull the cover, stick the capsule up one nostril, squeeze the ejector, and sniff. If you can leave this other dose sitting here on the desk you will live, and thus pass the test. If you can't, you die."

Samms sat, and pulled, and squeezed, and sniffed.

His forearms hit the desk with a thud. His hands clenched themselves into fists, the tight-stretched tendons standing boldly out. His face turned white. His eyes jammed themselves shut; his jaw-muscles sprang into bands and lumps as they clamped his teeth hard together. Every voluntary muscle in his body went into a rigor as extreme as that of death itself. His heart pounded; his breathing became stertorous.

This was the dreadful "muscle-lock" so uniquely characteristic of thionite; the frenzied immobility of the ultimately passionate satisfaction of every desire.

The Galactic Patrol became for him an actuality; a force for good pervading all the worlds of all the galaxies of all the universes of all existing space-time continua. He knew what the Lens was, and why. He understood time and space. He knew the absolute beginning and the ultimate end.

He also saw things and did things over which it is best to draw a kindly veil, for *every* desire—mental or physical, open or sternly suppressed, noble or base—that Virgil Samms had ever had was being *completely satisfied*. EVERY DESIRE.

As Samms sat there, straining motionlessly upon the verge of death through sheer ecstasy, a door opened and Senator Morgan entered the room. Herkimer started, almost imperceptibly, as he turned—had there been, or not, an instantaneously-suppressed flash of guilt in those now completely clear and frank brown eyes?

"Hi, Chief; come in and sit down. Glad to see you—this is not exactly my idea of fun."

"No? When did you stop being a sadist?" The senator sat down beside his minion's desk, the fingertips of his left hand began soundlessly to drum. "You wouldn't have, by any chance, been considering the idea of . . . ?" He paused significantly.

"What an idea!" Herkimer's act—if it was an act—was flawless. "He's too good a man to waste."

"I know it, but you didn't act as though you did. I've never seen you come out such a poor second in an interview . . . and it wasn't because you didn't know to start with just what kind of a tiger he was—that's why he was selected for this job. And it would have been so easy to give him just a wee bit more."

"That's preposterous, Chief, and you know it."

"Do I? However, it couldn't have been jealousy, because he isn't being considered for your job. He won't be over you, and there's plenty of room for everybody. What was the matter? Your bloodthirstiness wouldn't have taken you *that* far, under these circumstances. Come clean, Herkimer.''

"Okay—I hate the whole damned family!'' Herkimer burst out, viciously.

"I see. That adds up.'' Morgan's face cleared, his fingers became motionless. ''You can't make the Samms wench and aren't in position to skin her alive, so you get allergic to all her relatives. That adds up, but let me tell you something.'' His quiet, level voice carried more of menace than most men's loudest threats. ''Keep your love life out of business and keep that sadistic streak under control. Don't let anything like this happen again.''

"I won't, Chief. I got off the beam—but he made me so *damn* mad!''

"Certainly. That's exactly what he was trying to do. Elementary. If he could make you look small it would make him look big, and he just about did. But watch now, he's coming to.''

Samms' muscles relaxed. He opened his eyes groggily; then, as a wave of humiliated realization swept over his consciousness, he closed them again and shuddered. He had always thought himself pretty much of a man; how could he *possibly* have descended to such nauseous depths of depravity, of turpitude, of sheer moral degradation? And yet every cell of his being was shrieking its demand for more; his mind and his substance alike were permeated by an overmastering craving to experience again the ultimate thrills which they had so tremendously, so outrageously enjoyed.

There was another good jolt lying right there on the desk in front of him, even though thionite-sniffers always saw to it that no more of the drug could be obtained without considerable physical exertion; which exertion would bring them to their senses. If he took that jolt it would kill him. What of it? What was death? What good was life, except to enjoy such thrills as he had just had and was about to have again? And besides, thionite couldn't kill *him*. He was a super-man; he had just proved it!

He straightened up and reached for the capsule; and that effort, small as it was, was enough to bring First Lensman Virgil Samms back under control. The craving, however, did not decrease. Rather, it increased.

Months were to pass before he could think of thionite, or even of the color purple, without a spasmodic catching of the breath and a tightening of every muscle. Years were to pass before he could forget, even partially, the theretofore unsuspected dwellers in the dark recesses of his own mind. Nevertheless, from the store of whatever it was that made him what he was, Virgil Samms drew strength. Thumb and forefinger touched the capsule, but instead of picking it up, he pushed it across the desk toward Herkimer.

"Put it away, bub. One whiff of that stuff will last me for life." He stared unfathomably at the secretary, then turned to Morgan and nodded. "After all, he did not *say* that he ever passed this or any other test. He just didn't contradict me when I said it."

With a visible effort Herkimer remained silent, but Morgan did not.

"You talk too much, Olmstead. Can you stand up yet?"

Gripping the desk with both hands, Samms heaved himself to his feet. The room was spinning and gyrating; every individual thing in it was moving in a different and impossible orbit; his already splintered skull threatened more and more violently to emulate a fragmentation bomb; black and white spots and vari-colored flashes filled his cone of vision. He wrenched one hand free, then the other—and collapsed back into the chair.

"Not yet—quite," he admitted, through stiff lips.

Although he was careful not to show it, Morgan was amazed—not that the man had collapsed, but that he had been able so soon to lift himself even an inch. "Tiger" was not the word; this Olmstead must be seven-eighths dinosaur.

"It takes a few minutes; longer for some, not so long for others," Morgan said, blandly. "But what makes you think Herkimer here never took one of the same?"

"Huh?" Again two pairs of eyes locked and held; and this time the duel was longer and more pregnant. "What do *you* think? How do you suppose I lived to get as old as I am now? By being dumb?"

Morgan unwrapped a Venerian cigar, settled it comfortably between his teeth, lit it, and drew three slow puffs before replying.

"Ah, a student. An analytical mind," he said, evenly, and—apparently—irrelevantly. "Let's skip Herkimer for the moment. Try your hand on me."

"Why not? From what we hear out in the field, you have always been in the upper brackets, so you probably never had to prove that you could take it or let it alone. My guess would be, though, that you could."

"The good old oil, eh?" Morgan allowed his face and voice to register a modicum, precisely metered, of contempt. "How to get along in the world; Lesson One: Butter up the Boss."

"Nice try, Senator, but I'll have to score you a clean miss." Samms, now back almost to normal, grinned companionably. "We both know that if I were still in the kindergarten I wouldn't be here now."

"I'll let that one pass—this time." Under that look and tone Morgan's underlings were wont to cringe, but this Olmstead was not the cringing type. "Don't do it again. It might not be safe."

"Oh, it would be safe enough—for today, at least. There are two factors which you are very carefully ignoring. First, I haven't accepted the job yet."

"Are you innocent enough to think you'll get out of this building alive if I don't accept you?"

"If you want to call it innocence, yes. Oh, I know you've got gunnies all over the place, but they don't mean a thing."

"No?" Morgan's voice was silkily venemous.

"No." Olmstead was completely unimpressed. "Put yourself in my place. You know I've been around a long time; and not just around my mother. I was weaned quite a number of years ago."

"I see. You don't scare worth a damn. A point. And you are testing me, just as I am testing you. Another point. I'm beginning to like you, George. I think I know what your second point is, but let's have it, just for the record."

"I'm sure you do. Any man, to be my boss, has got to be at least as good a man as I am. Otherwise I take his job away from him."

"Fair enough. By God, I *do* like you, Olmstead!" Morgan, his big face wreathed in smiles, got up, strode over, and shook hands vigorously; and Samms, scan as he would, could not even hazard a guess as to how much—if any—of this enthusiasm was real. "Do you want the job? And when can you go to work?"

"Yes, sir. Two hours ago, sir."

"That's fine!" Morgan boomed. Although he did not comment upon it, he noticed and understood the change in the form of address. "Without knowing what the job is or how much it pays?"

"Neither is important, sir, at the moment." Samms, who had got up easily enough to shake hands, now shook his head experimentally. Nothing rattled. Good—he was in pretty good shape already. "As to the job, I can either do it or find out why it can't be done. As to pay, I've heard you called a lot of things, but 'piker' was never one of them."

"Very well. I predict that you will go far." Morgan again shook the Lensman's hand; and again Samms could not evaluate the Senator's sincerity. "Tuesday afternoon. New York Spaceport. Spaceship *Virgin Queen*. Report to Captain Willoughby in the dock office at fourteen hundred hours. Stop at the cashier's office on your way out. Goodbye."

9

TRENCO

Piracy was rife. There was no suspicion, however, nor would there be for many years, that there was anything of very large purpose about the business. Murgatroyd was simply a Captain Kidd of space; and even if he were actually connected with Galactic Spaceways, that fact would not be surprising. Such relationships had always existed; the most ferocious and dreaded pirates of the ancient world worked in full partnership with the First Families of that world.

Virgil Samms was thinking of pirates and of piracy when he left Senator Morgan's office. He was still thinking of them while he was reporting to Roderick Kinnison. Hence:

"But that's enough about this stuff and me, Rod. Bring me up to date on Operation Boskone."

"Branching out no end. Your guess was right that Spaceways' losses to pirates are probably phony. But it wasn't the *known* attacks—that is, those cases in which the ship was found, later, with some or most of the personnel alive—that gave us the real information. They were all pretty much alike. But when we studied the total disappearances we really hit the jack-pot."

"That doesn't sound just right, but I'm listening."

"You'd better, since it goes farther than even you suspected. It was no trouble at all to get the passenger lists and the names of the crews of the independent ships that were lost without a trace. Their relatives and friends—we concentrated mostly on wives—could be located, except for the usual few who moved around so much that they got lost. Spacemen average young, you know, and their wives are still younger. Well, these young women got jobs, most of them remarried, and so on. In short, normal."

"And in the case of Spaceways, not normal?"

"Decidedly not. In the first place, you'd be amazed at how little publication was ever done of passenger lists, and apparently crew lists were not published at all. No use going into detail as to how we got the stuff, but we got it. However, nine tenths of the wives had disappeared, and none had remarried. The only ones we could find were those who did not care, even when their husbands were alive, whether they ever saw them again or not. But the big break was—you remember the disappearance of that girls'-school cruise ship?"

"Of course. It made a lot of noise."

"An interesting point in connection with that cruise is that two days before the ship blasted off the school was robbed. The vault was opened with thermite and the whole Administration Building burned to the ground. All the school's records were destroyed. Thus, the list of missing had to be made up from statements made by friends, relatives, and what not."

"I remember something of the kind. My impression was, though, that the space-ship company furnished . . . Oh!" The tone of Samms' thought altered sharply. "That was Spaceways, under cover?"

"Definitely. Our best guess is that there were quite a few shiploads of women disappeared about that time, instead of one. Austine's College had more students that year than ever before or since. It was the extras, not the regulars, who went on that cruise; the ones who figured it would be more convenient to disappear in space than to become ordinary missing persons."

"But Rod! That would mean . . . but where?"

"It means just that. And finding out 'where' will run into a project. There are over two thousand million suns in this galaxy, and the best estimate is that there are more than that many planets habitable by beings more or less human in type. You know how much of the galaxy has been explored and how fast the work of exploring the rest of it is going. Your guess is just as good as mine as to where those spacemen and engineers and their wives and girl-friends are now. I am sure, though, of four things; none of which we can even begin to prove. One; they didn't die in space. Two; they landed on a comfortable and very well equipped Tellurian planet. Three; they built a fleet there. Four; that fleet attacked the Hill."

"Murgatroyd, do you suppose?" Although surprised by Kinnison's tremendous report, Samms was not dismayed.

"No idea. No data—yet."

"And they'll keep on building," Samms said. "They had a fleet much larger than the one they expected to meet. Now they'll build one larger than all our combined forces. And since the politicians will always know what we are doing . . . or it might be . . . I wonder . . . ?''

"You can stop wondering." Kinnison grinned savagely.

"What do you mean?"

"Just what you were going to think about. You know the edge of the galaxy closest to Tellus, where that big rift cuts in?''

"Yes."

"Across that rift, where it won't be surveyed for a thousand years, there's a planet that could be Earth's twin sister. No atomic energy, no space-drive, but heavily industrialized and anxious to welcome us. Project Bennett. Very, *very* hush-hush. Nobody except Lensmen know anything about it. Two friends of Dronvire's—smart, smooth operators—are in charge. It's going to be the Navy Yard of the Galactic Patrol."

"But Rod . . ." Samms began to protest, his mind leaping ahead to the numberless problems, the tremendous difficulties, inherent in the program which his friend had outlined so briefly.

"Forget it, Virge!" Kinnison cut in. "It won't be easy, of course, but we can do anything they can do, and do it better. You can go calmly ahead with your own chores, knowing that when—and notice that I say 'when,' not 'if'—we need it we'll have a fleet up our sleeves that will make the official one look like a task force. But I see you're at the rendezvous, and there's Jill. Tell her 'hi' for me. And as the Vegians say—'Tail high, brother!' ''

Samms was in the hotel's ornate lobby; a couple of uniformed "boys" and Jill Samms were approaching. The girl reached him first.

"You had no trouble in recognizing me, then, my dear?"

"None at all, Uncle George." She kissed him perfunctorily, the bell hops faded away. "So nice to see you—I've heard *so* much about you. The Marine Room, you said?"

"Yes. I reserved a table."

And in that famous restaurant, in the unequalled privacy of the city's noisiest and most crowded night spot, they drank sparingly; ate not-so-sparingly; and talked not sparingly at all.

"It's perfectly safe here, you think?" Jill asked first.

"Perfectly. A super-sensitive microphone couldn't hear anything, and its so dark that a lip-reader, even if he could read us, would need a pair of twelve-inch night-glasses."

"Goody! They did a marvelous job, Dad. If it weren't for your . . . well, your personality, I wouldn't recognize you even now."

"You think I'm safe, then?"

"Absolutely."

"Then we'll get down to business. You, Knobos, and DalNalten all have keen and powerful minds. You can't all be wrong. Spaceways, then, is tied in with both the Towne-Morgan gang and with thionite. The logical extension of that—Dal certainly thought of it, even though he didn't mention it—would be . . ." Samms paused.

"Check. That the notorious Murgatroyd, instead of being just another pirate chief, is really working for Spaceways and belongs to the Towne-Morgan-Isaacson gang. But dad—what an idea! Can things be *that* rotten, really?"

"They may be worse than that. Now the next thing. Who, in your opinion, is the real boss?"

"Well, it certainly is not Herkimer Herkimer Third." Jill ticked him off on a pink forefinger. She had been asked for an opinion; she set out to give it without apology or hesitation. "He could—just about—direct the affairs of a hot-dog stand. Nor is it Clander. He isn't even a little fish; he's scarcely a minnow. Equally certainly it is neither the Venerian nor the Martian. They may run planetary affairs, but nothing bigger. I haven't met Murgatroyd, of course, but I have had several evaluations and he does not rate up with Towne. And Big Jim—and this surprised me as much as it will you—is almost certainly not the prime mover." She looked at him questioningly.

"That would have surprised me tremendously yesterday; but after today—I'll tell you about that presently—it doesn't."

"I'm glad of that. I expected an argument, and I have been inclined to question the validity of my own results, since they do not agree with common knowledge—or, rather, what is supposed to be knowledge. That leaves Isaacson and Senator Morgan." Jill frowned in perplexity; seemed, for the first time, unsure. "Isaacson is of course a big man. Able. Well-informed. Extremely capable. A top-notch executive. Not only *is*, would *have* to be, to run Spaceways. On the other hand, I have always thought that Morgan was nothing but a windbag . . ." Jill stopped talking; left the thought hanging in air.

"So did I—until today," Samms agreed grimly. "I thought that he was simply an unusually corrupt, greedy, rabble-rousing politician. Our estimates of him may have to be changed very radically."

Samms' mind raced. From two entirely different angles of approach, Jill and he had arrived at the same conclusion. But, if Morgan were really the Big Shot, would he have deigned to interview personally such small fry as Olmstead? Or was Olmstead's job of more importance than he, Samms, had supposed?

"I've got a dozen more things to check with you," he went on, almost without a pause, "but since this leadership matter is the only one in which my experience would affect your judgment, I had better tell you about what happened today . . .''

Tuesday came, and hour fourteen hundred; and Samms strode into an office. There was a big, clean desk; a wiry, intense, gray-haired man.

"Captain Willoughby?"

"Yes."

"George Olmstead reporting."

"Fourth Officer." The captain punched a button; the heavy, sound-proof door closed itself and locked.

"*Fourth* Officer? New rank, eh? What does the ticket cover?"

"New, and special. Here's the articles; read it and sign it." He did not add "or else," it was not necessary. It was clearly evident that Captain Willoughby, never garrulous, intended to be particularly reticent with his new subordinate.

Samms read. ". . . Fourth Officer . . . shall . . . no duties or responsibilities in the operation or maintenance of said space-ship . . . cargo . . ." Then came a clause which fairly leaped from the paper and smote his eyes: "when in command of a detail outside the hull of said space-ship he shall enforce, by the infliction of death or such other penalty as he deems fit . . ."

The Lensman was rocked to the heels, but did not show it. Instead, he took the captain's pen—his own, as far as Willoughby was concerned, could have been filled with vanishing ink—and wrote George Olmstead's name in George Olmstead's bold, flowing script.

Willoughby then took him aboard the good ship *Virgin Queen* and led him to his cabin.

"Here you are, Mr. Olmstead. Beyond getting acquainted with the supercargo and the rest of your men, you will have no duties for a few days. You have full run of the ship, with one exception. Stay out of the control room until I call you. Is that clear?"

"Yes, sir." Willoughby turned away and Samms, after tossing his space-bag into the rack, took inventory.

The room was of course very small; but, considering the importance of mass, it was almost extravagantly supplied. There were shelves, or rather, tight racks, of books; there were sun-lamps and card-shelves and exercisers and games; there was a receiver capable of bringing in programs from almost anywhere in space. The room had only one lack; it did not have an ultra-wave visiplate. Nor was this lack surprising. "They" would scarcely let George Olmstead know where "they" were taking him.

Samms was surprised, however, when he met the men who were to be directly under his command; for, instead of one, or at most two, they numbered exactly forty. And they were all, he thought at first glance, the dregs and sweepings of the lowest dives in space. Before long, however, he learned that they were not all space-rats and denizens of Skid Rows. Six of them—the strongest physically and the hardest mentally of the lot—were fugitives from lethal chambers; murderers and worse. He looked at the biggest, toughest one of the six—a rock-drill-eyed, red-haired giant—and asked:

"What did they tell *you*, Tworn, that your job was going to be?"

"They didn't say. Just that it was dangerous, but if I done exactly what my boss would tell me to do, and nothing else, I might not even get hurt. An' I was due to take the deep breath the next week, see? That's just how it was, boss."

"I see," and one by one Virgil Samms, master psychologist, studied and analyzed his motley crew until he was called into the control room.

The navigating tank was covered; no charts were to be seen. The one "live" visiplate showed a planet and a fiercely blue-white sun.

"My orders are to tell you, at this point, all I know about what you've got to do and about that planet down there. Trenco, they call it." To Virgil Samms, the first adherent of Civilization ever to hear it, that name meant nothing whatever. "You are to take about five of your men, go down there, and gather all the green leaves you can. Not green in color; sort of purplish. What they call broadleaf is the best; leaves about two feet long and a foot wide. But don't be too choosy. If there isn't any broadleaf handy, grab anything you can get hold of."

"What is the opposition?" Samms asked, quietly. "And what have they got that makes them so tough?"

"Nothing. No inhabitants, even. Just the planet itself. Next to Arisia, it's the God damndest planet in space. I've never been any closer to it than this, and I never will, so I don't know anything about it except what I hear; but there's something about it that kills men or drives them crazy. We spend seven or eight boats every trip, and thirty-five or forty men, and the biggest load that anybody ever took away from here was just under two hundred pounds of leaf. A good many times we don't get any."

"They go crazy, eh?" In spite of his control, Samms paled. But it couldn't be like Arisia. "What are the symptoms? What do they say?"

"Various. Main thing seems to be that they lose their sight. Don't go blind, exactly, but can't see where anything is; or, if they do see it, it isn't there. And it rains over forty feet deep every night, and yet it all dries up by morning. The worst electrical storms in the universe, and wind-velocities—I can show you charts on that—of over eight hundred miles an hour.''

"Whew! How about time? With your permission, I would like to do some surveying before I try to land."

"A smart idea. A couple of the other boys had the same, but it didn't help—they didn't come back. I'll give you two Tellurian days—no, three—before I give you up and start sending out the other boats. Pick out your five men and see what you can do."

As the boat dropped away, Willoughby's voice came briskly from a speaker. "I know that you five men have got ideas. Forget 'em. Fourth Officer Olmstead has the authority and the orders to put a half-ounce slug through the guts of any or all of you that don't jump, and jump fast, to do what he tells you. And if that boat makes any funny moves I blast it out of the ether. Good harvesting!''

For forty-eight Tellurian hours, taking time out only to sleep, Samms scanned and surveyed the planet Trenco; and the more he studied it, the more outrageously abnormal it became.

Trenco was, and is, a peculiar planet indeed. Its atmosphere is not air as we know air; its hydrosphere does not resemble water. Half of that atmosphere and most of that hydrosphere are one chemical, a substance of very low heat of vaporization and having a boiling point of about seventy five degrees Fahrenheit. Trenco's days are intensely hot; its nights are bitterly cold.

At night, therefore, it rains; and by comparison a Tellurian downpour of one inch per hour is scarcely a drizzle. Upon Trenco it really rains— forty seven feet and five inches of precipitation, every night of every Trenconian year. And this tremendous condensation of course causes wind. Willoughby's graphs were accurate. Except at Trenco's very poles there is not a spot in which or a time at which an Earthly gale would not constitute a dead calm; and along the equator, at every sunrise and every sunset, the wind blows from the day side into the night side at a velocity which no Tellurian hurricane or cyclone, however violent, has even distantly approached.

Also, therefore, there is lightning. Not in the mild and occasional flashes which we of gentle Terra know, but in a continuous, blinding glare which outshines a normal sun; in battering, shattering, multi-billion-volt discharges which not only make darkness unknown there, but also distort beyond recognition and beyond function the warp and the woof of space itself. Sight is almost completely useless in that fan-tastically altered medium. So is the ultra-beam.

Landing on the daylight side, except possibly at exact noon, would be impossible because of the wind, nor could the ship stay landed for more than a couple of minutes. Landing on the night side would be practically as bad, because of the terrific charge the boat would pick up—unless the boat carried something that could be rebuilt into a leaker. Did it? It did.

Time after time, from pole to pole and from midnight around the clock, Samms stabbed visibeam and spy-ray down toward Trenco's falsely-visible surface, with consistently and meaninglessly impossible results. The planet tipped, lurched, spun, and danced. It broke up into chunks, each of which began insanely to follow mathematically impossible paths.

Finally, in desperation, he rammed a beam down and held it down. Again he saw the planet break up before his eyes, but this time he held on. He *knew* that he was well out of the stratosphere, a good two hundred miles up. Nevertheless, he *saw* a tremendous mass of jagged rock falling straight down, with terrific velocity, upon his tiny lifeboat!

Unfortunately the crew, to whom he had not been paying overmuch attention of late, saw it, too; and one of them, with a bestial yell, leaped toward Samms and the controls. Samms, reaching for pistol and blackjack, whirled around just in time to see the big red-head lay the would-be attacker out cold with a vicious hand's-edge chop at the base of the skull.

"Thanks, Tworn. Why?"

"Because I want to get out of this alive, and he'd've had us all in hell in fifteen minutes. You know a hell of a lot more than we do, so I'm playin' it your way. See?"

"I see. Can you use a sap?"

"An artist," the big man admitted, modestly. "Just tell me how long you want a guy to be out and I won't miss it a minute, either way. But you'd better blow that crumb's brains out, right now. He ain't no damn good."

"Not until after I see whether he can work or not. You're a Procian, aren't you?"

"Yeah. Midlands—North Central."

"What did you do?"

"Nothing much, at first. Just killed a guy that needed killing; but the goddam louse had a lot of money, so they give me twenty five years. I didn't like it very well, and acted rough, so they give me solitary—boot, bandage, and so on. So I tried a break—killed six or eight, maybe a dozen, guards—but didn't quite make it. So they slated me for the big whiff. That's all, boss."

"I'm promoting you, now, to squad leader. Here's the sap." He handed Tworn his blackjack. "Watch 'em—I'll be too busy to. This landing is going to be tough."

"Gotcha, boss." Tworn was calibrating his weapon by slugging himself experimentally on the leg. "Go ahead. As far as these crumbs are concerned, you've got this air-tank all to yourself."

Samms had finally decided what he was going to do. He located the terminator on the morning side, poised his little ship somewhat nearer to dawn than to midnight, and "cut the rope." He took one quick reading on the sun, cut off his plates, and let her drop, watching only his pressure gages and gyros.

One hundred millimeters of mercury. Three hundred. Five hundred. He slowed her down. He was going to hit a thin liquid, but if he hit it too hard he would smash the boat, and he had no idea what the atmospheric pressure at Trenco's surface would be. Six hundred. Even this late at night, it might be greater than Earth's . . . and it might be a lot less. Seven hundred.

Slower and slower he crept downward, his tension mounting infinitely faster than did the needle of the gage. This was an instrument landing with a vengeance! Eight hundred. How was the crew taking it? How many of them had Tworn had to disable? He glanced quickly around. None! Now that they could not see the hallucinatory images upon the plates, they were not suffering at all—he himself was the only one aboard who was feeling the strain!

Nine hundred . . . nine hundred forty. The boat "hit the drink" with a crashing, splashing impact. Its pace was slow enough, however, and the liquid was deep enough, so that no damage was done. Samms applied a little driving power and swung his craft's sharp nose into the line toward the sun. The little ship plowed slowly forward, as nearly just awash as Samms could keep her; grounded as gently as a river steamboat upon a mud-flat. The starkly incredible downpour slackened; the Lensman knew that the second critical moment was at hand.

"Strap down, men, until we see what this wind is going to do to us."

The atmosphere, moving at a velocity well above that of sound, was in effect not a gas, but a solid. Even a spaceboat's hard skin of alloy plate, with all its bracing, could not take what was coming next. Inert, she would be split open, smashed, flattened out, and twisted into pretzels. Samms' finger stabbed down; the Berg went into action; the lifeboat went free just as that raging blast of quasi-solid vapor wrenched her into the air.

The second descent was much faster and much easier than the first. Nor, this time, did Samms remain surfaced or drive toward shore. Knowing now that this ocean was not deep enough to harm his vessel, he let her sink to the bottom. More, he turned her on her side and drove her at a flat angle into the bottom; so deep that the rim of her starboard lock was flush with the ocean's floor. Again they waited; and this time the wind did not blow the lifeboat away.

Upon purely theoretical grounds Samms had reasoned that the weird distortion of vision must be a function of distance, and his observations so far had been in accord with that hypothesis. Now, slowly and cautiously, he sent out a visibeam. Ten feet . . . twenty . . . forty . . . all clear. At fifty the seeing was definitely bad; at sixty it became impossible. He shortened back to forty and began to study the vegetation, growing with such fantastic speed that the leaves, pressed flat to the ground by the gale and anchored there by heavy rootlets, were already inches long. There was also what seemed to be animal life, of sorts, but Samms was not, at the moment, interested in Trenconian zoology.

"Are them the plants we're going to get, boss?" Tworn asked, staring into the plate over Samms' shoulder. "Shall we go out now an' start pickin' 'em?"

"Not yet. Even if we could open the port the blast would wreck us. Also, it would shear your head off, flush with the coaming, as fast as you stuck it out. This wind should ease off after while; we'll go out a little before noon. In the meantime we'll get ready. Have the boys break out a couple of spare Number Twelve struts, some clamps and chain, four snatch blocks, and a hundred feet of heavy spaceline . . .

"Good," he went on, when the order had been obeyed. "Rig the line from the winch through snatch blocks here, and here, and here, so I can haul you back against the wind. While you are doing that I'll rig a remote control on the winch."

Shortly before Trenco's fierce, blue-white sun reached meridian, the six men donned space-suits and Samms cautiously opened the air-lock ports. They worked. The wind was now scarcely more than an Earthly hurricane; the wildly whipping broadleaf plants, struggling upward, were almost half-way to the vertical. The leaves were apparently almost fully grown.

Four men clamped their suits to the line. The line was paid out. Each man selected two leaves; the largest, fattest, purplest ones he could reach. Samms hauled them back and received the loot; Tworn stowed the leaves away. Again—again—again.

With noon there came a few minutes of "calm." A strong man could stand against the now highly variable wind; could move around without being blown beyond the horizon; and during those few minutes all six men gathered leaves. That time, however, was very short. The wind steadied into the reverse direction with ever-increasing fury; winch and space-line again came into play. And in a scant half hour, when the line began to hum an almost musical note under its load, Samms decided to call it quits.

"That'll be all for today, boys," he announced. "About twice more and this line will part. You've done too good a job to lose you. Secure ship."

"Shall I blow the air, sir?" Tworn asked.

"I don't think so." Samms thought for a moment. "No. I'm afraid to take the chance. This stuff, whatever it is, is probably as poisonous as cyanide. We'll keep our suits on and exhaust into space."

Time passed. "Night" came; the rain and the flood. The bottom softened. Samms blasted the lifeboat out of the mud and away from the planet. He opened the bleeder valves, then both airlock ports; the contaminated air was replaced by the ultra-hard vacuum of the interplanetary void. He signaled the *Virgin Queen;* the lifeboat was taken aboard.

"Quick trip, Olmstead," Willoughby congratulated him. "I'm surprised that you got back at all, to say nothing of with so much stuff and not losing a man. Give me the weight, mister, fast!"

"Three hundred and forty eight pounds, sir," the supercargo reported.

"My God! And all pure broadleaf! *Nobody* ever did *that* before! How did you do it, Olmstead?"

"I don't know whether that would be any of your business or not." Samms' mien was not insulting; merely thoughtful. "Not that I give a damn, but my way might not help anybody else much, and I think I had better report to the main office first, and let them do the telling. Fair enough?"

"Fair enough," the skipper conceded, ungrudgingly. "What a load! And no losses!"

"One boatload of air, is all; but air is expensive out here." Samms made a point, deliberately.

"Air!" Willoughby snorted. "I'll swap you a hundred flasks of air, any time, for any one of those leaves!" Which was what Samms wanted to know.

Captain Willoughby was smart. He knew that the way to succeed was to use and then to trample upon his inferiors; to toady to such superiors as were too strong to be pulled down and thus supplanted. He knew that this Olmstead had what it took to be a big shot. Therefore:

"They told me to keep you in the dark until we got to Trenco," he more than half apologized to his Fourth Officer shortly after the *Virgin Queen* blasted away from the Trenconian system. "But they didn't say anything about afterwards—maybe they figured you wouldn't be aboard any more, as usual—but anyway, you can stay right here in the control room if you want to."

"Thanks, Skipper, but mightn't it be just as well," he jerked his head inconspicuously toward the other officers, "to play the string out, this trip? I don't care where we're going, and we don't want anybody to get any funny ideas."

"That'd be a lot better, of course—as long as you know that your cards are all aces, as far as I'm concerned."

"Thanks, Willoughby. I'll remember that."

Samms had not been entirely frank with the pirate captain. From the time required to make the trip, he knew to within a few parsecs Trenco's distance from Sol. He did not know the direction, since the distance was so great that he had not been able to recognize any star or constellation. He did know, however, the course upon which the vessel then was, and he would know courses and distances from then on. He was well content.

A couple of uneventful days passed. Samms was again called into the control room, to see that the ship was approaching a three-sun solar system.

"This where we're going to land?" he asked, indifferently.

"We ain't going to land," Willoughby told him. "You are going to take the broadleaf down in your boat, close enough so that you can parachute it down to where it has to go. Way 'nuff, pilot, go inert and match intrinsics. Now, Olmstead, watch. You've seen systems like this before?"

"No, but I know about them. Those two suns over there are a hell of a lot bigger and further away than they look, and this one here, much smaller, is in the Trojan position. Have those big suns got any planets?"

"Five or six apiece, they say; all hotter and dryer than the brazen hinges of hell. This sun here has seven, but Number Two—'Cavenda,' they call it—is the only Tellurian planet in the system. The first thing we look for is a big, diamond-shaped continent . . . there's only one of that shape . . . there it is, over there. Notice that one end is bigger than the other—that end is north. Strike a line to split the continent in two and measure from the north end one-third of the length of the line. That's the point we're diving at now . . . see that crater?"

"Yes." The *Virgin Queen*, although still hundreds of miles up, was slowing rapidly. "It must be a big one."

"It's a good fifty miles across. Go down until you're dead sure that the box will land somewhere inside the rim of that crater. Then dump it. The parachute and the sender are automatic. Understand?"

"Yes, sir; I understand," and Samms took off.

He was vastly more interested in the stars, however, than in delivering the broadleaf. The constellation directly beyond Sol from wherever he was might be recognizable. Its shape would be smaller and more or less distorted; its smaller stars, brilliant to Earthly eyes only because of their nearness, would be dimmer, perhaps invisible; the picture would be further confused by intervening, nearby, brilliant strangers; but such giants as Canopus and Rigel and Betelgeuse and Deneb would certainly be highly visible if he could only recognize them. From Trenco his search had failed; but he was still trying.

There was something vaguely familiar! Sweating with the mental effort, he blocked out the too-near, too-bright stars and studied intensively those that were left. A blue-white and a red were most prominent. Rigel and Betelgeuse? Could that constellation be Orion? The Belt was very faint, but it was there. Then Sirius ought to be about there, and Pollux about there; and, at this distance, about equally bright. They were. Aldebaran would be orange, and about one magnitude brighter than Pollux; and Capella would be yellow, and half a magnitude brighter still. There they were! Not too close to where they should be, but close enough— it was Orion! And this thionite way-station, then, was somewhere near right ascension seventeen hours and declination plus ten degrees!

He returned to the *Virgin Queen*. She blasted off. Samms asked very few questions and Willoughby volunteered very little information; nevertheless the First Lensman learned more than anyone of his fellow pirates would have believed possible. Aloof, taciturn, disinterested to a degree, he seemed to spend practically all of his time in his cabin when he was not actually at work; but he kept his eyes and his ears wide open. And Virgil Samms, as has been intimated, had a brain.

The *Virgin Queen* made a quick flit from Cavenda to Vegia, arriving exactly on time; a proud, clean space-ship as high above suspicion as Calpurnia herself. Samms unloaded her cargo; replaced it with one for Earth. She was serviced. She made a fast, eventless run to Tellus. She docked at New York Spaceport. Virgil Samms walked unconcernedly into an ordinary-looking rest-room; George Olmstead, fully informed, walked as unconcernedly out.

As soon as he could, Samms Lensed Northrop and Jack Kinnison.

"We lined up a thousand and one signals, sir," Northrop reported for the pair, "but only one of them carried a message, and it didn't make sense."

"Why not?" Samms asked, sharply. "With a Lens, *any* kind of a message, however garbled, coded, or interrupted, makes sense."

"Oh, we understood what it *said*," Jack came in, "but it didn't say enough. Just 'READY—READY—READY'; over and over."

"What!" Samms exclaimed, and the boys could feel his mind work. "Did that signal, by any chance, originate anywhere near seventeen hours and plus ten degrees?"

"Very near. Why? How did you know?"

"Then it *does* make sense!" Samms exclaimed, and called a general conference of Lensmen.

"Keep working along these same lines," Samms directed, finally. "Keep Ray Olmstead in the Hill in my place. I am going to Pluto, and—I hope—to Palain Seven."

Roderick Kinnison of course protested; but, equally of course, his protests were over-ruled.

10

PALAINIANS ON PLUTO

Pluto is, on the average, about forty times as far away from the sun as is Mother Earth. Each square yard of Earth's surface receives about sixteen hundred times as much heat as does each of Pluto's. The sun as seen from Pluto is a dim, wan speck. Even at perihelion, an event which occurs only once in two hundred forty eight Tellurian years, and at noon and on the equator, Pluto is so bitterly cold that climatic conditions upon its surface simply cannot be described by or to warm-blooded, oxygen-breathing man.

As good an indication as any can be given, perhaps, by mentioning the fact that it had taken the Patrol's best engineers over six months to perfect the armor which Virgil Samms then wore. For no ordinary space-suit would do. Space itself is not cold; the only loss of heat is by radiation into or through an almost perfect vacuum. In contact with Pluto's rocky, metallic soil, however, there would be conduction; and the magnitude of the inevitable heat-loss made the Tellurian scientists gasp.

"Watch your feet, Virge!" had been Roderick Kinnison's insistent last thought. "Remember those psychologists—if they stayed in contact with that ground for five minutes they froze their feet to the ankles. Not that the boys aren't good, but slipsticks sometimes slip in more ways than one. If your feet ever start to get cold, drop whatever you're doing and drive back here at max!"

Virgil Samms landed. His feet stayed warm. Finally, assured that the heaters of his suit could carry the load indefinitely, he made his way on foot into the settlement near which he had come to ground. And there he saw his first Palainian.

Or, strictly speaking, he saw part of his first Palainian; for no three-dimensional creature has ever seen or ever will see in entirety any member of any of the frigid-blooded, poison-breathing races. Since life as we know it—organic, three-dimensional life—is based upon liquid water and gaseous oxygen, such life did not and could not develop upon planets whose temperatures are only a few degrees above absolute zero. Many, perhaps most, of these ultra-frigid planets have an atmosphere of sorts; some have no atmosphere at all. Nevertheless, with or without atmosphere and completely without oxygen and water, life—highly intelligent life—did develop upon millions and millions of such worlds. That life is not, however, strictly three-dimensional. Of necessity, even in the lowest forms, it possesses an extension into the hyper-dimension; and it is this metabolic extension alone which makes it possible for life to exist under such extreme conditions.

This extension makes it impossible for any human being to see anything of a Palainian except the fluid, amorphous, ever-changing thing which is his three-dimensional aspect of the moment; makes any attempt at description or portraiture completely futile.

Virgil Samms stared at the Palainian; tried to see what it looked like. He could not tell whether it had eyes or antennae; legs, arms, or tentacles; teeth or beaks; talons or claws or feet; skin, scales, or feathers. It did not even remotely resemble anything that the Lensman had ever seen, sensed, or imagined. He gave up; sent out an exploring thought.

"I am Virgil Samms, a Tellurian," he sent out slowly, carefully, after he made contact with the outer fringes of the creature's mind. "Is it possible for you, sir or madam, to give me a moment of your time?"

"Eminently possible, Lensman Samms, since my time is of completely negligible value." The monster's mind flashed into accord with Samms' with a speed and precision that made him gasp. That is, a part of it became en rapport with a part of his: years were to pass before even the First Lensman would know much more about the Palainian than he learned in that first contact; no human beings except the Children of the Lens ever were to understand even dimly the labyrinthine intricacies, the paradoxical complexities, of the Palainian mind.

" 'Madam' might be approximately correct," the native's thought went smoothly on. "My name, in your symbology, is Twelfth Pilinipsi; by education, training, and occupation I am a Chief Dexitroboper. I perceive that you are indeed a native of that hellish Planet Three, upon which it was assumed for so long that no life could possibly exist. But communication with your race has been almost impossible heretofore ... Ah, the Lens. A remarkable device, truly. I would slay you and take it, except for the obvious fact that only you can possess it."

"What!" Dismay and consternation flooded Samms' mind. "You already know the Lens?"

"No. Yours is the first that any of us has perceived. The mechanics, the mathematics, and the basic philosophy of the thing, however, are quite clear."

"What!" Samms exclaimed again. "You can, then, produce Lenses yourselves?"

"By no means, any more than you Tellurians can. There are magnitudes, variables, determinants, and forces involved which no Palainian will ever be able to develop, to generate, or to control."

"I see." The Lensman pulled himself together. For a First Lensman, he was making a wretched showing indeed . . .

"Far from it, sir," the monstrosity assured him. "Considering the strangeness of the environment into which you have voluntarily flung yourself so senselessly, your mind is well integrated and strong. Otherwise it would have shattered. If our positions were reversed, the mere thought of the raging heat of your Earth would—come no closer, please!" The thing vanished; reappeared many yards away. Her thoughts were a shudder of loathing, of terror, of sheer detestation. "But to get on. I have been attempting to analyze and to understand your purpose, without success. That failure is not too surprising, of course, since my mind is weak and my total power is small. Explain your mission, please, as simply as you can."

Weak? Small? In view of the power the monstrosity had just shown, Samms probed for irony, for sarcasm or pretense. There was no trace of anything of the kind.

He tried, then, for fifteen solid minutes, to explain the Galactic Patrol, but at the end the Palainian's only reaction was one of blank non-comprehension.

"I fail completely to perceive the use of, or the need for, such an organization," she stated flatly. "This altruism—what good is it? It is unthinkable that any other race would take any risks or exert any effort for us, any more than we would for them. Ignore and be ignored, as you must already know, is the Prime Tenet."

"But there is a little commerce between our worlds; your people did not ignore our psychologists; and you are not ignoring me," Samms pointed out.

"Oh, none of us is perfect," Pilinipsi replied, with a mental shrug and what seemed to be an airy wave of a multi-tentacled member. "That ideal, like any other, can only be approached asymptotically, never reached; and I, being somewhat foolish and silly, as well as weak and vacillant, am much less perfect than most."

Flabbergasted, Samms tried a new tack. "I might be able to make my position clearer if I knew you better. I know your name, and that you are a woman of Palain Seven"—it is a measure of Virgil Samms' real size that he actually thought "woman," and not merely "female"—"but all I can understand of your occupation is the name you have given it. What does a Chief Dexitroboper do?"

"She—or he—or, perhaps, it . . . is a supervisor of the work of dexitroboping." The thought, while perfectly clear, was completely meaningless to Samms, and the Palainian knew it. She tried again. "Dexitroboping has to do with . . . nourishment? No—with nutrients."

"Ah. Farming—agriculture," Samms thought; but this time it was the Palainian who could not grasp the concept. "Hunting? Fishing?" No better. "Show me, then, please."

She tried; but demonstration, too, was useless; for to Samms the Palainian's movements were pointless indeed. The peculiarly flowing, subtly changing thing darted back and forth, rose and fell, appeared and disappeared; undergoing the while cyclic changes in shape and form and size, in aspect and texture. It was now spiny, now tentacular, now scaly, now covered with peculiarly repellent feather-like fronds, each oozing a crimson slime. But it apparently did not *do* anything whatever. The net result of all its activity was, apparently, zero.

"There, it is done." Pilinipsi's thought again came clear. "You observed and understood? You did not. That is strange—baffling. Since the Lens did improve communication and understanding tremendously, I hoped that it might extend to the physical as well. But there must be some basic, fundamental difference, the nature of which is at present obscure. I wonder . . . if I had a Lens, too—but no . . . ."

"But yes!" Samms broke in, eagerly. "Why don't you go to Arisia and be tested for one? You have a magnificient, a really *tremendous* mind. It is of Lensman grade in every respect except one—you simply don't *want* to use it!"

"Me? Go to Arisia?" The thought would have been, in a Tellurian, a laugh of scorn. "How utterly silly—how abysmally stupid! There would be personal discomfort, quite possibly personal danger, and two Lenses would be little or no better than one in resolving differences between our two continua, which are probably in fact incommensurable."

"Well, then," Samms thought, almost viciously, "can you introduce me to someone who is stupider, sillier, and more foolish than you are?"

"Not here on Pluto, no." The Palainian took no offense. "That was why it was I who interviewed the earlier Tellurian visitors and why I am now conversing with you. The others avoided you."

"I see." Samms' thought was grim. "How about the home planet, then?"

"Ah. Undoubtedly. In fact, there is a group, a club, of such persons. None of them is, of course, as insane—as aberrant—as you are, but they are all much more so than I am."

"Who of this club would be most interested in becoming a Lensman?"

"Tallick was the least stable member of the New-Thought Club when I left Seven; Kragzex a close second. There may of course have been changes since then. But I cannot believe that even Tallick—even Tallick at his outrageous worst—would be crazy enough to join your Patrol."

"Nevertheless, I must see him myself. Can you and will you give me a chart or a routing from here to Palain Seven?"

"I can and I will. Nothing you have thought will be of any use to me; that will be the easiest and quickest way of getting rid of you." The Palainian spread a completely detailed chart in Samms mind, snapped the telepathic line, and went unconcernedly about her incomprehensible business.

Samms, mind reeling, made his way back to his boat and took off. And as the light-years and the parsecs screamed past, he sank deeper and deeper into a welter of unproductive speculation. What were—really—those Palainians? How could they—really—exist as they seemed to exist? And why had some of that dexitroboper's—whatever *that* meant!—thoughts come in so beautifully sharp and clear and plain, while others . . . ?

He knew that his Lens would receive and would convert into his own symbology any thought or message, however coded or garbled or however sent or transmitted. The Lens was not at fault; his symbology was. There were concepts—things—actualities—occurrences—so foreign to Tellurian experience that no referents existed. Hence the human mind lacked the channels, the mechanisms, to grasp them.

He and Roderick Kinnison had glibly discussed the possibility of encountering forms of intelligent life so alien that humanity would have no point whatever of contact with them. After what Samms had just gone through, that was more of a possibility than either he or his friend had believed; and he hoped grimly, as he considered how seriously this partial contact with the Palainian had upset him, that the possibility would never become a fact.

He found the Palainian system easily enough, and Palain Seven. That planet, of course, was almost as dark upon its sunward side as upon the other, and its inhabitants had no use for light. Pilinipsi's instructions, however, had been minute and exact; hence Samms had very little trouble in locating the principal city—or, rather, the principal village, since there were no real cities. He found the planet's one spaceport. What a thing to call a *port!* He checked back; recalled exactly this part of his interview with Pluto's Chief Dexitroboper.

"The place upon which space-ships land," had been her thought, when she showed him exactly where it was in relationship to the town. Just that, and nothing else. It had been his mind, not hers, that had supplied the docks and cradles, the service cars, the officers, and all the other things taken for granted in space-fields everywhere as Samms knew them. Either the Palainian had not perceived the trappings with which Samms had invested her visualization, or she had not cared enough about his misapprehension to go to the trouble of correcting it; he did not know which.

The whole area was as bare as his hand. Except for the pitted, scarred, slagged-down spots which showed so clearly what driving blasts would do to such inconceivably cold rock and metal, Palainport was in no way distinguishable from any other unimproved portion of the planet's utterly bleak surface.

There were no signals; he had been told of no landing conventions. Apparently it was everyone for himself. Wherefore Samms' tremendous landing lights blazed out, and with their aid he came safely to ground. He put on his armor and strode to the airlock; then changed his mind and went to the cargo-port instead. He had intended to walk, but in view of the rugged and deserted field and the completely unknown terrain between the field and the town, he decided to ride the "creep" instead.

This vehicle, while slow, could go—literally—anywhere. It had a cigar-shaped body of magnalloy; it had big, soft, tough tires; it had cleated tracks; it had air- and water-propellers; it had folding wings; it had driving, braking, and steering jets. It could traverse the deserts of Mars, the oceans and swamps of Venus, the crevassed glaciers of Earth, the jagged, frigid surface of an iron asteroid, and the cratered, fluffy topography of the moon; if not with equal speed, at least with equal safety.

Samms released the thing and drove it into the cargo lock, noting mentally that he would have to exhaust the air of that lock into space before he again broke the inner seal. The ramp slid back into the ship; the cargo port closed. Here he was!

Should he use his headlights, or not? He did not know the Palainians' reaction to or attitude toward light. It had not occurred to him while at Pluto to ask, and it might be important. The landing lights of his vessel might already have done his cause irreparable harm. He could drive by starlight if he had to . . . but he needed light and he had not seen a single living or moving thing. There was no evidence that there was a Palainian within miles. While he had known, with his brain, that Palain would be dark, he had expected to find buildings and traffic—ground-cars, planes, and at least a few space-ships—and not this vast nothingness.

If nothing else, there *must* be a road from Palain's principal city to its only spaceport; but Samms had not seen it from his vessel and he could not see it now. At least, he could not recognize it. Wherefore he clutched in the tractor drive and took off in a straight line toward town. The going was more than rough—it was really rugged—but the creep was built to stand up under punishment and its pilot's chair was sprung and cushioned to exactly the same degree. Hence, while the course itself was infinitely worse than the smoothly paved approaches to Rigelston, Samms found this trip much less bruising than the other had been.

Approaching the village, he dimmed his roadlights and slowed down. At its edge he cut them entirely and inched his way forward by starlight alone.

What a town! Virgil Samms had seen the inhabited places of almost every planet of Civilization. He had seen cities laid out in circles, sectors, ellipses, triangles, squares, parallelopipeds—practically every plan known to geometry. He had seen structures of all shapes and sizes— narrow skyscrapers, vast-spreading one-stories, polyhedra, domes, spheres, semi-cylinders, and erect and inverted full and truncated cones and pyramids. Whatever the plan or the shapes of the component units, however, those inhabited places had, without exception, been understandable. But this!

Samms, his eyes now completely dark-accustomed, could see fairly well, but the more he saw the less he grasped. There was no plan, no coherence or unity whatever. It was as though a cosmic hand had flung a few hundreds of buildings, of incredibly and senselessly varied shapes and sizes and architectures, upon an otherwise empty plain, and as though each structure had been allowed ever since to remain in whatever location and attitude it had chanced to fall. Here and there were jumbled piles of three or more utterly incongruous structures. There were a few whose arrangement was almost orderly. Here and there were large, irregularly-shaped areas of bare, untouched ground. There were no streets—at least, nothing that the man could recognize as such.

Samms headed the creep for one of those open areas, then stopped— declutched the tracks, set the brakes, and killed the engines.

"Go slow, fellow," he advised himself then. "Until you find out what a dexitroboper actually does while working at his trade, don't take chances of interfering or of doing damage!"

No Lensman knew—then—that frigid-blooded poison-breathers were not strictly three-dimensional; but Samms did know that he had actually seen things which he could not understand. He and Kinnison had discussed such occurrences calmly enough; but the actuality was enough to shake even the mind of Civilization's First Lensman.

He did not need to be any closer, anyway. He had learned the Palainians' patterns well enough to Lens them from a vastly greater distance than his present one; this personal visit to Palainopolis had been a gesture of friendliness, not a necessity.

"Tallick? Kragzex?" He sent out the questing, querying thought. "Lensman Virgil Samms of Sol Three calling Tallick and Kragzex of Palain Seven."

"Kragzex acknowledging, Virgil Samms," a thought snapped back, as diamond-clear, as precise, as Pilinipsi's had been.

"Is Tallick here, or anywhere on the planet?"

"He is here, but he is emmfozing at the moment. He will join us presently."

"Damnation! There it was again! First "dexitroboping," and now this!

"One moment, please," Samms requested. "I fail to grasp the meaning of your thought."

"So I perceive. The fault is of course mine, in not being able to attune my mind fully to yours. Do not take this, please, as any aspersion upon the character or strength of your own mind."

"Of course not. I am the first Tellurian you have met?"

"Yes."

"I have exchanged thoughts with one other Palainian, and the same difficulty existed. I can neither understand nor explain it; but it is as though there are differences between us so fundamental that in some matters mutual comprehension is in fact impossible."

"A masterly summation and undoubtedly a true one. This emmfozing, then—if I read correctly, your race has only two sexes?"

"You read correctly."

"I cannot understand. There is no close analogy. However, emmfozing has to do with reproduction."

"I see," and Samms saw, not only a frankness brand-new to his experience, but also a new view of both the powers and the limitations of his Lens.

It was, by its very nature, of precisionist grade. It received thoughts and translated them precisely into English. There was some leeway, but not much. If any thought was such that there was no extremely close counterpart or referent in English, the Lens would not translate it at all, but would simply give it a hitherto meaningless symbol—a symbol which would from that time on be associated, by all Lenses everywhere, with that one concept and no other. Samms realized then that he might, some day, learn what a dexitroboper actually did and what the act of emmfozing actually was; but that he very probably would not.

Tallick joined them then, and Samms again described glowingly, as he had done so many times before, the Galactic Patrol of his imaginings and plannings. Kragzex refused to have anything to do with such a thing, almost as abruptly as Pilinipsi had done, but Tallick lingered—and wavered.

"It is widely known that I am not entirely sane," he admitted, "which may explain the fact that I would very much like to have a Lens. But I gather, from what you have said, that I would probably not be given a Lens to use purely for my own selfish purposes?"

"That is my understanding," Samms agreed.

"I was afraid so." Tallick's mien was . . . "woebegone" is the only word for it. "I have work to do. Projects, you know, of difficulty, of extreme complexity and scope, sometimes even approaching danger. A Lens would be of tremendous use."

"How?" Samms asked. "If your work is of enough importance to enough people, Mentor would certainly give you a Lens."

"This would benefit me; only me. We of Palain, as you probably already know, are selfish, mean-spirited, small-souled, cowardly, furtive, and sly. Of what you call 'bravery' we have no trace. We attain our ends by stealth, by indirection, by trickery and deceit." Ruthlessly the Lens was giving Virgil Samms the uncompromisingly exact English equivalent of the Palainian's every thought. "We operate, when we must operate at all openly, with the absolutely irreducible minimum of personal risk. These attitudes and attributes will, I have no doubt, preclude all possibility of Lensmanship for me and for every member of my race."

"Not necessarily."

Not necessarily! Although Virgil Samms did not know it, this was one of the really critical moments in the coming into being of the Galactic Patrol. By a conscious, a tremendous effort, the First Lensman was lifting himself above the narrow, intolerant prejudices of human experience and was consciously attempting to see the whole through Mentor's Arisian mind instead of through his Tellurian own. That Virgil Samms was the first human being to be born with the ability to accomplish that feat even partially was one of the reasons why he was the first wearer of the Lens.

"Not necessarily," First Lensman Virgil Samms said and meant. He was inexpressibly shocked—revolted in every human fiber—by what this unhuman monster had so frankly and callously thought. There were, however, many things which no human being ever could understand, and there was not the shadow of a doubt that this Tallick had a really tremendous mind. "You have said that your mind is feeble. If so, there is no simple expression of the weakness of mine. I can perceive only one, the strictly human, facet of the truth. In a broader view it is distinctly possible that your motivation is at least as 'noble' as mine. And to complete my argument, you work with other Palainians, do you not, to reach a common goal?"

"At times, yes."

"Then you can conceive of the desirability of working with non-Palainian entities toward an end which would benefit both races?"

"Postulating such an end, yes; but I am unable to visualize any such. Have you any specific project in mind?"

"Not at the moment." Samms ducked. He had already fired every shot in his locker. "I am quite certain, however, that if you go to Arisia you will be informed of several such projects."

There was a period of silence. Then:

"I believe that I *will* go to Arisia, at that!" Tallick exclaimed, brightly. "I will make a deal with your friend Mentor. I will give him a share—say fifty percent, or forty—of the time and effort I save on my own projects!"

"Just so you *go*, Tallick." Samms concealed right manfully his real opinion of the Palainian's scheme. "When can you go? Right now?"

"By no means. I must first finish this project. A year, perhaps—or more; or possibly less. Who knows?"

Tallick cut communications and Samms frowned. He did not know the exact length of Seven's year, but he knew that it was long—*very* long.

11

ZABRISKAN FONTEMA

A small, black scout-ship, commanded jointly by Master Pilot John K. Kinnison and Master Electronicist Mason M. Northrop, was blasting along a course very close indeed to RA17: D+10. In equipment and personnel, however, she was not an ordinary scout. Her control room was so full of electronics racks and computing machines that there was scarcely footway in any direction; her graduated circles and vernier scales were of a size and a fineness usually seen only in the great vessels of the Galactic Survey. And her crew, instead of the usual twenty-odd men, numbered only seven—one cook, three engineers, and three watch officers. For some time the young Third Officer, then at the board, had been studying something on his plate; comparing it minutely with the chart clipped into the rack in front of him. Now he turned, with a highly exaggerated deference, to the two Lensmen.

"Sirs, which of your Magnificences is officially the commander of this here bucket of odds and ends at the present instant?"

"Him." Jack used his cigarette as a pointer. "The guy with the misplaced plucked eyebrow on his upper lip. I don't come on duty until sixteen hundred hours—one precious Tellurian minute yet in which to dream of the beauties of Earth, so distant in space and in both past and future time."

"Huh? Beauties? Plural? Next time I see a party whose pictures are cluttering up this whole ship I'll tell her about your polygamous ideas. I'll ignore that crack about my mustache, though, since you can't raise one of your own. I'm ignoring you, too—like this, see?" Ostentatiously turning his back upon the lounging Kinnison, Northrop stepped carefully over three or four breadboard hookups and stared into the plate over the watch officer's shoulder. He then studied the chart. "*Was ist los*, Stu? I don't see a thing."

"More Jack's line than yours, Mase. This system we're headed for is a triple, and the chart says it's a double. Natural enough, of course. This whole region is unexplored, so the charts are astronomicals, not surveys. But that makes us Prime Discoverers, and our Commanding Officer—and the book says 'Officer,' not 'Officers'—has got to . . ."

"That's me, now," Jack announced, striding grandly toward the plate. "Amscray, oobsbay. *I* will name the baby. *I* will report. *I* will go down in history . . ."

"Bounce back, small fry. You weren't at the time of discovery." Northrop placed a huge hand flat against Jack's face and pushed gently. "You'll go down, sure enough—not in history, but from a knock on the knob—if you try to steal any thunder away from *me*. And besides, you'd name it *'Dimples'*—what a *revolting* thought!"

"And what would you name it? *'Virgilia,'* I suppose?"

"Far from it, my boy." He had intended doing just that, but now he did not quite dare. "After our project, of course. The planet we're heading for will be Zabriska; the suns will be A-, B-, and C-Zabriskae, in order of size; and the watch officer then on duty, Lieutenant L. Stuart Rawlings, will engross these and all other pertinent data in the log. Can you classify 'em from here, Jack?"

"I can make some guesses—close enough, probably, for Discovery work." Then, after a few minutes: "Two giants, a blue-white and a bluish yellow; and a yellow dwarf."

"Dwarf in the Trojan?"

"That would be my guess, since that is the only place it could stay very long, but you can't tell much from one look. I can tell you one thing, though—unless your Zabriska is in a system straight beyond this one, it's got to be a planet of the big fellow himself; and brother, that sun is *hot!*"

"It's got to be here, Jack. I haven't made *that* big an error in reading a beam since I was a sophomore."

"I'll buy that . . . well, we're close enough, I guess." Jack killed the driving blasts, but not the Bergenholm; the inertialess vessel stopped instantaneously in open space. "Now we've got to find out which one of those twelve or fifteen planets was on our line when that last message was sent . . . There, we're stable enough, I hope. Open your cameras, Mase. Pull the first plate in fifteen minutes. That ought to give me enough track so I can start the job, since we're at a wide angle to their ecliptic."

The work went on for an hour or so. Then:

"Something coming from the direction of Tellus," the watch officer reported. "Big and fast. Shall I hail her?"

"Might as well," but the stranger hailed first.

"Space-ship *Chicago*, NA2AA, calling. Are you in trouble? Identify yourself, please."

"Space-ship NA774J acknowledging. No trouble . . ."

"Northrop! Jack!" came Virgil Samms' highly concerned thought. The superdreadnaught flashed alongside, a bare few hundred miles away, and stopped. "Why did you stop *here?*"

"This is where our signal came from, sir."

"Oh." A hundred thoughts raced through Samms' mind, too fast and too fragmentary to be intelligible. "I see you're computing. Would it throw you off too much to go inert and match intrinsics, so that I can join you?"

"No sir; I've got everything I need for a while."

Samms came aboard; three Lensmen studied the chart.

"Cavenda is there," Samms pointed out. "Trenco is there, off to one side. I felt sure that your signal originated on Cavenda; but Zabriska, here, while on almost the same line, is less than half as far from Tellus." He did not ask whether the two young Lensmen were sure of their findings. He knew. "This arouses my curiosity no end—does it merely complicate the thionite problem, or does it set up an entirely new problem? Go ahead, boys, with whatever you were going to do next."

Jack had already determined that the planet they wanted was the second out; A-Zabriskae Two. He drove the scout as close to the planet as he could without losing complete coverage; stationed it on the line toward Sol.

"Now we wait a bit," he answered. "According to recent periodicity, not less than four hours and not more than ten. With the next signal we'll nail that transmitter down to within a few feet. Got your spotting screens full out, Mase?"

"*Recent* periodicity?" Samms snapped. "It has improved, then, lately?"

"Very much, sir."

"That helps immensely. With George Olmstead harvesting broadleaf, it would. It is still one problem. While we wait, shall we study the planet a little?"

They explored, finding that A-Zabriskae Two was a disappointing planet indeed. It was small, waterless, airless, utterly featureless, utterly barren. There were no elevations, no depressions, no visible markings whatever—not even a meteor crater. Every square yard of its surface was apparently exactly like every other.

"No rotation," Jack reported, looking up from the bolometer. "That sand-pile is not inhabited and never will be. I'm beginning to wonder."

"So am I, now," Northrop admitted. "I still say that those signals came from this line and distance, but it looks as though they must have been sent from a ship. If so, now that we're here—particularly the *Chicago*—there will be no more signals."

"Not necessarily." Again Samms' mind transcended his Tellurian experience and knowledge. He did not suspect the truth, but he was not jumping at conclusions. "There may be highly intelligent life, even upon such a planet as this."

They waited, and in a few hours a communications beam snapped into life.

"READY—READY—READY . . ." it said briskly, for not quite one minute, but that was time enough.

Northrop yelped a string of numbers; Jack blasted the little vessel forward and downward; the three watch officers, keen-eyed at their plates, stabbed their visibeams, ultra-beams, and spy-rays along the indicated line.

"And bore straight through the planet if you have to—they may be on the other side!" Jack cautioned, sharply.

"They aren't—it's here, on this side!" Rawlings saw it first. "Nothing much to it, though . . . it looks like a relay station."

"A *relay!* I'll be a . . ." Jack started to express an unexpurgated opinion, but shut himself up. Young cubs did not swear in front of the First Lensman. "Let's land, sir, and look the place over, anyway."

"By all means."

They landed, and cautiously disembarked. The horizon, while actually quite a little closer than that of Earth, seemed much more distant because there was nothing whatever—no tree, no shrub, no rock or pebble, not even the slightest ripple—to break the geometrical perfection of that surface of smooth, hard, blindingly reflective, fiendishly hot white sand. Samms was highly dubious at first—a ground-tempertaure of four hundred seventy five degrees was not to be taken lightly; he did not at all like the looks of that ultra-fervent blue-white sun; and in his wildest imaginings he had never pictured such a desert. Their space-suits, however, were very well insulated, particularly as to the feet, and highly polished; and in lieu of atmosphere there was an almost perfect vacuum. They could stand it for a while.

The box which housed the relay station was made of non-ferrous metal and was roughly cubical in shape, perhaps five feet on a side. It was so buried that its upper edge was flush with the surface; its top, which was practically indistinguishable from the surrounding sand, was not bolted or welded, but was simply laid on, loose.

Previous spy-ray inspection having proved that the thing was not booby-trapped, Jack lifted the cover by one edge and all three Lensmen studied the mechanisms at close range; learning nothing new. There was an extremely sensitive nondirectional receiver, a highly directional sender, a beautifully precise uranium-clock director, and an "eternal" power-pack. There was nothing else.

"What next, sir?" Northrop asked. "There'll be an incoming signal, probably, in a couple of days. Shall we stick around and see whether it comes in from Cavenda or not?"

"You and Jack had better wait, yes." Samms thought for minutes. "I do not believe, now, that the signal will come from Cavenda, or that it will ever come twice from the same direction, but we will have to make sure. But I can't see any *reason* for it!"

"I think I can, sir." This was Northrop's specialty. "No space-ship could possibly hit Tellus from here except by accident with a single-ended beam, and they can't use a double-ender because it would have to be on all the time and would be as easy to trace as the Mississippi River. But this planet did all its settling ages ago—which is undoubtedly why they picked it out—and that director in there is a Marchanti—the second Marchanti I have ever seen."

"Whatever *that* is," Jack put in, and even Samms thought a question.

"The most precise thing ever built," the specialist explained. "Accuracy limited only by that of determination of relative motions. Give me an accurate enough equation to feed into it, like that tape is doing, and two sighting shots, and I'll guarantee to pour an eighteen-inch beam into any two foot cup on Earth. My guess is that it's aimed at some particular bucket-antenna on one of the Solar planets. I could spoil its aim easily enough, but I don't suppose that is what you're after."

"Decidedly not. We want to trace them, without exciting any more suspicion than is absolutely necessary. How often, would you say, do they have to come here to service this station—change tapes, and whatever else might be necessary?"

"Change tapes, is all. Not very often, by the size of those reels. If they know the relative motions exactly enough, they could compute as far ahead as they care to. I've been timing that reel—it's got pretty close to three months left on it."

"And more than that much has been used. It's no wonder we didn't see anything." Samms straightened up and stared out across the frightful waste. "Look there—I thought I saw something move—it *is* moving!"

"There's something moving closer than that, and it's really funny."

Jack laughed deeply. "Its like the paddle-wheels, shaft and all, of an old-fashioned river steamboat, rolling along as unconcernedly as you please. He won't miss me by over four feet, but he isn't swerving a hair. I think I'll block him off, just to see what he does."

"Be careful, Jack!" Samms cautioned, sharply. "Don't touch it—it may be charged, or worse."

Jack took the metal cover, which he was still holding, and by working it back and forth edgewise in the sand, made of it a vertical barrier squarely across the thing's path. The traveler paid no attention, did not alter its steady pace of a couple of miles per hour. It measured about twelve inches long over all; its paddle-wheel-like extremities were perhaps two inches wide and three inches in diameter.

"Do you think it's actually *alive*, sir? In a place like this?"

"I'm sure of it. Watch carefully."

It struck the barrier and stopped. That is, its forward motion stopped, but its rolling did not. Its rate of revolution did not change; it either did not know or did not care that its drivers were slipping on the smooth, hard sand; that it could not climb the vertical metal plate; that it was not getting anywhere.

"What a brain!" Northrop chortled, squatting down closer. "Why doesn't it back up or turn around? It may be alive, but it certainly isn't very bright."

The creature, now in the shadow of the 'Troncist's helmet, slowed down abruptly—went limp—collapsed.

"Get out of his light!" Jack snapped, and pushed his friend violently away; and as the vicious sunlight struck it, the native revived and began to revolve as vigorously as before. "I've got a hunch. Sounds screwy— never heard of such a thing—but it acts like an energy-converter. Eats energy, raw and straight. No storage capacity—on this world he wouldn't need it—a few more seconds in the shade would probably have killed him, but there's no shade here. Therefore, he can't be dangerous."

He reached out and touched the middle of the revolving shaft. Nothing happened. He turned it at right angles to the plate. The thing rolled away in a straight line, perfectly contented with the new direction. He recaptured it and stuck a test-prod lightly into the sand, just ahead of its shaft and just inside one paddle wheel. Around and around that slim wire the creature went: unable, it seemed, to escape from even such a simple trap; perfectly willing, it seemed, to spend all the rest of its life traversing that tiny circle.

" 'What a brain!' is right, Mase," Jack exclaimed. "*What* a brain!"

"This is wonderful, boys, really wonderful; something completely new to our science.'' Samms' thought was deep with feeling. "I am going to see if I can reach its mind or consciousness. Would you like to come along?''

"*Would* we!''

Samms tuned low and probed; lower and lower; deeper and deeper; and Jack and Mase stayed with him. The thing was certainly alive; it throbbed and vibrated with vitality: equally certainly, it was not very intelligent. But it had a definite consciousness of its own existence; and therefore, however tiny and primitive, a mind. Although its rudimentary ego could neither receive nor transmit thought, it knew that it was a fontema, that it must roll and roll and roll, endlessly, that by virtue of determined rolling its species would continue and would increase.

"Well, that's one for the book!'' Jack exclaimed, but Samms was entranced.

"I would like to find one or two more of them, to find out . . . I think I'll *take* the time. Can you see any more of them, either of you?''

"No, but we can find some—Stu!'' Northrop called.

"Yes?''

"Look around, will you? Find us a couple more of these fontema things and flick them over here with a tractor.''

"Coming up!'' and in a few seconds they were there.

"Are you photographing this, Lance?'' Samms called the Chief Communications Officer of the *Chicago*.

"We certainly are, sir—all of it. What are they, anyway? Animal, vegetable, or mineral?''

"I don't know. Probably no one of the three, strictly speaking. I'd like to take a couple back to Tellus, but I'm afraid that they'd die, even under an atomic lamp. We'll report to the Society.''

Jack liberated his captive and aimed it to pass within a few feet of one of the newcomers, but the two fontemas did not ignore each other. Both swerved, so that they came together wheel to wheel. The shafts bent toward each other, each into a right angle. The angles touched and fused. The point of fusion swelled rapidly into a double fist-sized lump. The half-shafts doubled in length. The lump split into four; became four perfect paddle-wheels. Four full-grown fontemas rolled away from the spot upon which two had met; their courses forming two mutually perpendicular straight lines.

"Beautiful!'' Samms exclaimed. "And notice, boys, the method of avoiding inbreeding. Upon a perfectly smooth planet such as this, no two of those four can ever meet, and the chance is almost vanishingly small that any of their first-generation offspring will ever meet. But I'm afraid I've been wasting time. Take me back out to the *Chicago*, please, and I'll be on my way.''

"You don't seem at all optimistic, sir." Jack ventured, as the NA774J approached the *Chicago*.

"Unfortunately, I am not. The signal will almost certainly come in from an unpredictable direction, from a ship so far away that even a super-fast cruiser could not get close enough to her to detect—just a minute. Rod!'' He Lensed the elder Kinnison so sharply that both young Lensmen jumped.

"What is it, Virge?''

Samms explained rapidly, concluding: "So I would like to have you throw a globe of scouts around this whole Zabriskan system. One detet* out and one detet apart, so as to be able to slap a tracer onto any ship laying a beam to this planet, from any direction whatever. It would not take too many scouts, would it?''

"No; but it wouldn't be worthwhile.''

"Why not?''

"Because it wouldn't prove a thing except what we already know— that Spaceways is involved in the thionite racket. The ship would be clean. Merely another relay.''

"Oh. You're probably right.'' If Virgil Samms was in the least put out at this cavalier dismissal of his idea, he made no sign. He thought intensely for a couple of minutes. "You *are* right. I will have to work from the Cavenda end. How are you coming with Operation Bennett?''

"Nice!'' Kinnison enthused. "When you get a couple of days, come over and see it grow. This is a fine world, Virge—it'll be ready!''

"I'll do that.'' Samms broke the connection and called Dronvire.

"The only change here is for the worse,'' the Rigellian reported, tersely. "The slight positive correlation between deaths from thionite and the arrival of Spaceways vessels has disappeared.''

There was no need to elaborate on that bare statement. Both Lensmen knew what it meant. The enemy, either in anticipation of statistical analysis or for economic reasons, was rationing his small supply of the drug.

And DalNalten was very much unlike his usual equable self. He was glum and unhappy; so much so that it took much urging to make him report at all.

"We have, as you know, put our best operatives to work on the interplanetary lines,'' he said finally, half sullenly. "We have secured quite a little data. The accumulating facts, however, point more and more definitely toward an utterly preposterous conclusion. Can you

---

*Detet—the distance at which one space-ship can detect another.   EES.

think of any valid reason why the exports and imports of thionite between Tellus and Mars, Mars and Venus, and Venus and Tellus, should all be exactly equal to each other?''

''*What!*''

''Precisely. That is why Knobos and I are not yet ready to present even a preliminary report.''

Then Jill. ''I can't prove it, any more than I could before, but I'm pretty sure that Morgan is the Boss. I have drawn every picture I can think of with Isaacson in the driver's seat, but none of them fit.'' She paused, questioningly.

''I am already reconciled to adopting that view, at least as a working hypothesis. Go ahead.''

''The fact seems to be that Morgan has always had all the left-wingers of the Nationalists under his thumb. Now he and his man Friday, Representative Flierce, are wooing all the radicals and so-called liberals on our side of both Senate and House—a new technique for him—and they're offering plenty of the right kind of bait. He has the commentators guessing, but there's no doubt whatever in my mind that he is aiming at next Election Day and our Galactic Council.''

''And you and Dronvire are sitting idly by, doing nothing, of course?''

''Of course!'' Jill giggled, but sobered quickly. ''He's a smooth, *smooth* worker, Dad. We are organizing, of course, and putting out propaganda of our own, but there's so pitifully little that we can actually *do*—look and listen to this for a minute, and you'll see what I mean.''

In her distant room Jill manipulated a reel and flipped a switch. A plate came to life, showing Morgan's big, sweating, passionately earnest face.

''. . . and who *are* these Lensmen, anyway?'' Morgan's voice bellowed, passionate conviction in every syllable. ''They are the hired minions of the classes, stabbers in the back, crooks and scoundrels, TOOLS OF RUTHLESS WEALTH! They are hirelings of the interplanetary bankers, those unspeakable excrescences on the body politic who are still grinding down into the dirt, under an iron heel, the face of the common man! In the guise of democracy they are trying to set up the worst, the most outrageous tyranny that this universe has ever . . .'' Jill snapped the switch viciously.

''And a lot of people *swallow* that . . . that *bilge!*'' she almost snarled. ''If they had the brains of a . . . of even that Zabriskan fontema Mase told me about, they wouldn't, but they *do!*''

''I know they do. We have known all along that he is a masterly actor; we now know that he is more than that.''

"Yes, and we're finding out that no appeal to reason, no psychological counter-measures, will work. Dronvire and I agree that you'll *have* to arrange matters so that you can do solid months of stumping yourself. Personally."

"It may come to that, but there's a lot of other things to do first."

Samms broke the connection and thought. He did not consciously try to exclude the two youths, but his mind was working so fast and in such a disjointed fashion that they could catch only a few fragments. The incomprehensible vastness of space—tracing—detection—Cavenda's one tiny, fast moving moon—back, and solidly, to DETECTION.

"Mase," Samms thought then, carefully. "As a specialist in such things, why is it that the detectors of the smallest scout—lifeboat, even—have practically the same range as those of the largest liners and battleships?"

"Noise level and hash, sir, from the atomics."

"But can't they be screened out?"

"Not entirely, sir, without blocking reception completely."

"I see. Suppose, then, that all atomics aboard were to be shut down; that for the necessary heat and light we use electricity, from storage or primary batteries or from a generator driven by an internal-combustion motor or a heat-engine. Could the range of detection then be increased?"

"Tremendously, sir. My guess is that the limiting factor would then be the cosmics."

"I hope you're right. While you are waiting for the next signal to come in, you might work out a preliminary design for such a detector. If, as I anticipate, this Zabriska proves to be a dead end, Operation Zabriska ends here—becomes a part of Zwilnik—and you two will follow me at max to Tellus. You, Jack, are very badly needed on Operation Boskone. You and I, Mase, will make appropriate alterations aboard a J-class vessel of the Patrol."

12

THIONITE AND URANIUM

Approaching Cavenda in his dead-black, converted scout-ship, Virgil Samms cut his drive, killed his atomics, and turned on his superpowered detectors. For five full detets in every direction—throughout a spherical volume over ten detets in diameter—space was void of ships. Some activity was apparent upon the planet dead ahead, but the First Lensman did not worry about that. The drug-runners would of course have atomics in their plants, even if there were no space-ships actually on the planet—which there probably were. What he did worry about was detection. There would be plenty of detectors, probably automatic; not only ordinary sub-ethereals, but electros and radars as well.

He flashed up to within one and a quarter detets, stopped, and checked again. Space was still empty. Then, after making a series of observations, he went inert and established an intrinsic velocity which, he hoped, would be close enough. He again shut off his atomics and started the sixteen-cylinder Diesel engine which would do its best to replace them.

That best was none too good, but it would do. Besides driving the Bergenholm it could furnish enough kilodynes of thrust to produce a velocity many times greater than any attainable by inert matter. It used a lot of oxygen per minute, but it would not run for very many minutes. With her atomics out of action his ship would not register upon the plates of the long-range detectors universally used. Since she was nevertheless traveling faster than light, neither electromagnetic detector-webs nor radar could "see" her. Good enough.

Samms was not the System's best computer, nor did he have the System's finest instruments. His positional error could be corrected easily enough; but as he drove nearer and nearer to Cavenda, keeping, toward the last, in line with its one small moon, he wondered more and more as to how much of an allowance he should make for error in his intrinsic, which he had set up practically by guess. And there was another variable, the cut-off. He slowed down to just over one light; but even at that comparatively slow speed an error of one millisecond at cut-off meant a displacement of two hundred miles! He switched the spotter into the Berg's cut-off circuit, set it for three hundred miles, and waited tensely at his controls.

The relays clicked, the driving force expired, the vessel went inert. Samms' eyes, flashing from instrument to instrument, told him that matters could have been worse. His intrinsic was neither straight up, as he had hoped, nor straight down, as he had feared, but almost exactly halfway between the two—straight out. He discovered that fact just in time; in another second or two he would have been out beyond the moon's protecting bulk and thus detectable from Cavenda. He went free, flashed back to the opposite boundary of his area of safety, went inert, and put the full power of the bellowing Diesel to the task of bucking down his erroneous intrinsic, losing altitude continuously. Again and again he repeated the maneuver; and thus, grimly and stubbornly, he fought his ship to ground.

He was very glad to see that the surface of the satellite was rougher, rockier, ruggeder, and more cratered even than that of Earth's Luna. Upon such a terrain as this, it would be next to impossible to spot even a moving vessel—if it moved carefully.

By a series of short and careful inertialess hops—correcting his intrinsic velocity after each one by an inert collision with the ground— he maneuvered his vessel into such a position that Cavenda's enormous globe hung directly overhead. Breathing a profoundly deep breath of relief he killed the big engine, cut in his fully-charged accumulators, and turned on detector and spy-ray. He would see what he could see.

His detectors showed that there was only one point of activity on the whole planet. He located it precisely; then, after cutting his spy-ray to minimum power, he approached it gingerly, yard by yard. Stopped! As he had more than half expected, there was a spy-ray block. A big one, almost two miles in diameter. It would be almost directly beneath him— or rather, almost straight overhead—in about three hours.

Samms had brought along a telescope, considerably more powerful than the telescopic visiplate of his scout. Since the surface gravity of this moon was low—scarcely one-fifth that of Earth—he had no difficulty in lugging the parts out of the ship or in setting the thing up.

But even the telescope did not do much good. The moon was close to Cavenda, as astronomical distances go—but really worthwhile astronomical optical instruments simply are not portable. Thus the Lensman saw something that, by sufficient stretch of the imagination, could have been a factory; and, eyes straining at the tantalizing limit of visibility, he even made himself believe that he saw a toothpick-shaped object and a darkly circular blob, either of which could have been the space-ship of the outlaws. He was sure, however, of two facts. There were no real cities upon Cavenda. There were no modern spaceports, or even airfields.

He dismounted the 'scope, stored it, set his detectors, and waited. He had to sleep at times, of course; but any ordinary detector rig can be set to sound off at any change in its status—and Samms' was no ordinary rig. Wherefore, when the drug-mongers' vessel took off, Samms left Cavenda as unobtrusively as he had approached it, and swung into that vessel's line.

Samms' strategy had been worked out long since. On his Diesel, at a distance of just over one detet, he would follow the outlaw as fast as he could; long enough to establish his line. He would then switch to atomic drive and close up to between one and two detets; then again go onto Diesel for a check. He would keep this up for as long as might prove necessary.

As far as any of the Lensmen knew, Spaceways always used regular liners or freighters in this business, and this scout was much faster than any such vessel. And even if—highly improbable thought!—the enemy ship was faster than his own, it would still be within range of *those* detectors when it got to wherever it was that it was going. But how wrong Samms was!

At his first check, instead of being not over two detets away the quarry was three and a half; at the second the distance was four and a quarter; at the third, almost exactly five. Scowling, Samms watched the erstwhile brilliant point of light fade into darkness. That circular blob that he had almost seen, then, had been the space-ship, but it had not been a sphere, as he had supposed. Instead, it had been a tear-drop; sticking, sharp tail down, in the ground. Ultra-fast. This was the result. But ideas had blown up under him before, they probably would again. He resumed atomic drive and made arrangements with the Port Admiral to rendezvous with him and the *Chicago* at the earliest possible time.

"What is there along that line?" he demanded of the superdreadnaught's Chief Pilot, even before junction had been made.

"Nothing, sir, that we know of," that worthy reported, after studying his charts.

He boarded the gigantic ship of war, and with Kinnison pored over those same charts.

"Your best bet is Eridan, I think," Kinnison concluded finally. "Not too near your line, but they could very easily figure that a one-day dogleg would be a good investment. And Spaceways owns it, you know, from core to planetary limits—the richest uranium mines in existence. Made to order. Nobody would suspect a uranium ship. How about throwing a globe around Eridan?"

Samms thought for minutes. "No . . . not yet, at least. We don't know enough yet."

"I know it—that's why it looks to me like a good time and place to learn something," Kinnison argued. "We know—almost know, at least—that a super-fast ship, carrying thionite, has just landed there. This is the hottest lead we've had. I say englobe the planet, declare martial law, and not let anything in or out until we find it. Somebody there must know something, a lot more than we do. I say hunt him out and make him talk."

"You're just popping off, Rod. You know as well as I do that nabbing a few of the small fry isn't enough. We can't move openly until we can strike high."

"I suppose not," Kinnison grumbled. "But we know so *damned* little, Virge!"

"Little enough," Samms agreed. "Of the three main divisions, only the political aspect is at all clear. In the drug division, we know where thionite comes from and where it is processed, and Eridan may be—probably is—another link. On the other end, we know a lot of peddlers and a few middlemen—nobody higher. We have no actual knowledge whatever as to who the higher-ups are or how they work; and it's the bosses we want. Concerning the pirates, we know even less. 'Murgatroyd' may be no more a man's name than 'zwilnik' is . . ."

"Before you get too far away from the subject, what are you going to do about Eridan?"

"Nothing, for the moment, would be best, I believe. However, Knobos and DalNalten should switch their attention from Spaceways' passenger liners to the uranium ships from Eridan to all three of the inner planets. Check?"

"Check. Particularly since it explains so beautifully the merry-go-round they have been on so long—chasing the same packages of dope backwards and forwards so many times that the corners of the boxes got worn round. We've got to get the top men, and they're smart. Which reminds me—Morgan as Big Boss does not square up with the Morgan that you and Fairchild smacked down so easily when he tried to investigate the Hill. A loud-mouthed, chiseling politician might have a lockbox full of documentary evidence about party bosses and power deals and chorus girls and Martian tekkyl coats, but the man we're after very definitely would not.''

"You're telling me?" This point was such a sore one that Samms relapsed into idiom. "The boys should have cracked that box a week ago, but they struck a knot. I'll see if they know anything yet. Tune in, Rod. Ray!" He Lensed a thought at his cousin.

"Yes, Virge?"

"Have you got a spy-ray into that lock-box yet?"

"Glad you called. Yes, last night. Empty. Empty as a sub-deb's skull—except for an atomic-powered gimmick that it took Bergenholm's whole laboratory almost a week to neutralize."

"I see. Thanks. Off." Samms turned to Kinnison. "Well?"

"Nice. A mighty smart operator." Kinnison gave credit ungrudgingly. "Now I'll buy your picture—what a man! But now—and I've got my ears pinned back—what was it you started to say about pirates?"

"Just that we have very little to go on, except for the kind of stuff they seem to like best, and the fact that even armed escorts have not been able to protect certain types of shipments of late. The escorts, too, have disappeared. But with these facts as bases, it seems to me that we could arrange something, perhaps like this . . .''

A fast, sleek freighter and a heavy battle-cruiser bored steadily through the inter-stellar void. The merchantman carried a fabulously valuable cargo: not bullion or jewels or plate of price, but things literally above price—machine tools of highest precision, delicate optical and electrical instruments, fine watches and chronometers. She also carried First Lensman Virgil Samms.

And aboard the war-ship there was Roderick Kinnison; for the first time in history a mere battle-cruiser bore a Port Admiral's flag.

As far as the detectors of those two ships could reach, space was empty of man-made craft; but the two Lensmen knew that they were not alone. One and one-half detets away, loafing along at the freighter's speed and paralleling her course, in a hemispherical formation open to the front, there flew six tremendous tear-drops; superdreadnaughts of whose existence no Tellurian or Colonial government had even an inkling. They were the fastest and deadliest craft yet built by man—the first fruits of Operation Bennett. And they, too, carried Lensmen—Costigan, Jack Kinnison, Northrop, Dronvire of Rigel Four, Rodebush, and Cleveland. Nor was there need of detectors: the eight Lensmen were in as close communication as though they had been standing in the same room.

"On your toes, men," came Samms' quiet thought. "We are about to pass within a few light-minutes of an uninhabited solar system. No Tellurian-type planets at all. This may be it. Tune to Kinnison on one side and to your captains on the other. Take over, Rod."

At one instant the ether, for one full detet in every direction, was empty. In the next, three intensely brilliant spots of detection flashed into being, in line with the dead planet so invitingly close at hand.

This development came as a surprise, since only two raiders had been expected: a battleship to take care of the escort, a cruiser to take the merchantman. The fact that the pirates had become cautious or suspicious and had sent three superdreadnaughts on the mission, however, did not operate to change the Patrol's strategy; for Samms had concluded, and Dronvire and Bergenholm and Rularion of Jupiter had agreed, that the real commander of the expedition would be aboard the vessel that attacked the freighter.

In the next instant, then—each Lensman saw what Roderick Kinnison saw, in the very instant of his seeing it—six more points of hard, white light sprang into being upon the plates of guileful freighter and decoying cruiser.

"Jack and Mase, take the leader!" Kinnison snapped out the thought. "Dronvire and Costigan, right wing—he's the one that's going after the freighter. Fred and Lyman, left wing. Hipe!"

The pirate ships flashed up, filling ether and sub-ether alike with a solid mush of interference through which no call for help could be driven; two superdreadnaughts against the cruiser, one against the freighter. The former, of course, had been expected to offer more than a token resistance. Battle cruisers of the Patrol were powerful vessels, both on offense and defense, and it was a known and recognized fact that the men of the Patrol were *men*. The pirate commander who attacked the freighter, however, was a surprised pirate indeed. His first beam, directed well forward, well ahead of the precious cargo, should have wrought the same havoc against screens and wall-shields and structure as a white-hot poker would against a pat of luke-warm butter. Practically the whole nose-section, including the control room, should have whiffed outward into space in gobbets and streamers of molten and gaseous metal. But nothing of the sort happened—this merchantman was *no* push-over!

No ordinary screens protected that particular freighter and the person of First Lensman Samms—Roderick Kinnison had very thoroughly seen to that. In sheer mass her screen generators outweighed her entire cargo, heavy as that cargo was, by more than two to one. Thus the pirate's beams stormed and struck and clawed and clung—uselessly. They did not penetrate. And as the surprised attacker shoved his power up and up, to his absolute ceiling of effort, the only result was to increase the already tremendous pyrotechnic display of energies cascading in all directions from the fiercely radiant defenses of the Tellurian freighter.

And in a few seconds the commanding officers of the other two attacking battleships were also surprised. The battle-cruiser's screens did not go down, even under the combined top effort of two superdreadnaughts! And she did not have a beam hot enough to light a match—she must be *all screen!* But before the startled outlaws could do anything about the realization that they, instead of being the trappers, were in cold fact the trapped, all three of them were surprised again—the last surprise that any one of them was ever to receive. Six mighty teardrops—vastly bigger, faster, more powerful than their own—were rushing upon them, blanketing all channels of communication as efficiently and as enthusiastically as they themselves had been doing an instant before.

Being out simply and ruthlessly to kill, and not to capture, four of the newcomers from Bennett polished off the cruiser's two attackers in very short order. They simply flashed in, went inert at the four corners of an imaginary tetrahedron, and threw everything they had—and they had plenty. Possibly—just barely possibly—there may have been, somewhere, a space-battle shorter than that one; but there certainly was never one more violent.

Then the four set out after their two sister-ships and the one remaining pirate, who was frantically devoting his every effort to the avoidance of engagement. But with six ships, each one of which was of vastly greater individual power than his own, at the six corners of an octahedron of which he was the geometrical center, his ability to cut tractor beams and to "squirt out" from between two opposed pressors did him no good whatever. He was englobed; or, rather, to apply the correct terminology to an operation involving so few units, he was "boxed."

To blow the one remaining raider out of the ether would have been easy enough, but that was exactly what the Patrolmen did not want to do. They wanted information. Wherefore each of the Patrol ships directed a dozen or so beams upon the scintillating protective screens of the enemy; enough so that every square yard of defensive web was under direct attack. As rapidly as it could be done without losing equilibrium or synchronization, the power of each beam was stepped up until the wildly violet incandescence of the pirate screen showed that it was hovering on the very edge of failure. Then, in the instant, needlebeamers went furiously to work. The screen was already loaded to its limit; no transfer of defensive energy was possible. Thus, tremendously overloaded locally, locally it flared through the ultra-violet into the black and went down; and the fiercely penetrant daggers of pure force stabbed and stabbed and stabbed.

The engine room went first, even though the needlers had to gnaw a hundred-foot hole straight through the pirate craft in order to find the vital installations. Then, enough damage done so that spy-rays could get in, the rest of the work was done with precision and dispatch. In a matter of seconds the pirate hulk lay helpless, and the Patrolmen peeled her like an orange—or, rather, more like an amateur cook very wastefully peeling a potato. Resistless knives of energy sheared off tail-section and nose-section, top and bottom, port and starboard sides; then slabbed off the corners of what was left, until the control room was almost bared to space.

Then, as soon as the intrinsic velocities could possibly be matched, board and storm! With Dronvire of Rigel Four in the lead, closely followed by Costigan, Northrop, Kinnison the Younger, and a platoon of armed and armored Space Marines!

Samms and the two scientists did not belong in such a melee as that which was to come, and knew it. Kinnison the Elder did not belong, either, but did not know it. In fact, he cursed fluently and bitterly at having to stay out—nevertheless, out he stayed.

Dronvire, on the other hand, did not like to fight. The very thought of actual, bodily, hand-to-hand combat revolted every fiber of his being. In view of what the spy-ray men were reporting, however, and of what all the Lensmen knew of pirate psychology, Dronvire had to get into that control room first, and he had to get there *fast*. And if he *had* to fight, he could; and, physically, he was wonderfully well equipped for just such activity. To his immense physical strength, the natural concomitant of a force of gravity more than twice Earth's, the armor which so encumbered the Tellurian battlers was a scarcely noticeable impediment. His sense of perception, which could not be barred by any material substance, kept him fully informed of every development in his neighborhood. His literally incredible speed enabled him not merely to parry a blow aimed at him, but to bash out the brains of the would-be attacker before that blow could be more than started. And whereas a human being can swing only one space-axe or fire only two ray-guns at a time, the Rigellian plunged through space toward what was left of the pirate vessel, swinging not one or two space-axes, but four; each held in a lithe and supple, but immensely strong, tentacular "hand."

Why axes? Why not Lewistons, or rifles, or pistols? Because the space armor of that day could withstand almost indefinitely the output of two or three hand-held projectors; because the resistance of its defensive fields varied directly as the cube of the velocity of any material projectile encountering them. Thus, and strangely enough, the advance of science had forced the re-adoption of that long-extinct weapon.

Most of the pirates had died, of course, during the dismemberment of their ship. Many more had been picked off by the needle-beam gunners. In the control room, however, there was a platoon of elite guards, clustered so closely about the commander and his officers that needles could not be used; a group that would have to be wiped out by hand.

If the attack had come by way of the only doorway, so that the pirates could have concentrated their weapons upon one or two Patrolmen, the commander might have had time enough to do what he was under compulsion to do. But while the Patrolmen were still in space a plane of force sheared off the entire side of the room, a tractor beam jerked the detached wall away, and the attackers floated in en masse.

Weightless combat is not at all like any form of gymnastics known to us ground-grippers. It is much more difficult to master, and in times of stress the muscles revert involuntarily and embarrassingly to their wonted gravity-field techniques. Thus the endeavors of most of the battlers upon both sides, while earnest enough and deadly enough of intent, were almost comically unproductive of result. In a matter of seconds frantically-struggling figures were floating from wall to ceiling to wall to floor; striking wildly, darting backward from the violence of their own fierce swings.

The Tellurian Lensman, however, had had more practice and remembered their lessons better. Jack Kinnison, soaring into the room, grabbed the first solid thing he could reach; a post. Pulling himself down to the floor, he braced both feet, sighted past the nearest foeman, swung his axe, and gave a tremendous shove. Such was his timing that in the instant of maximum effort the beak of his atrociously effective weapon encountered the pirate's helmet—and that was that. He wrenched his axe free and shoved the corpse away in such a direction that the reaction would send him against a wall at the floor line, in position to repeat the maneuver.

Since Mason Northrop was heavier and stronger than his friend, his technique was markedly different. He dove for the chart-table, which of course was welded to the floor. He hooked one steel-shod foot around one of the table's legs and braced the other against its top. Weightless but inert, it made no difference whether his position was vertical or horizontal or anywhere between; from this point of vantage, with his length of body and arm and axe, he could cover a lot of room. He reached out, hooked bill of axe into belt or line-snap or angle of armor, and pulled; and as the helplessly raging pirate floated past him, he swung and struck. And that, too, was that.

Dronvire of Rigel Four did not rush to the attack. He had never been and was not now either excited or angry. Indeed, it was only empirically that he knew what anger and excitement were. He had never been in any kind of a fight. Therefore he paused for a couple of seconds to analyze the situation and to determine his own most efficient method of operation. He would not have to be in physical contact with the pirate captain to go to work on his mind, but he would have to be closer than this and he would have to be free from physical attack while he concentrated. He perceived what Kinnison and Costigan and Northrop were doing, and knew why each was working in a different fashion. He applied that knowledge to his own mass, to his own musculature, to the length and strength of his arms—each one of which was twice as long and ten times as strong as the trunk of an elephant. He computed forces and leverages, actions and reactions, points of application, stresses and strains.

He threw away two of his axes. The two empty arms reached out, each curling around the neck of a pirate. Two axes flashed, grazing each pinioning arm so nearly that it seemed incredible that the sharp edges did not shear away the Rigellian's own armor. Two heads floated away from two bodies and Dronvire reached for two more. And two—and two—and two. Calm and dispassionate, but not wasting a motion or a millisecond, Dronvire accomplished more, in less time, than all the Tellurians in the room.

"Costigan, Northrop, Kinnison—attend!" he launched a thought. "I have no time to kill more of them. The commander is dying of a self-inflicted wound and I have important work to do. See to it, please, that these remaining creatures do not attack me while I am doing it."

Dronvire tuned his mind to that of the pirate and probed. Although dying, the pirate captain offered fierce resistance, but the Rigellian was not alone. Attuned to his mind, working smoothly with it, giving it strengths and qualities which no Rigellian ever had had or ever would have, were the two strongest minds of Earth: that of Rod the Rock Kinnison, with the driving force, the indomitable will, the transcendent urge of all human heredity; and that of Virgil Samms, with all that had made him First Lensman.

"TELL!" that terrific triple mind demanded, with a force which simply could not be denied. "WHERE ARE YOU FROM? Resistance is useless; yours or that of those whom you serve. Your bases and powers are smaller and weaker than ours, since Spaceways is only a corporation and we are the Galactic Patrol. TELL! WHO ARE YOUR BOSSES? TELL—TELL!"

Under that irresistible urge there appeared, foggily and without any hint of knowledge of name or of spatial coordinates, an embattled planet, very similar in a smaller way to the Patrol's own Bennett, and—

Even more foggily, but still not so blurred but that their features were unmistakably recognizable, the images of two men. That of Murgatroyd, the pirate chief, completely strange to both Kinnison and Samms; and—

Back of Murgatroyd and above him, that of—

BIG JIM TOWNE!

13

CANDIDATE KINNISON

"**F**irst, about Murgatroyd." In his office in The Hill Roderick Kinnison spoke aloud to the First Lensman. "What do you think should be done about him?"

"Murgatroyd. Hm . . . m . . . m." Samms inhaled a mouthful of smoke and exhaled it slowly; watched it dissipate in the air. "Ah, yes, Murgatroyd." He repeated the performance. "My thought, at the moment, is to let him alone."

"Check," Kinnison said. If Samms was surprised at his friend's concurrence he did not show it. "Why? Let's see if we check on that."

"Because he does not seem to be of fundamental importance. Even if we could find him . . . and by the way, what do you think the chance is of our spies finding him?"

"Just about the same chance that theirs have of finding out about the Samms-Olmstead switch or our planet Bennett. Vanishingly small. Zero."

"Right. And even if we could find him—even find their secret base, which is certainly as well hidden as ours is—it would do us no present good, because we could take no positive action. We have, I think, learned the prime fact; that Towne is actually Murgatroyd's superior."

"That's the way I see it. We can almost draw an organization chart now."

"I wouldn't say 'almost.' " Samms smiled half-ruefully. "There are gaping holes, and Isaacson is as yet a highly unknown quantity. I've tried to draw one a dozen times, but we haven't got enough information. An incorrect chart, you know, would be worse than none at all. As soon as I can draw a correct one, I'll show it to you. But in the meantime, the position of our friend James F. Towne is now clear. He is actually a Big Shot in both piracy and politics. That fact surprised me, even though it did clarify the picture tremendously.''

"Me, too. One good thing, we won't have to hunt for him. You've been working on him right along, though, haven't you?''

"Yes, but this new relationship throws light on a good many details which have been obscure. It also tends to strengthen our working hypothesis as to Isaacson—which we can't prove yet, of course—that he is the actual working head of the drug syndicate. Vice-President in charge of Drugs, so to speak.''

"Huh? That's a new one on me. I don't see it.''

"There is very little doubt that at the top there is Morgan. He is, and has been for some time, the real boss of North America. Under him, probably taking orders direct, is President Witherspoon.''

"Undoubtedly. The Nationalist party is strictly *a la* machine, and Witherspoon is one of the world's slimiest skinkers. Morgan is Chief Engineer of the Machine. Take it from there.''

"We know that Boss Jim is also in the top echelon—quite possibly the Commander-in-Chief—of the enemy's Armed Forces. By analogy, and since Isaacson is apparently on the same level as Towne, immediately below Morgan . . .''

"Wouldn't there be three? Witherspoon?''

"I doubt it. My present idea is that Witherspoon is at least one level lower. Comparatively small fry.''

"Could be—I'll buy it. A nice picture, Virge; and beautifully symmetrical. His Mightiness Morgan. Secretary of War Towne and Secretary of Drugs Isaacson; and each of them putting a heavy shoulder behind the political bandwagon. *Very* nice. That makes Operation Mateese tougher than ever—a triple-distilled toughie. Glad I told you it wasn't my dish—saves me the trouble of backing out now.''

"Yes, I have noticed how prone you are to duck tough jobs.'' Samms smiled quietly. "However, unless I am even more mistaken than usual, you will be in it up to your not-so-small ears, my friend, before it is over.''

"Huh? How?'' Kinnison demanded.

"That will, I hope, become clear very shortly.'' Samms stubbed out the butt of his cigarette and lit another. "The basic problem can be stated very simply. How are we going to persuade the sovereign countries of Earth—particularly the North American Continent—to grant the Galactic Patrol the tremendous power and authority it will have to have?''

"Nice phrasing, Virge, and studied. Not off the cuff. But aren't you over-drawing a bit? Little if any conflict. The Patrol would be pretty largely inter-systemic in scope . . . with of course the necessary inter-planetary and inter-continental . . . and . . . um . . . m . . ."

"Exactly."

"But it's logical enough, Virge, even at that, and has plenty of precedents, clear back to ancient history. 'Way back, before space-travel, when they first started to use atomic energy, and the only drugs they had to worry about were cocaine, morphine, heroin, and other purely Tellurian products. I was reading about it just the other day."

Kinnison swung around, fingered a book out of a matched set, and riffled its leaves. "Russia was the world's problem child then—put up what they called an iron curtain—wouldn't play with the neighbors' children, but picked up her marbles and went home. But yet—here it is. Original source unknown—some indications point to a report of somebody named Hoover, sometime in the nineteen forties or fifties, Gregorian calendar. Listen:

" 'This protocol'—he's talking about the agreement on world-wide Narcotics Control—'was signed by fifty-two nations, including the U.S.S.R.'—that was Russia—'and its satellite states. It was the only international agreement to which the Communist countries'—you know more about what Communism was, I suppose, than I do."

"Just that it was another form of dictatorship that didn't work out."

" '. . . to which the Communist countries ever gave more than lip service. This adherence is all the more surprising, in view of the political situation then obtaining, in that all signatory nations obligated themselves to surrender national sovereignty in five highly significant respects, as follows:

" 'First, to permit Narcotics agents of all other signatory nations free, secret, and unregistered entry into, unrestricted travel throughout, and exit from, all their lands and waters, wherever situate:

" 'Second, upon request, to allow known criminals and known contraband to enter and to leave their territories without interference:

" 'Third, to cooperate fully, and as a secondary and not as a prime mover, in any Narcotics Patrol program set up by any other signatory nation:

" 'Fourth, upon request, to maintain complete secrecy concerning any Narcotics operation: and

" 'Fifth, to keep the Central Narcotics Authority fully and continuously informed upon all matters hereinbefore specified.'

"And apparently, Virge, it worked. If they could do that, 'way back then, we certainly should be able to make the Patrol work now."

"You talk as though the situations were comparable. They aren't. Instead of giving up an insignificant fraction of their national sovereignty, all nations will have to give up practically all of it. They will have to change their thinking from a National to a Galactic viewpoint; will have to become units in a Galactic Civilization, just as counties used to be units of states, and states are units of the continents. The Galactic Patrol will not be able to stop at being the supreme and only authority in inter-systemic affairs. It is bound to become intra-systemic, intra-planetary, and intra-continental. Eventually, it must and it shall be the *sole* authority, except for such purely local organizations as city police."

"*What* a program!" Kinnison thought silently for minutes. "But I'm still betting that you can bring it off."

"We'll keep on driving until we do. What gives us our chance is that the all-Lensman Solarian Council is already in existence and is functioning smoothly; and that the government of North America has no jurisdiction beyond the boundaries of its continent. Thus, and even though Morgan has extra-legal powers both as Boss of North America and as the head of an organization which is in fact inter-systemic in scope, he can do nothing whatever about the fact that the Solarian Council has been enlarged into the Galactic Council. As a matter of fact, he was and is very much in favor of that particular move—just as much so as we are."

"You're going too fast for me. How do you figure that?"

"Unlike our idea of the Patrol as a coordinator of free and independent races, Morgan sees it as the perfect instrument of a Galactic dictatorship, thus: North America is the most powerful continent of Earth. The other continents will follow her lead—or else. Tellus can very easily dominate the other Solarian planets, and the Solar System can maintain dominance over all other systems as they are discovered and colonized. Therefore, whoever controls the North American Continent controls all space."

"I see. Could be, at that. Throw the Lensmen out, put his own stooges in. Wonder how he'll go about it? A *tour de force?* No. The next election, would be my guess. If so, that will be the most important election in history."

"If they decide to wait for the election, yes. I'm not as sure as you seem to be that they will not act sooner."

"They can't," Kinnison declared. "Name me one thing they think they can do, and I'll shoot it fuller of holes than a target."

"They can, and I am very much afraid that they will," Samms replied, soberly. "At any time he cares to do so, Morgan—through the North American Government, of course—can abrogate the treaty and name his own Council."

"Without my boys—the backbone and the guts of North America, as well as of the Patrol? Don't be stupid, Virge. They're *loyal*."

"Admitted—but at the same time they are being paid in North American currency. Of course, we will soon have our own Galactic credit system worked out, but . . ."

"What the hell difference would *that* make?" Kinnison wanted savagely to know. "You think they'd last until the next pay-day if they start playing that kind of ball? What in hell do you think *I'd* be doing? And Clayton and Schweikert and the rest of the gang? Sitting on our fat rumps and crying into our beers?"

"You would do nothing. I could not permit any illegal . . ."

"Permit!" Kinnison blazed, leaping to his feet. "Permit—hell! Are you loose-screwed enough to actually think I would ask or need your permission? Listen, Samms!" The Port Admiral's voice took on a quality like nothing his friend had ever before heard. "The first thing I would do would be to take off your Lens, wrap you up—especially your mouth—in seventeen yards of three-inch adhesive tape, and heave you into the brig. The second would be to call out everything we've got, including every half-built ship on Bennett able to fly, and declare martial law. The third would be a series of summary executions, starting with Morgan and working down. And if he's got any fraction of the brain I credit him with, Morgan knows damned well *exactly* what would happen."

"Oh." Samms, while very much taken aback, was thrilled to the center of his being. "I had not considered anything so drastic, but you probably would . . ."

"Not 'probably,'" Kinnison corrected him grimly. " 'Certainly.' "

". . . and Morgan does know . . . except about Bennett, of course . . . and he would not, for obvious reasons, bring in his secret armed forces. You're right, Rod, it will be the election."

"Definitely; and it's plain enough what their basic strategy will be." Kinnison, completely mollified, sat down and lit another cigar. "His Nationalist party is now in power, but it was our Cosmocrats of the previous administration who so basely slipped one over on the dear pee-pul—who betrayed the entire North American Continent into the claws of rapacious wealth, no less—by ratifying that unlawful, unhallowed, unconstitutional, and so on, treaty. Scoundrels! Bribe-takers! Betrayers of a sacred trust! *How* Rabble-Rouser Morgan will thump the tub on that theme—he'll make the welkin ring as it never rang before."

Kinnison mimicked savagely the demagogue's round and purple tones as he went on: " 'Since they had no mandate from the pee-pul to trade their birthright for a mess of pottage that nefarious and underhanded treaty is, *a prima vista* and *ipso facto* and *a priori*, completely and necessarily and positively null and void. People of Earth, arouse! Arise! Rise in your might and throw off this stultifying and degrading, this paralyzing yoke of the Monied Powers—throw out this dictatorial, autocratic, wealth-directed, illegal, monstrous Council of so-called Lensmen! Rise in your might at the polls! Elect a Council of your own choosing—not of Lensmen, but of ordinary folks like you and me. Throw *off* this hellish yoke, I say!'—and here he begins to positively froth at the mouth—'so that government of the people, by the people, and for the people shall not perish from the Earth!'

"He has used that exact peroration, ancient as it is, so many times that practically everybody thinks he originated it; and it's always good for so many decibels of applause that he'll keep on using it forever."

"Your analysis is vivid, cogent, and factual, Rod—but the situation is not at all funny."

"Did I act as though I thought it was? If so, I'm a damned poor actor. I'd like to kick the bloodsucking leech all the way from here to the Great Nebula in Andromeda, and if I ever get the chance I'm going to!"

"An interesting, but somewhat irrelevant idea." Samms smiled at his friend's passionate outburst. "But go on. I agree with you in principle so far, and your viewpoint is—to say the least—refreshing."

"Well, Morgan will have so hypnotized most of the dear pee-pul that they will think it their own idea when he renominates this spineless nincompoop Witherspoon for another term as President of North America, with a solid machine-made slate of hatchet-men behind him. They win the election. Then the government of the North American Continent—not the Morgan-Towne-Isaacson machine, but all nice and legal and by mandate and in strict accordance with the party platform—abrogates the treaty and names its own Council. And right then, my friend, the boys and I will do our stuff."

"Except that, in such a case, you wouldn't. Think it over, Rod."

"Why not?" Kinnison demanded, in a voice which, however, did not carry much conviction.

"Because we would be in the wrong; and we are even less able to go against united public opinion that is the Morgan crowd."

"We'd do *something*—I've got it!" Kinnison banged the desk with his fist. "That would be a strictly unilateral action. North America would be standing alone."

"Of course."

"So we'll pull all the Cosmocrats and all of our friends out of North America—move them to Bennett or somewhere—and make Morgan and Company a present of it. We won't declare martial law or kill anybody, unless they decide to call in their reserves. We'll merely isolate the whole damned continent—throw a screen around it and over it that a microbe won't be able to get through—one that would make that iron curtain I read about look like a bride's veil—and we'll *keep* them isolated until they beg to join up on our terms. Strictly legal, and the perfect solution. How about me giving the boys a briefing on it, right now?"

"Not yet." Samms' mien, however, lightened markedly. "I never thought of that way out . . . It *could* be done, and it would probably work, but I would not recommend it except as an ultimately last resort. It has at least two tremendous drawbacks."

"I know it, but . . ."

"It would wreck North America as no nation has ever been wrecked; quite possibly beyond recovery. Furthermore, how many people, including yourself and your children, would like to renounce their North American citizenship and remove themselves, permanently and irrevocably, from North American soil?"

"Um . . . m . . . m. Put that away, it doesn't sound so good, does it? But what the hell else can we do?"

"Just what we have been planning on doing. We must win the election."

"Huh?" Kinnison's mouth almost fell open. "You say it easy. How? With whom? By what stretch of the imagination do you figure that you can find anybody with a loose enough mouth to out-lie and out-promise Morgan? And can you duplicate his machine?"

"We can not only duplicate his machine; we can better it. The truth, presented to the people in language they can understand and appreciate, by a man whom they like, admire, and respect, will be more attractive than Morgan's promises. The same truth will dispose of Morgan's lies."

"Well, go on. You've answered my questions, after a fashion, except the stinger. Does the Council think it's got a man with enough dynage to lift the load?"

"Unanimously. They also agreed unanimously that we have only one. Haven't you any idea who he is?"

"Not a glimmering of one." Kinnison frowned in thought, then his face cleared into a broad grin and he yelled: *"What* a damn fool I am— *you*, of course!"

"Wrong. I was not even seriously considered. It was the consensus that I could not possibly win. My work has been such as to keep me out of the public eye. If the man in the street thinks of me at all, he thinks that I hold myself apart and above him—the ivory tower concept.''

"Could be, at that; but you've got my curiosity aroused. How can a man of that caliber have been kicking around so long without me knowing anything about him?''

"You do. That's what I've been working around to all afternoon. You.''

"Huh?'' Kinnison gasped as though he had received a blow in the solar plexus. "Me? ME? Hell's—Brazen—Hinges!''

"Exactly. You.'' Silencing Kinnison's inarticulate protests, Samms went on: "First, you'll have no difficulty in talking to an audience as you've just talked to me.''

"Of course not—but did I use any language that would burn out the transmitters? I don't remember whether I did or not.''

"I don't, either. You probably did, but that would be nothing new. Telenews has never yet cut you off the ether because of it. The point is this: while you do not realize it, you are a better tub-thumper and welkin-ringer than Morgan is, when something—such as just now—really gets you going. And as for a machine, what finer one is possible than the Patrol? Everybody in it or connected with it will support you to the hilt—you know that.''

"Why, I . . . I suppose so . . . probably they would, yes.''

"Do you know why?''

"Can't say that I do, unless it's because I treat them fair, so they do the same to me.''

"Exactly. I don't say that everybody likes you, but I don't know of anybody who doesn't respect you. And, most important, everybody—all over space—knows 'Rod the Rock' Kinnison, and why he is called that.''

"But that very 'man on horseback' thing may backfire on you, Virge.''

"Perhaps—slightly—but we're not afraid of that. And finally, you said you'd like to kick Morgan from here to Andromeda. How would you like to kick him from Panama City to the North Pole?''

"I said it, and I wasn't just warming up my jets, either. I'd like it.'' The big Lensman's nostrils flared, his lips thinned. "By God, Virge, I will!''

"Thanks, Rod.'' With no display whatever of the emotion he felt, Samms skipped deliberately to the matter next in hand. "Now, about Eridan. Let's see if they know anything yet.''

The report of Knobos and DalNalten was terse and exact. They had found—and that finding, so baldly put, could have filled and should fill a book—that Spaceways' uranium vessels were, beyond any reasonable doubt, hauling thionite from Eridan to the planets of Sol. Spy-rays being useless, they had considered the advisability of investigating Eridan in person, but had decided against such action. Eridan was closely held by Uranium, Incorporated. Its population was one hundred percent Tellurian human. Neither DalNalten nor Knobos could disguise himself well enough to work there. Either would be caught promptly, and as promptly shot.

"Thanks, fellows," Samms said, when it became evident that the brief report was done. Then, to Kinnison, "That puts it up to Conway Costigan. And Jack? Or Mase? Or both?"

"Both," Kinnison decided, "and anybody else they can use."

"I'll get them at it." Samms sent out thoughts. "And now, I wonder what that daughter of mine is doing? I'm a little worried about her, Rod. She's too cocky for her own good—or strength. Some of these days she's going to bite off more than she can chew, if she hasn't already. The more we learn about Morgan, the less I like the idea of her working on Herkimer Herkimer Third. I've told her so, a dozen times, and why, but of course it didn't do any good."

"It wouldn't. The only way to develop teeth is to bite with 'em. You had to. So did I. Our kids have got to, too. We lived through it. So will they. As for Herky the Third . . ." He thought for moments, then went on: "Check. But she's done a job so far that nobody else could do. In spite of that fact, if it wasn't for our Lenses I'd say to pull her, if you have to heave the insubordinate young jade into the brig. But with the Lenses, and the way you watch her . . . to say nothing of Mase Northrop, and he's a lot of man . . . I can't see her getting in either very bad or very deep. Can you?"

"No, I can't." Samms admitted, but the thoughtful frown did not leave his face. He Lensed her: finding, as he had supposed, that she was at a party; dancing, as he had feared, with Senator Morgan's Number One Secretary.

"Hi, Dad!" she greeted him gaily, with no slightest change in the expression of the face turned so engagingly to her partner's. "I have the honor of reporting that all instruments are still dead-centering the green."

"And have you, by any chance, been paying any attention to what I have been telling you?"

"Oh, lots," she assured him. "I've collected reams of data. He could be almost as much of a menace as he thinks he is, in some cases, but I haven't begun to slip yet. As I have told you all along, this is just a game, and we're both playing it strictly according to the rules."

"That's good. Keep it that way, my dear." Samms signed off and his daughter returned her full attention—never noticeably absent—to the handsome secretary.

The evening wore on. Miss Samms danced every dance; occasionally with one or another of the notables present, but usually with Herkimer Herkimer Third.

"A drink?" he asked. "A small, cold one?"

"Not so small, and *very* cold," she agreed, enthusiastically.

Glass in hand, Herkimer indicated a nearby doorway. "I just heard that our host has acquired a very old and very fine bronze—a Neptune. We should run an eye over it, don't you think?"

"By all means," she agreed again.

But as they passed through the shadowed portal the man's head perked to the right. "*There's* something you really ought to see, Jill!" he exclaimed. "Look!"

She looked. A young woman of her own height and build and with her own flamboyant hair, identical as to hairdo and as to every fine detail of dress and of ornamentation, glass in hand, was strolling back into the ball-room!

Jill started to protest, but could not. In the brief moment of inaction the beam of a snub-nosed P-gun had played along her spine from hips to neck. She did not fall—he had given her a very mild jolt—but, rage as she would, she could neither struggle nor scream. And, after the fact, she knew.

But he *couldn't*—couldn't *possibly!* Nevian paralysis-guns were as outlawed as was Vee Two gas itself! Nevertheless, he had.

And on the instant a woman, dressed in crisp and spotless white and carrying a hooded cloak, appeared—and Herkimer now wore a beard and heavy, horn rimmed spectacles. Thus, very shortly, Virgilia Samms found herself, completely helpless and completely unrecognizable, walking awkwardly out of the house between a businesslike doctor and a solicitous nurse.

"Will you need me any more, Doctor Murray?" The woman carefully and expertly loaded the patient into the rear seat of a car.

"Thank you, no, Miss Childs." With a sick, cold certainty Jill knew that this conversation was for the benefit of the doorman and the hackers, and that it would stand up under any examination. "Mrs. Harman's condition is . . . er . . . well, nothing at all serious."

The car moved out into the street and Jill, really frightened for the first time in her triumphant life, fought down an almost overwhelming wave of panic. The hood had slipped down over her eyes, blinding her. She could not move a single voluntary muscle. Nevertheless, she knew that the car traveled a few blocks—six, she thought—west on Bolton Street before turning left.

Why didn't somebody Lens her? Her father wouldn't, she knew, until tomorrow. Neither of the Kinnisons would, nor Spud—they never did except on direct invitation. But Mase would, before he went to bed— or would he? It was past his bed-time now, and she had been pretty caustic, only last night, because she was doing a particularly delicate bit of reading. But he would . . . he *must!*

"Mase! *Mase!* MASE!"

And, eventually, Mase did.

Deep under The Hill, Roderick Kinnison swore fulminantly at the sheer physical impossibility of getting out of that furiously radiating mountain in a hurry. At New York Spaceport, however, Mason Northrop and Jack Kinnison not only could hurry, but did.

"Where are you, Jill?" Northrop demanded presently. "What kind of a car are you in?"

"Quite near Stanhope Circle." In communication with her friends at last, Jill regained a measure of her usual poise. "Within eight or ten blocks, I'm sure. I'm in a black Wilford sedan, last year's model. I didn't get a chance to see its license plates."

"That helps a lot!" Jack grunted, savagely. "A ten-block radius covers a hell of a lot of territory, and half the cars in town are black Wilford sedans."

"Shut up, Jack! Go ahead, Jill—tell us all you can, and keep on sending us anything that will help at all."

"I kept the right and left turns and distances straight for quite a while—about twenty blocks—that's how I know it was Stanhope Circle. I don't know how many times he went around the circle, though, or which way he went when he left it. After leaving the Circle, the traffic was very light, and here there doesn't seem to be any traffic at all. That brings us up to date. You'll know as well as I do what happens next."

With Jill, the Lensmen knew that Herkimer drove his car up to the curb and stopped—parked without backing up. He got out and hauled the girl's limp body out of the car, displacing the hood enough to free one eye. Good! Only one other car was visible; a bright yellow convertible parked across the street, about half a block ahead. There was a sign—"NO PARKING ON THIS SIDE 7 TO 10." The building toward which he was carrying her was more than three stories high, and had a number—one, four—if he would *only* swing her a little bit more, so that she could see the rest of it—one-four-seven-nine!

"Rushton Boulevard, you think, Mase?"

"Could be. Fourteen seventy-nine would be on the down-town-traffic side. Blast!"

Into the building, where two masked men locked and barred the door behind them. "And keep it locked!" Herkimer ordered. "You know what to do until I come back down."

Into an elevator, and up. Through massive double doors into a room, whose most conspicuous item of furniture was a heavy steel chair, bolted to the floor. Two masked men got up and placed themselves behind that chair.

Jill's strength was coming back fast; but not fast enough. The cloak was removed. Her ankles were tied firmly, one to each front leg of the chair. Herkimer threw four turns of rope around her torso and the chair's back, took up every inch of slack, and tied a workmanlike knot. Then, still without a word, he stood back and lighted a cigarette. The last trace of paralysis disappeared, but the girl's mad struggles, futile as they were, were not allowed to continue.

"Put a double hammerlock on her," Herkimer directed, "but be damned sure not to break anything at this stage of the game. That comes later."

Jill, more furiously angry than frightened until now, locked her teeth to keep from screaming as the pressure went on. She could not bend forward to relieve the pain; she could not move; she could only grit her teeth and glare. She was beginning to realize, however, what was actually in store; that Herkimer Herkimer Third was in fact a monster whose like she had never known.

He stepped quietly forward, gathered up a handful of fabric, and heaved. The strapless and backless garment, in no way designed to withstand such stresses, parted; squarely across at the upper strand of rope. He puffed his cigarette to a vivid coal—took it in his fingers—there was an audible hiss and a tiny stink of burning flesh as the glowing ember was extinguished in the clear, clean skin below the girl's left armpit. Jill flinched then, and shrieked desperately, but her tormentor was viciously unmoved.

"That was just to settle any doubt as to whether or not I mean business. I'm all done fooling around with you. I want to know two things. First, everything you know about the Lens; where it comes from, what it really is, and what it does besides what your press-agents advertise. Second, what really happened at the Ambassadors' Ball. Start talking. The faster you talk, the less you'll get hurt."

"You can't get away with this, Herkimer." Jill tried desperately to pull her shattered nerves together. "I'll be missed—traced..." She paused, gasping. If she told him that the Lensmen were in full and continuous communication with her—and if he believed it—he would kill her right then. She switched instantly to another track. "That double isn't good enough to fool anybody who really knows me."

"She doesn't have to be." The man grinned venomously. "Nobody who knows you will get close enough to her to tell the difference. This wasn't done on the spur of the moment, Jill; it was planned—minutely. You haven't got the chance of the proverbial celluloid dog in hell."

"Jill!" Jack Kinnison's thought stabbed in. "It isn't Rushton—fourteen seventy-nine is a two-story. What other streets could it be?"

"I don't know . . ." She was not in very good shape to think.

"Damnation! Got to get hold of somebody who knows the streets. Spud, grab a hacker at the Circle and I'll Lens Parker . . ." Jack's thought snapped off as he tuned to a local Lensman.

Jill's heart sank. She was starkly certain now that the Lensmen could not find her in time.

"Tighten up a little, Eddie. You, too, Bob."

"Stop it! Oh, God, STOP IT!" The unbearable agony relaxed a little. She watched in horrified fascination a second glowing coal approach her bare right side. "Even if I do talk you'll kill me anyway. You couldn't let me go now."

"Kill you, my pet? Not if you behave yourself. We've got a lot of planets the Patrol never heard of, and you could keep a man interested for quite a while, if you really tried. And if you beg hard enough maybe I'll let you try. However, I'd get just as much fun out of killing you as out of the other, so it's up to you. Not sudden death, of course. Little things, at first, like we've been doing. A few more touches of warmth here and there—so . . .

"Scream as much as you please. I enjoy it, and this room is sound-proof. Once more, boys, about half an inch higher this time . . . up . . . steady . . . down. We'll have half an hour or so of this stuff"—Herkimer knew that to the quivering, sensitive, highly imaginative girl his words would be practically as punishing as the atrocious actualities themselves—"then I'll do things to your finger-nails and toe-nails, beginning with burning slivers of double-base flare powder and working up. Then your eyes—or no, I'll save them until last, so you can watch a couple of Venerian slasher-worms work on you, one on each leg, and a Martian digger on your bare belly."

Gripping her hair firmly in his left hand, he forced her head back and down; down almost to her hard-held hands. His right hand, concealing something which he had not mentioned and which was probably starkly unmentionable, approached her taut-stretched throat.

"Talk or not, just as you please." The voice was utterly callous, as chill as the death she now knew he was so willing to deal. "But listen. If you elect to talk, tell the truth. You won't lie twice. I'll count to ten. One."

Jill uttered a gurgling, strangling noise and he lifted her head a trifle. "Can you talk now?"

"Yes."

"Two."

Helpless, immobile, scared now to a depth of terror she had never imagined it possible to feel, Jill fought her wrenched and shaken mind back from insanity's very edge; managed with a pale tongue to lick bloodless lips. Pops Kinnison always said a man could die only once, but he didn't know . . . in battle, yes, perhaps . . . but she had already died a dozen times—but she'd keep on dying forever before she'd say a word. But—

"Tell him, Jill!" Northrop's thought beat at her mind. He, her lover, was unashamedly frantic; as much with sheer rage as with sympathy for her physical and mental anguish. "For the nineteenth time I say *tell him!* We've just located you—Hancock Avenue—we'll be there in two minutes!"

"Yes, Jill, quit being a damned stubborn jackass and *tell him!*" Jack Kinnison's thought bit deep; but this time, strangely enough, the girl felt no repugnance at his touch. There was nothing whatever of the lover; nor of the brother, except of the fraternity of arms. She belonged. She would come out of this brawl right side up or none of them would. "Tell the goddam rat the truth!" Jack's thought drove on. "It won't make any difference—he won't live long enough to pass it on!"

"But I can't—I won't!" Jill stormed. "Why, Pops Kinnison would . . ."

"Not this time I wouldn't, Jill!" Samms' thought tried to come in, too, but the Port Admiral's vehemence was overwhelming. "No harm— he's doing this strictly on his own—if Morgan had had any idea he'd've killed him first. Start talking or I'll spank you to a rosy blister!"

They were to laugh, later, at the incongruity of that threat, but it did produce results.

"Nine." Herkimer grinned wolfishly, in sadistic anticipation.

"Stop it—I'll tell!" she screamed. "Stop it—take that thing away—I can't *stand* it—I'll tell!" She burst into racking, tearing sobs.

"Steady." Herkimer put something in his pocket, then slapped her so viciously that fingers-long marks sprang into red relief upon the chalk-white background of her cheek. "Don't crack up; I haven't started to work on you yet. What about that Lens?"

She gulped twice before she could speak. "It comes from—ulp!—

Arisia. I haven't got one myself, so I don't know very much—ulp!—about it at first hand, but from what the boys tell me it must be . . .''

Outside the building three black forms arrowed downward. Northrop and young Kinnison stopped at the sixth level; Costigan went on down to take care of the guards.

"Bullets, not beams," the Irishman reminded his younger fellows. "We'll have to clean up the mess without leaving a trace, so don't do any more damage to the property than you absolutely have to."

Neither made any reply; they were both too busy. The two thugs standing behind the steel chair, being armed openly, went first; then Jack put a bullet through Herkimer's head. But Northrop was not content with that. He slid the pin to "full automatic" and ten more heavy slugs tore into the falling body before it struck the floor.

Three quick slashes and the girl was free.

"Jill!"

"Mase!"

Locked in each other's arms, straining together, no bystander would have believed that this was their first kiss. It was plainly—yes, quite spectacularly—evident, however, that it would not be their last.

Jack, blushing furiously, picked up the cloak and flung it at the oblivious couple.

"P-s-s-t! *P-s-s-t! Jill!* Wrap 'em up!" he whispered, urgently. "All the top brass in space is coming at full emergency blast—there'll be scrambled eggs all over the place any second now—*Mase! Damn* your thick, hard skull, snap out of it! He's always frothing at the mouth about her running around half naked and if he sees her like this—especially with *you*—he'll simply have a litter of lizards! You'll get a million black spots and seven hundred years in clink! That's better—'bye now—I'll see you up at New York Spaceport.''

Jack Kinnison dashed to the nearest window, threw it open, and dived headlong out of the building.

14

MINING AND DISASTER

The employment office of any concern with personnel running into the hundreds of thousands is a busy place indeed, even when its plants are all on Tellus and its working conditions are as nearly ideal as such things can be made. When that firm's business is Colonial, however, and its working conditions are only a couple of degrees removed from slavery, procurement of personnel is a first-magnitude problem; the Personnel Department, like Alice in Wonderland, must run as fast as it can go in order to stay where it is. Thus the "Help Wanted" advertisements of Uranium, Incorporated covered the planet Earth with blandishment and guile; and thus for twelve hours of every day and for seven days of every week the employment offices of Uranium, Inc. were filled with men—mostly the scum of Earth.

There were, of course, exceptions; one of which strode through the motley group of waiting men and thrust a card through the "Information" wicket. He was a chunky-looking individual, appearing shorter than his actual five feet nine because of a hundred and ninety pounds of weight—even though every pound was placed exactly where it would do the most good. He looked—well, slouchy—and his mien was sullen.

"Birkenfeld—by appointment," he growled through the wicket, in a voice which could have been pleasantly deep.

The coolly efficient blonde manipulated plugs. "Mr. George W. Jones, sir, by appointment . . . Thank you, sir," and Mr. Jones was escorted into Mr. Birkenfeld's private office.

"Have a chair, please, Mr. . . . er . . . Jones."

"So you know?"

"Yes. It is seldom that a man of your education, training, and demonstrated ability applies to us for employment of his own initiative, and a very thorough investigation is indicated.''

"What am I here for, then?'' the visitor demanded, truculently. "You could have turned me down by mail. Everybody else has, since I got out.''

"You are here because we who operate on the frontiers cannot afford to pass judgment upon a man because of his past, unless that past precludes the probability of a useful future. Yours does not; and in some cases, such as yours, we are very deeply interested in the future.'' The official's eyes drilled deep.

Conway Costigan had never been in the limelight. On the contrary, he had made inconspicuousness a passion and an art. Even in such scenes of violence as that which had occurred at the Ambassadors' Ball he managed to remain unnoticed. His Lens had never been visible. No one except Lensmen—and Clio and Jill—knew that he had one; and Lensmen—and Clio and Jill—did not talk. Although he was calmly certain that this Birkenfeld was not an ordinary interviewer, he was equally certain that the investigators of Uranium, Inc. had found out exactly and only what the Patrol had wanted them to find.

"So?'' Jones' bearing altered subtly, and not because of the penetrant eyes. "That's all I want—a chance. I'll start at the bottom, as far down as you say.''

"We advertise, and truthfully, that opportunity on Eridan is unlimited.'' Birkenfeld chose his words with care. "In your case, opportunity will be either absolutely unlimited or zero, depending entirely upon yourself.''

"I see.'' Dumbness had not been included in the fictitious Mr. Jones' background. "You don't need to draw a blue-print.''

"You'll do, I think.'' The interviewer nodded in approval. "Nevertheless, I must make our position entirely clear. If the slip was—shall we say accidental?—you will go far with us. If you try to play false, you will not last long and you will not be missed.''

"Fair enough.''

"Your willingness to start at the bottom is commendable, and it is a fact that those who come up through the ranks make the best executives; in our line at least. Just how far down are you willing to start?''

"How low do you go?''

"A mucker, I think would be low enough; and, from your build, and obvious physical strength, the logical job.''

"Mucker?''

"One who skoufers ore in the mine. Nor can we make any exception in your case as to the routines of induction and transportation.''

"Of course not."

"Take this slip to Mr. Calkins, in Room 6217. He will run you through the mill."

And that night, in an obscure boarding-house, Mr. George Washington Jones, after a meticulous Service Special survey in every direction, reached a large and somewhat grimy hand into a screened receptacle in his battered suit case and touched a Lens.

"Clio?" The lovely mother of their wonderful children appeared in his mind. "Made it, sweetheart, no suspicion at all. No more Lensing for a while—not too long, I hope—so . . . so-long, Clio."

"Take it easy, Spud darling, and *be careful.*" Her tone was light, but she could not conceal a stark background of fear. "Oh, I *wish* I could go, too!"

"I wish you could, Tootie." The linked minds flashed back to what the two had done together in the red opacity of Nevian murk; on Nevia's mighty, watery globe—but that kind of thinking would not do. "But the boys will keep in touch with me and keep you posted. And besides, you know how hard it is to get a baby-sitter!"

It is strange that the fundamental operations of working metalliferous veins have changed so little throughout the ages. Or is it? Ores came into being with the crusts of the planets; they change appreciably only with the passage of geologic time. Ancient mines, of course, could not go down very deep or follow a seam very far; there was too much water and too little air. The steam engine helped, in degree if not in kind, by removing water and supplying air. Tools improved—from the simple metal bar through pick and shovel and candle, through drill and hammer and low explosive and acetylene, through Sullivan slugger and high explosive and electrics, through skoufer and rotary and burley and sourceless glow, to the complex gadgetry of today—but what, fundamentally, is the difference? Men still crawl, snake-like, to where the metal is. Men still, by dint of sheer brawn, jackass the precious stuff out to where our vaunted automatics can get hold of it. And men still die, in horribly unknown fashions and in callously recorded numbers, in the mines which supply the stuff upon which our vaunted culture rests.

But to resume the thread of narrative, George Washington Jones went to Eridan as a common laborer; a mucker. He floated down beside the skip—a "skip" is a mine elevator—some four thousand eight hundred feet. He rode an ore-car a horizontal distance of approximately eight miles to the brilliantly-illuminated cavern which was the Station of the Twelfth and lowest level. He was assigned to the bunk in which he would sleep for the next fifteen nights: "Fifteen down and three up," ran the standard underground contract.

He walked four hundred yards, yelled "Nothing Down!" and inched his way up a rise—in many places scarcely wider than his shoulders—to the stope some three hundred feet above. He reported to the miner who was to be his immediate boss and bent his back to the skoufer—which, while not resembling a shovel at all closely, still meant hard physical labor. He already knew ore—the glossy, sub-metallic, pitchy black luster of uraninite or pitchblende; the yellows of autunite and carnotite; the variant and confusing greens of torbernite. No values went from Jones' skoufer into the heavily-timbered, steel-braced waste-pockets of the stope; very little base rock went down the rise.

He became accustomed to the work; got used to breathing the peculiarly lifeless, dry, oily compressed air. And when, after a few days, his stentorian "Nothing Down!" called forth a "Nothing but a little fine stuff!" and a handful of grit and pebbles, he knew that he had been accepted into the undefined, unwritten, and unofficial, yet nevertheless intensely actual, fellowship of hard-rock men. He belonged.

He knew that he must abandon his policy of invisibility; and, after several days of thought, he decided how he would do it. Hence, upon the first day of his "up" period, he joined his fellows in their descent upon one of the rawest, noisiest dives of Danopolis. The men were met, of course, by a bevy of giggling, shrieking, garishly painted and strongly perfumed girls—and at this point young Jones' behavior became exceedingly unorthodox.

"Buy me a drink, mister? And a dance, huh?"

"On your way, sister." He brushed the importunate wench aside. "I get enough exercise underground, an' you ain't got a thing I want."

Apparently unaware that the girl was exchanging meaningful glances with a couple of husky characters labelled "BOUNCER" in billposter type, the atypical mucker strode up to the long and ornate bar.

"Gimme a bottle of pineapple pop," he ordered bruskly, "an' a package of Tellurian cigarettes—Sunshines."

"P-p-pine . . . ?" The surprised bartender did not finish the word.

The bouncers were fast, but Costigan was faster. A hard knee took one in the solar plexus; a hard elbow took the other so savagely under the chin as to all but break his neck. A bartender started to swing a bung-starter, and found himself flying through the air toward a table. Men, table, and drinks crashed to the floor.

"I pick my own company an' I drink what I damn please," Jones announced, grittily. "Them lunkers ain't hurt none, to speak of . . ." His hard eyes swept the room malevolently, "but I ain't in no gentle mood an' the next jaspers that tackle me will wind up in the repair shop, or maybe in the morgue. See?''

This of course was much too much; a dozen embattled roughnecks leaped to mop up on the misguided wight who had so impugned the manhood of all Eridan. Then, while six or seven bartenders blew frantic blasts upon police whistles, there was a flurry of action too fast to be resolved into consecutive events by the eye. Conway Costigan, one of the fastest men with hands and feet the Patrol has ever known, was trying to keep himself alive; and he succeeded.

"What the hell goes on here?" a chorus of raucously authoritative voices yelled, and sixteen policemen—John Law did not travel singly in that district, but in platoons—swinging clubs and saps, finally hauled George Washington Jones out from the bottom of the pile. He had sundry abrasions and not a few contusions, but no bones were broken and his skin was practically whole.

And since his version of the affair was not only inadequate, but also differed in important particulars from those of several non-participating witnesses, he spent the rest of his holiday in jail; a development with which he was quite content.

The work—and time—went on. He became in rapid succession a head mucker, a miner's pimp (which short and rugged Anglo-Saxon word means simply "helper" in underground parlance), a miner, a top-miner, and then—a long step up the ladder!—a shift-boss.

And then disaster struck; suddenly, paralyzingly, as mine disasters do. Loud-speakers blared briefly—"Explosion! Cave-in! Flood! Fire! Gas! Radiation! Damp!"—and expired. Short-circuits; there was no way of telling which, if any, of those dire warnings were true.

The power failed, and the lights. The hiss of air from valves, a noise which by its constant and unvarying and universal presence soon becomes unheard, became noticeable because of its diminution in volume and tone. And then, seconds later, a jarring, shuddering rumble was felt and heard, accompanied by the snapping of shattered timbers and the sharper, utterly unforgettable shriek of rending and riven steel. And the men, as men do under such conditions, went wild; yelling, swearing, leaping toward where, in the rayless dark, each thought the rise to be.

It took a couple of seconds for the shift-boss to break out and hook up his emergency battery-lamp; and three or four more seconds, and by dint of fists, feet, and a two-foot length of air-hose, to restore any degree of order. Four men were dead; but that wasn't too bad—considering.

"Up there! Under the hanging wall!" he ordered, sharply. "*That* won't fall—unless the whole mountain slips. Now, how many of you jaspers have got your emergency kits on you? Twelve—out of twenty-six—what brains! Put on your masks. You without 'em can stay up here—you'll be safe for a while—I hope.''

Then, presently: "There, that's all for now. I guess." He flashed his light downward. The massive steel members no longer writhed; the crushed and tortured timbers were still.

"That rise may be open, it goes through solid rock, not waste. I'll see. Wright, you're all in one piece, aren't you?''

"I guess so—yes."

"Take charge up here. I'll go down to the drift. If the rise is open I'll give you a flash. Send the ones with masks down, one at a time. Take a jolly-bar and bash the brains out of anybody who gets panicky again.''

Jones was not as brave as he sounded: mine disasters carry a terror which is uniquely and peculiarly poignant. Nevertheless he went down the rise, found it open, and signalled. Then, after issuing brief orders, he led the way along the dark and silent drift toward the Station; wondering profanely why the people on duty there had not done something with the wealth of emergency equipment always ready there. The party found some cave-ins, but nothing they could not dig through.

The Station was also silent and dark. Jones, flashing his head-lamp upon the emergency panel, smashed the glass, wrenched the door open, and pushed buttons. Lights flashed on. Warning signals flared, bellowed and rang. The rotary air-pump began again its normal subdued, whickering whirr. But the water-pump! Shuddering, clanking, groaning, it was threatening to go out any second—but there wasn't a thing in the world Jones could do about it—yet.

The Station itself, so buttressed and pillared with alloy steel as to be little more compressible than an equal volume of solid rock, was unharmed; but in it nothing lived. Four men and a woman—the nurse— were stiffly motionless at their posts; apparently the leads to the Station had been blasted in such fashion that no warning whatever had been given. And smoke, billowing inward from the main tunnel, was growing thicker by the minute. Jones punched another button; a foot-thick barrier of asbestos, tungsten, and vitrified refractory slid smoothly across the tunnel's opening. He considered briefly, pityingly, those who might be outside, but felt no urge to explore. If any lived, there were buttons on the other side of the fire-door.

The eddying smoke disappeared, the flaring lights winked out, air-horns and bells relapsed into silence. The shift-boss, now apparently the Superintendent of the whole Twelfth Level, removed his mask, found the Station walkie-talkie, and snapped a switch. He spoke, listened, spoke again, then called a list of names—none of which brought any response.

"Wright, and you five others," picking out miners who could be depended upon to keep their heads, "take these guns. Shoot if you have to, but not unless you have to. Have the muckers clear the drift, just enough to get through. You'll find a shift-boss, with a crew of nineteen, up in Stope Sixty. Their rise is blocked. They've got light and power again now, and good air, and they're working on it, but opening the rise from the top is a damned slow job. Wright, you throw a chippie into it from the bottom. You others, work back along the drift, clear to the last glory hole. Be sure that all the rises are open—check all the stopes and glory holes—tell everybody you find alive to report to me here . . ."

"Aw, what good!" a man shrieked. "We're all goners anyway—I want *water* an' . . ."

"Shut up, fool!" There was a sound as of fist meeting flesh, the shriek was stilled. "Plenty of water—tanks full of the stuff." A grizzled miner turned to the self-appointed boss and twitched his head toward the laboring pump. "Too damn much water too soon, huh?"

"I wouldn't wonder—but get busy!"

As his now orderly and purposeful men disappeared, Jones picked up his microphone and changed the setting of a dial.

"On top, somebody," he said crisply. "On top . . ."

"Oh, there's somebody alive down in Twelve, after all!" a girl's voice screamed in his ear. "Mr. Clancy! Mr. Edwards!"

"To hell with Clancy, and Edwards, too," Jones barked. "Gimme the Chief Engineer and the Head Surveyor, and gimme 'em *fast*."

"Clancy speaking, Station Twelve." If Works Manager Clancy had heard that pointed remark, and he must have, he ignored it. "Stanley and Emerson will be here in a moment. In the meantime, who's calling? I don't recognize your voice, and it's been so long . . ."

"Jones. Shift-boss, Stope Fifty-Nine. I had a little trouble getting here to the Station."

"What? Where's Pennoyer? And Riley? And . . . ?"

"Dead. Everybody. Gas or damp. No warning."

"Not enough to turn on *anything*—not even the purifiers?"

"Nothing."

"Where were you?"

"Up in the stope."

"Good God!" That news, to Clancy, was informative enough.

"But to hell with all that. What happened, and where?"

"A skip-load, and then a magazine, of high explosive, right at Station

Seven—it's right at the main shaft, you know." Jones did not know, since he had never been in that part of the mine, but he could see the picture. "Main shaft filled up to above Seven, and both emergency shafts blocked. Number One at Six, Number Two at Seven—must have been a fault—But here's Chief Engineer Stanley." The works manager, not too unwillingly, relinquished the microphone.

A miner came running up and Jones covered his mouthpiece. "How about the glory holes?"

"Plugged solid, all four of 'em—by the vibro, clear up to Eleven."

"Thanks." Then, as soon as Stanley's voice came on:

"What I want to know is, why is this damned water-pump over-loading? What's the circuit?"

"You must be . . . yes, you are pumping against too much head. Five levels above you are dead, you know, so . . ."

"Dead? Can't you raise *anybody?*"

"Not yet. So you're pumping through dead boosters on Eleven and Ten and so on up, and when your overload-relief valve opens . . ."

"*Relief* valve!" Jones almost screamed. "Can I dog the damn thing down?"

"No, it's internal."

"Christ, what a design—I could eat a handful of iron filings and *puke* a better emergency pump than that!"

"When it opens," Stanley went stolidly on, "the water will go through the by-pass back into the sump. So you'd better rod out one of the glory holes and . . ."

"Get conscious, fat-head!" Jones blazed. "What would we use for time? Get off the air—gimme Emerson!"

"Emerson speaking."

"Got your maps?"

"Yes."

"We got to run a sag up to Eleven—fast—or drown. Can you give me the shortest possible distance?"

"Can do." The Head Surveyor snapped orders. "We'll have it for you in a minute. Thank God there was somebody down there with a brain."

"It doesn't take super-human intelligence to push buttons."

"You'd be surprised. Your point on glory holes was very well taken—you won't have much time after the pump quits. When the water reaches the Station . . ."

"Curtains. And it's all done now—running free and easy—recirculating. Hurry that dope!"

"Here it is now. Start at the highest point of Stope Fifty-Nine. Repeat."

"Stope Fifty-Nine." Jones waved a furious hand as he shouted the words; the tight-packed miners turned and ran. The shift-boss followed them, carrying the walkie-talkie, aiming an exasperated kick of pure frustration at the merrily-humming water pump as he passed it.

"Thirty-two degrees from the vertical—anywhere between thirty and thirty-five."

"Thirty to thirty-five off vertical."

"Direction—got a compass?"

"Yes."

"Set the blue on zero. Course two hundred seventy-five degrees."

"Blue on zero. Course two seven five."

"Dex sixty-nine point two zero feet. That'll put you into Eleven's class yard—so big you can't miss it."

"Distance sixty-nine point two—*that* all? Fine! Maybe we'll make it, after all. They're sinking a shaft, of course. From where?"

"About four miles in on Six. It'll take time."

"If we can get up into Eleven we'll have all the time on the clock—it'll take a week or more to flood Twelve's stopes. But this sag is sure as hell going to be touch and go. And say, from the throw of the pump and the volume of the sump, will you give me the best estimate you can of how much time we've got? I want at least an hour, but I'm afraid I won't have it."

"Yes. I'll call you back."

The shift-boss elbowed his way through the throng of men and, dragging the radio behind him, wriggled and floated up the rise.

"Wright!" he bellowed, the echoes resounding deafeningly all up and down the narrow tube. "You up there ahead of me?"

"Yeah!" that worthy bellowed back.

"More men left than I thought—how many—half of 'em?"

"Just about."

"Good. Sort out the ones you got up there by trades." Then, when he had emerged into the now brilliantly illuminated stope, "Where are the timber-pimps?"

"Over there."

"Rustle timbers. Whatever you can find and wherever you find it, grab it and bring it up here. Get some twelve-inch steel, too, six feet long. Timbermen, grab that stuff off of the face and start your staging right here. You muckers, rig a couple of skoufers to throw muck to bury the base and checkerwork up to the hanging wall. Doze a sluice-way down into that waste pocket there, so we won't clog ourselves up. Work fast, fellows, but make it *solid*—you know the load it'll have to carry and what will happen if it gives.''

They knew. They knew what they had to do and did it; furiously, but with care and precision.

''How wide a sag you figurin' on, Supe?'' the boss timberman asked. ''Eight-foot checkerwork to the hangin', anyway, huh?''

''Yes. I'll let you know in a minute.''

The surveyor came in. ''Forty-one minutes is my best guess.''

''From when?''

''From the time the pump failed.''

''That was four minutes ago—nearer five. And five more before we can start cutting. Forty-one less ten is thirty-one. Thirty-one into sixty-nine point two goes . . .''

''Two point two three feet per minute, my slip-stick says.''

''Thanks. Wright, what would you say is the biggest sag we can cut in this kind of rock at two and a quarter feet a minute?''

''Um . . . m . . . m.'' The miner scratched his whiskery chin. ''That's a tough one, boss. You'll hafta figure damn close to a hundred pounds of air to the foot on plain cuttin'—that's two hundred and a quarter. But without a burley to pimp for 'er, a rotary can't take that kind of air—she'll foul herself to a standstill before she cuts a foot. An' with a burley riggin' she's got to make damn near a double cut—seven foot inside figger—so any way you look at it you ain't goin' to cut no two foot to the minute.''

''I was hoping you wouldn't check my figures, but you do. So we'll cut five feet. Saw your timbers accordingly. We'll hold that burley by hand.''

Wright shook his head dubiously. ''We don't want to die down here any more than you do, boss, so we'll do our damndest—but how in *hell* do you figure you can hold her to her work?''

''Rig a yoke. Cut a stretcher up for canvas and padding. It'll pound, but a man can stand almost anything, in short enough shifts, if he's got to or die.''

And for a time—two minutes, to be exact, during which the rotary chewed up and spat out a plug of rock over five feet deep—things went very well indeed. Two men, instead of the usual three, could run the rotary; that is, they could tend the complicated pneumatic walking jacks which not only oscillated the cutting demon in a geometrical path, but also rammed it against the face with a steadily held and enormous pressure, even while climbing almost vertically upward under a burden of over twenty thousand pounds.

An armored hand waved a signal—voice was utterly useless—up! A valve was flipped; a huge, flat, steel foot arose; a timber slid into place, creaking and groaning as that big flat foot smashed down. Up—again! Up—a third time! Eighteen seconds—less than one-third of a minute— ten inches gained!

And, while it was not easy, two men could hold the burley—in one-minute shifts. As has been intimated, this machine "pimped" for the rotary. It waited on it, ministering to its every need with a singleness of purpose impossible to any except robotic devotion. It picked the rotary's teeth, it freed its linkages, it deloused its ports, it cleared its spillways of compacted debris, it even—and this is a feat starkly un-believable to anyone who does not know the hardness of neocarballoy and the tensile strength of ultra-special steels—it even changed, while in full operation, the rotary's diamond-tipped cutters.

Both burley and rotary were extremely efficient, but neither was either quiet or gentle. In their quietest moments they shrieked and groaned and yelled, producing a volume of sound in which nothing softer than a cannon-shot could have been heard. But when, in changing the rotary's cutting teeth, the burley's "fingers" were driven into and through the solid rock—a matter of merest routine to both machines—the resultant blasts of sound cannot even be imagined, to say nothing of being de-scribed.

And always both machines spewed out torrents of rock, in sizes rang-ing from impalpable dust up to chunks as big as a fist.

As the sag lengthened and the checkerwork grew higher, the work began to slow down. They began to lose the time they had gained. There were plenty of men, but in that narrow bore there simply was not room for enough men to work. Even through that storm of dust and hurtling rock the timbermen could get their blocking up there, but they could not place it fast enough—there were too many other men in the way. One of them had to get out. Since one man could not *possibly* run the rotary, one man would have to hold the burley.

They tried it, one after another. No soap. It hammered them flat. The rotary, fouled in every tooth and channel and vent under the terrific thrust of two hundred thirty pounds of air, merely gnawed and slid. The timbermen now had room—but nothing to do. And Jones, who had been biting at his mustache and ignoring the frantic walkie-talkie for minutes, stared grimly at watch and tape. Three minutes left, and over eight feet to go.

"Gimme that armor!" he rasped, and climbed the blocks. "Open the air wide open—give 'er the whole two-fifty! Get down, Mac—I'll take it the rest of the way!"

He put his shoulders to the improvised yoke, braced his feet, and heaved. The burley, screaming and yelling and clamoring, went joyously to work—both ways—God, what punishment! The rotary, free and clear, chewed rock more viciously than ever. An armored hand smote his leg. Lift! He lifted that foot, set it down two inches higher. The other one. Four inches. Six. One foot. Two. Three. Lord of the ancients! Was this lifetime of agony only one minute? Or wasn't he holding her— had the damn thing stopped cutting? No, it was still cutting—the rocks were banging against and bouncing off of his helmet as viciously and as numerously as ever; he could sense, rather than feel, the furious fashion in which the relays of timbermen were laboring to keep those high-stepping jacks in motion.

No, it had been only one minute. Twice that long yet to go. God! Nothing *could* be that brutal—a bull elephant couldn't take it—but by all the gods of space and all the devils in hell, he'd stay with it until that sag broke through. And grimly, doggedly, toward the end nine-tenths unconsciously, Lensman Conway Costigan stayed with it.

And in the stope so far below, a new and highly authoritative voice blared from the speaker.

"Jones! God damn it, Jones, answer me! If Jones isn't there, somebody else answer me—*anybody!*"

"Yes, sir?" Wright was afraid to answer that preemptory call, but more afraid not to.

"Jones? This is Clancy."

"No, sir. Not Jones. Wright, sir—top miner."

"Where's Jones?"

"Up in the sag, sir. He's holding the burley—alone."

"*Alone!* Hell's purple fires! Tell him to—how many men has he got on the rotary?"

"Two, sir. That's all they's room for."

"Tell him to quit it—put somebody else on it—I *won't* have him killed, damn it!"

"He's the only one strong enough to hold it, sir, but I'll send up word." Word went up via sign language, and came back down. "Beggin' your pardon, sir, but he says to tell you to go to hell, sir. He won't have no time for chit-chat, he says, until this goddam sag is through or the juice goes off, sir."

A blast of profanity erupted from the speaker, of such violence that the thoroughly scared Wright threw the walkie-talkie down the waste-chute, and in the same instant the rotary crashed through.

Dazed, groggy, barely conscious from his terrific effort, Jones stared owlishly through the heavy, steel-braced lenses of his helmet while the timbermen set a few more courses of wood and the rotary walked itself and the clinging burley up and out of the hole. He climbed stiffly out, and as he stared at the pillar of light flaring upward from the sag, his gorge began to rise.

"Wha's the idea of that damn surveyor lying to us like that?" he babbled. "We had oodles an' oodles of time—didn't have to kill ourselves—damn water ain't got there *yet*—wha's the big . . ." He wobbled weakly, and took one short step, and the lights went out. The surveyor's estimate had been impossibly, accidentally close. They had had a little extra time; but it was measured very easily in seconds.

And Jones, logical to the end in a queerly addled way, stood in the almost palpable darkness, and wobbled, and thought. If a man couldn't see anything with his eyes wide open, he was either blind or unconscious. He wasn't blind, therefore he must be unconscious and not know it. He sighed, wearily and gratefully, and collapsed.

Battery lights were soon reconnected, and everybody knew that they had holed through. There was no more panic. And, even before the shift-boss had recovered full consciousness, he was walking down the drift toward Station Eleven.

There is no need to enlarge upon the rest of that grim and grisly affair. Level after level was activated; and, since working upward in mines is vastly faster than working downward, the two parties met on the Eighth Level. Half of the men who would otherwise have died were saved, and—much more important from the viewpoint of Uranium, Inc.—the deeper and richer half of the biggest and richest uranium mine in existence, instead of being out of production for a year or more, would be back in full operation in a couple of weeks.

And George Washington Jones, still a trifle shaky from his ordeal, was called into the front office. But before he arrived:

"I'm going to make him Assistant Works Manager," Clancy announced.

"I think not."

"But listen, Mr. Isaacson—*please!* How do you expect me to build up a staff if you snatch every good man I find away from me?"

"You didn't find him. Birkenfeld did. He was here only on test. He is going into Department Q."

Clancy, who had opened his mouth to continue his protests, shut it wordlessly. He knew that Department Q was—

DEPARTMENT Q.

15

DEPARTMENT Q

Costigan was not surprised to see the man he had known as Birkenfeld in Uranium's ornate conference room. He had not expected however, to see Isaacson. He knew, of course, that Spaceways owned Uranium, Inc., and the planet Eridan, lock, stock, and barrel; but it never entered his modest mind that his case would be of sufficient importance to warrant the personal attention of the Big Noise himself. Hence the sight of that suave and unrevealing face gave the putative Jones a more than temporary qualm. Isaacson was top-bracket stuff, 'way out of his class. Virgil Samms ought to be taking this assignment, but since he wasn't—

But instead of being an inquisition, the meeting was friendly and informal from the start. They complimented him upon the soundness of his judgment and the accuracy of his decisions. They thanked him, both with words and with a considerable sum of expendable credits. They encouraged him to talk about himself, but there was nothing whatever of the star-chamber or of cross-examination. The last question was representative of the whole conference.

"One other thing, Jones, has me slightly baffled," Isaacson said, with a really winning smile. "Since you do not drink, and since you were not in search of feminine . . . er . . . companionship, just why did you go down to Roaring Jack's dive?"

"Two reasons," Jones said, with a somewhat shamefaced grin. "The minor one isn't easy to explain, but . . . well, I hadn't been having an exactly easy time of it on Earth . . . you all know about that, I suppose?"

They knew.

"Well, I was taking a very dim view of things in general, and a good fight would get it out of my system. It always does."

"I see. And the major reason?"

"I knew, of course, that I was on probation. I would have to get promoted, and fast, or stay sunk forever. To get promoted fast, a man can either be enough of a boot-licker to be pulled up from on high, or he can be shoved up by the men he is working with. The best way to get a crowd of hard-rock men to like you is to lick a few of 'em—off hours, of course, and according to Hoyle—and the more of 'em you can lick at once, the better. I'm pretty good at rough-and-tumble brawling, so I gambled that the cops would step in before I got banged up too much. I won."

"I see," Isaacson said again, in an entirely different tone. He did see, now. "The first technique is so universally used that the possibility of the second did not occur to me. Nice work—*very* nice." He turned to the other members of the Board. "This, I believe, concludes the business of the meeting?"

For some reason or other Isaacson nodded slightly as he asked the question; and one by one, as though in concurrence, the others nodded in reply. The meeting broke up. Outside the door, however, the magnate did not go about his own business nor send Jones about his. Instead:

"I would like to show you, if I may, the above-ground part of our Works?"

"My time is yours, sir. I am interested."

It is unnecessary here to go into the details of a Civilization's greatest uranium operation; the storage bins, the grinders, the Wilfley tables and slime tanks, the flotation sluices, the roasters and reducers, the processes of solution and crystallization and recrystallization, of final oxidation and reduction. Suffice it to say that Isaacson showed Jones the whole immensity of Uranium Works Number One. The trip ended on the top floor of the towering Administration Building, in a heavily-screened room containing a desk, a couple of chairs, and a tremendously massive safe.

"Smoke up." Isaacson indicated a package of Jones' favorite brand of cigarettes and lighted a cigar. "You knew that you were under test. I wonder, though, if you knew how much of it was testing?"

"All of it." Jones grinned. "Except for the big blow, of course."

"Of course."

"There were too many possibilities, of too many different kinds, too pat. I might warn you, though—I could have got away clear with that half-million."

"The possibility existed." Surprisingly, Isaacson did not tell him that the trap was more subtle than it had appeared to be. "It was, however, worth the risk. Why didn't you?"

"Because I figure on making more than that, a little later, and I might live longer to spend it."

"Sound thinking, my boy—really sound. Now—you noticed, of course, the vote at the end of the meeting?"

Jones had noticed it; and, although he did not say so, he had been wondering about it ever since. The older man strolled over to the safe and opened it, revealing a single, startlingly small package.

"You passed, unanimously; you are now learning what you have to know. Not that we trust you unreservedly. You will be watched for a long time, and before you can make one false step, you will die."

"That would seem to be good business, sir."

"Glad you look at it that way—we thought you would. You saw the Works. Quite an operation, don't you think?"

"Immense, sir. The biggest thing I ever saw."

"What would you say, then, to the idea of this office being our real headquarters, of that little package there being our real business?" He swung the safe door shut, spun the knob.

"It would have been highly surprising a couple of hours ago." Costigan could not afford to appear stupid, nor to possess too much knowledge. He had to steer an extremely difficult middle course. "After the climax of this build-up, though, it wouldn't seem at all impossible. Or that there were wheels—plenty of 'em!—within wheels."

"Smart!" Isaacson applauded. "And what would you think might be in that package? This room is ray-proof."

"Against anything the Galactic Patrol can swing?"

"Positively."

"Well, then, it *might* be something beginning with the letter" he flicked two fingers, almost invisibly fast, into a T and went on without a break "M, as in morphine."

"Your caution and restraint are commendable. If I had any remaining doubt as to your ability, it is gone." He paused, frowning. As belief in ability increased, that in sincerity lessened. This doubt, this questioning, existed every time a new executive was initiated into the mysteries of Department Q. The Board's judgment was good. They had slipped only twice, and those two errors had been corrected easily enough. The fellow had been warned once; that was enough. He took the plunge. "You will work with the Assistant Works Manager here until you understand the duties of the position. You will be transferred to Tellus as Assistant Works Manager there. Your principal duties will, however, be concerned with Department Q—which you will head up one day if you make good. And, just incidentally, when you go to Tellus, a package like that one in the safe will go with you."

"Oh . . . I see. I'll make good, sir." Jones let Isaacson see his jaw-muscles tighten in resolve. "It may take a little time for me to learn my way around, sir, but I'll learn it."

"I'm sure you will. And now, to go into greater detail . . ."

Virgil Samms had to be sure of his facts. More than that, he had to be able to prove them; not merely to the satisfaction of a law-enforcement officer, but beyond any reasonable doubt of the hardest-headed member of a cynical and skeptical jury. Wherefore Jack Kinnison and Mase Northrop took up the thionite trail at the exact point where, each trip, Ray Olmstead had had to abandon it; in the atmosphere of Cavenda. And fortunately, not too much preparation was required.

Cavenda was, as has been intimated, a primitive world. Its native people, humanoid in type, had developed a culture approximating in some respects that of the North American Indian at about the time of Columbus, in others that of the ancient Nomads of Araby. Thus a couple of wandering natives, unrecognizable under their dirty stormproof blankets and their scarcely thinner layers of grease and grime, watched impassively, incuriously, while a box floated pendant from its parachute from sky to ground. Mounted upon their uncouth steeds, they followed that box when it was hauled to the white man's village. Unlike many of the other natives, these two did not shuffle into that village, to lean silently against a rock or a wall awaiting their turns to exchange a few hours of simple labor for a container of a new and highly potent beverage. They did, however, keep themselves constantly and minutely informed as to everything these strange, devil-ridden white men did. One of these pseudo-natives wandered off into the wilderness two or three days before the huge thing-which-flies-without-wings left ground; the other immediately afterward.

Thus the departure of the space-ship from Cavenda was recorded, as was its arrival at Eridan. It had been extremely difficult for the Patrol's engineers to devise ways and means of tracing that ship from departure to arrival without exciting suspicion, but it had not proved impossible.

And Jack Kinnison, lounging idly and elegantly in the concourse of Danopolis Spaceport, seethed imperceptibly. Having swallowed a tiny Service Special capsule that morning, he knew that he had been under continuous spy-ray inspection for over two hours. He had not given himself away—practically everybody screened their inside coat pockets and hip pockets, and the cat-whisker lead from Lens to leg simply could not be seen—but for all the good they were doing him his ultra-instruments might just as well have been back on Tellus.

"Mase!" he sent, with no change whatever in the vapid expression then on his face. "I'm still covered. Are you?"

"Covered!" the answering thought was a snort. "They're covering me like water covers a submarine!"

"Keep tuned. I'll call Spud. Spud!"

"Come in, Jack." Conway Costigan, alone now in the sanctum of Department Q, did not seem to be busy, but he was.

"That red herring they told us to drag across the trail was too damned red. They must be touchier than fulminate to spy-work on their armed forces—neither Mase nor I can do a lick of work. Anybody else covered?"

"No. All clear."

"Good. Tell them the zwilnik blockers took us out."

"I'll do that. Distance only, or is somebody on your tail?"

"Somebody; and I mean *some body*. A slick chick with a classy chassis; a blonde, with great, big come-hither eyes. Too good to be true; especially the falsies. Wiring, my friend—and I haven't been able to get a close look, but I wouldn't wonder if her nostrils had a skillionth of a whillimeter too much expansion. I want a spy-ray op—is it safe to use Fred?" Kinnison referred to the grizzled engineer now puttering about in a certain space-ship; not the one in which he and Northrop had come to Eridan.

"Definitely not. I can do it myself and still stay very much in character . . . No, I don't know her. Not surprising, of course, since the policy here is never to let the right hand know what the left is doing. How about you, Mase? Have you got a little girl-friend, too?"

"Yea, verily, brother; but not little. More my size." Northrop pointed out a tall, trim brunette, strolling along with the effortless, consciously unconscious poise of the professional model.

"Hm . . . m . . . m. I don't know her, either," Costigan reported, "but both of them are wearing four-inch spy-ray blocks and are probably wired up like Christmas trees. By inference, P-gun proof. I can't penetrate, of course, but maybe I can get a viewpoint . . . You're right, Jack. Nostrils plugged. Anti-thionite, anti-Vee-Two, anti-everything. In fact, anti-social. I'll spread their pictures around and see if anybody knows either of them."

He did so, and over a hundred of the Patrol's shrewdest operatives—upon this occasion North America had invaded Eridan in force—studied and thought. No one knew the tall brunette, but—

"I know the blonde." This was Parker of Washington, a Service ace for twenty five years. " 'Hell-cat Hazel' DeForce, the hardest-boiled babe unhung. Watch your step around her; she's just as handy with a knife and knock-out drops as she is with a gun.''

"Thanks, Parker. I've heard of her." Costigan was thinking fast. "Free-lance. No way of telling who she's working for at the moment." This was a statement, not a question.

"Only that it would have to be somebody with a lot of money. Her price is high. That all?"

"That's all, fellows." Then, to Jack and Northrop: "My thought is that you two guys are completely out-classed—out-weighed, out-numbered, out-manned, and out-gunned. Undressed, you're sitting ducks; and if you put out any screens it'll crystallize their suspicions and they'll grab you right then—or maybe even knock you off. You'd better get out of here at full blast; you can't do any more good here, the way things are."

"Sure we can!" Kinnison protested. "You wanted a diversion, didn't you?"

"Yes, but you already . . ."

"What we've done already isn't a patch to what we can do next. We can set up such a diversion that the boys can walk right on the thionite-carrier's heels without anybody paying any attention. By the way, you don't know yet who is going to carry it, do you?"

"No. No penetration at all."

"You soon will, bucko. Watch our smoke!"

"What do you think you're going to do?" Costigan demanded, sharply.

"This." Jack explained. "And don't try to say no. We're on our own, you know."

"We . . . l . . . l . . . it sounds good, and if you can pull it off it will help no end. Go ahead."

The demurely luscious blonde stared disconsolately at the bulletin board, upon which another thirty minutes was being added to the time of arrival of a ship already three hours late. She picked up a book, glanced at its cover, put it down. Her hand moved toward a magazine, drew back, dropped idly into her lap. She sighed, stifled a yawn prettily, leaned backward in her seat—in such a position, Jack noticed, that he could not see into her nostrils—and closed her eyes. And Jack Kinnison, coming visibly to a decision, sat down beside her.

"Pardon me, miss, but I feel just like you look. Can you tell me why convention decrees that two people, stuck in this concourse by arrivals that nobody knows when will arrive, have got to suffer alone when they could have so much more fun suffering together?"

The girl's eyes opened slowly; she was neither startled, nor afraid, nor—it seemed—even interested. In fact, she gazed at him with so much disinterest and for so long a time that he began to wonder—was she going to play sweet and innocent to the end?

"Yes, conventions *are* stupid, sometimes," she admitted finally, her lovely lips curving into the beginnings of a smile. Her voice, low and sweet, matched perfectly the rest of her charming self. "After all, perfectly nice people do meet informally on shipboard; why not in concourses?"

"Why not, indeed? And I'm perfectly nice people, I assure you. Willi Borden is the name. My friends call me Bill. And you?"

"Beatrice Bailey; Bee for short. Tell me what you like, and we'll talk about it."

"Why talk, when we could be eating? I'm with a guy. He's out on the field somewhere—a big bruiser with a pencil-stripe black mustache. Maybe you saw him talking to me a while back?"

"I think so, now that you mention him. Too big—*much* too big." The girl spoke carelessly, but managed to make it very clear that Jack Kinnison was just exactly the right size. "Why?"

"I told him I'd have supper with him. Shall we hunt him up and eat together?"

"Why not? Is he alone?"

"He was, when I saw him last." Although Jack knew exactly where Northrop was, and who was with him, he had to play safe; he did not know how much this "Bee Bailey" really knew. "He knows a lot more people around here than I do, though, so maybe he isn't now. Let me carry some of that plunder?"

"You might carry those books—thanks. But the field is so *big*—how do you expect to find him? Or do you know where he is?"

"Uh-uh!" he denied, vigorously. This was the critical moment. She certainly wasn't suspicious—yet—but she was showing signs of not wanting to go out there, and if she refused to go . . . "To be honest, I don't care whether I find him or not—the idea of ditching him appeals to me more and more. So how about this? We'll dash out to the third dock—just so I won't have to actually lie about looking for him—and dash right back here. Or wouldn't you rather have it a twosome?"

"I refuse to answer, by advice of counsel." The girl laughed gaily, but her answer was plain enough.

Their rate of progress was by no means a dash, and Kinnison did not look—with his eyes—for Northrop. Nevertheless, just south of the third dock, the two young couples met.

"My cousin, Grace James," Northrop said, without a tremor or a quiver. "Wild Willi Borden, Grace—usually called Baldy on account of his hair."

The girls were introduced; each vouchsafing the other a completely meaningless smile and a colorlessly conventional word of greeting. Were they, in fact as in seeming, total strangers? Or were they in fact working together as closely as were the two young Lensmen themselves? If that was acting, it was a beautiful job; neither man could detect the slightest flaw in the performance of either girl.

"Whither away, pilot?" Jack allowed no lapse of time. "You know all the places around here. Lead us to a good one."

"This way, my old and fragrant fruit." Northrop led off with a flourish, and again Jack tensed. The walk led straight past the third-class, apparently deserted dock of which a certain ultra-fast vessel was the only occupant. If nothing happened for fifteen more seconds . . .

Nothing did. The laughing, chattering four came abreast of the portal. The door swung open and the Lensmen went into action.

They did not like to strong-arm women, but speed was their first consideration, with safety a close second; and it is impossible for a man to make speed while carrying a conscious, lithe, strong, heavily-armed woman in such a position that she cannot use fists, feet, teeth, gun or knife. An unconscious woman, on the other hand, can be carried easily and safely enough. Therefore Jack spun his partner around, forced both of her hands into one of his. The free hand flashed upward toward the neck; a hard finger pressed unerringly against a nerve; the girl went limp. The two victims were hustled aboard and the space-ship, surrounded now by full-coverage screen, took off.

Kinnison paid no attention to ship or course; orders had been given long since and would be carried out. Instead, he lowered his burden to the floor, spread her out flat, and sought out and removed item after item of wiring, apparatus, and offensive and defensive armament. He did not undress her—quite—but he made completely certain that the only weapons left to the young lady were those with which Nature had endowed her. And, Northrop having taken care of his alleged cousin with equal thoroughness, the small-arms were sent out and both doors of the room were securely locked.

"Now, Hell-cat Hazel DeForce," Kinnison said, conversationally, "You can snap out of it any time—you've been back to normal for at least two minutes. You've found out that your famous sex-appeal won't work. There's nothing loose you can grab, and you're too smart an operator to tackle me bare-handed. Who's the captain of your team— you or the clothes-horse?"

"Clothes-horse!" the statuesque brunette exclaimed, but her protests were drowned out. The blonde could—and did—talk louder, faster, and rougher.

"Do you think you can get away with *this?*" she demanded. "Why, you . . ." and the unexpurgated, trenchant, brilliantly detailed characterization could have seared its way through four-ply asbestos. "And just what do you think you're going to do with me?"

"As to the first, I think so," Kinnison replied, ignoring the deepspace verbiage. "As to the second—as of now I don't know. What would you do if our situations were reversed?"

"I'd blast you to a cinder—or else take a knife and . . ."

"Hazel!" the brunette cautioned sharply. "Careful! You'll touch them off and they'll . . ."

"Shut up, Jane! They won't hurt us any more than they have already; it's psychologically impossible. Isn't that true, copper?" Hazel lighted a cigarette, inhaled deeply, and blew a cloud of smoke at Kinnison's face.

"Pretty much so, I guess," the Lensman admitted, frankly enough, "but we can put you away for the rest of your lives."

"Space-happy? Or do you think I am?" she sneered. "What would you use for a case? We're as safe as if we were in God's pocket. And besides, our positions *will* be reversed pretty quick. You may not know it, but the fastest ships in space are chasing us, right now."

"For once you're wrong. We've got plenty of legs ourselves and we're blasting for rendezvous with a task-force. But enough of this chatter. I want to know what job you're on and why you picked on us. Give."

"Oh, does 'oo?" Hazel cooed, venomously. "Come and sit on mama's lap, itty bitty soldier boy, and she'll tell you everything you want to know."

Both Lensmen probed, then, with everything they had, but learned nothing of value. The women did not know what the Patrolmen were trying to do, but they were so intensely hostile that their mental blocks, unconscious although they were, were as effective as full-driven thought screens against the most insidious approaches the men could make.

"Anything in their hand-bags, Mase?" Jack asked, finally.

"I'll look . . . Nothing much—just this," and the very tonelessness of Northrop's voice made Jack look up quickly.

"Just a letter from the boy-friend." Hazel shrugged her shoulders. "Nothing hot—not even warm—go ahead and read it."

"Not interested in what it says, but it might be smart to develop it, envelope and all, for invisible ink and whatnot." He did so, deeming it a worth-while expenditure of time. He already knew what the hidden message was; but no one not of the Patrol should know that no transmission of intelligence, however coded or garbled or disguised or by whatever means sent, could be concealed from any wearer of Arisia's Lens.

"Listen, Hazel," Kinnison said, holding up the now slightly stained paper. " 'Three six two'—that's you, I suppose, and you're the squad leader—'Men mentioned previously being investigated stop assign three nine eight'—that must be you, Jane—'and make acquaintance stop if no further instructions received by eighteen hundred hours liquidate immediately stop party one.' "

The blonde operative lost for the first time her brazen control. "Why . . . that code is *unbreakable!*" she gasped.

"Wrong again, Gentle Alice. Some of us are specialists." He directed a thought at Northrop. "This changes things slightly, Mase. I was going to turn them loose, but now I don't know. Better we take it up with the boss, don't you think?"

"Pos-i-*tive*-ly!"

Samms was called, and considered the matter for approximately one minute. "Your first idea was right, Jack. Let them go. The message may be helpful and informative, but the women would not. They know nothing. Congratulations, boys, on the complete success of Operation Red Herring."

"Ouch!" Jack grimaced mentally to his partner after the First Lensman had cut off. "They know enough to be in on bumping you and me off, but that ain't important, says he!"

"And it ain't, bub," Northrop grinned back. "Moderately so, maybe, if they had got us, but not at all so now they can't. The Lensmen have landed and the situation is well in hand. It is written. Selah."

"Check. Let's wrap it up." Jack turned to the blonde. "Come on, Hazel. Out. Number Four lifeboat. Do you want to come peaceably or shall I work on your neck again?"

"You could think of other places that would be more fun." She got up and stared directly into his eyes, her lip curling. "That is, if you were a *man* instead of a sublimated Boy Scout."

Kinnison, without a word, wheeled and unlocked a door. Hazel swaggered forward, but the taller girl hung back. "Are you sure there's air— and they'll pick us up? Maybe they're going to make us breathe space . . ."

"Huh? They haven't got the guts," Hazel sneered. "Come on, Jane. Number Four, you said, darling?"

She led the way. Kinnison opened the portal. Jane hurried aboard, but Hazel paused and held out her arms.

"Aren't you even going to kiss mama goodbye, baby boy?'' she taunted.

"Better not waste much more time. We blow this boat, sealed or open, in fifteen seconds.'' By what effort Kinnison held his voice level and expressionless, he hoped the wench would never know.

She looked at him, started to say something, looked again. She had gone just about as far as it was safe to go. She stepped into the boat and reached for the lever. And as the valve was swinging smoothly shut the men heard a tinkling laugh, reminiscent of icicles breaking against steel bells.

"Hell's—Brazen—Hinges!'' Kinnison wiped his forehead as the lifeboat shot away. Hazel was something brand new to him; a phenomenon with which none of his education, training, or experience had equipped him to cope. "I've heard about the guy who got hold of a tiger by the tail, but . . .'' His thought expired on a wondering, confused note.

"Yeah.'' Northrop was in no better case. "We won—technically—I guess—or did we? That was a God-awful drubbing we took, mister.''

"Well, we got away alive, anyway . . . We'll tell Parker his dope is correct to the proverbial twenty decimals. And now that we've escaped, let's call Spud and see how things came out.''

And Costigan-Jones assured them that everything had come out very well indeed. The shipment of thionite had been followed without any difficulty at all, from the spaceship clear through to Jones' own office, and it reposed now in Department Q's own safe, under Jones' personal watch and ward. The pressure had lightened tremendously, just as Kinnison and Northrop had thought it would, when they set up their diversion. Costigan listened impassively to the whole story.

"Now *should* I have shot her, or not?'' Jack demanded. "Not whether I *could* have or not—I couldn't—but *should* I have, Spud?''

"I don't know.'' Costigan thought for minutes. "I don't think so. No—not in cold blood. I couldn't have, either, and wouldn't if I could. It wouldn't be worth it. Somebody will shoot her some day, but not one of us—unless, of course, it's in a fight.''

"Thanks, Spud; that makes me feel better. Off.''

Costigan-Jones' desk was already clear, since there was little or no paper-work connected with his position in Department Q. Hence his preparations for departure were few and simple. He merely opened the safe, stuck the package into his pocket, closed and locked the safe, and took a company ground-car to the spaceport.

Nor was there any more formality about his leaving the planet. Eridan had, of course, a Customs frontier of sorts; but since Uranium, Inc. owned Eridan in fee simple, its Customs paid no attention whatever to company ships or to low-number, gold-badge company men. Nor did Jones need ticket, passport, or visa. Company men rode company ships to and from company plants, wherever situate, without let or hindrance. Thus, wearing the aura of power of his new position—and Gold Badge Number Thirty-Eight—George W. Jones was whisked out to the uranium ship and was shown to his cabin.

Nor was it surprising that the trip from Eridan to Earth was completely without incident. This was an ordinary freighter, hauling uranium on a routine flight. Her cargo was valuable, of course—the sine qua non of inter-stellar trade—but in no sense precious. Not pirate-bait, by any means. And only two men knew that this flight was in any whit different from the one which had preceded it or the one which would follow it. If this ship was escorted or guarded the fact was not apparent: and no Patrol vessel came nearer to it than four detets—Virgil Samms and Roderick Kinnison saw to that.

The voyage, however, was not tedious. Jones was busy every minute. In fact, there were scarcely minutes enough in which to assimilate the material which Isaacson had given him—the layouts, flow-sheets, and organization charts of Works Number Eighteen, on Tellus.

And upon arrival at the private spaceport which was an integral part of Works Number Eighteen, Jones was not surprised (he knew more now than he had known a few weeks before; and infinitely more than the man on the street) to learn that the Customs men of this particular North American Port of Entry were just as complaisant as were those of Eridan. They did not bother even to count the boxes, to say nothing of inspecting them. They stamped the ship's papers without either reading or checking them. They made a perfunctory search, it is true, of crewmen and quarters, but a low number gold badge was still a magic talisman. Unquestioned, sacrosanct, he and his baggage were escorted to the ground-car first in line.

"Administration Building," Jones-Costigan told the hacker, and that was that.

16

OLMSTEAD GOES FISHING

It has been said that the basic drive of the Eddorians was a lust for power; a thought which should be elucidated and perhaps slightly modified. Their warrings, their strifes, their internicine intrigues and connivings were inevitable because of the tremendousness and capability—and the limitations—of their minds. Not enough *could* occur upon any one planet to keep such minds as theirs even partially occupied; and, unlike the Arisians, they could not satiate themselves in a static philosophical study of the infinite possibilities of the Cosmic All. They had to be *doing* something; or, better yet, making other and lesser beings do things to make the physical universe conform to their idea of what a universe should be.

Their first care was to set up the various echelons of control. The second echelon, immediately below the Masters, was of course the most important, and after a survey of both galaxies they decided to give this high honor to the Ploorans. Ploor, as is now well known, was a planet of a sun so variable that all Plooran life had to undergo radical cyclical changes in physical form in order to live through the tremendous climatic changes involved in its every year. Physical form, however, meant nothing to the Eddorians. Since no other planet even remotely like theirs existed in this, our normal plenum, physiques like theirs would be impossible; and the Plooran mentality left very little to be desired.

In the third echelon there were many different races, among which the frigid-blooded, poison-breathing Eich were perhaps the most efficient and most callous; and in the fourth there were millions upon millions of entities representing thousands upon thousands of widely-variant races.

Thus, at the pinpoint in history represented by the time of Virgil

Samms and Roderick Kinnison, the Eddorians were busy; and, if such a word can be used, happy. Gharlane of Eddore, second in authority only to the All-Highest, His Ultimate Supremacy himself, paid little attention to any one planet or to any one race. Even such a mind as his, when directing the affairs of twenty million and then sixty million and then a hundred million worlds, can do so only in broad, and not in fine.

And thus the reports which were now flooding in to Gharlane in a constantly increasing stream concerned classes and groups of worlds, and solar systems, and galactic regions. A planet might perhaps be mentioned as representative of a class, but no individual entity lower than a Plooran was named or discussed. Gharlane analyzed those tremendous reports; collated, digested, compared, and reconciled them; determined trends and tendencies and most probable resultants. Gharlane issued orders, the carrying out of which would make an entire galactic region fit more and ever more exactly into the Great Plan.

But, as has been pointed out, there was one flaw inherent in the Boskonian system. Underlings, then as now, were prone to gloss over their own mistakes, to cover up their own incompetences. Thus, since he had no reason to inquire specifically, Gharlane did not know that anything whatever had gone amiss on Sol Three, the pestiferous planet which had formerly caused him more trouble than all the rest of his worlds combined.

After the fact, it is easy to say that he should have continued his personal supervision of Earth, but can that view be defended? Egotistical, self-confident, arrogant, Gharlane *knew* that he had finally whipped Tellus into line. It was the same now as any other planet of its class. And even had he thought it worthwhile to make such a glaring exception, would not the fused Elders of Arisia have intervened?

Be those things as they may, Gharlane did not know that the newborn Galactic Patrol had been successful in defending Triplanetary's Hill against the Black Fleet. Nor did the Plooran Assistant Director in charge. Nor did any member of that dreadful group of Eich which was even then calling itself the Council of Boskone. The highest-ranking Boskonian who knew of the fiasco, calmly confident of his own ability, had not considered this minor reverse of sufficient importance to report to his immediate superior. He had already taken steps to correct the condition. In fact, as matters now stood, the thing was more fortunate than otherwise, in that it would lull the Patrol into believing themselves in a position of superiority—a belief which would, at election time, prove fatal.

This being, human to the limit of classification except for a faint but unmistakable blue coloration, had been closeted with Senator Morgan for a matter of two hours.

"In the matters covered, your reports have been complete and conclusive," the visitor said finally, "but you have not reported on the Lens."

"Purposely. We are investigating it, but any report based upon our present knowledge would be partial and inconclusive."

"I see. Commendable enough, usually. News of this phenomenon has, however, gone farther and higher than you think and I have been ordered to take cognizance of it; to decide whether or not to handle it myself."

"I am thoroughly capable of . . ."

"I will decide that, not you." Morgan subsided. "A partial report is therefore in order. Go ahead."

"According to the procedure submitted and approved, a Lensman was taken alive. Since the Lens has telepathic properties, and hence is presumably operative at great distances, the operation was carried out in the shortest possible time. The Lens, immediately upon removal from the Patrolman's arm, ceased to radiate and the operative who held the thing died. It was then applied by force to four other men—workers, these, of no importance. All four died, thus obviating all possibility of coincidence. An attempt was made to analyze a fragment of the active material, without success. It seemed to be completely inert. Neither was it affected by electrical discharges or by sub-atomic bombardment, nor by any temperatures available. Meanwhile, the man was of course being questioned, under truth-drug and beams. His mind denied any knowledge of the nature of the Lens; a thing which I am rather inclined to believe. His mind adhered to the belief that he obtained the Lens upon the planet Arisia. I am offering for your consideration my opinion that the high-ranking officers of the Patrol are using hypnotism to conceal the real source of the Lens."

"Your opinion is accepted for consideration."

"The man died during examination. Two minutes after his death his Lens disappeared."

"Disappeared? What do you mean? Flew away? Vanished? Was stolen? Disintegrated? Or what?"

"No. More like evaporation or sublimation, except that there was no gradual diminution in volume, and there was no detectable residue, either solid, liquid, or gaseous. The platinum-alloy bracelet remained intact."

"And then?"

"The Patrol attacked in force and our expedition was destroyed."

"You are sure of these observational facts?"

"I have the detailed records. Would you like to see them?"

"Send them to my office. I hereby relieve you of all responsibility in the matter of the Lens. In fact, even I may decide to refer it to a higher echelon. Have you any other material, not necessarily facts, which may have bearing?"

"None," Morgan replied; and it was just as well for Virgilia Samms' continued well-being that the Senator did not think it worthwhile to mention the traceless disappearance of his Number One secretary and a few members of a certain unsavory gang. To his way of thinking, the Lens was not involved, except perhaps very incidentally. Herkimer, in spite of advice and orders, had probably got rough with the girl, and Samms' mob had rubbed him out. Served him right.

"I have no criticism of any phase of your work. You are doing a particularly nice job on thionite. You are of course observing all specified precautions as to key personnel?"

"Certainly. Thorough testing and unremitting watchfulness. Our Mr. Isaacson is about to promote a man who has proved very capable. Would you like to observe the proceedings?"

"No. I have no time for minor matters. Your results have been satisfactory. Keep them that way. Goodbye." The visitor strode out.

Morgan reached for a switch, then drew his hand back. No. He would like to sit in on the forthcoming interview, but he did not have the time. He had tested Olmstead repeatedly and personally; he knew what the man was. It was Isaacson's department; let Isaacson handle it. He himself must work full time at the job which only he could handle; the Nationalists must and would win this forthcoming election.

And in the office of the president of Interstellar Space-ways, Isaacson got up and shook hands with George Olmstead.

"I called you in for two reasons. First, in reply to your message that you were ready for a bigger job. What makes you think that any such are available?"

"Do I need to answer that?"

"Perhaps not . . . no." The magnate smiled quietly. Morgan was right; this man could not be accused of being dumb. "There is such a job, you are ready for it, and you have your successor trained in the work of harvesting. Second, why did you cut down, instead of increasing as ordered, the weight of broadleaf per trip? This, Olmstead, is really serious."

"I explained why. It would have been more serious the other way. Didn't you believe I knew what I was talking about?"

"Your reasoning may have been distorted in transmittal. I want it straight from you."

"Very well. It isn't smart to be greedy. There's a point at which something that has been merely a nuisance becomes a thing that *has* to be wiped out. Since I didn't want to be in that ferry when the Patrol blows it out of the ether, I cut down the take, and I advise you to keep it down. What you're getting now is a lot more than you ever got before, and a *hell* of a lot more than none at all. Think it over."

"I see. Upon what basis did you arrive at the figure you established?"

"Pure guesswork, nothing else. I guessed that about three hundred percent of the previous average per month ought to satisfy anybody who wasn't too greedy to have good sense, and that more than that would ring a loud, clear bell right where we don't want any noise made. So I cut it down to three, and advised Ferdy either to keep it at three or quit while he was still all in one piece."

"You exceeded your authority . . . and were insubordinate . . . but it wouldn't surprise me if you were right. You are certainly right in principle, and the poundage can be determined by statistical and psychological analysis. But in the meantime, there is tremendous pressure for increased production."

"I know it. Pressure be damned. My dear cousin Virgil is, as you already know, a crackpot. He is visionary, idealistic, full of sweet and beautiful concepts of what the universe would be like if there weren't so many people like you and me in it; but don't ever make the mistake of writing him off as anybody's fool. And you know, probably better than I do, what Rod Kinnison is like. If I were you I'd tell whoever is doing the screaming to shut their damn mouths before they get their teeth kicked down their throats."

"I'm very much inclined to take your advice. And now as to this proposed promotion. You are of course familiar in a general way with our operation at Northport?"

"I could scarcely help knowing *something* about the biggest uranium works on Earth. However, I am not well enough qualified in detail to make a good technical executive."

"Nor is it necessary. Our thought is to make you a key man in a new and increasingly important branch of the business, known as Department Q. It is concerned neither with production nor with uranium."

"Q as in 'quiet,' eh? I'm listening with both ears. What duties would be connected with this . . . er . . . position? What would I really do?"

Two pairs of hard eyes locked and held, staring yieldlessly into each other's depths.

"You would not be unduly surprised to learn that substances other than uranium occasionally reach Northport?"

"Not *too* surprised, no," Olmstead replied dryly. "What would I do with it?"

"We need not go into that here or now. I offer you the position."

"I accept it."

"Very well. I will take you to Northport, and we will continue our talk en route."

And in a spy-ray-proof, sound-proof compartment of a Spaceways-owned stratoliner they did so.

"Just for my information, Mr. Isaacson, how many predecessors have I had on this particular job, and what happened to them? The Patrol get them?"

"Two. No; we have not been able to find any evidence that the Samms crowd has any suspicion of us. Both were too small for the job; neither could handle personnel. One got funny ideas, the other couldn't stand the strain. If you don't get funny ideas, and don't crack up, you will make out in a big—and I mean *really* big—way."

"If I do either I'll be more than somewhat surprised." Olmstead's features set themselves into a mirthless, uncompromising, somehow bitter grin.

"So will I." Isaacson agreed.

He knew what this man was, and just how case-hardened he was. He knew that he had fought Morgan himself to a scoreless tie after twisting Herkimer—and he was no soft touch—into a pretzel in nothing flat. At the thought of the secretary, so recently and so mysteriously vanished, the magnate's mind left for a moment the matter in hand. What was at the bottom of that affair—the Lens or the woman? Or both? If he were in Morgan's shoes ... but he wasn't. He had enough grief of his own, without worrying about any of Morgan's stinkeroos. He studied Olmstead's inscrutable, subtly sneering smile and knew that he had made a wise decision.

"I gather that I am going to be one of the main links in the primary chain of deliveries. What's the technique, and how do I cover up?"

"Technique first. You go fishing. You are an expert at that, I believe?"

"You might say so. I won't have to do any faking there."

"Some week-end soon, and *every* week-end later on, we hope, you will indulge in your favorite sport at some lake or other. You will take the customary solid and liquid refreshments along in a lunch-box. When you have finished eating you will toss the lunch-box overboard."

"That all?"

"That's all."

"The lunch-box, then, will be slightly special?"

"More or less, although it will look ordinary enough. Now as to the cover-up. How would 'Director of Research' sound?"

"I don't know. Depends on what the researchers are doing. Before I became an engineer I was a pure scientist of sorts; but that was quite a while ago and I was never a specialist."

"That is one reason why I think you will do. We have plenty of specialists—too many, I often think. They dash off in all directions, without rhyme or reason. What we want is a man with enough scientific training to know in general what is going on, but what he will need mostly is hard common sense, and enough ability—mental force, you might call it—to hold the specialists down to earth and make them pull together. If you can do it—and if I didn't think you could I wouldn't be talking to you—the whole force will know that you are earning your pay; just as we could not hide the fact that your two predecessors weren't."

"Put that way it sounds good. I wouldn't wonder if I could handle it."

The conversation went on, but the rest of it is of little importance here. The plane landed. Isaacson introduced the new Director of Research to Works Manager Rand, who in turn introduced him to a few of his scientists and to the svelte and spectacular red-head who was to be his private secretary.

It was clear from the first that the Research Department was not going to be an easy one to manage. The top men were defiant, the middle ranks were sullen, the smaller fry were apprehensive as well as sullen. The secretary flaunted chips on both shapely shoulders. Men and women alike expected the application of the old wheeze "a new broom sweeps clean" for the third time in scarcely twice that many months, and they were defying him to do his worst. Wherefore they were very much surprised when the new boss did nothing whatever for two solid weeks except read reports and get acquainted with his department.

"How d'ya like your new boss, May?" another secretary asked, during a break.

"Oh, not too bad . . . I guess." May's tone was full of reservations. "He's quiet—sort of reserved—no passes or anything like that—it'd be funny if I finally got a boss that had something on the ball, wouldn't it? But you know what, Molly?" The red-head giggled suddenly. "I had a camera-fiend first, you know, with a million credits' worth of stereocams and such stuff, and then a golf-nut. I wonder what this Dr. Olmstead does with his spare cash?"

"You'll find out, dearie, no doubt." Molly's tone gave the words a meaning slightly different from the semantic one of their arrangement.

"I intend to, Molly—I *fully* intend to." May's meaning, too, was not expressed exactly by the sequence of words used. "It must be tough, a boss's life. Having to sit at a desk or be in conference six or seven hours a day—when he isn't playing around somewhere—for a measly thousand credits or so a month. How do they get that way?"

"You said it, May. You *really* said it. But we'll get ours, huh?"

Time went on. George Olmstead studied reports, and more reports. He read one, and re-read it, frowning. He compared it minutely with another; then sent red-headed May to hunt up one which had been turned in a couple of weeks before. He took them home that evening, and in the morning he punched three buttons. Three stiffly polite young men obeyed his summons.

"Good morning, Doctor Olmstead."

"Morning, boys. I'm not up on the fundamental theory of any one of these three reports, but if you combine this, and this, and this," indicating heavily-penciled sections of the three documents, "would you, or would you not, be able to work out a process that would do away with about three-quarters of the final purification and separation processes?"

They did not know. It had not been the business of any one of them, or of all them collectively, to find out.

"I'm making it your business as of now. Drop whatever you're doing, put your heads together, and find out. Theory first, then a small-scale laboratory experiment. Then come back here on the double."

"Yes, sir," and in a few days they were back.

"Does it work?"

"In theory it should, sir, and on a laboratory scale it does." The three young men were, if possible, even stiffer than before. It was not the first time, nor would it be the last, that a Director of Research would seize credit for work which he was not capable of doing.

"Good. Miss Reed, get me Rand . . . Rand? Olmstead. Three of my boys have just hatched out something that may be worth quite a few million credits a year to us . . . Me? Hell, no! Talk to them. I can't understand any one of the three parts of it, to say nothing of inventing it. I want you to give 'em a class AAA priority on the pilot plant, as of right now. If they can develop it, and I'm betting they can, I'm going to put their pictures in the Northport News and give 'em a couple of thousand credits apiece and a couple of weeks vacation to spend it in . . . Yeah, I'll send 'em in." He turned to the flabbergasted three. "Take your dope in to Rand—now. Show him what you've got; then tear into that pilot plant.''

And, a little later, Molly and May again met in the powder room.

"So your new boss is a *fisherman!*" Molly snickered. "And they say he paid over *two hundred credits* for a *reel!* You were right, May; a boss's life must be mighty hard to take. And he sits around more and does less, they say, than any other exec in the plant.''

"*Who* says so, the dirty, sneaking liars?" the red-head blazed, completely unaware that she had reversed her former position. "And even if it *was* so, which it isn't, he can do more work sitting perfectly still than any other boss in the whole Works can do tearing around at forty parsecs a minute, so there!''

George Olmstead was earning his salary.

His position was fully consolidated when, a few days later, a tremor of excitement ran through the Research Department. "Heads up, everybody! Mr. Isaacson—himself—is coming—*here!* What for, I wonder? Y'don't s'pose he's going to take the Old Man away from us already, do you?"

He came. He went through, for the first time, the entire department. He observed minutely, and he understood what he saw.

Olmstead led the Big Boss into his private office and flipped the switch which supposedly rendered that sanctum proof against any and all forms of spying, eavesdropping, intrusion, and communication. It did not, however, close the deeper, subtler channels which the Lensmen used.

"Good work, George. So *damned* good that I'm going to have to take you out of Department Q entirely and make you Works Manager of our new plant on Vegia. Have you got a man you can break in to take your place here?''

"Including Department Q? No." Although Olmstead did not show it, he was disappointed at hearing the word "Vegia." He had been aiming much higher than that—at the secret planet of the Boskonian Armed Forces, no less—but there might still be enough time to win a transfer there.

"Excluding. I've got another good man here now for that. Jones. Not heavy enough, though, for Vegia.''

"In that case, yes. Dr. Whitworth, one of the boys who worked out the new process. It'll take a little time, though. Three weeks minimum.''

"Three weeks it is. Today's Friday. You've got things in shape, haven't you, so that you can take the week-end off?''

"I was figuring on it. I'm not going where I thought I was, though, I imagine.''

"Probably not. Lake Chesuncook, on Route 273. Rough country, and the hotel is something less than fourth rate, but the fishing can't be beat."

"I'm glad of that. When I fish, I like to catch something."

"It would smell if you didn't. They stock lunch-boxes in the cafeteria, you know. Have your girl get you one, full of sandwiches and stuff. Start early this afternoon, as soon as you can after I leave. Good-bye."

"Miss Reed, please send Whitworth in. Then skip down to the cafeteria and get me a lunch-box. Sandwiches and a thermos of coffee. Provender suitable for a wet and hungry fisherman."

"Yes, *sir!*" There were no chips now; the red-head's boss was the top ace of the whole plant.

"Hi, Ned. Take the throne." Olmstead waved his hand at the now vacant chair behind the big desk. "Hold it down 'til I get back. Monday, maybe."

"Going fishing, huh?" Gone was all trace of stiffness, of reserve, of unfriendliness. "You big, lucky stiff!"

"Well, my brilliant young squirt, maybe you'll get old and fat enough to go fishing yourself some day. Who knows? 'Bye."

Lunch-box in hand and encumbered with tackle, Olmstead walked blithely along the corridor to the office of Assistant Works Manager Jones. While he had not known just what to expect, he was not surprised to see a lunch-box exactly like his own upon the side-table. He placed his box beside it.

"Hi, Olmstead." By no slightest flicker of expression did either Lensman step out of character. "Shoving off early?"

"Yeah. Dropped by to let the Head Office know I won't be in 'til Monday."

"O.K. So'm I, but more speed for me. Chemquassabamticook Lake."

"Do you pronounce that or sneeze it? But have fun, my boy. I'm combining business with pleasure, though—breaking in Whitworth on my job. That Fairplay thing is going to break in about an hour, and it'll scare the pants off of him. But it'll keep until Monday, anyway, and if he handles it right he's just about in."

Jones grinned. "A bit brutal, perhaps, but a sure way to find out. 'Bye."

"So long." Olmstead strolled out, nonchalantly picking up the wrong lunch-box on the way, and left the building.

He ordered his Dillingham, and tossed the lunch-box aboard as carelessly as though it did not contain an unknown number of millions of credits' worth of clear-quill, uncut thionite.

"I hope you have a nice week-end, sir," the yard-man said, as he helped stow baggage and tackle.

"Thanks, Otto. I'll bring you a couple of fish Monday, if I catch that many," and it should be said in passing that he brought them. Lensmen keep their promises, under whatever circumstances or however lightly given.

It being mid-afternoon of Friday, the traffic was already heavy. Northport was not a metropolis, of course; but on the other hand it did not have metropolitan multi-tiered, one-way, non-intersecting streets. But Olmstead was in no hurry. He inched his spectacular mount—it was a violently iridescent chrome green in color, with highly polished chromium gingerbread wherever there was any excuse for gingerbread to be—across the city and into the north-bound side of the super-highway. Even then, he did not hurry. He wanted to hit the inspection station at the edge of the Preserve at dusk. Ninety miles an hour would do it. He worked his way into the ninety-mile lane and became motionless relative to the other vehicles on the strip.

It was a peculiar sensation; it seemed as though the cars themselves were stationary, with the pavement flowing backward beneath them. There was no passing, no weaving, no cutting in and out. Only occasionally would the formation be broken as a car would shift almost imperceptibly to one side or the other; speeding up or slowing down to match the assigned speed of the neighboring way.

The afternoon was bright and clear, neither too hot nor too cold. Olmstead enjoyed his drive thoroughly, and arrived at the turn-off right on schedule. Leaving the wide, smooth way, he slowed down abruptly; even a Dillingham Super-Sporter could not make speed on the narrow, rough, and hilly road to Chesuncook Lake.

At dusk he reached the Post. Instead of stopping on the pavement he pulled off the road, got out, stretched hugely, and took a few drum-major's steps to take the kinks out of his legs.

"A lot of road, eh?" the smartly-uniformed trooper remarked. "No guns?"

"No guns." Olmstead opened up for inspection. "From Northport. Funny, isn't it, how hard it is to stop, even when you aren't in any particular hurry? Guess I'll eat now—join me in a sandwich and some hot coffee or a cold lemon sour or cherry soda?"

"I've got my own supper, thanks; I was just going to eat. But did you say a *cold* lemon sour?"

"Uh-huh. Ice-cold. Zero degrees Centigrade."

"I *will* join you, in that case. Thanks."

Olmstead opened a frost-lined compartment; took out two half-liter bottles; placed them and his open lunch-box invitingly on the low stone wall.

"Hm . . . m . . . m. Quite a zipper you got there, mister." The trooper gazed admiringly at the luxurious, two-wheeled monster; listened appreciatively to its almost inaudible hum. "I've heard about those new supers, but that is the first one I ever saw. Nice. All the comforts of home, eh?"

"Just about. Sure you won't help me clean up on those sandwiches, before they get stale?"

Seated on the wall, the two men ate and talked. If that trooper had known what was in the box beside his leg he probably would have fallen over backward; but how was he even to suspect? There was nothing crass or rough or coarse about any of the work of any of Boskone's high-level operators.

Olmstead drove on to the lake and took up his reservation at the ramshackle hotel. He slept, and bright and early the next morning he was up and fishing—and this part of the performance he really enjoyed. He knew his stuff and the fish were there; big, wary, and game. He loved it.

At noon he ate, and quite openly and brazenly consigned the "empty" box to the watery deep. Even if he had not had so many fish to carry, he was not the type to lug a cheap lunch-box back to town. He fished joyously all afternoon, without getting quite the limit, and as the sun grazed the horizon he started his putt-putt and skimmed back to the dock.

The thing hadn't sent out any radiation yet, Northrop informed him tensely, but it certainly would, and when it did they'd be ready. There were Lensmen and Patrolmen all over the place, thicker than hair on a dog.

And George Olmstead, sighing wearily and yet blissfully anticipatory of one more day of enthralling sport, gathered up his equipment and his fish and strolled toward the hotel.

17

BENNETT THE ARSENAL

Forty thousand miles from Earth's center the *Chicago* loafed along a circular arc, inert, at a mere ten thousand miles an hour; a speed which, and not by accident, kept her practically stationary above a certain point on the planet's surface. Nor was it by chance that both Virgil Samms and Roderick Kinnison were aboard. And a dozen or so other craft, cruisers and such, whose officers were out to put space-time in their logs, were flitting aimlessly about; but never very far away from the flagship. And farther out—well out—a cordon of diesel-powered detector ships swept space to the full limit of their prodigious reach. The navigating officers of those vessels knew to a nicety the place and course of every ship lawfully in the ether, and the appearance of even one unscheduled trace would set in motion a long succession of carefully-planned events.

And far below, grazing atmosphere, never very far from the direct line between the *Chicago* and Earth's core, floated a palatial pleasure yacht. And this craft carried not one Lensman, or two, but eight; two of whom kept their eyes fixed upon their observation plates. They were watching a lunch-box resting upon the bottom of a lake.

"Hasn't it radiated *yet*?" Roderick Kinnison demanded. "Or been approached, or moved?"

"Not yet," Lyman Cleveland replied, crisply. "Neither Northrop's rig nor mine has shown any sign of activity."

He did not amplify the statement, nor was there need. Mason Northrop was a Master Electronicist; Cleveland was perhaps the world's greatest living expert. Neither of them had detected radiation. Ergo, none existed.

Equally certain the box had not moved, or been moved, or approached. "No change, Rod," Doctor Frederick Rodebush Lensed the assured thought. "Six of us have been watching the plates in five-minute shifts."

A few minutes later, however: "Here is a thought which may be of interest," DalNalten the Venerian announced, spraying himself with a couple pints of water. "It is natural enough, of course, for any Venerian to be in or on any water he can reach—I would enjoy very much being on or in that lake myself—but it may not be entirely by coincidence that one particular Venerian, Ossmen, is visiting this particular lake at this particular time."

"What!" Nine Lensmen yelled the thought practically as one.

"Precisely. Ossmen." It was a measure of the Venerian Lensman's concern that he used only two words instead of twenty or thirty. "In the red boat with the yellow sail."

"Do you see any detector rigs?" Samms asked.

"He wouldn't need any," DalNalten put in. "He will be able to see it. Or, if a little colane had been rubbed on it which no Tellurian could have noticed, any Venerian could smell it from one end of that lake to the other."

"True. I didn't think of that. It may not have a transmitter after all."

"Maybe not, but keep on listening, anyway," the Port Admiral ordered. "Bend a plate on Ossmen, and a couple more on the rest of the boats. But Ossmen is clean, you say, Jack? Not even a spy-ray block?"

"He couldn't have a block, Dad. It'd give too much away, here on our home grounds. Like on Eridan, where their ops could wear anything they could lift, but we had to go naked." He flinched mentally as he recalled his encounter with Hazel the Hell-cat, and Northrop flinched with him.

"That's right, Rod," Olmstead in his boat below agreed, and Conway Costigan, in his room in Northport, concurred. The top-drawer operatives of the enemy depended for safety upon perfection of technique, not upon crude and dangerous mechanical devices.

"Well, since you're all so sure of it, I'll buy it," and the waiting went on.

Under the slight urge of the light and vagrant breeze, the red boat moved slowly across the water. A somnolent, lackadaisical youth, who very evidently cared nothing about where the boat went, sat in its stern, with his left arm draped loosely across the tiller. Nor was Ossmen any more concerned. His only care, apparently, was to avoid interference with the fishermen; his under-water jaunts were long, even for a Venerian, and he entered and left the water as smoothly as only a Venerian—or a seal—could.

"However, he could have, and probably has got, a capsule spy-ray detector," Jack offered, presently. "Or, since a Venerian can swallow anything one inch smaller than a kitchen stove, he could have a whole analyzing station stashed away in his stomach. Nobody's put a beam on him yet, have you?"

Nobody had.

"It might be smart not to. Watch him with 'scopes . . . and when he gets up close to the box, better pull your beams off of it. DalNalten, I don't suppose it would be quite bright for you to go swimming down there too, would it?"

"Very definitely not, which is why I am up here and dry. None of them would go near it."

They waited, and finally Ossmen's purposeless wanderings brought him over the spot on the lake's bottom which was the target of so many Tellurian eyes. He gazed at the discarded lunch-box as incuriously as he had looked at so many other sunken objects, and swam over it as casually—and only the ultra-cameras caught what he actually did. He swam serenely on.

"The box is still there," the spy-ray men reported, "but the package is gone."

"Good!" Kinnison exclaimed. "Can you 'scopists see it on him?"

"Ten to one they can't," Jack said. "He swallowed it. I expected him to swallow it box and all."

"We can't see it, sir. He must have swallowed it."

"Make sure."

"Yes, sir . . . He's back on the boat now and we've shot him from all angles. He's clean—nothing outside."

"Perfect! That means he isn't figuring on slipping it to somebody else in a crowd. This will be an ordinary job of shadowing from here on in, so I'll pull in the umbrella."

The detector ships were recalled. The *Chicago* and the various other ships of war returned to their various bases. The pleasure craft floated away. But on the other hand there were bursts of activity throughout the forest for a mile or so back from the shores of the lake. Camps were struck. Hiking parties decided that they had hiked enough and began to retrace their steps. Lithe young men, who had been doing this and that, stopped doing it and headed for the nearest trails.

For Kinnison *pere* had erred slightly in saying that the rest of the enterprise was to be an ordinary job of shadowing. No ordinary job would do. With the game this nearly in the bag it must be made absolutely certain that no suspicion was aroused, and yet Samms had to have *facts*. Sharp, hard, clear facts; facts so self-evidently facts that no intelligence above idiot grade could possibly mistake them for anything but facts.

Wherefore Ossmen the Venerian was not alone thenceforth. From lake to hotel, from hotel to car, along the road, into and in and out of train and plane, clear to an ordinary-enough-looking building in an ordinary business section of New York, he was *never* alone. Where the traveling population was light, the Patrol operatives were few and did not crowd the Venerian too nearly; where dense, as in a metropolitan station, they ringed him three deep.

He reached his destination, which was of course spy-ray proofed, late Sunday night. He went in, remained briefly, came out.

"Shall we spy-ray him, Virge? Follow him? Or what?"

"No spy-rays. Follow him. Cover him like a blanket. At the usual time give him the usual spy-ray going-over, but not until then. This time, make it *thorough*. Make certain that he hasn't got it on him, in him, or in or around his house."

"There'll be nothing doing here tonight, will there?"

"No, it would be too noticeable. So you, Fred, and Lyman, take the first trick; the rest of us will get some sleep."

When the building opened Monday morning the Lensmen were back, with dozens of others, including Knobos of Mars. There were also present or nearby literally hundreds of the shrewdest, most capable detectives of Earth.

"So *this* is their headquarters—one of them at least," the Martian thought, studying the trickle of people entering and leaving the building. "It is as we thought, Dal, why we could never find it, why we could never trace any wholesaler backward. None of us has ever seen any of these persons before. Complete change of personnel per operation; probably inter-planetary. Long periods of quiescence. Check?"

"Check: but we have them now."

"Just like that, huh?" Jack Kinnison jibed; and from his viewpoint his idea was the more valid, for the wholesalers were very clever operators indeed.

From the more professional viewpoint of Knobos and DalNalten, however, who had fought a steadily losing battle so long, the task was not too difficult. Their forces were beautifully organized and synchronized; they were present in such overwhelming numbers that "tails" could be changed every fifteen seconds; long before anybody, however suspicious, could begin to suspect any one shadow. Nor was it necessary for the tails to signal each other, however inconspicuously, or to indicate any suspect at change-over time. Lensed thoughts directed every move, without confusion or error.

And there were tiny cameras with tremendous, protuberant lenses, the "long eyes" capable of taking wire-sharp close ups from five hundred feet; and other devices and apparatus and equipment too numerous to mention here.

Thus the wholesalers were traced and their transactions with the retail peddlers were recorded. And from that point on, even Jack Kinnison had to admit that the sailing was clear. These small fry were not smart, and their customers were even less so. None had screens or detectors or other apparatus; their every transaction could be and was recorded from a distance of many miles by the ultra-instruments of the Patrol. And not only the transactions. Clearly, unmistakably, the purchaser was followed from buying to sniffing; nor was the time intervening ever long. Thionite, then as now, was bought at retail only to use, and the whole ghastly thing went down on tape and film. The gasping, hysterical appeal; the exchange of currency for drug; the headlong rush to a place of solitude; the rigid muscle-lock and the horribly ecstatic transports; the shaken, soul-searing recovery or the entranced death. It all went on record. It was sickening to have to record such things. More than one observer did sicken in fact, and had to be relieved. But Virgil Samms had to have concrete, positive, irrefutable evidence. He got it. Any possible jury, upon seeing that evidence, would know it to be the truth; no possible jury, after seeing that evidence, could bring in any verdict other than "guilty."

Oddly enough, Jack Kinnison was the only casualty of that long and hectic day. A man—later proved to be a middle-sized potentate of the underworld—who was not even under suspicion at the time, for some reason or other got the idea that Jack was after him. The Lensman had, perhaps, allowed some part of his long eye to show; a fast and efficient long-range telephoto lens is a devilishly awkward thing to conceal. At any rate the racketeer sent out a call for help, just in case his bodyguards would not be enough, and in the meantime his personal attendants rallied enthusiastically around.

They had two objects in view; One, to pass a knife expeditiously and quietly through young Kinnison's throat from ear to ear; and: Two, to tear the long eye apart and subject a few square inches of super-sensitive emulsion to the bright light of day. And if the Big Shot had known that the photographer was not alone, that the big, hulking bruiser a few feet away was also a bull, they might have succeeded.

Two of the four hoods reached Jack just fractionally ahead of the other two; one to seize the camera, the other to swing the knife. But Jack Kinnison was fast; fast of brain and nerve and muscle. He saw them coming. In three flashing motions he bent the barrel of the telephoto into a neat arc around the side of the first man's head, ducked frantically under the fiercely-driven knife, and drove the toe of his boot into the spot upon which prize-fighters like to have their rabbit-punches land. Both of those attackers lost interest promptly. One of them lost interest permanently; for a telephoto lens in barrel is heavy, very rigid, and very, *very* hard.

While Battling Jack was still off balance, the other two guards arrived—but so did Mason Northrop. Mase was not quite as fast as Jack was; but, as has been pointed out, he was bigger and much stronger. When he hit a man, with either hand, that man dropped. It was the same as being on the receiving end of the blow of a twenty-pound hammer falling through a distance of ninety-seven and one-half feet.

The Lensmen had of course also yelled for help, and it took only a split second for a Patrol speedster to travel from any given point to any other in the same county. It took no time at all for that speedster to fill a couple of square blocks with patterns of force through which neither bullets nor beams could be driven. Therefore the battle ended as suddenly as it began; before more thugs, with their automatics and portables, could reach the scene.

Kinnison *fils* cursed and damned fulminantly the edict which had forbidden arms that day, and swore that he would never get out of bed again without strapping on at least two blasters; but he had to admit finally that he had nothing to squawk about. Kinnison *pere* explained quite patiently—for him—that all he had got out of the little fracas was a split lip, that young Northrop's hair wasn't even mussed, and that if everybody had been packing guns some scatter-brained young damn fool like him would have started blasting and blown everything higher than up—would have spoiled Samms' whole operation maybe beyond repair. Now would he please quit bellyaching and get to hell out?

He got.

"That buttons thionite up, don't you think?" Rod Kinnison asked. "And the lawyers will have plenty of time to get the case licked into shape and lined up for trial."

"Yes and no." Samms frowned in thought. "The *evidence* is complete, from original producer to ultimate consumer; but our best guess is that it will take years to get the really important offenders behind bars."

"Why? I thought you were giving them altogether too much time when you scheduled the blow-off for three weeks ahead of election."

"Because the drug racket is only a small part of it. We're going to break the whole thing at once, you know, and Mateese covers a lot more ground—murder, kidnapping, bribery, corruption, misfeasance—practically everything you can think of."

"I know. What of it?"

"Jurisdiction, among other things. With the President, over half of the Congress, much of the judiciary, and practically all of the political bosses and police chiefs of the Continent under indictment at once, the legal problem becomes incredibly difficult. The Patrol's Department of Law has been working on it twenty-four hours a day, and the only thing they seem sure of is a long succession of bitterly-contested points of law. There are no precedents whatever."

"Precedents be damned! They're guilty and everybody knows it. We'll change the laws so that . . ."

"We will *not!*" Samms interrupted, sharply. "We want and we will have government by law, not by men. We have had too much of that already. Speed is not of the essence; justice very definitely is."

" 'Crusader' Samms, now and forever! But I'll buy it, Virge—now let's get back down to earth. Operation Zwilnik is all set. Mateese is going good. Zabriska tied into Zwilnik. That leaves Operation Boskone, which is, I suppose, still getting nowhere fast."

The First Lensman did not reply. It was, and both men knew it. The shrewdest, most capable and experienced operatives of the Patrol had hit that wall with everything they had, and had simply bounced. Low-level trials had found no point of contact, no angle of approach. Middle level, ditto. George Olmstead, working at the highest possible level, was morally certain that he had found a point of contact, but had not been able to do anything with it.

"How about calling a Council conference on it?" Kinnison asked finally. "Or Bergenholm at least? Maybe he can get one of his hunches on it."

"I have discussed it with them all, just as I have with you. No one had anything constructive to offer, except to go ahead with Bennett as you are doing. The concensus is that the Boskonians know just as much about our military affairs as we know about theirs—no more."

"It *would* be too much to expect them to be dumb enough to figure us as dumb enough to depend only on our visible Grand Fleet, after the warning they gave us at The Hill," Kinnison admitted.

"Yes. What worries me most is that they had a running start."

"Not enough to count," the Port Admiral declared. "We can out-produce 'em and out-fight 'em."

"Don't be over-optimistic. You can't deny them the possession of brains, ability, man-power and resources at least equal to ours."

"I don't have to." Kinnison remained obstinately cheerful. "Morale, my boy, is what counts. Man-power and tonnage and fire-power are important, of course, but morale has won every war in history. And our morale right now is higher than a cat's back—higher than any time since John Paul Jones—and getting higher by the day."

"Yes?" The question was monosyllabic but potent.

"Yes. I mean just that—*yes*. From what we know of their system they *can't* have the morale we've got. Anything they can do we can do more of and better. What you've got, Virge, is a bad case of ingrowing nerves. You've never been to Bennett, in spite of the number of times I've asked you to. I say take time right now and come along—it'll be good for what ails you. It will also be a very fine thing for Bennett and for the Patrol—you'll find yourself no stranger there."

"You may have something there . . . I'll do it."

Port Admiral and First Lensman went to Bennett, not in the *Chicago* or other superdreadnaught, but in a two-man speedster. This was necessary because space-travel, as far as that planet was concerned, was a strictly one-way affair except for Lensmen. Only Lensmen could leave Bennett, under any circumstances or for any reason whatever. There was no outgoing mail, express, or freight. Even the war-vessels of the Fleet, while on practice maneuvers outside the bottle-tight envelopes surrounding the system, were so screened that no unauthorized communication could possibly be made.

"In other words," Kinnison finished explaining, "we slapped on everything anybody could think of, including Bergenholm and Rularion; and believe me, brother, that was a lot of stuff."

"But wouldn't the very fact of such rigid restrictions operate against morale? It is a truism of psychology that imprisonment, like everything else, is purely relative."

"Yeah, that's what I told Rularion, except I used simpler and rougher language. You know how sarcastic and superior he is, even when he's wrong?"

"*How* I know!"

"Well, when he's right he's too damned insufferable for words. You'd've thought he was talking to the prize boob of a class of half-wits. As long as nobody on the planet knew that there was any such thing as space-travel, or suspected that they were not the only form of intelligent life in the universe, it was all right. No such concept as being planet-bound could exist. They had all the room there was. But after they met us, and digested all the implications, they would develop the colly-wobbles no end. This, of course, is an extreme simplification of the way the old coot poured it into me; but he came through with the solution, so I took it like a little man."

"What was the solution?"

"It's a shame you were too busy to come in on it. You'll see when we land."

But Virgil Samms was quick on the uptake. Even before they landed, he understood. When the speedster slowed down for atmosphere he saw blazoned upon the clouds a welter of one many-times repeated signal; as they came to ground he saw that the same set of symbols was repeated, not only upon every available cloud, but also upon airships, captive balloons, streamers, roofs and sides of buildings—even, in multi-colored rocks and flower-beds, upon the ground itself.

"Twenty Haress," Samms translated, and frowned in thought. "A date of the Bennettan year. Would it by any chance happen to coincide with our Tellurian November fourteenth of this present year?"

"Bright boy!" Kinnison applauded. "I thought you'd get it, but not so fast. Yes—election day."

"I see. They know what is going on, then?"

"Everything that counts. They know what we stand to win—and lose. They've named it Liberation Day, and everything on the planet is building up to it in a grand crescendo. I was a little afraid of it at first, but if the screens are really tight it won't make any difference how many people know it, and if they aren't the beans would all be spilled anyway. And it really works—I get a bigger thrill every time I come here."

"I can see where it might work."

Bennett was a fully Tellurian world in mass, in atmosphere and in climate; her native peoples were human to the limit of classification, both physically and mentally. And First Lensman Samms, as he toured it with his friend, found a world aflame with a zeal and an ardor unknown to blasé Earth since the days of the Crusades. The Patrol's cleverest and shrewdest psychologists, by merely sticking to the truth, had done a marvelous job.

Bennett knew that it was the Arsenal and the Navy Yard of Civilization, and it was proud of it. Its factories were humming as they had never hummed before; every industry, every business, every farm was operating at one hundred percent of capacity. Bennett was dotted and spattered with spaceports already built, and hundreds more were being rushed to completion. The already staggering number of ships of war operating out of those ports was being augmented every hour by more and ever more ultra-modern, ultra-fast, ultra-powerful shapes.

It was an honor to help build those ships; it was a still greater one to help man them. Competitive examinations were being held constantly, nor were all or even most of the applicants native Bennettans.

Samms did not have to ask where these young people were coming from. He knew. From all the planets of Civilization, attracted by carefully-worded advertisements of good jobs at high pay on new and highly secret projects on newly discovered planets. There were hundreds of such ads. Most were probably the Patrol's, and led here; many were of Spaceways, Uranium, Incorporated, and other mercantile firms. The possibility that some of them might lead to what was now being called Boskonia had been tested thoroughly, but with uniformly negative results. Lensmen had applied by scores for those non-Patrol jobs and had found them bona-fide. The conclusion was unavoidable—Boskone was doing its recruiting on planets unknown to any wearer of Arisia's Lens. On the other hand, more than a trickle of Boskonians were applying for Patrol jobs, but Samms was almost certain that none had been accepted. The final screening was done by Lensmen, and in such matters Lensmen did not make many or serious mistakes.

Bennett had been informed of the First Lensman's arrival, and Kinnison had been guilty of a gross understatement indeed in telling Samms that he would not be regarded as a stranger. Wherever Samms went he was met by wildly enthusiastic crowds. He had to make speeches, each of which was climaxed by a tremendous roar of "TO LIBERATION DAY!"

"No Lensman material here, you say, Rod?" Samms asked, after the first city-shaking demonstration was over. One of his prime concerns, throughout his life, was this. "With all this enthusiasm? Sure?"

"We haven't found any good enough to refer to you yet. However, in a few years, when the younger generation gets a little older, there certainly will be."

"Check." The tour of inspection and acquaintance was finished, the two Lensmen started back to Earth.

"Well, my skeptical and pessimistic friend, was I lying, or not?" Kinnison asked, as soon as the speedster's ports were sealed. "Can they match that or not?"

"You weren't—and I don't believe they can. I have never seen anything like it. Autocracies have parades and cheers and demonstrations, of course, but they have always been forced—artificial. Those were spontaneous."

"Not only that, but the enthusiasm will carry through. We'll be piping hot and ready to go. But about this stumping—you said I'd better start as soon as we get back?"

"Within a few days, I'd say."

"I wouldn't wonder, so let's use this time in working out a plan of campaign. My idea is to start out like this . . ."

18

OPERATION ZUNK

Conway Costigan, leaving behind him scores of clues, all highly mis-
leading, severed his connection with Uranium, Inc. as soon as he dared
after Operation Zwilnik had been brought to a successful close. The
technical operation, that is; the legal battles in which it figured so largely
were to run on for enough years to make the word "zwilnik" a common
noun and adjective in the language.

He came to Tellus as unobtrusively as was his wont, and took an
inconspicuous but very active part in Operation Mateese, now in full
swing.

"Now is the time for all good men and true to come to the aid of
the party, eh?" Clio Costigan giggled.

"You can play that straight across the keyboard of your electric, pet,
and not with just two fingers, either. Did you hear what the boss told
'em today?"

"Yes." The girl's levity disappeared. "They're so *dirty*, Spud—I'm
really afraid."

"So am I. But we're not too lily-fingered ourselves if we have to be,
and we're covering 'em like a blanket—Kinnison and Samms both."

"Good."

"And in that connection, I'll have to be out half the night again
tonight. All right?"

"Of course. It's so nice having you home at all, darling, instead of
a million light-years away, that I'm practically delirious with delight."

It was sometimes hard to tell what impish Mrs. Costigan meant by
what she said. Costigan looked at her, decided she was taking him for
a ride, and smacked her a couple of times where it would do the most

good. He then kissed her thoroughly and left. He had very little time, these days, either to himself or for his lovely and adored wife.

For Roderick Kinnison's campaign, which had started out rough and not too clean, became rougher and rougher, and no cleaner, as it went along. Morgan and his crew were swinging from the heels, with everything and anything they could dig up or invent, however little of truth or even of plausibility it might contain, and Rod the Rock had never held even in principle with the gentle precept of turning the other cheek. He was rather an Old Testamentarian, and he was no neophyte at dirty fighting. As a young operative, skilled in the punishing, maiming techniques of hand-to-hand rough-and-tumble combat, he had brawled successfully in most of the dives of most of the solarian planets and of most of their moons. With this background, and being a quick study, and under the masterly coaching of Virgil Samms, Nels Bergenholm, and Rularion of North Polar Jupiter, it did not take him long to learn the various gambits and ripostes of this non-physical, but nevertheless no-holds-barred, political mayhem.

And the "boys and girls" of the Patrol worked like badgers, digging up an item here and a fact there and a bit of information somewhere else, all for the day of reckoning which was to come. They used ultra-wave scanners, spy-rays, long eyes, stool-pigeons—everything they could think of to use—and they could not *always* be blocked out or evaded.

"We've *got* it, boss—now let's *use* it!"

"No. Save it! Nail it down, solid! Get the facts—names, dates, places, and amounts. Prove it first—then save it!"

Prove it! Save it! The joint injunction was used so often that it came to be a slogan and was accepted as such. Unlike most slogans, however, it was carefully and diligently put to use. The operatives proved it and saved it, over and over, over and over again; by dint of what unsparing effort and selfless devotion only they themselves ever fully knew.

Kinnison stumped the Continent. He visited every state, all of the big cities, most of the towns, and many villages and hamlets; and always, wherever he went, a part of the show was to demonstrate to his audiences how the Lens worked.

"Look at me. You know that no two individuals are or ever can be alike. Robert Johnson is not like Fred Smith; Joe Jones is entirely different from John Brown. Look at me again. Concentrate upon whatever it is in your mind that makes me Roderick Kinnison, the individual. That will enable each of you to get into as close touch with me as though our two minds were one. I am not talking now; you are reading my mind. Since you are reading my very mind, you know exactly what

I am *really* thinking, for better or for worse. It is impossible for my mind to lie to yours, since I can change neither the basic pattern of my personality nor my basic way of thought; nor would I if I could. Being in my mind, you know that already; you know what my basic quality is. My friends call it strength and courage; Pirate Chief Morgan and his cut-throat crew call it many other things. Be that as it may, you now know whether or not you want me for your President. I can do nothing whatever to sway your opinion, for what your minds have perceived you know to be the truth. That is the way the Lens works. It bares the depths of my mind to yours, and in return enables me to understand your thoughts.

"But it is in no sense hypnotism, as Morgan is so foolishly trying to make you believe. Morgan knows as well as the rest of us do that even the most accomplished hypnotist, with all his apparatus, CAN NOT AFFECT A STRONG AND DEFINITELY OPPOSED WILL. He is therefore saying that each and every one of you now receiving this thought is such a spineless weakling that—but you may draw your own conclusions.

"In closing, remember—nail this fact down so solidly that you will never forget it—a sound and healthy mind CAN NOT LIE. The mouth can, and does. So does the typewriter. But the mind—NEVER! I can hide my thoughts from you, even while we are en rapport, like this . . . but I CAN NOT LIE TO YOU. That is why, some day, all of your highest executives will have to be Lensmen, and not politicians, diplomats, crooks and boodlers. I thank you."

As that long, bitter, incredibly vicious campaign neared its vitriolic end tension mounted higher and ever higher: and in a room in the Samms' home three young Lensmen and a red-haired girl were not at ease. All four were lean and drawn. Jack Kinnison was talking.

". . . not the party, so much, but Dad. He started out with bare fists, and now he's wading into 'em with spiked brass knuckles."

"You can play *that* across the board," Costigan agreed.

"He's really giving 'em hell," Northrop said, admiringly.

"Did you boys listen in on his Casper speech last night?"

They hadn't; they had been too busy.

"I could give it to you on your Lenses, but I couldn't reproduce the tone—the exquisite way he lifted large pieces of hide and rubbed salt into the raw places. When he gets excited you know he can't help but use voice, too, so I got some of it on a record. He starts out on voice, nice and easy, as usual; then goes onto his Lens without talking; then starts yelling as well as thinking. Listen:"

"You ought to have a Lensman president. You may not believe that any Lensman is, and as a matter of fact *must* be, incorruptible. That is my belief, as you can feel for yourselves, but I cannot *prove* it to you. Only time can do that. It is a self-evident fact, however, which you can feel for yourselves, that a Lensman president could not lie to you except by word of mouth or in writing. You could demand from him at any time a Lensed statement upon any subject. Upon some matters of state he could and should refuse to answer; but not upon any question involving moral turpitude. If he answered, you would know the truth. If he refused to answer, you would know why and could initiate impeachment proceedings then and there.

"In the past there have been presidents who used that high office for low purposes; whose very memory reeks of malfeasance and corruption. One was impeached, others should have been. Witherspoon never should have been elected. Witherspoon should have been impeached the day after he was inaugurated. Witherspoon should be impeached now. We know, and at the Grand Rally at New York Spaceport three weeks from tonight we are going to PROVE, that Witherspoon is simply a minor cog-wheel in the Morgan-Towne-Isaacson machine, 'playing footsie' at command with whatever group happens to be the highest bidder at the moment, irrespective of North America's or the System's good. Witherspoon is a gangster, a cheat, and a God damn liar, but he is of very little actual importance; merely a boodling nincompoop. Morgan is the real boss and the real menace, the Operating Engineer of the lowest-down, lousiest, filthiest, rottenest, most corrupt machine of murderers, extortionists, bribe-takers, panderers, perjurers, and other pimples on the body politic that has ever disgraced any so-called civilized government. Good night."

"Wow!" Jack Kinnison yelped. "That's high, even for him!"

"Just a minute, Jack," Jill cautioned. "The other side, too. Listen to this choice bit from Senator Morgan."

"It is not exactly hypnotism, but something infinitely worse; something that steals away your very minds; that makes anyone listening believe that white is yellow, red, purple, or pea-green. Until our scientists have checked this menace, until we have every wearer of that cursed Lens behind steel bars, I advise you in all earnestness not to listen to them at all. If you do listen your minds will surely be insidiously decomposed and broken; you will surely end your days gibbering in a padded cell.

"And murders? *Murders!* The feeble remnants of the gangs which our government has all but wiped out may perhaps commit a murder or so per year; the perpetrators of which are caught, tried, and punished. But how many of your sons and daughters has Roderick Kinnison mur-

dered, either personally or through his uniformed slaves? Think! Read
the record! Then make him explain, if he can; but do not listen to his
lying, mind-destroying Lens.

"Democracy? Bah! What does 'Rod the Rock' Kinnison—the hardest, most vicious tyrant, the most relentless and pitiless martinet ever
known to any Armed Force in the long history of our world—know of
democracy? Nothing! He understands only force. All who oppose him
in anything, however small, or who seek to reason with him, die without
record or trace; and if he is not arrested, tried, and executed, all such
will continue, tracelessly and without any pretense of trial, to die.

"But at bottom, even though he is not intelligent enough to realize
it, he is merely one more in the long parade of tools of ruthless and
predatory wealth, the MONIED POWERS. *They*, my friends, never
sleep; they have only one God, one tenet, one creed—the almighty
CREDIT. *That* is what they are after, and note how craftily, how stealth-
ily, they have done and are doing their grabbing. Where is your representation upon that so-called Galactic Council? How did this criminal,
this vicious, this outrageously unconstitutional, this irresponsible, uncontrollable, and dictatorial monstrosity come into being? How and
when did you give this bloated colossus the right to establish its own
currency—to have the immeasurable effrontery to debar the solidest
currency in the universe, the credit of North America, from interplanetary and interstellar commerce? Their aim is clear; they intend to tax
you into slavery and death. Do not forget for one instant, my friends,
that the power to tax is the power to destroy. THE POWER TO TAX
IS THE POWER TO DESTROY. Our forefathers fought and bled and
died to establish the principle that taxation without rep . . ."

"And so on, for one solid hour!" Jill snarled, as she snapped the
switch viciously. "How do you like *them* potatoes?"

"Hell's—Blazing—Pinnacles!" This from Jack, silent for seconds,
and:

"Rugged stuff . . . very, *very* rugged," from Northrop. "No wonder
you look sort of pooped, Spud. Being Chief Bodyguard must have developed recently into quite a chore."

"You ain't just snapping your choppers, bub," was Costigan's grimly
flippant reply. "I've yelled for help—in force."

"So have I, and I'm going to yell again, right now," Jack declared.
"I don't know whether Dad is going to kill Morgan or not—and don't
give a damn—but if Morgan isn't going all out to kill Dad it's because
they've forgotten how to make bombs."

He Lensed a call to Bergenholm.

"Yes, Jack? . . . I will refer you to Rularion, who has had this matter under consideration."

"Yes, John Kinnison, I have considered the matter and have taken action," the Jovian's calmly assured thought rolled into the minds of all, even Lensless Jill's. "The point, youth, was well taken. It was your thought that some thousands—perhaps five—of spy-ray operators and other operatives will be required to insure that the Grand Rally will not be marred by episodes of violence."

"It was," Jack said, flatly. "It still is."

"Not having considered all possible contingencies nor the extent of the field of necessary action, you err. The number will approach nineteen thousand very nearly. Admiral Clayton has been so advised and his staff is now at work upon a plan of action in accordance with my recommendation. Your suggestions, Conway Costigan, in the matter of immediate protection of Roderick Kinnison's person, are now in effect, and you are hereby relieved of that responsibility. I assume that you four wish to continue at work?"

The Jovian's assumption was sound.

"I suggest, then, that you confer with Admiral Clayton and fit yourselves into his program of security. I intend to make the same suggestion to all Lensmen and other qualified persons not engaged in work of more pressing importance."

Rularion cut off and Jack scowled blackly. "The Grand Rally is going to be held three weeks before election day. I *still* don't like it. I'd save it until the night before election—knock their teeth out with it at the last possible minute."

"You're wrong, Jack; the Chief is right," Costigan argued. "Two ways. One, we can't play that kind of ball. Two, this gives them just enough rope to hang themselves."

"Well . . . maybe." Kinnison-like, Jack was far from being convinced. "But that's the way it's going to be, so let's call Clayton."

"First," Costigan broke in. "Jill, will you please explain why they have to waste as big a man as Kinnison on such a piffling job as president? I was out in the sticks, you know—it doesn't make sense."

"Because he's the only man alive who can lick Morgan's machine at the polls," Jill stated a simple fact. "The Patrol can get along without him for one term, after that it won't make any difference."

"But Morgan works from the side-lines. Why couldn't he?"

"The psychology is entirely different. Morgan *is* a boss. Pops Kinnison isn't. He's a leader. See?"

"Oh . . . I guess so . . . Yes. Go ahead."

*   *   *

Outwardly, New York Spaceport did not change appreciably. At any given moment of day or night there were so many hundreds of persons strolling aimlessly or walking purposefully about that an extra hundred or so made no perceptible difference. And the spaceport was only the end-point. The Patrol's activities began hundreds or thousands or millions or billions of miles away from Earth's metropolis.

A web was set up through which not even a grain-of-sand meteorite could pass undetected. Every space-ship bound for Earth carried at least one passenger who would not otherwise have been aboard; passengers who, if not wearing Lenses, carried Service Special equipment amply sufficient for the work in hand. Geigers and other, vastly more complicated mechanisms flew toward Earth from every direction in space; streamed toward New York in Earth's every channel of traffic. Every train and plane, every bus and boat and car, every conveyance of every kind and every pedestrian approaching New York City was searched; with a search as thorough as it was unobtrusive. And every thing and every entity approaching New York Spaceport was combed, literally by the cubic millimeter.

No arrests were made. No package was confiscated, or even disturbed, throughout the ranks of public check boxes, in private offices, or in elaborate or casual hiding-places. As far as the enemy knew, the Patrol had no suspicion whatever that anything out of the ordinary was going on. That is, until the last possible minute. Then a tall, lean, space-tanned veteran spoke softly aloud, as though to himself:

"Spy-ray blocks—interference—umbrella—on. Report."

That voice, low and soft as it was, was picked up by every Service Special receiver within a radius of a thousand miles, and by every Lensman listening, wherever he might be. So were, in a matter of seconds, the replies.

"Spy-ray blocks on, sir."

"Interference on, sir."

"Umbrella on, sir."

No spy-ray could be driven into any part of the tremendous port. No beam, communicator or detonating, could operate anywhere near it. The enemy would now know that something had gone wrong, but he would not be able to do anything about it.

"Reports received," the tanned man said, still quietly. "Operation Zunk will proceed as scheduled."

And four hundred seventy-one highly skilled men, carrying duplicate keys and/or whatever other specialized apparatus and equipment would be necessary, quietly took possession of four hundred seventy-one objects, of almost that many shapes and sizes. And, out in the gathering crowd, a few disturbances occurred and a few ambulances dashed busily here and there. Some women had fainted, no doubt, ran the report. They always did.

And Conway Costigan, who had been watching, without seeming even to look at him, a porter loading a truck with opulent-looking hand-luggage from a locker, followed man and truck out into the concourse. Closing up, he asked:

"Where are you taking that baggage, Charley?"

"Up Ramp One, boss," came the unflurried reply. "Flight Ninety will be late taking off, on accounta this jamboree, and they want it right up there handy."

"Take it down to the . . ."

Over the years a good many men had tried to catch Conway Costigan off guard or napping, to beat him to the punch or to the draw—with a startlingly uniform lack of success. The Lensman's fist traveled a bare seven inches: the supposed porter gasped once and traveled—or rather, staggered backward—approximately seven feet before he collapsed and sprawled unconscious upon the pavement.

"Decontamination," Costigan remarked, apparently to empty air, as he picked the fellow up and draped him limply over the truckful of suitcases. "Deke. Front and center. Area forty-six. Class Eff-ex—hotter than the middle tailrace of hell."

"You called Deke?" A man came running up. Eff-ex six—nineteen. This it?"

"Check. It's yours, porter and all. Take it away."

Costigan strolled on until he met Jack Kinnison, who had a rapidly-developing mouse under his left eye.

"How did *that* happen, Jack?" he demanded sharply. "Something slip?"

"Not exactly." Kinnison grinned ruefully. "I have the *damndest* luck! A woman—an old lady at that—thought I was staging a hold-up and swung on me with her hand-bag—southpaw and from the rear. And if you laugh, you untuneful harp, I'll hang one right on the end of your chin, so help me!"

"Far be it from such," Costigan assured him, and did not—quite— laugh. "Wonder how we came out? They should have reported before this—p-s-s-t! Here it comes!"

Decontamination was complete; Operation Zunk had been a one-hundred-percent success; there had been no casualties.

"Except for one black eye," Costigan could not help adding; but his Lens and his Service Specials were off. Jack would have brained him if any of them had been on.

Linking arms, the two young Lensmen strode away toward Ramp Four, which was to be their station.

This was the largest crowd Earth had ever known. Everybody, particularly the Nationalists, had wondered why this climactic political rally had been set for three full weeks ahead of the election, but their curiosity had not been satisfied. Furthermore, this meeting had been advertised as no previous one had ever been; neither pains nor cash had been spared in giving it the greatest build-up ever known. Not only had every channel of communication been loaded for weeks, but also Samms' workers had been very busily engaged in starting rumors; which grew, as rumors do, into things which their own fathers and mothers could not recognize. And the baffled Nationalists, trying to play the whole thing down, made matters worse. Interest spread from North America to the other continents, to the other planets, and to the other solar systems.

Thus, to say that everybody was interested in, and was listening to, the Cosmocrats' Grand Rally would not be too serious an exaggeration.

Roderick Kinnison stepped up to the battery of microphones; certain screens were cut.

"Fellow entities of Civilization and others: while it may seem strange to broadcast a political rally to other continents and to beam it to other worlds, it was necessary in this case. The message to be given, while it will go into the political affairs of the North American Continent of Tellus, will deal primarily with a far larger thing; a matter which will be of paramount importance to all intelligent beings of every inhabited world. You know how to attune your minds to mine. Do it now."

He staggered mentally under the shock of encountering practically simultaneously so many minds, but rallied strongly and went on, via Lens:

"My first message is not to you, my fellow Cosmocrats, nor to you, my fellow dwellers on Earth, nor even to you, my fellow adherents to Civilization; but to THE ENEMY. I do not mean my political opponents, the Nationalists, who are almost all loyal fellow North Americans. I mean the entities who are using the leaders of that Nationalist party as pawns in a vastly larger game.

"I know, ENEMY, that you are listening. I know that you had goon squads in this audience, to kill me and my superior officer. Know now that they are impotent. I know that you had atomic bombs, with which to obliterate this assemblage and this entire area. They have been disassembled and stored. I know that you had large supplies of radioactive dusts. They now lie in the Patrol vaults near Weehauken. All the devices which you intended to employ are known, and all save one have been either nullified or confiscated.

"That one exception is your war-fleet, a force sufficient in your opinion to wipe out all the Armed Forces of the Galactic Patrol. You intended to use it in case we Cosmocrats win this forthcoming election; you may decide to use it now. Do so if you like; you can do nothing to interrupt or to affect this meeting. This is all I have to say to you, Enemy of Civilization.

"Now to you, my legitimate audience. I am not here to deliver the address promised you, but merely to introduce the real speaker—First Lensman Virgil Samms . . ."

A mental gasp, millions strong, made itself tellingly felt.

". . . Yes—First Lensman Samms, of whom you all know. He has not been attending political meetings because we, his advisers, would not let him. Why? Here are the facts. Through Archibald Isaacson, of Interstellar Space-ways, he was offered a bribe which would in a few years have amounted to some fifty billion credits; more wealth than any individual entity has ever possessed. Then there was an attempt at murder, which we were able—just barely—to block. Knowing there was no other place on Earth where he would be safe, we took him to The Hill. You know what happened; you know what condition The Hill is in now. This warfare was ascribed to pirates.

"The whole stupendous operation, however, was made in a vain attempt to kill one man—Virgil Samms. The Enemy knew, and we learned, that Samms is the greatest man who has ever lived. His name will last as long as Civilization endures, for it is he, and *only* he, who can make it possible for Civilization *to* endure.

"Why was I not killed? Why was I allowed to keep on making campaign speeches? Because I do not count. I am of no more importance to the cause of Civilization than is my opponent Witherspoon to that of the Enemy.

"I am a wheel-horse, a plugger. You all know me—'Rocky Rod' Kinnison, the hard-boiled egg. I've got guts enough to stand up and fight for what I *know* is right. I've got the guts and the inclination to stand up and slug it out, toe to toe, with man, beast, or devil. I would make and WILL MAKE a good president; I've got the guts and inclination to keep on slugging after you elect me; before God I promise to smash down every machine-made crook who tries to hold any part of our government down in the reeking muck in which it now is.

"I am a plugger and a slugger, with no spark of the terrific flame of inspirational genius which makes Virgil Samms what he so uniquely is. My *kind* may be important, but I individually am not. There are *so* many of us! If they had killed me another slugger would have taken my place and the effect upon the job would have been nil.

"Virgil Samms, however, *can not be replaced* and the Enemy knows it. He is unique in all history. No one else can do his job. If he is killed before the principles for which he is working are firmly established Civilization will collapse back into barbarism. It will not recover until another such mind comes into existence, the probability of which occurrence I will let you compute for yourselves.

"For those reasons Virgil Samms is not here in person. Nor is he in The Hill, since the Enemy may now possess weapons powerful enough to destroy not only that hitherto impregnable fortress, but also the whole Earth. And they would destroy Earth, without a qualm, if in so doing they could kill the First Lensman.

"Therefore Samms is now out in deep space. Our fleet is waiting to be attacked. If we win, the Galactic Patrol will go on. If we lose, we hope you shall have learned enough so that we will not have died uselessly."

"Die? Why should *you* die? *You* are safe on Earth!"

"Ah, one of the goons sent that thought. If our fleet is defeated no Lensman, anywhere, will live a week. The Enemy will see to that.

"That is all from me. Stay tuned. Come in, First Lensman Virgil Samms . . . take over, sir."

It was psychologically impossible for Virgil Samms to use such language as Kinnison had just employed. Nor was it either necessary or desirable that he should; the ground had been prepared. Therefore—coldly, impersonally, logically, tellingly—he told the whole terrific story. He revealed the most important things dug up by the Patrol's indefatigable investigators, reciting names, places, dates, transactions, and amounts. Only in the last couple of minutes did he warm up at all.

"Nor is this in any sense a smear campaign or a bringing of baseless charges to becloud the issue or to vilify without cause and upon the very eve of election a political opponent. These are facts. Formal charges are now being preferred; every person mentioned, and many others, will be put under arrest as soon as possible. If any one of them were in any degree innocent our case against him could be made to fall in less than the three weeks intervening before election day. That is why this meeting is being held at this time.

"Not one of them is innocent. Being guilty, and knowing that we can and will prove guilt, they will adopt a policy of delay and recrimination. Since our courts are, for the most part, just, the accused will be able to delay the trials and the actual presentation of evidence until after election day. Forewarned, however, you will know exactly why the trials will have been delayed, and in spite of the fog of misrepresentation you will know where the truth lies. You will know how to cast your votes. You will vote for Roderick Kinnison and for those who support him.

"There is no need for me to enlarge upon the character of Port Admiral Kinnison. You know him as well as I do. Honest, incorruptible, fearless, you know that he will make the best president we have ever had. If you do not already know it, ask any one of the hundreds of thousands of strong, able, clear-thinking young men and women who have served under him in our Armed Forces.

"I thank you, everyone who has listened, for your interest."

19

CYLINDER OF BATTLE

As long as they were commodores, Clayton of North America and Schweikert of Europe had stayed fairly close to the home planet except for infrequent vacation trips. With the formation of the Galactic Patrol, however, and their becoming Admiral and Lieutenant-Admiral of the First Galactic Region, and their acquisition of Lenses, the radius of their sphere of action was tremendously increased. One or the other of them was always to be found in Grand Fleet Headquarters at New York Spaceport, but only very seldom were both of them there at once. And if the absentee were not to be found on Earth, what of it? The First Galactic Region included all of the solar systems and all of the planets adherent to Civilization, and the absentee could, as a matter of business and duty, be practically anywhere.

Usually, however, he was not upon any of the generally-known planets, but upon Bennett—getting acquainted with the officers, supervising the drilling of Grand Fleet in new maneuvers, teaching classes in advanced strategy, and holding skill-practice generally. It was hard work, and not too inspiring, but in the end it paid off big. They knew their men; their men knew them. They could work together with a snap, a smoothness, a precision otherwise impossible; for imported top brass, unknown to and unacquainted with the body of command, can not have and does not expect the deep regard and the earned respect so necessary to high morale.

Clayton and Schweikert had both. They started early enough, worked hard enough, and had enough stuff, to earn both. Thus it came about that when, upon a scheduled day, the two admirals came to Bennett together, they were greeted as enthusiastically as though they had been Bennettans born and bred; and their welcome became a planet-wide celebration when Clayton issued the orders which all Bennett had been waiting so long and so impatiently to hear. Bennettans were at last to leave Bennett!

Group after group, sub-fleet after sub-fleet, the component units of the Galactic Patrol's Grand Fleet took off. They assembled in space; they maneuvered enough to shake themselves down into some semblance of unity; they practiced the new maneuvers; they blasted off in formation for Sol. And as the tremendous armada neared the Solar System it met—or, rather, was joined by—the Patrol ships about which Morgan and his minions already knew; each of which fitted itself into its long-assigned place. Every planet of Civilization had sent its every vessel capable of putting out a screen or of throwing a beam, but so immense was the number of war-ships in Grand Fleet that this increment, great as it intrinsically was, made no perceptible difference in its size.

On Rally Day Grand Fleet lay poised near Earth. As soon as he had introduced Samms to the intensely interested listeners at the Rally, Roderick Kinnison disappeared. Actually, he drove a bug to a distant corner of the spaceport and left the Earth in a light cruiser, but to all intents and purposes, so engrossed was everyone in what Samms was saying, Kinnison simply vanished. Samms was already in the *Boise*; the Port Admiral went out to his old flagship, the *Chicago*. Nor, in case any observer of the Enemy should be trying to keep track of him, could his course be traced. Cleveland and Northrop and Rularion and all they needed of the vast resources of the Patrol saw to that.

Neither Samms nor Kinnison had any business being with Grand Fleet in person, of course, and both knew it; but everyone knew why they were there and were glad that the two top Lensmen had decided to live or die with their Fleet. If Grand Fleet won, they would probably live; if Grand Fleet lost they would certainly die—if not in the pyrotechnic dissolution of their ships, then in a matter of days upon the ground. With the Fleet their presence would contribute markedly to morale. It was a chance very much worth taking.

Nor were Clayton and Schweikert together, or even near each other. Samms, Kinnison, and the two admirals were as far away from each other as they could get and still remain in Grand Fleet's fighting cylinder.

Cylinder? Yes. The Patrol's Board of Strategy, assuming that the enemy would attack in conventional cone formation and knowing that one cone could defeat another only after a long and costly engagement, had long since spent months and months at war-games in their tactical tanks, in search of a better formation. They had found it. Theoretically, a cylinder of proper composition could defeat, with negligible loss and in a very short time, the best cones they were able to devise. The drawback was that the ships composing a theoretically efficient cylinder would have to be highly specialized and vastly greater in number than any one power had ever been able to put into the ether. However, with all the resources of Bennett devoted to construction, this difficulty would not be insuperable.

This, of course, brought up the question of what would happen if cylinder met cylinder—if the Black strategists should also have arrived at the same solution—and this question remained unanswered. Or, rather, there were too many answers, no two of which agreed; like those to the classical one of what would happen if an irresistible force should strike an immovable object. There would be a lot of intensely interesting by-products!

Even Rularion of Jove did not come up with a definite solution. Nor did Bergenholm; who, although a comparatively obscure young Lensman-scientist and not a member of the Galactic Council, was frequently called into consultation because of his unique ability to arrive at correct conclusions via some obscurely short-circuiting process of thought.

"Well," Port Admiral Kinnison had concluded, finally, "*If* they've got one, too, we'll just have to shorten ours up, widen it out, and pray."

"Clayton to Port Admiral Kinnison," came a communication through channels. "Have you any additional orders or instructions?"

"Kinnison to Admiral Clayton. None," the Port Admiral replied, as formally, then went on via Lens: "No comment or criticism to make, Alex. You fellows have done a job so far and you'll keep on doing one. How much detection have you got out?"

"Twelve detets—three globes of Diesels. If we sit here and do nothing the boys will get edgy and go stale, so if you and Virge agree we'll give 'em some practice. Lord knows they need it, and it'll keep 'em on their toes. But about the Blacks—they may be figuring on delaying any action until we've had time to crack from boredom. What's your idea on that?"

"I've been worried about the same thing. Practice will help, but whether enough or not I don't know. What do you think, Virge? Will they hold it up deliberately or strike fast?"

"Fast," the First Lensman replied, promptly and definitely. "As soon as they possibly can, for several reasons. They don't know our real strength, any more than we know theirs. They undoubtedly believe, however, the same as we do, that they are more efficient than we are and have the larger force. By their own need of practice they will know ours. They do not attach nearly as much importance to morale as we do; by the very nature of their regime they can't. Also, our open challenge will tend very definitely to force their hands, since face-saving is even more important to them than it is to us. They will strike as soon as they can and as hard as they can.''

Grand Fleet maneuvers were begun, but in a day or so the alarms came blasting in. The enemy had been detected; coming in, as the previous Black Fleet had come, from the direction of Coma Berenices. Calculating machines clicked and whirred; orders were flashed, and a brief string of numbers; ships by the hundreds and the thousands flashed into their assigned positions.

Or, more precisely, *almost* into them. Most of the navigators and pilots had not had enough practice yet to hit their assigned positions exactly on the first try, since a radical change in axial direction was involved, but they did pretty well; a few minutes of juggling and jockeying were enough. Clayton and Schweikert used a little caustic language—via Lens and to their fellow Lensmen only, of course—but Samms and Kinnison were well enough pleased. The time of formation had been very satisfactorily short and the cone was smooth, symmetrical, and of beautifully uniform density.

The preliminary formation was a cone, not a cylinder. It was not a conventional Cone of Battle in that it was not of standard composition, was too big, and had altogether too many ships for its size. It was, however, of the conventional shape, and it was believed that by the time the enemy could perceive any significant differences it would be too late for him to do anything about it. The cylinder would be forming about that time, anyway, and it was almost believed—at least it was strongly hoped—that the enemy would not have the time or the knowledge or the equipment to do anything about that, either.

Kinnison grinned to himself as his mind, en rapport with Clayton's, watched the enemy's Cone of Battle enlarge upon the Admiral's conning plate. It was big, and powerful; the Galactic Patrol's publicly-known forces would have stood exactly the chance of the proverbial snowball in the nether regions. It was not, however, the Port Admiral thought, big enough to form an efficient cylinder, or to handle the Patrol's real force in any fashion—and unless they shifted within the next second or two it would be too late for the enemy to do anything at all.

As though by magic about ninety-five percent of the Patrol's tremendous cone changed into a tightly-packed double cylinder. This maneuver was much simpler than the previous one, and had been practiced to perfection. The mouth of the cone closed in and lengthened; the closed end opened out and shortened. Tractors and pressors leaped from ship to ship, binding the whole myriad of hitherto discrete units into a single structure as solid, even comparatively as to size, as a cantilever bridge. And instead of remaining quiescent, waiting to be attacked, the cylinder flashed forward, inertialess, at maximum blast.

Throughout the years the violence, intensity, and sheer brute power of offensive weapons had increased steadily. Defensive armament had kept step. One fundamental fact, however, had not changed throughout the ages and has not changed yet. Three or more units of given power have always been able to conquer one unit of the same power, if engagement could be forced and no assistance could be given; and two units could practically always do so. Fundamentally, therefore, strategy always has been and still is the development of new artifices and techniques by virtue of which two or more of our units may attack one of theirs; the while affording the minimum of opportunity for them to retaliate in kind.

The Patrol's Grand Fleet flashed forward, almost exactly along the axis of the Black cone; right where the enemy wanted it—or so he thought. Straight into the yawning mouth, erupting now a blast of flame beside which the wildest imaginings of Inferno must pale into insignificance; straight along that raging axis toward the apex, at the terrific speed of the two directly opposed velocities of flight. But, to the complete consternation of the Black High Command, nothing much happened. For, as has been pointed out, that cylinder was not of even approximately normal composition. In fact, there was not a normal warvessel in it. The outer skin and both ends of the cylinder were purely defensive. Those vessels, packed so closely that their repellor fields actually touched, were all screen; none of them had a beam hot enough to light a match. Conversely, the inner layer, or "Liner," was composed of vessels that were practically all offense. They had to be protected at every point—but *how* they could ladle it out!

The leading and trailing edges of the formation—the ends of the gigantic pipe, so to speak—would of course bear the brunt of the Black attack, and it was this factor that had given the Patrol's strategists the most serious concern. Wherefore the first ten and the last six double rings of ships were special indeed. They were *all* screen—nothing else. They were drones, operated by remote control, carrying no living thing. If the Patrol losses could be held to eight double rings of ships at the first pass and four at the second—theoretical computations indicated losses of six and two—Samms and his fellows would be well content.

All of the Patrol ships had, of course, the standard equipment of socalled "violet," "green," and "red" fields, as well as duodecaplylatomate and ordinary atomic bombs, dirigible torpedoes and transporters, slicers, polycyclic drills, and so on; but in this battle the principal reliance was to be placed upon the sheer, brutal, overwhelming power of what had been called the "macro beam"—now simply the "beam." Furthermore, in the incredibly incandescent frenzy of the chosen field of action—the cylinder was to attack the cone at its very strongest part—no conceivable material projectile could have lasted a single microsecond after leaving the screens of force of its parent vessel. It could have flown fast enough; ultra-beam trackers could have steered it rapidly enough and accurately enough; but before it could have traveled a foot, even at ultra-light speed, it would have ceased utterly to be. It would have been resolved into its sub-atomic constituent particles and waves. Nothing material could exist, except instantaneously, in the field of force filling the axis of the Black's Cone of Battle; a field beside which the exact center of a multi-billion-volt flash of lightning would constitute a dead area.

That field, however, encountered no material object. The Patrol's "screeners," packed so closely as to have a four hundred percent overlap, had been designed to withstand precisely that inconceivable environment. Practically all of them withstood it. And in a fraction of a second the hollow forward end of the cylinder engulfed, pipe-wise, the entire apex of the enemy's war-cone, and the hitherto idle "sluggers" of the cylinder's liner went to work.

Each of those vessels had one heavy pressor beam, each having the same push as every other, directed inward, toward the cylinder's axis, and backward at an angle of fifteen degrees from the perpendicular line between ship and axis. Therefore, wherever any Black ship entered the Patrol's cylinder or however, it was driven to and held at the axis and forced backward along that axis. None of them, however, got very far. They were perforce in single file; one ship opposing at least one solid ring of giant sluggers who did not have to concern themselves with defense, but could pour every iota of their tremendous resources into offensive beams. Thus the odds were not merely two or three to one; but never less than eighty, and very frequently over two hundred to one.

Under the impact of those unimaginable torrents of force the screens of the engulfed vessels flashed once, practically instantaneously through the spectrum, and went down. Whether they had two or three or four courses made no difference—in fact, even the ultra-speed analyzers of the observers could not tell. Then, a couple of microseconds later, the wall-shields—the strongest fabrics of force developed by man up to that time—also failed. Then those ravenous fields of force struck bare, unprotected metal, and every molecule, inorganic and organic, of ships and contents alike, disappeared in a bursting flare of energy so raw and so violent as to stagger even those who had brought it into existence. It was certainly vastly more than a mere volatilization; it was deduced later that the detonating unstable isotopes of the Black's own bombs, in the frightful temperatures already existing in the Patrol's quasi-solid beams, had initiated a chain reaction which had resulted in the fissioning of a considerable proportion of the atomic nuclei of usually completely stable elements!

The cylinder stopped; the Lensmen took stock. The depth of erosion of the leading edge had averaged almost exactly six double rings of drones. In places the sixth ring was still intact; in others, which had encountered unusually concentrated beaming, the seventh was gone. Also, a fraction of one percent of the manned war-vessels had disappeared. Brief though the time of engagement had been, the enemy had been able to concentrate enough beams to burn a few holes through the walls of the attacking cylinder.

It had not been hoped that more than a few hundreds of Black vessels could be blown out of the ether at this first pass. General Staff had been sure, however, that the heaviest and most dangerous ships, including those carrying the enemy's High Command, would be among them. The midsection of the apex of the conventional Cone of Battle had always been the safest place to be; therefore that was where the Black admirals had been and therefore they no longer lived.

In a few seconds it became clear that if any Black High Command existed, it was not in shape to function efficiently. Some of the enemy ships were still blasting, with little or no concerted effort, at the regulation cone which the cylinder had left behind; a few were attempting to get into some kind of a formation, possibly to attack the Patrol's cylinder. Indecision was visible and rampant.

To turn that tremendous cylindrical engine of destruction around would have been a task of hours, but it was not necessary. Instead, each vessel cut its tractors and pressors, spun end for end, re-connected, and retraced almost exactly its previous course; cutting out and blasting into nothingness another "plug" of Black warships. Another reversal, another dash; and this time, so disorganized were the foes and so feeble the beaming, not a single Patrol vessel was lost. The Black fleet, so proud and so conquering of mien a few minutes before, had fallen completely apart.

"That's enough, Rod, don't you think?" Samms thought then. "Please order Clayton to cease action, so that we can hold a parley with their senior officers."

"Parley, hell!" Kinnison's answering thought was a snarl. "We've got 'em going—mop 'em up before they can pull themselves together! Parley be damned!"

"Beyond a certain point military action becomes indefensible butchery, of which our Galactic Patrol will never be guilty. That point has now been reached. If you do not agree with me, I'll be glad to call a Council meeting to decide which of us is right."

"That isn't necessary. You're right—that's one reason I'm not First Lensman." The Port Admiral, fury and fire ebbing from his mind, issued orders; the Patrol forces hung motionless in space. "As President of the Galactic Council, Virge, take over."

Spy-rays probed and searched; a communicator beam was sent. Virgil Samms spoke aloud, in the lingua franca of deep space.

"Connect me, please, with the senior officer of your fleet."

There appeared upon Samms' plate a strong, not unhandsome face; deep-stamped with the bitter hopelessness of a strong man facing certain death.

"You've got us. Come on and finish us."

"Some such indoctrination was to be expected, but I anticipate no trouble in convincing you that you have been grossly misinformed in everything you have been told concerning us; our aims, our ethics, our morals, and our standards of conduct. There are, I assume, other surviving officers of your rank, although of lesser seniority?"

"There are ten other vice-admirals, but I am in command. They will obey my orders or die."

"Nevertheless, they shall be heard. Please go inert, match our intrinsic velocity, and come aboard, all eleven of you. We wish to explore with all of you the possibilities of a lasting peace between our worlds."

"Peace? Bah! Why lie?" The Black commander's expression did not change. "I know what you are and what you do to conquered races. We prefer a clean, quick death in your beams to the kind you deal out in your torture rooms and experimental laboratories. Come ahead—I intend to attack you as soon as I can make a formation."

"I repeat, you have been grossly, terribly, *shockingly* misinformed." Samms' voice was quiet and steady; his eyes held those of the other. "We are civilized men, not barbarians or savages. Does not the fact that we ceased hostilities so soon mean anything to you?"

For the first time the stranger's face changed subtly, and Samms pressed the slight advantage.

"I see it does. Now if you will converse with me mind to mind . . ." The First Lensman felt for the man's ego and began to tune to it, but this was too much.

"I will not!" The Black put up a solid block. "I will have nothing to do with your cursed Lens. I know what it is and will have none of it!''

''Oh, what's the use, Virge!'' Kinnison snapped. ''Let's get on with it!''

''A great deal of use, Rod,'' Samms replied, quietly. ''This is a turning-point. I *must* be right—I *can't* be that far wrong,'' and he again turned his attention to the enemy commander.

''Very well, sir, we will continue to use spoken language. I repeat, please come aboard with your ten fellow vice-admirals. You will not be asked to surrender. You will retain your side-arms—as long as you make no attempt to use them. Whether or not we come to any agreement, you will be allowed to return unharmed to your vessels before the battle is resumed.''

''What? Side-arms? Returned? You swear it?''

''As President of the Galactic Council, in the presence of the highest officers of the Galactic Patrol as witnesses, I swear it.''

''We will come aboard.''

''Very well. I will have ten other Lensmen and officers here with me.''

The *Boise*, of course, inerted first; followed by the *Chicago* and nine of the tremendous tear-drops from Bennett. Port Admiral Kinnison and nine other Lensmen joined Samms in the *Boise*'s con room; the tight formation of eleven Patrol ships blasted in unison in the space-courtesy of meeting the equally tight formation of Black warships half-way in the matter of intrinsic velocity.

Soon the two little sub-fleets were motionless in respect to each other. Eleven Black gigs were launched. Eleven Black vice-admirals came aboard, to the accompaniment of the full military honors customarily granted to visiting admirals of friendly powers. Each was armed with what seemed to be an exact duplicate of the Patrol's own current blaster; Lewiston, Mark Seventeen. In the lead strode the tall, heavy, gray-haired man with whom Samms had been dealing; still defiant, still sullen, still concealing sternly his sheer desperation. His block was still on, full strength.

The man next in line was much younger than the leader, much less wrought up, much more intent. Samms felt for this man's ego, tuned to it, and got the shock of his life. This Black vice-admiral's mind was not at all what he had expected to encounter—it was, in every respect, of Lensman grade!

''Oh . . . how? You are not speaking, and . . . I see . . . the Lens . . . THE LENS!'' The stranger's mind was for seconds an utterly indescribable turmoil in which relief, gladness, and high anticipation struggled for supremacy.

In the next few seconds, even before the visitors had reached their places at the conference table, Virgil Samms and Corander of Petrine exchanged thoughts which would require many thousands of words to express; only a few of which are necessary here.

"The LENS . . . I have dreamed of such a thing, without hope of realization or possibility. *How* we have been misled! They are, then, actually available upon your world, Samms of Tellus?"

"Not exactly, and not at all generally," and Samms explained as he had explained so many times before. "You will wear one sooner than you think. But as to ending this warfare. You survivors are practically all natives of your own world. Petrine?"

"Not 'practically,' we are Petrinos all. The 'teachers' were all in the Center. Many remain upon Petrine and its neighboring worlds, but none remain alive here."

"Ohlanser, then, who assumed command, is also a Petrino? So hard-headed, I had assumed otherwise. He will be a stumbling-block. Is he actually in supreme command?"

"Only by and with our consent, under such astounding circumstances as these. He is a reactionary, of the old, diehard, war-dog school. He would ordinarily be in supreme command and would be supported by the teachers if any were here; but I will challenge his authority and theirs; standing upon my right to command my own fleet as I see fit. So will, I think, several others. So go ahead with your meeting."

"Be seated, gentlemen." All saluted punctiliously and sat down. "Now, Vice-Admiral Ohlanser . . ."

"How do you, a stranger, know my name?"

"I know many things. We have a suggestion to offer which, if you Petrinos will follow it, will end this warfare. First, please believe that we have no designs upon your planet, nor any quarrel with any of its people who are not hopelessly contaminated by the ideas and the culture of the entities who are back of this whole movement; quite possibly those whom you refer to as the 'teachers.' You did not know whom you were to fight, or why." This was a statement, with no hint of question about it.

"I see now that we did not know all the truth," Ohlanser admitted, stiffly. "We were informed, and given proof sufficient to make us believe, that you were monsters from outer space—rapacious, insatiable, senselessly and callously destructive to all other forms of intelligent life."

"We suspected something of the kind. Do you others agree? Vice-Admiral Corander?"

"Yes. We were shown detailed and documented proofs; stereos of battles, in which no quarter was given. We saw system after system conquered, world after world laid waste. We were made to believe that our only hope of continued existence was to meet you and destroy you in space; for if you were allowed to reach Petrine every man, woman, and child on the planet would either be killed outright or tortured to death. I see now that those proofs were entirely false; completely vicious."

"They were. Those who spread that lying propaganda and all who support their organization must be and shall be weeded out. Petrine must be and shall be given her rightful place in the galactic fellowship of free, independent, and cooperative worlds. So must any and all planets whose peoples wish to adhere to Civilization instead of to tyranny and despotism. To further these ends, we Lensmen suggest that you re-form your fleet and proceed to Arisia . . ."

"Arisia!" Ohlanser did not like the idea.

"Arisia," Samms insisted. "Upon leaving Arisia, knowing vastly more than you do now, you will return to your home planet, where you will take whatever steps you will then know to be necessary."

"We were told that your Lenses are hypnotic devices," Ohlanser sneered, "designed to steal away and destroy the minds of any who listen to you. I believe *that*, fully. I will not go to Arisia, nor will any part of Petrine's Grand Fleet. I will not attack my home planet. I will not do battle against my own people. This is final."

"I am not saying or implying that you should. But you continue to close your mind to reason. How about you, Vice-Admiral Corander? And you others?"

In the momentary silence Samms put himself en rapport with the other officers, and was overjoyed at what he learned.

"I do not agree with Vice-Admiral Ohlanser," Corander said, flatly. "He commands, not Grand Fleet, but his sub-fleet merely, as do we all. I will lead my sub-fleet to Arisia."

"Traitor!" Ohlanser shouted. He leaped to his feet and drew his blaster, but a tractor beam snatched it from his grasp before he could fire.

"You were allowed to wear side-arms, not to use them," Samms said, quietly. "How many of you others agree with Corander; how many with Ohlanser?"

All nine voted with the younger man.

"Very well. Ohlanser, you may either accept Corander's leadership or leave this meeting now and take your sub-fleet directly back to Petrine. Decide now which you prefer to do.''

"You mean you aren't going to kill me, even now? Or even degrade me, or put me under arrest?''

"I mean exactly that. What is your decision?''

"In that case . . . I was—must have been—wrong. I will follow Corander.''

"A wise choice. Corander, you already know what to expect; except that four or five other Petrinos now in this room will help you, not only in deciding what must be done upon Petrine, but also in the doing of it. This meeting will adjourn.''

"But . . . no reprisals?'' Corander, in spite of his newly acquired knowledge, was dubious, almost dumbfounded. "No invasion or occupation? No indemnities to your Patrol, or reparations? No punishment of us, our men, or our families?''

"None.''

"That does not square up even with ordinary military usage.''

"I know it. It does conform, however, to the policy of the Galactic Patrol which is to spread throughout our island universe.''

"You are not even sending your fleet, or heavy units of it, with us, to see to it that we follow your instructions?''

"It is not necessary. If you need any form of help you will inform us of your requirements via Lens, as I am conversing with you now, and whatever you want will be supplied. However, I do not expect any such call. You and your fellows are capable of handling the situation. You will soon know the truth, and know that you know it; and when your housecleaning is done we will consider your application for representation upon the Galactic Council. Goodbye.''

Thus the Lensmen—particularly First Lensman Virgil Samms—brought another sector of the galaxy under the aegis of Civilization.

20

THE ELECTION

After the Rally there were a few days during which neither Samms nor Kinnison was on Earth. That the Cosmocrats' presidential candidate and the First Lensman were both with the Fleet was not a secret; in fact, it was advertised. Everyone was told why they were out there, and almost everyone approved.

Nor was their absence felt. Developments, fast and terrific, were slammed home. Cosmocratic spellbinders in every state of North America waved the flag, pointed with pride, and viewed with alarm, in the very best tradition of North American politics. But above all, there appeared upon every news-stand and in every book-shop of the Continent, at opening time of the day following Rally Day, a book of over eighteen hundred pages of fine print; a book the publication of which had given Samms himself no little concern.

"But I'm afraid of it!" he had protested. "*We* know it's true; but there's material on almost every page for the biggest libel and slander suits in history!"

"I know it," the bald and paunchy Lensman-attorney had replied. "Fully. I hope they *do* take action against us, but I'm absolutely certain they won't."

"You hope they *do?*"

"Yes. If they take the initiative they can't prevent us from presenting our evidence in full; and there is no court in existence, however corrupt, before which we could not win. What they want and must have is delay; avoidance of any issue until after the election."

"I see." Samms was convinced.

The location of the Patrol's Grand Fleet had been concealed from all inhabitants of the Solarian system, friends and foes alike; but the climactic battle—liberating as it did energies sufficient to distort the very warp and woof of the fabric of space itself—could not be hidden or denied, or even belittled. It was not, however, advertised or blazoned abroad. Then as now the newshawks wanted to know, instantly and via long-range communicators, vastly more than those responsible for security cared to tell; then as now the latter said as little as it was humanly possible to say.

Everyone knew that the Patrol had won a magnificent victory; but nobody knew who or what the enemy had been. Since the rank and file knew it, everyone knew that only a fraction of the Black fleet had actually been destroyed; but nobody knew where the remaining vessels went or what they did. Everyone knew that about ninety-five percent of the Patrol's astonishingly huge Grand Fleet had come from, and was on its way back to, the planet Bennett, and knew—since Bennettans would in a few weeks be scampering gaily all over space—in general *what* Bennett was; but nobody knew *why* it was.

Thus, when the North American Contingent landed at New York Spaceport, everyone whom the newsmen could reach was literally mobbed. However, in accordance with the aphorism ascribed to the wise old owl, those who knew the least said the most. But the Telenews ace who had once interviewed both Kinnison and Samms wasted no time upon small fry. He insisted on seeing the two top Lensmen, and kept on insisting until he did see them.

"Nothing to say," Kinnison said curtly, leaving no doubt whatever that he meant it. "All talking—if any—will be done by First Lensman Samms."

"Now, all you millions of Telenews listeners, I am interviewing First Lensman Samms himself. A little closer to the mike, please, First Lensman. Now, sir, what everybody wants to know is—who are the Blacks?"

"I don't know."

"You don't know? On the Lens, sir?"

"On the Lens. I still don't know."

"I see. But you have suspicions or ideas? You can guess?"

"I can guess; but that's all it would be—a guess."

"And my guess, folks, is that his guess would be a very highly informed guess. Will you tell the public, First Lensman Samms, what your guess is?"

"I will." If this reply astonished the newshawk, it staggered Kinnison and the others who knew Samms best. It was, however, a coldly calculated political move. "While it will probably be several weeks before we can furnish detailed and unassailable proof, it is my considered opinion that the Black fleet was built and controlled by the Morgan-Towne-Isaacson machine. That they, all unknown to any of us, enticed, corrupted, and seduced a world, or several worlds, to their program of domination and enslavement. That they intended by armed force to take over the Continent of North America and through it the whole Earth and all the other planets adherent to Civilization. That they intended to hunt down and kill every Lensman, and to subvert the Galactic Council to their own ends. This is what you wanted?"

"That's fine, sir—*just* what we wanted. But just one more thing, sir." The newsman had obtained infinitely more than he had expected to get; yet, good newsmanlike, he wanted more. "Just a word, if you will, Mr. Samms, as to these trials and the White Book?"

"I can add very little, I'm afraid, to what I have already said and what is in the book; and that little can be classed as 'I told you so.' We are trying, and will continue to try, to force those criminals to trial; to break up, to prohibit, an unending series of hair-splitting delays. We want, and are determined to get, legal action; to make each of those we have accused defend himself in court and under oath. Morgan and his crew, however, are working desperately to avoid any action at all, because they know that we can and will prove every allegation we have made."

The Telenews ace signed off, Samms and Kinnison went to their respective offices, and Cosmocratic orators throughout the nation held a field-day. They glowed and scintillated with triumph. They yelled themselves hoarse, leather-lunged tub-thumpers though they were, in pointing out the unsullied purity, the spotless perfection of their own party and its every candidate for office; in shuddering revulsion at the never-to-be-sufficiently-condemned, proved and demonstrated villainy and blackguardy of the opposition.

And the Nationalists, although they had been dealt a terrific and entirely unexpected blow, worked near-miracles of politics with what they had. Morgan and his minions ranted and raved. They were being jobbed. They were being crucified by the Monied Powers. All those allegations and charges were sheerest fabrications—false, utterly vicious, containing nothing whatever of truth. They, not the Patrol, were trying to force a show-down; to vindicate themselves and to confute those unspeakably unscrupulous Lensmen before Election Day. And they were succeeding! Why, otherwise, had not a single paper been served? Why had not any single one of the thousands of accused even been arrested? Ask that lying First Lensman, Virgil Samms! Ask that rock-hearted, iron-headed, conscienceless murderer, Roderick Kinnison! But do not, at peril of your sanity, submit your minds to their Lenses!

And why, the reader asks, were not at least some of those named persons arrested before Election Day? And your historian must answer frankly that he does not know. He is not a lawyer. It would be of interest—to some few of us—to follow in detail at least one of those days of legal battling in one of the high courts of the land; to quote verbatim at least a few of the many thousands of pages of transsscript: but to most of us the technicalities involved would be boring in the extreme.

But couldn't the voters tell easily enough which side was on the offensive and which on the defensive? Which pressed for action and which insisted on postponement and delay? They could have, easily enough, if they had cared enough about the basic issues involved to make the necessary mental effort, but almost everyone was too busy doing something else. And it was so much easier to take somebody else's word for it. And finally, *thinking* is an exercise to which all too few brains are accustomed.

But Morgan neither ranted nor raved nor blustered when he sat in conference with his faintly-blue superior, who had come storming in as soon as he had learned of the crushing defeat of the Black fleet. The Kalonian was very highly concerned; so much so that the undertone of his peculiar complexion was turning slowly to a delicate shade of green.

"How did *that* happen? How *could* it happen? Why was I not informed of the Patrol's real power—how could you be guilty of such stupidity? Now I'll have to report to Scrwan of the Eich. He's pure, undiluted poison—and if word of this catastrophe ever gets up to Ploor . . . !!!"

"Come down out of the stratosphere, Fernald," Morgan countered, bitingly. "Don't try to make *me* the goat—I won't sit still for it. It happened because they could build a bigger fleet than we could. You were in on that—all of it. You knew what we were doing, and approved it—all of it. You were as badly fooled as I was. You were not informed because I could find out nothing—I could learn no more of their Bennett than they could of our Petrine. As to reporting, you will of course do as you please; but I would advise you not to cry too much before you're really hurt. This battle isn't over yet, my friend."

The Kalonian had been a badly shaken entity; it was a measure of his state of mind that he did not liquidate the temerarious Tellurian then and there. But since Morgan was as undisturbed as ever, and as sure of himself, he began to regain his wonted aplomb. His color became again its normal pale blue.

"I will forgive your insubordination this time, since there were no witnesses, but use no more such language to me," he said, stiffly. "I fail to perceive any basis for your optimism. The only chance now remaining is for you to win the election, and how can you do that? You are—must be—losing ground steadily and rapidly.''

"Not as much as you might think.'' Morgan pulled down a large, carefully-drawn chart. "This line represents the hide-bound Nationalists, whom nothing we can do will alienate from the party; this one the equally hide-bound Cosmocrats. The balance of power lies, as always, with the independents—these here. And many of them are not as independent as is supposed. We can buy or bring pressure to bear on half of them—that cuts them down to this size here. So, no matter what the Patrol does, it can affect only this relatively small block here, and it is this block we are fighting for. We are losing a little ground, and steadily, yes; since we can't conceal from anybody with half a brain the fact that we're doing our best to keep the cases from ever coming to trial. But here's the actual observed line of sentiment, as determined from psychological indices up to yesterday; here is the extrapolation of that line to Election Day. It forecasts us to get just under forty-nine percent of the total vote.''

"And is there anything cheerful about that?'' Fernald asked, frostily.

"I'll say there is!'' Morgan's big face assumed a sneering smile, an expression never seen by any voter. "This chart deals only with living, legally registered, bona-fide voters. Now if we can come that close to winning an absolutely honest election, how do you figure we can possibly lose the kind this one is going to be? We're in power, you know. We've got the machine and we know how to use it.''

"Oh, yes, I remember—vaguely. You told me about North American politics once, a few years ago. Dead men, ringers, repeaters, ballot-box stuffing, and so on, you said?''

" 'And so on' is right, Chief!'' Morgan assured him, heartily. "Everything goes, this time. It'll be one of the biggest land-slides in North American history.''

"I will, then, defer any action until after the election.''

"That will be the smart thing to do, Chief; then you won't have to take any, or make any report at all,'' and upon this highly satisfactory note the conference closed.

And Morgan was actually as confident as he had appeared. His charts were actual and factual. He knew the power of money and the effectiveness of pressure; he knew the capabilities of the various units of his machine. He did not, however, know two things: Jill Samms' insidious, deeply-hidden Voters' Protective League and the bright flame of loyalty pervading the Galactic Patrol. Thus, between times of bellowing and screaming his carefully-prepared, rabble-rousing speeches, he watched calmly and contentedly the devious workings of his smooth and efficient organization.

Until the day before election, that is. Then hordes of young men and young women went suddenly and briefly to work; at least four in every precinct of the entire nation. They visited, it seemed, every residence and every dwelling unit, everywhere. They asked questions, and took notes, and vanished; and the machine's operatives, after the alarm was given, could not find man or girl or notebook. And the Galactic Patrol, which had never before paid any attention to elections, had given leave and ample time to its every North American citizen. Vessels of the North American Contingent were grounded and practically emptied of personnel; bases and stations were depopulated; and even from every distant world every Patrolman registered in any North American precinct came to spend the day at home.

Morgan began then to worry, but there was nothing he could do about the situation—or was there? If the civilian boys and girls were checking the registration books—and they were—it was as legally-appointed checkers. If the uniformed boys and girls were all coming home to vote—and they were—that, too, was their inalienable right. But boys and girls were notoriously prone to accident and to debauchery . . . but again Morgan was surprised; and, this time, taken heavily aback. The web which had protected Grand Rally so efficiently, but greatly enlarged now, was functioning again; and Morgan and his minions spent a sleepless and thoroughly uncomfortable night.

Election Day dawned clear, bright, and cool; auguring a record turn-out. Voting was early and extraordinarily heavy; the polls were crowded. There was, however, very little disorder. Surprisingly little, in view of the fact that the Cosmocratic watchers, instead of being the venal wights of custom, were cold-eyed, unreachable men and women who seemed to know by sight every voter in the precinct. At least they spotted on sight and challenged without hesitation every ringer, every dead one, every repeater, and every imposter who claimed the right to vote. And those challenges, being borne out in every case by the carefully-checked registration lists, were in every case upheld.

Not all of the policemen on duty, especially in the big cities, were above suspicion, of course. But whenever any one of those officers began to show a willingness to play ball with the machine a calm, quiet-eyed Patrolman would remark, casually:

"Better see that this election stays straight, bud, and strictly according to the lists and signatures—or you're apt to find yourself listed in the big book along with the rest of the rats."

It was not that the machine liked the way things were going, or that it did not have goon squads on the job. It was that there were, every-where and always, more Patrolmen than there were goons. And those Patrolmen, however young in years some of them might have appeared to be, were space-bronzed veterans, space-hardened fighting men, armed with the last word in blasters—Lewiston, Mark Seventeen.

To the boy's friends and neighbors, of course, his Lewiston was prac-tically invisible. It was merely an article of clothing, the same as his pants. It carried no more of significance, of threat or of menace, than did the pistol and the club of the friendly Irish cop on the beat. But the goon did not see the Patrolman as a friend. He saw the keen, clear, sharply discerning eyes; the long, strong fingers; the smoothly flowing muscles, so eloquent of speed and of power. He saw the Lewiston for what it was; the deadliest, most destructive hand-weapon known to man. Above all, he saw the difference in numbers: six or seven or eight Patrolmen to four or five or six of his own kind. If more hoods arrived, so did more spacemen; if some departed, so did a corresponding number of the wearers of the space-black and silver.

"Ain't you getting tired of sticking around here, George?" One mob-ster asked confidentially of one Patrolman. "I am. What say we and some of you fellows round up some girls and go have us a party?"

"Uh-uh," George denied. His voice was gay and careless, but his eyes were icy cold. "My uncle's cousin's stepson is running for second assistant dog-catcher, and I can't leave until I find out whether he wins or not."

Thus nothing happened; thus the invisible but nevertheless terrific tension did not erupt into open battle; and thus, for the first time in North America's long history, a presidential election was ninety-nine and ninety-nine one-hundredths percent pure!

Evening came. The polls closed. The Cosmocrats' headquarters for the day, the Grand Ballroom of the Hotel van der Voort, became the goal of every Patrolman who thought he stood any chance at all of getting in. Kinnison had been there all day, of course. So had Joy, his wife, who for lack of space has been sadly neglected in these annals. Betty, their daughter, had come in early, accompanied by a husky and personable young lieutenant, who has no other place in this story. Jack Kinnison arrived, with Dimples Maynard—dazzlingly blonde, wearing a screamingly red wisp of silk. She, too, has been shamefully slighted here, although she was never slighted anywhere else.

"The first time I ever saw her," Jack was wont to say, "I went right into a flat spin, running around in circles and biting myself in the small of the back, and couldn't pull out of it for four hours!"

That Miss Maynard should be a very special item is not at all surprising, in view of the fact that she was to become the wife of one of THE Kinnisons and the mother of another.

The First Lensman, who had been in and out, came in to stay. So did Jill and her inseparable, Mason Northrop. And so did others, singly or by twos or threes. Lensmen and their wives. Conway and Clio Costigan, Dr. and Mrs. Rodebush, and Cleveland, Admiral and Mrs. Clayton, ditto Schweikert, and Dr. Nels Bergenholm. And others. Nor were they all North Americans, or even human. Rularion was there; and so was blocky, stocky Dronvire of Rigel Four. No outsider could tell, ever, what any Lensman was thinking, to say nothing of such a monstrous Lensman as Dronvire—but that hotel was being covered as no political headquarters had ever been covered before.

The returns came in, see-sawing maddeningly back and forth. Faster and faster. The Maritime Provinces split fifty-fifty. Maine, New Hampshire, and Vermont, Cosmocrat. New York, upstate, Cosmocrat. New York City, on the basis of incomplete but highly significant returns, was piling up a huge Nationalist majority. Pennsylvania—labor—Nationalist. Ohio—farmers—Cosmocrat. Twelve southern states went six and six. Chicago, as usual, solidly for the machine; likewise Quebec and Ottawa and Montreal and Toronto and Detroit and Kansas City and St. Louis and New Orleans and Denver.

Then northern and western and far southern states came in and evened the score. Saskatchewan, Alberta, Britcol, and Alaska, all went Cosmocrat. So did Washington, Idaho, Montana, Oregon, Nevada, Utah, Arizona, Newmex, and most of the states of Mexico.

At three o'clock in the morning the Cosmocrats had a slight but definite lead and were, finally, holding it. At four o'clock the lead was larger, but California was still an unknown quantity—California could wreck everything. *How* would California go? Especially, how would California's two metropolitan districts—the two most independent and freethinking and least predictable big cities of the nation—how *would* they go?

At five o'clock California seemed safe. Except for Los Angeles and San Francisco, the Cosmocrats had swept the state, and in those two great cities they held a commanding lead. It was still mathematically possible, however, for the Nationalists to win.

"It's in the bag! Let's start the celebration!" someone shouted, and others took up the cry.

"Stop it! No!" Kinnison's parade-ground voice cut through the noise. "No celebration is in order or will be held until the result becomes certain or Witherspoon concedes!"

The two events came practically together: Witherspoon conceded a couple of minutes before it became mathematically impossible for him to win. Then came the celebration, which went on and on interminably. At the first opportunity, however, Kinnison took Samms by the arm, led him without a word into a small office, and shut the door. Samms, also saying nothing, sat down in the swivel chair, put both feet up on the desk, lit a cigarette, and inhaled deeply.

"Well, Virge—satisfied?" Kinnison broke the silence at last. His Lens was off. "We're on our way."

"Yes, Rod. Fully. At last." No more than his friend did he dare to use his Lens; to plumb the depths he knew so well were there. "Now it will roll—under its own power—no one man now is or ever will be indispensable to the Galactic Patrol—*nothing* can stop it now!"

EPILOGUE

The murder of Senator Morgan, in his own private office, was never solved. If it had occurred before the election, suspicion would certainly have fallen upon Roderick Kinnison, but as it was it did not. By no stretch of the imagination could anyone conceive of "Rod the Rock" kicking a man after he had knocked him down. Not that Morgan did not have powerful and vindictive enemies in the underworld: he had so many that it proved impossible to fasten the crime to any one of them.

Officially, Kinnison was on a five-year leave of absence from the Galactic Patrol, the office of Port Admiral had been declared vacant, and the superdreadnaught *Chicago* had been detached entirely from the fleet and assigned to the Office of the President of North America. Actually, however, in every respect that counted, Roderick Kinnison was still Port Admiral, and would remain so until he died or until the Council retired him by force.

Officially, Kinnison was taking a short, well-earned vacation from the job in which he had been so outstandingly successful. Actually, he was doing a quick flit to Petrine, to get personally acquainted with the new Lensmen and to see what kind of a job they were doing. Besides, Virgil Samms was already there.

He arrived. He got acquainted. He saw. He approved.

"How about coming back to Tellus with me, Virge?" he asked, when the visiting was done. "I've got to make a speech, and it'd be nice to have you hold my head."

"I'd be glad to," and the *Chicago* took off.

Half of North America was dark when they neared Tellus; all of it, apparently, was obscured by clouds. Only the navigating officers of the vessel knew where they were, nor did either of the two Lensmen care.

They were having too much fun arguing about the talents and abilities of their respective grandsons.

The *Chicago* landed. A bug was waiting. The two Lensmen, without an order being given, were whisked away. Samms had not asked where the speech was to be given, and Kinnison simply did not realize that he had not told him all about it. Thus Samms had no idea that he was just leaving Spokane Spaceport, Washington.

After a few miles of fast, open-country driving the bug reached the city. It slowed down, swung into brightly-lighted Maple Street, and passed a sign reading "Cannon Hill" something-or-other—neither of which names meant anything to either Lensman.

Kinnison looked at his friend's red-thatched head and glanced at his watch.

"Looking at you reminds me—I need a haircut," he remarked. "Should have got one aboard, but didn't think of it. Joy told me if I come home without it she'll braid it in pigtails and tie it up with pink ribbons, and you're shaggier than I am. You've got to get one or else buy yourself a violin. What say we do it now?"

"Have we got time enough?"

"Plenty." Then, to the driver: "Stop at the first barber shop you see, please."

"Yes, sir. There's a good one a few blocks further along."

The bug sped down Maple Street, turned sharply into plainly-marked Twelfth Avenue. Neither Lensman saw the sign.

"Here you are, sir."

"Thanks."

There were two barbers and two chairs, both empty. The Lensmen, noticing that the place was neatly kept and meticulously clean, sat down and resumed their discussion of two extremely unusual infants. The barbers went busily to work.

"Just as well, though—better, really—that the kids didn't marry each other, at that," Kinnison concluded finally. "The way it is, we've each got a grandson—it'd be tough to have to share one with *you*."

Samms made no reply to this sally, for something was happening. The fact that this fair-skinned, yellow-haired, blue-eyed barber was left-handed had not rung any bells—there were lots of left-handed barbers. He had neither seen nor heard the cat—a less-than-half-grown, gray, tiger-striped kitten—which, after standing up on its hind legs to sniff ecstatically at his nylon-clad ankles, had uttered a couple of almost inaudible "meows" and had begun to purr happily. Crouching, tensing its strong little legs, it leaped almost vertically upward. Its tail struck the barber's elbow.

Hastily brushing the kitten aside, and beginning profuse apologies both for his awkwardness and for the presence of the cat—he had never done such a thing before and he would drown him forthwith—the barber applied a styptic pencil and recollection hit Samms a pile-driver blow.

"Well, I'm a . . . !" He voiced three highly un-Samms-like, highly specific expletives which, as Mentor had foretold so long before, were both self-derogatory and profane. Then, as full realization dawned, he bit a word squarely in two.

"Excuse me, please, Mr. Carbonero, for this outrageous display. It was not the scratch, nor was any of it your fault. Nothing you could have done would have . . ."

"You know my name?" the astonished barber interrupted.

"Yes. You were . . . ah . . . recommended to me by a . . . a friend . . ." Whatever Samms could say would make things worse. The truth, wild as it was, would have to be told, at least in part. "You do not look like an Italian, but perhaps you have enough of that racial heritage to believe in prophecy?"

"Of course, sir. There have always been prophets—*true* prophets."

"Good. This event was foretold in detail; in such complete detail that I was deeply, terribly shocked. Even to the kitten. You call it Thomas."

"Yes, sir. Thomas Aquinas."

"It is actually a female. In here, Thomasina!" The kitten had been climbing enthusiastically up his leg; now, as he held a pocket invitingly open, she sprang into it, settled down, and began to purr blissfully. While the barbers and Kinnison stared pop-eyed Samms went on:

"She is determined to adopt me, and it would be a shame not to requite such affection. Would you part with her—for, say, ten credits?"

"*Ten credits!* I'll be glad to give her to you for nothing!"

"Ten it is, then. One more thing. Rod, you always carry a pocket rule. Measure this scratch, will you? You'll find it's mighty close to three millimeters long."

"Not 'close,' Virge—it's *exactly* three millimeters, as near as this vernier can scale it."

"And just above and parallel to the cheek-bone."

"Check. Just above and as parallel as though it had been ruled there by a draftsman."

"Well, that's that. Let's get finished with the haircuts, before you're late for your speech," and the barbers, with thoughts which will be left to the imagination, resumed their interrupted tasks.

"Spill it, Virge!" Kinnison Lensed the pent-up thought. If Carbonero, who did not know Samms at all, had been amazed at what had been happening, Kinnison, who had known him so long and so well, had been literally and completely dumbfounded. "What in hell's behind this? What's the story? GIVE!"

Samms told him, and a mental silence fell; a silence too deep for intelligible thought. Each was beginning to realize that he never would and never could know what Mentor of Arisia really was.

Galactic Patrol

To
Clarrissa M. MacD. Hamnett
and
Clarrissa MacD. S. Wilcox

Contents

1. Graduation 493
2. In Command 503
3. In the Lifeboats 512
4. Escape 522
5. Worsel to the Rescue 531
6. Delgonian Hypnotism 540
7. The Passing of the Overlords 549
8. The Quarry Strikes Back 559
9. Breakdown 568
10. Trenco 577
11. Grand Base 587
12. Kinnison Brings Home the Bacon 596
13. Maulers Afloat 605
14. Unattached 612
15. The Decoy 622
16. Kinnison Meets the Wheelmen 630
17. Nothing Serious at All 640
18. Advanced Training 649
19. Judge, Jury, and Executioner 659
20. Mac Is a Bone of Contention 668
21. The Second Line 677
22. Preparing for the Test 686
23. Tregonsee Turns Zwilnik 695
24. Kinnison Bores from Within 702

1

GRADUATION

Dominating twice a hundred square miles of campus, parade-ground, airport, and spaceport, a ninety-story edifice of chromium and glass sparkled dazzlingly in the bright sunlight of a June morning. This monumental pile was Wentworth Hall, in which the Tellurian candidates for the Lens of the Galactic Patrol live and move and have their being. One wing of its topmost floor seethed with tense activity, for that wing was the habitat of the lordly Five-Year Men, this was Graduation Day, and in a few minutes Class Five was due to report in Room A.

Room A, the private office of the Commandant himself; the dreadful lair into which an undergraduate was summoned only to disappear from the Hall and from the Cadet Corps; the portentous chamber into which each year the handful of graduates marched and from which they emerged, each man in some subtle fashion changed.

In their cubicles of steel the graduates scanned each other narrowly, making sure that no wrinkle or speck of dust marred the space-black and silver perfection of the dress uniform of the Patrol; that not even the tiniest spot of tarnish or dullness violated the glittering golden meteors upon their collars or the resplendently polished ray-pistols and other equipment at their belts. The microscopic mutual inspection over, the kit-boxes were snapped shut and racked, and the embryonic Lensmen made their way out into the assembly hall.

In the wardroom Kimball Kinnison, Captain of the Class by virtue of graduating at its head, and his three lieutenants, Clifford Maitland, Raoul LaForge, and Widel Holmberg, had inspected each other minutely and were now simply awaiting, in ever-increasing tension, the zero minute.

"Now, fellows, remember that drop!" the young Captain jerked out. "We're dropping the shaft free, at higher velocity and in tighter for-

mation than any class ever tried before. If anybody hashes the formation—our last show and with the whole Corps looking on . . ."

"Don't worry about the drop, Kim," advised Maitland. "All three
platoons will take that like clockwork. What's got me all of a dither is
what is really going to happen in Room A."

"Uh-*huh*!" exclaimed LaForge and Holmberg as one.

"You can play that across the board for the whole Class," Kinnison
agreed. "Well, we'll soon know—it's time to get going," and the four
officers stepped out into the assembly hall; the Class springing to attention at their approach.

Kinnison, now all brisk Captain, stared along the mathematically exact lines and snapped:

"Report!"

"Class Five present in full, sir!" The sergeant-major touched a stud
at his belt and all vast Wentworth Hall fairly trembled under the impact
of an all-pervading, lilting, throbbing melody as the world's finest military band crashed into "Our Patrol."

"Squads left—March!" Although no possible human voice could
have been heard in that gale of soul-stirring sound and although Kinnison's lips scarcely moved, his command was carried to the very bones
of those for whom it was intended—and to no one else—by the tight-
beam ultra-communicators strapped upon their chests. "Close formation—forward—March!"

In perfect alignment and cadence the little column marched down the
hall. In their path yawned the shaft—a vertical pit some twenty feet
square extending from main floor to roof of the Hall; more than a thousand sheer feet of unobstructed air, cleared now of all traffic by flaring
red lights. Five left heels clicked sharply, simultaneously upon the lip
of the stupendous abyss. Five right legs swept out into emptiness. Five
right hands snapped to belts and five bodies, rigidly erect, arrowed
downward at such an appalling velocity that to unpractised vision they
simply vanished.

Six-tenths of a second later, precisely upon a beat of the stirring
march, those ten heels struck the main floor of Wentworth Hall, but not
with a click. Dropping with a velocity of almost two thousand feet per
second though they were at the instant of impact, yet those five husky
bodies came from full speed to an instantaneous, shockless, effortless
halt at contact, for the drop had been made under complete neutralization of inertia—"free," in space parlance. Inertia restored, the march
was resumed—or rather continued—in perfect time with the band. Five
left feet swung out, and as the right toes left the floor the second rank,

with only bare inches to spare, plunged down into the space its predecessor had occupied a moment before.

Rank after rank landed and marched away with machine-like precision. The dread door of Room A opened automatically at the approach of the cadets and closed behind them.

"Column right—March!" Kinnison commanded inaudibly, and the Class obeyed in clockwork perfection. "Column left—March! Squad right—March! Company—Halt! Salute!"

In company front, in a huge, square room devoid of furniture, the Class faced the Ogre—Lieutenant-Marshal Fritz von Hohendorff, Commandant of Cadets. Martinet, tyrant, dictator—he was known throughout the System as the embodiment of soullessness; and, insofar as he had ever been known to show emotion or feeling before any undergraduate, he seemed to glory in his repute of being the most pitilessly rigid disciplinarian that Earth had ever known. His thick, white hair was roached fiercely upward into a stiff pompadour. His left eye was artificial and his face bore dozens of tiny, threadlike scars; for not even the marvelous plastic surgery of that age could repair entirely the ravages of space-combat. Also, his right leg and left arm, although practically normal to all outward seeming, were in reality largely products of science and art instead of nature.

Kinnison faced, then, this reconstructed potentate, saluted crisply, and snapped:—

"Sir, Class Five reports to the Commandant."

"Take your post, sir." The veteran saluted as punctiliously, and as he did so a semi-circular desk rose around him from the floor—a desk whose most striking feature was an intricate mechanism surrounding a splint-like form.

"Number One, Kimball Kinnison!" von Hohendorff barked. "Front and center—March! . . . The oath, sir."

"Before the Omnipotent Witness I promise never to lower the standard of the Galactic Patrol," Kinnison said reverently; and, baring his arm, thrust it into the hollow form.

From a small container labelled "#1, Kimball Kinnison," the Commandant shook out what was apparently an ornament—a lenticular jewel fabricated of hundreds of tiny, dead-white gems. Taking it up with a pair of insulated forceps he touched it momentarily to the bronzed skin of the arm before him, and at that fleeting contact a flash as of many-colored fire swept over the stones. Satisfied, he dropped the jewel into a recess provided for it in the mechanism, which at once burst into activity.

The forearm was wrapped in thick insulation, molds and shields snapped into place, and there flared out an instantly-suppressed flash of brilliance intolerable. Then the molds fell apart, the insulation was removed, and there was revealed the LENS. Clasped to Kinnison's brawny wrist by a bracelet of imperishable, almost unbreakable, metal in which it was imbedded it shone in all its lambent splendor—no longer a whitely inert piece of jewelry, but a lenticular polychrome of writhing, almost fluid radiance which proclaimed to all observers in symbols of ever-changing flame that here was a Lensman of the GALACTIC PATROL.

In similar fashion each man of the Class was invested with the symbol of his rank. Then the stern-faced Commandant touched a button and from the bare metal floor there arose deeply-upholstered chairs, one for each graduate.

"Fall out!" he commanded, then smiled almost boyishly—the first intimation any of the Class ever had that the hard-boiled old tyrant *could* smile—and went on in a strangely altered voice:

"Sit down, men, and smoke up. We have an hour in which to talk things over, and now I can tell you what it is all about. Each of you will find his favorite refreshment in the arm of his chair.

"No, there's no catch to it," he continued in answer to amazedly doubtful stares, and lighted a huge black cigar of Venerian tobacco as he spoke. "You are Lensmen now. Of course you have yet to go through the formalities of Commencement, but they don't count. Each of you really graduated when his Lens came to life.

"We know your individual preferences, and each of you has his favorite weed, from Tilotson's Pittsburgh stogies up to Snowden's Alsakanite cigarettes—even though Alsakan is just about as far away from here as a planet can be and still lie within the galaxy.

"We also know that you are all immune to the lure of noxious drugs. If you were not, you would not be here today. So smoke up and break up—ask any questions you care to, and I will try to answer them. Nothing is barred now—this room is shielded against any spy-ray or communicator beam operable upon any known frequency."

There was a brief and rather uncomfortable silence, then Kinnison suggested, diffidently:

"Might it not be best, sir, to tell us all about it, from the ground up? I imagine that most of us are in too much of a daze to ask intelligent questions."

"Perhaps. While some of you undoubtedly have your suspicions, I will begin by telling you what is behind what you have been put through during the last five years. Feel perfectly free to break in with questions at any time. You know that every year one million eighteen-year-old boys of Earth are chosen as cadets by competitive examinations. You know that during the first year, before any of them see Wentworth Hall, that number shrinks to less than fifty thousand. You know that by Graduation Day there are only approximately one hundred left in the class. Now I am allowed to tell you that you graduates are those who have come with flying colors through the most brutally rigid, the most fiendishly thorough process of elimination that it has been possible to develop.

"Every man who can be made to reveal any real weakness is dropped. Most of these are dismissed from the Patrol. There are many splendid men, however, who, for some reason not involving moral turpitude, are not quite what a Lensman must be. These men make up our organization, from grease-monkeys up to the highest commissioned officers below the rank of Lensman. This explains what you already know—that the Galactic Patrol is the finest body of intelligent beings yet to serve under one banner.

"Of the million who started, you few are left. As must every being who has ever worn or who ever will wear the Lens, each of you has proven repeatedly, to the cold verge of death itself, that he is in every respect worthy to wear it. For instance, Kinnison here once had a highly adventurous interview with a lady of Aldebaran II and her friends. He did not know that we knew all about it, but we did."

Kinnison's very ears burned scarlet, but the Commandant went imperturbably on:

"So it was with Voelker and the hypnotist of Karalon; with LaForge and the bentlam-eaters; with Flewelling when the Ganymede-Venus thionite smugglers tried to bribe him with ten million in gold . . ."

"Good Heavens, Commandant!" broke in one outraged youth. "Do you—did you—know everything that happened?"

"Not quite everything, perhaps, but it is my business to know enough. No man who can be cracked has ever worn, or ever will wear, the Lens. And none of you need be ashamed, for you have passed every test. Those who did not pass them were those who were dropped.

"Nor is it any disgrace to have been dismissed from the Cadet Corps. The million who started with you were the pick of the planet, yet we knew in advance that of that selected million scarcely one in ten thousand would measure up in every essential. Therefore it would be manifestly unfair to stigmatize the rest of them because they were not born with that extra something, that ultimate quality of fiber which does, and of necessity *must*, characterize the wearers of the Lens. For that reason not even the man himself knows why he was dismissed, and no one save those who wear the Lens knows why they were selected—and a Lensman does not talk.

"It is necessary to consider the history and background of the Patrol in order to bring out clearly the necessity for such care in the selection of its personnel. You are all familiar with it, but probably very few of you have thought of it in that connection. The Patrol is of course an outgrowth of the old Planetary Police systems; and, until its development, law enforcement always lagged behind law violation. Thus, in the old days following the invention of the automobile, state troopers could not cross state lines. Then when the National Police finally took charge, they could not follow the rocket-equipped criminals across the national boundaries.

"Still later, when interplanetary flight became a commonplace, the Planetary Police were at the same old disadvantage. They had no authority off their own worlds, while the public enemies flitted unhampered from planet to planet. And finally, with the invention of the inertialess drive and the consequent traffic between the worlds of many solar systems, crime became so rampant, so utterly uncontrollable, that it threatened the very foundations of Civilization. A man could perpetrate any crime imaginable without fear of consequences, for in an hour he could be so far away from the scene as to be completely beyond the reach of the law.

"And helping powerfully toward utter chaos were the new vices which were spreading from world to world; among others the taking of new and horrible drugs. Thionite, for instance; occurring only upon Trenco; a drug as much deadlier than heroin as that compound is than coffee, and which even now commands such a fabulous price than a man can carry a fortune in one hollow boot-heel.

"Thus the Triplanetary Patrol and the Galactic Patrol came into being. The first was a pitiful enough organization. It was handicapped from without by politics and politicians, and honey-combed from within by the usual small but utterly poisonous percentage of the unfit—grafters, corruptionists, bribe-takers, and out-and-out criminals. It was hampered by the fact that there was then no emblem or credential which could not be counterfeited—no one could tell with certainty that the man in uniform was a Patrolman and not a criminal in disguise.

"As everyone knows, Virgil Samms, then Head of the Triplanetary Patrol, became First Lensman Samms and founded our Galactic Patrol. The Lens, which, being proof against counterfeiting or even imitation, makes identification of Lensmen automatic and positive, was what made our Patrol possible. Having the Lens, it was easy to weed out the few unfit. Standards of entrance were raised ever higher, and when it had been proved beyond question that every Lensman was in fact incorruptible, the Galactic Council was given more and ever more authority. More and ever more solar systems, having developed Lensmen of their own, voted to join Civilization and sought representation on the Galactic Council, even though such a course meant giving up much of their systemic sovereignty.

"Now the power of the Council and its Patrol is practically absolute. Our armament and equipment are the ultimate; we can follow the lawbreaker wherever he may go. Furthermore, any Lensman can commandeer any material or assistance, wherever and whenever required; upon any planet of any solar system adherent to Civilization; and the Lens is so respected throughout the galaxy that any wearer of it may be called upon at any time to be judge, jury, and executioner. Wherever he goes, upon, in, or through any land, water, air, or space anywhere within the confines of our Island Universe, his word is LAW.

"That explains what you have been forced to undergo. The only excuse for its severity is that it produces results—no wearer of the Lens has ever disgraced it.

"Now as to the Lens itself. Like every one else, you have known *of* it ever since you could talk, but you know nothing of its origin or its nature. Now that you are Lensmen, I can tell you what little I know about it. Questions?"

"We have all wondered about the Lens, sir, of course," Maitland ventured. "The outlaws apparently keep up with us in science. I have always supposed that what science can build, science can duplicate. Surely more than one Lens has fallen into the hands of the outlaws?"

"If it had been a scientific invention or discovery it would have been duplicated long ago," the Commandant made surprising answer. "It is, however, not essentially scientific in nature. It is almost entirely philosophical, and was developed for us by the Arisians.

"Yes, each of you was sent to Arisia quite recently," von Hohendorff went on, as the newly commissioned officers stared, dumbfounded, at him and at each other. "What did you think of them, Murphy?"

"At first, sir, I thought that they were some new kind of dragon; but dragons with brains that you could actually *feel*. I was glad to get away, sir. They fairly gave me the creeps, even though I never did see one of them so much as move."

"They are a peculiar race," the Commandant went on. "Instead of being mankind's worst enemies, as is generally believed, they are the *sine qua non* of our Patrol and of Civilization. I cannot understand them; I do not know of anyone who can. They gave us the Lens; yet Lensmen must not reveal that fact to any others. They make a Lens to fit each candidate; yet no two candidates, apparently, have ever seen the same things there, nor is it believed that anyone has ever seen them as they really are. To all except Lensmen they seem to be completely anti-social; and even those who become Lensmen go to Arisia only once in their lives. They seem—although I caution you that this seeming may contain no more of reality than the physical shapes you thought you saw—to be supremely indifferent to all material things.

"For more generations than you can understand they have devoted themselves to thinking; mainly of the essence of life. They say that they know scarcely anything fundamental concerning it; but even so they know more about it than does any other known race. While ordinarily they will have no intercourse whatever with outsiders, they did consent to help the Patrol, for the good of all intelligence.

"Thus, each being about to graduate into Lensmanship is sent to Arisia, where a Lens is built to match his individual life force. While no mind other than that of an Arisian can understand its operation, thinking of your Lens as being synchronized with, or in exact resonance with, your own vital principle or ego will give you a rough idea of it. The Lens is not really alive, as we understand the term. It is, however, endowed with a sort of pseudo-life, by virtue of which it gives off its strong, characteristically changing light as long as it is in metal-to-flesh circuit with the living mentality for which it was designed. Also by virtue of that pseudo-life, it acts as a telepath through which you may converse with other intelligences, even though they may possess no organs of speech or of hearing.

"The Lens cannot be removed by anyone except its wearer without dismemberment; it glows as long as its rightful owner wears it; it ceases to glow in the instant of its owner's death and disintegrates shortly thereafter. Also—and here is the thing that renders completely impossible the impersonation of a Lensman—not only does the Lens not glow if worn by an imposter; but if a Lensman be taken alive and his Lens removed, that Lens kills in a space of seconds any living being who attempts to wear it. As long as it glows—as long as it is in circuit with its living owner—it is harmless; but in the dark condition its pseudo-life interferes so strongly with any life to which it is not attuned that that life is destroyed forthwith."

A brief silence fell, during which the young men absorbed the stunning import of what their Commandant had been saying. More, there was striking into each young consciousness a realization of the stark heroism of the grand old Lensman before them; a man of such fiber that although physically incapacitated and long past the retirement age, he had conquered his human emotions sufficiently to accept deliberately his ogre's role because in that way he could best further the progress of his Patrol!

"I have scarcely broken the ground," von Hohendorff continued. "I have merely given you an introduction to your new status. During the next few weeks, before you are assigned to duty, other officers will make clear to you the many things about which you are still in the dark. Our time is growing short, but we perhaps have time for one more question."

"Not a question, sir, but something more important," Kinnison spoke up. "I speak for the Class when I say that we have misjudged you grievously, and we wish to apologize."

"I thank you sincerely for the thought, although it is unnecessary. You could not have thought otherwise of me than as you did. It is not a pleasant task that we old men have; that of weeding out those who do not measure up. But we are too old for active duty in space—we no longer have the instantaneous nervous responses that are for that duty imperative—so we do what we can. However, the work has its brighter side, since each year there are about a hundred found worthy of the Lens. This, my one hour with the graduates, more than makes up for the year that precedes it; and the other oldsters have somewhat similar compensations.

"In conclusion, you are now able to understand what kind of mentalities fill our ranks. You know that any creature wearing the Lens is in every sense a Lensman, whether he be human or, hailing from some strange and distant planet, a monstrosity of a shape you have as yet not even imagined. Whatever his form, you may rest assured that he has been tested even as you have been; that he is as worthy of trust as are you yourselves. My last word is this—Lensmen die, but they do not fold up: individuals come and go, but the Galactic Patrol goes on!"

Then, again all martinet:

"Class Five, attention!" he barked. "Report upon the stage of the main auditorium!" ·

The Class, again a rigidly military unit, marched out of Room A and down the long corridor toward the great theater in which, before the massed Cadet Corps and a throng of civilians, they were formally to be graduated.

And as they marched along the graduates realized in what way the wearers of the Lens who emerged from Room A were different from the candidates who had entered it such a short time before. They had gone in as boys; nervous, apprehensive, and still somewhat unsure of themselves, in spite of their survival through the five long years of grueling tests which now lay behind them. They emerged from Room

A as men: men knowing for the first time the real meaning of the physical and mental tortures they had undergone; men able to wield justly the vast powers whose scope and scale they could even now but dimly comprehend.

2

IN COMMAND

Barely a month after his graduation, even before he had entirely completed the post-graduate tours of duty mentioned by von Hohendorff, Kinnison was summoned to Prime Base by no less a personage than Port Admiral Haynes himself. There, in the Admiral's private aero, whose flaring lights cut a right-of-way through the swarming traffic, the novice and the veteran flew slowly over the vast establishment of the Base.

Shops and factories, city-like barracks, landing-fields stretching beyond the far horizon; flying craft ranging from tiny one-man helicopters through small and large scouts, patrol-ships and cruisers up to the immense, globular superdreadnaughts of space—all these were observed and commented upon. Finally the aero landed beside a long, comparatively low building—a structure heavily guarded, inside Base although it was—within which Kinnison saw a thing that fairly snatched away his breath.

A space-ship it was—but what a ship!* In bulk it was vastly larger even than the superdreadnaughts of the Patrol; but, unlike them, it was in shape a perfect teardrop, streamlined to the ultimate possible degree.

"What do you think of her?" the Port Admiral asked.

"Think of her!" The young officer gulped twice before he attained

---

*In the "big teardrops"—cruisers and battleships—the driving force is always directed upward, along the geometrical axis of the ship, and the artificial gravity is always downward along that same line. Thus, throughout any possible maneuvering, free or inert, "down" and "up" have the same significance as within any Earthly structure.

These vessels are ordinarily landed only in special docks, but in emergencies can be landed almost anywhere, sharp stern down, as their immense weight drives them deep enough into even the hardest ground to keep them upright. They sink in water, but are readily maneuverable, even under water. E. E. S.

coherence. "I can't put it in words, sir; but some day, if I live long enough and develop enough force, I hope to command a ship like that."

"Sooner than you think, Kinnison," Haynes told him, flatly. "You are in command of her beginning tomorrow morning."

"Huh? Me?" Kinnison exclaimed, but sobered quickly. "Oh, I see, sir. It takes ten years of proved accomplishment to rate command of a first-class vessel, and I have no rating at all. You have already intimated that this ship is experimental. There is, then, something about her that is new and untried, and so dangerous that you do not want to risk an experienced commander in her. I am to give her a work-out, and if I can bring her back in one piece I turn her over to her real captain. But that's all right with me, Port Admiral—thanks a lot for picking me out. What a chance—*What* a chance!" and Kinnison's eyes gleamed at the prospect of even a brief command of such a creation.

"Right—and wrong," the old Admiral made surprising answer. "It is true that she is new, untried, and dangerous, so much so that we are unwilling to give her to any of our present captains. No, she is not really new, either. Rather, her basic idea is so old that it has been abandoned for centuries. She uses explosives; of a type that cannot be tried out fully except in actual combat. Her primary weapon is what we have called the 'Q-gun.' The propellant is heptadetonite: the shell carries a charge of twenty metric tons of duodecaplylatomate."

"But, sir . . ." Kinnison began.

"Just a minute, I'll go into that later. While your premises were correct, your conclusion is not. You graduated Number One, and in every respect save experience you are as well qualified to command as is any captain of the Fleet; and since the *Brittania* is such a radical departure from any conventional type, battle experience is not a prerequisite. Therefore if she holds together through one engagement she is yours for good. In other words, to make up for the possibility of having yourself scattered all over space, you have a chance to win that ten years' rating you mentioned a minute ago, all in one trip. Fair enough?"

"Fair? It's fine—wonderful! And thanks a . . ."

"Never mind the thanks until you get back. You were about to comment, I believe, upon the impossibility of using explosives against a free opponent?"

"It can't be impossible, of course, since the *Brittania* has been built. I just don't quite see how it could have been made effective."

"You lock to the pirate with tractors, screen to screen—dex about ten kilometers. You blast a hole through his screens to his wall-shield. The muzzle of the Q-gun mounts as annular multiplex projector which puts out a Q-type tube of force—Q47SM9, to be exact. As you can see from the type formula, this helix extends the gun-barrel from ship to ship and confines the propellent gases behind the projectile, where they belong. When the shell strikes the wall-shield of the pirate and detonates, *something* will have to give way—all the Brains agree that twenty tons of duodec, attaining a temperature of about forty million degrees absolute in less than one micro-second, simply cannot be confined.

"The tube and tractors, being pure force and computed for this particular combination of explosions, will hold; and our physicists have calculated that the ten-kilometer column of inert propellent gases will offer so much inertia and resistance that any possible wall-shield will have to go down. That is the point that cannot be tried out experimentally—it is quite within the bounds of possibility that the pirates may have been able to develop wall-screens as powerful as our Q-type helices, even though we have not.

"It should not be necessary to point out to you that if they *have* been able to develop a wall-shield that will stand up under those conditions, the back-blast through the breech of the Q-gun will blow the *Brittania* apart as though she were so much matchwood. That is only one of the chances—and perhaps not the greatest one—that you and your crew will have to take. They are all volunteers, by the way, and will get plenty of extra rating if they come through alive. Do you want the job?"

"You don't have to ask me that, Chief—you *know* I want it!"

"Of course, but I had to go through the formality of asking, sometime. But to get on with the discussion, this pirate situation is entirely out of control, as you already know. We don't even know whether Boskone is a reality, a figurehead, a symbol, or simply a figment of an old-time Lensman's imagination. But whoever or whatever Boskone really is, some being or some group of beings has perfected a mighty efficient organization of outlaws; so efficient that we haven't even been able to locate their main base.

"And you may as well know now a fact that is not yet public property—that even conveyed vessels are no longer safe. The pirates have developed ships of a new and extraordinary type; ships that are much faster than our heavy battleships, and yet vastly more heavily armed than our fast cruisers. Thus, they can outfight any Patrol vessel that can catch them, and can out-run anything of ours armed heavily enough to stand up against their beams."

"That accounts for the recent heavy losses," Kinnison mused.

"Yes," Haynes went on, grimly. "Ship after ship of our best has been blasted out of the ether, doomed before it pointed a beam, and more will be. We cannot force an engagement on our terms; we must fight them where and when they please.

"That is the present intolerable situation. We *must* learn what the pirates' new power-system is. Our scientists say that it may be anything, from cosmic-energy receptors and converters down to a controlled space-warp—whatever that may be. Anyway, they haven't been able to duplicate it, so it is up to us to find out what it is. The *Brittania* is the tool our engineers have designed to get that information. She is the fastest thing in space, developing at full blast an inert acceleration of *ten gravities*. Figure out for yourself what velocity that means free in open space!"

"You have just said that we can't have everything in one ship," Kinnison said, thoughtfully. "What did they sacrifice to get that speed?"

"All the conventional offensive armament," Haynes replied frankly. "She has no long-range beams at all, and only enough short-range stuff to help drive the Q-helix through the enemy's screens. Practically her only offense is the Q-gun. But she has plenty of defensive screens, she has speed enough to catch anything afloat, and she has the Q-gun— which we hope will be enough.

"Now we'll go over the general plan of action. The engineers will go into all the technical details with you, during a test flight that will last as long as you like. When you and your crew are thoroughly familiar with every phase of her operation, bring the engineers back here to Base and go out on patrol.

"Now we'll go over the general plan of action. Then engineers will go into all the technical details with you, during a test flight that will last as long as you like. When you and your crew are thoroughly familiar with every phase of her operation, bring the engineers back here to Base and go out on patrol.

"Somewhere in the galaxy you will find a pirate vessel of the new type. You lock to him, as I said before. You attach the Q-gun well forward, being sure that the point of attachment is far enough away from the power-rooms so that the essential mechanisms will not be destroyed. You board and storm—another revival of the technique of older times. Specialists in your crew, who will have done nothing much up to that time, will then find out what our scientists want to know. If at all possible they will send it in instantly via tight-beam communicator. If for any reason it should be impossible for them to communicate, the whole thing is again up to you."

The Port Admiral paused, his eyes boring into those of the younger man, then went on impressively:

"That information MUST get back to Base. If it does not, the *Brittania* is a failure; we will be back right where we started from; the slaughter of our men and the destruction of our ships will continue unchecked. As to how you are to do it we cannot give even general instructions. All I can say is that you have the most important assignment in the Universe today, and repeat—*that information* MUST GET BACK TO BASE. Now come aboard and meet your crew and the engineers.''

Under the expert tutelage of the designers and builders of the *Brittania* Lieutenant Kinnison drove her hither and thither through the trackless wastes of the galaxy.* Inert and free, under every possible degree of power he maneuvered her; attacking imaginary foes and actual meteorites with equal zeal. Maneuvered and attacked until he and his ship were one; until he reacted automatically to her slightest demand; until he and every man of his eager and highly trained crew knew to the final volt and to the ultimate ampere her gargantuan capacity both to give it and to take it.

Then and only then did he return to Base, unload the engineers, and set out upon the quest. Trail after trail he followed, but all were cold. Alarm after alarm he answered, but always he arrived too late: arrived to find gutted merchantman and riddled Patrol vessel, with no life in either and with nothing to indicate in which direction the marauders might have gone.

Finally, however:

"QBT! Calling QBT!" The *Brittania*'s code call blared from the sealed-band speaker, and a string of numbers followed—the spatial coordinates of the luckless vessel's position.

Chief Pilot Henry Henderson punched the figures upon his locator, and in the "tank"—the enormous, minutely cubed model of the galaxy—there appeared a redly brilliant point of light. Kinnison rocketed out of his narrow bunk, digging sleep out of his eyes, and shot himself into place beside the pilot.

"Right in our laps!" he exulted. "Scarcely ten light-years away! Start

*Navigation. Each ship has as reference sphere a galactic-inductor compass. This instrument, swinging freely in an almost frictionless mount, is held in one position relative to the galaxy as a whole by galactic lines of force, analogous to the Terrestrial lines of magnetic force which affect Terrestrial compasses. Its equator is always parallel to the galactic equator; its line of zeroes is always parallel to the line joining Centralia, the central solar system of the First Galaxy, with the system of Vandemar, which is on its very rim.

The position of the ship in the galaxy is known at all times by that of a moving dot in the tank. This dot is shifted automatically by calculating machines coupled inductively to the leads of the drives. When the ship is inert this device is inoperative, as any distance traversed in inert flight is entirely negligible in galactic computations. Due to various perturbations and other slight errors, cumulative discrepancies occur, for which the pilot must from time to time correct manually the position of the dot in the tank representing his ship. E. E. S.

scrambling the ether!'' and as the vengeful cruiser darted toward the scene of depredation all space became filled with blast after blast of static interference through which, it was hoped, the pirate could not summon the help he was so soon to need.

But that howling static gave the pirate commander pause. Surely this was something new? Before him lay a richly-laden freighter, its two convoying ships already practically out of action. A few more minutes and the prize would be his. Nevertheless he darted away, swept the ether with his detectors, saw the *Brittania*, and turned in headlong flight. For if this streamlined fighter was sufficiently convinced of its prowess to try to blanket the ether against *him*, that information was something that Boskone would value far above one shipload of material wealth.

But the pirate craft was now upon the visiplates of the *Brittania*, and, entirely ignoring the crippled space-ships, Henderson flung his vessel after the other. Manipulating his incredibly complex controls purely by touch, the while staring into his plate not only with his eyes, but with every fiber of his being as well, he hurled his huge mount hither and thither in frantic leaps. After what seemed an age he snapped down a toggle switch and relaxed long enough to grin at Kinnison.

"Holding 'em?" the young commander demanded.

"Got 'em, Skipper," the pilot replied, positively. "It was touch and go for ninety seconds, but I've got a CRX tracer on him now at full pull. He can't put out enough jets to get away from *that*—I can hold him forever!"

"Fine work, Hen!" Kinnison strapped himself into his seat and donned his headset. "General call! Attention! Battle stations! By stations, report!"

"Station One, tractor beams—hot!"

"Station Two, repellors—hot!"

"Station Three, projector One—hot!"

Thus station after station of the warship of the void reported, until:

"Station Fifty-Eight, the Q-gun—hot!" Kinnison himself reported; then gave to the pilot the words which throughout the spaceways of the galaxy had come to mean complete readiness to face any emergency.

"Hot and tight, Hen—let's take 'em!"

The pilot shoved his blast-lever, already almost at maximum, clear out against its stop and hunched himself even more intently over his instruments, varying by infinitesimals the direction of the thrust that was driving the *Brittania* toward the enemy at the unimaginable velocity of ninety parsecs an hour*—a velocity possible only to inertialess matter

---

*With the neutralization of inertia it was discovered that there is no limit whatever to the velocity of inertialess matter. A free ship takes on instantaneously the velocity at which the force of her drive is exactly equalled by the friction of the medium.   E. E. S.

being urged through an almost perfect vacuum by a driving blast capable of lifting the stupendous normal tonnage of the immense sky-rover against a gravity ten times that of her native Earth.

Unimaginable? Completely so—the ship of the Galactic Patrol was hurling herself through space at a pace in comparison with which any speed that the mind can grasp would be the merest crawl: a pace to make light itself seem stationary.

Ordinary vision would have been useless, but the observers of that day used no antiquated optical systems. Their detector beams, converted into light only at their plates, were heterodyned upon and were carried by subetheral ultra-waves; vibrations residing far below the level of the ether and thus possessing a velocity and a range infinitely greater than those of any possible ether-borne wave.

Although stars moved across the visiplates in flaming, zig-zag lines of light as pursued and pursuer passed solar system after solar system in fantastic, light-years-long hops, yet Henderson kept his cruiser upon the pirate's tail and steadily cut down the distance between them. Soon a tractor beam licked out from the Patrol ship, touched the fleeing marauder lightly, and the two space-ships flashed toward each other.

Nor was the enemy unprepared for combat. One of the crack raiders of Boskone, master pirate of the known Universe, she had never before found difficulty in conquering any vessel fleet enough to catch her. Therefore, her commander made no attempt to cut the beam. Or rather, since the two inertialess vessels flashed together to repellor-zone contact in such a minute fraction of a second that any human action within that time was impossible, it would be more correct to say that the pirate captain changed his tactics instantly from those of flight to those of combat.

He thrust out tractor beams of his own, and from the already white-hot refractory throats of his projectors there raved out horribly potent beams of annihilation; beams of dreadful power which tore madly at the straining defensive screens of the Patrol ship. Screens flared vividly, radiating all the colors of the spectrum. Space itself seemed a rainbow gone mad, for there were being exerted there forces of a magnitude to stagger the imagination; forces to be yielded only by the atomic might from which they sprang; forces whose neutralization set up visible strains in the very fabric of the ether itself.

The young commander clenched his fists and swore a startled deep-space oath as red lights flashed and alarmbells clanged. His screens were leaking like sieves—practically down—needle after needle of force incredible stabbing at and through his wall-shield—four stations gone already and more going!

"Scrap the plan!" he yelled into his microphone. "Open everything to absolute top—short out all resistors—give 'em everything you can put through the bare bus-bars. Dalhousie, cut all your repellors; bring us right up to their zone. All you beamers, concentrate on Area Five. *Break down those screens!*" Kinnison was hunched rigidly over his panel, his voice came grittily through locked teeth. *"Get through to that wall-shield so I can use this Q-gun!"*

Under the redoubled force of the *Brittania*'s attack the defenses of the enemy began to fail. Kinnison's hands flew over his controls. A port opened in the Patrol-ship's armored side and an ugly snout protruded— the projector-ringed muzzle of a squat and monstrous cannon. From its projector bands there leaped out with the velocity of light a tube of quasi-solid force which was in effect a continuation of the gun's grim barrel; a tube which crashed through the weakened third screen of the enemy with a space-wracking shock and struck savagely, with writhing, twisting thrusts, at the second. Aided by the massed concentration of the *Brittania*'s every battery of short-range beams, it went through. And through the first. Now it struck the very-wall-shield of the outlaw—that impregnable screen which, designed to bear the brunt of any possible inert collision, had never been pierced or ruptured by any material substance, however applied.

To this inner defense the immaterial gun-barrel clung. Simultaneously the tractor beams, hitherto exerting only a few dynes of force, stiffened into unbreakable, inflexible rods of energy, binding the two ships of space into one rigid system; each, relative to the other, immovable.

Then Kinnison's flying finger tip touched a button and the Q-gun spoke. From its sullen throat there erupted a huge torpedo. Slowly the giant projectile crept along, watched in awe and amazement by the officers of both vessels. For to those space-hardened veterans the velocity of light was a veritable crawl; and here was a thing that would require four or five whole seconds to cover a mere ten kilometers of distance!

But, although slow, this bomb *might* prove dangerous, therefore the pirate commander threw his every resource into attempts to cut the tube of force, to blast away from the tractor beams, to explode the sluggish missile before it could reach his wall-shield. In vain; for the *Brittania*'s every beam was set to protect the torpedo and the mighty rods of energy without whose grip the inertialess mass of the enemy vessel would offer no resistance whatever to the force of the proposed explosion.

Slowly, *so* slowly, as the age-long seconds crawled into eternity, there extended from Patrol ship almost to pirate wall a raging, white-hot pillar—the gases of combustion of the propellant heptadetonite—ahead of which there rushed the Q-gun's tremendous shell with its horridly destructive freight. What would happen? Could even the almost immeasurable force of that frightful charge of atomic explosive break down a wall-shield designed to withstand the cosmic assaults of meteoric missiles? And what would happen if that wall-screen held?

In spite of himself Kinnison's mind insisted upon painting the ghastly picture: the awful explosion; the pirate's screen still intact; the forward-rushing gases driven backward along the tube of force. The bare metal of the Q-gun's breech, he knew, was not and could not be reenforced by the infinitely stronger, although immaterial shields of pure energy which protected the hull; and no conceivable substance, however resistant, could impede save momentarily the unimaginable forces about to be unleashed.

Nor would there be time to release the Q-tube after the explosion but before the *Brittania*'s own destruction; for if the enemy's shield stayed up for even a fraction of a second the unthinkable pressure of the blast would propagate backward through the already densely compressed gases in the tube, would sweep away as though it were nothing the immensely thick metallic barrier of the gun-breech, and would wreak within the bowels of the Patrol vessel a destruction even more complete than that intended for the foe.

Nor were his men in better case. Each knew that this was the climactic instant of his existence; that life itself hung poised upon the issue of the next split second. Hurry it up! Snap into it! Will that crawling, creeping thing *never* strike?

Some prayed briefly, some swore bitterly; but prayers and curses were alike unconscious and had precisely the same meaning—each man, white of face and grim of jaw, clenched his hands and waited, tense and straining, for the impact.

3

IN THE LIFEBOATS

The missile struck, and in the instant of its striking the coldly brilliant stars were blotted from sight in a vast globe of intolerable flame. The pirate's shield had failed, and under the cataclysmic force of that horrific detonation the entire nose-section of the enemy vessel had flashed into incandescent vapor and had added itself to the rapidly expanding cloud of fire. As it expanded the cloud cooled. Its fierce glare subsided to a rosy glow, through which the stars again began to shine. It faded, cooled, darkened—revealing the crippled hulk of the pirate ship. She was still fighting; but ineffectually, now that all her heavy forward batteries were gone.

"Needlers, fire at will!" barked Kinnison, and even that feeble resistance was ended. Keen-eyed needle-ray men, working at spy-ray visiplates, bored hole after hole into the captive, seeking out and destroying the control-panels of the remaining beams and screens.

"Pull 'er up!" came the next order. The two ships of space flashed together, the yawning, blasted-open fore-end of the raider solidly against the *Brittania*'s armored side. A great port opened.

"Now, Bus, it's all yours. Classification to six places, straight A's—they're human or approximately so. Board and storm!"

Back of that port there had been massed a hundred fighting men; dressed in full panoply of space armor, armed with the deadliest weapons known to the science of the age, and powered by the gigantic accumulators of their ship. At their head was Sergeant vanBuskirk, six and a half feet of Dutch Valerian dynamite, who had fallen out of Valeria's Cadet Corps only because of an innate inability to master the intricacies of higher mathematics. Now the attackers swept forward in a black-and-silver wave.

Four squatly massive semi-portable projectors crashed down upon their magnetic clamps and in the fierce ardor of their beams the thick bulkhead before them ran the gamut of the spectrum and puffed outward. Some score of defenders were revealed, likewise clad in armor, and battle again was joined. Explosive and solid bullets detonated against and ricocheted from that highly efficient armor, the beams of De-Lameter hand-projectors splashed in torrents of man-made lightning off its protective fields of force. But that skirmish was soon over. The semi-portables, whose vast energies no ordinary personal armor could withstand, were brought up and clamped down; and in their holocaust of vibratory destruction all life vanished from the pirates' compartment.

"One more bulkhead and we're in their control room!" vanBuskirk cried. "Beam it down!"

But when the beamers pressed their switches nothing happened. The pirates had managed to jury-rig a screen generator, and with it had cut the power-beams behind the invading forces. Also they had cut loopholes in the bulkhead, through which in frantic haste they were trying to bring heavy projectors of their own into alignment.

"Bring up the ferral paste," the sergeant commanded. "Get up as close to that wall as you can, so they can't blast us!"

The paste—successor to thermite—was brought up and the giant Dutchman troweled it on in furious swings, from floor up and around in a huge arc and back down to floor. He fired it, and simultaneously some of the enemy gunners managed to angle a projector sharply enough to reach the further ranks of the Patrolmen. Then mingled the flashing, scintillating, gassy glare of the thermite and the raving energy of the pirates' beam to make of that confined space a veritable inferno.

But the paste had done its work, and as the semi-circle of wall fell out the soldiers of the Lens leaped through the hole in the still-glowing wall to struggle hand-to-hand against the pirates, now making a desperate last stand. The semi-portables and other heavy ordnance powered from the *Brittania* were of course useless. Pistols were ineffective against the pirates' armor of hard alloy; hand-rays were equally impotent against its defensive shields. Now heavy hand-grenades began to rain down among the combatants, blowing Patrolmen and pirates alike to bits—for the outlaw chiefs cared nothing that they killed many of their own men if in so doing they could take toll of the Law. And worse, a crew of gunners was swiveling a mighty projector around upon its hastily-improvised mount to cover that sector of the compartment in which the policemen were most densely massed.

But the minions of the Law had one remaining weapon, carried expressly for this eventuality. The space-axe—a combination and sublimation of battle-axe, mace, bludgeon, and lumberman's picaroon, a massively needle-pointed implement of potentialities limited only by the physical strength and bodily agility of its wielder.

Now all the men of the *Brittania*'s storming party were Valerians, and therefore were big, hard, fast, and agile; and of them all their sergeant leader was the biggest, hardest, fastest, and most agile. When the space-tempered apex of that thirty-pound monstrosity, driven by the four-hundred-odd pounds of rawhide and whalebone that was his body, struck pirate armor that armor gave way. Nor did it matter whether or not that hellish beak of steel struck a vital part after crashing through the armor. Head or body, leg or arm, the net result was the same; a man does not fight effectively when he is breathing space in lieu of atmosphere.

VanBuskirk perceived the danger to his men in the slowly turning projector and for the first time called his chief.

"Kim," he spoke in level tones into his microphone. "Blast that delta-ray, will you? . . . Or have they cut this beam, so you can't hear me? . . . Guess they have."

"They've cut our communication," he informed his troopers then. "Keep them off me as much as you can and I'll attend to that delta-ray outfit myself."

Aided by the massed interference of his men he plunged toward the threatening mechanism, hewing to right and to left as he strode. Beside the temporary projector-mount at last, he aimed a tremendous blow at the man at the delta-ray controls; only to feel the axe flash instantaneously to its mark and strike it with a gentle push, and to see his intended victim float effortless away from the blow. The pirate commander had played his last card: vanBuskirk floundered, not only weightless, but inertialess as well!

But the huge Dutchman's mind, while not mathematical, was even faster than his muscles, and not for nothing had he spent arduous weeks in inertialess tests of strength and skill. Hooking feet and legs around a convenient wheel he seized the enemy operator and jammed his helmeted head down between the base of the mount and the long, heavy steel lever by means of which it was turned. Then, throwing every ounce of his wonderful body into the effort, he braced both feet against the projector's grim barrel and heaved. The helmet flew apart like an eggshell, blood and brains gushed out in nauseous blobs: but the delta-ray projector was so jammed that it would not soon again become a threat.

Then vanBuskirk drew himself across the room toward the main control panel of the warship. Officer after officer he pushed aside, then reversed two double-throw switches, restoring gravity and inertia to the riddled cruiser.

In the meantime the tide of battle had continued in favor of the Patrol. Few survivors though there were of the black-and-silver force, of the pirates there were still fewer; fighting now a desperate and hopeless defensive. But in this combat quarter was not, *could* not be thought of, and Sergeant vanBuskirk again waded into the fray. Four times more his horribly effective hybrid weapon descended like the hammer of Thor, cleaving and crushing its way through steel and flesh and bone. Then, striding to the control board, he manipulated switches and dials, then again spoke evenly to Kinnison.

"You can hear me now, can't you? . . . All mopped up—come and get the dope!"

The specialists, headed by Master Technician LaVerne Thorndyke, had been waiting strainingly for that word for minutes. Now they literally flew at their tasks; in furious haste, but following rigidly and in perfect coordination a prearranged schedule. Every control and lead, every bus-bar and immaterial beam of force was traced and checked. Instruments and machines were dismantled, sealed mechanisms were ruthlessly torn apart by jacks or sliced open with cutting beams. And everywhere, every thing and every movement was being photographed, charted, and diagrammed.

"Getting the idea now, Kim," Thorndyke said finally, during a brief lull in his work. "A sweet system . . ."

"Look at this!" a mechanic interrupted. "Here's a machine that's all shot to hell!"

The shielding cover had been torn from a monstrous fabrication of metal, apparently a motor or generator of an exceedingly complex type. The insulation of its coils and windings had fallen away in charred fragments, its copper had melted down in sluggish, viscous streams.

"That's what we're looking for!" Thorndyke shouted. "Check those leads! Alpha!"

"Seven-three-nine-four!" and the minutely careful study went on until:

"That's enough; we've got everything we need now. Have you draftsmen and photographers got everything down solid?"

"On the boards!" and "In the cans!" rapped out the two reports as one.

"Then let's go!"

"And go *fast!*" Kinnison ordered, briskly. "I'm afraid we're going to run out of time as it is!"

All hands hurried back into the *Brittania*, paying no attention to the bodies littering the decks. So desperate was the emergency, each man knew, that nothing could be done about the dead, whether friend or foe. Every resource of mechanism, of brain and of brawn, must needs be strained to the utmost if they themselves were not soon to be in similar case.

"Can you talk, Nels?" demanded Kinnison of his Communications Officer, even before the air-lock had closed.

"No, sir, they're blanketing us solid," that worthy replied instantly. "Space's so full of static you couldn't drive a power-beam through it, let alone a communicator. Couldn't talk direct, anyway—look where we are," and he pointed out in the tank their present location.

"Hm . . . m . . . m. Couldn't have got much farther away without jumping the galaxy entirely. Boskone got a warning, either from that ship back there or from the disturbance. They're undoubtedly concentrating on us now . . . One of them will spear us with a tractor, just as sure as hell's a man-trap . . ."

The fledgling commander rammed both hands into his pockets and thought in black intensity. He *must* get this data back to Base—but how? *HOW*? Henderson was already driving the vessel back toward Sol with every iota of her inconceivable top speed, but it was out of the question even to hope that she would ever get there. The life of the *Brittania* was now, he was coldly certain, to be measured in hours—and all too scant measure, even of them. For there must be hundreds of pirate vessels even now tearing through the void, forming a gigantic net to cut off her return to Base. Fast though she was, one of that barricading horde would certainly manage to clamp on a tractor—and when that happened her flight was done.

Nor could she fight. She had conquered one first-class war-vessel of the public enemy, it was true; but at what awful cost! One fresh vessel could blast his crippled mount out of space; nor would there be only one. Within a space of minutes after the attachment of a tracer the *Brittania* would be surrounded by the cream of Boskone's fighters. There was only one chance; and slowly, thoughtfully, and finally grimly, young Lieutenant Kinnison—now and briefly Captain Kinnison—decided to take it.

"Listen, everybody!" he ordered. "We *must* get this in formation back to Base, and we can't do it in the *Brittania* The pirates are bound to catch us, and our chance in an other fight is exactly zero. We'll have to abandon ship and take to the lifeboats, in the hope that at least one will be able to get through.

"The technicians and specialists will take all the data they got— information, descriptions, diagrams, pictures, everything—boil it down, and put it on a spool of tape. They will make about a hundred copies of it. The crew and the Valerian privates will man boats starting with Number Twenty One and blast off as soon as you can get your tapes. Once away, use very little detectable power, or better yet no power at all, until you're sure the pirates have chased the *Brittania* a good many parsecs away from where you are.

"The rest of us—specialists and the Valerian non-coms—will go last. Twenty boats, two men to a boat, and each man will have a spool. We'll start launching when we're as far as it's safe to go. Each boat will be strictly on its own. Do it any way you can; but some way, *any* way, get your spool back to Base. There's no use in me trying to impress you with the importance of this stuff; you know what it means as well as I do.

"Boatmates will be drawn by lot. The quartermaster will write all our names—and his own, to make it forty even—on slips of paper and draw them out of a helmet two at a time. If two navigators, such as Henderson and I, are drawn together, both names go back into the pot. Get to work!"

Twice the name of "Kinnison" came out together with that of another skilled in astronautics and was replaced. The third time, however, it came out paired with "vanBuskirk," to the manifest joy of the giant Valerian and to the approval of the crowd as well.

"That was a break for me, Kim!" the sergeant called over the cheers of his fellows. "I'm *sure* of getting back now!"

"That's throwing the oil, big fellow—but I don't know of anybody I'd rather have at my back than you," Kinnison replied, with a boyish grin.

The pairings were made; DeLameters, spare batteries, and other equipment were checked and tested; the spools of tape were sealed in their corrosion-proof containers and distributed; and Kinnison sat talking with the Master Technician.

"So they've solved the problem of the really efficient reception and conversion of cosmic radiation!" Kinnison whistled softly through his teeth. "And a sun—even a small one—radiates the energy given off by the annihilation of one-to-several million tons of matter per second! SOME power!"

"That's the story, Skipper, and it explains completely why their ships have been so much superior to ours. They could have installed faster drives even than the *Brittania*'s—they probably will, now that it has become necessary. Also, if the bus-bars in that receptor-convertor had been a few square centimeters larger in cross-section, they could have held their wall-shield, even against our duodec bomb. Then what? . . . They had plenty of intake, but not quite enough distribution.''

"They have atomic motors, the same as ours; just as big and just as efficient," Kinnison coagitated. "But those motors are all we *have* got, while they use them, and at full power, too, simply as first-stage exciters for the cosmic-energy screens. Blinding blue blazes, what power! Some of us have *got* to get back, Verne. If we don't, Boskone's got the whole galaxy by the tail, and civilization is sunk without a trace."

"I'll say so; but also I'll say this for those of us who don't get back— it won't be for lack of trying. Well, better I go check my boat. If I don't see you again, Kim old man, clear ether!"

They shook hands briefly and Thorndyke strode away. Enroute, however, he paused beside the quartermaster and signalled to him to disconnect his communicator.

"Clever lad, Allerdyce!" Thorndyke whispered, with a grin. "Kinda loaded the dice a trifle once or twice, didn't you? I don't think anybody but me smelled a rat, though. Certainly neither the skipper nor Henderson did, or you'd've had it to do over again."

"At least one team has got to get through," Allerdyce replied, quietly and obliquely, "and the strongest teams we can muster will find the going none too easy. Any team made up of strength and weakness is a weak team. Kinnison, our only Lensman, is of course the best man aboard this buzz-buggy. Who would you pick for number two?"

"VanBuskirk, of course, the same as you did. I wasn't criticising you, man, I was complimenting you, and thanking you, in a roundabout way, for giving me Henderson. He's got plenty of what it takes, too."

"It wasn't 'vanBuskirk, of course,' by any means," the quartermaster rejoined. "It's mighty hard to figure either you or Henderson third, to say nothing of fourth, in any kind of company, however fast—mentally and physically. However, it seemed to me that you fitted in better with the pilot. I could hand-pick only two teams without getting caught at it—you spotted me as it was—but I think I picked the two strongest teams possible. One of you will get through—if none of you four can make it, nobody could."

"Well, here's hoping, anyway. Thanks again. See you again some time, maybe—clear ether!"

Chief Pilot Henderson had, a few minutes since, changed the course of the cruiser from right-line flight to fantastic, zig-zag leaps through space, and now he turned frowningly to Kinnison.

"We'd better begin dumping them out pretty soon now, I think," he suggested. "We haven't detected anything yet, but according to the figures it won't be long now; and after they get their traps set we'll run out of time mighty quick.''

"Right," and one after another, but even so several light-years apart in space, eighteen of the small boats were launched into the void. In the control room there were left only Henderson and Thorndyke with vanBuskirk and Kinnison, who were of course to be the last to leave the vessel.

"All right, Hen, now we'll try out your roulette-wheel director-by-chance," Kinnison said, then went on, in answer to Thorndyke's questioning glance: "A bouncing ball on an oscillating table. Every time the ball carroms off a pin it shifts the course through a fairly large, but unpredictable angle. Pure chance—we thought it might cross them up a little."

Hairline beams were connected from panels to pins, and soon four interested spectators looked on while, with no human guidance, the *Brittania* lurched and leaped even more erratically than she had done under Henderson's direction. Now, however, the ever-changing vectors of her course were as unexpected and surprising to her passengers as to any possible external observer.

One more lifeboat left the vessel, and only the Lensman and his giant aide remained. While they were waiting the required few minutes before their own departure, Kinnison spoke.

"Bus, there's one more thing we ought to do, and I've just figured out how to do it. We don't want this ship to fall into the pirates' hands intact, as there's a lot of stuff in her that would probably be as new to them as it was to us. They know we got the best of that ship of theirs, but they don't know what we did or how. On the other hand, we want her to drive on as long as possible after we leave her—the farther away from us she gets, the better our chance of getting away. We should have something to touch off those duodec torpedoes we have left—all seven at once—at the first touch of a spy beam; both to keep them from studying her and to do a little damage if possible—they'll go inert and pull her up close as soon as they get a tracer on her. Of course we can't do it by stopping the spy-ray altogether, with a spy-screen, but I think I can establish an R7TX7M field outside our regular screens that will interfere with a TX7 just enough—say one-tenth of one percent—to actuate a relay in the field-supporting beam.''

"One-tenth of one percent of one milliwatt is one microwatt, isn't it? Not much power, I'd say, but that's a little out of my line. Go ahead— I'll observe while you're busy.''

Thus it came about that, a few minutes later, the immense sky-rover of the Galactic Patrol darted along entirely untenanted. And it was her non-human helmsman, operating solely by chance, that prolonged the chase far more than even the most optimistic member of her crew could have hoped. For the pilots of the pirate pursuers were intelligent, and assumed that their quarry also was directed by intelligence. Therefore they aimed their vessels for points toward which the *Brittania* should logically go; only and maddeningly to watch her go somewhere else. Senselessly she hurled herself directly toward enormous suns, once grazing one so nearly that the harrying pirates gasped at the foolhardiness of such exposure to lethal radiation. For no reason at all she shot straight backward, almost into a cluster of pirate craft, only to dash off on another unexpected tangent before the startled outlaws could lay a beam against her.

But finally she did it once too often. Flying between two vessels, she held her line the merest fraction of a second too long. Two tractors lashed out and the three vessels flashed together, zone to zone to zone. Then, instantly, the two pirate ships became inert, to anchor in space their wildly fleeing prey. Then spy-beams licked out, to explore the *Brittania*'s interior.

At the touch of those beams, light and delicate as they were, the relay clicked and the torpedoes let go. Those frightful shells were so designed and so charged that one of them could demolish any inert structure known to man: what of seven? There was an explosion to stagger the imagination and which must be left to the imagination, since no words in any language of the galaxy can describe it adequately.

The *Brittania*, literally blown to bits, more-than-half fused and partially volatilized by the inconceivable fury of the outburst, was hurled in all directions in streamers, droplets, chunks, and masses; each component part urged away from the center of pressure by the ragingly compressed gases of detonation. Furthermore, each component was now of course inert and therefore capable of giving up its full measure of kinetic energy to any inert object with which it should come in contact.

One mass of wreckage, so fiercely sped that its victim had time neither to dodge nor become inertialess, crashed full against the side of the nearer attacker. Meteorite screens flared brilliantly violet and went down. The full-driven wall-shield held; but so terrific was the concussion that what few of the crew were not killed outright would take no interest in current events for many hours to come.

The other, slightly more distant attacker was more fortunate. Her commander had had time to render her inertialess, and as she rode lightly away, ahead of the outermost, most tenuous fringe of vapor, he reported succinctly to his headquarters all that had transpired. There was a brief interlude of silence, then a speaker gave tongue.

"Helmuth, speaking for Boskone," snapped from it. "Your report is neither complete nor conclusive. Find, study, photograph, and bring in to headquarters every fragment and particle pertaining to the wreckage, paying particular attention to all bodies or portions thereof."

"Helmuth, speaking for Boskone!" roared from the general wave unscrambler. "Commanders of all vessels, of every class and tonnage, upon whatever mission bound, attention! The vessel referred to in our previous message has been destroyed, but it is feared that some or all of her personnel were allowed to escape. Every unit of that personnel must be killed before he has opportunity to communicate with any Patrol base. Therefore cancel your present orders, whatever they may be, and proceed at maximum blast to the region previously designated. Scour that entire volume of space. Beam out of existence every vessel whose papers do not account unquestionably for every intelligent being aboard. Investigate every possible avenue of escape. More detailed orders will be given each of you upon your nearer approach to the neighborhood under search."

4

ESCAPE

Space-suited complete except for helmets, and with those ready to hand, Kinnison and vanBuskirk sat in the tiny control room of their lifeboat as it drifted inert through inter-stellar space. Kinnison was poring over charts taken from the *Brittania*'s pilot room; the sergeant was gazing idly into a detector plate.

"No clear ether yet, I don't suppose," the captain remarked, as he rolled up a chart and tossed it aside.

"No let-up for a second; they're not taking any chances at all. Found out where we are? Alsakan ought to be hereabouts somewhere, hadn't it?"

"Yeah. Not close, though, even for a ship—out of the question for us. Nothing much inhabited around here, either, to say nothing of being civilized. Scarcely one to the block. Don't think I've ever been out here before; have you?"

"Off my beat entirely. How long do you figure it'll be before it's safe for us to blast off?"

"Can't start blasting until your plates are clear. Anything we can detect can detect us as soon as we start putting out power."

"We may be in for a spell of waiting, then . . ." VanBuskirk broke off suddenly and his tone changed to one of tense excitement. "Help, Noshabkeming, help! Look at that!"

"Blinding blue blazes!" Kinnison exclaimed, staring into the plate. "With all macro-universal space and all eternity to play around in, why in all space's hells did she have to come back here and now?"

For there, right in their laps, not a hundred miles away, lay the *Brittania* and her two pirate captors!

"Better go free, hadn't we?" whispered vanBuskirk.

"Daren't!" Kinnison grunted. "At this range they'd spot us in a split second. Acting like a hunk of loose metal's our only chance. We'll be able to dodge any flying chunks, I think . . . there she goes!"

From their coign of vantage the two Patrolmen saw their gallant ship's terrific end; saw the one pirate vessel suffer collision with the flying fragment; saw the other escape inertialess; saw her disappear.

The inert pirate vessel had now almost exactly the same velocity as the lifeboat, both in speed and in direction; only very slowly were the large craft and the small approaching each other. Kinnison stood rigid, staring into his plate, his nervous hands grasping the switches whose closing, at the first sign of detection, would render them inertialess and would pour full blast into their driving projectors. But minute after minute passed and nothing happened.

"Why don't they *do* something?" he burst out, finally. "They know we're here—there isn't a detector made that could be badly enough out of order to miss us at this distance. Why, they can *see* us from there, with no detectors at all!"

"Asleep, unconscious, or dead," vanBuskirk diagnosed, "and they're not asleep. Believe me, Kim, that ship was nudged. She must've been hit hard enough to lay her whole crew out cold . . . and say, she's got a standard emergency inlet port—how about it, huh?"

Kinnison's mind leaped eagerly at the daring suggestion of his subordinate, but he did not reply at once. Their first, their *only* duty, concerned the safety of two spools of tape. But if the lifeboat lay there inert until the pirates regained control of their craft, detection and capture were certain. The same fate was as certain should they attempt flight with all nearby space so full of enemy fliers. Therefore, harebrained though it appeared at first glance, vanBuskirk's wild idea was actually the safest course!

"All right, Bus, we'll try it. We'll take a chance on going free and using a tenth of a dyne of drive for a hundredth of a second. Get into the lock with your magnets."

The lifeboat flashed against the pirate's armored side and the sergeant, by deftly manipulating his two small hand-magnets, worked it rapidly along the steel plating, toward the driving jets. There, in the conventional location just forward of the main driving projectors, was indeed the emergency inlet port, with its Galactic Standard controls.

In a few minutes the two warriors were inside, dashing toward the control room. There Kinnison glanced at the board and heaved a sigh of relief.

"Fine! Same type as the one we studied. Same race, too," he went on, eyeing the motionless forms scattered about the floor. Seizing one of the bodies, he propped it against a panel thus obscuring a multiple lens.

"That's the eye overlooking the control room," he explained unnecessarily. "We can't cut their headquarters visi-beams without creating suspicion, but we don't want them looking around in here until after we've done a little stage-setting."

"But they'll get suspicious anyway when we go free," vanBuskirk protested.

"Sure, but we'll arrange for that later. First thing we've got to do is to make sure that all the crew except possibly one or two in here, are really dead. Don't beam unless you have to; we want to make it look as though everybody got killed or fatally injured in the crash."

A complete tour of the vessel, with a grim and distasteful accompaniment, was made. Not all of the pirates were dead, or even disabled; but, unarmored as they were and taken completely by surprise, the survivors could offer but little resistance. A cargo port was opened and the *Brittania*'s lifeboat was drawn inside. Then back to the control room, where Kinnison picked up another body and strode to the main panels.

"This fellow," he announced, "was hurt badly, but managed to get to the board. He threw in the free switch, like this, and then full-blast drive, so. Then he pulled himself over to the steering globe and tried to lay course back toward headquarters, but couldn't quite make it. He died with the course set right there. Not exactly toward Sol, you notice—that would be too much of a coincidence—but close enough to help a lot. His bracelet got caught in the guard, like this. There is clear evidence as to exactly what happened. Now we'll get out of range of that eye, and let the body that's covering it float away naturally."

"Now what?" asked vanBuskirk, after the two had hidden themselves.

"Nothing whatever until we have to," was the reply. "Wish we could go on like this for a couple of weeks, but no chance. Headquarters will get curious pretty quick as to why we're shoving off."

Even as he spoke a furious burst of noise erupted from the communicator; a noise which meant:

"Vessel F47U596! Where are you going, and why? Report!"

At that brusk command one of the still forms struggled weakly to its knees and tried to frame words, but fell back dead.

"Perfect!" Kinnison breathed into vanBuskirk's ear. "Couldn't have been better. Now they'll probably take their time about rounding us up ... maybe we can get back to somewhere near Tellus, after all ... Listen, here comes some more." The communicator was again sending. "See if you can get a line on their transmitter."

"If there are any survivors able to report, do so at once!" Kinnison understood the dynamic cone to say. Then, the voice moderating as though the speaker had turned from his microphone to someone nearby, it went on, "No one answers, sir. This, you know, is the ship that was lying closest to the new Patrol ship when she exploded; so close that her navigator did not have time to go free before collision with the debris. The crew were apparently all killed or incapacitated by the shock."

"If any of the officers survive have them brought in for trial," a more distant voice commanded, savagely. "Boskone has no use for bunglers except to serve as examples. Have the ship seized and returned here as soon as possible."

"Could you trace it, Bus?" Kinnison demanded. "Even one line on their headquarters would be mighty useful."

"No, it came in scrambled—couldn't separate it from the rest of the static out there. Now what?"

"Now we eat and sleep. Particularly and most emphatically, we sleep."

"Watches?"

"No need; I'll be awakened in plenty of time if anything happens. My Lens, you know."

They ate ravenously and slept prodigiously; then ate and slept again. Rested and refreshed, they studied charts, but vanBuskirk's mind was very evidently not upon the maps before them.

"You understand that jargon, and it doesn't even sound like a language to me," he pondered. "It's the Lens, of course. Maybe it's something that shouldn't be talked about?"

"No secret—not among us, at least," Kinnison assured him. "The Lens receives as pure thought any pattern of force which represents, or is in any way connected with, thought. My brain receives this thought in English, since that is my native language. At the same time my ears are practically out of circuit, so that I actually hear the English language instead of whatever noise is being made. I do not hear the foreign sounds at all. Therefore I haven't the slightest idea what the pirates' language sounds like, since I have never heard any of it.

"Conversely, when I want to talk to someone who doesn't know any language I do, I simply think into the Lens and direct its force at him, and he thinks I am talking to him in his own mother tongue. Thus, you are hearing me now in perfect Valerian Dutch, even though you know that I can speak only a dozen or so words of it, and those with a vile American accent. Also, you are hearing it in my voice, even though you know I am actually not saying a word, since you can see that my mouth is wide open and that neither my lips, tongue, nor vocal cords are moving. If you were a Frenchman you would be hearing this in French; or, if you were a Manarkan and couldn't talk at all, you would be getting it as regular Manarkan telepathy.''

"Oh . . . I see . . . I think,'' the astounded Dutchman gulped. "Then why couldn't you talk back to them through their phones?''

"Because the Lens, although a mighty fine and versatile thing, is not omnipotent,'' Kinnison replied, dryly. "It sends out only thought; and thought-waves, lying below the level of the ether, cannot affect a microphone. The microphone, not being itself intelligent, cannot receive thought. Of course I can broadcast a thought—everybody does, more or less—but without a Lens at the other end I can't reach very far. Power, they tell me, comes with practice—I'm not so good at it yet.''

"You can receive a thought . . . everybody broadcasts . . . Then you can read minds?'' vanBuskirk stated, rather than asked.

"When I want to, yes. That was what I was doing while we were mopping up. I demanded the location of their base from every one of them alive, but none of them knew it. I got a lot of pictures and descriptions of the buildings, layout, arrangements and personnel of the base, but not a hint as to where it is in space. The navigators were all dead, and not even the Arisians understand death. But that's getting pretty deep into philosophy and it's time to eat again. Let's go!''

Days passed uneventfully, but finally the communicator again began to talk. Two pirate ships were closing in upon the supposedly derelict vessel; discussing with each other the exact point of convergence of the three courses.

"I was hoping we'd be able to communicate with Prime Base before they caught up with us,'' Kinnison remarked. "But I guess it's no dice—I can't get anybody on my Lens and the ether's as full of interference as ever. They're a suspicious bunch, and they aren't going to let us get away with a single thing if they can help it. You've got that duplicate of their communications unscrambler built?''

"Yes—that was it you just listened to. I built it out of our own stuff, and I've gone over the whole ship with a cleaner. There isn't a trace, not even a finger-print, to show that anybody except her own crew has ever been aboard.''

"Good work! This course takes us right through a planetary system in a few minutes and we'll have to unload there. Let's see . . . this chart marks planets two and three as inhabited, but with a red reference number, eleven twenty-seven. Um . . . m . . . that means practically unexplored and unknown. No landing ever made . . . no patrol representation or connection . . . no commerce . . . state of civilization unknown . . .

scanned only once, in the Third Galactic Survey, and that was a hell of a long time ago. Not so good, apparently—but maybe all the better for us, at that. Anyway, it's a forced landing, so get ready to shove off.''

They boarded their lifeboat, placed it in the cargo-lock, opened the outer port upon its automatic block, and waited. At their awful galactic speed the diameter of a solar system would be traversed in such a small fraction of a second that observation would be impossible, to say nothing of computation. They would have to act first and compute later.

They flashed into the strange system. A planet loomed terrifyingly close; at their frightful velocity almost invisible even upon their ultra-vision plates. The lifeboat shot out, becoming inert as it passed the screen. The cargo-port swung shut. Luck had been with them; the planet was scarcely a million miles away. While vanBuskirk drove toward it, Kinnison made hasty observations.

"Could have been better—but could have been a lot worse," he reported. "This is planet four. Uninhabited, which is very good. Three, though, is clear over across the sun, and Two isn't any too close for a space-suit flight—better than eighty million miles. Easy enough as far as distance goes—we've all made longer hops in our suits—but we'll be open to detection for about fifteen minutes. Can't be helped, though . . . here we are!''

"Going to land her free, huh?" vanBuskirk whistled. "What a chance!''

"It'd be a bigger one to take the time to land her inert. Her power will hold—I hope. We'll inert her and match intrinsics with her when we come back—we'll have more time then.''

The lifeboat stopped instantaneously, in a free landing, upon the uninhabited, desolate, rocky soil of the strange world. Without a word the two men leaped out, carrying fully packed knapsacks. A portable projector was then dragged out and its fierce beam directed into the base of the hill beside which they had come to earth. A cavern was quickly made, and while its glassy walls were still smoking hot the lifeboat was driven within it. With their DeLameters the two wayfarers then undercut the hill, so that a great slide of soil and rock obliterated every sign of the visit. Kinnison and vanBuskirk could find their vessel again, from their accurately-taken bearings; but, they hoped, no one else could.

Then, still without a word, the two adventurers flashed upward. The atmosphere of the planet, tenuous and cold though it was, nevertheless so sorely impeded their progress that minutes of precious time were required for the driving projectors of their suits to force them through its thin layer. Eventually, however, they were in interplanetary space and were flying at quadruple the speed of light. Then vanBuskirk spoke.

"Landing the boat, hiding it, and this trip are the danger spots. Heard anything yet?"

"No, and I don't believe we will. I think probably we've lost them completely. Won't know definitely, though, until after they catch the ship, and that won't be for ten minutes yet. We'll be landed by then."

A world now loomed beneath them; a pleasant, Earthly-appearing world of scattered clouds, green forests, rolling plains, wooded and snow-capped mountain-ranges, and rolling oceans. Here and there were to be seen what looked like cities, but Kinnison gave them a wide berth; electing to land upon an open meadow in the shelter of a black and glassy cliff.

"Ah, just in time: they're beginning to talk," Kinnison announced. "Unimportant stuff yet, opening the ship and so on. I'll relay the talk as nearly verbatim as possible when it gets interesting." He fell silent, then went on in a singsong tone, as though he were reciting from memory, which in effect he was:

" 'Captains of ships P4J263 and EQ69B47 calling Helmuth! We have stopped and have boarded the F47U596. Everything is in order and as deduced and reported by your observers. Everyone aboard is dead. They did not all die at the same time, but they all died from the effects of the collision. There is no trace of outside interference and all the personnel are accounted for.'

" 'Helmuth, speaking for Boskone. Your report is inconclusive. Search the ship minutely for tracks, prints, scratches. Note any missing supplies or misplaced items of equipment. Study carefully all mechanisms, particularly converters and communicators, for signs of tampering or dismantling.'

"Whew!" whistled Kinnison. "They'll find where you took that communicator apart, Bus, just as sure as hell's a mantrap!"

"No, they won't," declared vanBuskirk as positively. "I did it with rubber-nosed pliers, and if I left a scratch or a scar or a print on it I'll eat it, tubes and all!"

A pause.

" 'We have studied everything most carefully, Oh Helmuth, and find no trace of tampering or visit.'

"Helmuth again: 'Your report is still inconclusive. Whoever did what has been done is probably a Lensman, and certainly has *brains*. Give me the present recorded serial number of all port openings, and the exact number of times you have opened each port.'

"Ouch!" groaned Kinnison. "If that means what I think it does, all hell's out for noon. Did you see any numbering recorders on those ports? I didn't—of course neither of us thought of such a thing. Hold it—here comes some more stuff.

" 'Port-opening recorder serial numbers are as follows' . . . don't mean a thing to us . . . 'we have opened the emergency inlet port once and the starboard main lock twice. No other port at all.'

"And here's Helmuth again: 'Ah, as I thought. The emergency port was opened once by outsiders, and the starboard cargo port twice. The Lensman came aboard, headed the ship toward Sol, took his lifeboat aboard, listened to us, and departed at his leisure. And this in the very midst of our fleet, the entire personnel of which was supposed to be looking for him! How supposedly intelligent spacemen could be guilty of such utter and indefensible stupidity. . . .' He's tellin' 'em plenty, Bus, but there's no use repeating it. The tone can't be reproduced, and it's simply taking the hide right off their backs . . . here's some more . . . 'General broadcast! Ship F47U596 in its supposedly derelict condition flew from the point of destruction of the Patrol ship, on course . . .' No use quoting, Bus, he's simply giving directions for scouring our whole line of flight . . . Fading out—they're going on, or back. This outfit, of course, is good for only the closest kind of close-up work."

"And we're out of the frying pan into the fire, huh?"

"Oh, no; we're a lot better off than we were. We're on a planet and not using any power they can trace. Also, they've got to cover so much territory that they can't comb it very fine, and that gives the rest of the fellows a break. Furthermore . . ."

A crushing weight descended upon his back, and the Patrolmen found themselves fighting for their lives. From the bare, supposedly evidently safe rack face of the cliff there had emerged rope-tentacled monstrosities in a ravenously attacking swarm. In the savage blasts of DeLameters hundreds of the gargoyle horde vanished in vivid flares of radiance, but on they came; by thousands and, it seemed, by millions. Eventually the batteries energizing the projectors became exhausted. Then flailing coil met shearing steel, fierce-driven parrot beaks clanged against space-tempered armor, bulbous heads pulped under hard-swung axes; but not for the fractional second necessary for inertialess flight could the two win clear. Then Kinnison sent out his SOS.

"A Lensman calling help! A Lensman calling help!" he broadcast with the full power of mind and Lens, and immediately a sharp, clear voice poured into his brain:

"Coming, wearer of the Lens! Coming at speed to the cliff of the Catlats. Hold until I come! I arrive in thirty . . ."

Thirty what? What possible intelligible relative measure of that unknown and unknowable concept, Time, can be conveyed by thought alone?

"Keep slugging, Bus!" Kinnison panted. "Help is on the way. A local cop—voice sounds like it could be a woman—will be here in thirty somethings. Don't know whether it's thirty minutes or thirty days; but we'll still be there."

"Maybe so and maybe not," grunted the Dutchman. "Something's coming besides help. Look up and see if you see what I think I do."

Kinnison did so. Through the air from the top of the cliff there was hurtling downward toward them a veritable dragon: a nightmare's horror of hideously reptilian head, of leathern wings, of viciously fanged jaws, of frightfully taloned feet, of multiple knotty arms, of long, sinuous, heavily-scaled serpent's body. In fleeting glimpses through the writhing tentacles of his opponents Kinnison perceived little by little the full picture of that unbelievable monstrosity: and, accustomed as he was to the outlandish denizens of worlds scarcely known to man, his very senses reeled.

5

WORSEL TO THE RESCUE

As the quasi-reptilian organism descended the cliff-dwellers went mad. Their attack upon the two Patrolmen, already vicious, became insanely frantic. Abandoning the gigantic Dutchman entirely, every Catlat within reach threw himself upon Kinnison and so enwrapped the Lensman's head, arms, and torso that he could scarcely move a muscle. Then entwining captors and helpless man moved slowly toward the largest of the openings in the cliff's obsidian face.

Upon that slowly moving mass vanBuskirk hurled himself, deadly space-axe swinging. But, hew and smite as he would, he could neither free his chief from the grisly horde enveloping him nor impede measurably that horde's progress toward its goal. However, he could and did cut away the comparatively few cables confining Kinnison's legs.

"Clamp a leg-lock around my waist, Kim," he directed, the flashing thought in no whit interfering with his prodigious axe-play, "and as soon as I get a chance, before the real tussle comes, I'll couple us together with all the belt-snaps I can reach—wherever we're going we're going together! Wonder why they haven't ganged up on me, too, and what that lizard is doing? Been too busy to look, but thought he'd've been on my back before this."

"He won't be on your back. That's Worsel, the lad who answered my call. I told you his voice was funny? They can't talk or hear—use telepathy, like the Manarkans. He's cleaning them out in great shape. If you can hold me for three minutes he'll have the lot of them whipped."

"I can hold you for three minutes against all the vermin between here and Andromeda," vanBuskirk declared. "There, I've got four snaps on you."

"Not too tight, Bus," Kinnison cautioned. "Leave enough slack so you can cut me loose if you have to. Remember that the spools are more important than any one of us. Once inside that cliff we'll be all washed up—even Worsel can't help us there—so drop me rather than go in yourself."

"Um," grunted the Dutchman, non-committally. "There, I've tossed my spool out onto the ground. Tell Worsel that if they get us he's to pick it up and carry on. We'll go ahead with yours, inside the cliff if necessary."

"I said cut me loose if you can't hold me!" Kinnison snapped, and I meant it. That's an official order. Remember it!"

"Official order be damned!" snorted vanBuskirk, still plying his ponderous mace. "They won't get you into that hole without breaking me in two, and that will be a job of breaking in anybody's language. Now shut your pan," he concluded grimly. "We're here, and I'm going to be too busy, even to think, very shortly."

He spoke truly. He had already selected his point of resistance, and as he reached it he thrust the head of his mace into the crack behind the open trap-door, jammed its shaft into the shoulder-socket of his armor, set blocky legs and Herculean arms against the cliffside, arched his mighty back, and held. And the surprised Catlats, now inside the gloomy fastness of their tunnel, thrust anchoring tentacles into crevices in the wall and pulled; harder, ever harder.

Under the terrific stress Kinnison's heavy armor creaked as its airtight joints accommodated themselves to their new and unusual positions. That armor, or space-tempered alloy, of course would not give way—but what of its anchor?

Well it was for Kimball Kinnison that day, and well for our present civilization, that the *Brittania*'s quartermaster had selected Peter vanBuskirk for the Lensman's mate; for death, inevitable and horrible, resided within that cliff, and no human frame of Earthly growth, however armored, could have borne for even a fraction of a second the violence of the Catlats' pull.

But Peter vanBuskirk, although of Earthly-Dutch ancestry, had been born and reared upon the planet Valeria, and that massive planet's gravity—over two and one half times Earth's—had given him a physique and a strength almost inconceivable to us life-long dwellers upon small, green Terra. His head, as has been said, towered seventy-eight inches above the ground; but at that he appeared squatty because of his enormous spread of shoulder and his startling girth. His bones were elephantine—they had to be, to furnish adequate support and leverage for the incredible masses of muscle overlaying and surrounding them. But even vanBuskirk's Valerian strength was now being taxed to the uttermost.

The anchoring chains hummed and snarled as the clamps bit into the rings. Muscles writhed and knotted, tendons stretched and threatened to snap; sweat rolled down his mighty back. His jaws locked in agony and his eyes started from their sockets with the effort; but still vanBuskirk held.

"Cut me loose!" commanded Kinnison at last. "Even you can't take much more of that. No use letting them break your back . . . *Cut*, I tell you . . . I said *CUT*, you big, dumb, Valerian ape!"

But if vanBuskirk heard or felt the savagely-voiced commands of his chief he gave no heed. Straining to the very ultimate fiber of his being, exerting every iota of loyal mind and every atom of Brobdingnagian frame: grimly, tenaciously, stubbornly the gigantic Dutchman held.

Held while Worsel of Velantia, that grotesquely hideous, that fantastically reptilian ally, plowed toward the two Patrolmen through the horde of Catlats; a veritable tornado of rending fang and shearing talon, of beating wing and crushing snout, of mailed hand and trenchant tail:

Held while that demon incarnate drove closer and closer, hurling entire Catlats and numberless dismembered fragments of Catlats to the four winds as he came:

Held until Worsel's snake-like body, a supple and sentient cable of living steel, tipped with its double-edged, razor-keen, scimitar-like sting, slipped into the tunnel beside Kinnison and wrought grisly havoc among the Catlats close-packed there!

As the terrific tension upon him was suddenly released vanBuskirk's own efforts hurled him away from the cliff. He fell to the ground, his overstrained muscles twitching uncontrollably, and on top of him fell the fettered Lensman. Kinnison, his hands now free, unfastened the clamps linking his armor to that of vanBuskirk and whirled to confront the foe—but the fighting was over. The Catlats had had enough of Worsel of Velantia; and, screaming and shrieking in baffled rage, the last of them were disappearing into their caves.

VanBuskirk got shakily to his feet. "Thanks for the help, Worsel, we were just about to run out of time . . ." he began, only to be silenced by an insistent thought from the grotesquely monstrous stranger.

"Stop that radiating! Do not think at all if you cannot screen your minds!" came urgent mental commands. "These Catlats are a very minor pest of this planet Delgon. There are others worse by far. Fortunately, your thoughts are upon a frequency never used here—if I had not been so very close to you I would not have heard you at all—but should the Overlords have a listener upon that band your unshielded thinking may already have done irreparable harm. Follow me. I will slow my speed to yours, but hurry all possible!"

"You tell 'im, Chief," vanBuskirk said, and fell silent; his mind as nearly a perfect blank as his iron will could make it.

"This is a screened thought, through my Lens," Kinnison took up the conversation. "You don't need to slow down on our account—we can develop any speed you wish. Lead on!"

The Velantian leaped into the air and flashed away in headlong flight. Much to his surprise the two human beings kept up with him effortlessly upon their inertialess drives, and after a moment Kinnison directed another thought.

"If time is an object, Worsel, know that my companion and I can carry you anywhere you wish to go at a speed hundreds of times greater than this that we are using," he vouchsafed.

It developed that time was of the utmost possible importance and the three closed in. Mighty wings folded back, hands and talons gripped armor chains, and the group, inertialess all, shot away at a pace that Worsel of Velantia had never imagined even in his wildest dreams of speed. Their goal, a small, featureless tent of thin sheet metal, occupying a barren spot in a writhing, crawling expanse of lushly green jungle, was reached in a space of minutes. Once inside, Worsel sealed the opening and turned to his armored guests.

"We can now think freely in open converse. This wall is the carrier of a screen through which no thought can make its way."

"This world you call by a name I have interpreted as Delgon," Kinnison began, slowly. "You are a native of Velantia, a planet now beyond the sun. Therefore I assumed that you were taking us to your space-ship. Where is that ship?"

"I have no ship," the Velantian replied, composedly, "nor have I need of one. For the remainder of my life—which is now to be measured in a few of your hours—this tent is my only . . ."

"No ship!" vanBuskirk broke in. "I hope we won't have to stay on this Noshabkeming-forgotten planet forever—and I'm not very keen on going much further in that lifeboat, either."

"We may not have to do either of those things," Kinnison reassured his sergeant. "Worsel comes of a long-lived tribe, and the fact that he thinks his enemies are going to get him in a few hours doesn't make it true, by any means—there are three of us to reckon with now. Also, when we need a spaceship we'll get one, if we have to build it. Now, let's find out what this is all about. Worsel, start at the beginning and don't skip a thing. Between us we can surely find a way out, for all of us."

Then the Velantian told his story. There was much repetition, much roundabout thinking, as some of the concepts were so bizarre as to defy transmission, but finally the Patrolmen had a fairly complete picture of the situation then obtaining within that strange solar system.

The inhabitants of Delgon were bad, being characterized by a type and a depth of depravity impossible for a human mind to visualize. Not only were the Delgonians enemies of the Velantians in the ordinary sense of the word; not only were they pirates and robbers; not only were they their masters, taking them both as slaves and as food-cattle; but there was something more, something deeper and worse, something only partially transmissible from mind to mind—a horribly and repulsively Saturnalian type of mental and intellectual, as well as biological, parasitism. This relationship had gone on for ages, and during those ages rebellion was impossible, as any Velantian capable of leading such a movement disappeared before he could make any headway at all.

Finally, however, a thought screen had been devised, behind which Velantia developed a high science of her own. The students of this science lived with but one purpose in life, to free Velantia from the tyranny of the Overlords of Delgon. Each student, as he reached the zenith of his mental power, went to Delgon, to study and if possible to destroy the tyrants. And after disembarking upon the soil of that dread planet no Velantian, whether student or scientist or private adventurer, had ever returned to Velantia.

"But why don't you lay a complaint against them before the Council?" demanded vanBuskirk. "They'd straighten things out in a hurry."

"We have not heretofore known, save by the most unreliable and roundabout reports, that such an organization as your Galactic Patrol really exists," the Velantian replied, obliquely. "Nevertheless, many years since, we launched a space-ship toward its nearest reputed base. However, since that trip requires three normal lifetimes, with deadly peril in every moment, it will be a miracle if the ship ever completes it. Furthermore, even if the ship should reach its destination, our complaint will probably not even be considered because we have not a single shred of real evidence with which to support it. No living Velantian has even seen a Delgonian, nor can anyone testify to the truth of anything I have told you. While we believe that that is the true condition of affairs, our belief is based, not upon evidence admissible in a court of law, but upon deductions from occasional thoughts radiated from this planet. Nor were these thoughts alike in tenor . . ."

"Skip that for a minute—we'll take the picture as correct," Kinnison broke in. "Nothing you have said so far shows any necessity for you to die in the next few hours."

"The only object in life for a trained Velantian is to liberate his planet from the horrors of subjection to Delgon. Many such have come here, but not one has found a workable idea; not one has either returned to or even communicated with Velantia after starting work here. I am a Velantian. I am here. Soon I shall open that door and get in touch with the enemy. Since better men than I am have failed, I do not expect to succeed. Nor shall I return to my native planet. As soon as I start to work the Delgonians will command me to come to them. In spite of myself I will obey that command, and very shortly thereafter I shall die, in what fashion I do not know."

"Snap out of it, Worsel!" Kinnison ordered, bruskly. "That's the rankest kind of defeatism, and you know it. Nobody ever got to the first check-station on that kind of fuel."

"You are talking about something now about which you know nothing whatever." For the first time Worsel's thoughts showed passion. "Your thoughts are idle—ignorant—vain. You know nothing whatever of the mental power of the Delgonians."

"Maybe not—I make no claim to being a mental giant—but I do know that mental power alone cannot overcome a definitely and positively opposed *will*. An Arisian could probably break my will, but I'll stake my life that no other mentality in the known Universe can do it!"

"You think so, Earthling?" and a seething sphere of mental force encompassed the Tellurian's brain. Kinnison's senses reeled at the terrific impact, but he shook off the attack and smiled.

"Come again, Worsel. That one jarred me to the heels, but it didn't quite ring the bell."

"You flatter me," the Velantian declared in surprise. "I could scarcely touch your mind—could not penetrate even its outermost defenses, and I exerted all my force. But that fact gives me hope. My mind is of course inferior to theirs, but since I could not influence you at all, even in direct contact and at full power, you may be able to resist the minds of the Delgonians. Are you willing to hazard the stake you mentioned a moment ago? Or rather, I ask you, by the Lens you wear, so to hazard it—with the liberty of an entire people dependent upon the outcome."

"Why not? The spools come first, of course—but without you our spools would both be buried now inside the cliff of the Catlats. Fix it so your people will find these spools and carry on with them in case we fail, and I'm your man. There—now tell me what we're apt to be up against, and then let loose your dogs."

"That I cannot do. I know only that they will direct against us mental forces such as you have never even imagined—I cannot forewarn you in any respect whatever as to what forms those forces may appear to assume. I know, however, that I shall succumb to the first bolt of force. Therefore bind me with these chains before I open the shield. Physically I am extremely strong, as you know; therefore be sure to put on enough chains so that I cannot possibly break free, for if I can break away I shall undoubtedly kill both of you."

"How come all these things here, ready to hand?" asked vanBuskirk, as the two Patrolmen so loaded the passive Velantian with chains, manacles, hand-cuffs, leg-irons and straps that he could not move even his tail.

"It has been tried before, many times," Worsel replied bleakly, "but the rescuers, being Velantians, also succumbed to the force and took off the irons. Now I caution you, with all the power of my mind—no matter what you see, no matter what I may command you or beg of you, no matter how urgently you yourself may wish to do so—DO NOT LIBERATE ME UNDER ANY CIRCUMSTANCES unless and until things appear exactly as they do now and that door is shut. Know fully and ponder well the fact that if you release me while that door is open it will be because you have yielded to Delgonian force; and that not only will all three of us die, lingeringly and horribly; but also and worse, that our deaths will not have been of any benefit to civilization. Do you understand? Are you ready?"

"I understand—I am ready," thought Kinnison and vanBuskirk as one.

"Open that door."

Kinnison did so. For a few minutes nothing happened. Then three-dimensional pictures began to form before their eyes—pictures which they knew existed only in their own minds, yet which were composed of such solid substance that they obscured from vision everything else in the material world. At first hazy and indistinct, the scene—for it was in no sense now a picture—became clear and sharp. And, piling horror upon horror, sound was added to sight. And directly before their eyes, blotting out completely even the solid metal of the wall only a few feet distant from them, the two outlanders saw and heard something which can be represented only vaguely by imagining Dante's Inferno an actuality and raised to the Nth power!

In a dull and gloomy cavern there lay, sat, and stood hordes of *things*. These beings—the "nobility" of Delgon—had reptilian bodies, somewhat similar to Worsel's, but they had no wings and their heads were distinctly apish rather than crocodilian. Every greedy eye in the vast throng was fixed upon an enormous screen which, like that in a motion-picture theater, walled off one end of the stupendous cavern.

Slowly, shudderingly, Kinnison's mind began to take in what was happening upon that screen. And it was really happening, Kinnison was sure of that—this was not a picture any more than this whole scene was an illusion. It was all an actuality—somewhere. Upon that screen there were stretched out victims. Hundreds of these were Velantians, more hundreds were winged Delgonians, and scores were creatures whose like Kinnison had never seen. And all these were being tortured: tortured to death both in fashions known to the Inquisitors of old and in ways of which even those experts had never an inkling. Some were being twisted outrageously in three-dimensional frames. Others were being stretched upon racks. Many were being pulled horribly apart, chains intermittently but relentlessly extending each helpless member. Still others were being lowered into pits of constantly increasing temperature or were being attacked by gradually increasing concentrations of some foully corrosive vapor which ate away ate away their tissues, little by little. And, apparently the pièce de résistance of the hellish exhibition, one luckless Velantian, in a spot of hard, cold light, was being pressed out flat against the screen, as an insect might be pressed between two panes of glass. Thinner and thinner he became under the influence of some awful, invisible force; in spite of every exertion of inhumanly powerful muscles driving body, tail, wings, arms, legs, and head in every frantic maneuver which grim and imminent death could call forth.

Physically nauseated, brain-sick at the atrocious visions blasting his mind and at the screaming of the damned assailing his ears, Kinnison strove to wrench his mind away, but was curbed savagely by Worsel.

"You *must* stay! You *must* pay attention!" commanded the Velantian. "This is the first time any living being has seen so much—you *must* help me now! They have been attacking me from the first; but, braced by the powerful negatives in your mind, I have been able to resist and have transmitted a truthful picture so far. But they are surprised at my resistance and are concentrating more force . . . I am slipping fast . . . you *must* brace my mind! And when the picture changes— as change it must, and soon—do not believe it. Hold fast, brothers of the Lens, for your own lives and for the people of Velantia. There is more—and worse!"

Kinnison stayed. So did vanBuskirk, fighting with all his stubborn Dutch mind. Revolted, outraged, nauseated as they were at the sights and sounds, they stayed. Flinching with the victims as they were fed into the hoppers of slowly turning mills; wincing at the unbelievable acts of the boilers, the beaters, the scourgers, the flayers; suffering themselves every possible and many apparently impossible nightmares of slow and hideous torture—with clenched fists and locked teeth, with sweating foreheads over white and straining faces, Kinnison and vanBuskirk stayed.

The light in the cavern now changed to a strong, greenish-yellow glare; and in that hard illumination it was to be seen that each dying being was surrounded by a palely glowing aura. And now, crowning horror of that unutterably horrible orgy of Sadism resublimed, from the eyes of each one of the monstrous audience there leaped out visible beams of force. These beams touched the auras of the dying prisoners; touched and clung. And as they clung, the auras shrank and disappeared.

The Overlords of Delgon were actually FEEDING upon the ebbing life-forces of their tortured, dying victims!

6

DELGONIAN HYPNOTISM

Gradually and so insidiously that the Velantian's dire warnings might as well never have been uttered, the scene changed. Or rather, the scene itself did not change, but the observers' perception of it slowly underwent such a radical transformation that it was in no sense the same scene it had been a few minutes before; and they felt almost abjectly apologetic as they realized how unjust their previous ideas had been.

For the cavern was not a torture-chamber, as they had supposed. It was in reality a hospital, and the beings they had thought victims of brutalities unspeakable were in reality patients undergoing treatments and operations for various ills. In proof whereof the patients—who should have been dead by this time were the early ideas well-founded—were now being released from the screen-like operating theater. And not only was each one completely whole and sound in body, but he was also possessed of a mental clarity, power, and grasp undreamed-of before his hospitalization and treatment by Delgon's super-surgeons!

Also the intruders had misunderstood completely the audience and its behavior. They were really medical students, and the beams which had seemed to be devouring rays were simply visibeams, by means of which each student could follow, in close-up detail, each step of the operation in which he was most interested. The patients themselves were living, vocal witnesses of the visitors' mistakenness, for each, as he made his way through the assemblage of students, was voicing his thanks for the marvelous results of his particular treatment or operation.

Kinnison now became acutely aware that he himself was in need of immediate surgical attention. His body, which he had always regarded so highly, he now perceived to be sadly inefficient; his mind was in even worse shape than his physique; and both body and mind would be improved immeasurably if he could get to the Delgonian hospital before the surgeons departed. In fact, he felt an almost irresistible urge to rush away toward that hospital; instantly, without the loss of a single precious second. And, since he had had no reason to doubt the evidence of his own senses, his conscious mind was not aroused to active opposition. However in his—in his subconscious, or his essence, or whatever you choose to call that ultimate something of his that made him a Lensman—a "dead slow bell" began to sound.

"Release me and we'll all go, before the surgeons leave the hospital," came an insistent thought from Worsel. "But hurry—we haven't much time!"

VanBuskirk, completely under the influence of the frantic compulsion, leaped toward the Velantian, only to be checked bodily by Kinnison, who was foggily trying to isolate and identify one thing about the situation that did not ring quite true.

"Just a minute, Bus—shut that door first!" he commanded.

"Never mind the door!" Worsel's thought came in a roaring crescendo. "Release me instantly! Hurry! Hurry, or it will be too late, for all of us!"

"All this terrific rush doesn't make any kind of sense at all," Kinnison declared, closing his mind resolutely to the clamor of the Velantian's thoughts. "I want to go just as badly as you do, Bus, or maybe more so—but I can't help feeling that there's something screwy somewhere. Anyway, remember the last thing Worsel said, and let's shut the door before we unsnap a single chain."

Then something clicked in the Lensman's mind.

"Hypnotism, through Worsel!" he barked, opposition now aflame. "So gradual that it never occurred to me to build up a resistance. Holy Klono, what a fool I've been! Fight 'em, Bus—*fight 'em!* Don't let 'em kid you any more, and pay no attention to anything Worsel sends at you!" Whirling around, he leaped toward the open door of the tent.

But as he leaped his brain was invaded by such a concentration of force that he fell flat upon the floor, physically out of control. He must *not* shut the door. He *must* release the Velantian. They *must* go to the Delgonian cavern. Fully aware now, however, of the source of the waves of compulsion, he threw the sum total of his mental power into an intense negation and struggled, inch-wise, toward the opening.

Upon him now, in addition to the Delgonians' compulsion, beat at point-blank range the full power of Worsel's mighty mind, demanding release and compliance. Also, and worse, he perceived that some powerful mentality was being exerted to make vanBuskirk kill him. One blow of the Valerian's ponderous mace would shatter helmet and skull, and all would be over—once more the Delgonians would have triumphed. But the stubborn Dutchman, although at the very verge of surrender, was still fighting. One step forward he would take, bludgeon poised aloft, only to throw it convulsively backward. Then in spite of himself, he would go over and pick it up, again to step toward his crawling chief.

Again and again vanBuskirk repeated his futile performance while the Lensman struggled nearer and nearer the door. Finally he reached it and kicked it shut. Instantly the mental turmoil ceased and the two white and shaking Patrolmen released the limp, unconscious Velantian from his bonds.

"Wonder what we can do to help him revive?" gasped Kinnison, but his solicitude was unnecessary—the Velantian recovered consciousness as he spoke.

"Thanks to your wonderful power of resistance, I am alive, unharmed, and know more of our foes and their methods than any other of my race has ever learned," Worsel thought, feelingly. "But it is of no value whatever unless I can send it back to Velantia. The thought-screen is carried only by the metal of these walls; and if I make an opening in the wall to think through, however small, it will now mean death. Of course the science of your Patrol has not perfected an apparatus to drive thought through such a screen?"

"No. Anyway, it seems to me that we'd better be worrying about something besides thought-screens," Kinnison suggested. "Surely, now that they know where we are, they'll be coming out here after us, and we haven't got much of any defense."

"They don't know where we are, or care . . ." began the Velantian.

"Why not?" broke in vanBuskirk. "Any spy-ray capable of such scanning as you showed us—I never saw anything like it before—would certainly be as easy to trace as an out-and-out atomic blast!"

"I sent out no spy-ray or anything of the kind," Worsel thought, carefully. "Since our science is so foreign to yours, I am not sure that I can explain satisfactorily, but I shall try to do so. First, as to what you saw. When that door is open, no barrier to thought exists. I merely broadcast a thought, placing myself en rapport with the Delgonian Overlords in their retreat. This condition established, of course I heard and saw exactly what they heard and saw—and so, equally of course, did you, since you were also en rapport with me. That is all."

"That's all!" echoed vanBuskirk. "What a system! You can do a thing like that, without apparatus of any kind, and yet say 'that's all'!"

"It is results that count," Worsel reminded him gently. "While it is true that we have done much—this is the first time in history that any

Velantian has encountered the mind of a Delgonian Overlord and lived—it is equally true that it was the will-power of you Patrolmen that made it possible; not my mentality. Also, it remains true that we cannot leave this room and live.''

"Why won't we need weapons?" asked Kinnison, returning to his previous line of thought.

"Thought-screens are the only defense we will require," Worsel stated positively, "for they use no weapons except their minds. By mental power alone they make us come to them; and, once there, their slaves do the rest. Of course, if my race is ever to rid the planet of them, we must employ offensive weapons of power. We have such, but we have never been able to use them. For, in order to locate the enemy, either by telepathy or by spy-ray, we must open our metallic shields— and the instant we release those screens we are lost. From those conditions there is no escape," Worsel concluded, hopelessly.

"Don't be such a pessimist," Kinnison commanded. "There's a lot of things not tried yet. For instance, from what I have seen of your generator equipment and the pattern of that screen, you don't need a metallic conductor any more than a snake needs hips. Maybe I'm wrong, but I think we're a bit ahead of you there. If a deVilbiss projector can handle that screen—and I think it can, with special tuning—vanBuskirk and I can fix things in an hour so that all three of us can walk out of here in perfect safety—from mental interference, at least. While we're trying it out, tell us all the new stuff you got on them just now, and anything else that by any possibility may prove useful. And remember you said this is the first time any of you had been able to cut them off. That fact ought to make them sit up and take notice—probably they'll stir around more than they ever did before. Come on, Bus—let's tear into it!"

The deVilbiss projectors were rigged and tuned. Kinnison had been right—they worked. Then plan after plan was made, only to be discarded as its weaknesses were pointed out.

"Whichever way we look there are too many 'ifs' and 'buts' to suit me," Kinnison summed up the situation finally. "*If* we can find them, and *if* we can get up close to them without losing our minds to them, we could clean them out *if* we had some power in our accumulators. So I'd say the first thing for us to do is to get our batteries charged. We saw some cities from the air, and cities always have power. Lead us to power, Worsel—almost *any* kind of power—and we'll soon have it in our guns."

"There are cities, yes," Worsel was not at all enthusiastic, "dwelling-places of the ordinary Delgonians; the people you saw being eaten in

the cavern of the Overlords. As you saw, they resemble us Velantians
to a certain extent. Since they are of a lower culture and are much
weaker in life force than we are, however, the Overlords prefer us to
their own slave races.

"To visit any city of Delgon is out of the question. Every inhabitant
of every city is an abject slave and his brain is an open book. Whatever
he sees, whatever he thinks, is communicated instantly to his master.
And I now perceive that I may have misinformed you as to the Overlords' ability to use weapons. While the situation has never arisen, it is
only logical to suppose that as soon as we are seen by any Delgonian
the controllers will order all the inhabitants of the city to capture us and
bring us to them."

"What a guy!" interjected vanBuskirk. "Did you ever see his top
for looking at the bright side of life?"

"Only in conversation," the Lensman replied. "When the ether gets
crowded, you notice, he's right in there, blasting away and not saying
a word. But to get back to the question of power. I've got only a few
minutes of free flight left in my battery; and with your mass, you must
be just about out. Come to think of it, didn't you land a trifle hard when
we sat down here?"

"Fairly—I went into the ground up to my knees."

"I thought so. We've *got* to get some power, and the nearest city—
out of the question or not—is the best place to get it. Luckily, it isn't
far."

VanBuskirk grunted. "As far as I'm concerned it might as well be
on Mars, considering what's between here and there. You can take my
batteries and I'll wait here."

"On your emergency food, water, and air? That's out!"

"What else, then?"

"I can spread my field to cover all three of us," proposed Kinnison.
"That will give us at least one minute of free flight—almost, if not
quite, enough to clear the jungle. They have night here; and, like us,
the Delgonians are night-sleepers. We start at dusk, and tonight we
recharge our batteries."

The following hour, during which the huge, hot sun dropped to the
horizon, was spent in intense discussion, but no significant improvement
upon the Lensman's plan could be devised.

"It is time to go," Worsel announced, curling out one extensile eye
toward the vanishing orb. "I have recorded all my findings. Already I
have lived longer and, through you, have accomplished more, than anyone has ever believed possible. I am ready to die—I should have been
dead long since."

"Living on borrowed time's a lot better than not living at all," Kinnison replied, with a grin. "Link up . . . Ready? . . . Go!"

He snapped his switches and the close-linked group of three shot into the air and away. As far as the eye could reach in any direction extended the sentient, ravenous growth of the jungle; but Kinnison's eyes were not upon that fantastically inimical green carpet. His whole attention was occupied by two all-important meters and by the task of so directing their flight as to gain the greatest possible horizontal distance with the power at his command.

Fifty seconds of flashing flight, then:

"All right, Worsel, get out in front and get ready to pull!" Kinnison snapped. "Ten seconds of drive left, but I can hold us free for five seconds after my driver quits. Pull!"

Kinnison's driver expired, its small accumulator completely exhausted; and Worsel, with his mighty wings, took up the task of propulsion. Inertialess still, with Kinnison and vanBuskirk grasping his tail, each beat a mile-long leap, he struggled on. But all too soon the battery powering the neutralizers also went dead and the three began to plummet downward at a sharper and sharper angle, in spite of the Velantian's Herculean efforts to keep them aloft.

Some distance ahead of them the green of the jungle ended in a sharply cut line, beyond which there was a heavy growth of fairly open forest. A couple of miles of this and there was the city, their objective— so near and yet so far!

"We'll either just make the timber or we just won't," Kinnison, mentally plotting the course, announced dispassionately. "Just as well if we land in the jungle, I think. It'll break our fall, anyway—hitting solid ground inert at this speed would be bad."

"If we land in the jungle we will never leave it," Worsel's thought did not slow the incredible tempo of his prodigious pinions, "but it makes little difference whether I die now or later."

"It does to us, you pessimistic croaker!" flared Kinnison. "Forget that dying complex of yours for a minute! Remember the plan, and follow it! We're going to strike the jungle, about ninety or a hundred meters in. If you come in with us you die at once, and the rest of our scheme is all shot to hell. So when we let go, you go ahead and land in the woods. We'll join you there, never fear: our armor will hold long enough for us to cut our way through a hundred meters of any jungle that ever grew—even this one . . . Get ready, Bus . . . Leggo!"

They dropped. Through the lush succulence of close-packed upper leaves and tentacles they crashed; through the heavier, woodier main branches below; through to the ground. And there they fought for their lives; for those voracious plants nourished themselves not only upon the soil in which their roots were imbedded, but also upon anything organic unlucky enough to come within their reach. Flabby but tough tentacles encircled them; ghastly sucking disks, exuding a potent corrosive, slobbered wetly at their armor; knobbed and spiky bludgeons whanged against tempered steel as the monstrous organisms began dimly to realize that these particular tid-bits were encased in something far more resistant than skin, scales, or bark.

But the Lensman and his giant companion were not quiescent. They came down oriented and fighting. VanBuskirk, in the van, swung his frightful space-axe as a reaper swings his scythe—one solid, short step forward with each swing. And close behind the Valerian strode Kinnison, his own flying axe guarding the giant's head and back. Forward they pressed, and forward—not the strongest, toughest stems of that monstrous weed could stay vanBuskirk's Herculean strength; not the most agile of the striking tendrils and curling tentacles could gain a manacling hold in the face of Kinnison's flashing speed in cut, thrust, and slash.

Masses of the obscene vegetation crashed down upon their heads from above, revoltingly cupped orifices sucking and smacking; and they were showered continually with floods of the opaque, corrosive sap, to the action of which even their armor was not entirely immune. But, hampered as they were and almost blinded, they struggled on; while behind them an ever-lengthening corridor of demolition marked their progress.

"Ain't we got fun?" grunted the Dutchman, in time with his swing. "But we're quite a team at that, chief—brains and brawn, huh?"

"Uh uh," dissented Kinnison, his weapon flying. "Grace and poise; or, if you want to be really romantic, ham and eggs."

"Rack and ruin will be more like it if we don't break out before this confounded goo eats through our armor. But we're making it—the stuff's thinning out and I think I can see trees up ahead."

"It is well if you can," came a cold, clear thought from Worsel, "for I am sorely beset. Hasten or I perish!"

At that thought the two Patrolmen forged ahead in a burst of even more furious activity. Crashing through the thinning barriers of the jungle's edge, they wiped their lenses partially clear, glanced quickly about, and saw the Velantian. That worthy was "sorely beset" indeed. Six animals—huge, reptilian, but lithe and active—had him down. So helplessly immobile was Worsel that he could scarcely move his tail, and the monsters were already beginning to gnaw at his scaly, armored hide.

"I'll put a stop to that, Worsel!" called Kinnison; referring to the fact, well known to all us moderns, that any real animal, no matter how savage, can be controlled by any wearer of the Lens. For, no matter how low in the scale of intelligence the animal is, the Lensman can get in touch with whatever mind the creature has, and reason with it.

But these monstrosities, as Kinnison learned immediately, were not really animals. Even though of animal form and mobility, they were purely vegetable in motivation and behavior, reacting only to the stimuli of food and of reproduction. Weirdly and completely inimical to all other forms of created life, they were so utterly noisome, so completely alien that the full power of mind and Lens failed entirely to gain rapport.

Upon that confusedly writhing heap the Patrolmen flung themselves, terrible axes destructively a-swing. In turn they were attacked viciously, but this battle was not long to endure. VanBuskirk's first terrific blow knocked one adversary away, almost spinning end over end. Kinnison took out one, the Dutchman another, and the remaining three were no match at all for the humiliated and furiously raging Velantian. But it was not until the monstrosities had been gruesomely carved and torn apart, literally to bits, that they ceased their insensately voracious attacks.

"They took me by surprise," explained Worsel, unnecessarily, as the three made their way through the night toward their goal, "and six of them at once were too much for me. I tried to hold their minds, but apparently they have none."

"How about the Overlords?" asked Kinnison. "Suppose they have received any of our thoughts? Bus and I may have done some unguarded radiating."

"No," Worsel made positive reply. "The thought-screen batteries, while small and of very little actual power, have a very long service life. Now let us go over again the next steps of our plan of action."

Since no more untoward events marred their progress toward the Delgonian city, they soon reached it. It was for the most part dark and quiet, its somber buildings merely blacker blobs against a background of black. Here and there, however, were to be seen automotive vehicles moving about, and the three invaders crouched against a convenient wall, waiting for one to come along the "street" in which they were. Eventually one did.

As it passed them Worsel sprang into headlong, gliding flight, Kinnison's heavy knife in one gnarled fist. And as he sailed he struck—lethally. Before that luckless Delgonian's brain could radiate a single thought it was in no condition to function at all; for the head containing it was bouncing in the gutter. Worsel backed the peculiar conveyance along the curb and his two companions leaped into it, lying flat upon its floor and covering themselves from sight as best they could.

Worsel, familiar with things Delgonian and looking enough like a native of the planet to pass a casual inspection in the dark, drove the car. Streets and thoroughfares he traversed at reckless speed, finally drawing up before a long, low building; entirely dark. He scanned his surrounding with care, in every direction. Not a creature was in sight. "All is clear, friends," he thought, and the three adventurers sprang to the building's entrance. The door—it had a door, of sorts—was locked, but vanBuskirk's axe made short work of that difficulty. Inside, they braced the wrecked door against intrusion, then Worsel led the way into the unlighted interior. Soon he flashed his lamp about him and stepped upon a black, peculiarly-marked tile set into the floor, whereupon a harsh, white light illuminated the room.

"Cut it, before somebody takes alarm!" snapped Kinnison.

"No danger of that," replied the Velantian. "There are no windows in any of these rooms; no light can be seen from outside. This is the control room of the city's power plant. If you can convert any of this power to your uses, help yourselves to it. In this building is also a Delgonian arsenal. Whether or not anything in it can be of service to you is of course for you to say. I am now at your disposal."

Kinnison had been studying the panels and instruments. Now he and vanBuskirk tore open their armor—they had already learned that the atmosphere of Delgon, while not as wholesome for them as that in their suits, would for a time at least support human life—and wrought diligently with pliers, screw-drivers, and other tools of the electrician. Soon their exhausted batteries were upon the floor beneath the instrument panel, absorbing greedily the electrical fluid from the bus-bars of the Delgonians.

"Now, while they're getting filled up, let's see what these people use for guns. Lead on, Worsel!"

7

THE PASSING OF THE OVERLORDS

With worsel in the lead, the three interlopers hastened along a corridor, past branching and intersecting hallways, to a distant wing of the structure. There, it was evident, manufacturing of weapons was carried on; but a quick study of the queer-looking devices and mechanisms upon the benches and inside the storage racks lining the walls convinced Kinnison that the room could yield them nothing of permanent benefit. There were high-powered beam-projectors, it was true; but they were so heavy that they were not even semi-portable. There were also hand-weapons of various peculiar patterns, but without exception they were ridiculously inferior to the DeLameters of the Patrol in every respect of power, range, controllability, and storage capacity. Nevertheless, after testing them out sufficiently to make certain of the above findings, he selected an armful of the most powerful models and turned to his companions.

"Let's go back to the power room," he urged. "I'm nervous as a cat. I feel stark naked without my batteries; and if anyone should happen to drop in there and do away with them, we'd be sunk without a trace."

Loaded down with Delgonian weapons they hurried back the way they had come. Much to Kinnison's relief he found that his forebodings had been groundless; the batteries were still there, still absorbing myriawatt-hour after myriawatt-hour from the Delgonian generators. Staring fixedly at the innocuous-looking containers, he frowned in thought.

"Better we insulate those leads a little heavier and put the cans back in our armor," he suggested finally. "They'll charge just as well in place, and it doesn't stand to reason that this drain of power can go on for the rest of the night without *somebody* noticing it. And when that happens those Overlords are bound to take plenty of steps—none of which we have any idea what are going to be.''

''You must have power enough now so that we can all fly away from any possible trouble,'' Worsel suggested.

''But that's just exactly what we're *not* going to do!'' Kinnison declared, with finality. ''Now that we've found a good charger, we aren't going to leave it until our accumulators are chock-a-block. It's coming in faster than full draft will take it out, and we're going to get a full charge if we have to stand off all the vermin of Delgon to do it.''

Far longer than Kinnison had thought possible they were unmolested, but finally a couple of Delgonian engineers came to investigate the unprecedented shortage in the output of their completely automatic generators. At the entrance they were stopped, for no ordinary tools could force the barricade vanBuskirk had erected behind that portal. With leveled weapons the Patrolmen stood, awaiting the expected attack, but none developed. Hour by hour the long night wore away, uneventfully. At daybreak, however, a storming party appeared and massive battering rams were brought into play.

As the dull, heavy concussions reverberated throughout the building the Patrolmen each picked up two of the weapons piled before them and Kinnison addressed the Velantian.

''Drag a couple of those metal benches across that corner and coil up behind them,'' he directed. ''They'll be enough to ground any stray charges—if they can't see you they won't know you're here, so probably nothing much will come your way direct.''

The Velantian demurred, declaring that he would not hide while his two companions were fighting his battle, but Kinnison silenced him fiercely.

''Don't be a fool!'' the Lensman snapped. ''One of these beams would fry you to a crisp in ten seconds, but the defensive fields of our armor could neutralize a thousand of them, from now on. Do as I say, and do it quick, or I'll shock you unconscious and toss you in there myself!''

Realizing that Kinnison meant exactly what he said, and knowing that, unarmored as he was, he was utterly unable to resist either the Tellurian or their common foe, Worsel unwillingly erected his metallic barrier and coiled his sinuous length behind it. He hid himself just in time.

The outer barricade had fallen, and now a wave of reptilian forms flooded into the control room. Nor was this any ordinary investigation. The Overlords had studied the situation from afar, and this wave was one of heavily-armed—for Delgon—soldiery. On they came, projectors fiercely aflame; confident in their belief that nothing could stand before their blasts. But how wrong they were! The two repulsively erect bipeds before them neither burned nor fell. Beams, no matter how powerful, did not reach them at all, but spent themselves in crackingly incandescent fury, inches from their marks. Nor were these outlandish beings inoffensive. Utterly careless of the service-life of the pitifully weak Delgonian projectors, they were using them at maximum drain and at extreme aperture—and in the resultant beams the Delgonian soldier-slaves fell in scorched and smoking heaps. On came reserves, platoon after platoon, only and continuously to meet the same fate; for as soon as one projector weakened the invincibly armored man would toss it aside and pick up another. But finally the last commandeered weapon was exhausted and the beleaguered pair brought their own DeLameters—the most powerful portable weapons known to the military scientists of the Galactic Patrol—into play.

And what a difference! In *those* beams the attacking reptiles did not smoke or burn. They simply vanished in a blaze of flaming light, as did also the nearby walls and a good share of the building beyond! The Delgonian hordes having disappeared, vanBuskirk shut off his projector. Kinnison, however, left his on, angling its beam sharply upward; blasting into fiery vapor the ceiling and roof over their heads; remarking:

"While we're at it we might as well fix things so that we can make a quick get-away if we want to."

Then they waited. Waited, watching the needles of their meters creep ever closer to the "full-charge" marks; waited while, as they suspected, the distant, cowardly-hiding Overlords planned some other, more promising line of physical attack.

Nor was it long in developing. Another small army appeared, armored this time; or, more accurately, advancing behind metallic shields. Knowing what to expect, Kinnison was not surprised when the beam of his DeLameter not only failed to pierce one of those shields, but did not in any way impede the progress of the Delgonian column.

"Well, we're all done here, anyway, as far as I'm concerned," Kinnison grinned at the Dutchman as he spoke. "My cans've been showing full back pressure for the last two minutes. How about yours?"

"Same here," vanBuskirk reported, and the two leaped lightly into the Velantian's refuge. Then, inertialess all, the three shot into the air at such a pace that to the slow senses of the Delgonian slaves they simply disappeared. Indeed, it was not until the barrier had been blasted away and every room, nook, and cranny of the immense structure had been literally and minutely combed that the Delgonians—and through their enslaved minds the Overlords—became convinced that their prey had in some uncanny and unknown fashion eluded them.

Now high in air, the three allies traversed in a matter of minutes the same distance that had cost them so much time and strife the day before. Over the monster-infested forest they sped, over the deceptively peaceful green lushness of the jungle, to slant down toward Worsel's thought-proof tent. Inside that refuge they snapped off their thought screens and Kinnison yawned prodigiously.

"Working days and nights both is all right for a while, but it gets monotonous in time. Since this seems to be the only really safe spot on the planet, I suggest that we take a day or so off and catch up on our eats and sleeps."

They slept and ate; slept and ate again.

"The next thing on the program," Kinnison announced then, "is to clean out that den of Overlords. Then Worsel will be free to help us get going about our own business."

"You speak lightly indeed of the impossible," Worsel, all glum despondency, reproved him. "I have already explained why the task is, and must remain, beyond our power."

"Yes, but you don't quite grasp the possibilities of the stuff we've got now to work with," the Tellurian replied. "Listen: you could never do anything because you couldn't see through or work through your thought screens. Neither we nor you could, even now, enslave a Delgonian and make him lead us to the cavern, because the Overlords would know all about it 'way ahead of time and the slave would lead us anywhere else except to the cavern. However, one of us can cut his screen and surrender; possibly keeping just enough screen up to keep the enemy from possessing his mind fully enough to learn that the other two are coming along. The big question is—which of us is to surrender?"

"That is already decided," Worsel made instant reply. "I am the logical—in fact, the *only* one—to do it. Not only would they think it perfectly natural that they should overpower me, but also I am the only one of us three sufficiently able to control his thoughts as to keep from them the knowledge that I am being accompanied. Furthermore, you both know that it would not be good for your minds, unaccustomed as they are to the practice, to surrender their control voluntarily to an enemy."

"I'll say it wouldn't!" Kinnison agreed, feelingly. "I might do it if I had to, but I wouldn't like it and I don't think I'd ever quite get over it. I hate to put such a horrible job off onto you, Worsel, but you're undoubtedly the best equipped to handle it—and even you may have your hands full.''

"Yes . . .'' the Velantian said, thoughtfully. "While the undertaking is no longer an absolute impossibility, it is difficult . . . very. In any event you will probably have to beam me yourselves if we succeed in reaching the cavern . . . The Overlords will see to that. If so, do it without regret—know that I expect it and am well content to die in that fashion. Any one of my fellows would be only too glad to be in my place; meaning what it does to all Velantia. Know also that I have already reported what is to occur, and that your welcome to Velantia is assured, whether or not I accompany you there.''

"I don't think I'll have to kill you, Worsel," Kinnison replied, slowly, picturing in detail exactly what that steel-hard reptilian body would be capable of doing when, unshackled, its directing mind was completely taken over by an utterly soulless and conscienceless Overlord. "If you can't keep from going off the deep end, of course you'll get tough and I know you're mighty hard to handle. However, as I told you back there, I think I can beam you unconscious without killing you. I may have to burn off a few scales, but I'll try not to do any damage that can't be repaired.''

"If you can so stop me it will be wonderful indeed. Are we ready?''

They were ready. Worsel opened the door and in a moment was hurtling through the air, his giant wings arrowing him along at a pace no winged creature of Earth could even approach. And, following him easily at a little distance, floated the two Patrolmen upon their inertialess drives.

During that long flight scarcely a thought was exchanged, even between Kinnison and vanBuskirk. To direct a thought at the Velantian was of course out of the question. All lines of communication with him had been cut; and furthermore his mind, able as it was, was being taxed to the ultimate cell in doing what he had set out to do. And the two Patrolmen were reluctant to converse with each other, even upon their tight-beams, radios, or sounders, for fear that some slight leakage of thought-energy might reveal their presence to the everwatchful Overlords. If this opportunity were lost, they knew, another chance to wipe out that hellish horde might never present itself.

Land was traversed, and sea; but finally a stupendous range of mountains reared before them and Worsel, folding back his tireless wings, shot downward in a screaming, full-weight dive. In his line of flight Kinnison saw the mouth of a cave, a darker spot of blackness in the black rock of the mountain's side. Upon the ledged approach there lay a Delgonian—a guard or lookout, of course.

The Lensman's DeLameter was already in his hand, and at sight of the guardian reptile he sighted and fired in one fast motion. But, rapid as it was, it was still too slow—the Overlords had seen that the Velantian had companions of whom he had been able to keep them in ignorance theretofore.

Instantly Worsel's wings again began to beat, bearing him off at a wide angle; and, although the Patrolmen were insulated against his thought, the meaning of his antics was very plain. He was telling them in every possible way that the hole below was *not* the cavern of the Overlords; that it was over this way; that they were to keep on following him to it. Then, as they refused to follow him, he rushed upon Kinnison in mad attack.

"Beam him down, Kim!" vanBuskirk yelled. "Don't take any chances with that bird!" and leveled his own DeLameter.

"Lay off, Bus!" the Lensman snapped. "I can handle him—a lot easier out here than on the ground."

And so it proved. Inertialess as he was, the buffetings of the Velantian affected him not at all; and when Worsel coiled his supple body around him and began to apply pressure, Kinnison simply expanded his thought screen to cover them both, thus releasing the mind of his temporarily inimical friend from the Overlord's grip. Instantly the Velantian became himself, snapped on his own shield, and the three continued as one their interrupted downward course.

Worsel came to a halt upon the ledge, beside the practically incinerated corpse of the lookout; knowing, unarmored as he was, that to go further meant sudden death. The armored pair, however, shot on into the gloomy passage. At first they were offered no opposition—the Overlords had had no time to muster an adequate defense. Scattering handfuls of slaves rushed them, only to be blasted out of existence as their hand weapons proved useless against the armor of the Galactic Patrol. Defenders became more numerous as the cavern itself was approached, but neither were they allowed to stay the Patrolman's progress. Finally a palely shimmering barrier of metal appeared to bar their way. Its fields of force neutralized or absorbed the blasts of the DeLameters, but its material substance offered but little resistance to a thirty-pound sledge, swung by one of the strongest men ever produced by any planet colonized by the humanity of Earth.

Now they were in the cavern itself—the sanctum sanctorum of the Overlords of Delgon. There was the hellish torture screen; now licked clean of life. There was the audience which had been so avid, now milling about in a mob frenzy of panic. There, upon a raised balcony, were the "big shots" of this nauseous clan; now doing their utmost to marshal some force able to cope effectively with this unheard-of violation of their ages-old immunity.

A last wave of Delgonian slaves hurled themselves forward, futile projectors furiously aflame, only to disappear in the DeLameters' fans of force. The Patrolmen hated to kill those mindless slaves, but it was a nasty job that had to be done. The slaves out of the way, those ravening beams bored on into the massed Overlords.

And now Kinnison and vanBuskirk killed, if not joyously, at least relentlessly, mercilessly, and with neither sign nor sensation of compunction. For this unbelievably monstrous tribe needed killing, root and branch—not a scion or shoot of it should be allowed to survive, to continue to contaminate the civilization of the galaxy. Back and forth, to and fro, up and down swept the raging beams; playing on until in all the vast volume of that gruesome chamber nothing lived save the two grim figures in its portal.

Assured of this fact, but with DeLameters still in hand, the two destroyers retraced their way to the tunnel's mouth, where Worsel anxiously awaited them. Lines of communication again established, Kinnison informed the Velantian of all that had taken place and the latter gradually cut down the power of his thought-screen. Soon it was at zero strength and he reported jubilantly that for the first time in untold ages, the Overlords of Delgon were off the air!

"But surely the danger isn't over yet!" protested Kinnison. "We couldn't have got them all in this one raid. Some of them must have escaped, and there must be other dens of them on this planet somewhere?"

"Possibly, possibly;" the Velantian waved his tail airily—the first sign of joyousness he had shown. "But their power is broken, definitely and forever. With these new screens, and with the arms and armament which, thanks to you, we can now fabricate, the task of wiping them out completely will be comparatively simple. Now you will accompany me to Velantia; where, I assure you, the resources of the planet will be put solidly behind you in your own endeavors. I have already summoned a space-ship—in less than twelve days we will be back in Velantia and at work upon your projects. In the meantime . . ."

"Twelve *days!* Noshabkeming the Radiant!" vanBuskirk exploded, and Kinnison put in:

"Sure—you forget they haven't got free drive. We'd better hop over and get our lifeboat, I think. It's not so good, either way, but in our own boat we'll be open to detection less than an hour, as against twelve days in the Velantians'. And the pirates may be here any minute. It's as good as certain that their ship will be stopped and searched long before it gets back to Velantia, and if we were aboard it'd be just too bad.''

"And, since the crew knows about us, the pirates soon will, and it'll be just too bad, anyway," vanBuskirk reasoned.

"Not at all," interposed Worsel. "The few of my people who know of you have been instructed to seal that knowledge. I must admit, however, that I am greatly disturbed by your conceptions of these pirates of space. You see, until I met you I knew nothing more of the pirates than I did of your Patrol.''

"What a world!" vanBuskirk exclaimed. "No Patrol and no pirates! But at that, life might be simpler without both of them and without the free space-drive—more like it used to be in the good old airplane days that the novelists rave about.''

"Of course I could not judge as to that." The Velantian was very serious. "This in which we live seems to be an out-of-the-way section of the galaxy; or it may be that we have nothing the pirates want.''

"More likely it's simply that, like the Patrol, they haven't got organized into this district yet," suggested Kinnison. "There are so many thousands of millions of solar systems in the galaxy that it will probably be thousands of years yet before the Patrol gets into them all.''

"But about these pirates," Worsel went back to his point. "If they have such minds as those of the Overlords, they will be able to break the seals of our minds. However, I gather from your thoughts that their minds are not of that strength?''

"Not so far as I know," Kinnison replied. "You folks have the most powerful brains I ever heard of, short of the Arisians. And speaking of mental power, you can hear thoughts a lot farther than I can, even with my Lens or with this pirate receiver I've got. See if you can find out whether there are any pirates in space around here, will you?''

While the Velantian was concentrating, vanBuskirk asked:

"Why, if his mind is so strong, could the Overlords put him under so much easier than they could us 'weak-minded' human beings?''

"You are confusing 'mind' with 'will,' I think. Ages of submission to the Overlords made the Velantians' willpower zero, as far as the bosses were concerned. On the other hand, you and I could raise stubbornness to sell to most people. In fact, if the Overlords had succeeded in really breaking us down, back there, the chances are we'd have gone insane.''

"Probably you're right—we break, but don't bend, huh?" and the Velantian was ready to report.

"I have scanned space to the nearer stars—some eleven of your light-years—and have encountered no intruding entities," he announced.

"Eleven light-years—what a range!" Kinnison exclaimed. "However, that's only a shade over two minutes for a pirate ship at full blast. But we've got to take a chance sometime, and the quicker we get started the sooner we'll get back. We'll pick you up here, Worsel. No use in you going back to your tent—we'll be back here long before you could reach it. You'll be safe enough, I think, especially with our spare DeLameters. Let's get going, Bus!"

Again they shot into the air, again they traversed the airless depths of interplanetary space. To locate the temporary tomb of their lifeboat required only a few minutes, to disinter her only a few more. Then again they braved detection in the void; Kinnison tense at his controls, vanBuskirk in strained attention listening to and staring at his unscramblers and detectors. But the ether was still blank as the lifeboat struck Delgon's atmosphere; it remained blank while the lifeboat, inert, blasted frantically to match Worsel's intrinsic velocity.

"All right, Worsel, snap it up!" Kinnison called, and went on to vanBuskirk, "Now, you big, flat-footed Valerian spacehound, I hope that spaceman's god of yours will see to it our luck holds good for just fourteen minutes more. We've had more luck already than we had any right to expect, but we can put a little more to most God-awful good use!"

"Noshabkeming *does* bring spacemen luck," insisted the giant, grimacing a peculiar salute toward a small, golden image set inside his helmet, "and the fact that you warty, runty, atheistic little space-fleas of Tellus haven't got sense enough to know it—not even enough sense to really believe in your own gods, even Klono—doesn't change matters at all."

"That's tellin' 'em, Bus!" Kinnison applauded. "But if it helps charge your batteries, go to it . . . Ready to blast! Lift!"

The Velantian had come aboard, the tiny airlock was again tight, and the little vessel shot away from Delgon toward far Velantia. And still the ether remained empty as far as the detectors could reach. Nor was this fact surprising, in spite of the Lensman's fears to the contrary; for the Patrolmen had given the pirates such an extremely long line to cover that many days must yet elapse before the minions of Boskone would get around to visit that unimportant, unexplored, and almost unknown solar system. En route to his home planet Worsel got in touch with the crew of the Velantian vessel already in space, ordering them to return to port post-haste and instructing them in detail what to think and how to act should they be stopped and searched by one of Boskone's raiders. By the time these instructions had been given, Velantia loomed large beneath the flying midget. Then, with Worsel as guide, Kinnison drove over a mighty ocean upon whose opposite shore lay the great city in which Worsel lived.

"But I would like to have them welcome you as befits what you have done, and have you go to the Dome!" mourned the Velantian. "Think of it! You have done a thing which for ages the massed power of the planet has been trying vainly to accomplish, and yet you insist that I alone take credit for it!"

"I don't insist on any such thing," argued Kinnison, "even though it's practically all yours, anyway. I insist only on your keeping us and the Patrol out of it, and you know as well as I do why you've got to do that. Tell them anything else you want to. Say that a couple of pink-haired Chickladorians helped you and then beat it back home. *That* planet's far enough away so that if the pirates chase them they'll get a real run for their money. After this blows over you can tell the truth— but *not until then.*

"And as for us going to the Dome for a grand hocus-pocus, that is completely and definitely OUT. We're not going anywhere except to the biggest airport you've got. You're not going to give us anything except a lot of material and a lot of highly-trained help that can keep their thoughts sealed.

"We've got to build a lot of heavy stuff fast; and we've got to get started on it just as quick as Klono and Noshabkeming will let us!"

8

THE QUARRY STRIKES BACK

Worsel knew his council of scientists, as well he might; since it developed that he himself ranked high in that select circle. True to his promise, the largest airport of the planet was immediately emptied of its customary personnel, which was replaced the following morning by an entirely new group of workmen.

Nor were these replacements ordinarily laborers. They were young, keen, and highly trained; taken to a man from behind the thought-screens of the Scientists. It is true that they had no inkling of what they were to do, since none of them had ever dreamed of the possibility of such engines as they were to be called upon to construct.

But, on the other hand, they were well versed in the fundamental theories and operations of mathematics, and from pure mathematics to applied mechanics is but a step. Furthermore, they had *brains*; knew how to think logically, coherently, and effectively; and needed neither driving nor supervision—only instruction. And best of all, practically every one of the required mechanisms already existed, in miniature, within the *Brittania*'s lifeboat; ready at hand for their dissection, analysis, and enlargement. It was not lack of understanding which was to slow up the work; it was simply that the planet did not boast machine tools and equipment large enough or strong enough to handle the necessarily huge and heavy parts and members required.

While the construction of this heavy machinery was being rushed through, Kinnison and vanBuskirk devoted their efforts to the fabrication of an ultra-sensitive receiver, tunable to the pirates' scrambled wave-bands. With their exactly detailed knowledge, and with the cleverest technicians and the choicest equipment of Velantia at their disposal, the set was soon completed.

Kinnison was giving its exceedingly delicate coils their final alignment when Worsel wriggled blithely into the radio laboratory.

"Hi, Kimball Kinnison of the Lens!" he called gaily. Throwing a few yards of his serpent's body in lightning loops about a convenient pillar, he made a horizontal bar of the rest of himself and dropped one wing-tip to the floor. Then, nonchalantly upside down, he thrust out three or four eyes and curled their stalks over the Lensman's shoulder, the better to inspect the results of the mechanics' efforts. Gone was the morose, pessimistic, death-haunted Worsel entirely; gay, happy, care-free, and actually frolicsome—if you can imagine a thirty-foot-long, crocodile-headed, leather-winged python as being frolicsome!

"Hi, your royal snakeship!" Kinnison retorted in kind. "Still here, huh? Thought you'd be back on Delgon by this time, cleaning up the rest of that mess."

"The equipment is not ready, but there's no hurry about that," the playful reptile unwrapped ten or twelve feet of tail from the pillar and waved it airily about. "Their power is broken, their race is done. You are about to try out the new receiver?"

"Yes—going out after them right now," and Kinnison began deftly to manipulate the micrometric verniers of his dials.

Eyes fixed upon meters and gauges, he listened . . . listened. Increased his power and listened again. More and more power he applied to his apparatus, listening continually. Suddenly he stiffened, his hands becoming rock-still. He listened, if possible even more intently than before; and as he listened his face grew grim and granite-hard. Then the micrometers began again crawlingly to move, as though he were tracing a beam.

"Bus! Hook on the focusing beam-antenna!" he snapped. "It's going to take every milliwatt of power we've got in this hookup to tap his beam, but I think I've got Helmuth direct instead of through a pirate-ship relay!"

Again and again he checked the readings of his dials and of the directors of his antenna; each time noting the exact time of the Velantian day.

"There! As soon as we get some time, Worsel, I'd like to work out these figures with some of your astronomers. They'll give me a right line through Helmuth's headquarters—I hope. Some day, if I'm spared, I'll get another!"

"What kind of news did you get, chief?" asked vanBuskirk.

"Good and bad both," replied the Lensman. "Good in that Helmuth doesn't believe that we stayed with his ship as long as we did. He's a suspicious devil, you know, and is pretty well convinced that we tried to run the same kind of a blazer on him that we did the other time. Since he hasn't got enough ships on the job to work the whole line, he's concentrating on the other end. That means that we've got plenty of days left yet. The bad part of it is that they've got four of our boats already and are bound to get more. Lord, how I wish I could call the rest of them! Some of them could certainly make it here before they got caught."

"Might I then offer a suggestion?" asked Worsel, of a sudden diffident.

"Surely!" the Lensman replied in surprise. "Your ideas have never been any kind of poppycock. Why so bashful all at once?"

"Because this one is so . . . ah . . . so peculiarly personal, since you men regard so highly the privacy of your minds. Our two sciences, as you have already observed, are vastly different. You are far beyond us in mechanics, physics, chemistry, and the other applied sciences. We, on the other hand, have delved much deeper than you have into psychology and the other introspective studies. For that reason I know positively that the Lens you wear is capable of enormously greater things than you are at present able to make it perform. Of course I cannot use your Lens directly, since it is attuned to your own ego. However, if the idea appeals to you, I could, with your consent, occupy your mind and use your Lens to put you en rapport with your fellows. I have not volunteered the suggestion before because I know how averse your mind is to any foreign control."

"Not necessarily to foreign control," Kinnison corrected him. "Only to *enemy* control. The idea of friendly control never even occurred to me. That would be an entirely different breed of cats. Go to it!"

Kinnison relaxed his mind completely, and that of the Velantian came welling in; wave upon friendly, surging wave of benevolent power. And not only—or not precisely—power. It was more than power; it was a dynamic poignancy, a vibrant penetrance, a depth and clarity of perception that Kinnison in his most cogent moments had never dreamed a possibility. The possessor of that mind knew things, cameo-clear in microscopic detail, which the keenest minds of Earth could perceive only as chaotically indistinct masses of mental light and shade, of no recognizable pattern whatever!

"Give me the thought-pattern of him with whom you wish first to converse," came Worsel's thought, this time from deep within the Lensman's own brain.

Kinnison felt a subtle thrill of uneasiness at that new and ultra-strange dual personality, but thought back steadily: "Sorry—I can't."

"Excuse me, I should have known that you cannot think in our patterns. Think, then, of him as a person—as an individual. That will give me, I believe, sufficient data.''

Into the Earthman's mind there leaped a picture of Henderson, sharp and clear. He felt his Lens actually tingle and throb as a concentration of vital force such as he had never known poured through his whole being and into that almost-living creation of the Arisians; and immediately thereafter he was in full mental communication with the Master Pilot! And there, seated across the tiny mess-table of their lifeboat, was LaVerne Thorndyke, the Master Technician.

Henderson came to his feet with a yell as the telepathic message bombshelled into his brain, and it required several seconds to convince him that he was not the victim of space-insanity or suffering from any other form of hallucination. Once convinced, however, he acted—his lifeboat shot toward far Velantia at maximum blast.

Then: "Nelson! Allerdyce! Thompson! Jenkins! Uhlenhuth! Smith! Chatway! . . ." Kinnison called the roll.

Nelson, the specialist in communications, answered his captain's call. So did Allerdyce, the juggling quartermaster. So did Uhlenhuth, a technician. So did those in three other boats. Two of these three were apparently well within the danger zone and might get nipped in their dash, but their crews elected without hesitation to take the chance. Four boats, it was already known, had been captured by the pirates. The others . . .

"Only eight boats," Kinnison mused. "Not so good—but it could have been a lot worse—they might have got us all by this time—and maybe some of them are just out of our reach." Then, turning to the Velantian, who had withdrawn his mind as soon as the job was done:

"Thanks, Worsel," he said simply. "Some of those lads coming in have got plenty of just what it takes, and *how* we can use them!"

One by one the lifeboats made port, where their crews were welcomed briefly but feelingly before they were put to work. Nelson, one of the last pair to arrive, was particularly welcome.

"Nels, we need you badly," Kinnison informed him as soon as greetings had been exchanged. "The pirates have a beam, carrying a peculiarly scrambled signal, that they can receive and decode through any ordinary kind of blanketing interference, and you're the best man we've got to study their system. Some of these Velantian scientists can probably help you a lot on that—any race that can develop a screen against thought figures ought to know more than somewhat about vibration in general. We've got working models of the pirates' instruments, so you can figure out their patterns and formulas. When you've done that, I want you and your Velantians to design something that will scramble all the pirates' communicator beams in space, as far as you can reach. If you can fix things so they can't talk, any more than we can, it'll help a lot, believe me!''

"QX, Chief, we'll give it the works," and the radio man called for tools, apparatus, and electricians.

Then throughout the great airport the many Velantians and the handful of Patrolmen labored mightily, side by side, and to very good effect indeed. Slowly the port became ringed about by, and studded everywhere with, monstrous mechanisms. Everywhere there were projectors: refractory-throated demons ready to vomit forth every force known to the expert technicians of the Patrol. There were absorbers, too, backed by their bleeder resistors, air-gaps, ground-rods, and racks for discharged accumulators. There, too, were receptors and converters for the cosmic energy which was to empower many of the devices. There were, of course, atomic motor-generators by the score, and battery upon battery of gigantic accumulators. And Nelson's high-powered scrambler was ready to go to work.

These machines appeared crude, rough, unfinished; for neither time nor labor had been wasted upon non-essentials. But inside each one the moving parts fitted with micrometric accuracy and with hair-spring balance. All, without exception, functioned perfectly.

At Worsel's call, Kinnison climbed up out of a great beam-proof pit, the top of whose wall was practically composed of tractor-beam projectors. Pausing only to make sure that a sticking switch on one of the screen-dome generators had been replaced, he hurried to the heavily armored control room, where his little force of fellow Patrolmen awaited him.

"They're coming, boys," he announced. "You all know what to do. There are a lot more things we could have done if we'd had more time, but as it is we'll just go to work on them with what we've got," and Kinnison, again all brisk Captain, bent over his instruments.

In the ordinary course of events the pirate would have flashed up to the planet with spy-rays out and issuing a preemptory demand for the planet to show a clean bill of health or to surrender instantly such fugitives as might lately have landed upon it. But Kinnison did not—could not—wait for that. The spy-rays, he knew, would reveal the presence of his armament; and such armament most certainly did not belong to this planet. Therefore he acted first, and everything happened practically at once.

A tracer lashed out, the pilot-ray of the rim-battery of extraordinarily powerful tractors. Under their terrific pull the inertialess ship flashed toward their center of action. At the same moment there burst into activity Nelson's scrambler, a dome-screen against cosmic-energy intake, and a full circle of super-powered projectors.

All these things occurred in the twinkling of an eye, and the vessel was being slowed down by the atmosphere of Velantia before her startled commander could even realize that he was being attacked. Only the automatically-reacting defensive screens saved that ship from instant destruction; but they did so save it and in seconds the pirates' every weapon was furiously ablaze.

In vain. The defenses of that pit could take it. They were driven by mechanisms easily able to absorb the output of any equipment mountable upon a mobile base, and to his consternation the pirate found that his cosmic-energy intake was at, and remained at, zero. He sent out call after call for help, but could not make contact with any other pirate station—ether and sub-ether alike were closed to him, his signals were blanketed completely. Nor could his drivers, even though operating at ruinous overload, move him from the geometrical center of that incandescently flaming pit, so inconceivably rigid were the tractors' clamps upon him.

And soon his power began to fail. His vessel, designed to operate upon cosmic-energy intake, carried only enough accumulators for stablization of power-flow, an amount ridiculously inadequate for a combat as profligate of energy as this. But strangely enough, as his defenses weakened, so lessened the power of the attack. It was no part of the Lensman's plan to destroy this superdreadnaught of the void.

"That was one good thing about the old *Brittania*," he gritted, as he cut down step by step the power of his beams, "what power she had, nobody could block her off from!"

Soon the stored-up energy of the battleship was exhausted and she lay there, quiescent. Then giant pressers went into action and she was lifted over the wall of the pit, to settle down in an open space beside it—open, but still under the domes of force.

Kinnison had no needle-rays as yet, the time at his disposal having been sufficient only for the construction of the absolutely essential items of equipment. Now, while he debated with his fellows as to what part of the vessel to destroy in order to wipe out its crew, the pirates themselves ended the debate. Ports yawned in the vessel's side and they came out fighting.

For they were not a breed to die like rats in a trap, and they knew that to remain inside their vessel was to die whenever and however their captors willed. They knew also that die they must if they could not conquer. Their surrender, even if it should be accepted, would mean only a somewhat later death in the lethal chambers of the Law. In the open, they could at least take some of their foes with them.

Furthermore, not being men as we know men, they had nothing in common with either human beings or Velantians. Both to them were vermin, as they themselves were to the beings manning this surprisingly impregnable fortress here in this waste corner of the galaxy. Therefore, space-hardened veterans all, they fought, with the insane ferocity and desperation of the ultimately last stand; but they did not conquer. Instead, and to the last man, they died.

As soon as the battle was over, before the interference blanketing the pirates' communicators was cut off, Kinnison went through the captured vessel, destroying the headquarters visiplates and every automatic sender which could transmit any kind of a message to any pirate base. Then the interference was stopped, the domes were released, and the ship was removed from the field of operations. Then, while Thorndyke and his reptilian aides—themselves now radio experts of no mean attainments—busied themselves at installing a high-powered scrambler aboard her, Kinnison and Worsel scanned space in search of more prey. Soon they found it, more distant than the first one had been—two solar systems away—and in an entirely different direction. Tracers and tractors and interference and domes of force again became the order of the day. Projectors again raved out in their incandescent might, and soon another immense cruiser of the void lay beside her sister ship. Another, and another; then for a long time space was blank.

The Lensman then energized his ultra-receiver, pointing his antenna carefully into the galatic line to Helmuth's base, as laid down for him by the Velantian astronomers. Again, so tight and hard was Helmuth's beam, he had to drive his apparatus so unmercilly that the tube-noise almost drowned out the signals, but again he was rewarded by hearing faintly the voice of the pirate Director of Operations:

". . . four vessels, all within or near one of those five solar systems, have ceased communicating; each cessation being accompanied by a period of blanketing interference of a pattern never before registered. You two vessels who are receiving these orders are instructed to investigate that region with the utmost care. Go with screens out and everything on the trips, and with automatic recorders set on me here. It is not believed that the Patrol has anything to do with this, as ability has been shown transcending anything it has been known to possess. As a working hypothesis it is assumed that one of the solar systems, hitherto practically unexplored and unknown, is in reality the seat of a highly advanced race, which perhaps has taken offense at the attitude or conduct of our first ship to visit them. Therefore proceed with extreme caution, with a thorough spy-ray search at extreme range before approaching at all. If you land, use tact and diplomacy instead of the customary tactics. Find out whether our ships and crews have been destroyed, or are only being held: and remember, automatic reporters on me at all times. Helmuth speaking for Boskone—off!''

For minutes Kinnison manipulated his controls in vain—he could not get another sound.

"What are you trying to get, Kim?" asked Thorndyke. "Wasn't that enough?"

"No, that's only half of it," Kinnison returned. "Helmuth's nobody's fool. He's certainly trying to plot the boundaries of our interference, and I want to see how he's coming out with it. But no dice. He's so far away and his beam's so hard I can't work him unless he happens to be talking almost directly toward us. Well, it won't be long now until we'll give him some real interference to plot. Now let's see what we can do about those two other ships that are heading this way."

Carefully as those two ships investigated, and sedulously as they sought to obey Helmuth's instructions, all their precautions amounted to exactly nothing. As ordered, they began to spy-ray survey at extreme range; but even at that range Kinnison's tracers were effective and those pirates also ceased communicating in a blaze of interference. Then recent history repeated itself. The details were changed somewhat, since there were two vessels instead of one; but the pit was of ample size to accommodate two ships, and the tractors could hold two as well and as rigidly as one. The conflict was a little longer, the beaming a little hotter and more coruscant, but the ending was the same. Scramblers and other special appartus were installed and Kinnison called his men together.

"We're about ready to shove off again. Running away has worked twice so far and should work once more, if we can ring in enough variations on the theme to keep Helmuth guessing a while longer. Maybe, if the supply of pirate ships holds up, we can make Helmuth furnish us transportation clear back to Prime Base!

"Here's the idea. We've got six ships, and enough Velantians have volunteered to man them—in spite of the fact that they probably won't get back. Six ships, of course, isn't enough of a task force to fight its way through Helmuth's fleets; so we'll spread out, covering plenty of parsecs and broadcasting every watt of interference we can put out, in as many different shapes and sizes as our generators can figure. We won't be able to talk to each other, but nobody else can talk, either, anywhere near us, and that ought to give us a chance. Each ship will be on its own, like we were before, in the boats; the big difference being that we'll be in superdreadnaughts.

"Question—should we split up again or stick together? We'd better all go in one ship, I think—with spools aboard the others, of course. What do you think?"

They agreed with him to a man and he directed a thought at the Velantian.

"Now, Worsel, about you fellows here—you probably won't have it so easy, either. Sooner or later—and sooner would be my guess—Helmuth's boys will be coming to see you. In force and cocked and primed and with blood in their eyes. It'll be a battle, not a slaughter."

"Let them come, in whatever force they care to bring. The more who attack here, the less there will be to halt your progress. This armament represents the best of that possessed by both your Patrol and the pirates, with improvements developed by your scientists and ours in full cooperation. We understand thoroughly its construction, operation, and maintenance. You may rest assured that the pirates will never levy tribute upon us, and that any pirate visiting this system will remain in it—permanently!"

"At-a-snake, Worsel—long may you wiggle!" Kinnison exclaimed. Then, more seriously, "Maybe, after this is all over, I'll see you again sometime. If not, goodbye. Good-bye, all Velantia. All set, everybody? Clear ether—blast off!"

Six ships, one pirate craft, now vessels of the Galactic Patrol, hurled themselves into and through Velantian air; into and through interplanetary space; out into the larger, wider, opener emptiness of the interstellar void. Six ships, each broadcasting with prodigious power and volume an all-inclusive interference through which not even a CRX tracer could be driven.

9

BREAKDOWN

Kimball Kinnison sat at the controls, smoking a rare festive cigarette and smiling; at peace with the entire universe. For this new picture was in every element a different one from the old. Instead of being in a pitifully weak and defenseless lifeboat, skulking and hiding, he was in one of the most powerful battleships afloat, driving boldly at full blast almost directly toward home. While the Patrolmen were so terribly few in number that most of them had to work double shifts—Kinnison and Henderson had to do all the piloting and navigating—they had under them a full crew of alert and highly-trained Velantians. And the enemy, instead of being a close-knit group, keeping Helmuth informed moment by moment of the situation and instantly responsive to his orders, were now entirely out of communication with each other and with their head-quarters; groping helplessly. Literally as well as figuratively the pirates were in the dark; the absolute blackness of interstellar space.

Thorndyke entered the room, frowning slightly. "You look like the fabled Cheshire cat, Kim. I hate to spoil such perfect bliss, but I'm here to tell you that we ain't out of the woods yet, by seven thousand rows of big, green, peppermint trees."

"Maybe not," the Lensman returned blithely, "but compared to the jam we were in a little while back we're not only sitting on top of the world; we're perched right on the exact apex of the universe. They can't send or receive reports or orders, and they can't communicate. Even their detectors are mighty lame—you know how far they can get on electromagnetics and visual apparatus. Furthermore, there isn't an identification number, symbol, or name on the outside of this buzz-buggy. If it ever had one the friction and attrition have worn it off, clear down to the armor. What can happen that we can't cope with?"

"These engines can happen," the technician responded, bluntly. "The Bergenholm is developing a meter-jump that I don't like a little bit."

"Does she knock? Or even tick?" demanded Kinnison.

"Not yet," Thorndyke confessed, reluctantly.

"How big a jump?"

"Pretty near two thousandths maximum. Average a thousandth and a half."

"That's hardly a wiggle on the recorder line. Drivers run for months with bigger jumps than that."

"Yeah—drivers. But of all the troubles anybody ever had with Bergenholms, a meter-kick was never one of them, and that's what's got me guessing as to the whichness of the why. I'm not trying to scare you—yet. I'm just telling you."

The machine referred to was the neutralizer of inertia, the sine qua non of interstellar speed, and it was not to be wondered at that the slightest irregularity in its performance was to the technician a matter of grave concern. Day after day passed, however, and the huge converter continued to function; taking in and sending out its wonted torrents of power. It developed not even a tick, and the meter-jump did not grow worse. And during those days they put an inconceivable distance behind them.

During all this time their visual instruments remained blank; to all optical apparatus space was empty save for the normal tenancy of celestial bodies. From time to time something invisible or beyond the range of vision registered upon one of the electromagnet detectors, but so slow were these instruments that nothing came of their signals. In fact, by the time the warnings were recorded, the objects causing the disturbance were probably far astern.

One day, however, the Bergenholm quit—cold. There was no laboring, no knocking, no heating up, no warning at all. One instant the ship was speeding along in free flight, the next she was lying inert in space. Practically motionless, for any possible velocity built up by inert acceleration is scarcely a crawl, as free space-speeds go.

Then the whole crew labored like mad. As soon as they had the massive covers off, Thorndyke scanned the interior of the machine and turned to Kinnison.

"I think we can patch her up, but it'll take quite a while. Maybe you'd be of more use in the control room—this ain't quite as safe as church, is it, lying here inert?"

"Most of the stuff is on automatic trip, but maybe I'd better keep an eye on things, at that. Let me know occasionally how you're getting along," and the Lensman went back to his controls—none too soon.

For one pirate ship was already beaming him viciously. Only the fact that his defensive armament was upon its automatic trips had saved the stolen battleship from practically instantaneous destruction. And as the surprised Lensman began to check his other instruments another space-ship flashed into being upon his other side and also went to work.

As Kinnison had already remarked more than once, Helmuth was far from being a fool, and that new and amazingly effective blanketing of his every means of communication was a problem whose solution was of paramount importance. Almost every available ship had been for days upon the fringe of that interference; observing and reporting continuously. So rapidly was it moving, however, so peculiar was its apparent shape, and so contradictory were the directional readings obtained, that Helmuth's computers had been baffled.

Then Kinnison's Bergenholm failed and his ship went inert. In a space of minutes the location of one center of interference was known. Its coordinates were determined and half a dozen warships were ordered to rush that spot. The raider first to arrive had signalled, visually and audibly; then, obtaining no response, had anchored with a tractor and had loosed his bolts. Nor would the result have been different had everyone aboard, instead of no one, been in the control room at the time of the signalling. Kinnison could have read the messages, but neither he nor anyone else then aboard the erstwhile pirate craft could have answered them in kind.

The two space-ships attacking the turncoat became three, and still the Lensman sat unworried at his board. His meters showed no dangerous overload; his noble craft was taking everything her sister-ships could send.

Then Thorndyke stepped into the room, no longer a natty officer of space. Instead, he was stripped to sweat-soaked undershirt and overalls, he was covered with grease and grime, and what of his thickly smeared face was visible was almost haggard with fatigue. He opened his mouth to say something, then snapped it shut as his eye was caught by a flaring visiplate.

"Holy Klono's claws!" he exclaimed, "At us already? Why didn't you yell?"

"How much good would that have done?" Kinnison wanted to know. "Of course, if I had known that you were loafing on the job and could have snapped it up a little, I would have. But there's no particular hurry about this. It'll take at least four of them to break us down, and I was hoping you'd have us travelling before they overload us. What was on your mind?''

''I came up here—One, to tell you that we're ready to blast; Two, to suggest that you hit her easy at first; and Three, to ask if you know where there's any grease-soap. But you can cancel Two and Three. We don't want to play around with these boys much longer—they play too rough—and I ain't going to wash up until I see whether she holds together or not. Blast away—and won't those guys be surprised!''

''I'll say so—some of this stuff is NEW!''

The Lensman twirled a couple of knobs, then punched down hard upon three buttons. As he did so the flaring plates became dark; they were again alone in space. To the dumbfounded pirates it was as though their prey had slipped off into the fourth dimension. Their tractors gripped nothing whatever; their ravening beams bored unimpeded through the space occupied an instant before by resisting screens; tracers were useless. They did not know what had happened, or how, and they could neither report to nor be guided by the master mind of Boskone.

For minutes Thorndyke, vanBuskirk, and Kinnison waited tensely for they knew not what to happen; but nothing happened and then the tension gradually relaxed.

''What was the matter with it?'' Kinnison asked, finally.

''Overloaded,'' was Thorndyke's terse reply.

''Overloaded—hooey!'' snapped the Lensman. ''How *could* they overload a Bergenholm? And, even if they could, why in all the nine hells of Valeria would they want to?''

''They *could* do it easily enough, in just the way they *did* do it; by banking accumulators onto it in series-parallel. As to why, I'll let you do the guessing. With no load on the Bergenholm you've got full inertia, with full load you've got zero inertia—you can't go any further. It looks just plain dumb to me. But then, I think all pirates are short a few jets somewhere—if they weren't they wouldn't be pirates.''

''I don't know whether you're right or not. Hope so, but afraid not. Personally, I don't believe these folks are pirates at all, in the ordinary sense of the word.''

''Huh? What are they, then?''

''Piracy implies similarity of culture, I would think,'' the Lensman said, thoughtfully. ''Ordinary pirates are usually renegades, deficient somehow, as you suggested; rebelling against a constituted authority which they themselves have at one time acknowledged and of which they are still afraid. That pattern doesn't fit into this matrix at all, anywhere.''

"So what? Now I say 'hooey' right back at you. Anyway, why worry about it?"

"Not worrying about it exactly, but somebody has got to do something about it, or else . . ."

"I don't like to think; it makes my head ache," interrupted van-Buskirk. "Besides, we're getting away from the Bergenholm."

"You'll get a real headache there," laughed Kinnison, "because I'll bet a good Tellurian beefsteak that the pirates were trying to set up a negative inertia when they overloaded the Bergenholm; and thinking about that state of matter is enough to make *anybody's* head ache!"

"I knew that some of the dippier Ph.D.'s in higher mechanics have been speculating about it," Thorndyke offered, "but it can't be done that way, can it?"

"Nor any other way that anybody has tried yet, and if such a thing is possible the results may prove really startling. But you two had better shove off, you're dead from the neck up. The Berg's spinning like a top—as smooth as that much green velvet. You'll find a can of soap in my locker, I think."

"Maybe she'll hold together long enough for us to get some sleep." The technician eyed a meter dubiously, although its needle was not wavering a hair's breadth from the green line. "But I'll tell the cockeyed Universe that we gave her a jury rigging if there ever was one. You can't depend on it for an hour until after it's been pulled and gone over; and that, you know as well as I do, takes a real shop, with plenty of equipment: If you take my advice you'll sit down somewhere while you can and as soon as you can. That Bergenholm is in bad shape, believe me. We can hold her together for a while by main strength and awkwardness, but before very long she's going out for keeps—and when she does you don't want to find yourself fifty years from a machine shop instead of fifty minutes."

"I'll say not," the Lensman agreed. "But on the other hand, we don't want those birds jumping us the minute we land, either. Let's see, where are we? And where are the bases? Um . . . um . . . Sector bases are white rings, you know, sub-sector bases red stars . . ." Three heads bent over charts.

"The nearest red-star marker seems to be in System 240-16-37," Kinnison finally announced. "Don't know the name of the planet— never been there . . ."

"Too far," interrupted Thorndyke. "We'll never make it—might as well try direct for Prime Base on Tellus. If you can't find a red closer than that, look for an orange or a yellow."

"Bases of any kind seem to be scarce around here," the Lensman commented. "You'd think they'd be thicker. Here's a violet triangle, but that wouldn't help us—just an outpost.... How about this blue square? It's just about on our line to Tellus, and I can't see anything any better that we can possibly reach."

"That looks like our best bet," Thorndyke concurred, after a few minutes of study. "It's probably several breakdowns away, but maybe we can make it—sometime. Blues are pretty low-grade space-ports, but they've got tools, anyway. What's the name of it, Kim—or is it only a number?"

"It's that very famous planet, Trenco," the Lensman announced, after looking up the reference numbers in the atlas.

"*Trenco!*" exclaimed Thorndyke in disgust. "The nuttiest dopiest, wooziest planet in the galaxy—we *would* draw something like that to sit down on for repairs, wouldn't we? Well, I'm on plus time for sleep. Call me if we go inert before I wake up, will you?"

"I sure will; and I'll try to figure out a way of getting down to ground without bringing all the pirates in space along with us."

Then Henderson came in to stand his watch, Kinnison slept, and the mighty Bergenholm continued to hold the vessel inertialess. In fact, all the men were thoroughly rested and refreshed before the expected breakdown came. And when it did come they were more or less prepared for it. The delay was not sufficiently long to enable the pirates to find them again; but from that point in space to the ill-famed planet which was their destination, progress was one long series of hops.

The sweating, grunting, swearing engineers made one seemingly impossible repair after another, by dint of what dodge, improvisation, and makeshift only the fertile brain of LaVerne Thorndyke ever did know. The Master Technician, one of the keenest and most highly trained engineers of the whole Solarian System, was not used to working with his hands. Although young in years, he was wont to use only his head, in directing the labors and the energies of others.

Nevertheless, he was now working like a stevedore. He was permanently grimy and greasy—their one can of mechanics' soap had been used up long since—his finger-nails were black and broken, his hands and face were burned, blistered, and cracked. His muscles ached and shrieked at the unaccustomed effort, until now they were on the build. But through it all he had stuck uncomplainingly, even buoyantly, to his task. One day, during an interlude of free flight, he strode into the control-room and glanced at the course-plotting goniometer, then started into the "tank."

"Still on the original course, I see. Have you got anything doped out yet?"

"Nothing very good, that's why I'm staying on this course until we reach the point closest to Trenco. I've figured until my alleged brain backfired on me, and here's all I can get:

"I've been shrinking and expanding our interference zone, changing its shape as much as I could, and cutting it off entirely now and then; to cross up their surveyors as much as I could. When we come to the jumping-off place we'll simply cut off everything that is sending out traceable vibrations. The Berg will have to run, of course, but it doesn't radiate much and we can ground out practically all of that. The drive is the bad feature—it looks as though we'll have to cut down to where we can ground out the radiation."

"How about the flare?" Thorndyke took the inevitable slide-rule from a pocket of his overalls.

"I've already had the Velantians build us some baffles—we've got lots of spare tantalum, tungsten, carballoy, and refractory, you know— just in case we should want to use them."

"Radiation . . . detection . . . decrement . . . cosine squared theta . . . um . . . call it point zero zero three eight," the engineer mumbled, squinting at his "slip-stick." "Times half a million . . . about nineteen hundred lights will have to be tops. Mighty slow, but we would get there sometime—maybe. Now about the baffles," and he went into another bout of computation during which could be distinguished a few such words as "temperature . . . inert corpuscles . . . velocity . . . fusion-point . . . Weinberger's Constant. . . ." Then:

"It figures that at about eighteen hundred lights your baffles go out," he announced. "Pretty close check with the radiation limit. QX, I guess—but I shudder to think of what we may have to do to that Bergenholm to hold it together that long."

"It's not so hot. I don't think much of the scheme myself," admitted Kinnison frankly. "Probably you can think up something better before. . . ."

"Who, me? What with?" Thorndyke interrupted, with a laugh. "Looks to me like our best bet—anyway, ain't you the master mind of this outfit? Blast off!"

Thus it came about that, long later, the Lensman cut off his interference, cut off his driving power, cut off every mechanism whose operation generated vibrations which would reveal to enemy detectors the location of his cruiser. Space-suited mechanics emerged from the stern lock and fitted over the still white-hot vents of the driving projectors the baffles they had previously built.

It is of course well known that all ships of space are propelled by the inert projection, by means of high-potential static fields, of nascent fourth-order particles or "corpuscles," which are formed, inert, inside the inertialess projector, by the conversion of some form of energy into matter. This conversion liberates some heat, and a vast amount of light. This light, or "flare," shining as it does directly upon and through the highly tenuous gas formed by the projected corpuscles, makes of a speeding space-ship one of the most gorgeous spectacles known to man; and it was this very spectacular effect that Kinnison and his crew must do away with if their bold scheme were to have any chance at all of success.

The baffles were in place. Now, instead of shooting out in tell-tale luminescence, the light was shut in—but so, alas, was approximately three percent of the heat. And the generation of heat *must* be cut down to a point at which the radiation-equilibrium temperature of the baffles would be below the point of fusion of the refractories of which they were composed. This would cut down their speed tremendously; but on the other hand, they were practically safe from detection and would reach Trenco eventually—if the Bergenholm held out.

Of course there was still the chance of visual or electromagnetic detection, but that chance was vanishingly small. The proverbial task of finding a needle in a haystack would be an easy one indeed, compared to that of seeing in a telescope or upon visiplate or magneplate a dead-black, lightless ship in the infinity of space. No, the Bergenholm was their great, their only concern; and the engineers lavished upon that monstrous fabrication of metal a devotion to which could be likened only that of a corps of nurses attending the ailing baby of a multi-millionaire.

This concentration of attention did get results. The engineers still found it necessary to sweat and to grunt and to swear, but they did somehow keep the thing running—most of the time. Nor were they detected—then.

For the attention of the pirate high command was very much taken up with that fast-moving, that ever-expanding, that peculiarly-fluctuating volume of interference; utterly enigmatic as it was and impenetrable to their every instrument of communcation. In that system was the Prime Base of the Galactic Patrol. Therefore it *was* the Lensman's work—undoubtedly the same Lensman who had conquered one of their super-ships and, after having learned its every secret, had escaped in a lifeboat through the fine-meshed net set to catch him! And, piling Ossa upon Pelion, this same Lensman had—*must* have—captured ship after un-conquerable ship of their best and was even now sailing calmly home with them! It was intolerable, unbearable, an insult that could not and would not be borne.

Therefore, using as tools every pirate ship in that sector of space, Helmuth and his computers and navigators were slowly but grimly solving the equations of motion of that volume of interference. Smaller and smaller became the uncertainties. Then ship after ship bored into the subethereal murk, to match course and velocity with, and ultimately to come to grips with, each focus of disturbance as it was determined.

Thus in a sense and although Kinnison and his friends did not then know it, it was only the failure of the Bergenholm that was to save their lives, and with those lives our present Civilization.

Slowly, hatingly, and, for reasons already given, undetected, Kinnison made pitiful progress toward Trenco; cursing impatiently and impartially his ship, the crippled generator, its designer and its previous operators as he went. But at long last Trenco loomed large beneath them and the Lensman used his Lens.

"Lensman of Trenco space-port, or any other Lensman within call!" he sent out clearly. "Kinnison of Tellus—Sol III—calling. My Bergenholm is almost out and I must sit down at Trenco space-port for repairs. I have avoided the pirates so far, but they may be either behind me or ahead of me, or both. What is the situation there?"

"I fear that I can be of no help," came back a weak thought, without the customary identification. "I am out of control. However, Tregonsee is in the . . . "

Kinnison felt a poignant, unbearably agonizing mental impact that jarred him to the very core: a shock that, while of sledge-hammer force, was still of such a keenly penetrant timbre that it almost exploded every cell of his brain. It seemed as though some mighty fist, armed with yard-long needles, had slugged an actual blow into the most vitally sensitive nerve-centers of his being.

Communication ceased, and the Lensman knew, with a sick, shuddering certainty, that while in the very act of talking to him a Lensman had died.

10

TRENCO

Judged by any earthly standards the planet Trenco was—and is—a peculiar one indeed. Its atmosphere, which is not air, and its liquid, which is not water, are its two outstanding peculiarities and the sources of most of its others. Almost half of that atmosphere and by far the greater part of the liquid phase of the planet is a substance of extremely low latent heat of vaporization, with a boiling-point such that during the daytime it is a vapor and at night a liquid. To make matters worse, the other constituents of Trenco's gaseous envelope are of very feeble blanketing power, low specific heat, and of high permeability, so that its days are intensely hot and its nights are bitterly cold.

At night, therefore, it rains. Words are entirely inadequate to describe to anyone who has never been there just how it does rain during Trenco's nights. Upon Earth one inch of rainfall in an hour is a terrific downpour. Upon Trenco that amount of precipitation would scarcely be considered a mist; for along the equatorial belt, in less than thirteen Tellurian hours, it rains exactly forty-seven feet and five inches every night—no more no less, each and every night of every year.

Also there is lightning. Not in Terra's occasional flashes, but in one continuous, blinding glare which makes night as we know it unknown there; in nerve-wracking, battering, sense-destroying discharges which make ether and sub-ether alike impenetrable to any ray or signal short of a full-driven power beam. The days are practically as bad. The lightning is not violent then, but the bombardment of Trenco's monstrous sun, through that outlandishly peculiar atmosphere, produces almost the same effect.

Because of the difference in pressure set up by the enormous precipitation, always and everywhere upon Trenco there is wind—and what a wind! Except at the very poles, where it is too cold for even Trenconian life to exist, there is hardly a spot in which or a time at which an Earthly gale would not be considered a dead calm; and along the equator, at every sunrise and at every sunset, the wind blows from the day side to the night side at the rate of well over eight hundred miles an hour!

Through countless thousands of years wind and wave have planed and scoured the planet Trenco to a geometrically perfect oblate spheroid. It has no elevations and no depressions. Nothing fixed in an Earthly sense grows or exists upon its surface; no structure has ever been built there able to stay in one place through one whole day of the cataclysmic meteorological phenomena which constitute the natural Trenconian environment.

There live upon Trenco two types of vegetation, each type having innumerable sub-divisions. One type sprouts in the mud of morning; flourishes flatly, by dint of deeply sent and powerful roots, during the wind and the heat of the day; comes to full fruit in later afternoon; and at sunset dies and is swept away by the flood. The other type is free-floating. Some of its genera are remotely like footballs, others resemble tumbleweeds, still others thistledowns, hundreds of others have not their remotest counterparts upon Earth. Essentially, however, they are alike in habits of life. They can sink in the "water" of Trenco; then can burrow in its mud, from which they derive part of their sustenance; they can emerge therefrom into the sunlight; they can, undamaged float in or roll along before the ever-present Trenconian wind; and they can enwrap, entangle, or otherwise seize and hold anything with which they come in contact which by any chance may prove edible.

Animal life, too, while abundant and diverse, is characterized by three qualities. From lowest to very highest it is amphibious, it is streamlined, and it is omnivorous. Life upon Trenco is hard, and any form of life to evolve there must of stern necessity be willing, yes, even anxious, to eat literally *anything* available. And for that reason all surviving forms of life, vegetable and animal, have a voracity and a fecundity almost unknown anywhere else in the galaxy.

Thionite, the noxious drug referred to earlier in this narrative, is the sole reason for Trenco's galactic importance. As chlorophyll is to Earthly vegetation, so is thionite to that of Trenco. Trenco is the only planet thus far known upon which this substance occurs, nor have our scientists even yet been able either to analyze or to synthesize it. Thionite is capable of affecting only those races who breathe oxygen and possess warm blood, red with hæmoglobin. However, the planets peopled by such races are legion, and very shortly after the drug's discovery hordes of addicts, smugglers, peddlers, and out-and-out pirates were rushing toward the new Bonanza. Thousands of these adventurers died, either from each other's ray-guns or under an avalanche of hungry Trenconian life; but, thionite being what it is, thousands more kept coming. Also came the Patrol, to curb the evil traffic at its source by beaming down ruthlessly any being attempting to gather any Trenconian vegetation.

Thus between the Patrol and the drug syndicate there rages a bitterly continuous battle to the death. Arrayed against both factions is the massed life of the noisome planet, omnivorous as it is, eternally ravenous, and of an individual power and ferocity and a collective aggregate of numbers by no means to be despised. And eternally raging against all these contending parties are the wind, the lightning, the rain, the flood, and the hellish vibratory output of Trenco's enormous, malignant, blue-white sun.

This, then, was the planet upon which Kinnison had to land in order to repair his crippled Bergenholm—and in the end how well it was to be that such was the case!

"Kinnison of Tellus, greetings. Tregonsee of Rigel IV calling from Trenco space-port. Have you ever landed on this planet before?"

"No, but what . . ."

"Skip that for a time; it is most important that you land here quickly and safely. Where are you in relation to this planet?"

"Your apparent diameter is a shade under six degrees. We are near the plane of your ecliptic and almost in the plane of your terminator, on the morning side."

"That is well, you have ample time. Place your ship between Trenco and the sun. Enter the atmosphere exactly fifteen G-P minutes from the present moment, at twenty degrees after meridian, as nearly as possible on the ecliptic, which is also our equator. Go inert as you enter atmosphere, for a free landing upon this planet is impossible. Synchronize with our rotation, which is twenty six point two G-P hours. Descend vertically until the atmospheric pressure is seven hundred millimeters of mercury, which will be at an altitude of approximately one thousand meters. Since you rely largely upon that sense called sight, allow me to caution you now not to trust it. When your external pressure is seven hundred millimeters of mercury your altitude will be one thousand meters, whether you believe it or not. Stop at that pressure and inform me of the fact, meanwhile holding yourself as nearly stationary as you can. Check so far?"

"QX—but do you mean to tell me that we can't locate each other at a *thousand meters?*'' Kinnison's amazed thought escaped him. "What kind of..."

"I can locate you, but you cannot locate me,'' came the dry reply. "Everyone knows that Trenco is peculiar, but no one who has never been here can realize even dimly how peculiar it really is. Detectors and spy-rays are useless, electro-magnetics are practically paralyzed, and optical apparatus is distinctly unreliable. You cannot trust your vision here—do not believe anything you see. It used to require days to land a ship at this port, but with our Lenses and my 'sense of perception,' as you call it, it will be a matter of minutes."

Kinnison flashed his ship to the designated position.

"Cut the Berg, Thorndyke, we're all done with it. We've got to build up an inert velocity to match the rotation, and land inert."

"Thanks be to all the gods of space for that." The engineer heaved a sigh of relief. "I've been expecting it to blow its top for the last hour, and I don't know whether we'd ever have got it meshed in again or not."

"QX on location and orbit,'' Kinnison reported to the as yet invisible space-port a few minutes later. "Now, what about that Lensman? What happened?"

"The usual thing,'' came the emotionless response. "It happens to altogether too many Lensmen who can see, in spite of everything we can tell them. He insisted upon going out after his zwilniks in a ground car, and of course we had to let him go. He became confused, lost control, let something—possibly a zwilnik's bomb—get under his leading edge, and the wind and the trencos did the rest. He was Lageston of Mercator V—a good man, too. What is your pressure now?"

"Five hundred millimeters."

"Slow down. Now, if you cannot conquer the tendency to believe your eyes, you had better shut off your visiplates and watch only the pressure gauge."

"Being warned, I can disbelieve my eyes, I think,'' and for a minute or so communication ceased.

At a startled oath from vanBuskirk, Kinnison glanced into the plate and it needed all his nerve to keep from wrenching savagely at the controls. For the whole planet was tipping, lurching, spinning; gyrating madly in a frenzy of impossible motions; and even as the Patrolmen stared a huge mass of something shot directly toward the ship!

"Sheer off, Kim!'' yelled the Valerian.

"Hold it, Bus,'' cautioned the Lensman. "That's what we've got to expect, you know—I passed all the stuff along as I got it. Everything, that is, except that a 'zwilnik' is anything or anybody that comes after thionite, and that a 'trenco' is anything, animal or vegetable, that lives on the planet. QX, Tregonsee—seven hundred, and I'm holding steady—I hope!''

"Steady enough, but you are too far away for our landing beam to grasp you. Apply a little drive . . . Shift course to your left and down . . . more left . . . up a trifle . . . that's it . . . slow down . . . QX.''

There was a gentle, snubbing shock, and Kinnison again translated to his companions the stranger's thoughts:

"We have you. Cut off all power and lock all controls in neutral. Do nothing more until I instruct you to come out.''

Kinnison obeyed; and, released from all duty, the visitors stared in fascinated incredulity into the visiplate. For that at which they stared was and must forever remain impossible of duplication upon Earth, and only in imagination can it be even faintly pictured. Imagine all the fantastic and monstrous creatures of a delirium-tremens vision incarnate and actual. Imagine them being hurled through the air, borne by a dust-laden gale more severe than any the great American dust-bowl or Africa's Sahara Desert ever endured. Imagine this scene as being viewed, not in an ordinary, solid distorting mirror, but in one whose falsely reflecting contours were changing constantly, with no logical or intelligible rhythm, into new and ever more grotesque warps. If imagination has been equal to the task, the resultant is what the visitors tried to see.

At first they could make nothing whatever of it. Upon nearer approach, however, the ghastly distortion grew less and the flatly level expanse took on a semblance of rigidity. Directly beneath them they made out something that looked like an immense, flat blister upon the otherwise featureless terrain. Toward this blister their ship was drawn.

A port opened, dwarfed in apparent size to a mere window by the immensity of the structure one of whose entrances it was. Through this port the vast bulk of the spaceship was wafted upon the landing-bars, and behind it the mighty bronze-and-steel gates clanged shut. The lock was pumped to a vacuum, there was a hiss of entering air, a spray of vaporous liquid bathed every inch of the vessel's surface, and Kinnison felt again the calm thought of Tregonsee, the Rigellian Lensman:

"You may now open your air-lock and emerge. If I have read aright our atmosphere is sufficiently like your own in oxygen content so that you will suffer no ill effects from it. It may be well, however, to wear your armor until you have become accustomed to its considerably greater density.''

"That'll be a relief!'' growled vanBuskirk's deep bass, when his chief had transmitted the thought. "I've been breathing this thin stuff so long I'm getting light-headed.''

"That's gratitude!" Thorndyke retorted. "We've been running our air so heavy that all the rest of us are thick-headed now. If the air in this space-port is any heavier than what we've been having, I'm going to wear armor as long as we stay here!"

Kinnison opened the air-lock, found the atmosphere of the space-port satisfactory, and stepped out; to be greeted cordially by Tregonsee the Lensman.

This—this apparition was at least erect, which was something. His body was the size and shape of an oil-drum. Beneath this massive cylinder of a body were four short, blocky legs upon which he waddled about with surprising speed. Midway up the body, above each leg, there sprouted out a ten-foot-long, writhing, boneless, tentacular arm, which toward the extremity branched out into dozens of lesser tentacles, ranging in size from hair-like tendrils up to mighty fingers two inches or more in diameter. Tregonsee's head was merely a neckless, immobile, bulging dome in the center of the flat upper surface of his body—a dome bearing neither eyes nor ears, but only four equally-spaced toothless mouths and four single, flaring nostrils.

But Kinnison felt no qualm of repugnance at Tregonsee's monstrous appearance, for embedded in the leathery flesh of one arm was the Lens. Here, the Lensman knew, was in every essential a MAN—and probably a super-man.

"Welcome to Trenco, Kinnison of Tellus," Tregonsee was saying. "While we are near neighbors in space, I have never happened to visit your planet. I have encountered Tellurians here, of course, but they were not of a type to be received as guests."

"No, a zwilnik is not a high type of Tellurian," Kinnison agreed. "I have often wished that I could have your sense of perception, if only for a day. It must be wonderful indeed to be able to perceive a thing as a whole, inside and out, instead of having vision stopped at its surface, as is ours. And to be independent of light or darkness, never to be lost or in need of instruments; to know definitely where you are in relation to every other object or thing around you—that, I think, is the most marvelous sense in the Universe."

"Just as I have wished for sight and hearing, those two remarkable and to us entirely unexplainable senses. I have dreamed, I have studied volumes, on color and sound. Color in art and in nature; sound in music and in the voices of loved ones; but they remain meaningless symbols upon a printed page. However, such thoughts are vain. In all probability neither of us would enjoy the other's equipment if he had it, and this interchange is of no material assistance to you."

In flashing thoughts Kinnison then communicated to the other Lens-man everything that had transpired since he left Prime Base.

"I perceive that your Bergenholm is of standard fourteen rating," Tregonsee said, as the Tellurian finished his story. "We have several spares here; and, while they all have regulation Patrol mountings, it would take much less time to change mounts than to overhaul your machine."

"That's so, too—I never thought of the possibility of your having spares on hand—and we've lost a lot of time already. How long will it take?"

"One shift of labor to change mounts; at least eight to rebuild yours enough to be sure that it will get you home."

"We'll change mounts, then, by all means. I'll call the boys . . ."

"There is no need of that. We are amply equipped, and neither you humans nor the Velantians could handle our tools." Tregonsee made no visible motion nor could Kinnison perceive a break in his thought, but while he was conversing with the Tellurian half a dozen of his blocky Rigellians had dropped whatever they had been doing and were scuttling toward the visiting ship. "Now I must leave you for a time, as I have one more trip to make this afternoon."

"Is there anything I can do to help you?" asked Kinnison.

"No," came the definite negative. "I will return in three hours, as well before sunset the wind makes it impossible to get even a ground-car into the port. I will then show you why you can be of little assistance to us."

Kinnison spent those three hours watching the Rigellians work upon the Bergenholm; there was no need for direction or advice. They knew what to do and they did it. Those tiny, hairlike fingers, literally hundreds of them at once, performed delicate tasks with surpassing nicety and dispatch; when it came to heavy tasks the larger digits or even whole arms wrapped themselves around the work and, with the solid bracing of the four block-like legs, exerted forces that even vanBuskirk's giant frame could not have approached.

As the end of the third hour neared, Kinnison watched with a spy-ray—there were no windows in Trenco space-port—the leeward groundway of the structure. In spite of the weird antics of Trenco's sun—gyrating, jumping, appearing and disappearing—he knew that it was going down. Soon he saw the ground-car coming in, scuttling crab-wise, nose into the wind but actually moving backward and sidewise. Although the "seeing" was very poor, at this close range the distortion was minimized and he could see that, like its parent craft, the ground-car was a blister. Its edges actually touched the ground all around, sloping upward and over the top in such a smooth reverse curve that the harder the wind blew the more firmly was the vehicle pressed downward. The ground-flap came up just enough to clear the car's top and the tiny craft crept up. But before the landing bars could seize her the ground-car struck an eddy from the flap—an eddy in a medium which, although gaseous, was at that velocity practically solid. Earth blasted away in torrents from the leading edge, the car leaped bodily into the air and was flung away, end over end. But Tregonsee, with consummate craftsmanship, forced her flat again, and again she crawled up toward the flap. This time the landing-bars took hold and, although the little vessel fluttered like a leaf in a gale, she was drawn inside the port and the flap went down behind her. She was then sprayed, and Tregonsee came out.

"Why the spray?" thought Kinnison, as the Rigellian entered his control-room.

"Trencos. Much of the life of this planet starts from almost imperceptible spores. It develops rapidly, attains considerable size, and consumes anything organic it touches. This port was depopulated time after time before the lethal spray was developed. Now turn your spy-ray again to the lee of the port."

During the few minutes that had elapsed the wind had increased in fury to such an extent that the very ground was boiling away from the trailing edge in the tumultuous eddy formed there, ultra-streamlined though the space-port was. And that eddy, far surpassing in violence any storm known to Earth, was to the denizens of Trenco a miraculously appearing quiet spot in which they could stop and rest, eat and be eaten.

A globular monstrosity had thrust pseudopodia deep into the boiling dirt. Other limbs now shot out, grasping a tumbleweedlike growth. The latter fought back viciously, but could make no impression upon the rubbery integument of the former. Then a smaller creature, slipping down the polished curve of the shield, was enmeshed by the tumbleweed. There ensued the amazing spectacle of one-half of the tumbleweed devouring the newcomer, even while its other half was being devoured by the globe!

"Now look out farther . . . still farther," directed Tregonsee.

"I can't. Things take on impossible motions and become so distorted as to be unrecognizable."

"Exactly. If you saw a zwilnik out there, where would you shoot?"

"At him, I suppose—why?"

"Because if you shot at where you think you see him, not only would you miss him, but the beam might very well swing around and enter your own back. Many men have been killed by their own weapons in precisely that fashion. Since we know, not only what the object is, but exactly where it is, we can correct our lines of aim for the then existing values of distortion. This is of course the reason why we Rigellians and other races possessing the sense of perception are the only ones who can efficiently police this planet.''

"Reason enough, I'd say, from what I've seen," and silence fell.

For minutes the two Lensmen watched, while creatures of a hundred kinds streamed into the lee of the space-port and killed and ate each other. Finally something came crawling up wind, against that unimaginable gale; a flatly streamlined creature resembling somewhat a turtle, but shaped as was the ground-car. Thrusting down long, hooked flippers into the dirt it inched along, paying no attention to the scores of lesser creatures who hurled themselves upon its armored back, until it was close beside the largest football-shaped creature in the eddy. Then, lightning-like, it drove a needle-sharp organ at least eight inches into the leathery mass of its victim. Struggling convulsively, the stricken thing lifted the turtle a fraction of an inch—and both were hurled instantly out of sight; the living ball still eating a luscious bit of prey despite the fact that it was impaled upon the poniard of the turtle and was certainly doomed.

"Good Lord, what was that?" exclaimed Kinnison.

"The flat? That was a representative of Trenco's highest life-form. It may develop a civilization in time—it is quite intelligent now."

"But the difficulties!" protested the Tellurian. "Building cities, even homes . . .''

"Neither cities nor homes are necessary here, nor even desirable. Why build? Nothing is or can be fixed on this planet, and since one place is exactly like every other place, why wish to remain in any one particular spot? They do very well, in their own mobile way. Here, you will notice, comes the rain.''

The rain came—forty-four inches per hour of rain—and the incessant lightning. The dirt became first mud, then muddy water being driven in fiercely flying gouts and masses. Now, in the lee of the space-port, the outlandish denizens of Trenco were burrowing down into the mud— still eating each other and anything else that came within reach.

The water grew deeper and deeper, its upper surface now whipped into frantic sheets of spray. The structure was now afloat, and Kinnison saw with astonishment that, small as was the exposed surface and flatly curved, yet it was pulling through the water at frightful speed the widespreading steel sea-anchors which were holding its head to the gale.

"With no reference points how do you know where you're going?" he demanded.

"We neither know nor care," responded Tregonsee, with a mental shrug. "We are like the natives in that. Since one spot is like every other spot, why choose between them?"

"What a world—*what* a world! However, I am beginning to understand why thionite is so expensive," and, overwhelmed by the ever-increasing fury raging outside, Kinnison sought his bunk.

Morning came, a reversal of the previous evening. The liquid evaporated, the mud dried, the flat-growing vegetation sprang up with shocking speed, the animals emerged and again ate and were eaten.

And eventually came Tregonsee's announcement that it was almost noon, and that now, for half an hour or so, it would be calm enough for the space-ship to leave the port.

"You are sure that I would be of no help to you?" asked the Rigellian, half-pleadingly.

"Sorry, Tregonsee, but I'm afraid you wouldn't fit into my matrix any better than I would into yours. But here's the spool I told you about. If you will take it to your base on your next relief you will do civilization and the Patrol more good than you could by coming with us. Thanks for the Bergenholm, which is covered by credits, and thanks a lot for your help and courtesy, which can't be covered. Goodbye," and the now entirely space-worthy craft shot out through the port, through Trenco's noxiously peculiar atmosphere, and into the vacuum of space.

11

GRAND BASE

At some little distance from the galaxy, yet shackled to it by the flexible yet powerful bonds of gravitation, the small but comfortable planet upon which was Helmuth's base circled about its parent sun. This planet had been chosen with the utmost care, and its location was a secret guarded jealously indeed. Scarcely one in a million of Boskone's teeming myriads knew even that such a planet existed; and of the chosen few who had ever been asked to visit it, fewer still by far had been allowed to leave it.

Grand Base covered hundreds of square miles of that planet's surface. It was equipped with all the arms and armament known to the military genius of the age; and in the exact center of that immense citadel there arose a glittering metallic dome.

The inside surface of that dome was lined with visiplates and communicators, hundreds of thousands of them. Miles of catwalks clung precariously to the inward-curving wall. Control panels and instrument boards covered the floor in banks and tiers, with only narrow runways between them. And what a personnel! There were Solarians, Crevenians, Sirians. There were Antareans, Vandemarians, Arcturians. There were representatives of scores, yes, hundreds of other solar systems of the galaxy.

But whatever their external form they were all breathers of oxygen and they were all nourished by warm, red blood. Also, they were all alike mentally. Each had won his present high place by trampling down those beneath him and by pulling down those above him in the branch to which he had first belonged of the "pirate" organization. Each was characterized by a total lack of scruple; by a coldly ruthless passion for power and place.

Kinnison had been eminently correct in his belief that Boskone's was not a "pirate outfit" in any ordinary sense of the word, but even his ideas of its true nature fell far short indeed of the truth. It was a culture already inter-galactic in scope, but one built upon ideals diametrically opposed to those of the civilization represented by the Galactic Patrol.

It was a tyranny, an absolute monarchy, a despotism not even remotely approximated by the dictatorships of earlier ages. It had only one creed—"The end justifies the means." Anything—literally *anything at all*—that produced the desired result was commendable; to fail was the only crime. The successful named their own rewards; those who failed were disciplined with an impersonal, rigid severity exactly proportional to the magnitude of their failures.

Therefore no weaklings dwelt within that fortress; and of all its cold, hard, ruthless crew far and away the coldest, hardest, and most ruthless was Helmuth, the "speaker for Boskone," who sat at the great desk in the dome's geometrical center. This individual was almost human in form and build, springing as he did from a planet closely approximating Earth in mass, atmosphere, and climate. Indeed, only his general, all-pervasive aura of blueness bore witness to the fact that he was not a native of Tellus.

His eyes were blue, his hair was blue, and even his skin was faintly blue beneath its coat of ultra-violet tan. His intensely dynamic personality fairly radiated blueness—not the gentle blue of an Earthly sky, not the sweetly innocuous blue of an Earthly flower; but the keenly merciless blue of a delta-ray, the cold and bitter blue of a Polar iceberg, the unyielding, inflexible blue of quenched and drawn tungsten-chromium steel.

Now a frown sat heavily upon his arrogantly patrician face as his eyes bored into the plate before him, from the base of which were issuing the words being spoken by the assistant pictured in its deep surface:

"... the fifth dove into the deepest ocean of Corvina II, in the depths of which all rays are useless. The ships which followed have not as yet reported, but they will do so as soon as they have completed their mission. No trace of the sixth has been found, and it is therefore assumed that it was destroyed. ..."

"Who assumes so?" demanded Helmuth, coldly. "There is no justification whatever for such an assumption. Go on!"

"The Lensman, if there is one and if he is alive, must therefore be in the fifth ship, which is about to be taken."

"Your report is neither complete nor conclusive, and I do not at all approve of your intimation that the Lensman is simply a figment of my imagination. That it was a Lensman is the only possible logical conclusion—none other of the Patrol forces could have done what has been done. Postulating his reality, it seems to me that instead of being a bare possibility, it is highly probable that he has again escaped us, and again in one of our own vessels—this time in the one you have so conveniently assumed to have been destroyed. Have you searched the line of flight?''

''Yes, sir. Everything in space and every planet within reach of that line has been examined with care; except, of course, Velantia and Trenco.''

''Velantia is, for the time being, unimportant. The sixth ship left Velantia and did not go back there. Why Trenco?'' and Helmuth pressed a series of buttons. ''Ah, I see . . . To recapitulate, one ship, the one which in all probability is now carrying the Lensman, is still unaccounted for. *Where is it?* We know that it has not landed upon or near any Solarian planet, and measures are being taken to see to it that it does not land upon or near any planet of 'Civilization.' Now, I think, it has become necessary to comb that planet Trenco, inch by inch.''

''But sir, how . . .'' began the anxious-eyed underling.

''When did it become necessary to draw diagrams and make blueprints for you?'' demanded Helmuth, harshly. ''We have ships manned by Ordoviks and other races having the sense of perception. Find out where they are and get them there at full blast!'' and he punched a button, to replace the image upon his plate by another.

''It has now become of paramount importance that we complete our knowledge of the Lens of the Patrol,'' he began, without salutation or preamble. ''Have you traced its origin yet?''

''I believe so, but I do not certainly know. It has proved to be a task of such difficulty . . .''

''If it had been an easy one I would not have made a special assignment of it to you. Go on!''

''Everything seems to point to the planet Arisia, of which I can learn nothing definite whatever except. . . .''

''Just a moment!'' Helmuth punched more buttons and listened. ''Unexplored . . . unknown . . . shunned by all spacemen . . .

''Superstition, eh?'' he snapped. ''Another of those haunted planets?''

''Something more than ordinary spacemen's superstition, sir, but just what I have not been able to discover. By combing my department I managed to make up a crew of those who either were not afraid of it or had never heard of it. That crew is now en route there.''

"Whom have we in that sector of space? I find it desirable to check your findings."

The department head reeled off a list of names and numbers, which Helmuth considered at length.

"Gildersleeve, the Valerian," he decided. "He is a good man, coming along fast. Aside from a firm belief in his own peculiar gods, he has shown no signs of weakness. You considered him?"

"Certainly." The henchman, as cold as his icy chief, knew that explanations would not satisfy Helmuth, therefore he offered none. "He is raiding at the moment, but I will put you on him if you like."

"Do so," and upon Helmuth's plate there appeared a deep-space scene of rapine and pillage.

The convoying Patrol cruiser had already been blasted out of existence; only a few idly drifting masses of debris remained to show that it had ever been. Needle-beams were at work, and soon the merchant-man hung inert and helpless. The pirates, scorning to use the emergency inlet port, simply blasted away the entire entrance panel. Then they boarded, an armored swarm; flaming DeLameters spreading death and destruction before them.

The sailors, outnumbered as they were and over-armed, fought heroically—but uselessly. In groups and singly they fell; those who were not already dead being callously tossed out into space in slitted spacesuits and with smashed drivers. Only the younger women—the stewardesses, the nurses, the one or two such among the few passengers—were taken as booty; all others shared the fate of the crew.

Then, the ship plundered from nose to after-jets and every article or thing of value trans-shipped, the raider drew off, bathed in the blue-white glare of the bombs that were destroying every trace of the merchant-ship's existence. Then and only then did Helmuth reveal himself to Gildersleeve.

"A good, clean job of work, Captain," he commended. "Now, how would you like to visit Arisia for me—for *me*, direct?"

A pallor overspread the normally ruddy face of the Valerian and an uncontrollable tremor shook his giant frame. But as he considered the implications resident in Helmuth's concluding phrase he licked his lips and spoke.

"I hate to say no, sir, if you order me to and if there was any way of making my crew do it. But we were near there once, sir, and we . . . I . . . they . . . it well, sir, I *saw* things, sir, and I was . . . was *warned*, sir!"

"Saw what? And was warned of what?"

"I can't describe what I saw, sir. I can't even think of it in thoughts that mean anything. As for the warning, though, it was very definite, sir. I was told very plainly that if I ever go near that planet again I will die a worse death than any I have dealt out to any other living being."

"But you will go there again?"

"I tell you, sir, that the crew will not do it," Gildersleeve replied, doggedly. "Even if I were anxious to go, every man aboard will mutiny if I try it."

"Call them in right now and tell them that you have been ordered to Arisia."

The captain did so, but he had scarcely started to talk when he was stopped in no uncertain fashion by his first officer—also of course a Valerian—who pulled his DeLameter and spoke savagely:

"Cut it, Gil! We are not going to Arisia. I was with you before, you know. Set course within five points of that accursed planet and I blast you where you sit!"

"Helmuth, speaking for Boskone!" ripped from the headquarters speaker. "This is rankest mutiny. You know the penalty, do you not?"

"Certainly I do—what of it?" The first officer snapped back.

"Suppose that I *tell* you to go to Arisia?" Helmuth's voice was now soft and silky, but instinct with deadly menace.

"In that case *I* tell *you* to go to the ninth hell—or to Arisia, a million times worse!"

"What? You dare speak thus to *me*?" demanded the arch-pirate, sheer amazement at the fellow's audacity blanketing his rising anger.

"I so dare," declared the rebel, brazen defiance and unalterable resolve in every line of his hard body and in every lineament of his hard face. "All you can do is kill us. You can order out enough ships to blast us out of the ether, but that's all you *can* do. That would be only death and we'd have the fun of taking a lot of the boys along with us. If we go to Arisia, though, it would be different—very, *very* different. No, Helmuth, and I throw this in your teeth: if I ever go near Arisia again it will be in a ship in which you, Helmuth, in person, are sitting at the controls. If you think this is an empty dare and don't like it, don't take it. Send on your dogs!"

"That will do! Report yourselves to Base D under . . ." Then Helmuth's flare of anger passed and his cold reason took charge. Here was something utterly unprecedented; an entire crew of the hardest-bitten marauders in space offering open and barefaced mutiny—no, not mutiny, but actual rebellion—to him, Helmuth, in his very person. And not a typical, skulking, carefully planned uprising, but the immovably brazen desperation of men making an ultimately last-ditch stand. Truly, it must be a powerful superstition indeed, to make that crew of hard-boiled hellions choose certain death rather than face again the imaginary—they *must* be imaginary—perils of a planet unknown to and unexplored by Boskone's planetographers. But they were, after all, ordinary space-men, of little mental force and of small real ability. Even so, it was clearly indicated that in this case precipitate action was to be avoided. Therefore he went on calmly and almost without a break. "Cancel all this that has been spoken and that has taken place. Continue with your original orders pending further investigation," and switched his plate back to the department head.

"I have checked your conclusions and have found them correct," he announced, as though nothing at all out of the way had transpired. "You did well in sending a ship to investigate. No matter where I am or what I am doing, notify me instantly at the first sign of irregularity in the behavior of any member of that ship's personnel."

Nor was that call long in coming. The carefully-selected crew—selected for complete lack of knowledge of the dread planet which was their objective—sailed along in blissful ignorance, both of the real meaning of their mission and of what was to be its ghastly end. Soon after Helmuth's unsatisfactory interview with Gildersleeve and his mate, the luckless exploring vessel reached the barrier which the Arisians had set around their system and through which no uninvited stranger was allowed to pass.

The free-flying ship struck that frail barrier and stopped. In the instant of contact a wave of mental force flooded the mind of the captain, who, gibbering with sheer, stark, panic terror, flashed his vessel away from that horror-impregnated wall and hurled call after frantic call along his beam, back to headquarters. His first call, in the instant of reception, was relayed to Helmuth at his central desk.

"Steady, man; report intelligently!" that worthy snapped, and his eyes, large now upon the cowering captain's plate, bored steadily, hypnotically into those of the expedition's leader. "Pull yourself together and tell me exactly what happened. Everything!"

"Well, sir, when we struck something—a screen of some sort—and stopped, something came aboard. It was . . . oh . . . ay-ay-e-e!" his voice rose to a shriek, but under Helmuth's dominating glare he subsided quickly and went on. "A monster, sir, if there ever was one. A fire-breathing demon, sir, with teeth and claws and cruelly barbed tail. He spoke to me in my own Crevenian language. He said . . ."

"Never mind what he said. I did not hear it, but I can guess what it was. He threatened you with death in some horrible fashion, did he not?" and the coldly ironical tones did more to restore the shaking man's equilibrium than reams of remonstrance could have done.

"Well, yes, that was about the size of it, sir," he admitted.

"And does that sound reasonable to you, the commander of a first class battleship of Boskone's Fleet?" sneered Helmuth.

"Well, sir, put on that way, it does seem a bit farfetched," the captain replied, sheepishly.

"It *is* far-fetched." The director, in the safety of his dome, could afford to be positive. "We do not know exactly what caused that hallucination, apparition, or whatever it was—you were the only one who could see it, apparently; it certainly was not visible on our master-plates. It was probably some form of suggestion or hypnotism; and you know as well as we do that any suggestion can be thrown off by a definitely opposed will. But you did not oppose it, did you?"

"No, sir, I didn't have time."

"Nor did you have your screens out, nor automatic recorders on the trip. Not much of anything, in fact . . . I think that you had better report back here, at full blast."

"Oh, no, sir—please!" He knew what rewards were granted to failures, and Helmuth's carefully chosen words had already produced the effect desired by their speaker. "They took me by surprise then, but I'll go through this next time."

"Very well, I will give you one more chance. When you get close to the barrier, or whatever it is, go inert and put out all your screens. Man your plates and weapons, for whatever can hypnotize can be killed. Go ahead at full blast, with all the acceleration you can get. Crash through anything that opposes you, and beam anything that you can detect or see. Can you think of anything else?"

"That should be sufficient, sir." The captain's equanimity was completely restored, now that the warlike preparations were making more and more nebulous the sudden, but single, thought wave of the Arisian. "Proceed!"

The plan was carried out to the letter. This time the pirate craft struck the frail barrier inert, and its slight force offered no tangible bar to the prodigious mass of metal. But this time, since the barrier was actually passed, there was no mental warning and no possibility of retreat.

Many men have skeletons in their closets. Many have phobias, things of which they are consciously afraid. Many others have them, not consciously, but buried deep in the subconscious; specters which seldom or never rise above the threshold of perception. Every sentient being has, if not such specters as these, at least a few active or latent dislikes, dreads, or outright fears. This is true, no matter how quiet and peaceful a life the being has led.

These pirates, however, were the scum of space. They were beings of hard and criminal lives and of violent and lawless passions. Their hates and conscience-searing deeds had been legion, their count of crimes long, black, and hideous. Therefore, slight indeed was the effort required to locate in their conscious minds—to say nothing of the noxious depths of their subconscious ones—visions of horror fit to blast stronger intellects than theirs. And that is exactly what the Arisian Watchman did. From each pirate's total mind, a veritable charnel pit, he extracted the foulest, most unspeakable dregs, the deeply hidden things of which the subject was in the greatest fear. Of these things he formed a whole of horror incomprehensible and incredible, and this ghastly whole he made incarnate and visible to the pirate who was its unwilling parent; as visible as though it were composed of flesh and blood, of copper and steel. Is it any wonder that each member of that outlaw crew, seeing such an abhorrent materialization, went instantly mad?

It is of no use to go into the horribly monstrous shapes of the things, even were it possible; for each of them was visible to only one man, and none of them was visible to those who looked on from the safety of the distant base. To them the entire crew simply abandoned their posts and attacked each other, senselessly and in insane frenzy, with whatever weapons came first to hand. Indeed, many of them fought bare-handed, weapons hanging unused in their belts, gouging, beating, clawing, biting until life had been rived horribly away. In other parts of the ship DeLameters flamed briefly, bars crashed crunchingly, knives and axes sheared and trenchantly bit. And soon it was over—almost. The pilot was still alive, unmoving and rigid at his controls.

Then he, too, moved; rapidly and purposefully. He cut in the Bergenholm, spun the ship around, shoved her drivers up to maximum blast, and steadied her into an exact course—and when Helmuth read that course even his iron nerves failed him momentarily. For the ship was flying, not for its own home port, but directly toward Grand Base, the jealously secret planet whose spatial coordinates neither that pilot nor any other creature of the pirates' rank and file had ever known!

Helmuth snapped out orders, to which the pilot gave no heed. His voice—for the first time in his career—rose to a howl, but the pilot still paid no attention. Instead, eyes bulging with horror and fingers curved tensely into veritable talons, he reared upright upon his bench and leaped as though to clutch and to rend some unutterably appalling foe. He leaped over his board into thin and empty air. He came down a-sprawl in a maze of naked, high-potential bus-bars. His body vanished in a flash of searing flame and a cloud of thick and greasy smoke.

The bus-bars cleared themselves of their gruesome "short" and the great ship, manned now entirely by corpses, bored on.

". . . stinking klebots, the lily-livered cowards!" the department head, who had also been yelling orders, was still pounding his desk and yelling. "If they're *that* afraid—go crazy and kill each other without being touched—I'll have to go myself. . . ."

"No, Sansteed," Helmuth interrupted curtly. "You will not have to go. There is, after all, I think, something there—something that you may not be able to handle. You see, you missed the one essential key fact." He referred to the course, the setting of which had shaken him to the very core.

"Let be," he silenced the other's flood of question and protest. "It would serve no purpose to detail it to you now. Have the ship taken back to port."

Helmuth knew now that it was not superstition that made spacemen shun Arisia. He knew that, from his standpoint at least, there was something very seriously amiss. But he had not the faintest conception of the real situation, nor of the real and terrible power which the Arisians could, and upon occasion would, wield.

12

KINNISON BRINGS HOME THE BACON

Helmuth sat at his desk, thinking; thinking with all the coldly analytical precision of which he was capable.

This Lensman was both powerful and tremendously resourceful. The cosmic-energy drive, developed by the science of a world about which the Patrol knew nothing, was Boskone's one great item of superiority. If the Patrol could be kept in ignorance of that drive the struggle would be over in a year; the culture of the iron hand would be unchallenged throughout the galaxy. If, however, the Patrol should succeed in learning Boskone's top secret, the war between the two cultures might well be prolonged indefinitely. This Lensman knew that secret and was still at large, of that he was all too certain. Therefore the Lensman must be destroyed. And that brought up the Lens.

What was it? A peculiar bauble indeed; impossible of duplication because of some subtlety of intra-atomic arrangement, and possessing peculiar and dire potentialities. The old belief that no one except a Lensman could wear a Lens was true—he had proved it. The Lens must account in some way for the outstanding ability of the Lensman, and it must tie in, somehow, with both Arisia and the thought-screens. The Lens was the one thing possessed by the Patrol which his own forces did not have. He must and would have it, for it was undoubtedly a powerful arm. Not to be compared, of course, with their own monopoly of cosmic energy—but that monopoly was now threatened, and seriously. That Lensman *must be destroyed.*

But how? It was easy to say "Comb Trenco, inch by inch," but doing it would prove a Herculean task. Suppose that the Lensman should again escape, in that volume of so fantastically distorted media? He had already escaped twice, in much clearer ether than Trenco's. However, if his information should never get back to Prime Base little harm would be done, and ships had been thrown around every solar system the Lensman could reach. Not even a grain-of-dust meteorite could pass those screens without detection. So much for the Lensman. Now about getting the secret of the Lens.

Again, how? There was *something* upon Arisia; something connected in some way with the Lens and with thought—possibly also with those thought-screens . . .

His mind flashed back over the unorthodox manner of his acquirement of those devices—unorthodox in that he had neither stolen them nor murdered their inventor. A person had come to him with pass-words and credentials which could not be ignored; had handed him a heavily-sealed container, which, he said, had come from a planet named Ploor; had remarked casually "Thought-screen data—you'll know when you need 'em"; and had gone.

Whatever the Arisian was, it had mental power; of that fact there could be no doubt. Out of the full sphere of space, what was the mathematical probability that the pilot of that deathship would have set by accident his course so exactly upon Grand Base? Vanishingly small. Treachery would not explain the facts—not only had the pilot been completely insane when he laid the course, but also *he did not know where Grand Base was.*

As an explanation mental force alone seemed fantastic, but no other as yet presented itself as a possibility. Also, it was supported by the unbelievable, the absolutely definite refusal of Gildersleeve's normally fearless crew even to approach the planet. It would take an unheard-of mental force so to affect such crime-hardened veterans.

Helmuth was not one to underestimate an enemy. Was there a man beneath that dome, save himself, of sufficient mental caliber to undertake the now necessary mission to Arisia? There was not. He himself had the finest mind on the planet; else that other had deposed him long since and had sat at the control desk himself. He was sublimely confident that no outside thought could break down *his* definitely opposed will—and besides, there were the thought-screens, the secret of which he had not as yet shared with anyone. The time had come to use those screens.

It has already been made clear that Helmuth was not a fool. No more was he a coward. If he himself could best of all his force do a thing, that thing he did; with the coldly ruthless efficiency that marked alike his every action and his every thought.

How should he go? Should he accept that challenge, and take Gildersleeve's rebellious crew of cutthroats to Arisia? No. In the event of an outcome short of complete success, it would not do to lose face before that band of ruffians. Moreover, the idea of such a crew going insane behind him was not one to be relished. He would go alone.

"Wolmark, come to the center," he ordered. When that worthy appeared he went on: "Be seated, as this is to be a serious conference. I have watched with admiration and appreciation, as well as some mild amusement, the development of your lines of information; especially those concerning affairs which are most distinctly not in your department. They are, however, efficient—you already know exactly what has happened." A statement this, in no wise a question.

"Yes, sir," quietly. Wolmark was somewhat taken aback, but not at all abashed.

"That is the reason you are here now. I thoroughly approve of you. I am leaving the planet for a few days, and you are the best man in the organization to take charge in my absence."

"I suspected that you would be leaving, sir."

"I know you did: but I am now informing you, merely to make sure that you develop no peculiar ideas in my absence, that there are at least a few things which you do not suspect at all. That safe, for instance," nodding toward a peculiarly shimmering globe of force anchoring itself in air. "Even your highly efficient spy system has not been able to learn a thing about that."

"No, sir, we have not—yet," he could not forbear adding.

"Nor will you, with any skill or force known to man. But keep on trying, it amuses me. I know, you see, of all your attempts. But to get on. I now say, and for your own good I advise you to believe, that failure upon my part to return to this desk will prove highly unfortunate for you."

"I believe that, sir. Any man of intelligence would make such arrangement, if he could. But sir, suppose that the Arisians . . ."

"If your 'if he could' implies a doubt, act upon it and learn wisdom," Helmuth advised him coldly. "You should know by this time that I neither gamble nor bluff. I have made arrangements to protect myself, both from enemies, such as the Arisians and the Patrol, and from friends, such as ambitious youngsters who are trying to supplant me. If I were not entirely confident of getting back here safely, my dear Wolmark, I would not go."

"You misunderstand me, sir. Really, I have no idea of supplanting you."

"Not until you get a good opportunity, you mean—I understand you thoroughly; and, as I have said before, I approve of you. Go ahead with all your plans. I have kept at least one lap ahead of you so far, and if the time should ever come when I can no longer do so, I shall no longer be fit to speak for Boskone. You understand, of course, that the most important matter now in work is the search for the Lensman, of which the combing of Trenco and the screening of the Patrol's systems are only two phases?"

"Yes, sir."

"Very well. I can, I think, leave matters in your hands. If anything really serious comes up, such as a development in the Lensman case, let me know at once. Otherwise do not call me. Take the desk," and Helmuth strode away.

He was whisked to the space-port, where there awaited him his special speedster, equipped long since with divers and sundry items of equipment whose functions were known only to himself.

For him the trip to Arisia was neither long nor tedious. The little racer was fully automatic, and as it tore through space he worked as coolly and efficiently as he was wont to do at his desk. Indeed, more so, for here he could concentrate without interruption. Many were the matters he planned and the decisions he made, the while his portfolio of notes grew thicker and thicker.

As he neared his destination he put away his work, actuated his special mechanisms, and waited. When the speedster struck the barrier and stopped Helmuth wore a faint, hard smile; but that smile disappeared with a snap as a thought crashed into his supposedly shielded brain.

"You are surprised that your thought-screens are not effective?" The thought was coldly contemptuous. "I know in essence what the messenger from Ploor told you concerning them when he gave them to you; but he spoke in ignorance. We of Arisia know thought in a way that no member of his race is now or ever will be able to understand.

"Know, Helmuth, that we Arisians do not want and will not tolerate uninvited visitors. Your presence is particularly distasteful, representing as you do a despotic, degrading, and antisocial culture. Evil and good are of course purely relative, so it cannot be said in absolute terms that your culture is evil. It is, however, based upon greed, hatred, corruption, violence, and fear. Justice it does not recognize, nor mercy, nor truth except as a scientific utility. It is basically opposed to liberty. Now liberty—of person, of thought, of action—is the basic and the goal of the civilization to which you are opposed, and with which any really philosophical mind must find itself in accord.

"Inflated overweeningly by your warped and perverted ideas, by your momentary success in dominating your handful of minions, tied to you by bonds of greed, of passion, and of crime, you come here to wrest from us the secret of the Lens; from us, a race as much abler than yours as we are older—a ratio of millions to one.

"You consider yourself cold, hard, ruthless. Compared to me, you are weak, soft, tender; as helpless as a newborn child. That you may learn and appreciate that fact is one reason why you are living at this present moment. Your lesson will now begin."

Then Helmuth, starkly rigid, unable to move a muscle, felt delicate probes enter his brain. One at a time they pierced his innermost being, each to a definitely selected center. It seemed that each thrust carried with it the ultimate measure of exquisitely poignant anguish possible of endurance, but each successive needle carried with it an even more keenly unbearable thrill of agony.

Helmuth was not now calm and cold. He could have screamed in wild abandon, but even that relief was denied him. He could not even scream; all he could do was sit there and suffer.

Then he began to see things. There, actually materializing in the empty air of the speedster, he saw in endless procession things he had done, either in person or by proxy, both during his ascent to his present high place in the pirates' organization and since the attainment of that place. Long was the list, and black. As it unfolded his torment grew more and ever more intense, until finally, after an interval that might have been a fraction of a second or might have been untold hours, he could stand no more. He fainted, sinking beyond the reach of pain into a sea of black unconsciousness.

He awakened white and shaking, wringing wet with perspiration and so weak that he could scarcely sit erect, but with a supremely blissful realization that, for the time being at least, his punishment was over.

"This, you will observe, has been a very mild treatment," the cold Arisian accents went on inside his brain. "Not only do you still live, you are even still sane. We now come to the second reason why you have not been destroyed. Your destruction by us would not be good for that struggling young civilization which you oppose.

"We have given that civilization an instrument by virtue of which it should become able to destroy you and everything for which you stand. If it cannot do so it is not yet ready to become a civilization and your obnoxious culture shall be allowed to conquer and to flourish for a time.

"Now go back to your dome. Do not return. I know that you will not have the temerity to do so in person. Do not attempt to do so by any form whatever of proxy."

There were no threats, no warnings, no mention of consequences; but the level and incisive tone of the Arisian put a fear into Helmuth's cold heart the like of which he had never before known.

He whirled his speedster about and hurled her at full blast toward his home planet. It was only after many hours that he was able to regain even a semblance of his customary poise, and days elapsed before he could think coherently enough to consider as a whole the shocking, the unbelievable thing that had happened to him.

He wanted to believe that the creature, whatever it was, had been bluffing—that it could not kill him, that it had done its worst. In similar case he would have killed without mercy, and that course seemed to him the only logical one to pursue. His cold reason, however, would not allow him to entertain that comforting belief. Deep down he *knew* that the Arisian could have killed him as easily as it had slain the lowest member of his band, and the thought chilled him to the marrow.

What could he do? What *could* he do? Endlessly, as the miles and light-years reeled off behind his hurtling racer, this question reiterated itself; and when his home planet loomed close it was still unanswered.

Since Wolmark believed implicitly his statement that it would be poor technique to oppose his return, the planet's screens went down at Helmuth's signal. His first act was to call all the department heads to the center, for an extremely important council of war. There he told them everything that had happened, calmly and concisely, concluding:

"They are aloof, disinterested, unpartisan to a degree I find it impossible to understand. They disapprove of us on purely philosophical grounds, but they will take no active part against us as long as we stay away from their solar system. Therefore we cannot obtain knowledge of the Lens by direct action, but there are other methods which shall be worked out in due course.

"The Arisians do approve of the Patrol, and have helped them to the extent of giving them the Lens. There, however, they stop. If the Lensmen do not know how to use their Lenses efficiently—and I gather that they do not—we 'shall be allowed to conquer and to flourish for a time.' We *will* conquer, and we will see to it that the time of our flourishing will be a long one indeed.

"The whole situation, then, boils down to this: our cosmic energy against the Lens of the Patrol. Ours is the much more powerful arm, but our only hope of immediate success lies in keeping the Patrol in ignorance of our cosmic-energy receptors and converters. One Lensman already has that knowledge. Therefore, gentlemen, it is very clear that the death of that Lensman has now become absolutely imperative. We *must* find him, if it means the abandonment of our every other enterprise throughout this galaxy. Give me a full report upon the screening of the planets upon which the Lensman may try to land."

"It is done, sir," came quick reply. "They are completely blockaded.

Ships are spaced so closely that even the electromagnetic detectors have a five hundred percent overlap. Visual detectors have at least two hundred fifty percent overlap. Nothing as large as one millimeter in any dimension can get through without detection and observation."

"And how about the search of Trenco?"

"Results are still negative. One of our ships, with papers all in order, visited Trenco space-port openly. No one was there except the regular force of Rigellians. Our captain was in no position to be too inquisitive, but the missing ship was certainly not in the port and he gathered that he was the first visitor they had had in a month. We learned on Rigel IV that Tregonsee, the Lensman on duty on Trenco, has been there for a month and will not be relieved for another month. He was the only Lensman there. We are of course carrying on the search of the rest of the planet. About half the personnel of each vessel to land has been lost, but they started with double crews and replacements are being sent."

"The Lensman Tregonsee's story may or may not be true," Helmuth mused. "It makes little difference. It would be impossible to hide that ship in Trenco space-port from even a casual inspection, and if the ship is not there the Lensman is not. He may be in hiding elsewhere on the planet, but I doubt it. Continue to search nevertheless. There are many things he may have done . . . I will have to consider them, one by one."

But Helmuth had very little time to consider what Kinnison might have done, for the Lensman had left Trenco long since. Because of the flare-baffles upon his driving projectors his pace was slow; but to compensate for this condition the distance to be covered was not too long. Therefore, even as Helmuth was cogitating upon what next to do, the Lensman and his crew were approaching the far-flung screen of Boskonian war-vessels investing the entire Solarian System.

To approach that screen undetected was a physical impossibility, and before Kinnison realized that he was in a danger zone six tractors had flicked out, had seized his ship, and had jerked it up to combat range. But the Lensman was ready for anything, and again everything happened at once.

Warnings screamed into the distant pirate base and Helmuth, tense at his desk, took personal charge of his mighty fleet. On the field of action Kinnison's screens flamed out in stubborn defense, tractors snapped under his slashing shears, the baffles disappeared in an incandescent flare as he shot maximum blast into his drive, and space again became suffused with the output of his now ultra-powered multiplex scramblers.

And through that murk the Lensman directed a thought, with the full power of mind and Lens.

"Port Admiral Haynes—Prime Base! Port Admiral Haynes—Prime Base! Urgent! Kinnison calling from the direction of Sirius—urgent!" he sent out the fiercely-driven message.

It so happened that at Prime Base it was deep night, and Port Admiral Haynes was sound asleep; but, trigger-nerved old space-cat that he was, he came instantly and fully awake. Scarcely had an eye flicked open than his answer had been hurled back:

"Haynes acknowledging—send it, Kinnison!"

"Coming in, in a pirate ship. All the pirates in space are on our necks, but we're coming in, in spite of hell and high water! Don't send up any ships to help us down—they could blast you out of space in a second, but they can't stop us. Get ready—it won't be long now!"

Then, after the Port Admiral had sounded the emergency alarm, Kinnison went on:

"Our ship carries no markings, but there's only one of us and you'll know which one it is—we'll be doing the dodging. They'd be crazy to follow us down into atmosphere, with all the stuff you've got, but they act crazy enough to do almost anything. If they do follow us down, get ready to give 'em hell—here we are!"

Pursued and pursuers had touched the outermost fringe of the stratosphere; and, slowed down to optical visibility by even that highly rarified atmosphere, the battle raged in incandescent splendor. One ship was spinning, twisting, looping, gyrating, jumping and darting hither and thither—performing every weird maneuver that the fertile and agile minds of the Patrolmen could improvise—to shake off the horde of attackers.

The pirates, on the other hand, were desperately determined that, whatever the cost, THE Lensman should not land. Tractors would not hold and the inertialess ship could not be rammed. Therefore their strategy was that which had worked so successfully four times before in similar case—to englobe the ship completely and thus beam her down. And while attempting this englobement they so massed their forces as to drive the Lensman's vessel as far as possible away from the grim and tremendously powerful fortifications of Prime Base, almost directly below them.

But the four ships which the pirates had recaptured had been manned by Velantians; whereas in this one Kinnison the Lensman and Henderson the Master Pilot were calling upon their every resource of instantaneous nervous reaction, of brilliant brain and of lightning hand to avoid that fatal trap. And avoid it they did, by series after series of fantastic maneuvers never set down in any manual of space combat.

Powerful as were the weapons of Prime Base, in that thick atmosphere their effective range was less than fifty miles. Therefore the gunners, idle at their controls, and the officers of the superdreadnaughts, chained by definite orders to the ground, fumed and swore as, powerless to help their battling fellows, they stood by and watched in their plates the furious engagement so high overhead.

But slowly, *so* slowly, Kinnison won his way downward, keeping as close over Base as he could without being englobed, and finally he managed to get within range of the gigantic projectors of the Patrol. Only the heaviest of the fixed-mount guns could reach that mad whirlpool of ships, but each one of them raved out against the same spot at precisely the same instant. In the inferno which that spot instantly became, not even a full-driven wall-shield could endure, and a vast hole yawned where pirate ships had been. The beams flicked off, and, timed by his Lens, Kinnison shot his ship through that hole before it could be closed and arrowed downward at maximum blast.

Ship after ship of the pirate horde followed him down in madly suicidal last attempts to blast him out of the ether; down toward the terrific armament of the base. Prime Base itself, the most dreaded, the most heavily armed, the most impregnable fortress of the Galactic Patrol! Nothing afloat could even threaten that citadel—the overbold attackers simply disappeared in brief flashes of coruscant vapor.

Kinnison, even before inerting his ship preparatory to landing, called his commander.

"Did any of the other boys beat us in, sir?" he asked.

"No, sir," came the curt response. Congratulations, felicitations, and celebration would come later; Haynes was now the Port Admiral receiving an official report.

"Then, sir, I have the honor to report that the expedition has succeeded," and he could not help adding informally, youthfully exultant at the success of his first real mission, "We've brought home the bacon!"

13

MAULERS AFLOAT

A powerful fleet had been sent to rescue those of the *Brittania*'s crew who might have managed to stay out of the clutches of the pirates. The wildly enthusiastic celebration inside Prime Base was over. Outside the force-walls of the Reservation, however, it was just beginning. The specialists and the Velantians were in the thick of it. No one on Earth knew anything about Velantia, and those highly intelligent reptilian beings knew just as little of Tellus. Nevertheless, simply because they had aided the Patrolmen, the visitors were practically given the keys to the planet, and they were enjoying the experience tremendously.

"We want Kinnison—we want Kinnison!" the festive crowd, led by Universal Telenews men, had been yelling; and finally the Lensman came out. But after one pose before a lens and a few words into a microphone, he pleaded, "There's my call, now—urgent!" and fled back inside Reservation. Then the milling tide of celebrants rolled back toward the city, taking with it every Patrolman who could get leave.

Engineers and designers were swarming through and over the pirate ship Kinnison had driven home, each armed with a sheaf of blue-prints already prepared from the long-cherished data-spool, each directing a corps of mechanics in dismantling some mechanism of the great space-rover. To this hive of bustling activity it was that Kinnison had been called. He stood there, answering as best he could the multitude of questions being fired at him from all sides, until he was rescued by no less a personage than Port Admiral Haynes.

"You gentlemen can get your information from the data sheets better than you can from Kinnison," he remarked with a smile, "and I want to take his report without any more delay."

Hand under arm, the old Lensman led the young one away, but once inside his private office he summoned neither secretary nor recorder. Instead, he pushed the buttons which set up a complete-coverage shield and spoke.

"Now, son, open up. Out with it—everything that you have been holding back ever since you landed. I got your signal."

"Well, yes, I have been holding back," Kinnison admitted. "I haven't got enough jets to be sticking my neck out in fast company, even if it were something to be discussed in public, which it isn't. I'm glad you could give me this time so quick. I want to go over an idea with you, and with *no one else*. It may be as cockeyed as Trenco's ether—you're to be the sole judge of that—but you'll know I mean well, no matter how goofy it is."

"That certainly is not an overstatement," Haynes replied, dryly. "Go ahead."

"The great peculiarity of space combat is that we fly free, but fight inert," Kinnison began, apparently irrelevantly, but choosing his phraseology with care. "To force an engagement one ship locks to the other first with tracers, then with tractors, and goes inert. Thus, relative speed determines the ability to force or to avoid engagement; but it is relative power that determines the outcome. Heretofore the pirates—"

"And by the way, we are belittling our opponents and building up a disastrous overconfidence in ourselves by calling them pirates. They are not—they can't be. Boskonia must be more than a race or a system— it is very probably a galaxy-wide culture. It is an absolute despotism, holding its authority by means of a rigid system of rewards and punishments. In our eyes it is fundamentally wrong, but it works—*how* it works! It is organized just as we are, and is apparently as strong in bases, vessels, and personnel.

"Boskonia has had the better of us, both in speed—except for the *Brittania*'s momentary advantage—and in power. That advantage is now lost to them. We will have, then, two immense powers, each galactic in scope, each tremendously powerful in arms, equipment, and personnel; each having exactly the same weapons and defenses, and each determined to wipe out the other. A stalemate is inevitable; an absolute deadlock; a sheerly destructive war of attrition which will go on for centuries and which must end in the annihilation of both Boskonia and civilization."

"But our new projectors and screens!" protested the older man. "They give us an overwhelming advantage. We can force or avoid engagement, as we please. You know the plan to crush them—you helped to develop it."

"Yes, I know the plan. I also know that we will not crush them. So do you. We both know that our advantage will be only temporary.'' The young Lensman, unimpressed, was in deadly earnest.

The Admiral did not reply for a time. Deep down, he himself had felt the doubt; but neither he nor any other of his school had ever mentioned the thing that Kinnison had now so baldly put into words. He knew that whatever one side had, of weapon or armor or equipment, would sooner or later become the property of the other; as was witnessed by the desperate venture which Kinnison himself had so recently and so successfully concluded. He knew that the devices installed in the vessels captured upon Velantia had been destroyed before falling into the hands of the enemy, but he also knew that with entire fleets so equipped the new arms could not be kept secret indefinitely. Therefore he finally replied:

"That may be true." He paused, then went on like the indomitable veteran that he was. "But we have the advantage now and we'll drive it while we've got it. After all, we *may* be able to hold it long enough."

"I've just thought of one more thing that would help—communication," Kinnison did not argue the previous point, but went ahead. "It seems to be impossible to drive any kind of a communicator beam through the double interference . . ."

"*Seems* to be!" barked Haynes. "It *is* impossible! Nothing but a thought . . ."

"That's it exactly—*thought!*" interrupted Kinnison in turn. "The Velantians can do things with a Lens that nobody would believe possible. Why not examine some of them for Lensmen? I'm sure that Worsel could pass, and probably many others. They can drive thoughts through anything except their own thought-screens—and what communicators they would make!"

"That idea has distinct possibilities and will be followed up. However, it is not what you wanted to discuss. Go ahead."

"QX." Kinnison went into Lens-to-Lens communication. "I want some kind of a shield or screen that will neutralize or nullify a detector. I asked Hotchkiss, the communications expert, about it—under seal. He said it had never been investigated, even as an academic problem in research, but that it was theoretically possible."

"This room is shielded, you know." Haynes was surprised at the use of the Lenses. "Is it *that* important?"

"I don't know. As I said before, I may be cockeyed; but if my idea is any good at all that nullifier is the most important thing in the universe, and if word of it gets out it may be useless. You see, sir, over the long route, the only really permanent advantage that we have over Boskonia, the one thing they can't get, is the Lens. There must be some way to use it. If that nullifier is possible, and if we can keep it secret for a while, I believe I've found it. At least, I want to try something. It may not work—probably it won't, it's a mighty slim chance—but if it does, we may be able to wipe out Boskonia in a few months instead of carrying on forever a war of attrition. First, I want to go . . ."

"Hold on!" Haynes snapped. "I've been thinking, too. I can't see any possible relation between such a device and any real military weapon, or the Lens, either. If I can't, not many others can, and that's a point in your favor. If there's anything at all in your idea, it's too big to share with anyone, even me. Keep it to yourself."

"But it's a peculiar hook-up, and may not be any good at all," protested Kinnison. "You might want to cancel it."

"No danger of that," came the positive statement. "You know more about the pirates—pardon me, about Boskonia—than any other Patrolman. You believe that your idea has some slight chance of success. Very well—that fact is enough to put every resource of the Patrol back of you. Put your idea on a tape under Lensman's Seal, so that it will not be lost in case of your death. Then go ahead. If it is possible to develop that nullifier you shall have it. Hotchkiss will take charge of it, and have any other Lensmen he wants. No one except Lensmen will work on it or know anything about it. No records will be kept. It will not even exist until you yourself release it to us."

"Thanks, sir," and Kinnison left the room.

Then for weeks Prime Base was the scene of an activity furious indeed. New apparatus was designed and tested—new shears, new generators, new scramblers, and many other new things. Each item was designed and tested, redesigned and retested, until even the most skeptical of the Patrol's engineers could no longer find in it anything to criticize. Then throughout the galaxy the ships of the Patrol were recalled to their sector bases to be rebuilt.

There were to be two great classes of vessels. Those of the first—special scouting cruisers—were to have speed and defense—nothing else. They were to be the fastest things in space, and able to defend themselves against attack—that was all. Vessels of the second class had to be built from the keel upward, since nothing even remotely like them had theretofore been conceived. They were to be huge, ungainly, slow—simply storehouses of incomprehensibly vast powers of offense. They carried projectors of a size and power never before set upon movable foundations, nor were they dependent upon cosmic energy. They carried their own, in bank upon bank of stupendous accumulators. In fact, each of these monstrous floating fortresses was to be able to generate screens of such design and power that no vessel anywhere near them could receive cosmic energy!

This, then, was the bolt which civilization was preparing to hurl against Boskonia. In theory the thing was simplicity itself. The ultra-fast cruisers would catch the enemy, lock on with tractors so hard that they could not be sheared, and go inert, thus anchoring the enemy in space. Then, while absorbing and dissipating everything that the opposition could send, they would put out a peculiarly patterned interference, the center of which could easily be located. The mobile fortresses would then come up, cut off the Boskonians' power intake, and finish up the job.

Not soon was that bolt forged; but in time civilization was ready to launch its terrific and, it was generally hoped and believed, conclusive attack upon Boskonia. Every sector base and sub-base was ready; the zero hour had been set.

At Prime Base Kimball Kinnison, the youngest Tellurian ever to wear the four silver bars of captain, sat at the conning-plate of the heavy battle cruiser *Brittania*, so named at his own request. He thrilled inwardly as he thought of her speed. Such was her force of drive that, streamlined to the ultimate degree although she was, she had special wall-shields, and special dissipators to radiate into space the heat of friction of the medium through which she tore so madly. Otherwise she would have destroyed herself in an hour of full blast, even in the hard vacuum of interstellar space!

And in his office Port Admiral Haynes watched a chronometer. Minutes to go—then seconds.

"Clear ether!" His deep voice was gruff with unexpressed emotion. "Five seconds—four—three—two—one—Lift!" and the Fleet shot into the air.

The first objective of this Tellurian fleet was very close indeed to home, for the Boskonians had established a base upon Neptune's moon, right here in the Solarian System. So close to Prime Base that only intensive screening and constant vigilance had kept its spy-rays out; so powerful that the ordinary battleships of the Patrol had not been sent against it. Now it was to be reduced.

Short as was the time necessary to traverse any interplanetary distance, the Solarians were detected and were met in force by the ships of Boskone. But scarcely had battle been joined when the enemy began to realize that this was to be a battle the like of which they had never before seen; and when they began to understand it, it was too late. They could not run, and all space was so full of interference that they could not even report to Helmuth what was going on. These first, peculiarly tear-drop-shaped vessels of the Patrol did not fight at all. They simply held on like bull-dogs, taking without response everything that the white-hot projectors could throw at them. Their defensive screens radiated fiercely, high into the violet, under the appalling punishment being dealt out to them by the batteries of ship and shore, but they did not go down. Nor did the grip of a single tractor loosen from its anchorage. And in minutes the squat and monstrous maulers came up. Out went their cosmic-energy blocking screens, out shot their tractor beams, and out from the refractory throats of their stupendous projectors raved the most terrifically destructive forces ever generated by mobile machinery.

Boskonian outer screens scarcely even flickered as they went down before the immeasurable, the incredible violence of that thrust. The second course offered a briefly brilliant burst of violet radiance as it gave way. The inner screen resisted stubbornly as it ran the spectrum in a wildly coruscant display of pyrotechnic splendor; but it, too, went through the ultra-violet and into the black. Now the wall-shield itself—that inconceivably rigid fabrication of pure force which only the detonation of twenty metric tons of duodec had ever been known to rupture—was all that barred from the base metal of Boskonian walls the utterly indescribable fury of the maulers' beams. Now force was streaming from that shield in veritable torrents. So terrible were the conflicting energies there at grips that their neutralization was actually visible and tangible. In sheets and masses, in terrific, ether-wracking vortices, and in miles-long, pillaring streamers and flashes, those energies were being hurled away. Hurled to all the points of the sphere's full compass, filling and suffusing all nearby space.

The Boskonian commanders stared at their instruments, first in bewildered amazement and then in sheer, stark, unbelieving horror as their power-intake dropped to zero and their wall-shields began to fail—and still the attack continued in never-lessening power. Surely that beaming *must* slacken down soon—no conceivable mobile plant could throw such a load for long!

But those mobile plants could—and did. The attack kept up, at the terrifically high level upon which it had begun. No ordinary storage cells fed those mighty projectors; along no ordinary bus-bars were their Titanic amperages borne. Those maulers were designed to do just one thing—to *maul*—and that one thing they did well; relentlessly and thoroughly.

Higher and higher into the spectrum the defending wall-shields began to radiate. At the first blast they had leaped almost through the visible spectrum, in one unbearably fierce succession of red, orange, yellow, green, blue, and indigo; up to a sultry, coruscating, blindingly hard violet. Now the doomed shields began leaping erratically into the ultra-violet. To the eye they were already invisible; upon the recorders they were showing momentary flashes of black.

Soon they went down; and in the instant of each failure one vessel of Boskonia was no more. For, that last defense gone, nothing save unresisting metal was left to withstand the ardor of those ultra-powerful, ravening beams. As has already been said, no substance, however refractory or resistant or inert, can endure even momentarily in such a field of force. Therefore every atom, alike of vessel and of contents, went to make up the searing, seething burst of brilliant, incandescently luminous vapor which suffused all circumambient space.

Thus passed out of the Scheme of Things the vessels of the Solarian Detachment of Boskonia. Not a single vessel escaped; the cruisers saw to that. And then the attack thundered on to the base. Here the cruisers were useless; they merely formed an observant fringe, the while continuing to so blanket all channels of communication that the doomed pirates could send out no word of what was happening. The maulers moved up and grimly, doggedly, methodically went to work.

Since a base is always much more powerfully armored than is a battleship, the reduction of the fortresses took longer than had the destruction of the fleet. But their receptors could no longer draw power from the sun or from any other heavenly body, and their other sources of power were comparatively weak. Therefore their defenses also failed under that incessant assault. Course after course their screens went down, and with the last ones went every structure. The maulers' beams went through metal and masonry as effortlessly as steel-jacketed bullets go through butter, and bored on, deep into the planet's bed-rock, before their frightful force was spent.

Then around and around they spiralled until nothing whatever was left of the Boskonian works; until only a seething, white-hot lake of molten lava in the midst of the satellite's frigid waste was all that remained to show that anything had ever been built there.

Surrender had not been thought of. Quarter or clemency had not been asked or offered. Victory of itself was not enough. This was, and of stern necessity had to be, a war of utter, complete, and merciless extinction.

14

UNATTACHED

The enemy stronghold so insultingly close to prime Base having been obliterated, Regional Fleets, in loose formations, began to scour the various Galactic Regions. For a few weeks game was plentiful enough. Hundreds of raiding vessels were overtaken and held by the Patrol cruisers, then blasted to vapor by the maulers.

Many Boskonian bases were also reduced. The locations of most of these had long been known to the Intelligence Service, others were detected or discovered by the fast-flying cruisers themselves. Marauding vessels revealed the sites of others by succeeding in reaching them before being overtaken by the cruisers. Others were found by the tracers and loops of the Signal Corps.

Very few of these bases were hidden or in any way difficult of access, and most of them fell before the blasts of a single mauler. But if one mauler was not enough, others were summoned until it did fall. One fortress, a hitherto unknown and surprisingly strong Secor Base, required the concentration of every mauler of Tellus, but they were brought up and the fortress fell. As had been said, this was a war of extinction and every pirate base that was found was wiped out.

But one day a cruiser found a base which had not even a spy-ray shield up, and a cursory inspection showed it to be completely empty. Machinery, equipment, stores, and personnel had all been evacuated. Suspicious, the Patrol vessels stood off and beamed it from afar, but there were no untoward occurrences. The structures simply slumped down into lava, and that was all.

Every base discovered thereafter was in the same condition, and at the same time the ships of Boskone, formerly so plentiful, disappeared utterly from space. Day after day the cruisers sped hither and thither throughout the vast reaches of the void, at the peak of their unimaginably high pace, without finding a trace of any Boskonian vessel. More remarkable still, and for the first time in years, the ether was absolutely free from Boskonian interference.

Following an impulse, Kinnison asked and received permission to take his ship on scouting duty. At maximum blast he drove toward the Velantian system, to the point at which he had picked up Helmuth's communication line. Along that line he drove for days, halting only when well outside the galaxy. Ahead of him there was nothing reachable except a few star-clusters. Behind him there extended the immensity of the galactic lens in all its splendor, but Captain Kinnison had no eye for astronomical beauty that day.

He held the *Brittania* there for an hour, while he mulled over in his mind what the apparent facts could mean. He knew that he had covered the line, from its point of determination out beyond the galaxy's edge. He knew that his detectors, operating as they had been in clear and undistorted ether, could not possibly have missed a thing as large as Helmuth's base must be, if it had been anywhere near that line; that their effective range was immensely greater than the largest possible error in the determination or the following of the line. There were, he concluded, four possible explanations, and only four.

First, Helmuth's base might also have been evacuated. This was unthinkable. From what he himself knew of Helmuth that base would be as nearly impregnable as anything could be made, and it was no more apt to be vacated than was Prime Base of the Patrol. Second, it might be subterranean; buried under enough metal-bearing rock to ground out all radiation. This possibility was just as unlikely as the first. Third, Helmuth might already have the device he himself wanted so badly, and upon which Hotchkiss and the other experts had been at work so long, a detector nullifier. This was possible, distinctly so. Possible enough, at least, to warrant filing the idea for future consideration. Fourth, that base might not be in the galaxy at all, but in that star-cluster out there straight ahead of him, or possibly in one even farther away. That idea seemed the best of the four. It would necessitate ultra-powerful communicators, of course, but Helmuth could very well have them. It squared up in other ways—its pattern fitted into the matrix very nicely.

But if that base were out there ... it could stay there—for a while ... a battle cruiser just wasn't enough ship for that job. Too much opposition out there, and not—enough—ship ... Or too much ship? But he wasn't ready, yet, anyway. He needed, and would get, another line on Helmuth's base. Therefore, shrugging his shoulders, he whirled his vessel about and set out to rejoin the fleet.

While a full day short of junction, Kinnison was called to his plate, to see upon its lambent surface the visage of Port Admiral Haynes.

"Did you find out anything on your trip?" he asked.

"Nothing definite, sir. Just a couple of things to think about, is all. But I can say that I don't like this at all—I don't like anything about it or any part of it."

"No more do I," agreed the admiral. "It looks very much as though your forecast of a stalemate might be about to eventuate. Where are you headed for now?"

"Back to the Fleet."

"Don't do it. Stay on scouting duty for a while longer. And, unless something more interesting turns up, report back here to me—we have something that may interest you. The boys have been . . ."

The admiral's picture was broken up into flashes of blinding light and his words became a meaningless, jumbled roar of noise. A distress call had begun to come in, only to be blotted out by a flood of Boskonian static interference, of which the ether had for so long been clear. The young Lensman used his Lens.

"Excuse me, sir, while I see what this is all about?"

"Certainly, son."

"Got its center located?" Kinnison yelped at his communications officer. "They're close—right in our laps!"

"Yes, sir!" and the radio man snapped out numbers.

"Blast!" the captain commanded, unnecessarily; for the alert pilot had already set the course and was kicking in full-blast drive. "If that baby is what I think it is, all hell's out for noon."

Toward the center of disturbance the *Brittania* flashed, emitting now a scream of peculiarly patterned interference which was not only a scrambler of all un-Lensed communication throughout that whole part of the galaxy, but also an imperative call for any mauler within range. So close had the cruiser been to the scene of depredation that for her to reach it required only minutes.

There lay the merchantman and her Boskonian assailant. Emboldened by the cessation of piratical activities, some shipping concern had sent out a freighter, loaded probably with highly "urgent" cargo; and this was the result. The marauder, inert now, had gripped her with his tractors and was beaming her into submission. She was resisting, but feebly now; it was apparent that her screens were failing. Her crew must soon open ports in token of surrender or roast to a man; and they would probably prefer to roast.

Thus the situation obtaining in one instant. The next instant it was changed; the Boskonian discovering suddenly that his beams, instead of boring through the weak defenses of the freighter, were not even exciting to a glow the mighty protective envelopes of a battle-cruiser of the Patrol. He switched from the diffused heat-beam he had been using upon the merchantman to the hardest, hottest, most penetrating beam of annihilation he mounted—with but little more to show for it and with no better results. For the *Brittania*'s screens had been designed to stand up almost indefinitely against the most potent beams of any ordinary warship, and they stood up.

Kinnison had tremendously powerful beams of his own, but he did not use them. It would take the super-powerful offense of a mauler to produce a definite answer to the question seething in his mind.

Increase power as the pirate would, to whatever ruinous overload, he could not break down Kinnison's screens; nor, dodge as he would, could he again get in position to attack his former prey. And eventually the mauler arrived; fortunately it, too, had been fairly close by. Out reached its mighty tractors. Out raved one of its tremendous beams, striking the Boskonian's defenses squarely amidships.

That beam struck and the pirate ship disappeared—but not in a hazily incandescent flare of volatilized metal. The raider disappeared bodily, and still all in one piece. He had put out super-shears of his own, snapping the mauler's supposedly unbreakable tractors like threads; and the velocity of his departure was due almost as much to the pressor effect of the Patrol beam as it was to the thrust of his own drivers.

It was the beginning of the stalemate Kinnison had foreseen.

"I was afraid of that," the young captain muttered; and, paying no attention whatever to the merchantman, he called the commander of the mauler. At this close range, of course, no ether scrambler could interfere with visual apparatus, and there on his plate he saw the face of Clifford Maitland, the man who had graduated number two in his own class.

"Hi, Kim, you old space-flea!" Maitland exclaimed in delight. "Oh, pardon me, sir," he went on in mock deference, with an exaggerated salute. "To a guy with four jets, I should say. . . ."

"Seal that, Cliff, or I'll climb up you like a squirrel, first chance I get!" Kinnison retorted. "So they've got you skippering an El Ponderoso, huh? Think of a mere infant like you being let play with so much high-power! What'll we do about this heap here?"

"Damfino. It isn't covered, so you'll have to tell me, Captain."

"Who'm I to be passing out orders? As you say, it isn't covered in the book—it's against G I regs for them to be cutting our tractors. But he's all yours, not mine—I've got to flit. You might find out what he's carrying, from where, to where, and why. Then, if you want to, you can escort him either back where he came from or on to where he's going;

whichever you think best. If this interference doesn't let up, maybe you'd better Lens Prime Base for orders. Or use your own judgment, if any. Clear ether, Cliff, I've got to buzz along."

"Clear ether, spacehound!"

"Now, Hank," Kinnison turned to his pilot, "we've got urgent business at Prime Base—and when I say 'urgent' I don't mean perchance. Let's see you burn a hole in the ether."

The *Brittania* streaked Earthward, and scarcely had she touched ground when Kinnison was summoned to the office of the Port Admiral. As soon as he was announced, Haynes bruskly cleared his office and sealed it against any possible form of intrusion or eavesdropping. He had aged noticeably since these two had had that memorable conference in this same room. His face was lined and care-worn, his eyes and his entire mien bore witness to days and nights of sleeplessly continuous work.

"You were right, Kinnison," he began, Lens to Lens. "A stalemate it is; a hopeless deadlock. I called you in to tell you that Hotchkiss has your nullifier done, and that it works perfectly against all long-range stuff. Against electromagnetics, however, it is not very effective. About all that can be done, it seems, is to shorten the range; and it doesn't interfere with vision at all."

"I can get by with that, I think—I will be out of electromagnetic range most of the time, and nobody watches their electos very close, anyway. Thanks a lot. It's ready to install?"

"Doesn't need installation. It's such a little thing you can put it in your pocket. It's self-contained and will work anywhere."

"Better and better. In that case I'll need two of them—and a ship. I would like to have one of those new automatic speedsters.* Lots of legs,

---

*Unlike the larger war-vessels of the Patrol, speedsters are very narrow in proportion to their length, and in their design nothing is considered save speed and maneuverability. Very definitely they are not built for comfort. Thus, although their gravity plates are set for horizontal flight, they have braking jets, under jets, side jets, and top jets, as well as driving jets; so that in inert maneuvering any direction whatever may seem "down," and that direction may change with bewildering rapidity.

Nothing can be loose in a speedster—everything, even to food-supplies in the refrigerators, must be clamped into place. Sleeping is done in hammocks, not in beds. All seats and resting-places have heavy safety-straps, and there are no loose items of furniture or equipment anywhere on board.

Because they are designed for the utmost possible speed in the free condition, speedsters are extremely cranky and tricky in inert flight unless they are being handled upon their under jets, which are designed and placed specifically and only for inert flight.

Some of the ultra-fast vessels of the pirates, as will be brought out later, were also of this shape and design. E.E.S.

cruising range, and screens. Only one beam, but I probably won't use even that one . . ."

"Going *alone*?" interrupted Haynes. "Better take your battle-cruiser, at least. I don't like the idea of you going into deep space alone."

"I don't particularly relish the prospect, either, but it's got to be that way. The whole fleet, maulers and all, isn't enough to do by force what's got to be done, and even two men is too many to do it in the only way it can be done. You see, sir . . ."

"No explanations, please. It's on the spool, where we can get it if we need it. Are you informed as to the latest developments?"

"No, sir. I heard a little coming in, but not much."

"We are almost back where we were before you took off in the first *Brittania*. Commerce is almost at a standstill. All shipping firms are practically idle, but that is neither all of it nor the worst of it. You may not realize how important interstellar trade is; but as a result of its stoppage general business has slowed down tremendously. As is only to be expected, perhaps, complaints are coming in by the thousand because we have not already blasted the pirates out of space, and demands that we do so at once. They do not understand the true situation, nor realize that we are doing everything we can. We cannot send a mauler with every freighter and liner, and mauler-escorted vessels are the only ones to arrive at their destinations."

"But why? With tractor shears on all ships, how can they hold them?" asked Kinnison.

"Magnets!" snorted Haynes. "Plain, old-fashioned electromagnets. No pull to speak of, at a distance, of course, but with the raider running free they don't need much. Close up—lock on—board and storm—all done!"

"Hm . . . m . . . m. That changes things. I've got to find a pirate ship. I was planning on following a freighter or liner out toward Alsakan, but if there aren't any to follow . . . I'll have to hunt around . . ."

"That is easily arranged. Lots of them want to go. We will let one go, with a mauler accompanying her, but well outside detector range."

"That covers everything, then, except the assignment. I can't very well ask for leave, but maybe I could be put on special assignment, reporting direct to you?"

"Something better than that," and Haynes smiled broadly, in genuine pleasure. "Everything is fixed. Your Release has been entered in the books. Your commission as captain has been cancelled, so leave your uniform in your former quarters. Here is your credit book and here is the rest of your kit. You are now an Unattached Lensman."

The Release! The goal toward which—all Lensmen strive, but which so few attain! He was now a free agent, responsible to no one and to nothing save his own conscience. He was no longer of Earth, nor of the Solarian System, but of the galaxy as a whole. He was no longer a tiny cog in the immense machine of the Galactic Patrol; wherever he might go, throughout the immensity of the entire Island Universe, he *would be* the Galactic Patrol!

"Yes, it's real." The older man was enjoying the youngster's stupefaction at his Release, reminding him as it did of the time, long years before, when he had won his own. "You go anywhere you please and do anything you please, for as long as you please. You take anything you want, whenever you want it, with or without giving reasons—although you will usually give a thumb-printed credit slip in return. You report if, as, when, where, how, and to whom you please—or not, as you please. You don't even get a salary any more. You help yourself to that, too, wherever you may be; as much as you want, whenever you want it."

"But, sir . . . I . . . you . . . I mean . . . that is . . ." Kinnison gulped three times before he could speak coherently. "I'm not ready, sir. Why, I'm nothing but a kid—I haven't got enough jets to swing it. Just the bare thought of it scares me into hysterics!"

"It would—it always does." Haynes was very much in earnest now, but it was a glad, proud earnestness. "You are to be as nearly absolutely free an agent as it is possible for a living, flesh-and-blood creature to be. To the man on the street that would seem to spell a condition of perfect bliss. Only a Gray Lensman knows what a frightful load it really is; but it is a load that such a Lensman is glad and proud to carry."

"Yes, sir, he would be, of course, if he . . ."

"That thought will bother you for a time—if it did not, you would not be here—but don't worry about it any more than you can help. All I can say is that in the opinion of those who should know, not only have you proved yourself ready for Release, but also you have earned it."

"How do they figure that out?" Kinnison demanded, hotly. "All that saved my bacon on that trip was luck—a burned-out Bergenholm—and at the time I thought it was bad luck, at that. And vanBuskirk and Worsel and the other boys and the Lord knows who else pulled me out of jam after jam. I'd like awfully well to believe that I'm ready, sir, but I'm not. I can't take credit for pure dumb luck and for other men's abilities."

"Well, cooperation is to be expected, and we like to make Gray Lensmen out of the lucky ones." Haynes laughed deeply. "It may make you feel better, though, if I tell you two more things. First, that so far you have made the best showing of any man yet graduated from Wentworth Hall. Second, that we of the Court believe that you would have succeeded in that almost impossible mission without vanBuskirk, without Worsel, and without the lucky failure of the Bergenholm. In a different, and now of course unguessable fashion, but succeeded, nevertheless. Nor is this to be taken as in any sense a belittlement of the very real abilities of those others, nor a denial that luck, or chance, does exist. It is merely our recognition of the fact that you have what it takes to be an Unattached Lensman.

"Seal it now, and buzz off!" he commanded, as Kinnison tried to say something; and, clapping him on the shoulder, he turned him around and gave him a gentle shove toward the door. "Clear ether, lad!"

"Same to you, sir—all of it there is. I still think that you and all the rest of the Court are cockeyed; but I'll try not to let you down," and the newly unattached Lensman blundered out. He stumbled over the threshold, bumped against a stenographer who was hurrying along the corridor, and almost barged into the jamb of the entrance door instead of going through the opening. Outside he regained his physical poise and walked on air toward his quarters; but he never could remember afterward what he did or whom he met on that long, fast hike. Over and over the one thought pounded in his brain: unattached! *Unattached!!* UNATTACHED!!!

And behind him, in the Port Admiral's office, that high official sat and mused, smiling faintly with lips and eyes, staring unseeingly at the still open doorway through which Kinnison had staggered. The boy had measured up in every particular. He would be a good man. He would marry. He did not think so now, of course—in his own mind his life was consecrate—but he would. If necessary, the Patrol itself would see to it that he did. There were ways, and such stock was altogether too good not to be propagated. And, fifteen years from now—if he lived— when he was no longer fit for the grinding, grueling life to which he now looked forward so eagerly, he would select the Earth-bound job for which he was best fitted and would become a good executive. For such were the executives of the Patrol. But this day-dreaming was getting him nowhere, fast: he shook himself and plunged again into his work.

Kinnison reached his quarters at last, realizing with a thrill that they were no longer his. He now had no quarters, no residence, no address. Wherever he might be, throughout the whole of illimitable space, there was his home. But, instead of being dismayed by the thought of the life he faced, he was filled by a fierce eagerness to be actually living it.

There was a tap at his door and an orderly entered, carrying a bulky package.

"Your Grays, sir," he announced, with a crisp salute.

"Thanks." Kinnison returned the salute as smartly; and, almost before the door had closed, he was yanking off the space-black-and-silver-and-gold gorgeousness of the uniform he wore.

Stripped bare, he made the quick, meaningful gesture he had not really expected ever to be able to make. Gray Seal. No entity has ever donned or ever will don the Gray unmoved, nor without dedicating himself anew to that for which it stands.

The Gray—the unadorned, neutral-colored leather that was the proud garb of that branch of the Patrol to which he was thenceforth to belong. It had been tailored to his measurements, and he could not help studying with approval his reflection in the mirror. The round, almost visorless cap, heavily and softly quilted in protection against the helmet of his armor. The heavy goggles, opaque to all radiation harmful to the eyes. The short jacket, emphasizing broad shoulders and narrow waist. The trim breeches and high boots, encasing powerful, tapering legs.

"What an outfit—*what* an outfit!" he breathed. "And maybe I ain't such a bad-looking ape, at that, in these Grays!"

He did not then, and never did realize that he was wearing the plainest, drabbest, most strictly utilitarian uniform in existence; for to him, as to all others who knew it, the sheer, stark simplicity of the Unattached Lensman's plain gray leather transcended by far the gaudy trappings of the other branches of the Service. He had admired himself boyishly, as men do, feeling a trifle ashamed in so doing; but he did not then and never did appreciate what a striking figure of a man he really was as he strode out of Quarters and down the wide avenue toward the *Brittania*'s dock.

He was glad indeed that there had been no ceremony or public show connected with this, his real and only important graduation. For as his fellows—not only his own crew, but also his friends from all over the Reservation—thronged about him, mauling and pummeling him in congratulation and acclaim, he knew that he couldn't stand much more. If there were to be much more of it, he discovered suddenly, he would either pass out cold or cry like a baby—he didn't quite know which.

That whole howling, chanting mob clustered about him; and, considering it an honor to carry the least of his personal belongings, formed a yelling, cap-tossing escort. Traffic meant nothing whatever to that pleasantly mad crew; nor, temporarily, did regulations. Let traffice detour—let pedestrians, no matter how august, cool their heels—let cars, trucks, yes, even trains, wait until they got past—let everything wait, or turn around and go back, or go some other way. Here comes Kinnison! Kimball Kinnison! Kimball Kinnison, Gray Lensman! Make way! And way was made; from the *Brittania*'s dock clear across the base to the slip in which the Lensman's new speedster lay.

And what a ship this little speedster was! Trim, trig, streamlined to the ultimate she lay there; quiescent but surcharged with power. Almost sentient she was, this power-packed, ultraracy little fabrication of space-toughened alloy; instantly ready at his touch to liberate those tremendous energies which were to hurl him through the infinite reaches of the cosmic void.

None of the mob came aboard, of course. They backed off, still frantically waving and throwing whatever came closest to hand; and as Kinnison touched a button and shot into the air he swallowed several times in a vain attempt to dispose of an amazing lump which had somehow appeared in his throat.

15

THE DECOY

It so happened that for many long weeks there had been lying in New York Spaceport an urgent shipment for Alsakan, and that urgency was not merely a one-way affair. For, with the possible exception of a few packets whose owners had locked them in vaults and would not part with them at any price, there was not a single Alsakanite cigarette left on Earth!

Luxuries, then as now, soared feverishly in price with scarcity. Only the rich smoked Alsakanite cigarettes, and to those rich the price of anything they really wanted was a matter of almost complete indifference. And plenty of them wanted, and wanted badly, their Alsakanite cigarettes—there was no doubt of that. The current market report upon them was:

"Bid, one thousand credits per packet of ten. Offered, none at any price."

With that ever-climbing figure in mind, a merchant prince named Matthews had been trying to get an Alsakan-bound ship into the ether. He knew that one cargo of Alsakanite cigarettes safely landed in any Tellurian spaceport would yield more profit than could be made by his entire fleet in ten years of normal trading. Therefore he had for weeks been pulling every wire, and even every string, that he could reach; political, financial, even at times verging altogether too close for comfort upon the criminal—but without results.

For, even if he could find a crew willing to take the risk, to launch the ship without an escort would be out of the question. There would be no profit in a ship that did not return to Earth. The ship was his, to do with as he pleased, but the escorting maulers were assigned solely by the Galactic Patrol, and the Patrol would not give his ship an escort.

In answer to his first request, he had been informed that only cargoes classed as "necessary" were being escorted at all regularly; that "semi-necessary" loads were escorted occasionally, when of a particularly useful or desirable commodity and if opportunity offered; that "luxury" loads such as his were not being escorted at all; that he would be notified if, as, and when the *Prometheus* could be given escort. Then the merchant prince began his siege.

Politicians of high rank, local and national, sent in "requests" of varying degrees of diplomacy. Financiers first offered inducements, then threatened to "bear down," then put on all the various kinds of pressure known to their pressure-loving ilk. Pleas, demands, threats, and pressures were alike, however, futile. The Patrol could not be coaxed or bullied, cajoled, bribed, or cowed; and all further communications upon the subject, from whatever source originating were ignored.

Having exhausted his every resource of diplomacy, politics, guile, and finance, the merchant prince resigned himself to the inevitable and stopped trying to get his ship off the ground. Then New York Base received from Prime Base an open message, not even coded, which read:

"Authorize space-ship *Prometheus* to clear for Alsakan at will, escorted by Patrol ship B 42 TC 838, whose present orders are hereby cancelled. Signed, Haynes."

A demolition bomb dropped into that sub-base would not have caused greater excitement than did that message. No one could explain it—the base commander, the mauler's captain, the captain of the *Prometheus*, or the highly pleased but equally surprised Matthews—but all of them did whatever they could to expedite the departure of the freighter. She was, and had been for a long time, practically ready to sail.

As the base commander and Matthews sat in the office, shortly before the scheduled time of departure, Kinnison arrived—or, more correctly, let them know that he was there. He invited them both into the control-room of his speedster; and invitations from Gray Lensmen were accepted without question or demur.

"I suppose you are wondering what this is all about," he began. "I'll make it as short as I can. I asked you in here because this is the only convenient place in which I *know* that what we say will not be overheard. There are lots of spy-rays around here, whether you know it or not. The *Prometheus* is to be allowed to go to Alsakan, because that is where pirates seem to be most numerous, and we do not want to waste time hunting all over space to find one. Your vessel was selected, Mr. Matthews, for three reasons, and in spite of the attempts you have been making to obtain special privileges, not because of them. First, because there is no necessary or semi-necessary freight waiting for clearance into that region. Second, because we do not want your firm to fail. We do not know of any other large shipping line in such a shaky position as yours, nor of any firm anywhere to which one single cargo would make such an immense financial difference.''

"You are certainly right there, Lensman!" Matthews agreed, whole-heartedly. "It means bankruptcy on the one hand and a fortune on the other.''

"Here's what is to happen. The ship and the mauler blast off on schedule, fourteen minutes from now. They get about to Valeria, when they are both recalled—urgent orders for the mauler to go on rescue work. The mauler comes back, but your captain will, in all probability, keep on going, saying that he started out for Alsakan and that's where he's going . . .''

"But he wouldn't—he wouldn't *dare!*" gasped the shipowner.

"Sure he would," Kinnison insisted, cheerfully enough. "That is the third good reason your vessel is being allowed to set out, because it certainly will be attacked. You didn't know it until now, but your captain and over half of your crew are pirates themselves, and are going to . . .''

"What? Pirates!" Matthews bellowed. "I'll go down there and . . .''

"You'll do nothing whatever, Mr. Matthews, except watch things, and you will do that from here. The situation is under control.''

"But my ship! My cargo!" the shipper wailed. "We'll be ruined if they . . .''

"Let me finish, please," the Lensman interrupted. "As soon as the mauler turns back it is practically certain that your captain will send out a message, letting the pirates know that he is easy prey. Within a minute after sending that message, he dies. So does every other pirate aboard. Your ship lands on Valeria and takes on a crew of space-fighting wild-cats, headed by Peter vanBuskirk. Then it goes on toward Alsakan, and when the pirates board that ship, after its pre-arranged half-hearted re-sistance and easy surrender, they are going to think that all hell's out for noon. Especially since the mauler, back from her 'rescue work,' will be tagging along, not too far away.''

"Then my ship will really go to Alsakan, and back, safely?" Matthews was almost dazed. Matters were entirely out of his hands, and things had moved so rapidly that he hardly knew what to think. "But if my own crews are pirates, some of them may . . . but I can of course get police protection if necessary.''

"Unless something entirely unforeseen happens, the *Prometheus* will make the round trip in safety, cargoes and all—under mauler escort all the way. You will of course have to take the other matter up with your local police.''

''When is the attack to take place, sir?'' asked the base commander.

''That's what the mauler skipper wanted to know when I told him what was ahead of him,'' Kinnison grinned. ''He wanted to sneak up a little closer about that time. I'd like to know, myself, but unfortunately that will have to be decided by the pirates after they get the signal. It will be on the way out, though, because the cargo she has aboard now is a lot more valuable to Boskone than a load of Alsakanite cigarettes would be.''

''But do you think you can take the pirate ship that way?'' asked the commander, dubiously.

''No, but we will cut down his personnel to such an extent that he will have to head back for his base.''

''And that's what you want—the base. I see.''

He did not see—quite—but the Lensman did not enlighten him further.

There was a brilliant double flare as freighter and mauler lifted into the air, and Kinnison showed the ship-owner out.

''Hadn't I better be going, too?'' asked the commander. ''Those orders, you know.''

''A couple of minutes yet. I have another message for you—official. Matthews won't need a police escort long—if any. When that ship is attacked it is to be the signal for cleaning out every pirate in Greater New York—the worst pirate hot-bed on Tellus. Neither you nor your force will be in on it directly, but you might pass the word around, so that our own men will be informed ahead of the Telenews outfits.''

''Good! That has needed doing for a long time.''

''Yes, but you know it takes a long time to line up every man in such a big organization. They want to get them all, without getting any innocent bystanders.''

''Who's doing it—Prime Base?''

''Yes. Enough men will be thrown in here to do the whole job in an hour.''

''That *is* good news—clear ether, Lensman!'' and the base commander went back to his post.

As the air-lock toggles rammed home, sealing the exit behind the departing visitor, Kinnison eased his speedster into the air and headed for Valeria. Since the two vessels ahead of him had left atmosphere inertialess, as would he, and since several hundred seconds had elapsed since their take-off, he was of course some ten thousand miles off their line as well as being uncounted millions of miles behind them. But the larger distance meant no more than the smaller, and neither of them meant anything at all to the Patrol's finest speedster. Kinnison, on easy touring blast, caught up with them in minutes. Closing up to less than one light-year, he slowed his pace to match theirs and held his distance.

Any ordinary ship would have been detected long since, but Kinnison rode no ordinary ship. His speedster was immune to all detection save electromagnetic or visual, and therefore, even at that close range—the travel of half a minute for even a slow space-ship in open space—he was safe. For electromagnetics are useless at that distance: and visual apparatus, even with subether converters, is reliable only up to a few mere thousands of miles, unless the observer knows exactly what to look for and where to look for it.

Kinnison, then, closed up and followed the *Prometheus* and her mauler escort; and as they approached the Valerian solar system the recall message came booming in. Also, as had been expected, the renegade captain of the freighter sent his defiant answer and his message to the pirate high command. The mauler turned back, the merchantman kept on. Suddenly, however, she stopped, inert, and from her ports were ejected discrete bits of matter—probably the bodies of the Boskonian members of her crew. Then the *Prometheus*, again inertialess, flashed directly toward the planet Valeria.

An inertialess landing is, of course, highly irregular, and is made only when the ship is to take off again immediately. It saves all the time ordinarily lost in spiraling and deceleration, and saves the computation of a landing orbit, which is no task for an amateur computer. It is, however, dangerous. It takes power, plenty of it, to maintain the force which neutralizes the inertia of mass, and if that force fails even for an instant while a ship is upon a planet's surface, the consequences are usually highly disastrous. For in the neutralization of inertia there is no magic, no getting of something for nothing, no violation of Nature's law of the conservation of matter and energy. The instant that force becomes inoperative the ship possesses exactly the same velocity, momentum, and inertia that it possessed at the instant the force took effect. Thus, if a space-ship takes off from Earth, with its orbital velocity of about eighteen and one-half miles per second relative to the sun, goes free, dashes to Mars, lands free, and then goes inert, its original velocity, both in speed and in direction, is instantly restored; with consequences better imagined than described. Such a velocity of course *might* take the ship harmlessly into the air; but it probably would not.

Inertialess vessels do not ordinarily load freight. They do, however, take on passengers, especially military personnel accustomed to open-space maneuvers in powered space-suits. Men and ship must go inert—

separately, of course—immediately after leaving the planet, so that the men can match their intrinsic velocity to the ship's; but that takes only a very small fraction of the time required for an inert landing.

Hence the *Prometheus* landed free, and so did Kinnison. He stepped out, fully armored against Valeria's extremely heavy atmosphere, and laboring a trifle under its terrific gravitation, to be greeted cordially by *Lieutenant* vanBuskirk, whose fighting men were already streaming aboard the freighter.

"Hi, Kim!" the Dutchman called, gaily. "Everything went off like clockwork. Won't hold you up long—be blasting off in ten minutes."

"Ho, Lefty!" the Lensman acknowledged, as cordially, but saluting the newly commissioned officer with an exaggerated formality. "Say, Bus, I've been doing some thinking. Why wouldn't it be a good idea to . . ."

"Uh-uh, it would *not*," denied the fighter, positively. "I know what you're going to say—that you want in on this party—but don't say it."

"But I . . ." Kinnison began to argue.

"Nix," the Valerian declared flatly. "You've got to stay with your speedster. No room for her inside; she's clear full of cargo and my men. You can't clamp on outside, because that would give the whole thing away. And besides, for the first and last time in my life I've got a chance to give a Gray Lensman orders. Those orders are to stay out of and away from this ship—and I'll see to it that you do, too, you little Tellurian shrimp! Boy, what a kick I get out of that!"

"You would, you big, dumb Valerian ape—you always were a small-souled type!" Kinnison retorted. "Piggy-piggy . . . Haynes, huh?"

"Uh-huh." VanBuskirk nodded. "How else could I talk so rough to *you* and get away with it? However, don't feel too bad—you aren't missing a thing, really. It's in the cans already, and your fun is up ahead somewhere. And by the way, Kim, congratulations. You had it coming. We're all behind you, from here to the Magellanic Clouds and back."

"Thanks. The same to you, Bus, and many of 'em. Well, if you won't let me stow away, I'll tag along behind, I guess. Clear ether—or rather, I hope it's full of pirates by tomorrow morning. Won't be, though, probably; don't imagine they'll move until we're almost there."

And tag along Kinnison did, through thousands and thousands of parsecs of uneventful voyage.

Part of the time he spent in the speedster dashing hither and yon. Most of it, however, he spent in the vastly more comfortable mauler; to the armored side of which his tiny vessel clung with its magnetic clamps while he slept and ate, gossiped and read, exercised and played with the mauler's officers and crew, in deep-space comradery. It so happened, however, that when the long-awaited attack developed he was out in his speedster, and thus saw and heard everything from the beginning.

Space was filled with the old, familiar interference. The raider flashed up, locked on with magnets, and began to beam. Not heavily—scarcely enough to warm up the defensive screens—and Kinnison probed into the pirate with his spy-ray.

"Terrestrials—North Americans!" he exclaimed, half-aloud, startled for an instant. "But naturally they would be, since this is a put-up job and over half the crew were New York gangsters."

"The blighter's got his spy-ray screens up," the pilot was grumbling to his captain. The fact that he spoke in English was immaterial to the Lensman; he would have understood equally well any other possible form of communication or of thought exchange. "That wasn't part of the plan, was it?"

If Helmuth or one of the other able minds at Grand Base had been directing that attack it would have stopped right there. The pilot had shown a flash of feeling that, with a little encouragement, might have grown into a suspicion. But the captain was not an imaginative man. Therefore:

"Nothing was said about it, either way," he replied. "Probably the mate's on duty—he isn't one of us, you know. The captain will open up. If he doesn't do it pretty quick I'll open her up myself . . . there, the port's opening. Slide a little forward . . . hold it! Go get 'em, men!"

Men, hundreds of them, armed and armored, swarmed through the freighter's locks. But as the last man of the boarding party passed the portal something happened that was most decidedly not on the program. The outer port slammed shut and its toggles drove home!

"Blast those screens! Knock them down—get in there with a spray-ray!" barked the pirate captain. He was not one of those hardy and valiant souls who, like Gildersleeve, led in person the attacks of his cut-throats. He emulated instead the higher Boskonian officials and directed his raids from the safety of his control-room; but, as has been intimated, he was not exactly like those officials. It was only after it was too late that he became suspicious. "I wonder if somebody could have double-crossed us? . . . Highjackers?"

"We'll bally soon know," the pilot growled, and even as he spoke the spy-ray got through, revealing a very shambles.

For vanBuskirk and his Valerians had not been caught napping, nor were they a crew—unarmored, partially armed, and rendered even more impotent by internal mutiny, strife, and slaughter—such as the pirates had expected to find.

Instead, the boarders met a force that was overwhelmingly superior to their own. Not only in the strength and agility of its units, but also in that at least one semi-portable projector commanded every corridor of the freighter. In the blasts of those projectors most of the pirates died instantly, not knowing what struck them.

They were the fortunate ones. The others knew what was coming and saw it as it came, for the Valerians did not even draw their DeLameters. They knew that the pirates' armor could withstand for minutes any hand-weapon's beams, and they disdained to remount the heavy semi-portables. They came in with their space-axes, and at the sight the pirates broke and ran screaming in panic fear. But they could not escape. The toggles of the exit port were socketed and locked.

Therefore the storming party died to the last man; and, as vanBuskirk had foretold, it was scarcely even a struggle. For ordinary armor is so much tin-plate against a Valerian swinging a space-axe.

The spy-ray of the pirate captain got through just in time to see the ghastly finale of the massacre, and his face turned first purple, then white.

"The Patrol!" he gasped. "Valerians—a whole company of them! I'll say we've been double-crossed!"

"Righto—we've been jolly well had," the pilot agreed. "You don't know the half of it, either. Somebody's coming, and it isn't a boy scout. If a mauler should suck us in, we'd be very much a spent force, what?"

"Cut the gabble!" snapped the captain. "Is it a mauler, or not?"

"A bit too far away yet to say, but it probably is. They wouldn't have sent those jaspers out without cover, old bean—they know we can burn that freighter's screens down in an hour. Better get ready to run, what?"

The commander did so, wild thoughts racing through his mind. If a mauler got close enough to him to use magnets, he was done. His heaviest beams wouldn't even warm up a mauler's screens; his defenses wouldn't stand up for a second against a mauler's blasts . . . and he'd be ordered back to base . . .

"Tally ho, old fruit!" The pilot slammed on maximum blast. "It's a mauler and we've been bloody well jobbed. Back to base?"

"Yes," and the discomfited captain energized his communicator, to report to his immediate superior the humiliating outcome of the supposedly carefully-planned coup.

16

KINNISON MEETS THE WHEELMEN

As the pirate fled into space Kinnison followed, matching his quarry in course and speed. He then cut in the automatic controller on his drive, the automatic recorder on his plate, and began to tune in his beam-tracer; only to be brought up short by the realization that the spy-ray's point would not stay in the pirate's control room without constant attention and manual adjustment. He had known that, too. Even the most precise of automatic controllers, driven by the most carefully stabilized electronic currents, are prone to slip a little at even such close range as ten million miles, especially in the bumpy ether near solar systems, and there was nothing to correct the slip. He had not thought of that before; the pilot always made those minor corrections as a matter of course.

But now he was torn between two desires. He wanted to listen to the conversation that would ensue as soon as the pirate captain got into communication with his superior officers; and, especially should Helmuth put in his beam, he very much wanted to trace it and thus secure another line on the headquarters he was so anxious to locate. He now feared that he could not do both—a fear that soon was to prove well grounded—and wished fervently that for a few minutes he could be two men. Or at least a Velantian; they had eyes and hands and separate brain-compartments enough so that they could do half-a-dozen things at once and do each one well. He could not; but he could try. Maybe he should have brought one of the boys along, at that. No, that would wreck everything, later on; he would have to do the best he could.

Communication was established and the pirate captain began to make his report; and by using one hand on the ray and the other on the tracer, he managed to get a partial line and to record scraps of the conversation. He missed, however, the essential part of the entire episode, that part

in which the base commander turned the unsuccessful captain over to Helmuth himself. Therefore Kinnison was surprised indeed at the disappearance of the beam he was so laboriously trying to trace, and to hear Helmuth conclude his castigation of the unlucky captain with:

". . . not entirely your fault, I will not punish you at all severely this time. Report to our base on Aldebaran I, turn your vessel over to commander there, and do anything he tells you to for thirty of the days of that planet."

Frantically Kinnison drew back his tracer and searched for Helmuth's beam; but before he could synchronize with it the message of the pirates' high chief was finished and his beam was gone. The Lensman sat back in thought.

Aldebaran! Practically next door to his own Solarian System, from which he had come so far. How had they possibly managed to keep concealed, or to re-establish, a base so close to Sol, through all the intensive searching that had been done? But they *had*—that was the important thing. Anyway, he knew where he was going, and that helped. One other thing he hadn't thought of, and one that might have spoiled everything, was the fact that he couldn't stay awake indefinitely to follow that ship! He had to sleep sometime, and while he was asleep his quarry was bound to escape. He of course had a CRX tracer, which would hold a ship without attention as long as it was anywhere within even extreme range; and it would have been a simple enough matter to have had a photo-cell relay put in between the plate of the CRX and the automatic controls of the spacer and driver—but he had not asked for it. Well, luckily, he now knew where he was going, and the trip Aldebaran would be long enough for him to build a dozen such contr He had all the necessary parts and plenty of tools.

Therefore, following the pirate ship easily as it tore through Kinnison built his automatic "chaser," as he called it. During the first four or five "nights" he lost the vessel he was pursu found it without any great difficulty upon awakening. Thereafte it continuously; improving day by day the performance of his until it could do almost anything except talk. After that he time to an intensive study of the general problem before him were highly unsatisfactory; for in order to solve any probl have enough data to set it up, either in actual equations sequences, and Kinnison did not have enough data. He too many unknowns and not enough knowns.

The first specific problem was that of getting into Since the searchers of the Patrol had not found it, very well hidden indeed. And hiding anything as

Aldebaran I, as he remembered it, would be quite a feat in itself. He had been in that system only once, but . . .

Alone in his ship, and in deep space although he was, he blushed painfully as he remembered what had happened to him during that visit. He had chased a couple of dope runners to Aldebaran II, and there he had encountered the most vividly, the most flawlessly, the most remarkably and intriguingly beautiful girl he had ever seen. He had seen beautiful women, of course, before and in plenty. He had seen beauties amateur and professional; social butterflies, dancers, actresses, models, and posturers; both in the flesh and in Telenewscasts; but he had never supposed that such an utterly ravishing creature as she was could exist outside of a thionite dream. As a timidly innocent damsel in distress she had been perfect, and if she had held that pose a little longer Kinnison shuddered to think of what might have happened.

But, having known too many dope-runners and too few Patrolmen, she misjudged entirely, not only the cadet's sentiments, but also his reactions. For, even as she came amorously into his arms, he had known that there was something screwy. Women like that did not play that kind of game for nothing. She must be mixed up with the two he had been chasing. He got away from her, with only a couple of scratches, just in time to capture her confederates as they were making their escape—and he had been afraid of beautiful women ever since. He'd like to see that Aldebaranian hell-cat again—just once. He'd been just a kid then, but now . . .

But that line of thought was getting him nowhere, fast. It was Aldebaran I that he had better be thinking of. Barren, lifeless, desolate, airless, waterless. Bare as his hand, covered with extinct volcanoes, cratered, jagged, and torn. To hide a base on that planet would take plenty of doing, and, conversely, it would be correspondingly difficult to approach. If on the surface at all, which he doubted very strongly, it would be covered. In any event, all its approaches would be thoroughly screened and equipped with lookouts on the ultra-violet and on the infrared, as well as on the visible. His detector nullifier wouldn't help him much there. Those screens and lookouts were bad—very, very bad. Question—could *anything* get into that base without setting off an alarm?

His speedster could not even get close, that was certain. Could he, alone? He would have to wear armor, of course, to hold his air, and it would radiate. Not necessarily—he could land out of range and walk, without power; but there were still the screens and the lookouts. If the gates were on their toes it simply wasn't in the cards; and he had to assume that they would be alert.

What, then, could pass those barriers? Prolonged consideration of every fact of the situation gave definite answer and marked out clearly the course he must take. Something admitted by the pirates themselves was the only thing that could get in. The vessel ahead of his was going in. Therefore he must and would enter that base within the pirate vessel itself. With that point decided there remained only the working out of a method, which proved to be almost ridiculously simple.

Once inside the base, what should he—or rather, what *could* he—do? For days he made and discarded plans, but finally he tossed them all out of his mind. So much depended upon the location of the base, its personnel, its arrangement, and its routine, that he could develop not even the rough draft of a working plan. He knew what he wanted to do, but he had not even the remotest idea as to how he could go about doing it. Of the openings that appeared, he would have to choose the most feasible and fit his actions to whatever situation then and there obtained.

So deciding, he shot his spy-ray toward the planet and studied it with care. It was indeed as he had remembered it, or worse. Bleakly, hotly arid, it had no soil whatever, its entire surface being composed of igneous rock, lava, and pumice. Stupendous ranges of mountains criss-crossed and intersected each other at random, each range a succession of dead volcanic peaks and blown-off craters. Mountainside and rocky plain, crater-wall and valley floor, alike and innumerably were pock-marked with sub-craters and with immensely yawning shell-holes, as though the whole planet had been throughout geologic ages the target of an incessant cosmic bombardment.

Over its surface and through and through its volume he drove his spy-ray; finding nothing. He bored into its substance with his detectors and his tracers; with results completely negative. Of course, closer up, his electromagnetics would report iron—plenty of it—but that information would also be meaningless. Practically all planets had iron cores. As far as his instruments could tell—and he had given Aldebaran I a more thorough going-over by far than any ordinary surveying ship would have given it—there was no base of any kind upon or within the planet. Yet he *knew* that a base was there. So what?—maybe—Helmuth's base might be inside the galaxy after all, protected from detection in the same way; probably by solid miles of iron or of iron ore. A second line upon that base had now become imperative. But they were approaching the system fast; he had better get ready.

He belted on his personal equipment, including a nullifier, then inspected his armor, checking its supplies and apparatus carefully before he hooked it ready to his hand. Glancing into the plate, he noted with approval that his "chaser" was functioning perfectly. Pursued and pursuer were now both well inside the solar system of Aldebaran; and, as slowed the pirate so slowed the speedster. Finally the leader went inert in preparation for his spiral, but Kinnison was no longer following. Before he went inert he flashed down to within fifty thousand miles of the planet's forbidding surface. He then cut his Bergenholm, threw the speedster into an almost circular orbit, well away from the landing orbit selected by the pirate, cut off all his power, and drifted. He stayed in the speedster, observing and computing, until he had so exactly defined its path that he could find it unerringly at any future instant. Then he went into the airlock, stepped out into space, and, waiting only to be sure that the portal had snapped shut behind him, set his course toward the pirate's spiral.

Inert now, his progress was so slow as to seem imperceptible, but he had plenty of time. And it was only relatively that his speed was low. He was actually hurtling through space at the rate of well over two thousand miles an hour, and his powerful little driver was increasing that speed constantly by an acceleration of two Earth gravities.

Soon the vessel crept up, beneath him now, and Kinnison, increasing his drive to five gravities, shot toward it in a long, slanting dive. This was the most ticklish minute of the trip, but the Lensman had assumed correctly that the ship's officers would be looking ahead of them and down, not backward and up. They were, and he made his approach unseen. The approach itself, the boarding of an inert spaceship at its frightful landing-spiral velocity, was elementary to any competent space-man. There was not even a flare to bother him or to reveal him to sight, as the braking jets were now doing all the work. Matching course and velocity ever more closely, he crept up—flung his magnet— pulled up, hand over hand—opened the emergency inlet lock—and there he was.

Unconcernedly he made his way along the sternway and into the now deserted quarters of the fighters. There he lay down in a hammock, snapped the acceleration straps, and shot his spy-ray into the control room. And there, in the pirate captain's own visiplate, he observed the rugged and torn topography of the terrain below as the pilot fought his ship down, mile by mile. Tough going, this, Kinnison reflected, and the bird was doing a nice job, even if he was taking it the hard way, bringing her down straight on her nose instead of taking one more spiral around the planet and then sliding in on her under jets, which were designed and placed specifically for such work. But taking it the hard way he was, and his vessel was bucking, kicking, bouncing and spinning on the terrific blasts of her braking jets. Down she came, fast; and it was only after she was actually inside one of those stupendous craters, well below the level of its rim, that the pilot flattened her out and assumed normal landing position.

They were still going too fast, Kinnison thought, but the pirate pilot knew what he was doing. Five miles the vessel dropped, straight down that Titanic shaft, before the bottom was reached. The shaft's wall was studded with windows; in front of the craft loomed the outer gate of a gigantic airlock. It opened, the ship was trundled inside, landing-cradle and all, and the massive gate closed behind it. This was the pirates' base, and Kinnison was inside it!

"Men, attention!" The pirate commander snapped then. "The air is deadly poison, so put on your armor and be sure your tanks are full. They have rooms for us, having good air, but don't open your suits a crack until I tell you to. Assemble! All of you that are not here in this control room in five minutes will stay on board and take your own chances!"

Kinnison decided instantly to assemble with the crew. He could do nothing in the ship, and it would be inspected, of course. He had plenty of air, but space-armor all looked alike, and his Lens would warn him in time of any unfriendly or suspicious thought. He had better go. If they called a roll . . . but he would cross that bridge when he came to it.

No roll was called; in fact, the captain paid no attention at all to his men. They would come along or not, just as they pleased. But since to stay in the ship meant death, every man was prompt. At the expiration of the five minutes the captain strode away, followed by the crowd. Through a doorway, left turn, and the captain was met by a creature whose shape Kinnison could not make out. A pause, a straggling forward, then a right turn.

Kinnison decided that he would not take that turn. He would stay here, close to the shaft, where he could blast his way out if necessary, until he had studied the whole base thoroughly enough to map out a plan of campaign. He soon found an empty and apparently unused room, and assured himself that through its heavy, crystal-clear window he could indeed look out into the vastly cylindrical emptiness of a volcanic shaft.

Then with his spy-ray he watched the pirates as they were escorted to the quarters prepared for them. Those might have been rooms of state, but it looked to Kinnison very much as though his former shipmates were being jailed ignominiously, and he was glad that he had taken leave of them. Shooting his ray here and there throughout the structure, he finally found what he was looking for; the communicator room. That room was fairly well lighted, and at what he saw there his jaw dropped in sheerest amazement.

He had expected to see men, since Aldebaran II, the only inhabited planet in the system, had been colonized from Tellus and its people were as truly human and Caucasian as those of Chicago or of Paris. But there . . . these *things* . . . he had been around quite a bit, but he had never seen nor heard of their like. They were wheels, really. When they went anywhere they rolled. Heads where hubs ought to be . . . eyes . . . arms, dozens of them, and very capable-looking hands . . .

"Vogenar!" a crisp thought flashed from one of the peculiar entities to another, impinging also upon Kinnison's Lens. "Someone—some outsider—is looking at me. Relieve me while I abate this intolerable nuisance."

"One of those creatures from Tellus? We will teach them very shortly that such intrusion is not to be borne."

"No, it is not one of them. The touch is similar, but the tone is entirely different. Nor could it be one of them, for not one of them is equipped with the instrument which is such a clumsy substitute for inherent power of mind. There, I will now. . . ."

Kinnison snapped on his thought-screen, but the damage had already been done. In the violated Communications Room the angry observer went on:

". . . attune myself and trace the origin of that prying look. It has disappeared now, but its sender cannot be distant, since our walls are shielded and screened . . . Ah, there is a blank space, which I cannot penetrate, in the seventh room of the fourth corridor. In all probability it is one of our guests, hiding now behind a thought screen." Then his orders boomed out to a corps of guards. "Take him and put him with the others!"

Kinnison had not heard the order, but he was ready for anything, and those who came to take him found that it was much easier to issue such orders than to carry them out.

"Halt!" snapped the Lensman, his Lens carrying the crackling command deep into the Wheelmen's minds. "I do not wish to harm you, but come no closer!"

"You? Harm us?" came a cold, clear thought, and the creatures vanished. But not for long. They or others like them were back in moments, this time armed and armored for strife.

Again Kinnison found that DeLameters were useless. The armor of the foe mounted generators as capable as his own; and, although the air in the room soon became one intolerably glaring field of force, in which the very walls themselves began to crumble and to vaporize, neither he nor his attackers were harmed. Again, then, the Lensman had recourse to his mediæval weapon; sheathing his DeLameter and wading in with his axe. Although not a vanBuskirk, he was, for an Earthman, of unusual strength, skill, and speed: and to those opposing him he was a very Hercules.

Therefore, as he struck and struck and struck again, the cell became a gorily reeking slaughter-pen, its every corner high-piled with the shattered corpses of the Wheelmen and its floor running with blood and slime. The last few of the attackers, unwilling to face longer that irresistible steel, wheeled away, and Kinnison thought flashingly of what he should do next.

This trip was a bust so far. He couldn't do himself a bit of good here now, and he'd better flit while he was still in one piece. How? The door? No. Couldn't make it—he'd run out of time quick that way. His screens would stop small-arms projectiles, but they knew that as well as he did. They'd use a young cannon—or, more probably, a semi-portable. Better take out the wall. That would give them something else to think about, too, while he was doing his flit.

Only a fraction of a second was taken up by these thoughts, then Kinnison was at the wall. He set his DeLamater to minimum aperture and at maximum blast, to throw an irresistible cutting pencil. Through the wall that pencil pierced; up, over, and around.

But, fast as the Lensman had acted, he was still too late. There came trundling into the room behind him a low, four-wheeled truck, bearing a complex and monstrous mechanism. Kinnison whirled to face it. As he turned the section of the wall upon which he had been at work blew outward with a crash. The ensuing rush of escaping atmosphere swept the Lensman up and whisked him out through the opening and into the shaft. In the meantime the mechanism upon the truck had begun a staccato, grinding roar, and as it roared Kinnison felt slugs ripping through his armor and tearing through his flesh; each as crushing, crunching, paralyzing a blow as though it had been inflicted by vanBuskirk's space axe.

This was the first time Kinnison had ever been really badly wounded, and it made him sick. But, sick and numb, senses reeling at the shock of his slug-torn body, his right hand flashed to the external controller of his neutralizer. For he was falling inert. Only ten or fifteen meters to the bottom, as remembered it—he had mightly little time to waste if he were not to land inert. He snapped the controller. Nothing happened. Something had been shot away. His driver, too, was dead. Snapping the sleeve of his armor into its clamp he began to withdraw his arm in order to operate the internal controls, but he ran out of time. He crashed; on the top of a subsiding pile of masonry which had preceded him, but which had not yet attained a state of equilibrium; underneath a shower of similar material which rebounded from his armor in a boiler-shop clangor of noise.

Well it was that that heap of masonry had not yet had time to settle into form, for in some slight measure it acted as a cushion to break the Lensman's fall. But an inert fall of forty feet, even cushioned by sliding rocks, is in no sense a light one. Kinnison crashed. It seemed as though a thousand pile-drivers struck him at once. Surges of almost unbearable agony swept over him as bones snapped and bruised flesh gave way; and he knew dimly that a merciful tide of oblivion was reaching up to engulf his shrieking, suffering mind.

But, foggily at first in the stunned confusion of his entire being, something stirred; that unknown and unknowable something, that indefinable ultimate quality that had made him what he was. He lived, and while a Lensman lived he did not quit. To quit was to die then and there, since he was losing air fast. He had plastic in his kit, of course, and the holes were small. He *must* plug those leaks, and plug them quick. His left arm, he found, he could not move at all. It must be smashed pretty badly. Every shallow breath was a searing pain—that meant a rib or two gone out. Luckily, however, he was not breathing blood, therefore his lungs must still be intact. He could move his right arm, although it seemed like a lump of clay or a limb belonging to someone else. But, mustering all his power of will, he made it move. He dragged it out of the armor's clamped sleeve; and forced the leaden hand to slide through the welter of blood that seemed almost to fill the bulge of his armor. He found his kit-box, and, after an eternity of pain-wracked time, he compelled his sluggish hand to open it and to take out the plastic.

Then, in a continuously crescendo throbbing of agony, he forced his maimed, crushed, and broken body to writhe and to wriggle about, so that his one sound hand could find and stop the holes through which his precious air was whistling out and away. Find them he did, and quickly, and seal them tight; but when he had plugged the last one he slumped down, spent and exhausted. He did not hurt so much, now; his suffering had mounted to such terrific heights of intolerable keenness that the nerves themselves, in outraged protest at carrying such a load, had blocked it off.

There was much more to do, but he simply could not do it without a rest. Even his iron will could not drive his tortured muscles to any further effort until they had been allowed to recuperate a little from what they had gone through.

How much air did he have left, if any, he wondered: foggily and with an entirely detached and disinterested impersonality. Maybe his tanks were empty. Of course it couldn't have taken him so long to plug those leaks as it had seemed to, or he wouldn't have had any air left at all, in tanks or suit. He couldn't, however, have much left. He would look at his gauges and see.

But now he found that he could not move even his eyeballs, so deep was the coma that was enveloping him. Away off somewhere there was a billowy expanse of blackness, utterly heavenly in its deep, softly-cushioned comfort; and from that sea of peace and surcease there came reaching to embrace him huge, soft, tender arms. Why suffer, something crooned at him. It was so much easier to let go!

17

NOTHING SERIOUS AT ALL

Kinnison did not lose consciousness—quite. There was too much to do, too much that *had* to be done. He *had* to get out of here. He *had* to get back to his speedster. He *had*, by hook or by crook, to get back to Prime Base! Therefore, grimly, doggedly, teeth tight-locked in the enhancing agony of every movement, he drew again upon those hidden, those deeply buried resources which even he had no idea he possessed. His code was simple: the code of the Lens. While a Lensman lived he did not quit. Kinnison was a Lensman. Kinnison lived. Kinnison did not quit.

He fought back that engulfing tide of blackness, wave by wave as it came. He beat down by sheer force of will those tenderly beckoning, those sweetly seducing arms of oblivion. He forced the mass of pro-testing putty that was his body to do what *had* to be done. He thrust styptic gauze into the most copiously bleeding of his wounds. He was burned, too, he discovered then—they must have had a high-powered needle-beam on that truck, as well as the rifle—but he could do nothing about burns. There simply wasn't time.

He found the power lead that had been severed by a bullet. Stripping the insulation was an almost impossible job, but it was finally accom-plished, after a fashion. Bridging the gap proved to be even a worse one. Since there was no slack, the ends could not be twisted together, but had to be joined by a short piece of spare wire, which in turn had to be stripped and then twisted with each end of the severed lead. That task, too, he finally finished; working purely by feel although he was, and half-conscious withal in a wracking haze of pain.

Soldering those joints was of course out of the question. He was afraid even to try to insulate them with tape, lest the loosely-twined strands should fall apart in the attempt. He did have some dry hand-kerchiefs, however, if he could reach them. He could, and did; and wrapped one carefully about the wires' bare joints. Then, apprehensively, he tried his neutralizer. Wonder of wonder, it worked! So did his driver!

In moments then he was rocketing up the shaft, and as he passed the opening out of which he had been blown he realized with amazement that what had seemed to him like hours must have been minutes only, and few even of them. For the frantic Wheelmen were just then lifting into place the temporary shield which was to stem the mighty out-rush of their atmosphere. Wonderingly, Kinnison looked at his air-gauges. He had enough—if he hurried.

And hurry he did. He *could* hurry, since there was practically no atmosphere to impede his flight. Up the five-miles-deep shaft he shot and out into space. His chronometer, built to withstand even severer shocks than that of his fall, told him where his speedster was to be found, and in a matter of minutes he found her. He forced his rebellious right arm into the sleeve of his armor and fumbled at the lock. It yielded. The port swung open. He was inside his own ship again.

Again the encroaching universe of blackness threatened, but again he fought it off. He *could not* pass out—yet! Dragging himself to the board, he laid his course upon Sol, too distant by far to permit of the selection of such a tiny objective as its planet Earth. He connected the automatic controls.

He was weakening fast, and he knew it. But from somewhere and in some fashion he *must* get strength to do what *must* be done—and somehow he did it. He cut in the Berg, cut in maximum blast. Hang on, Kim! Hang on for just a second more! He disconnected the spacer. He killed the detector nullifiers. Then, with the utterly last remnant of his strength he thought into his Lens.

"Haynes." The thought went out blurred, distorted, weak. "Kinniston. I'm coming . . . com . . ."

He was done. Out, cold. Utterly spent. He had already done too much—far, far too much. He had driven that pitifully mangled body of his to its ultimately last possible movement; his wracked and tortured mind to its ultimately last possible thought. The last iota of even his tremendous reserve of vitality was consumed and he plunged, parsecs deep, into the black depths of oblivion which had so long and so unsuccessfully been trying to engulf him. And on and on the speedster flashed at the very peak of her unimaginably high speed; carrying the insensible, the utterly spent, the sorely wounded, the abysmally unconscious Lensman toward his native Earth.

$*$ $*$ $*$

But Kimball Kinnison, Gray Lensman, had done everything that had *had* to be done before he blacked out. His final thought, feeble though it was, and incomplete, did its work.

Port Admiral Haynes was seated at his desk, discussing matters of import with an office-full of executives, when that thought arrived. Hardened old spacehound that he was, and survivor of many encounters and hospitalizations, he knew instantly what that thought connoted and from the depths of what dire need it had been sent.

Therefore, to the amazement of the officers in the room, he suddenly leaped to his feet, seized his microphone, and snapped out orders. Orders, and still more orders. Every vessel in seven sectors, of whatever class or tonnage, was to shove its detectors out to the limit. Kinnison's speedster is out there somewhere. Find her—get her—kill her drive and drag her in here, to number ten landing field. Get a pilot here, fast— no, two pilots, in armor. Get them off the top of the board, too—Henderson and Watson or Schermerhorn if they're anywhere within range. He then Lensed his lifelong friend Surgeon-Marshal Lacy, at Base Hospital.

"Sawbones, I've got a boy out that's badly hurt. He's coming in free—you know what that means. Send over a good doctor. And have you got a nurse who knows how to use a personal neutralizer and who isn't afraid to go into the net?"

"Coming myself. Yes." The doctor's thought was as crisp as the admiral's. "When do you want us?"

"As soon as they get their tractors on that speedster—you'll know when that happens."

Then, neglecting all other business, the Port Admiral directed in person the far-flung screen of ships searching for Kinnison's flying midget.

Eventually she was found; and Haynes, cutting off his plates, leaped to a closet, in which was hanging his own armor. Unused for years, nevertheless it was kept in readiness for instant service; and now, at long last, the old space-hound had a good excuse to use it again. He could have sent out one of the younger men, of course, but this was one job that he was going to do himself.

Armored, he strode out into the landing field across the paved way. There awaiting him were two armored figures, the two top-bracket pilots. There were the doctor and the nurse. He barely saw—or, rather, he saw without noticing—a saucy white cap atop a riot of red-bronze-auburn curls; a symmetrical young body in its spotless white. He did not notice the face at all. What he saw was that there was a neutralizer strapped snugly into the curve of her back, that it was fitted properly, and that it was not yet functioning.

For this that faced them was no ordinary job. The speedster would land free. Worse, the admiral feared—and rightly—that Kinnison would also be free, but independently; with an intrinsic velocity different from that of his ship. They must enter the speedster, take her out into space, and inert her. Kinnison must be taken out of the speedster, inerted, his velocity matched to that of the flier, and brought back aboard. Then and only then could doctor and nurse begin to work on him. Then they would have to land as fast as a landing could be made—the boy should have been in hospital long ago.

And during all these evolutions and until their return to ground the rescuers themselves would remain inertialess. Ordinarily such visitors left the ship, inerted themselves, and came back to it inert, under their own power. But now there was no time for that. They had to get Kinnison to the hospital; and besides, the doctor and the nurse—particularly the nurse—could not be expected to be space-suit navigators. They would all take it in the net, and that was another reason for haste. For while they were gone their intrinsic velocity would remain unchanged, while that of their present surroundings would be changing constantly. The longer they were gone the greater would become the discrepancy. Hence the net.

The net—a leather-and-canvas sack, lined with sponge-rubber-padded coiled steel, anchored to ceiling and to walls and to floor through every shock-absorbing artifice of beryllium-copper springs and of rubber and nylon cable that the mind of man had been able to devise. It takes something to absorb and to dissipate the kinetic energy which may reside within a human body when its intrinsic velocity does not match the intrinsic velocity of its surroundings—that is, if that body is not to be mashed to a pulp. It takes something, also, to enable any human being to face without flinching the prospect of going into that net, especially in ignorance of exactly how much kinetic energy will have to be dissipated. Haynes cogitated, studying the erect, supple young back, then spoke:

"Maybe we'd better cancel the nurse, Lacy, or get her a suit . . ."

"Time is too important," the girl herself put in, crisply. "Don't worry about me, Port Admiral; I've been in the net before."

She turned toward Haynes as she spoke, and for the first time he really saw her face. Why, she was a real beauty—a knockout—a seven-sector callout . . .

"Here she is!" In the grip of a tractor the speedster flashed to ground in front of the waiting five, and they hurried aboard.

They hurried, but there was no flurry, no confusion. Each knew exactly what to do, and each did it.

Out into space shot the little vessel, jerking savagely downward and sidewise as one of the pilots cut the Bergenholm. Out of the airlock flew the Port Admiral and the helpless, unconscious Kinnison, inertialess both and now chained together. Off they darted, in a new direction and with tremendous speed as Haynes cut Kinnison's neutralizer. There was a mighty double flare as the drivers of both space-suits went to work.

As soon as it was safe to do so, out darted an armored figure with a space-line, whose grappling end clinked into a socket of the old man's armor as the pilot rammed it home. Then, as an angler plays a fish, two husky pilots, feet wide-braced against the steel portal of the air-lock and bodies sweating with effort, heaving when they could and giving line only when they must, helped the laboring drivers to overcome the difference in velocity.

Soon the Lensmen, young and old, were inside. Doctor and nurse went instantly to work, with the calmness and precision so characteristic of their highly-skilled crafts. In a trice they had him out of his armor, out of his leather, and into a hammock; perceiving at once that except for a few pads of gauze they could do nothing for their patient until they had him upon an operating table. Meanwhile the pilots, having swung the hammocks, had been observing, computing and conferring.

"She's got a lot of speed, Admiral—most of it straight down," Henderson reported. "On her landing jets it'll take close to two G's on a full revolution to bring her in. Either one of us can balance her down, but it'll have to be straight on her tail and it'll mean over five G's most of the way. Which do you want?"

"Which is more important, Lacy, time or pressure?" Haynes transferred decision to the surgeon.

"Time." Lacy decided instantly. "Fight her down!" His patient had been through so much already of force and pressure that a little more would not do additional hurt, and time was most decidedly of the essence. Doctor, nurse, and admiral leaped into hammocks; pilots at their controls tightened safety belts and acceleration straps—five gravities for over half an hour is no light matter—and the fight was on.

Starkly incandescent flares ripped and raved from driving jets and side jets. The speedster spun around viciously, only to be curbed, skilfully if savagely, at the precisely right instant. Without an orbit, without even a corkscrew or other spiral, she was going down—straight down. And not upon her under jets was this descent to be, nor upon her even more powerful braking jets. Master Pilot Henry Henderson, Prime Base's best, was going to kill the awful inertia of the speedster by "balancing her down on her tail." Or, to translate from the jargon of space, he was going to hold the tricky, cranky little vessel upright upon the terrific blasts of her main driving projectors, against the Earth's gravitation and against all other perturbing forces, while her driving force counteracted, overcame, and dissipated the full frightful measure of the kinetic energy of her mass and speed!

And balance her down he did. Haynes was afraid for a minute that that intrepid wight was actually going to *land* the speedster on her tail. He didn't—quite—but he had only a scant hundred feet to spare when he nosed her over and eased her to ground on her under-jets.

The crash-wagon and its crew were waiting, and as Kinnison was rushed to the hospital the others hurried to the net room. Doctor Lacy first, of course, then the nurse; and, to Haynes' approving surprise, she took it like a veteran. Hardly had the surgeon let himself out of the "cocoon" than she was in it; and hardly had the terrific surges and recoils of her own not inconsiderable one hundred and forty-five pounds of mass abated than she herself was out and sprinting across the sward toward the hospital.

Haynes went back to his office and tried to work, but he could not concentrate, and made his way back to the hospital. There he waited, and as Lacy came out of the operating room he buttonholed him.

"How about it, Lacy, will he live?" he demanded.

"Live? Of course he'll live." the surgeon replied, gruffly. "Can't tell you details yet—we won't know, ourselves, for a couple of hours yet. Do a flit, Haynes. Come back at sixteen forty—not a second before— and I'll tell you all about it."

Since there was no help for it the Port Admiral did go away, but he was back promptly on the tick of the designated hour.

"How is he?" he demanded without preamble. "Will he really live, or were you just giving me a shot in the arm?"

"Better than that, much better," the surgeon assured him. "Definitely so; yes. He's in much better shape than we dared hope. Must have been a very light crash indeed—nothing seriously the matter with him at all. We won't even have to amputate, from what we can see now. He should make a one hundred percent recovery, not only without artificial members, but with scarcely a scar. He couldn't have been in a space crack-up at all, or he wouldn't have come out with so little injury."

"Fine, Doc—wonderful! Now the details."

"Here's the picture." The doctor unrolled a full-length X-ray print, showing every anatomical detail of the Lensman's interior structure. "First, just notice that skeleton. It is really remarkable. Slightly out of true here and there right now, of course, but I believe it's going to turn out to be the first absolutely perfect male skeleton I have ever seen. That young man will go far, Haynes.''

''Sure he will. Why else do you suppose we put him in Gray? But I didn't come over here to be told that—show me the damage.''

''Look at the picture—see for yourself. Multiple and compound fractures, you notice, of legs and arm; and a few ribs. Scapula, of course—there. Oh, yes, there's a skull fracture, too, but it doesn't amount to much. That's all—the spine, you see, isn't injured at all.''

''What d'you mean, 'that's all'? How about his wounds? I saw some of them myself, and they were *not* pin-pricks.''

''Nothing of the least importance. A few punctured wounds and a couple of incised ones, but nothing even close to a vital part. He won't need even a transfusion, since he stopped the major hemorrhages himself, shortly after he was wounded. There are a few burns, of course, but they are mostly superficial—none that will not yield quite readily to treatment.''

''Mighty glad of that. He'll be here six weeks, then?''

''Better call it twelve, I think—ten at least. You see, some of the fractures, especially those in the left leg, and a couple of burns, are rather severe, as such things go. Then, too, the length of time elapsing between injury and treatment didn't do anything a bit of good.''

''In two weeks he'll be wanting to get up and go places and do things; and in six he'll be tearing down your hospital, stone by stone.''

''Yes.'' The surgeon smiled. ''He isn't the type to make an ideal patient; but, as I have told you before, I like to have patients that we do not like.''

''And another thing. I want the files on his nurses, particularly the red-headed one.''

''I suspected that you would, so I had them sent down. Here you are. Glad you noticed MacDougall—she's by way of being my favorite. Clarissa MacDougall—Scotch, of course, with that name—twenty years old. Height, five feet six; weight, one forty-five and a half. Here are her pictures, conventional and X-ray. Man, look at that skeleton! Beautiful! The only really perfect skeleton I ever saw in a woman . . .''

''It isn't the skeleton I'm interested in,'' grunted Haynes. ''It's what is outside the skeleton that my Lensman will be looking at.''

''You needn't worry about MacDougall,'' declared the surgeon. ''One good look at that picture will tell you that. She classifies—with that skeleton she has to. She couldn't leave the beam a millimeter, even if she wanted to. Good, bad, or indifferent; male or female; physical, mental, moral, and psychological; the skeleton tells the whole story.''

''Maybe it does to you, but not to me,'' and Haynes took up the "conventional" photograph a stereoscope in full, true color; an almost living duplicate of the girl in question. Her thick, heavy hair was not red, but was a vividly intense and brilliant auburn; a coppery bronze, flashed with red and gold. Her eyes ... bronze was all that he could think of, with flecks of topaz and of tawny gold. Her skin, too, was faintly bronze, glowing with even more than healthy youth's normal measure of sparkling vitality. Not only was she beautiful, the Port Admiral decided; in the words of the surgeon, she "classified."

"Hm ... m. Dimples, too," Haynes muttered. "Worse even than I thought—she's a menace to civilization," and he went on to read the documents. "Family ... hm. History ... experiences ... reactions and characteristics ... behavior patterns ... psychology ... mentality ..."

"She'll do, Lacy," he advised the surgeon finally. "Keep her on with him ..."

"Do!" Lacy snorted. "It isn't a question of whether *she* rates. Look at that hair—those eyes. Pure Samms. A man to match her would have to be one in a hundred thousand million. With that skeleton, though, he is."

"Of course he is. You don't seem to realize, you myopic old appendix-snatcher, that *he's* pure *Kinnison!*"

"Ah ... so maybe we could ... but he won't be falling for anybody yet, since he's just been unattached. He'll be bullet-proof for quite a while. You ought to know that young Lensmen—especially young Gray Lensmen—can't see anything but their jobs; for a couple of years, anyway."

"His skeleton tells you that, too, huh?" Haynes grunted, skeptically. "Ordinarily, yes; but you never can tell, especially in hospitals ..."

"More of your layman's misinformation!" Lacy snapped. "Contrary to popular belief, romance does not thrive in hospitals; except, of course, among the staff. Patients oftentimes think that they fall in love with nurses, but it takes two people to make one romance. Nurses do not fall in love with patients, because a man is never at his best under hospitalization. In fact, the better a man is, the poorer a showing he is apt to make."

"And, as I forget who said, a long time ago, 'no generalization is true, not even this one'," retorted the Port Admiral. "When it does hit him it will hit hard, and we'll take no chances. How about the black-haired one?"

"Well, I just told you that MacDougall has the only perfect skeleton I ever saw in a woman. Brownlee is very good, too, of course, but ..."

"But not good enough to rate Lensman's Mate, eh?" Haynes completed the thought. "Then take her out. Pick the best skeletons you've got for this job, and see that no others come anywhere near him. Transfer them to some other hospital—to some other floor of this one, at least. Any woman that he ever falls for will fall for him, in spite of your ideas as to the one-wayness of hospital romance; and I don't want him to have such a good chance of making a dive at something that doesn't rate up. Am I right or wrong, and for how much?''

"Well, I haven't had time yet to really study his skeleton, but . . .''

"Better take a week off and study it. I've studied a lot of people in the last sixty-five years, and I'll match my experience against your knowledge of bones, any time. Not saying that he *will* fall this trip, you understand—just playing safe.''

18

ADVANCED TRAINING

Kinnison came to—or, rather, to say that he came half-to would be a more accurate statement—with a yell directed at the blurrily-seen figure in white which he knew must be a nurse.

"Nurse!" Then, as a searing stab of pain shot through him at the effort, he went on, thinking at the figure in white through his Lens: "My speedster! I must have landed her free! Get the space-port . . ."

"There, there, Lensman," a low, rich voice crooned, and a red head bent over him. "The speedster has been taken care of. Everything is on the green; go to sleep and rest."

"Never mind your ship," the unctuous voice went on. "It was landed and put away. . . ."

"Listen, dumb-bell!" snapped the patient, speaking aloud now, in spite of the pain, the better to drive home his meaning. "Don't try to soothe me! What do you think I am, delirious? Get this and get it straight. I said I landed that speedster *free*. If you don't know what that means, tell somebody that does. Get the space-port—get Haynes—get . . ."

"We got them, Lensman, long ago." Although her voice was still creamily, sweetly soft, an angry color burned into the nurse's face. "I said everything is on zero. Your speedster was inerted; how else could you be here, inert? I helped do it myself, so I *know* she's inert."

"QX." The patient relapsed instantly into unconsciousness and the nurse turned to an interne standing by—wherever *that* nurse was, at least one doctor could almost always be found.

"But my ship . . ."

"Dumb-bell!" she flared. "What a sweet mess *he's* going to be to take care of! Not even conscious yet, and he's calling names and picking fights already!''

In a few days Kinnison was fully and alertly conscious. In a week most of the pain had left him, and he was beginning to chafe under restraint. In ten days he was "fit to be tied," and his acquaintance with his head nurse, so inauspiciously begun, developed even more inauspiciously as time went on. For, as Haynes and Lacy had each more than anticipated, the Lensman was by no means an ideal patient.

Nothing that could be done would satisfy him. All doctors were fatheads, even Lacy, the man who had put him together. All nurses were dumb-bells, even—or especially?—''Mac,'' who with almost superhuman skill, tact, and patience had been holding him together. Why, even fat-heads and dumb-bells, even high-grade morons, ought to know that a man needed food!

Accustomed to eating everything he could reach, three or four or five times a day, he did not realize—nor did his stomach—that his now quiescent body could no longer use the five thousand or more calories that it had been wont to burn up, each twenty-four hours, in intense effort. He was always hungry, and he was forever demanding food.

And food, to him, did not mean orange juice or grape juice or tomato juice or milk. Nor did it mean weak tea and hard, dry toast and an occasional anemic soft-boiled egg. If he ate eggs at all he wanted them fried; three or four of them, accompanied by two or three thick slices of ham.

He wanted—and demanded in no uncertain terms, argumentatively and persistently—a big, thick, rare beefsteak. He wanted baked beans, with plenty of fat pork. He wanted bread in thick slices, piled high with butter, and not this quadruply-and-unmentionably-qualified toast. He wanted roast beef, rare, in big, thick slabs. He wanted potatoes and thick brown gravy. He wanted corned beef and cabbage. He wanted pie— any kind of pie—in large, thick quarters. He wanted peas and corn and asparagus and cucumbers, and also various other-worldly staples of diet which he often and insistently mentioned by name.

But above all he wanted beefsteak. He thought about it days and dreamed about it nights. One night in particular he dreamed about it—an especially luscious porterhouse, fried in butter and smothered in mushrooms—only to wake up, mouth watering, literally starved, to face again the weak tea, dry toast, and, horror of horrors, this time a flabby, pallid, flaccid *poached* egg! It was the last straw.

"Take it away," he said, weakly; then, when the nurse did not obey, he reached out and pushed the breakfast, tray and all, off the table.

Then, as it crashed to the floor, he turned away, and, in spite of all his efforts, two hot tears forced themselves between his eyelids.

It was a particularly trying ordeal, and one requiring all of even Mac's skill, diplomacy, and forbearance, to make the recalcitrant patient eat the breakfast prescribed for him. She was finally successful, however, and as she stepped out into the corridor she met the ubiquitous interne.

"How's your Lensman?" he asked, in the privacy of the diet kitchen.

"Don't call him *my* Lensman!" she stormed. She was about to explode with the pent-up feelings which she of course could not vent upon such a pitiful, helpless thing as her star patient. "Beefsteak! I almost wish they *would* give him a beefsteak, and that he'd choke on it—which of course he would. He's worse than a baby. I never saw such a . . . such a *brat* in my life. I'd like to spank him—he needs it. I'd like to know how *he* ever got to be a Lensman, the big cantankerous clunker! I'm *going* to spank him, too, one of these days, see if I don't!"

"Don't take it so hard, Mac," the interne urged. He was, however, very much relieved that relations between the handsome young Lensman and the gorgeous red-head were not upon a more cordial basis. "He won't be here very long. But I never saw a patient clog *your* jets before."

"You probably never saw a patient like *him* before, either. I certainly hope he never gets cracked up again."

"Huh?"

"Do I have to draw you a chart?" she asked, sweetly. "Or, if he does get cracked up again, I hope they send him to some other hospital," and she flounced out.

Nurse MacDougall thought that when the Lensman could eat the meat he craved her troubles would be over; but she was mistaken. Kinnison was nervous, moody, brooding; by turns irritable, sullen, and pugnacious. Nor is it to be wondered at. He was chained to that bed, and in his mind was the gnawing consciousness that he had failed. And not only failed—he had made a complete fool of himself. He had underestimated an enemy, and as a result of his own stupidity the whole Patrol had taken a setback. He was anguished and tormented. Therefore:

"Listen, Mac," he pleaded one day. "Bring me some clothes and let me take a walk. I need exercise."

"Uh uh, Kim, not yet," she denied him gently, but with her entrancing smile in full evidence. "But pretty quick, when that leg looks a little less like a Chinese puzzle, you and nursie go bye-bye."

"Beautiful, but dumb!" the Lensman growled. "Can't you and those cockeyed croakers realize that I'll never get any strength back if you keep me in bed all the rest of my life? And don't talk baby-talk at me, either. I'm well enough at least so you can wipe that professional smile off your pan and cut that soothing bedside manner of yours.''

"Very well—I think so, too!" she snapped, patience at long last gone. "Somebody should tell you the truth. I always supposed that Lensmen had to have *brains*, but you've been a perfect *brat* ever since you've been here. First you wanted to eat yourself sick, and now you want to get up, with bones half-knit and burns half-healed, and undo everything that has been done for you. Why don't you snap out of it and act your age for a change?"

"I never did think nurses had much sense, and now I know they haven't." Kinnison eyed her with intense disfavor, not at all convinced. "I'm not talking about going back to work. I mean a little gentle exercise, and I know what I need."

"You'd be surprised at what you don't know," and the nurse walked out, chin in air. In five minutes, however, she was back, her radiant smile again flashing.

"Sorry, Kim, I shouldn't have blasted off that way—I know that you're bound to back-fire and to have brainstorms. I would, too, if I were . . ."

"Cancel it, Mac," he began, awkwardly. "I don't know why I have to be crabbing at you all the time."

"QX, Lensman," she replied, entirely serene now. "I do. You're not the type to stay in bed without it griping you; but when a man has been ground up into such hamburger as you are, he has to stay in bed whether he likes it or not, and no matter how much he pops off about it. Roll over here, now, and I'll give you an alcohol rub. But it won't be long now, really—pretty soon we'll have you out in a wheel-chair . . ."

Thus it went for weeks. Kinnison knew his behavior was atrocious, abominable; but he simply could not help it. Every so often the accumulated pressure of his bitterness and anxiety *would* blow off; and, like a jungle tiger with a toothache, he would bite and claw anything or anybody within reach.

Finally, however, the last picture was studied, the last bandage removed, and he was discharged as fit. And he was not discharged, bitterly although he resented his "captivity," as he called it, until he really *was* fit. Haynes saw to that. And Haynes had allowed only the most sketchy interviews during that long convalescence. Discharged, however, Kinnison sought him out.

"Let me talk first," Haynes instructed him at sight. "No self-reproaches, no destructive criticism. Everything constructive. Now, Kimball, I'm mighty glad to hear that you made a perfect recovery. You were in bad shape. Go ahead.''

"You have just about shut my mouth by your first order." Kinnison smiled sourly as he spoke. "Two words—flat failure. No, let me add two more—as yet."

"That's the spirit!" Haynes exclaimed. "Nor do we agree with you that it was a failure. It was merely not a success—so far—which is an altogether different thing. Also, I may add that we had very fine reports indeed on you from the hospital."

"Huh?" Kinnison was amazed to the point of being inarticulate.

"You just about tore it down, of course, but that was only to be expected."

"But, sir, I made such a. . . ."

"Exactly. As Lacy tells me quite frequently, he likes to have patients over there that they don't like. Mull that one over for a bit—you may understand it better as you get older. The thought, however, may take some of the load off your mind."

"Well, sir, I am feeling a trifle low, but if you and the rest of them still think . . ."

"We do so think. Cheer up and get on with the story."

"I've been doing a lot of thinking, and before I go around sticking out my neck again I'm going to . . ."

"You don't need to tell me, you know."

"No, sir, but I think I'd better. I'm going to Arisia to see if I can get me a few treatments for swell-head and lame-brain. I still think that I know how to use the Lens to good advantage, but I simply haven't got enough jets to do it. You see, I . . ." he stopped. He would not offer anything that might sound like an alibi: but his thoughts were plain as print to the old Lensman.

"Go ahead, son. We know you wouldn't."

"If I thought at all, I assumed that I was tackling men, since those on the ship were men, and men were the only known inhabitants of the Aldebaranian system. But when those wheelers took me so easily and so completely, it became very evident that I didn't have enough stuff. I ran like a scared pup, and I was lucky to get home at all. It wouldn't have happened if . . ." he paused.

"If what? Reason it out, son," Haynes advised, pointedly. "You are wrong, dead wrong. You made no mistake, either in judgment or in execution. You have been blaming yourself for assuming that they were men. Suppose you had assumed that they were the Arisians themselves. Then what? After close scrutiny, even in the light of after-knowledge, we do not see how you could have changed the outcome." It did not occur, even to the sagacious old admiral, that Kinnison need not have gone in. Lensmen always went in.

"Well, anyway, they licked me, and that hurts," Kinnison admitted, frankly. "So I'm going back to Arisia for more training, if they'll give it to me. I may be gone quite a while, as it may take even Mentor a long time to increase the permeability of my skull enough so that an idea can filter through it in something under a century."

"Didn't Mentor tell you never to go back there?"

"No, sir." Kinnison grinned boyishly. "He must've forgot it in my case—the only slip he ever made, I guess. That's what gives me an out."

"Um . . . m . . . m." Haynes pondered this startling bit of information. He knew, far better than young Kinnison could, the Arisian power of mind: he did not believe that Mentor of Arisia had ever forgotten anything, however tiny or unimportant. "It has never been done . . . they are a peculiar race; incomprehensible . . . but not vindictive. He may refuse you, but nothing worse—that is, if you do not cross the barrier without invitation. It's a splendid idea, I think; but be very careful to strike that barrier free and at almost zero power—or else don't strike it at all."

They shook hands, and in a space of minutes the speedster was again tearing through space. Kinnison now knew exactly what he wanted to get, and he utilized every waking hour of that long trip in physical and mental exercise to prepare himself to take it. Thus the time did not seem long. He crept up to the barrier at a snail's pace, stopping instantly as he touched it, and through that barrier he sent a thought.

"Kimball Kinnison of Sol Three calling Mentor of Arisia. Is it permitted that I approach your planet?" He was neither brazen nor obsequious, but was matter-of-factly asking a simple question and expecting a simple reply.

"It is permitted, Kimball Kinnison of Tellus," a slow, deep, measured voice resounded in his brain. "Neutralize your controls. You will be landed."

He did so, and the inert speedster shot forward, to come to ground in a perfect landing at a regulation space-port. He strode into the office, to confront the same grotesque entity who had measured him for his Lens not so long ago. Now, however, he stared straight into that entity's unblinking eyes, in silence.

"Ah, you have progressed. You realize now that vision is not always reliable. At our previous interview you took it for granted that what you saw must really exist, and did not wonder as to what our true shapes might be."

"I am wondering now, seriously," Kinnison replied, "and if it is permitted, I intend to stay here until I can see your true shapes."

"This?" and the figure changed instantly into that of an old, white-bearded, scholarly gentleman.

"No. There is a vast difference between seeing something myself and having you show it to me. I realize fully that you can make me see you as anything you choose. You could appear to me as a perfect copy of myself, or as any other thing, person or object conceivable to my mind."

"Ah; your development has been eminently satisfactory. It is now permissible to tell you, youth, that your present quest, not for mere information, but for real knowledge, was expected."

"Huh? How could that be? I didn't decide definitely, myself, until only a couple of weeks ago."

"It was inevitable. When we fitted your Lens we knew that you would return if you lived. As we recently informed that one known as Helmuth . . ."

"*Helmuth!* You know, then, where . . ." Kinnison choked himself off. He would not ask for help in that—he would fight his own battles and bury his own dead. If they volunteered the information, well and good; but he would not ask it. Nor did the Arisian furnish it.

"You are right," the sage remarked, imperturbably. "For proper development it is essential that you secure that information for yourself." Then he continued his previous thought:

"As we told Helmuth recently, we have given your civilization an instrumentality—the Lens—by virtue of which it should be able to make itself secure throughout the galaxy. Having given it, we could do nothing more of real or permanent benefit until you Lensmen yourselves began to understand the true relationship between mind and Lens. That understanding has been inevitable; for long we have known that in time a certain few of your minds would become strong enough to discover that theretofore unknown relationship. As soon as any mind made that discovery it would of course return to Arisia, the source of the Lens, for additional instruction; which, equally of course, that mind could not have borne previously.

"Decade by decade your minds have become stronger. Finally you came to be fitted with a Lens. Your mind, while pitifully undeveloped, had a latent capacity and a power that made your return here certain. There are several others who will return. Indeed, it has become a topic of discussion among us as to whether you or one other would be the first advanced student."

"Who is that other, if I may ask?"

"Your friend, Worsel the Velantian."

"He's got a real mind—'way, 'way ahead of mine," the Lensman stated, as a matter of self-evident fact.

"In some ways, yes. In other and highly important characteristics, no."

"Huh?" Kinnison exclaimed. "In what possible way have I got it over him?"

"I am not certain that I can explain it exactly in thoughts which you can understand. Broadly speaking, his mind is the better trained, the more fully developed. It is of more grasp and reach, and of vastly greater present power. It is more controllable, more responsive, more adaptable than is yours—now. But your mind, while undeveloped, is of considerable greater capacity than his, and of greater and more varied latent capabilities. Above all, you have a driving force, a will to do, an undefeatable mental urge that no one of his race will ever be able to develop. Since I predicted that you would be the first to return, I am naturally gratified that you have developed in accordance with that prediction."

"Well, I have been more or less under pressure, and I got quite a few lucky breaks. But at that, it seemed to me that I was progressing backward instead of forward."

"It is ever thus with the really competent. Prepare yourself!"

He launched a mental bolt, at the impact of which Kinnison's mind literally turned inside out in a wildly gyrating spiral vortex of dizzyingly confused images.

"Resist!" came the harsh command.

"Resist! How?" demanded the writhing, sweating Lensman. "You might as well tell a fly to resist an inert spaceship!"

"Use your will—your force—your adaptability. Shift your mind to meet mine at every point. Apart from these fundamentals neither I nor anyone else can tell you how; each mind must find its own medium and develop its own technique. But this is a very mild treatment indeed; one conditioned to your present strength. I will increase it gradually in severity, but rest assured that I will at no time raise it to the point of permanent damage. Constructive exercises will come later; the first step must be to build up your resistance. Therefore resist!"

The force, which had not slackened for an instant, waxed slowly to the very verge of intolerability; and grimly, doggedly, the Lensman fought it. Teeth locked, muscles straining, fingers digging savagely into the hard leather upholstery of his chair he fought it; mustering his every ultimate resource to the task . . .

Suddenly the torture ceased and the Lensman slumped down, a mental and physical wreck. He was white, trembling, sweating: shaken to the very core of his being. He was ashamed of his weakness. He was humiliated and bitterly disappointed at the showing he had made; but from the Arisian there came a calm, encouraging thought.

"You need not feel ashamed; you should instead feel proud, for you have made a start which is almost surprising, even to me, your sponsor. This may seem to you like needless punishment, but it is not. This is the only possible way in which that which you seek may be found."

"In that case, go to it," the Lensman declared. "I can take it."

The "advanced instruction" went on, with the pupil becoming ever stronger; until he was taking without damage thrusts that would at first have slain him instantly. The bouts became shorter and shorter, requiring as they did such terrific outpourings of mental force that no human mind could stand the awful strain for more than half an hour at a time.

And now these savage conflicts of wills and minds were interspersed with real instruction; with lessons neither painful nor unpleasant. In these the aged scientists probed gently into the youngster's mind, opening it out and exposing to its owner's gaze vast caverns whose very presence he had never even suspected. Some of these storehouses were already partially or completely filled; needing only arrangement and connection. Others were nearly empty. These were catalogued and made accessible. And in all, permeating everything, was the Lens.

"Just like clearing out a clogged-up water system; with the Lens the pump that couldn't work!" exclaimed Kinnison one day.

"More like that than you at present realize," assented the Arisian. "You have observed, of course, that I have not given you any detailed instructions nor pointed out any specific abilities of the Lens which you have not known how to use. You will have to operate the pump yourself; and you have many surprises awaiting you as to what your Lens will pump, and how. Our sole task is to prepare your mind to work with the Lens, and that task is not yet done. Let us on with it."

After what seemed to Kinnison like weeks the time came when he could block out Mentor's suggestions completely; nor, now blocked out, should the Arisian be able to discern that fact. The Lensman gathered all his force together, concentrated it, and hurled it back at his teacher; and there ensued a struggle none the less Titanic because of its essential friendliness. The very ether seethed and boiled with the fury of the mental forces there at grips, but finally the Lensman beat down the other's screens. Then, boring deep into his eyes, he willed with all his force to see that Arisian as he really was. And instantly the scholarly old man subsided into a . . . a BRAIN! There were a few appendages, of course, and appurtenances, and incidentalia to nourishment, loco-motion, and the like, but to all intents and purposes the Arisian was simply and solely a brain.

Tension ended, conflict ceased, and Kinnison apologized.

"Think nothing of it," and the brain actually smiled into Kinnison's mind. "Any mind of power sufficient to neutralize the forces which I have employed is of course able to hurl no feeble bolts of its own. See to it, however, that you thrust no such force at any lesser mind, or it dies instantly."

Kinnison started to stammer a reply, but the Arisian went on:

"No, son, I knew and know that the warning is superfluous. If you were not worthy of this power and were you not able to control it properly you would not have it. You have obstained that which you sought. Go, then, with power."

"But this is only one phase, barely a beginning!" protested Kinnison.

"Ah, you realize even that? Truly, youth, you have come far, and fast. But you are not yet ready for more, and it is a truism that the reception of forces for which a mind is not prepared will destroy that mind. Thus, when you came to me you knew exactly what you wanted. Do you know with equal certainty what more you want from us?"

"No."

"Nor will you for years, if ever. Indeed, it may well be that only your descendants will be ready for that for which you now so dimly grope. Again I say, young man, go with power."

Kinnison went.

19

JUDGE, JURY, AND EXECUTIONER

It had taken the Lensman a long time to work out in his mind exactly what it was that he had wanted from the Arisians, and from no single source had the basic idea come. Part of it had come from his own knowledge of ordinary hypnosis; part from the ability of the Overlords of Delgon to control from a distance the minds of others; part from Worsel, who, working through Kinnison's own mind, had done such surprising things with a Lens; and a great part indeed from the Arisians themselves, who had the astounding ability literally and completely to super-impose their own mentalities upon those of others, wherever situate. Part by part and bit by bit the Tellurian Lensman had built up his plan, but he had not had the sheer power of intellect to make it work. Now he had that, and was ready to go.

Where? His first impulse was to return to Aldebaran I and to invade again the stronghold of the Wheelmen, who had routed him so ignominiously in his one encounter with them. Ordinary prudence, however, counseled against that course.

"You'd better lay off them a while, Kim, old boy," he told himself quite frankly. "They've got a lot of jets and you don't know how to use this new stuff of yours yet. Better pick out something easier to take!"

Ever since leaving Arisia he had been subconsciously aware of a difference in his eyesight. He was seeing things much more clearly than he had ever seen them before; more sharply and in greater detail. Now this awareness crept into his consciousness and he glanced toward his tube-lights. They were out—except for the tiny lamps and bulls-eyes of his instrument board the vessel must be in complete darkness. He remembered then with a shock that when he entered the speedster he had not turned on his lights—he could see, and had not thought of them at all!

This, then, was the first of the surprises the Arisian had promised him. He now had the sense of perception of the Rigellians. Or was it that of the Wheelmen? Or both? Or were they the same sense? Intently aware now, he focused his attention upon a meter before him. First upon its dial, noting that the needle was exactly upon the green hair-line of normal operation. Then deeper. Instantly the face of the instrument disappeared—moved behind his point of sight, or so it seemed—so that he could see its coils, pivots, and other interior parts. He could look into and study the grain and particle-size of the dense, hard condensite of the board itself. His vision was limited, apparently, only by his will to see!

"Well—ain't—that—something?" he demanded of the universe at large; then, as a thought struck him; "I wonder if they blinded me in the process?"

He switched on his lamps, discovering that his vision was unimpaired and normal in every respect; and a rigid investigation proved to him conclusively that in addition to ordinary vision he now had an extra sense—or perhaps two of them—and that he could change from one to the other, or use them simultaneously, at will! But the very fact of this discovery gave Kinnison pause.

He hadn't better go anywhere, or do anything, until he had found out something about his new equipment. The fact was that he didn't even know what he had, to say nothing of knowing how to use it. If he had the sense of a Zabriskan fontema he would go somewhere where he could do a little experimenting without getting his jets burned off in case something slipped at a critical moment. Where was the nearest Patrol base? A big one, fully defended . . . Let's see . . . Radelix would be about the closest Sector Base, he guessed—he'd find out if he could raid that outfit without getting caught at it.

Off he shot, and in due course a fair, green, Earthlike planet lay beneath his vessel's keel. Since it was Earthlike in climate, age, atmosphere, and mass, its people were of course more or less similar to humanity in general characteristics, both of body and of mind. If anything, they were even more intelligent than Earthlings, and their Patrol base was a very strong one indeed. His spy-ray would be useless, since all Patrol bases were screened thoroughly and continuously—he would see what a sense of perception would do. From Tregonsee's explanation, it ought to work at this range.

It did. When Kinnison concentrated his attention upon the base he saw it. He advanced toward it at the speed of thought and entered it;

passing through screens and metal walls without hindrance and without giving alarm. He saw men at their accustomed tasks and heard, or rather sensed, their conversation: the everyday chat of their professions. A thrill shot through him at a dazzling possibility thus revealed.

If he could make one of those fellows down there do something without his knowing that he was doing it, the problem was solved. That computer, say; make him uncover that calculator and set up a certain integral on it. It would be easy enough to get into touch with him and have him do it, but this was something altogether different.

Kinnison got into the computer's mind easily enough, and willed intensely what he was to do; but the officer did not do it. He got up; then, staring about him in bewilderment, sat down again.

"What's the matter?" asked one of his fellows. "Forget something?"

"Not exactly," the computer still stared. "I was going to set up an integral. I didn't want it, either—I could swear that somebody *told* me to set it up."

"Nobody did," grunted the other, "and you'd better start staying home nights—then maybe you wouldn't get funny ideas."

This wasn't so good, Kinnison reflected. The guy should have done it, and shouldn't have remembered a thing about it. Well, he hadn't really thought he could put it across at that distance, anyway—he didn't have the brain of an Arisian. He'd have to follow his original plan, of close-up work.

Waiting until the base was well into the night side of the planet and making sure that his flare-baffles were in place, he allowed the speedster to drop downward, landing at some little distance from the fortress. There he left the ship and made his way toward his objective in a rapid series of long, inertialess hops. Lower and shorter became the hops. Then he cut off his power entirely and walked until he saw before him, rising from the ground and stretching interminably upward, an almost invisibly shimmering web of force. This, the prowler knew, was the curtain which marked the border of the Reservation; the trigger upon which a touch, either of solid object or of beam, would initiate a succession of events which he was in no position to stop.

To the eye that base was not impressive, being merely a few square miles of level ground, outlined with low, broad pill-boxes and studded here and there with harmless-looking, bulging domes. There were a few clusters of buildings. That was all—to the eye—but Kinnison was not deceived. He knew that the base itself was a thousand feet underground; that the pill-boxes housed lookouts and detectors; and that those domes were simply weathershields which, rolled back, would expose projectors second in power not even to those of Prime Base itself.

Far to the right, between two tall pylons of metal, was a gate; the nearest opening in the web. Kinnison had avoided it purposely; it was no part of his plan to subject himself yet to the scrutiny of the all-inclusive photo-cells of that entrance. Instead, with his new sense of perception, he sought out the conduits leading to those cells and traced them down, through concrete and steel and masonry, to the control room far below. He then superimposed his mind upon that of the man at the board and flew boldly toward the entrance. He now actually had a dual personality; since one part of his mind was in his body, darting through the the air toward the portal, while the other part was deep in the base below, watching him come and acknowledging his signals!

A trap lifted, revealing a sloping, tunneled ramp, down which the Lensman shot. He soon found a convenient storeroom; and, slipping within it, he withdrew his control carefully from the mind of the observer, wiping out all traces of that control as he did so. He then watched apprehensively for a possible reaction. He was almost sure that he had performed the operation correctly, but he had to be absolutely certain; more than his life depended upon the outcome of this test. The observer, however, remained calm and placid at his post; and a close reading of his thoughts showed that he had not the faintest suspicion that anything out of the ordinary had occurred.

One more test and he was through. He must find out how many minds he could control simultaneously, but he'd better do that openly. No use making a man feel like a fool needlessly—he'd done that once already, and once was one time too many.

Therefore, reversing the procedure by which he had come, he went back to his speedster, took her out into the ether, and slept. Then, when the light of morning flooded the base, he cut his detector nullifier and approached it boldly.

"Radelix base! Lensman Kinnison of Tellus, Unattached, asking permission to land. I wish to confer with your commanding officer, Lensman Gerrond."

A spy-ray swept through the speedster, the web disappeared, and Kinnison landed, to be greeted with a quiet and cordial respect. The base commander knew that his visitor was not there purely for pleasure—Gray Lensmen did not take pleasure jaunts. Therefore he led the way into his private office and shielded it.

"My announcement was not at all informative," Kinnison admitted then, "but my errand is nothing to be advertised. I've got to try out something, and I want to ask you and three of your best and—'stubbornest,' if I may use the term—officers to cooperate with me for a few minutes. QX?"

"Of course."

Three officers were called in and Kinnison explained. "I've been working for a long time on a mind-controller, and I want to see if it works. I'll put your books on this table, one in front of each of you. Now I would like to try to make two or three of you—all four of you if I can—each bend over, pick up his book, and hold it. Your part of the game will be for each of you to try not to pick it up, and to put it back as soon as you possibly can if I do make you obey. Will you?"

"Sure!" three of them chorused, and "There will be no mental damage, of course?" asked the commander.

"None whatever, and no after-effects. I've had it worked on myself, a lot."

"Do you want any apparatus?"

"No, I have everything necessary. Remember, I want top resistance."

"Let her come! You'll get plenty of resistance. If you can make any one of us pick up a book, after all this warning, I'll say you've got something."

Officer after officer, in spite of strainingly resisting mind and body, lifted his book from the table, only to drop it again as Kinnison's control relaxed for an instant. He could control two of them—*any* two of them—but he could not quite handle three. Satisfied, he ceased his efforts; and, as the base commander poured long, cold drinks for the sweating five, one of his fellows asked:

"What did you do, anyway, Kinnison—oh, pardon me, I shouldn't have asked."

"Sorry," the Tellurian replied uncomfortably, "but it isn't ready yet. You'll all know about it as soon as possible, but not just now."

"Sure," the Radeligian replied. "I knew I shouldn't have blasted off as soon as I spoke."

"Well, thanks a lot, fellows." Kinnison set his empty glass down with a click. "I can make a nice progress report on this do-jig now. And one more thing. I did a little long-range experimenting on one of your computers last night . . ."

"Desk Twelve? The one who thought he wanted to integrate something?"

"That's the one. Tell him I was using him for a mindray subject, will you, and give him this fifty-credit bill? Don't want the boys needling him *too* much."

"Yes, and thanks . . . and . . . I wonder . . ." the Radeligian Lensman had something on his mind. "Well . . . can you make a man tell the truth with that? And if you can, will you?"

"I think so. Certainly I will, if I can. Why?" Kinnison knew that he could, but did not wish to seem cocksure.

"There's been a murder." The other three glanced at each other in understanding and sighed with profound relief. "A particularly fiendish murder of a woman—a girl, rather. Two men stand accused. Each has a perfect alibi, supported by honest witnesses; but you know how much an alibi means now. Both men tell perfectly straight stories, even under a lie-detector, but neither will let me—or any other Lensman so far— touch his mind." Gerrond paused.

"Uh-huh." Kinnison understood. "Lots of innocent people simply can't stand Lensing and have mighty strong blocks."

"Glad you've seen such. One of those men is lying with a polish I wouldn't have believed possible, or else both are innocent. And one of them *must* be guilty; they are the only suspects. If we try them now we make fools of ourselves, and we can't put the trial off very much longer without losing face. If you can help us out you'll be doing a lot for the Patrol, throughout this whole sector."

"I can help you," Kinnison declared. "For this, though, better have some props. Make me a box—double Burbank controls, with five baby spots on it—orange, blue, green, purple, and red. The biggest set of headphones you've got, and a thick, black blindfold. How soon can you try 'em?"

"The sooner the better. It can be arranged for this afternoon."

The trial was announced, and long before the appointed hour the great court-room of that world's largest city was thronged. The hour struck. Quiet reigned. Kinnison, in his somber gray, strode to the judge's desk and sat down behind the peculiar box upon it. In dead silence two Patrol officers approached. The first invested him reverently with the head-phones, the second so enwrapped his head in black cloth that it was apparent to all observers that his vision was completely obscured.

"Although from a world far distant in space, I have been asked to try two suspects for the crime of murder," Kinnison intoned. "I do not know the details of the crime nor the identity of the suspects. I do know that they and their witnesses are within these railings. I shall now select those who are about to be examined."

Piercing beams of intense, vari-colored light played over the two groups, and the deep, impressive voice went on:

"I know now who the suspects are. They are about to rise, to walk, and to seat themselves as I shall direct."

They did so; it being plainly evident to all observers that they were under some awful compulsion.

"The witnesses may be excused. Truth is the only thing of importance here; and witnesses, being human and therefore frail, obstruct truth more frequently than they further its progress. I shall now examine these two accused.''

Again the vivid, weirdly distorting glares of light lashed out; bathing in intense monochrome and in various ghastly combinations first one prisoner, then the other; the while Kinnison drove his mind into theirs, plumbing their deepest depths. The silence, already profound, became the utter stillness of outer space as the throng, holding its very breath now, sat enthralled by that portentous examination.

"I have examined them fully. You are all aware that any Lensman of the Galactic Patrol may in case of need serve as judge, jury, and executioner. I am, however, none of these; nor is this proceeding to be a trial as you may have understood the term. I have said that witnesses are superfluous. I will now add that neither judge nor jury are necessary. All that is required is to discover the truth; since truth is all-powerful. For that same reason no executioner is needed here—the discovered truth will in and of itself serve us in that capacity.

"One of these men is guilty, the other is innocent. From the mind of the guilty one I am about to construct a composite, not of this one fiendish crime alone, but of all the crimes he has ever committed. I shall project that composite into the air before him. No innocent mind will be able to see any iota of it. The guilty man, however, will perceive its every revolting detail; and, so perceiving, he will forthwith cease to exist in this plane of life.''

One of the men had nothing to fear—Kinnison had told him so, long since. The other had been trembling for minutes in uncontrollable paroxysms of terror. Now this one leaped from his seat, clawing savagely at his eyes and screaming in mad abandon.

"I did it! Help! Mercy! Take her away! Oh . . . h . . . h!!'' he shrieked, and died, horribly, even as he shrieked.

Nor was there noise in the court-room after the thing was over. The stunned spectators slunk away, scarcely daring even to breathe until they were safely outside.

Nor was the Radeligian officers in much better case. Not a word was said until the five were back in the base commander's office. Then Kinnison, still white of face and set of jaw, spoke. The others knew that he had found the guilty man, and that he had in some peculiarly terrible fashion executed him. He knew that they knew that the man was hideously guilty. Nevertheless:

"He was guilty,'' the Tellurian jerked out. "Guilty as all the devils in hell. I never had to do that before and it gripes me—but I couldn't shove the job off onto you fellows. I wouldn't want anybody to see that picture that didn't have to, and without it you could never begin to understand just how atrociously and damnably guilty that hell-hound really was."

"Thanks, Kinnison," Gerrond said, simply. "Kinnison. Kinnison of Tellus. I'll remember that name, in case we ever need you as badly again. But, after what you just did, it will be a long time—if ever. You didn't know, did you, that all the inhabitants of four planets were watching you?"

"Holy Klono, no! Were they?"

"They were; and if the way you scared *me* is any criterion, it will be a long, cold day before anything like that comes up again in this system. And thanks again, Gray Lensman. You have done something for our whole Patrol this day."

"Be sure to dismantle that box so thoroughly that nobody will recognize any of its component parts," and Kinnison managed a rather feeble grin. "One more thing and I'll buzz along. Do you fellows happen to know where there's a good, strong pirate base around here anywhere? And, while I don't want to seem fussy, I would like it all the better if they were warm-blooded oxygen-breathers, so I won't have to wear armor all the time."

"What are you trying to do, give us the needle, or something?" This is not precisely what the Radeligian said, but it conveys the thought Kinnison received as the base commander stared at him in amazement.

"Don't tell me that there *is* such a base around here!" exclaimed the Tellurian in delight. "Is there, really?"

"There is. So strong that we haven't been able to touch it; manned and staffed by natives of your own planet, Tellus of Sol. We reported it to Prime Base some eighty-three days ago, just after we discovered it. You're direct from there . . ." He fell silent. This was no way to be talking to a Gray Lensman.

"I was in the hospital then, fighting with my nurse because she wouldn't give me anything to eat," Kinnison explained with a laugh. "When I left Tellus I didn't check up on the late data—didn't think I'd need it quite so soon. If you've got it, though . . ."

"Hospital! You?" queried one of the younger Radeligians.

"Yeah—bit off more than I could chew," and the Tellurian described briefly his misadventure with the Wheelmen of Aldebaran I. "This other thing has come up since then, though, and I won't be sticking my neck out that way again. If you've got such a made-to-order base as that in this region, it'll save me a long trip. Where is it?"

They gave him its coordinates and what little information they had been able to secure concerning it. They did not ask him why he wanted that data. They may have wondered at his temerity in daring to scout alone a fortress whose strength had kept at bay the massed Patrol forces of the sector: but if they did so they kept their thoughts well screened. For this was a Gray Lensman, and very evidently a super-powered individual, even of that select group whose weakest members were powerful indeed. If he felt like talking they would listen; but Kinnison did not talk. He listened; then, when he had learned everything they knew of the Boskonian base:

"Well, I'd better be flitting. Clear ether, fellows!" and he was gone.

20

MAC IS A BONE OF CONTENTION

Out from Radelix and into deep space shot the speedster, bearing the Gray Lensman toward Boyssia II, where the Boskonian base was situated. The Patrol forces had not been able to locate it definitely, therefore it must be cleverly hidden indeed. Manned and staffed by Tellurians—and this was fairly close to the line first taken by the pilot of the pirate vessel whose crew had been so decimated by vanBuskirk and his Valerians. There couldn't be so many Boskonian bases with Tellurian personnel, Kinnison reflected. It was well within the bounds of possibility, even of probability, that he might encounter here his former, but unsuspecting, shipmates again.

Since the Boyssian system was less than a hundred parsecs from Radelix, a couple of hours found the Lensman staring down upon another strange planet; and this one was a very Earthly world indeed. There were polar ice-caps, areas of intensely dazzling white. There was an atmosphere, deep and sweetly blue, filled for the most part with sunlight, but flecked here and there with clouds, some of which were slow-moving storms. There were continents, bearing mountains and plains, lakes and rivers. There were oceans, studded with islands great and small.

But Kinnison was no planetographer, nor had he been gone from Tellus sufficiently long so that the sight of this beautiful and home-like world aroused in him any qualm of nostalgia. He was looking for a pirate base; and, dropping his speedster as low into the night side as he dared, he began his search.

Of man or of the works of man he at first found little enough trace. All human or near-human life was apparently still in a savage state of development; and, except for a few scattered races, or rather tribes, of burrowers and of cliff-or cave-dwellers, it was still nomadic, wandering here and there without permanent habitation or structure. Animals of scores of genera and species were there in myriads, but neither was Kinnison a biologist. He wanted pirates; and, it seemed, that was the one form of life which he was *not* going to find!

But finally, through sheer, grim, bull-dog pertinacity, he was successful. That base was there, somewhere. He would find it, no matter how long it took. He would find it, if he had to examine the entire crust of the planet, land and water alike, kilometer by plotted cubic kilometer! He set out to do just that; and it was thus that he found the Boskonian stronghold.

It had been built directly beneath a towering range of mountains, protected from detection by mile upon mile of native copper and of iron ore.

Its entrances, invisible before, were even now not readily perceptible, camouflaged as they were by outer layers of rock which matched exactly in form, color, and texture the rocks of the cliffs in which they were placed. Once those entrances were located, the rest was easy. Again he set his speedster into a carefully-observed orbit and came to ground in his armor. Again he crept forward, furtively and skulkingly, until he could perceive again a shimmering web of force.

With minor variations his method of entry into the Boskonian base was similar to that he had used in making his way into the Patrol base upon Radelix. He was, however, working now with a surety and a precision which had then been lacking. His practise with the Patrolmen had given him knowledge and technique. His sitting in judgment, during which he had touched almost every mind in the vast assemblage, had taught him much. And above all, the grisly finale of that sitting, horribly distasteful and soulwracking as it had been, had given him training of inestimable value; necessitating as it had the infliction of the ultimate penalty.

He knew that he might have to stay inside that base for some time, therefore he selected his hiding-place with care. He could of course blank out the knowledge of his presence in the mind of anyone chancing to discover him; but since such an interruption might come at a critical instant, he preferred to take up his residence in a secluded place. There were, of course, many vacant suites in the officers' quarters—all bases must have accommodations for visitors—and the Lensman decided to occupy one of them. It was a simple matter to obtain a key, and, inside the bare but comfortable little room, he stripped off his armor with a sigh of relief.

Leaning back in a deeply upholstered leather arm-chair, he closed his eyes and let his sense of perception roam throughout the great establishment. With all his newly developed power he studied it, hour after hour and day after day. When he was hungry the pirate cooks fed him, not knowing that they did so—he had lived on iron rations long enough. When he was tired he slept, with his eternally vigilant Lens on guard.

Finally he knew everything there was to be known about that stronghold and was ready to act. He did not take over the mind of the base commander, but chose instead the chief communications officer as the one most likely and most intimately to have dealings with Helmuth. For Helmuth, he who spoke for Boskone, had for many months been the Lensman's definite objective.

But this game could not be hurried. Bases, no matter how important, did not call Grand Base except upon matters of the most dire urgency, and no such matter eventuated. Nor did Helmuth call that base, since nothing out of the ordinary was happening—to any pirates' knowledge, that is—and his attention was more necessary elsewhere.

One day, however, there came crackling in a triumphant report—a ship working out of that base had taken noble booty indeed; no less a prize than a fully-supplied hospital ship of the Patrol itself! As the report progressed Kinnison's heart went down into his boots and he swore bitterly to himself. How in all the nine hells of Valeria had they managed to take such a ship as that? Hadn't she been escorted?

Nevertheless, as chief communications officer he took the report and congratulated heartily, through the ship's radio man, its captain, its officers, and its crew.

"Mighty fine work; Helmuth himself shall hear of this," he concluded his words of praise. "How did you do it? With one of the new maulers?"

"Yes, sir," came the reply. "Our mauler, accompanying us just out of range, came up and engaged theirs. That left us free to take this ship. We locked on with magnets, cut our way in, and here we are."

There they were indeed. The hospital ship was red with blood; patients, doctors, internes, officers and operating crew alike had been butchered with the horribly ruthless savagery which was the customary technique of all the agencies of Boskone. Of all that ship's personnel only the nurses lived. They were not to be put to death—yet. In fact, and under certain conditions, they need not die at all.

They huddled together, a little knot of white-clad misery in that corpse-littered room, and even now one of them was being dragged away. She was fighting viciously, with fists and feet, with nails and teeth. No one pirate could handle her; it took two strong men to subdue that struggling fury. They hauled her upright and she threw back her head, in panting defiance. There was a cascade of red-bronze hair and Kinnison saw—Clarrissa MacDougall! And remembered that there *had* been some talk that they were going to put her back into space service! The Lensman decided instantly what to do.

"Stop, you swine!" he roared through his pirate mouth-piece. "Where do you think you're going with that nurse?"

"To the captain's cabin, sir." The huskies stopped short in amazement as that roar filled the room, but answered the question concisely.

"Let her go!" Then, as the girl fled back to the huddled group in the corner: "Tell the captain to come out here and assemble every officer and man of the crew. I want to talk to you all at once."

He had a minute or two in which to think, and he thought furiously, but accurately. He had to do something, but whatever he did must be done strictly according to the pirates' own standards of ethics; if he made one slip it might be Aldebaran I all over again. He knew how to keep from making that slip, he thought. But also, and this was the hard part, he must work in something that would let those nurses know that there was still hope; that there were more acts of this drama yet to come. Otherwise he knew with a stark, cold certainty what would happen. He knew of what stuff the space-nurses of the Patrol were made; knew that they could be driven just so far, and no farther—alive.

There was a way out of that, too. In the childishness of his hospitalization he had called Nurse MacDougall a dumbbell. He had thought of her, and had spoken to her quite frankly, in uncomplimentary terms. But he knew that there was a real brain back of that beautiful face, that a quick and keen intelligence resided under that red-bronze thatch. Therefore when the assembly was complete he was ready, and in no uncertain or ambiguous language he opened up.

"Listen, you—all of you" he roared. "This is the first time in months that we have made such a haul as this, and you fellows have the brazen gall to start helping yourselves to the choicest stuff before anybody else gets a look at it. I tell you now to lay off, and that goes exactly as it lays. I, personally, will kill any man that touches one of those women before they arrive here at base. Now you, captain, are the first and worst offender of the lot," and he stared directly into the eyes of the officer whom he had last seen entering the dungeon of the Wheelmen.

"I admit that you're a good picker." Kinnison's voice was now venomously soft, his intonation distinct with thinly veiled sarcasm. "Unfortunately, however, your taste agrees too well with mine. You see, captain, I'm going to need a nurse myself. I think I'm coming down with something. And, since I've got to have a nurse, I'll take that red-headed one. I had a nurse once with hair just that color, who insisted on feeding me tea and toast and a soft-boiled egg when I wanted beef-steak; and I'm going to take my grudge out on this one here for all the red-headed nurses that ever lived. I trust that you will pardon the length of this speech, but I want to give you my reasons in full for cautioning you that that particular nurse is my own particular personal property. Mark her for me, and see to it that she gets here—exactly as she is now.''

The captain had been afraid to interrupt his superior, but now he erupted.

"But see here, Blakeslee!" he stormed. "She's mine, by every right. I captured her, I saw her first, I've got her here . . ."

"Enough of that back-talk, captain!" Kinnison sneered elaborately. "You know, of course, that you are violating every rule by taking booty for yourself before division at base, and that you can get shot for doing it."

"But everybody does it!" protested the captain.

"Except when a superior officer catches him at it. Superiors get first pick, you know," the Lensman reminded him suavely.

"But I protest, sir! I'll take it up with . . ."

"Shut up!" Kinnison snarled, with cold finality. "Take it up with whom you please, but remember this, my last warning. Bring her in to me as she is and you live. Touch her and you die! Now, you nurses, come over here to the board!"

Nurse MacDougall had been whispering furtively to the others and now she led the way, head high and eyes blazing defiance. She was an actress, as well as a nurse.

"Take a good, long look at this button, right here, marked 'Relay 46,' " came curt instructions. "If anybody aboard this ship touches any one of you, or even looks at you as though he wants to, press this button and I'll do the rest. Now, you big, red-headed dumb-bell, look at me. Don't start begging—yet. I just want to be sure you'll know me when you see me."

"I'll know you, never fear, you . . . you *brat!*" she flared, thus informing the Lensman that she had received his message. "I'll not only know you—I'll scratch your eyes out on sight!"

"That'll be a good trick if you can do it," Kinnison sneered, and cut off.

"What's it all about, Mac? What has got into you?" demanded one of the nurses, as soon as the women were alone.

"I don't know," she whispered. "Watch out, they may have spy-rays on us. I don't know anything, really, and the whole thing is too wildly impossible, too utterly fantastic to make sense. But pass the word along to all the girls to ride this out, because my Gray Lensman is in on it, somewhere and somehow. I don't see how he can be, possibly, but I just know he is."

For, at the first mention of tea and toast, before she perceived even an inkling of the true situation, her mind had flashed back instantly to Kinnison, the most stubborn and rebellious patient she had ever had. More, the only man she had ever known who had treated her precisely as though she were a part of the hospital's very furniture. As is the way of women—particularly of beautiful women—she had orated of women's rights and of women's status in the scheme of things. She had decried all special privileges, and had stated, often and with heat, that she asked no odds of any man living or yet to be born. Nevertheless, and also beautiful-womanlike, the thought had bitten deep that here was a man who had never even realized that she *was* a woman, to say nothing of realizing that she was an extraordinarily beautiful one! And deep within her and sternly suppressed the thought had still rankled.

At the mention of beefsteak she had all but screamed, gripping her knees with frantic hands to keep her emotion down. For she had had no real hope; she was simply fighting with everything she had until the hopeless end, which she had known could not long be delayed. Now she gathered herself together and began to act.

When the word "dumb-bell" boomed from the speaker she knew, beyond doubt or peradventure, that it was Kinnison, the Gray Lensman, who was really doing that talking. It was crazy—it didn't make any kind of sense at all—but it was, it must be, true. And, again womanlike, she knew with a calm certainty that as long as that Gray Lensman were alive and conscious, he would be completely the master of any situation in which he might find himself. Therefore she passed along her illogical but cheering thought, and the nurses, being also women, accepted it without question as the actual and accomplished fact.

They carried on, and when the captured hospital ship had docked at base, Kinnison was completely ready to force matters to a conclusion. In addition to the chief communications officer, he now had under his control a highly capable observer. To handle two such minds was child's play to the intellect which had directed, against their full fighting wills, the minds of two and three quarters alert, powerful, and fully warned officers of the Galactic Patrol!

"Good girl, Mac" he put his mind en rapport with hers and sent his message. "Glad you got the idea. You did a good job of acting, and if you can do some more as good we'll be all set. Can do?"

"I'll say I can!" she assented fervently. "I don't know what you are doing, how you can possibly do it, or where you are, but that can wait. Tell me what to do and I'll do it!''

"Make passes at the base commander," he instructed her. "Hate me—the ape I'm working through, you know; Blakeslee, his name is—like poison. Go into it big—all jets wide open. You maybe could love him, but if I get you you'll blow out your brains—if any. You know the line—play up to him with everything you can bring to bear, and hate me to hell and back. Help all you can to start a fight between us. If he falls for you hard enough the blow-off comes then and there. If not, he'll be able to do us all plenty of dirt. I can kill a lot of them, but not enough of them quick enough."

"He'll fall," she promised him gleefully, "like ten thousand bricks falling down a well. Just watch my jets!"

And fall he did. He had not even seen a woman for months, and he expected nothing except bitter-end resistance and suicide from any of these women of the Patrol. Therefore he was rocked to the heels—set back upon his very haunches—when the most beautiful woman he had ever seen came of her own volition into his arms, seeking in them sanctuary from his own chief communications officer.

"I hate him!" she sobbed, nestling against the huge bulk of the commander's body and turning upon him the full blast of the high powered projectors which were her eyes. "*You* wouldn't be so mean to me, I just know you wouldn't!" and her subtly perfumed head sank upon his shoulder. The outlaw was just so much soft wax.

"I'll say I wouldn't be mean to you" his voice dropped to a gentle bellow. "Why, you little sweetheart, I'll *marry* you. I will so, by all the gods of space!"

It thus came about that nurse and base commander entered the control room together, arms about each other.

"There he is!" she shrieked, pointing at the chief communications officer. "He's the one! Now let's see you start something, you rat-faced clunker! There's one real man around here, and he won't let you touch me—ya-a-a!" She gave him a resounding Bronx cheer, and her escort swelled visibly.

"Is—that—so?" Kinnison sneered. "Get this, glamor-puss, and get it straight. I marked you for mine as soon as I saw you, and mine you're going to be, whether you like it or not and no matter what anybody says or does about it. As for you, captain, you're too late—I saw her first. And now, you red-headed tomato, come over here where you belong."

She snuggled closer into the commander's embrace and the big man turned purple.

"What d'you mean, too late!" he roared. "You took her away from the ship's captain, didn't you? You said that superior officers get first choice, didn't you? I'm the boss here and I'm taking her away from you, get me? You'll stand for it, too, Blakeslee, and like it. One word out of you and I'll have you spread-eagled across the mouth of number six projector!''

''Superior officers don't *always* get first choice,'' Kinnison replied; with bitter, cold ferocity, but choosing his words with care. ''It depends entirely on who the two men are.''

Now was the time to strike. Kinnison knew that if the commander kept his head, the lives of those valiant women were forfeit, and his own whole plan seriously endangered. He himself could get away, of course—but he could not see himself doing it under these conditions. No, he must goad the commander to a frenzy. And without swearing would be better—the ape was used to invectives that would raise blisters on armor plate. Mac would help. In fact, and without his suggestion, she was even then hard at work fomenting trouble between the two men.

''You don't have to take that kind of stuff off of anybody, big boy,'' she was whispering, urgently. ''Don't call in a crew to spread-eagle him, either; beam him out yourself. You're a better man than he is, any time. Blast him down—that'll show him who's who around here!''

''When the inferior is such a man as I am, and the superior such a louse as you are;'' the biting, contemptuously sneering voice went on without a break, ''Such a bloated swine; such a mangy, low-down cur; such a pussy-gutted tub of lard; such a brainless, filthy spawn of the lowest dregs of the rottenest scum of space; such an utterly incompetent, self-opinionated, misbegotten abortion as you are ...''

The outraged pirate, bellowing profanity in wildly mounting rage, tried to break in; but Kinnison-Blakeslee's voice, if no louder than his, was far more penetrant.

''... then, in that case, the inferior keeps the redheaded wench himself. Put that on a tape, you white-livered coward, and eat it!''

Still bellowing, the fat man had turned and was leaping toward the arms cabinet.

''Blast him! Blast him down!'' the nurse had been shrieking; and, as the raging commander neared the cabinet, no one noticed that her latest and loudest scream was ''Kim! Blast him down! Don't wait any longer—beam him before he gets a gun!''

But the Lensman did not act—yet. Although almost every man of the pirate crew stared spell-bound, Kinnison's enslaved observer had for many seconds been jamming the sub-ether with Helmuth's personal and urgent call. It was of almost vital importance to his plan that Helmuth himself should see the climax of this scene. Therefore Blakeslee stood immobile while his profanely raving superior reached the cabinet and tore it open.

21

THE SECOND LINE

Blakeslee was already armed—Kinnison had seen to that—and as the base commander wrenched open the arms cabinet Helmuth's private look-out set began to draw current. Helmuth himself was now looking on and the enslaved observer had already begun to trace his beam. Therefore as the furious pirate whirled around with raised DeLameter he faced one already ablaze; and in a matter of seconds there was only a charred and smoking heap where he had stood.

Kinnison wondered that Helmuth's cold voice was not already snapping from the speaker, but he was soon to discover the reason for that silence. Unobserved by the Lensman, one of the observers had recovered sufficiently from his shocked amazement to turn in a riot alarm to the guard-room. Five armed men answered that call on the double, stopped and glanced around.

"Guards! Blast Blakeslee down!" Helmuth's unmistakable voice blared from his speaker.

Obediently and manfully enough the five guards tried; and, had it actually been Blakeslee confronting them so defiantly, they probably would have succeeded. It was the body of the communications officer, it is true. The mind operating the muscles of that body, however, was the mind of Kimball Kinnison, Gray Lensman, the fastest man with a hand-gun old Tellus had ever produced; keyed up, expecting the move, and with two DeLameters out and poised at hip! *This* was the being whom Helmuth was so nonchalantly ordering his minions to slay! Faster than any watching eye could follow, five bolts of lightning flicked from Blakeslee's DeLameters. The last guard went down, his head a shrivelled cinder, before a single pirate bolt could be loosed. Then:

"You see, Helmuth," Kinnison spoke conversationally to the board, his voice dripping vitriol, "Playing it safe from a distance, and making other men pull your chestnuts out of the fire, is a very fine trick as long as it works. But when it fails to work, as now, it puts you exactly where I want you. I, for one, have been for a long time completely fed up with taking orders from a mere voice; especially from the voice of one whose entire method of operation proves him to be the prize coward of the galaxy."

"Observer! You other at the board!" snarled Helmuth, paying no attention to Kinnison's barbed shafts. "Sound the assembly—armed!"

"No use, Helmuth, he's stone deaf," Kinnison explained, voice smoothly venomous. "I'm the only man in this base you can talk to, and you won't be able to do even that very much longer."

"And you really think that you can get away with this mutiny—this barefaced insubordination—this defiance of *my authority?*"

"Sure I can—that's what I've been telling you. If you were here in person, or ever had been; if any of the boys had ever seen you, or had ever known you as anything except a disembodied voice; maybe I couldn't. But, since nobody has ever seen even your face, that gives me a chance . . . ."

In his distant base Helmuth's mind had flashed over every aspect of this unheard-of situation. He decided to play for time; therefore, even as his hands darted to buttons here and there, he spoke:

"Do *you* want to see my face?" he demanded. "If you do see it, no power in the galaxy . . ."

"Skip it, Chief," sneered Kinnison. "Don't try to kid me into believing you wouldn't kill me now, under any conditions, if you possibly could. As for your face, it makes no difference to me whether I ever see your ugly pan or not."

"Well, you shall!" and Helmuth's visage appeared; concentrating upon the rebellious officer a glare of such fury and such power that any ordinary man must have quailed. But not Blakeslee-Kinnison!

"Well! Not so bad, at that—the guy looks almost human!" Kinnison exclaimed, in the tone most carefully designed to drive even more frantic the helpless and inwardly raging pirate leader. "But I've got things to do. You can guess at what goes on around here from now on," and in the blaze of a DeLameter Helmuth's plate, set, and "eye" disappeared. Kinnison had also been playing for time, and his observer had checked and rechecked this second and highly important line to Helmuth's ultra-secret base.

Then, throughout the fortress, there blared out the urgent assembly call, to which the Lensman added, verbally:

"This is a one hundred percent callout, including crews of ships in dock, regular base personnel, and all prisoners. Come as you are and come fast—the doors of the auditorium will be locked in five minutes and any man outside those doors will be given ample reason to wish that he had been inside.''

The auditorium was immediately off the control room, and was so arranged that when a partition was rolled back the control room became its stage. All Boskonian bases were arranged thus, in order that the supervising officers at Grand Base could oversee through their instruments upon the main panel just such assemblies as this one was supposed to be. Every man hearing that call assumed that it came from Grand Base, and every man hurried to obey it.

Kinnison rolled back the partition between the two rooms and watched for weapons as the men came streaming into the auditorium. Ordinarily only the guards went armed, but possibly a few of the ships' officers would be wearing their DeLameters . . . four—five—six. The captain and the pilot of the battleship that had taken the hospital ship, Vice-Commander Krimsky of the base, and three guards. Knives, billies, and such did not count.

"Time's up. Lock the doors. Bring the keys and the nurses up here,'' he ordered the six armed men, calling each by name. "You women take these chairs over here, you men sit there.''

Then, when all were seated, Kinnison touched a button and the steel partition slid smoothly into place.

"What's coming off here?'' demanded one of the officers. "Where's the commander? How about Grand Base? Look at that board!''

"Sit tight.'' Kinnison directed. "Hands on knees—I'll burn any or all of you that make a move. I have already burned the old man and five guards, and have put Grand Base out of the picture. Now I want to find out just how us seven stand.'' The Lensman already knew, but he was not tipping his hand.

"Why us seven?''

"Because we are the only ones who happened to be wearing sidearms. Everyone else of the entire personnel is unarmed and is now locked in the auditorium. You know how apt they are to get out until one of us lets them out.''

"But Helmuth—he'll have you blasted for this!''

"Hardly—my plans were not made yesterday. How many of you fellows are with me?''

"What's your scheme?''

"To take these nurses to some Patrol base and surrender. I'm sick of this whole game; and, since none of them have been hurt, I figure they're good for a pardon and a fresh start—a light sentence at least.''

"Oh, so *that's* the reason . . ." growled the captain.

"Exactly—but I don't want anyone with me whose only thought would be to burn me down at the first opportunity."

"Count me in," declared the pilot. "I've got a strong stomach, but enough of these jobbies is altogether too much. If you wangle anything short of a life sentence for me I'll go along, but I bloody well won't help you against . . ."

"Sure not. Not until after we're out in space. I don't need any help here."

"Do you want my DeLameter?"

"No, keep it. You won't use it on me. Anybody else?"

One guard joined the pilot, standing aside; the other four wavered.

"Time's up!" Kinnison snapped. "Now, you four fellows, either go for your DeLameters or turn your backs, and do it right now!"

They elected to turn their backs and Kinnison collected their weapons, one by one. Having disarmed them, he again rolled back the partition and ordered them to join the wondering throng in the auditorium. He then addressed the assemblage, telling them what he had done and what he had it in mind to do.

"A good many of you must be fed up on this lawless game of piracy and anxious to resume association with decent men, if you can do so without incurring too great a punishment," he concluded. "I feel quite certain that those of us who man the hospital ship in order to return these nurses to the Patrol will get light sentences, at most. Miss MacDougall is a head nurse—a commissioned officer of the Patrol. We will ask her what she thinks."

"I can say more than that," she replied clearly. "I am not 'quite certain,' either—I am absolutely sure that whatever men Mr. Blakeslee selects for his crew will not be given any sentences at all. They will be pardoned, and will be given whatever jobs they can do best."

"How do you know, Miss?" asked one. "We're a black lot."

"I know you are." The head nurse's voice was serenely positive. "I won't say *how* I know, but you can take my word for it that I *do* know."

"Those of you who want to take a chance with us line up over here," Kinnison directed, and walked rapidly down the line, reading the mind of each man in turn. Many of them he waved back into the main group, as he found thoughts of treachery or signs of inherent criminality. Those he selected were those who were really sincere in their desire to quit forever the ranks of Boskone, those who were in those ranks because of some press of circumstance rather than because of a mental taint. As each man passed inspection he armed himself from the cabinet and stood at ease before the group of women.

Having selected his crew, the Lensman operated the controls that opened the exit nearest the hospital ship, blasted away the panel, so that that exit could not be closed, unlocked a door, and turned to the pirates.

"Vice-Commander Krimsky, as senior officer, you are now in command of this base," he remarked. "While I am in no sense giving you orders, there are a few matters about which you should be informed. First, I set no definite time as to when you may leave this room—I merely state that you will find it decidedly unhealthy to follow us at all closely as we go from here to the hospital ship. Second, you haven't a ship fit to take the ether; your main injector toggles have all been broken off at the pivots. If your mechanics work at top speed, new ones can be put on in exactly two hours. Third, there is going to be a severe earthquake in precisely two hours and thirty minutes, one which should make this base merely a memory."

"An earthquake! Don't bluff, Blakeslee—you couldn't do *that!*"

Well, perhaps not a regular earthquake, but something that will do just as well. If you think I'm bluffing, wait and find out. But common sense should give you the answer to that—I know exactly what Helmuth is doing now, whether you do or not. At first I intended to wipe you all out without warning, but I changed my mind. I decided to leave you alive, so that you could report to Helmuth exactly what happened. I wish I could be watching him when he finds out how easily one man took him, and how far from foolproof his system is—but we can't have everything. Let's go!"

As the group hurried away, Mac loitered until she was near Blakeslee, who was bringing up the rear.

"Where are you, Kim?" she whispered urgently.

"I'll join up at the next corridor. Keep farther ahead, and get ready to run when we do!"

As they passed that corridor a figure in gray leather, carrying an extremely heavy object, stepped out of it. Kinnison himself set his burden down, yanked a lever, and ran—and as he ran fountains of intolerable heat erupted and cascaded from the mechanism he had left upon the floor. Just ahead of him, but at some distance behind the others, ran Blakeslee and the girl.

"Gosh, I'm glad to see you, Kim!" she panted as the Lensman caught up with them and all three slowed down. "What is that thing back there?"

"Nothing much—just a KJ4Z hot-shot. Won't do any real damage—just melt this tunnel down so they can't interfere with our get-away."

"Then you *were* bluffing about the earthquake?" she asked, a shade of disappointment in her tone.

"Hardly," he reproved her. "That isn't due for two hours and a half yet, but it'll happen on scheduled time."

"How?"

"You remember about the curious cat, don't you? However, no particular secret about it, I guess—three lithiumhydride bombs placed where they'll do the most good and timed for exactly simultaneous detonation. Here we are—don't tell anybody I'm here."

Aboard the vessel, Kinnison disappeared into a stateroom while Blakeslee continued in charge. Men were divided into watches, duties were assigned, inspections were made, and the ship shot into the air. There was a brief halt to pick up Kinnison's speedster; then, again on the way, Blakeslee turned the board over to Crandall, the pilot, and went into Kinnison's room.

There the Lensman withdrew his control, leaving intact the memory of everything that had happened. For minutes Blakeslee was almost in a daze, but struggled through it and held out his hand.

"Mighty glad to meet you, Lensman. Thanks. All I can say is that after I got sucked in I couldn't . . ."

"Sure, I know all about it—that was one of the reasons I picked you out. Your subconscious didn't fight back a bit, at any time. You're to be in charge, from here to Tellus. Please go and chase everybody out of the control room except Crandall."

"Say, I just thought of something!" exclaimed Blakeslee when Kinnison joined the two officers at the board. "You must be that particular Lensman who has been getting in Helmuth's hair so much lately!"

"Probably—that's my chief aim in life."

"I'd like to see Helmuth's face when he gets the report of this. I've said that before, haven't I? But I mean it now, even more than I did before."

"I'm thinking of Helmuth, too, but not that way." The pilot had been scowling at his plate, and now turned to Blakeslee and the Lensman, glancing curiously from one to the other. "Oh I say . . . A Lensman, what? A bit of good old light begins to dawn; but that can wait. Helmuth is after us, foot, horse, and marines. Look at that plate!"

"Four of 'em already!" exclaimed Blakeslee. "And there's another! And we haven't got a beam hot enough to light a cigarette, nor a screen strong enough to stop a fire-cracker. We've got legs, but not as many as they've got. You knew all about that, though, before we started; and from what you've pulled off so far you've got something left on the hooks. What is it? What's the answer?"

"For some reason or other they can't detect us. All you have to do is to stay out of range of their electros and drill for Tellus."

"Some reason or other, eh? Nine ships on the plate now—all Boskonians and all looking for us—and not seeing us—*some* reason! But I'm not asking questions . . ."

"Just as well not to. I'd rather you'd answer one. Who or what is Boskone?"

"Nobody knows. Helmuth speaks for Boskone, and nobody else ever does, not even Boskone himself—if there is such a person. Nobody can prove it, but everybody knows that Helmuth and Boskone are simply two names for the same man. Helmuth, you know, is only a voice—nobody ever saw his face until today."

"I'm beginning to think so, myself," and Kinnison strode away, to call at the office of Head Nurse MacDougall.

"Mac, here's a small, but highly important box," he told her, taking the neutralizer from his pocket and handing it to her. "Put it in your locker until you get to Tellus. Then take it, yourself, in person, and give it to Haynes, himself, in person, and to nobody else. Just tell him I sent it—he knows all about it."

"But why not keep it and give it to him yourself? You're coming with us, aren't you?"

"Probably not all the way. I imagine I'll have to do a flit before long."

"But I want to talk to you!" she exclaimed. "Why, I've got a million questions to ask you!"

"That would take a long time," he grinned at her, "and time is just what we ain't got right now, neither of us," and he strode back to the board.

There he labored for hours at a calculating machine and in the tank; finally to squat down upon his heels, staring at two needle-like rays of light in the tank and whistling softly between his teeth. For those two lines, while exactly in the same plane, did not intersect in the tank at all! Estimating as carefully as he could the point of intersection of the lines, he punched the "cancel" key to wipe out all traces of his work and went to the chart-room. Chart after chart he hauled down, and for many minutes he worked with calipers, compass, goniometer, and a carefully-set adjustable triangle. Finally he marked a point—exactly upon a numbered dot already upon the chart—and again whistled. Then:

"Huh!" he grunted. He rechecked all his figures and retraversed the chart, only to have his needle pierce again the same tiny hole. He stared at it for a full minute, studying the map all around his marker.

"Star cluster AC 257-4736," he ruminated. "The smallest most insignificant, least-known star-cluster he could find, and my largest possible error can't put it anywhere else . . . kind of thought it might be in a cluster, but I never would have looked *there*. No wonder it took a lot of stuff to trace his beam—it would have to be four numbers Brinnell harder than a diamond drill to work from there.''

Again whistling tunelessly to himself he rolled up the chart upon which he had been at work, stuck it under his arm, replaced the others in their compartments, and went back to the control room.

"How's tricks, fellows?" he asked.

"QX," replied Blakeslee. "We're through them and into clear ether. Not a ship on the plate, and nobody gave us even a tumble."

"Fine! You won't have any trouble, then, from here in to Prime Base. Glad of it, too—I've got to flit. That'll mean long watches for you two, but it can't very well be helped."

"But I say, old bird, I don't mind the watches, but . . ."

"Don't worry about that, either. This crew can be trusted, to a man. Not one of you joined the pirates of your own free will, and not one of you has ever taken active part . . ."

"What are you, a mind-reader or something?" Crandall burst out.

"Something like that," Kinnison assented with a grin, and Blakeslee put in:

"More than that, you mean. Something like hypnosis, only more so. You think I had something to do with this, but I didn't—the Lensman did it all himself."

"Um . . . m." Crandall stared at Kinnison, new respect in his eyes. "I knew that Unattached Lensmen were good, but I had no idea they were *that* good. No wonder Helmuth has been getting his wind up about you. I'll string along with any one who can take a whole base, single-handed, and make such a bally ass to boot out of such a keen old bird as Helmuth is. But I'm in a bit of a dither, not so say a funk, about what's going to happen when we pop into Prime Base without you. Every man jack of us, you know, is slated for the lethal chamber without trial. Miss MacDougall will do her bit, of course, but what I mean is has she enough jets to swing it, what?"

"She has, but to avoid all argument I've fixed that up, too. Here's a tape, telling all about what happened. It ends up with my recommendation for a full pardon for each of you, and for a job at whatever he is found best fitted for. Signed with my thumb-print. Give it or send it to Port Admiral Haynes as soon as you land. I've got enough jets, I think, so that it will go as it lays."

"Jets? You? Right-o! You've got jets enough to lift fourteen freighters off the North Pole of Valeria. What next?"

"Stores and supplies for my speedster. I'm doing a long flit and this ship has supplies to burn, so load me up, Plimsoll down."

The speedster was stocked forthwith. Then, with nothing more than a casually waved salute in the way of farewell, Kinnison boarded his tiny space-ship and shot away toward his distant goal. Crandall, the pilot, sought his bunk; while Blakeslee started his long trick at the board. In an hour or so the head nurse strolled in.

"Kim?" she queried, doubtfully.

"No, Miss MacDougall—Blakeslee. Sorry . . ."

"Oh, I'm glad of that—that means that everything's settled. Where's the Lensman—in bed?"

"He has gone, Miss."

"Gone! Without a word? Where?"

"He didn't say."

"He wouldn't, of course." The nurse turned away, exclaiming inaudibly; "Gone! I'd like to cuff him for that, the lug! GONE! Why, the great, big, lobsterly clunker!"

22

PREPARING FOR THE TEST

But Kinnison was not heading for Helmuth's base—yet. He was splitting the ether toward Aldebaran instead, as fast as his speedster could go; and she was one of the fastest things in the galaxy. He had two good reasons for going there before tackling Boskone's Grand Base. First, to try out his skill upon non-human intellects. If he could handle the Wheelmen he was ready to take the far greater hazard. Second, he owed those wheelers something, and he did not like to call in the whole Patrol to help him pay his debts. He could, he thought, handle that base himself.

Knowing exactly where it was, he had no difficulty in finding the volcanic shaft which was its entrance. Down that shaft his sense of perception sped. He found the lookout plates and followed their power leads. Gently, carefully, he insinuated his mind into that of the Wheelman at the board; discovering, to his great relief, that that monstrosity was no more difficult to handle than had been the Radeligian observer. Mind or intellect, he found, were not affected at all by the shape of the brains concerned; quality, reach, and power were the essential factors. Therefore he let himself in and took position in the same room from which he had been driven so violently. Kinnison examined with interest the wall through which he had been blown, noting that it had been repaired so perfectly that he could scarcely find the joints which had been made.

These wheelers, the Lensman knew, had explosives; since the bullets which had torn their way through his armor and through his flesh had been propelled by that agency. Therefore, to the mind within his grasp he suggested "the place where explosives are kept?" and the thought of that mind flashed to the store-room in question. Similarly, the thought of the one who had access to that room pointed out to the Lensman the particular Wheelman he wanted. It was as easy as that, and since he took care not to look at any of the weird beings, he gave no alarm.

Kinnison withdrew his mind delicately, leaving no trace of its occupancy, and went to investigate the arsenal. There he found a few cases of machine-rifle cartridges, and that was all. Then into the mind of the munitions officer, where he discovered that the heavy bombs were kept in a distant crater, so that no damage would be done by any possible explosion.

"Not quite as simple as I thought," Kinnison ruminated, "but there's a way out of that, too."

There was. It took an hour or so of time; and he had to control two Wheelmen instead of one, but he found that he could do that. When the munitions master took out a bombscow after a load of H.E., the crew had no idea that it was anything except a routine job. The only Wheelman who would have known differently, the one at the lookout board, was the other whom Kinnison had to keep under control. The scow went out, got its load, and came back. Then, while the Lensman was flying out into space, the scow dropped down the shaft. So quietly was the whole thing done that not a creature in that whole establishment knew that anything was wrong until it was too late to act—and then none of them knew anything at all. Not even the crew of the scow realized that they were dropping too fast.

Kinnison did not know what would happen if a mind—to say nothing of two of them—died while in his mental grasp, and he did not care to find out. Therefore, a fraction of a second before the crash, he jerked free and watched.

The explosion and its consequences did not look at all impressive from the Lensman's coign of vantage. The mountain trembled a little, then subsided noticeably. From its summit there erupted an unimportant little flare of flame, some smoke, and an insignificant shower of rock and debris.

However, when the scene had cleared there was no longer any shaft leading downward from that crater; a floor of solid rock began almost at its lip. Nevertheless the Lensman explored thoroughly all the region where the stronghold had been, making sure that the clean-up had been one hundred percent effective.

Then, and only then, did he point the speedster's streamlined nose toward star cluster AC 257–4736.

In his hidden retreat so far from the galaxy's crowded suns and worlds, Helmuth was in no enviable or easy frame of mind. Four times he had declared that that accursed Lensman, whoever he might be, must be destroyed; and had mustered his every available force to that end; only to have his intended prey slip from his grasp as effortlessly as a droplet of mercury eludes the clutching fingers of a child.

That Lensman, with nothing except a speedster and a bomb, had taken and had studied one of Boskone's new battleships, thus obtaining for his Patrol the secret of cosmic energy. Abandoning his own vessel, then crippled and doomed to capture or destruction, he had stolen one of the ships searching for him and in it he had calmly sailed to Velantia right through Helmuth's screen of blockading vessels. He had in some way so fortified Velantia as to capture six Boskonian battleships. In one of those ships he had won his way back to Prime Base, with information of such immense importance that it had robbed the Boskonian organization of its then overwhelming superiority. More, he had found or had developed new items of equipment which, save for Helmuth's own success in obtaining them, would have given the Patrol a definite and decisive superiority over Boskonia. Now both sides were equal, except for that Lensman and . . . the Lens.

Helmuth still quailed inwardly whenever he thought of what he had undergone at the Arisian barrier, and he had given up all thought of securing the secret of the Lens by force or from Arisia. But there must be other ways of getting it . . .

And just then there came in the urgent call from Boyssia II, followed by the stunningly successful revolt of the hitherto innocuous Blakeslee, culminating as it did in the destruction of Helmuth's every Boyssian device of vision or of communication. Blue-white with fury, the Boskonian flung his net abroad to take the renegade; but as he settled back to await results a thought struck him like a blow from a fist. Blakeslee *was* innocuous. He never had had, did not now have and never would have, the cold nerve and the sheer, dominating power he had just shown. Toward what conclusion did that fact point?

The furious anger disappeared from Helmuth's face as though it had been wiped therefrom with a sponge, and he became again the cold calculating mechanism of flesh and blood that he ordinarily was. This conception changed matters entirely. This was not an ordinary revolt of an ordinary subordinate. The man had done something which he could not possibly do. So what? The Lens again . . . again that accursed Lensman, the one who had somehow learned really to *use* his Lens!

"Wolmark, call every vessel at Boyssia base," he directed crisply. "Keep on calling them until someone answers. Get whoever is in charge there now and put him on me here."

A few minutes of silence followed, then Vice-Commander Krimsky reported in full everything that had happened and told of the threatened destruction of the base.

"You have an automatic speedster there, have you not?"

"Yes, sir."

"Turn over command to the next in line, with orders to move to the nearest base, taking with him as much equipment as is possible. Caution him to leave on time, however, for I very strongly suspect that it is now too late to do anything to prevent the destruction of the base. You, alone, take the speedster and bring away the personal files of the men who went with Blakeslee. A speedster will meet you at a point to be designated later and relieve you of the records."

An hour passed. Two, then three.

"Wolmark! Blakeslee and the hospital ship have vanished, I presume?"

"They have." The underling, expecting a verbal flaying, was greatly surprised at the mildness of his chief's tone and at the studious serenity of his face.

"Come to the center." Then, when the lieutenant was seated, "I do not suppose that you as yet realize what—or rather, who—it is that is doing this?"

"Why, Blakeslee is doing it, of course."

"I thought so, too, at first. That was what the one who really did it wanted us to think."

"It must have been Blakeslee. We saw him do it, sir—how could it have been anyone else?"

"I do not know. I do know, however, and so should you, that he could not have done it. Blakeslee, of himself, is of no importance whatever."

"We'll catch him, sir, and make him talk. He can't get away."

"You will find that you will not catch him and that he can get away. Blakeslee alone, of course, could not do so, any more than he could have done the things he apparently did do. No. Wolmark, we are not dealing with Blakeslee."

"Who then, sir?"

"Haven't you deduced that yet? The Lensman, fool—the same Lensman who has been thumbing his nose at us ever since he took one of our first-class battleships with a speed-boat and a firecracker."

"But—how *could* he?"

"Again I admit that I do not know—yet. The connection, however, is quite evident. Thought. Blakeslee was thinking thoughts utterly beyond him. The Lens comes from Arisia. The Arisians are masters of thought—of mental forces and processes incomprehensible to any of us.

These are the elements which, when fitted together, will give us the complete picture.''

"I don't see how they fit.''

"Neither do I—yet. However, surely he can't trace . . .''

"Just a moment! The time has come when it is no longer safe to say what that Lensman can or cannot do. Our communicator beams are hard and tight, yes. But any beam can be tapped if enough power be applied to it, and any beam that can be tapped can be traced. I expect him to visit us here, and we shall be prepared for his visit. That is the reason for this conference with you. Here is a device which generates a field through which no thought can penetrate. I have had this device for some time, but for obvious reasons have not released it. Here are the diagrams and complete constructional data. Have a few hundred of them made with all possible speed, and see to it that every being upon this planet wears one continuously. Impress upon everyone, and I will also, that it is of the utmost importance that absolutely continuous protection be maintained, even while changing batteries.

"Experts have been working for some time upon the problem of protecting the entire planet with a screen, and there is some little hope of success in the near future; but individual protection will still be of the utmost importance. We cannot impress it too forcibly upon everyone that every man's life is dependent upon each one maintaining his thought-screen in full operation at all times. That is all.''

When the messenger brought in the personal files of Blakeslee and the other deserters, Helmuth and his psychologists went over them with minutely painstaking care. The more they studied them the clearer it became that the chief's conclusion was the correct one. THE Lensman could read minds.

Reason and logic told Helmuth that the Lensman's only purpose in attacking the Boyssian base was to get a line on Grand Base; that Blakeslee's flight and the destruction of the base were merely diversions to obscure the real purpose of the visit; that the Lensman had staged that theatrical performance especially to hold him, Helmuth, while his beam was being traced, and that that was the only reason why the visiset was not sooner put out of action; and finally, that the Lensman had scored another clean hit.

He, Helmuth himself, had been caught flat-footed; and his face hardened and his jaw set at the thought. But he had not been taken in. He was forewarned and he would be ready, for he was coldly certain that Grand Base and he himself were the real objectives of the Lensman. That Lensman knew full well that any number of ordinary bases, ships, and men could be destroyed without damaging materially the Boskonian cause.

Steps must be taken to make Grand Base as impregnable to mental forces as it already was to physical ones. Otherwise, it might well be that even Helmuth's own life would presently be at stake—a thing precious indeed. Therefore council after council was held, every contingency that could be thought of was brought up and discussed, every possible precaution was taken. In short, every resource of Grand Base was devoted to the warding off of any possible mental threat which might be forthcoming.

Kinnison approached that star cluster with care. Small though it was, as cosmic groups go, it yet was composed of some hundreds of stars and an unknown number of planets. Any one of those planets might be the one he sought, and to approach it unknowingly might prove disastrous. Therefore he slowed down to a crawl and crept up, light-year by light-year, with his ultra-powered detectors fanning out before him to the limit of their unimaginable reach.

He had more than half expected that he would have to search that cluster, world by world; but in that, at least, he was pleasantly disappointed. One corner of one of his plates began to show a dim glow of detection. A bell tinkled and Kinnison directed his most powerful master plate into the region indicated. This plate, while of very narrow field, had tremendous resolving power and magnification; and in it he saw that there were eighteen small centers of radiation surrounding one vastly larger one.

There was no doubt then as to the location of Helmuth's base, but there arose the question of approach. The Lensman had not considered the possibility of a screen of lookout ships—if they were close enough together so that the electromagnetics had even a fifty percent overlap, he might as well go back home. What were those outposts, and exactly how closely were they spaced? He observed, advanced, and observed again; computing finally that, whatever they were, they were so far apart that there could be no possibility of any electro overlap at all. He could get between them easily enough—he wouldn't even have to baffle his flares They could not be guards at all, Kinnison concluded, but must be simply outposts, set far outside the solar system of the planet they guarded; not to ward off one-man speedsters, but to warn Helmuth of the possible approach of a force large enough to threaten Grand Base.

Closer and closer Kinnison flashed; discovering that the central object was indeed a base, startling in its immensity and completely and intensively fortified; and that the outposts were huge, floating fortresses, practically stationary in space relative to the sun of the solar system they surrounded. The Lensman aimed at the center of the imaginary square formed by four of the outposts and drove in as close to the planet as he dared. Then, going inert, he set his speedster into an orbit—he did not care particularly about its shape, provided that it was not too narrow an ellipse—and cut off all his power. He was now safe from detection. Leaning back in his seat and closing his eyes, he hurled his sense of perception into and through the massed fortifications of Grand Base.

For a long time he did not find a single living creature. Hundreds of miles he traversed, perceiving only automatic machinery, bank after towering, miles-square bank of accumulators, and remote-controlled projectors and other weapons and apparatus. Finally, however, he came to Helmuth's dome; and in that dome he received another severe shock. The personnel in that dome were to be numbered by the hundreds, but he could not make mental contact with any one of them. He could not touch their minds at all; he was stopped cold. Every member of Helmuth's band was protected by a thought-screen as effective as the Lensman's own!

Around and around the planet the speedster circled, while Kinnison struggled with this new and entirely unexpected setback. This looked as though Helmuth knew what was coming. Helmuth was nobody's fool, Kinnison knew; but how could he possibly have suspected that a mental attack was in the book? Perhaps he was just playing safe. If so, the Lensman's chance would come. Men would be careless; batteries weakened and would have to be changed.

But this hope was also vain, as continued watching revealed that each battery was listed, checked, and timed. Nor was any screen released, even for an instant, when its battery was changed; the fresh power source being slipped into service before the weakening one was disconnected.

"Well, that tears it—Helmuth *knows*," Kinnison cogitated, after watching vainly several such changes. "He's a wise old bird. The guy really has jets—I still don't see what I did that could have put him wise to what was going on."

Day after day the Lensman studied every detail of construction, operation, and routine of that base, and finally an idea began to dawn. He shot his attention toward a barracks he had inspected frequently of late, but stopped, irresolute.

"Uh uh, Kim, maybe better not," he advised himself. "Helmuth's mighty quick on the trigger, to figure out that Boyssian thing so fast . . ."

His projected thought was sheared off without warning, thus settling the question definitely. Helmuth's big apparatus was at work, the whole planet was screened against thought.

"Oh well, probably better, at that," Kinnison went on arguing with himself. "If I'd tried it out maybe he'd've got onto it and laid me a stymie next time, when I really need it."

He went free and hurled his speedster toward Earth, now distant indeed. Several times during that long trip he was sorely tempted to call Haynes through his Lens and get things started; but he always thought better of it. This was altogether too important a thing to be sent through so much sub-ether, or even to be thought about except inside an absolutely thought-tight room. And besides, every waking hour of even that long trip could be spent very profitably in digesting and correlating the information he had obtained and in mapping out the salient features of the campaign that was to come. Therefore, before time began to drag, Kinnison landed at Prime Base and was taken directly to Port Admiral Haynes.

"Mighty glad to see you, son," Haynes greeted the young Lensman cordially as he sealed the room thought-tight. "Since you came in under your own power, I assume that you are here to make a constructive report?"

"Better than that, sir—I'm here to start something in a big way. I know at last where their Grand Base is, and have detailed plans of it. I think I know who and where Boskone is. I know where Helmuth is, and I have worked out a plan whereby, if it works, we can wipe out that base. Boskone, Helmuth, and all the lesser master minds, at one wipe."

"Mentor *did* come through, huh?" For the first time since Kinnison had known him the old man lost his poise. He leaped to his feet and seized Kinnison by the arm. "I knew you were good, but not *that* good! He gave you what you wanted?"

"He sure did," and the younger man reported as briefly as possible everything that had happened.

"I'm just as sure that Helmuth is Boskone as I can be of anything that can't be proved," Kinnison continued, unrolling a sheaf of drawings. "Helmuth speaks for Boskone, and nobody else ever does, not even Boskone himself. None of the other big shots know anything about Boskone or ever heard him speak; but they all jump through their hoops when Helmuth, 'speaking for Boskone,' cracks the whip. And I couldn't get a trace of Helmuth ever taking anything up with any higher-ups. Therefore I'm dead certain that when we get Helmuth we get Boskone.

"But that's going to be a job of work. I scouted his headquarters from stem to gudgeon, as I told you; and Grand Base is absolutely impregnable as it stands. I never imagined anything like it—it makes Prime Base here look like a deserted cross-roads after a hard winter. They've got screens, pits, projectors, accumulators, all on a gigantic scale. In fact, they've got everything—but you can get all that from the tape and these sketches. They simply can't be taken by any possible direct frontal attack. Even if we used every ship and mauler we've got they could stand us off. And they can match us, ship for ship—we'd never get near Grand Base at all if they knew we were coming . . ."

"Well, if it's such an impossible job, what . . ."

"I'm coming to that. It's impossible as it stands; but there's a good chance that I'll be able to soften it up," and the young Lensman went on to outline the plan upon which he had been working so long. "You know, like a worm—bore from within. That's the only possible way to do it. You'll have to put detector nullifiers on every ship assigned to the job, but that'll be easy. We'll need everything we've got."

"The important thing, as I gather it, is timing."

"Absolutely. To the minute, since I won't be able to communicate, once I get inside their thought-screens. How long will it take to assemble our stuff and put it in that cluster?"

"Seven weeks—eight at the outside."

"Plus two for allowances. QX—at exactly hour 20, ten weeks from today, let every projector of every vessel you can possibly get there cut loose on that base with everything they can pour in. There's a detailed drawing in here somewhere . . . here—twenty-six main objectives, you see. Blast them all, simultaneously to the second. If they all go down, the rest will be possible—if not, it'll be just too bad. Then work along these lines here, straight from those twenty-six stations to the dome, blasting everything as you go. Make it last exactly fifteen minutes, not a minute more or less. If, by fifteen minutes after twenty, the main dome hasn't surrendered by cutting its screen, blast that, too, if you can—it'll take a lot of blasting, I'm afraid. From then on you and the five-star admirals will have to do whatever is appropriate to the occasion."

"Your plan doesn't cover that, apparently. Where will you be—how will *you* be fixed—if the main dome does not cut its screens?"

"I'll be dead, and you'll be just starting the damndest war that this galaxy ever saw."

23

TREGONSEE TURNS
ZWILNIK

While servicing and checking the speedster required only a couple of hours, Kinnison did not leave Earth for almost two days. He had requisitioned much special equipment, the construction of one item of which—a suit of armor such as had never been seen before—caused almost all of the delay. When it was ready the greatly interested Port Admiral accompanied the young Lensman out to the steel-lined, sand-filled concrete dugout, in which the suit had already been mounted upon a remote-controlled dummy. Fifty feet from that dummy there was a heavy, water-cooled machine rifle, with its armored crew standing by. As the two approached the crew leaped to attention.

"As you were," Haynes instucted, and:

"You checked those cartridges against those I brought in from Aldebaran I?" asked Kinnison of the officer in charge, as, accompanied by the Port Admiral, he crouched down behind the shields of the control panel.

"Yes, sir. These are twenty-five percent over, as you specified."

"QX—commence firing" Then, as the weapon clamored out its stuttering, barking roar, Kinnison made the dummy stoop, turn, bend, twist, and dodge, so as to bring its every plate, joint, and member into that hail of steel. The uproar stopped.

"One thousand rounds, sir," the officer reported.

"No holes—no dents—not a scratch or a scar," Kinnison reported, after a minute examination, and got into the thing. "Now give me two thousand rounds, unless I tell you to stop. Shoot!"

Again the machine rifle burst into its ear-shattering song of hate; and, strong as Kinnison was and powerfully braced by the blast of his drivers, he could not stand against the awful force of those bullets. Over he went, backward, and the firing ceased.

"Keep it up!" he snapped. "Think they're going to quit shooting at me because I fall down?"

"But you had had nineteen hundred!" protested the officer.

"Keep on pecking until you run out of ammunition or until I tell you to stop," ordered Kinnison. "I've got to learn how to handle this thing under fire," and the storm of metal again began to crash against the reverberating shell of steel.

It hurled the Lensman down, rolled him over and over, slammed him against the back-stop. Again and again he struggled upright, only to be hurled again to ground as the riflemen, really playing the game now, swung their leaden hail from part to part of the armor, and varied their attack from steady fire to short but savage bursts. But finally, in spite of everything the gun crew could do, Kinnison learned his controls.

Then, drivers flaring, he faced that howling, chattering muzzle and strode straight into the stream of smoke and flame-enshrouded steel. Now the air was literally full of metal. Bullets and fragments of bullets whined and shrieked in mad abandon as they ricocheted in all directions off that armor. Sand and bits of concrete flew hither and yon, filling the atmosphere of the dugout. The rifle yammered at maximum, with its sweating crew laboring mightily to keep its voracious maw full-fed. But, in spite of everything, Kinnison held his line and advanced. He was barely six feet from that yelling, steel-vomiting muzzle when the firing again ceased.

"Twenty thousand, sir," the officer reported, crisply. "We'll have to change barrels before we can give you any more."

"That's enough!" snapped Haynes. "Come out of there!"

Out Kinnison came. He removed heavy ear-plugs, swallowed four times, blinked and grimaced. Finally he spoke.

"It works perfectly, sir, except for the noise. 'Sa good thing I've got a Lens—in spite of the plugs I won't be able to hear anything for three days!"

"How about the springs and shock-absorbers? Are you bruised anywhere? You took some real bumps."

"Perfect—not a bruise. Let's look her over."

Every inch of that armor's surface was now marked by blurs, where the metal of the bullets had rubbed itself off upon the shining alloy, but that surface was neither scratched, scored, nor dented.

"QX, boys—thanks," Kinnison dismissed the riflemen. They probably wondered how any man could see out through a helmet built up of inches-thick laminated alloys, with neither window nor port through which to look; but if so, they made no mention of their curiosity. They, too, were Patrolmen.

"Is that thing an armor or a personal tank?" asked Haynes, "I aged ten years while that was going on; but at that I'm glad you insisted on testing it. You can get away with anything now."

"It's much better technique to learn things among friends than enemies," Kinnison laughed. "It's heavy, of course—pretty close to a ton. I won't be walking around in it, though; I'll be flying it. Well, sir, since everything's all set, I think I'd better fly it over to the speedster and start flitting, don't you? I don't know exactly how much time I'm going to need on Trenco."

"Might as well," the Port Admiral agreed, as casually, and Kinnison was gone.

"What a man!" Haynes stared after the monstrous figure until it vanished in the distance, then strolled slowly toward his office, thinking as he went.

Nurse MacDougall had been highly irked and incensed at Kinnison's casual departure, without idle conversation or formal leave-takings. Not so Haynes. That seasoned campaigner knew that Gray Lensmen—especially young Gray Lensmen—were prone to get that way. He knew, as she would one day learn, that Kinnison was no longer of Earth.

He was now only of the galaxy, not of any one tiny dust-grain of it. He was of the Patrol. He *was* the Patrol, and he was taking his new responsibilities very seriously indeed. In his fierce zeal to drive his campaign through to a successful end he would use man or woman, singly or in groups; ships; even Prime Base itself; exactly as he had used them: as pawns, as mere tools, as means to an end. And, having used them, he would leave them as unconcernedly and as unceremoniously as he would drop pliers and spanner, and with no more realization that he had violated any of the nicer amenities of life as it is lived!

And as he strolled along and thought, the Port Admiral smiled quietly to himself. He knew, as Kinnison would learn in time, that the universe was vast, that time was long, and that the Scheme of Things, comprising the whole of eternity and the Cosmic All, was a something incomprehensibly immense indeed: with which cryptic thought the space-hardened veteran sat down at his desk and resumed his interrupted labors.

But Kinnison had not yet attained Haynes' philosophic viewpoint, any more than he had his age, and to him the trip to Trenco seemed positively interminable. Eager as he was to put his plan of campaign to the test, he found that mental urgings, or even audible invective, would not make the speedster go any faster than the already incomprehensible top speed of her drivers' maximum blast. Nor did pacing up and down the little control room help very much. Physical exercise he had to perform, but it did not satisfy him. Mental exercise was impossible; he could think of nothing except Helmuth's base.

Eventually, however, he approached Trenco and located without difficulty the Patrol's space-port. Fortunately, it was then at about eleven o'clock, so that he did not have to wait long to land. He drove downward inert, sending ahead of him a thought:

"Lensman of Trenco Space-port—Tregonsee or his relief? Lensman Kinnison of Sol III asking permission to land."

"It is Tregonsee," came back the thought. "Welcome, Kinnison. You are on the correct line. You have, then, perfected an apparatus to see truly in this distorting medium?"

"I didn't perfect it—it was given to me."

The landing bars lashed out, seized the speedster, and eased her down into the lock; and, as soon as she had been disinfected, Kinnison went into consultation with Tregonsee. The Rigellian was a highly important factor in the Tellurian's scheme; and, since he was also a Lensman, he was to be trusted implicitly. Therefore Kinnison told him briefly what occurred and what he had it in mind to do, concluding:

"So you see, I need about fifty kilograms of thionite. Not fifty milligrams, or even grams, but fifty *kilograms*; and, since there probably isn't that much of the stuff loose in the whole galaxy, I came over here to ask you to make it for me."

Just like that. Calmly asking a Lensman, whose duty it was to kill any being even attempting to gather a single Treconian plant, to make for him more of the prohibited drug than was ordinarily processed throughout the galaxy during a Solarian month! It would be just such an errand were one to walk into the Treasury Department at Washington and inform the Chief of the Narcotics Bureau, quite nonchalantly, that he had dropped in to pick up ten tons of heroin! But Tregonsee did not flinch or question—he was not even surprised. This was a Gray Lensman.

"That should not be too difficult," Tregonsee replied, after a moment's study. "We have several thionite processing units, confiscated from zwilnik outfits and not yet sent in; and all of us are of course familiar with the technique of extracting and purifying the drug."

He issued orders and shortly Trenco Space-port presented the astounding spectacle of a full crew of the Galactic Patrol devoting its every energy to the whole-hearted breaking of the one law it was supposed most rigidly, and without fear or favor, to enforce!

It was a little after noon, the calmest hour of Trenco's day. The wind had died to "nothing"; which, on the planet, meant that a strong man could stand against it; could even, if he were agile as well as strong, walk about in it. Therefore Kinnison donned his light armor and was soon busily harvesting broad-leaf, which, he had been informed, was the richest source of thionite.

He had been working for only a few minutes when a flat came crawling up to him; and, after ascertaining that his armor was not good to eat, drew off and observed him intently. Here was another opportunity for practice and in a flash the Lensman availed himself of it. Having practiced for hours upon the minds of various Earthly animals, he entered this mind easily enough, finding that the trenco was considerably more intelligent than a dog. So much so, in fact, that the race had already developed a fairly comprehensive language. Therefore it did not take long for the Lensman to learn to use his subject's peculiar limbs and other members, and soon the flat was working as though he were in the business for himself. And, since he was ideally adapted to his wildly raging Trenconian environment, he actually accomplished more than all the rest of the force combined.

"It's a dirty trick I'm playing on you, Spike," Kinnison told his helper after a while. "Come on into the receiving room and I'll see if I can square it with you."

Since food was the only logical tender, Kinnison brought out from his speedster a small can of salmon, a package of cheese, a bar of chocolate, a few lumps of sugar, and a potato, offering them to the Trenconian in order. The salmon and cheese were both highly acceptable fare. The morsel of chocolate was a delightfully surprising delicacy. The lump of sugar, however, was what really rang the bell—Kinnison's own mind felt the shock of pure ecstasy as that wonderful substance dissolved in the trenco's mouth. He also ate the potato, of course—any Trenconian animal will, at any time, eat practically anything—but it was merely food; nothing to rave about.

Knowing now what to do, Kinnison led his assistant out into the howling, shrieking gale and released him from control, throwing a lump of sugar up-wind as he did so. The trenco seized it in the air, ate it, and went into a very hysteria of joy.

"More! More!" he insisted, attempting to climb up the Lensman's armored leg.

"You must work for more of it, if you want it," Kinnison explained. "Break off broad-leaf plants and carry them over into that empty thing over there, and you get more."

This was an entirely new idea to the native, but after Kinnison had taken hold of his mind and had shown him how to do consciously that which he had been doing unconsciously for an hour, he worked willingly enough. In fact, before it started to rain, thereby putting an end to the labor of the day, there were a dozen of them toiling at the harvest and the crop was coming in as fast as the entire crew of Rigellians could process it. And even after the spaceport was sealed they crowded up, paying no attention to the rain, bringing in their small loads of leaves and plaintively asking admittance.

It took some little time for Kinnison to make them understand that the day's work was done, but that they were to come back tomorrow morning. Finally, however, he succeeded in getting the idea across; and the last disconsolate turtle-man swam reluctantly away. But sure enough, next morning, even before the mud had dried, the same twelve were back on the job; and the two Lensmen wondered simultaneously—how *could* those trencos have found the space-port? Or had they stayed near it through the storm and flood of the night.

"I don't know," Kinnison answered the unasked question, "but I can find out." Again and more carefully he examined the minds of two or three of them. "No, they didn't follow us," he reported then. "They're not as dumb as I thought they were. They have a sense of perception, Tregonsee, about the same thing, I judge, as yours—perhaps even more so. I wonder . . . why couldn't they be trained into mighty efficient police assistants on this planet?"

"The way *you* handle them, yes. I can converse with them a little, of course, but they have never before shown any willingness to cooperate with us."

"You never fed them sugar," Kinnison laughed. "You have sugar, of course—or do you? I was forgetting that many races do not use it at all."

"We Rigellians are one of those races. Starch is so much tastier and so much better adapted to our body chemistry that sugar is used only as a chemical. We can, however, obtain it easily enough. But there is something else—you can tell these trencos what to do and make them really understand you. I can not."

"I can fix that up with a simple mental treatment that I can give you in five minutes. Also, I can let you have enough sugar to carry on with until you can get in a supply of your own."

In the few minutes during which the Lensman had been discussing their potential allies, the mud had dried and the amazing coverage of vegetation was springing visibly into being. So incredibly rapid was its growth that in less than an hour some species were large enough to be gathered. The leaves were lush and rank in color or a vivid crimsonish purple.

"These early morning plants are the richest of any in thionite—much richer than broad-leaf—but the zwilniks can never get more than a handful of them because of the wind," remarked the Rigellian. "Now, if you will give me that treatment, I will see what I can do with the flats."

Kinnison did so, and the trencos worked for Tregonsee as industriously as they had for Kinnison—and ate his sugar as rapturously.

"That's enough," decided the Rigellian presently. "This will finish your fifty kilograms and to spare."

He then paid off his now enthusiastic helpers, with instructions to return when the sun was directly overhead, for more work and more sugar. And this time they did not complain, nor did they loiter around or bring in unwanted vegetation. They were learning fast.

Well before noon the last kilogram of impalpable, purplish blue powder was put into its impermeable sack. The machinery was cleaned; and untouched leaves, the waste, and the contaminated air were blown out of the space-port; and the room and its occupants were sprayed with anti-thionite. Then and only then did the crew remove their masks and air-filters. Trenco Space-port was again a Patrol post, no longer a zwilnik's paradise.

"Thanks, Tregonsee and all you fellows . . ." Kinnison paused, then went on, dubiously, "I don't suppose that you will . . ."

"We will not," declared Tregonsee. "Our time is yours, as you know, without payment; and time is all that we gave you, really."

"Sure—that and a thousand million credits' worth of thionite."

"That, of course, does not count, as you also know. You have helped us, I think, even more than we have helped you."

"I hope I've done you some good, anyway. Well, I've got to flit. Thanks again—I'll see you again sometime, maybe," and again the Tellurian Lensman was on his way.

24

KINNISON BORES FROM WITHIN

Kinnison approached star cluster AC 257-4736 warily, as before; and as before he insinuated his speedster through the loose outer cordon of guardian fortresses. This time, however, he did not steer even remotely near Helmuth's world. He would be there too long—there was altogether too much risk of electromagnetic detection to set his ship into any kind of an orbit around *that* planet. Instead, he had computed a long, narrow, elliptical orbit around its sun; well inside the zone guarded by the maulers. He could compute it only approximately, of course, since he did not know exactly either the masses involved or the perturbing forces; but he thought that he could find his ship again with an electro. If not, she would not be an irreplaceable loss. He set the speedster, then, into the outward leg of that orbit and took off in his new armor.

He knew that there was a thought-screen around Helmuth's planet, and suspected that there might be other screens as well. Therefore, shutting off every watt of power, he dropped straight down into the night side, almost halfway around the planet from Grand Base. His flares were of course heavily baffled, but even so he did not put on his brakes until it was absolutely necessary. He landed heavily, then sprang away in long, free hops, until he reached his previously-selected destination; a great cavern thickly shielded with iron ore and within working range of his objective. Deep within the cavern he hid himself, then searched intently for any sign that his approach had been observed. There was no such sign—so far, so good.

But during his search he had perceived with a slight shock that Helmuth had tightened his defenses even more. Not only was every man in the dome screened against thought, but also each was now wearing full armor. Had he protected the dogs, too? Or killed them? No real matter if he had—any kind of a pet animal would do; or, in a pinch, even a wild rock-lizard! Nevertheless he shot his perception into the particular barracks he had noted so long before, and found with some relief that the dogs were still there, and that they were still unprotected. It had not occurred, even to Helmuth's cautious mind, that a dog could be a source of mental danger.

With all due precaution against getting even a single grain of the stuff into his own system, Kinnison transferred his thionite into the special container in which it was to be used. Another day sufficed to observe and to memorize the personnel of the gateway observers, their positions, and the sequence in which they took the boards. Then the Lensman, still almost a week ahead of schedule, settled down to wait the time when he should make his next move. Nor was this waiting unduly irksome; now that everything was ready he could be as patient as a cat on duty at a mouse-hole.

The time came to act. Kinnison took over the mind of the dog, which at once moved over to the bunk in which one particular observer lay asleep. There would be no chance whatever of gaining control of any observer while he was actually on the board, but here in barracks it was almost ridiculously easy. The dog crept along on soundless paws—a long, slim nose reached out and up—sharp teeth closed delicately upon a battery lead—out came the plug. The thought-screen went down, and instantly Kinnison was in charge of the fellow's mind.

And when that observer went on duty his first act was to let Kimball Kinnison, Gray Lensman, into Boskone's Grand Base! Low and fast Kinnison flew, while the observer so placed his body as to shield from any chance passer-by the all too revealing surface of his visiplate. In a few minutes the Lensman reached a portal of the dome itself. That door also opened—and closed behind him. He released the mind of the observer and watched briefly. Nothing happened. All was still well!

Then, in every barracks save one, using whatever came to hand in the way of dog or other unshielded animal, Kinnison wrought briefly but effectively. He did not slay by mental force—he did not have enough of that to spare—but the mere turn of an inconspicuous valve would do just as well. Some of those now idle men would probably live to answer Helmuth's call to extra duty, but not too many—nor would those who obeyed that summons live long thereafter.

Down stairway after stairway he dove, down to the compartment in which was housed the great air-purifier. Now let them come! Even if they had a spy-ray on him now it would be too late to do them a bit of good. And now, by Klono's golden gills, that fleet had better be out there, getting ready to blast!

It was. From all over the galaxy Grand Fleet had come; every Patrol base had been stripped of almost everything mobile that could throw a beam. Every vessel carried either a Lensman or some other highly trusted officer; and each such officer had two detector nullifiers—one upon his person, the other in his locker—either of which would protect his whole ship from detection.

In long lines, singly and at intervals, those untold thousands of ships had crept between the vessels guarding Grand Base. Nor were the outpost crews to blame. They had been on duty for months, and not even an asteroid had relieved the monotony. Nothing had happened or would. They watched their plates steadily enough—and, if they did nothing more, why should they have? And what could they have done? How could they suspect that such a thing as a detector nullifier had been invented?

The Patrol's Grand Fleet, then, was already massing over its primary objectives, each vessel in a rigidly assigned position. The pilots, captains, and navigators were chatting among themselves; jerkily and in low tones, as though even to raise their voices might reveal prematurely to the enemy the concentration of the Patrol forces. The firing officers were already at their boards, eyeing hungrily the small switches which they could not throw for so many long minutes yet.

And far below, beside the pirates' air-purifier, Kinnison released the locking toggles of his armor and leaped out. To burn a hole in the primary duct took only a second. To drop into that duct his container of thionite; to drench that container with the reagent which would in sixty seconds dissolve completely the container's substance without affecting either its contents or the metal of the duct; to slap a flexible adhesive patch over the hole in the duct; and to leap back into his armor: all these things required only a trifle over one minute. Eleven minutes to go—QX.

In the nearest barracks, even while the Lensman was arrowing up the stairways, a dog again deprived a sleeping man of his thought-screen. That man, however, instead of going to work, took up a pair of pliers and proceeded to cut the battery leads of every sleeper in the barracks; severing them so closely that no connection could be made without removing the armor.

As those leads were severed men woke up and dashed into the dome. Along catwalk after catwalk they raced, and apparently that was all they were doing. But each runner, as he passed a man on duty, flicked a battery plug out of its socket; and that observer, at Kinnison's command, opened the face-plate of his armor and breathed deeply of the now drug-laden atmosphere.

Thionite, as has been intimated, is perhaps the worst of all known habit-forming drugs. In almost infinitesimal doses it gives rise to a state in which the victim seems actually to experience the gratification of his every desire, whatever that desire may be. The larger the dose, the more intense the sensation, until—and very quickly—the dosage is reached at which he passes into an ecstasy so unbearable that death ensues forthwith.

Thus there was no alarm, no outcry, no warning. Each observer sat or stood entranced, holding exactly the pose he had been in at the instant of opening his face-plate. But now, instead of paying attention to his duty, he was plunging deeper and deeper into the paroxysmally ecstatic profundity of a thionite debauch from which there was to be no awakening. Therefore half of that mighty dome was unmanned before Helmuth even realized that anything out of order was going on.

As soon as he realized that something was amiss, however, he sounded the "all hands on duty" alarm and rapped out instructions to the officers in the barracks. But the cloud of death had arrived there first, and to his consternation not one-quarter of those officers responded. Quite a number of men did get into the dome, but every one of them collapsed before reaching the catwalks. And three-fourths of his working force died before he located Kinnison's speeding messengers.

"Blast them down!" Helmuth shrieked, pointing, gesticulating madly.

Blast whom down? The minions of the Lensmen were themselves blasting away now, right and left, shouting contradictory but supposedly authoritative orders.

"Blast those men not on duty!" Helmuth's raging voice now filled the dome. "You, at board 479! Blast that man on catwalk 28, at board 495!"

With such detailed instructions, Kinnison's agents one by one ceased to be. But as one was beamed down another took his place, and soon every one of the few remaining living pirates in the dome was blasting indiscriminately at every other one. And then, to cap the Saturnalian climax, came the zero second.

The Galactic Patrol's Grand Fleet had assembled. Every cruiser, every battleship, every mauler hung poised above its assigned target. Every vessel was stripped for action. Every accumulator cell was full to its ultimate watt, every generator and every arm was tuned and peaked to its highest attainable efficiency. Every firing officer upon every ship sat tensely at his board; his hand hovering near, but not touching, his firing key; his eyes fixed glaringly upon the second-hand of his precisely synchronized timer; his ears scarcely hearing the droning, soothing voice of Port Admiral Haynes.

For the Old Man had insisted upon giving the firing order himself, and he now sat at the master timer, speaking into the master microphone. Beside him sat von Hohendorff, the grand old Commandant of Cadets. Both of these veterans had thought long since that they were done with space-war forever, but only an order of the full Galactic Council could have kept either of them at home. They were grimly determined that they were going to be in at the death, even though they were not at all certain whose death it was to be. If it should turn out that it was to be Helmuth's, well and good—everything would be on the green. If, on the other hand, young Kinnison had to go, they would in all probability have to go, too—and so be it.

"Now, remember, boys, keep your hands off of those keys until I give you the word," Haynes' soothing voice droned on, giving no hint of the terrific strain he himself was under. "I'll give you lots of warning . . . I am going to count the last five seconds for you. I know that you all want to shoot the first bolt, but remember that I personally will strangle any and every one of you who beats my signal by a thousandth of a second. It won't be long now, the second hand is starting around on its last lap . . . Keep your hands off of those keys . . . keep away from them, I tell you, or I'll smack you down . . . fifteen seconds yet . . . stay away, boys, let 'em alone . . . going to start counting now." His voice dropped lower and lower. "Five—four—three—two—one—FIRE!" he yelled.

Perhaps some of the boys did beat the gun a trifle; but not many, or much. To all intents and purposes it was one simultaneous blast of destruction that flashed down from a hundred thousand projectors, each delivering the maximum blast of which it was capable. There was no thought now of service life of equipment or of holding anything back for a later effort. They had to hold that blast for only fifteen minutes; and if the task ahead of them could not be done in those fifteen minutes it probably could not be done at all.

Therefore it is entirely useless even to attempt to describe what happened then, or to portray the spectacle that ensued when beam met screen. Why try to describe pink to a man born blind? Suffice it to say that those Patrol beams bored down, and that Helmuth's automatic screens resisted to the limit of their ability. Nor was that resistance small.

Had Helmuth's customary staff of keen-eyed, quick-witted lieutenants been at their posts, to reenforce those primary screens with the practically unlimited power which could have been put behind them, his defense would not have failed under even the unimaginable force of that Titanic thrust; but those lieutenants were not at their posts. The screens of the twenty-six primary objectives failed, and the twenty-six stupendous flotillas moved slowly, grandly, voraciously, each along its designated line.

Every alarm in Helmuth's dome had burst into frantic warning as the massed might of the Galactic Patrol was hurled against the twenty-six vital points of Grand Base, but those alarms clamored in vain. No hands were raised to the switches whose closing would unleash the hellish energies of Boskone's irresistible projectors, no eyes were upon the sighting devices which would align them against the attacking ships of war. Only Helmuth, in his inner-shielded control compartment, was left; and Helmuth was the directing intelligence, the master mind, and not a mere operator. And, now that he had no operators to direct, he was utterly helpless. He could see the stupendous fleet of the Patrol, he could understand fully its dire menace; but he could neither stiffen his screens nor energize a single beam. He could only sit, grinding his teeth in helpless fury, and watch the destruction of the armament which, if it could only have been in operation, would have blasted those battleships and maulers from the skies as though they had been so many fluffy bits of thistledown.

Time after time he leaped to his feet, as if about to dash across to one of the control stations, but each time he sank back into his seat at the desk. One firing-station would be little, if any, better than none at all. Besides, that accursed Lensman was back of this. He was—must be—right here in the dome, somewhere. He *wanted* him to leave this desk—that was what he was waiting for! As long as he stayed at the desk he himself was safe. For that matter, this whole dome was safe. The projector had never been mounted that could break down *those* screens. No—no matter what happened, he would stay at the desk!

Kinnison, watching, marveled at his fortitude. He himself could not have stayed there, he knew; and he also knew now that Helmuth was going to stay. Time was flying; five of the fifteen minutes were gone. He had hoped that Helmuth would leave that well-protected inner sanctum, with its unknown potentialities; but if the pirate would not come out, the Lensman would go in. The storming of that inner stronghold was what his new armor was for.

In he went, but he did not catch Helmuth napping. Even before he

crashed the screens his own defensive zones burst into furiously coruscant activity, and through that flame there came tearing the metallic
slugs of a high-power machine rifle.

Ha! There *was* a rifle, even though he had not been able to find it!
Clever guy, that Helmuth! And what a break that he had taken time to
learn how to hold this suit up against the trickiest kind of machine-rifle
fire!

Kinnison's screens were almost those of a battleship; his armor almost, relatively, as strong. And he could hold that armor upright.
Therefore through the raging beam of the semi-portable projector he
plowed and straight up that torrent of raging steel he drove his way.
And now from his own mighty projector, against Helmuth's armor, there
raved out a beam carcely less potent than that of a semi-portable. The
Lensman's armor did not mount a water-cooled machine rifle—there
was a limit to what even that powerful structure could carry—but
grimly, with every faculty of his newly enlarged mind concentrated
upon that thought-screened, armored head behind the belching gun, Kinnison held his line and forged ahead.

Well it was that the Lensman *was* concentrating upon that screened
head; for when the screen weakened slightly and a thought began to
seep through it toward an enigmatically sparkling ball of force, Kinnison
was ready. He blanketed the thought savagely, before it could take form,
and attacked the screen so viciously that Helmuth had either to restore
full coverage instantly or die then and there. For the Lensman had studied that ball long and earnestly. It was the one thing about the whole
base that he could not understand; the one thing, therefore, of which he
had been afraid.

But he was afraid of it no longer. It was operated, he now knew, by
thought; and, no matter how terrific its potentialities might be, it now
was and would remain perfectly harmless; for if the pirate chief softened
his screen enough to emit a thought, he would never think again.

Therefore he rushed. At full blast he hurdled the rifle and crashed full
against the armored figure behind it. Magnetic clamps locked and held;
and, driving projectors furiously ablaze, he whirled around and forced
the madly struggling Helmuth back, toward the line along which the
bellowing rifle was still spewing forth a continuous storm of metal.

Helmuth's utmost efforts sufficed only to throw the Lensman out of
balance, and both figures crashed to the floor. And now the madly fighting armored pair rolled over and over—straight into the line of fire.

First Kinnison; the bullets whining, shrieking off the armor of his
personal battleship and crashing through or smashing ringingly against

whatever happened to be in the ever-changing line or ricochet. Then Helmuth; and as the fierce-driven metal slugs tore in their multitudes through his armor and through and through his body, riddling his every vital organ, that was THE END